RAGE … IST HEAVEN

‘Is this it?’ he asked.

‘This is it,’ said Burt.

Lew looked around. The woods were deserted.

‘But there’s no one here.’

‘I know.’

Lew turned back to Thomson. He was holding a gun.

‘The general has told me to kill you,’ said Thomson, ‘and it’s a real pleasure. I hate your good-looking Frog guts.’

And he fired at his heart, point-blank.

Burt Thomson stuck his pistol back in his holster, then spurred his horse and started back up the hill.

He looked pleased with himself.

A Rage Against Heaven

Fred M. Stewart

THE SHERIDAN
BOOK COMPANY

This edition published in 1993 by
The Sheridan Book Company

First published by Hutchinson 1978
Arrow edition 1979

Printed and bound in Great Britain by
Cox & Wyman Ltd, Reading, Berkshire

ISBN 1–85501–440–8

To my wife, Joan,
who, when I told her the idea,
said, 'Write it.'

Contents

Author's note

Although it is, for some reason, unusual for authors of historical fiction to mention their sources, I do want, since this fiction is based on fact, to thank the hundreds of authors and editors whose books guided me through the past. I also wish to thank John Ransom, who lived through the horror of Andersonville, and whose excellent diary was invaluable to me (and Hank Gaynor). I will also add, as a personal note, that although the Civil War. the Mexican Empire, the French Second Empire, the Franco-Prussian War, the Siege of Paris and the Commune are wars and empires in the dust, reading about them helped me to clarify not only the past but the present as well.

F.M.S.

Prologue

Elizabeth Butterfield thought the baseball game was the most exciting thing she had ever seen. Her lover was standing on the pitcher's mound, the hot sun burning his thick hair even more golden as he eyed the umpire, who was sitting on a stool near first base looking pompous in a top hat and frock coat. Her lover's tall, lanky body relaxed to one side as he fondled the ball, which he held in both hands in front of his mouth. His white shirt was open at the chest, and his black trousers were tucked into the tops of his high canvas shoes. He wore a thick patent-leather belt with the buckle on his right hip, a brass plate with his team insignia on it in front. How magnificent he looked, Elizabeth thought, bursting with pride. She couldn't imagine anyone in the world being more in love than she was.

Now he turned to eye the batter. Then, suddenly, the windup, and his powerful right arm fired lightning. It was an overhand pitch, which had startled the team from nearby Trenton, who were used to underhand pitching.

'Strrr-ike three! You're out!'

The crowd of parents, sweethearts, and members of the Class of 1860 went wild. The Princeton team went wild. They rushed their captain and pitcher, grabbed him, and started throwing him in the air. Elizabeth Butterfield threw her white parasol in the air.

'He won! He did it! He *won!*' she practically screamed. Her father, Dr Ward Butterfield, caught the parasol.

'Elizabeth, get hold of yourself,' he growled. He had a thick black beard and a thin Scots burr, a fading remnant of his Edinburgh childhood.

'Oh, but Father, he was magnificent! Wasn't he magnificent? Admit he was magnificent!'

'But you mustn't make a spectacle of yourself, girl. People will think you're not proper.'

'I'm not! I mean, I am, but . . . Isn't he the most handsome man you've ever seen in your life?'

'Aye, the lad's good-looking, there's no denying that. But physical beauty is a thing that passes. . . .'

Elizabeth rolled her eyes at her father's constant dour moralizing.

'Aye, it passes,' she mimicked his burr. 'But while it's there, it's sure wondrous to behold!'

Her father, Philadelphia's leading surgeon, looked shocked.

'Elizabeth! You'll remember you're my daughter!'

She sighed and looked back at her lover, who really was not.

'It's hard to forget, Father. Oh, that overhand pitch! It's twice as fast as the old way, and twice as exciting. . . . They didn't have a chance. . . . Poor Lew, they're still throwing him around . . . he'll get seasick. . . .'

Indeed, Lew was being tossed like a shuttlecock by his jubilant teammates. But he wasn't getting sick. He was laughing. He had won! It was June! Elizabeth was here to see him win, and it was June and life was wonderful! June, summer, love, baseball, youth . . . everything was beautiful!

'I love you,' said Lew. 'No, that's too unoriginal. I *adore* you! I worship you! How's that?'

Elizabeth purred. They were lying in the grass next to a pond at the edge of the campus. It was an hour after the game, and Dr Butterfield had conveniently left his daughter unchaperoned for forty-five minutes while he went off to discuss 'some peculiarities of the pancreas gland', as he had put it, with the college surgeon, Dr Brown. Elizabeth knew that, for all her father's moralizing, he wasn't adverse to letting young people be by themselves periodically. But only forty-five minutes, mind. . . .

'That's very good,' she said, 'I like "adore" much better than "love".' She smiled. 'But I'll settle for love.'

He leaned over her and kissed her. She didn't resist.

'I'll settle for love, too,' he said. 'Will you marry me, Elizabeth?'

She looked up into his blue eyes. How she loved those blue eyes!

'Silly goose, we've been engaged since we were ten.'

'I know, but that was games. This is a *real* proposal. I want you to be my wife.'

Her brown eyes widened.

'Better say yes before I change my mind.'

'Yes!' she blurted out. Yes, yes, YES!'

They kissed and hugged each other and rolled around in the grass like antic colts. After a while they stopped, and she felt his hand on her breast.

'No,' she whispered.

'I want you,' he whispered back. He was on top of her, and she felt something hardening against her. She became frightened.

'No!' She tried to push him off. For a moment, he fought her. Then he relented. He got to his feet and went to a tree. Leaning against it, his back to her, he let the rising sap in him descend, and he thought he would go crazy. Then she was next to him, her hand on his arm.

'Later, my darling,' she said. 'And it will be so wonderful.' She didn't know what 'it' would be.

He looked at her and smiled. 'It better be.'

'I love you, Lew,' she said. 'I've always loved you, and I always will love you. Forever.'

'And I'll love you forever.'

'Do you swear?'

'Of course I swear. Do you?'

'I swear with all my heart.'

'Swear you'll never forget me or never leave me?'

Tears welled in her eyes at the very suggestion.

'I could *never* forget you and *never* leave you.'

He kissed the end of her nose. 'Nor I you. Do you think your father will object?'

'Father *object?* To *you?* He thinks you're the best catch in Philadelphia, which you *are* . . . as you well know.'

'He doesn't like my mother.'

'Oh, but he does!'

'Liar.'

'Well, he doesn't *dis*like her. But don't worry. Father will be ecstatic. And so will Mother. She adores you . . . but not as much as I do.'

They stood for a while next to each other, watching two ducks splash in the pond.

'What are you thinking about?' she finally asked. 'The wedding?'

He turned and grinned. 'Nope. I was thinking about how great my pitching was today.'

'Oh, you're awful!'

He laughed, took her in his arms, and kissed her again. She revelled in the warmth and strength and smell of his body. Good Lord, she thought. If all life is half as wonderful as this moment, how wonderful life will be. . . .

They were both twenty-two.

'I'm jealous, jealous, jealous!' cried Deborah Butterfield, Elizabeth's fourteen-year-old sister. She was in Elizabeth's bedroom in their big brick house on Locust Street in Philadelphia. Elizabeth and her father had returned from the Princeton game in time for a late supper. Now it was nine o'clock. The tall windows were open, and a slight evening breeze fluttered the lace curtains as Elizabeth gave her chestnut hair its nightly hundred strokes with her silver brush.

'Jealous of me? Don't be silly. How can you be jealous of your sister?'

'Easily.' Debbie sniffed. She, like Elizabeth, had the sharp Butterfield nose. It was called a Butterfield nose even though they had inherited it from their mother, who was one of the numerous and aristocratic Burlington clan, so by all rights it was a Burlington nose. 'I'm in love with Lew too. And since I'm three times more beautiful than you, he *should* be marrying me.'

Elizabeth giggled.

'You *are* modest. But don't worry, Debbie. Some day a Prince Charming will come along and sweep you off your feet. That is, until he finds out what a brat you are.'

Debbie, who was wearing a white nightgown, began waltzing around the bedroom.

'And he'll be tall and dark and handsome, and he'll swoon every time he looks at me because I'm so *dev*astatingly attractive. . . .'

'And witty, too. Don't forget witty.'

'Yes, witty. And mysterious . . . I have a deep, dark secret he'll *never* guess.'

'What's the deep, dark secret?'

Debbie stopped waltzing and flopped on the bed. She sighed. 'My secret is that I'm in love with my future brother-in-law. Oh dear. I wish I were older.' She looked tragic. 'Lew Crandall is the most wonderful man in Philadelphia – no, the world! – and who gets him? You.' Sigh. 'It's not fair.'

'Well, don't get *too* upset. Besides, you're going to be in the wedding.'

Debbie brightened. 'Yes, that's *something*. But it won't be till next summer. Why does Father think you have to wait till Lew gets his medical degree?'

Elizabeth put down her brush, and now it was her turn to look tragic.

'Oh, he says marriage will "distract" Lew from his studies, which is silly. Actually, it's worse than silly. I think it's rotten of him.'

Debbie got off the bed and came over to her sister's dressing table. 'Well, a year's not *that* long,' she said.

'A year's forever.'

'Have you let him kiss you?'

Elizabeth frowned and started brushing again. 'That's none of your business.'

'Bet you have.'

Debbie looked smugly worldly-wise. Her sister gave her a smack on the tail with her hairbrush.

'You *are* a brat!'

Debbie giggled and skipped across the room to the door.

'Liz has kissed Lew-ew,' she sang. 'Liz has kissed Lew-ew!'

'Don't you dare sing that around Mother!'

'Oh, I wouldn't *think* of it!' said Debbie, all mock innocence at the door. She stuck out her tongue, then skipped out of the room, singing, 'Liz has kissed Lew-ew, Liz has kissed Lew-ew. . . .'

Elizabeth gave up brushing, since she had lost count of the strokes. She put the brush down on the dressing table and stared moodily into the mirror. A year! It sounded like a century, but her father had been adamant.

A whole year!

She thought of that thing she had felt harden against her that afternoon when Lew had kissed her. What in the world was it? Did it have something to do with kissing?

She had often toyed with the idea of sneaking into her father's library downstairs and looking at the big book on the third shelf. The book on anatomy. One of her classmates at Miss Devon's School had whispered that they ought to look at her father's anatomy book because it was supposed to have drawings. . . .

Well, why not look? Why shouldn't she know? This ridiculous conspiracy of silence about a subject that obviously was important, and certainly was fascinating. . . .

She straightened, and her face in the mirror frowned with determination. Yes, why not look? In fact, why not look now?

She turned and listened. The house was still, but it was too early for her parents to have gone to bed. She would wait. . . .

Two hours later, she pulled the heavy book from the shelf. Her hands were trembling as she set it on the table and opened it. The oil lamp spilled its soft light on the pages as she turned them. The Ear. The Eye. The Nose. The Throat. The Heart. The Lungs.

The Organs of Reproduction.

She stared at the drawings, amazed and slightly sickened.

So *that's* what was there. . . .

She heard the library door open and looked up to see her father. He was wearing a velvet bathrobe.

'I thought I heard someone . . .' he began. Then he saw the book. He came across the room, looked down at the page then looked up at his daughter. He raised his hand and slapped her. She cringed and stepped back, holding her cheek. Her father had never struck her in his life, and it was the action that hurt rather than the slap.

'I've always trusted you,' he said softly, as he closed the book. 'I've left you and Lew alone because I think that is proper. I've fought with your mother about constant chaperones, because I think that is cruel to young people. But *this* . . .'

'What have I done wrong?' she said.

'Do I have to tell you? Do I have to lock this room?'

'But Father, why can't I *know?* Isn't it natural? Isn't it God's way?'

He glared, and for a moment she thought he was going to strike her again.

'My daughter will be pure in body and mind and spirit till her wedding night,' he whispered. 'And *that's* God's way! Now go to bed. And don't tell anyone what's happened here.'

'No, I *won't* go to bed!' she exclaimed, amazed at her nerve. 'And I refuse to feel like a criminal because of a natural curiosity about something. . . .'

He slapped her again, even harder. She burst into tears.

'Go to *bed!*'

She ran out of the room and up the stairs, almost hysterical. It wasn't fair! She hadn't done anything wrong! All she wanted was to *know*. . . .

She ran in her room, slammed the door, and threw herself on the bed. Lew, Lew, Lew . . . she wanted Lew. . . .

She stared up at the canopy, her eyes swimming. It wasn't fair. . . . She wanted Lew *now*, not a year from now. . . .

It wasn't fair. . . .

Lew, Lew, Lew, my beautiful golden prince. . . .

It wasn't fair. . . .

1

THE GOLDEN PRINCE 1860

1

He came across the letter that was to change his life while searching the attic for a sea shell. It was a blustery December afternoon, and he had a cold. Bored with his chemistry textbooks, Lew had gone to the attic of the big new four-storey house on Rittenhouse Square to look for part of his shell collection. The house had been completed only three months before, having taken over two years to build, and much was still unpacked. Lew was looking for an old carpet-bag in which he had put part of his collection of sea shells before leaving the old house on Spruce Street, the house he had grown up in and much preferred to this new Italianate mansion his mother had built when she became Philadelphia's wealthiest widow. Still, he had to admit the new house had advantages – including the first completely equipped bathrooms to be installed in the city of William Penn – and one of the advantages was its large, airy attic, which was illuminated by several skylights. It was filled with cartons, trunks, and packing cases. He poked around for a while before spotting the trunk in the corner, the battered trunk with his father's name on it. He remembered it and, filled with a sudden nostalgia, went over to look inside. It wasn't locked. He lifted the lid and found it was filled with part of his father's collection of legal texts. Of course. He remembered the argument he had had with his mother about these calf-bound tomes. She didn't want to put them in the new library downstairs because, she had said, they would remind her of the judge and make her melancholy. The real reason, Lew knew, was that she wanted to fill the shelves of the new walnut-panelled room with nothing but deluxe editions of the most fashionable English and French novels. He had thought it callous of his mother – Nicole Louise could be callous – but he had given in. After all, it was her house. Now he felt ashamed that he hadn't made more of a stand. His father had loved these books.

He picked the top one up, blew the dust off, and opened it. On the gilt-swirled inside cover was his father's bookplate: Jefferson Shippen Crandall. What a distinguished career he had had! thought Lew. After all, he could have done nothing with his life, like so many rich men. But Jefferson Crandall, the grandson of one of the Signers of the Declaration of Independence and an heir to a shipping fortune, had read for the law and become one of Philadelphia's leading attorneys. In 1845 he had been named to the Federal bench, where he served with distinction until his death in 1857. A distinguished judge and a wonderful father, thought Lew: what a challenge for him to live up to! He remembered with warm fondness the long hikes his father had taken him on, the fishing trips; even the trip to the Eastern Penitentiary, taken because the judge had wanted his son to see criminals, to see a prison, to see that life even in the best country in the world (for the judge had been an unabashed patriot, as was his son) had its ugly side; and the point had been taken by Lew.

A wonderful father, whose death had caused Lew great anguish. And was the son going to be equally wonderful? Louis de Rochefort Crandall had his serious doubts about that. True, at Princeton everything had seemed rosy. He had gotten good grades, if not the best. He had been popular with his classmates, and certainly he had been the top athlete, which he was proud of. Baseball, boxing, fencing, running – he was one of those fortunate human beings who could do anything physical with superlative ease.

But now he was six months out of college, and everything seemed to be going sour. He had thought medicine would be interesting, but the Philadelphia Academy of Medical Science, where he was just completing his first of two six-month terms, was not only a bore but something of a joke. The professors obviously knew very little about what they professed to teach, and even Dr Butterfield, his future father-in-law, admitted that medicine was 'sixty per cent guesswork'. Did he want to spend the rest of his life in a profession that was mostly guessing, in a profession that seemed to cause more pain and suffering than it cured? He was beginning to wonder.

Then there was his whoremongering, about which he crawled with guilt. Was sneaking down to Mrs Simpson's in South Philadelphia proper conduct for the son of a distinguished judge? Hardly. Yet the rutty lust that seemed to be his constant companion had to have some outlet, and old man Butterfield had been such a stick about making him get his diploma before marrying Elizabeth. . . .

But worst of all, he wasn't sure of what he wanted out of life. He had been given so much, he should have felt supremely lucky. Instead, he felt he wasn't fulfilling his potential. But his potential what? He didn't know. All he knew was that life was supposed to be an adventure. So far, his had been anything but.

He leafed through his father's book. Coke on something dull. And then the letter dropped out.

He picked it up off the floor and examined it. It was beginning to turn yellow; he noticed the U.S. Senate mark on the envelope. He pulled the letter out and opened it. It was dated March 1845 – fifteen years before – and the engraved letterhead read in florid Gothic characters: 'United States Senate, Chambers of the Hon. Simon Cameron of Pennsylvania.' Simon Cameron. The notorious Boss Cameron. Lew felt a queasy turn in his stomach.

The letter was addressed to his father. Lew reread it three times, the implication of its text sinking gradually into his consciousness.

Then he felt his gut slowly twist.

He went downstairs to the ornate first-floor salon to wait for his mother. Lew Crandall didn't know it, but his life was beginning to be an adventure.

Rain or shine, hot or cold, Nicole Louise de Rochefort Crandall never failed to take her afternoon drive through Fairmount Park, the lovely park with handsome waterworks on the bank of the Schuylkill River. She said it reminded her of the Bois de Boulogne, although of course it was not as beautiful. Nothing in Philadelphia was as beautiful as Paris, as far as Nicole Louise was concerned. Although born in New York in 1810, she thought of herself as an *émigrée* and was more French than the French. She had even imported her staff of twelve servants from France because she preferred speaking French (even though English was her native tongue: she claimed that when her father took her from New York back to Paris in 1816, hoping to retrieve his family's lost estates from the returned Bourbons, she had almost totally forgotten her English and had had to relearn it when she came back to New York in 1826. She now spoke with a thick French accent). She also didn't like American servants. She said they didn't know 'their place'. She abominated American cooking.

Philadelphia had returned her dislike. In fairness, when she first came to the town as the bride of the young Jefferson Crandall (who had fallen in love at first sight with the daughter of his Princeton room-mate's impoverished French tutor) Nicole Louise had tried her best to make friends. Hadn't she even abandoned her Catholic religion to make the marriage work? But the City of Brotherly Love disliked foreigners, and Nicole Louise was foreign with a vengeance. She was also ravishingly beautiful, with her black hair, violet eyes, and flawless complexion, and this did little to make the Philadelphia matrons take her to their hearts. Perhaps worst of all, she was 'showy', which was terribly un-Philadelphia. She imported her clothes from France and wore too many jewels. If they had known the cold, roachy rooms she had grown up in, the constant 'making-do' with hand-me-downs and castoffs from the families that had employed her father, they might have had more compassion for her extravagances. But Nicole Louise was sensitive about her impoverished background. When she talked of her family, she conveniently skipped the years of poverty and spoke of her grandfather instead, the glorious Sieur de Rochefort. The Sieur de Rochefort had owned vineyards in Burgundy, a château outside Dijon and another near Tours, an exquisite hôtel in the Faubourg St Germain. He had been a leader of society, an intimate of the queen herself – or so Nicole Louise insisted. Then had come 1789, and the Sieur de Rochefort lost everything, including his head. His son, Nicole Louise's father, had fled to New York to begin forty years of grinding poverty, forty years of surviving by drumming irregular French verbs into the ears of rich American children, forty years of futile dreaming and scheming to get back the great inheritance that had long since been bought by new-rich Napoleonic generals and dukes. After Nicole Louise married the rich Jefferson Crandall, she didn't like to dwell on those forty years. Naturally, her Philadelphia acquaintances came to the conclusion she was not only showy but a braggart and liar as well.

They tolerated her while the judge was alive – they almost had to – but she knew if he died, the city would drop her like a fallen soufflé. For herself, she didn't care. But she couldn't allow her son to be ostracized. Thus, when Jefferson did die she decided on a bold stroke, an act of blazing defiance that, had she any insight into the character of Philadelphian society, she would have seen as the worst possible move to make. She was now very rich: the estate amounted to the then staggering sum of three million. Since the more than doubling of her husband's inheritance had been due to her own shrewd investments in railroad bonds and real estate, she considered it her privilege to splurge some of the capital on her own comfort. She bought two houses on Rittenhouse Square, demolished them (to the howls of conservative neighbours), and put up the four-storey house in the new Italianate style. It had an elaborate cornice, pedimented windows, and was as outrageously 'foreign' as Nicole Louise. But she loved it. Now, as her elegant carriage pulled up in front of it, she looked out the window at the beige stone walls and glowed with pride. She would show them. Three nights hence, on the evening of December twentieth, she was giving a ball for Louis and his fiancée, Elizabeth Butterfield (Nicole Louise insisted on calling her son 'Lou-ee', which Lew hated. Lew liked plain 'Lou', which he Anglicized to 'Lew'). She had sent out a hundred invitations and had received only twenty regrets. They were coming, she knew, mainly because they couldn't afford to snub the Butterfields. But they were also coming out of curiosity to see the new house with its big ballroom in the back that had caused so much gossip, its Bohemian crystal chandeliers, its red velvet portières. She would show them, the bigoted imbeciles.

Guy, her outrider, climbed down from the box to open the carriage door. He was a tall Auvergnat and looked splendid in his shiny boots, cinnamon and green livery (they were Nicole Louise's favourite colours), and top hat. Now he held the door and helped Madame down to the brick sidewalk. Lew, standing at the tall triple-hung window in the salon, watched his mother make her way up the short walk to the entrance and, as always, felt a twinge of pride. She was exasperatingly French, vain and stubborn, but she was a magnificent-looking woman, even at fifty. In her huge green skirt and the sable-lined, black velvet hooded cape, she looked like an empress. As he heard Eugène, the butler, admit her to the cavernous marble entrance hall with its splendid staircase and brass lantern hanging from the coffered ceiling, he told himself to remain cool. But every time he looked at that incredible letter in his right hand, he got hot.

He heard her order tea in the library. Then the click of the tall doors as she went into her favourite room. He waited a moment, then left the salon, crossed the empty entrance hall, and went into the library. She was seated in a black leather Voltaire chair before a snapping fire, her Siamese cat, Hyacinthe, curled in her green taffeta lap, her sleek borzoi, André, dozing at her booted feet. She looked up at her son and smiled.

'Louis, *mon cher fils*,' she said. '*Es-tu encore enrhumé?*'

'The cold's better,' he said, forcing the conversation into English, just as she always tried to force it into French.

Nicole Louise had raised her son to be bilingual, which Lew didn't mind. She had also tried to raise him to be binational, which he minded very much. She was determined her son would be essentially French. Her son was even more determined to be American. Now he came up to her chair and handed her the letter.

'I found this in the attic,' he said quietly. 'Did you ever see it before?'

She took it with her ring-heavy hand and examined it. Her face became expressionless. She handed it back.

'Perhaps. I can't remember. This was sent to your father fifteen years ago.'

'Let me read it – to refresh your memory.' He opened the faded stationery.

'My dear Jefferson,

I have received your bank draft for ten thousand dollars, which will be placed in the Party's general fund. As we discussed, I will now proceed to ensure your appointment to the Federal bench in Philadelphia. With your distinguished record in the legal profession, I foresee no difficulties with either the President or my colleagues in the Senate. I predict the appointment will be approved within the month.

'As to your suggestion of appointing your cousin, Mr Winant, to the post of Collector of the Port of Philadelphia, I am having more difficulty with that matter. The objection is that Mr Winant is without apparent qualifications. Also, there is the fact that he has not been a regular Party contributor, though, as you pointed out, he is without funds and part of your ten thousand dollar contribution was to be construed as coming from him. The Secretary of the Treasury remains reluctant (he has obligations of his own in Philadelphia) but I will continue to pressure him. As always, your devoted friend, Simon Cameron. P.S.' [and here Lew's voice became harsh] 'P.S. For obvious reasons, I would suggest you destroy this correspondence. S.C.'

Lew looked up from the letter.

'Father got his judgeship in the spring of forty-five,' he said. 'Cousin Andrew became Collector of the Port the following year and died six years later a rich man.'

'So?' said his mother. 'What are you trying to say?'

'I can see why he wanted Father to burn the letter: there were a lot of strings attached to that ten thousand dollars.'

'But my dear Louis,' she laughed, 'this happens all the time! You're a sophisticated young man – surely you know this! It's not something one talks about, but it's done. I can tell you're shocked, but there's no reason to be. This is politics. And your father was an excellent judge, wasn't he?'

'Yes . . .'

She shrugged. 'So it cost him ten thousand dollars to get what he wanted, and the people got what they *say* they want – an honest judge. Everyone came out ahead.'

'But ten thousand dollars is a fortune! You could buy the Presidency for ten thousand!'

'Simon Cameron's price is very high, but it was worth it. Now throw that letter in the fire and forget it. Something that happened fifteen years ago is hardly of any consequence now.'

Lew folded the letter and put it in the pocket of his well-cut checkered trousers. His mother picked up the edition of the *Argus* that Eugène had placed on the brass trivet by the fire and perused the ads on the front page, evidently dismissing the subject of the family honour from her mind. 'Are you taking Elizabeth to the Academy of Music tonight?'

She looked up to see that her son had left her side and gone to the door. She frowned.

'Louis!'

He turned and looked at her.

'You are being very rude,' she said, 'and more than a little stupid.'

'You asked Senator Cameron to the ball Saturday night,' said Lew, his voice still quiet. 'Did he accept?'

'Of course. He's even bringing the mayor of Harrisburg. Simon Cameron remains a dear friend of mine, as he was of your father's.'

'He's also the biggest thief in the Republican Party. If we're to judge people by the company they keep, then my father doesn't look quite so honourable any more, does he?'

She stiffened.

'Your father was a fine man! I will not tolerate hearing his memory slurred this way....'

'If he'd buy a judgeship,' interrupted Lew, his voice rising, 'and buy Cousin Andrew a licence to steal money – which is what that job is – what else did he buy? How honest a judge could he have been when he's supposed to destroy the letter that tells him he's got the job?'

'This is absurd! Your father only did what he had to do to get the Federal bench. You're not only being ridiculous, you're being unbearably self-righteous.'

'And you're being unbearably casual!' he shouted. 'Don't you realize what my father meant to me? And now I find out that my great god of a father had clay feet. I'm not feeling self-righteous: I'm feeling *sick*.'

He opened the door and left the room, slamming the heavy mass of carved walnut with its gleaming brass knob behind him.

His mother stared at the door, her luxuriant black brows raised in an attempt to mask her shock and anger with hauteur. Then she eased back in the chair, stroking Hyacinthe's silky back. After a while, her face relaxed into a smile.

'*Pauvre garçon*,' she told the cat. 'He thinks he must make this great show of wounded pride to protect his honour. Men!' She shook her head, then held Hyacinthe up to her cheek. 'Oh well, it will all pass in time. He'll grow up. *Mon petit, as-tu faim? Hm? Tu veux ton lait maintenant?*'

Hyacinthe's tongue reached out and licked her cheek. Yes, he was hungry. Hyacinthe was always hungry.

The pretty, plump woman's pink tongue reached out and licked the smooth skin of the young man's belly, then moved up to his chest, which had a light carpet of golden hair. Irene loved the taste of this man's skin. Some men tasted of dirt and sweat, but this golden god tasted clean and good, and was there any taste better than fine human skin? The only problem was, he wasn't responding. He was lying on the rickety bed in the small bedroom on Mrs Simpson's second floor, staring at the cracked ceiling, lost in one of his moods.

She pulled in her tongue and rested her head against his arm, arranging her fat, beautiful breasts so that the left one squished against his naked side.

'You've only got fifteen more minutes,' she said.

'I know.'

'What's the matter with my Lew?'

'Your Lew's feeling like a horse's ass.'

She looked down his flat belly at his organs. 'You're built like a horse, honey. Did you know my father had a horse with a thing fifteen inches long? Imagine that!'

'And you measured it, I suppose.'

She giggled. 'I thought about it.' She screwed her finger in his navel and turned it slowly to the right, then to the left. 'Now are you going to tell Irene why you feel like a horse's ass?'

'Oh, it's something about my father. Something that happened a long time ago, and I just found out about it this afternoon.'

'Did he do something bad?'

'Well, that's the question. My mother obviously doesn't think it's bad, but I do. Or did. Now, I don't know.'

'What was it? Or don't you want to tell me?'

He hesitated, then thought, Why not? 'He bribed a politician to get something he wanted – not only for himself, but for his drunk, no-good cousin. It really was a political contribution, not a bribe, but it still stinks. I never thought he'd do something like that. And that's why I feel like a horse's ass. Live and learn.'

'What's a bribe to a politician? Everybody does it.'

'Exactly. But one doesn't like to think one's father is "everybody". At least I don't.'

She sat up. 'But why blame your father? It wasn't his fault. It was the politician's fault.'

He looked at her sceptically. 'That's a nice rationalization.'

'A what?'

'My father *gave* the money. So he's as wrong as the man who took it.'

'Oh pooh. I don't believe that. If you have an ache, you go to a doctor. You pay him to give you the pill you need.

It's the same with politicians. You want what they have to sell, you buy it. It's simple.'

'But a judgeship shouldn't be for sale!'

'But it is.' She reached to the bed table, where, standing in a blue and white china bidet, was a bottle of cheap perfume labelled 'Honeymoon Love Drops'. 'If it's wrong that it's for sale, it's not the buyer's fault, it's the seller's fault.' She dabbed a few Honeymoon Love Drops on her fingers, raised her left arm, and smeared the perfume on the hair in her armpit. 'I sell sex,' she went on, 'but people don't say you're wrong for buying it. They say *I'm* wrong for selling it. So shouldn't it be the same with politicians?'

Lew watched her Rubenesque body with awakening interest.

'You know, you have a point,' he said. 'If my father *had* to buy it, I shouldn't be so upset, should I? It's Simon Cameron's fault.'

'Oh my God, was *he* the politician? No wonder your father had to pay up. I wouldn't let Cameron touch my left tit unless he paid cash first.'

Lew laughed and reached over, putting his arms around her plump waist and pulling her back down on top of him.

'Put that perfume away.'

'Oh, you're waking up? It's about time.'

He started kissing her, revelling in her cheap smell and her expensive, expansive flesh. Her huge breasts and round thighs were the incarnation of thousands of his teen-age dreams, and now that her whorehouse cynicism had erased his father's guilt from his mind, his constant companion – lust – returned with full force. It occurred to him that Irene had said essentially the same thing his mother had. But Lew was always leery of his mother's French cynicism, while Irene's variety seemed earthily fresh. Moreover, he *wanted* to exonerate his father: and he was beginning to see a way to pay back the man he now considered his father's corrupter.

His mouth moved down to suck her huge nipples as his fingers dug into her plump buttocks.

'Mm,' purred Irene, eyeing the clock on the wall. 'Seven minutes left.'

Lew rolled over on top of her and straddled her, his throbbing penis jutting out below his belly like the bowsprit of a Yankee clipper. She looked up at him and smiled. 'Well, let's say ten. Three minutes on the house for an old customer.'

2

Elizabeth Butterfield finished the last 'unison' movement of the second Chopin sonata and got up from the piano thinking a word she didn't sare say aloud in front of her parents. Lew was late – almost an hour late! They had missed half the concert at the Academy of Music, and she was furious at missing the Beethoven. Now she snatched her fan from the top of the rosewood Pleyel piano and went to the front window of the parlour to look out at gaslit Locust Street. Her father, who had been listening attentively in his chair by the fire, applauded.

'That was beautiful, Elizabeth,' said Dr Butterfield, who came from a musical family and was himself an accomplished violinist. 'But it's strange music for Chopin, isn't it?'

'Very,' she said tersely. The street was empty.

Debbie, who was working on a quilt with her mother, snickered.

'Liz has been stood up,' she sang. 'Liz has been sto-od u-u-up!'

'You shut up, loudmouth!'

'Elizabeth!' clucked her mother, Hermione Butterfield. 'That's no way to talk to your sister!'

'Well, she *is* a loudmouth,' retorted Elizabeth, opening her fan and fluttering it angrily, trying to cool her face. She was a tall, thin girl whose rich chestnut hair had been slicked back from her narrow face with a shell comb. Then it reversed its direction to cascade down in a series of thick curls. It was slightly out of date now, but she liked the look because it filled her face out and she knew her features were a shade too sharp – especially her Butterfield nose. Still, she had felt beautiful that evening as she put on her new white dress for the concert. Now, with Lew nowhere in sight, she felt ugly, hurt, and furious. She lifted the lid of a white china confectionary jar and popped a chocolate in her mouth.

'You'll get pimples!' called Debbie gleefully.

Elizabeth resisted an impulse to jerk her sister's curls.

'Deborah, stop teasing,' said her mother. 'I'm sure there's some perfectly good reason why Lew is late.'

'Bet he's out with another girl,' trilled Debbie, and Elizabeth rolled her eyes wearily.

'Nonsense,' said Dr Butterfield. 'Lew is a gentleman.'

'Lots of gentlemen have other girls, even when they're married.'

'Deborah!' gasped her mother. 'What a dreadful thing to say! I have half a mind to send you straight to bed.'

'Well, it's true,' sniffed Debbie cautiously.

'Nevertheless, it's not something ladies say, though you certainly wouldn't qualify as a lady tonight! Now, mind your manners.'

'Yes, Mamma.'

Waiting for her mother's eyes to return to her quilting, she stuck her tongue out at Elizabeth, then went back to her sewing. Elizabeth pretended to ignore her by turning back to look again at the street. Where *was* he? How could he be so rude? Anxiety swept over her as she wondered if he were down in Moyamensing with one of those 'women'. Sarah Bramwell had whispered to her that her brother Ben, who was Lew's best friend, had gotten drunk one night recently and told his horrified sister that he and Lew Crandall had been to Mrs Simpson's. Well, it was possible it might have been male braggadocio – particularly in the case of Ben, who was hardly a lady-killer – but it just as possibly was true. Elizabeth knew many of the young men in town went to the 'houses' in South Philadelphia, and she knew why. If she were a man, she'd probably go herself, though it was maddening that her sex was supposed to adhere to the code of 'respectability' while the young bucks got away with paying it lip service. She had an excellent mind – as good as any man's she knew of – why should she remain ignorant of something that was so obviously natural? Why should God's method of reproducing the race be a subject no woman was supposed to discuss or even think of? Why should she have to feel ashamed of the desire she had in her body to touch Lew, caress him, kiss him? Wasn't it natural? Oh, she knew about unwed mothers and all that, but still there was something suffocatingly hypocritical about the way her world regarded the world's way of conquering time. She would never forget those slaps her father had given her for looking in the anatomy book.

Since that night, their relationship had returned to its former closeness. She knew her father respected her intelligence, and she even suspected he had come to regret his attitude (to her surprise, he had even continued to champion her against her mother's demands that she be constantly chaperoned when with Lew. 'The girl's engaged!' he had said. 'And if she's got sense enough to get a husband, she's got sense enough to behave with him.') But though things had returned to normal, she would resent those slaps till her dying day. They were badges of inferiority. Lew could go to Mrs Simpson's and get away with it. But if she so much as opened an anatomy book – ! It was infuriating and insulting, and the result had been to strengthen her determination to try to make a career for herself in music.

Her heroine was Clara Schumann, the celebrated pianist and widow of the composer who had died four years previously. Frau Schumann had conquered Europe with her keyboard mastery, becoming the first woman to do so. Well, Elizabeth couldn't be a lawyer or a doctor or a politician.

She couldn't go into business, she couldn't vote, and she couldn't even look in an anatomy book. But she could try to be America's Frau Schumann. Thank God she had inherited talent from her father's musical family, a talent that her teacher, Professor Ernst Schlessing (who had studied with Czerny and had actually met Beethoven) said was very good. Her father had encouraged the talent, buying her the best piano available, even playing chamber music with her and other musicians when she became accomplished enough. Whether Dr Butterfield would encourage her to become a professional pianist – to appear in public, for money! – she wasn't sure of, as she wasn't sure of her own ability to do it. She hadn't told her father she was toying with the idea, but she had told Lew. He had thought the plan splendid, and for this she adored him even more. How many men would be willing to have their wives try for a public career? He was unique – a wonder.

He was also maddeningly late. She looked at her handsome diamond engagement ring and told herself to be patient. She popped another chocolate in her mouth and stared out the window (whenever she was mad, she ate. It was miraculous that she stayed thin). Nothing except the leafless branches of the trees writhing before the December wind, groping at the gaslights. And then she heard the clip-clop of hooves on cobblestones, and a hack pulled up in front of the house. Lew jumped out and ran toward the door.

'He's here!' she exclaimed, sticking her tongue out at her sister. 'I *wasn't* stood up and you *are* a brat!'

She ran through the double doors into the foyer and unlatched the front door even before he could ring the bell. The wind gusted in as he hurried inside, taking her in his arms and kissing her. She wanted to cry with joy until she smelled the Honeymoon Love Drops.

'Sorry I'm late,' he was saying, 'but I went over to Independence Square to take a look at the rally and lost track of the time. . . .'

She had backed away, staring at him, trying to fight down her anger, which was welling again. How dare he lie so glibly? The cheap perfume – he stank of it! She closed her eyes, telling herself she had to be realistic, she mustn't show her anger and jealousy, she must ignore the insult to her. Then she opened her eyes and glared at him.

'If you're ready, we can still catch the second half of the concert,' he went on, wondering why she was looking at him so strangely. Then he thought of the perfume. God, had she smelled it? The Honeymoon Love Drops! It was so wonderfully tacky, he wanted to laugh despite his fear of having his clandestine sex life suddenly exposed. But the look on Elizabeth's face indicated laughter wouldn't be appreciated.

'It's too late for the concert,' she replied coolly. 'Why don't we go back to the rally? I'd like to hear the mayor speak.'

His face brightened as he realized that she wasn't going to make a scene. He loved Elizabeth, but she had a temper.

'Not a bad idea! It's a real show – the whole town's there.'

'Then let's go.'

He helped her on with her cloak, stuck his head in the parlour to say hello to her parents, then escorted her out to the cab. 'Independence Square,' he said to the hackman. Then he climbed inside after Elizabeth and took her in his arms, trying to kiss her. She pushed him away.

'What's wrong?' he asked.

'You reek of something I *assume* isn't eau de cologne,' she snapped, forgetting her resolve not to bring the subject up.

'Well, it *is* cologne. My cousin gave it to me last Christmas.'

'Oh, stop lying. I know where you've been and why you're late. I *suppose* I don't blame you for going down there, but I hate lies.' She turned to look at him. 'Are you going to lie to me when we're married? Is that the sort of relationship we're going to have? If it is, maybe we should forget the whole thing.'

He took a deep breath and sank down in the seat. He had turned red, and felt crawly with misery. The brim of his top hat caught on the back of the seat, which tilted the hat over his forehead.

'Caught,' he said.

'I know you men think it's howlingly funny, and I suppose

it has its humorous side, though I can't say *I'm* amused. . . .'

'It's not funny.'

'I'm glad to hear you think so. I don't intend to be a nagging wife, but Lew' – and her voice became less harsh, more warm, almost plaintive – 'it's so beneath you. It makes you so *dirty*. I always want to be proud of you, because I think you're the most wonderful man on earth. But how can I be proud of you when I think of you being with one of those disgusting women?'

'She's not disgusting.'

'Oh, there's just *one*?'

'Yes. She's smart and funny. And how did you find out, anyway?'

'Ben Bramwell talks too much when he drinks.'

'Ben. I should have known. The big mouth.'

'See? You *do* think it's a joke! Oh, damn you – and damn men!'

He sat up, amazed to hear her say 'damn'.

'When did you start talking like a sailor?'

'Since I became engaged to one! It makes me furious that I have to be a vision of purity while *you* can run around town like a tomcat and get away with it. The whole rotten thing's so hypocritical.'

He reached over and took her hand again. 'I know, but don't hate her. She was a great help to me tonight.'

'A help? How?'

'She helped me see what I have to do to a certain politician.'

'Who?'

'You'll find out Saturday night. And meanwhile, why don't we make up?'

She said nothing. He leaned over and kissed her cheek.

She moved her face away. 'The next time you feel you need "help" from a woman, why don't you come to me? That's what a wife's supposed to be for.'

'You're not my wife yet.'

It was so simple, so obvious – and so true. She deflated. She wasn't his wife. She couldn't give him what he needed.

'Oh Lew, let's get married *now*,' she said suddenly. 'Let's not wait till June. I'll lose you if we wait till June!'

'You won't lose me – that's silly. And your father says . . .'

'I know what Father says, but he's wrong! We love each other and we should be married *now*, so you'll come to me instead of going down to South Philadelphia.'

'You worry too much about that.'

'Well, shouldn't I?'

'All right, I swear I won't do it again.'

'That's not the point! I don't want you to take vows that you'll hate me for the minute you get those . . . urges again. *I* get the urge, for heaven's sake! I want us to be able to . . . to satisfy each other that way.'

He looked at her in wonderment, never dreaming that Elizabeth had the same animal instincts he agonized over in himself.

'*You* get the urge?' he asked.

'Well, of course, It works both ways, you know.'

'But you're a lady!'

'Oh, that word! I've come to hate it! Yes, I'm a "lady", but does that mean I'm not built the same way every other woman is? The whole thing is not only hypocritical, it's so amazingly stupid! It absolutely dumbfounds me, the assumptions men make about women and women make about men. It's a miracle babies ever get born in Philadelphia!'

He laughed. 'But they do, thank God. All right: I'll talk to your father Saturday night at the ball. If I can get him to agree to it, we'll get married . . . well, next month?'

She turned, her face suddenly radiant. 'Oh yes, next month! The sooner the better!'

'Do you have that urge *now*?' he whispered mischievously.

'I'd be lying if I said no,' she whispered back.

'We could go to a hotel – the Continental, maybe.'

She was tempted. Very tempted. But she shook her head. 'No. Next month.'

He took her in his arms and kissed her. This time she didn't push him away.

Independence Square was jammed.

'There must be five thousand people here,' said Elizabeth in an awed tone as she looked out the cab window at the sea of burning torches. In the distance, in front of Independence Hall, a wooden platform had been put up to seat the dignitaries, and she could see the small figure of Mayor Henry, who was addressing the throng. There were many hand-printed placards in evidence bearing such slogans as 'Save the Union!', 'Sesechies Are Traitors!' and 'Abolish the Evil!' A few other signs announced different opinions: 'States' Rights', 'Niggers Aren't Worth a War', and so forth. The crowd was quiet, straining to hear the distant voice of the mayor, but there was tension in the air.

'You'd better stay in the cab,' said Lew.

'Why? I can't hear anything. Let's get closer.'

And before he could remonstrate further, she was out of the cab. He got out his side, told the cabby to wait, then hurried to catch up with his fiancée, who had already started into the crowd. He could see now that the crowd was a mixed bag socially, as was to be expected. Well-dressed men and women in furs were squeezed beside working-class types huddled in shawls and homespun coats, shivering against the gusty north wind.

Lew took Elizabeth's arm and whispered, 'Don't go too far. I don't like the look of this bunch.'

'But I can't *hear*,' she insisted, wriggling between two black men who looked at her with curiously cold eyes. In a few minutes, they had shoved their way almost twenty feet into the crowd, at which point the sea of humanity became so thick they could go no further. They stopped and listened.

'And what better place than here at the very birthplace of our nation,' the mayor was shouting, 'where eighty-four years ago the Declaration of Independence was signed and the Liberty Bell rung signalling to the world the creation of a nation dedicated to the principles of liberty and equality – what better place than here for us to reaffirm our dedication to those noble principles and raise our voice to God in one mighty shout, crying "We will not tolerate slavery for the black man! We will not tolerate this evil to exist on our soil!" '

He paused for applause, which he got. The crowd, so quiet, suddenly burst into a cheer, though it was not unanimous. Lew noted a group of men not far from them who remained silent. He judged them to be from the south wards.

'This coming Saturday,' the mayor went on after the noise subsided, 'the South Carolina Legislature is meeting to vote on a bill of secession from the Union. Can there be any doubt as to the outcome of this meeting? South Carolina has sworn that if the nation elected Mr Lincoln, she would renege on the Constitution and secede! And I say to you, ladies and gentlemen, that if South Carolina commits this act of treason, she must take the consequences! Our forefathers did not write the Constitution to have it torn up by selfish slaveowners. . . .'

A burly man behind Lew suddenly cupped his hands around his mouth and yelled, 'Niggers ain't worth a war!'

Mayor Henry stopped as people turned to stare at the shouter. There were some angry mumbles of 'Tell him to shut up,' 'Who's he?' Elizabeth gave the man a haughty stare and said, 'That was a repulsive remark.' The man looked at her as another voice, closer to the speaker's platform, yelled, 'If South Carolina wants slaves, it's no one's business but her own!'

Mayor Henry raised his hands to quiet the hubbub.

'Someone says South Carolina has the right to do what she wants!' he cried. 'But is this true? Doesn't Saint Matthew say, "If thy right eye offend thee, pluck it out and cast it from thee, and if thy right hand offend thee, cut it off"? Slavery offends me, sir, and I say cut it off! South Carolina offends me. . . .'

But he was being drowned out by the noise. Chants of 'Niggers aren't worth a war' were being met with opposing cries to shut up. The opposers were in the majority, but it was quickly evident the chanters were organized and part of a planned attempt to break up the antislavery rally. Lew grabbed Elizabeth's hand and started pulling her to the rear.

'Wait a minute!' she cried.

'Shut up.'

'But I want to see it!'

The big man behind them stopped Lew's progress. He grinned and said, 'Let her see the fight, nigger-lover.'

'There's not going to be any fight.'

'The hell there ain't!'

And he smashed his fist into Lew's nose, sending him flying back into Elizabeth, almost knocking her over. There were screams from the bystanders. Lew got to his feet, his nose starting to trickle blood. He took off his top hat and lowered his head. Then he charged into the man, holding his hat up to cover the man's face and blind him as his skull rammed into his belly. The man 'oofed' and staggered as the crowd cheered. Then, roaring, 'Son of a bitch!' the man grabbed Lew's neck in a hammerlock and jerked him around and down, forcing him to his knees as he plowed his hairy fist into his eyes.

'Stop it!' screamed Elizabeth, but just then her fiancé grabbed the man's ankles and jerked them from under him. The man fell down as Lew rolled over backward on top of him. Then with a speed that amazed and thrilled the onlookers, he got to his feet on the man's belly, jumped in the air, and landed with both feet full force on his enormous gut. The man roared like a gored bull as the crowd, which had quickly chosen Lew's side, cheered. Lew stepped off and picked up his top hat, which he dusted. His left eye was black and his nose was bleeding badly now, dripping blood onto his snow-white shirt front, but he was grinning.

'Pick on someone your own size,' he said, glowing inwardly at his bravura. He turned to give Elizabeth his arm when someone yelled, 'Watch out!' Instinctively, he ducked and turned. The man had gotten to his feet. Lew handed Elizabeth his hat and raised his fists in the classic boxing stance as the crowd pushed back to give the two men room. Other brawls were going on elsewhere, because the rally was turning into pandemonium, and Mayor Henry had given up any attempt to make himself heard. In the distance, police whistles were shrilling. But Lew was oblivious of all that. Whereas he was cautious enough to avoid a fight, once the lines were drawn he was in his element. He was not indifferent to the great slavery question that was tearing the country apart at the seams. At Princeton there had been many arguments over it, and he had sided with the Northerners against the Southern students (many of whom brought their personal slaves north to college with them). But while intellectually he agreed with Mayor Henry that slavery was an evil, emotionally he wasn't sure it was worth going to war over. However, right now he wasn't thinking of slavery or secession or the Constitution. It was the thrill of action that was making him glow, and it wouldn't have mattered if their political positions had been reversed: he was on stage. He had always adored the theatre and had at one point even toyed with the idea of becoming an actor – though his shocked father had made him swear not to. Still, he had a streak of the ham in him. Now he was conscious of all eyes on him, conscious his 'audience' was rooting for him, and he was galvanized. He could feel every muscle in his body tense; his mind was amazingly clear. He was not an enormously vain man, but he owned eyes and mirrors and knew he was good-looking. Now, despite his black eye and bloody nose, he knew he never looked better. He was David confronting Goliath. Even more to the point, he was cock strutting his feathers before his hen. He knew Elizabeth was rapt.

He danced around the furious man, who kept turning like a lumbering bear. Finally the bear lunged, his hammy fists smashing out at his elusive prey. It was what Lew had expected. Trained boxer that he was, he easily ducked the fists, darted in and under and ploughed his right fist into the man's mouth while his left clobbered his stomach. Then, like lightning, he was out again, dancing, dancing, while the man bellowed and stumbled, putting one hand to his bloody mouth. The hand pulled out a yellow tooth and held it up.

'You little prick!' roared the bear, and the wives blanched. 'I lost a toof!'

Wham! Lew was in again, his fist aiming at the vulnerable mouth, finding its bloody target. The man swung wildly, this time his left fist hitting its mark, delivering a hard cuff to Lew's ear. Out again, dancing, dancing, dancing, the ear stinging and ringing, the nose bleeding, sweat flying from his face despite the cold, his mind elated, the wine of action making him drunk, his wrinkled tail coat flapping. He waited for the opening, then ploughed in for the knockout blow. His fist smashed into the man's nose and he felt crunching cartilage. Goliath staggered back, moaning, his hands to his face. He bumped into the crowd, and his legs gave out. He slumped down on his rear, leaving him in a ridiculous sitting position, staring at David with hurt incredulity. The onlookers burst into cheers: they loved it. Like Lew, they too had forgotten slavery and secession and were lost in admiration at the spectacle that has always dazzled Americans, the athlete in action.

They crowded around Lew, clapping his back, pumping his hands, cheering him in a babble of love. He found a handkerchief and wiped his dirty face, grinning, loving it. Elizabeth pushed through and threw her arms around him, kissing him: he loved that too. Then, somehow, they made their way out of the crowd back to the hack. By now, police were everywhere, trying to bring some order to Independence Square, but it seemed a lost cause. Everyone was shouting, running, fighting, throwing torches, banging one another's heads with placards. Lew took a look back as he held the door for Elizabeth.

'If South Carolina could see this,' and he laughed, 'she'd think twice about seceding.'

Then he was inside, next to Elizabeth, and the hack was clip-clopping away from the battleground, headed for Locust Street.

'You were wonderful!' She glowed.

'I know it.' He grinned.

'Aren't you modest? But you *were* wonderful. I never knew you were so good!'

'Middleweight champion at Princeton,' he puffed, holding the handkerchief to his bloody nose.

'I loved it when that big bully landed on his . . .' She stopped and lowered her voice, a look of confusion on her face. 'Lew,' she whispered, 'what's a "prick"?'

He went into such convulsive laughter that she looked amazed.

'Well? What *is* it?'

'Wait till next month and you'll see!' He guffawed.

She understood and turned red.

'Oh,' she said, remembering the sketch in her father's anatomy book. She sat up straight and stared out the window, trying to think pure thoughts.

It was difficult.

3

Nicole Louise de Rochefort Crandall didn't give a damn about the sufferings of the slaves in the South or preserving the Union or noble principles, and she couldn't understand why so many Americans did. What she did give a damn about was her son, Lou-ee. The following Saturday at six o'clock in the evening, she sat at her chintz-flounced vanity in her green silk-lined dressing room off her bedroom and thought about Louis as she held a diamond eardrop to her ear – an eardrop so pendulous it almost touched her naked shoulder. It was fashionable but wrong, she decided, handing it back to her Strasbourgeoise maid, Liselotte, who weighed two hundred pounds and had an incipient moustache.

'Let's try the emeralds,' she said in French. 'These people think I'm ostentatious, so I might as well give them something to talk about.'

'Ah, but madame is always dressed in perfect taste!' said Liselotte, replacing the diamonds in the big red velvet jewel case with the de Rochefort coat of arms on the top. 'It is the Pheel-a-del-*phee*-ans who have no taste.'

'That'll be our secret,' replied her mistress, studying her reflection. Louis: headstrong, irritating, and yet irresistible Louis. Getting in a fight in Independence Square like some common guttersnipe! It was monstrous. On the other hand, he had won, and she liked that. It was so important to win in life . . . that was why she thought perhaps he had forgotten that stupid letter (so thoughtless of Jefferson to have kept it rather than burning it! But then, he had often been impractical . . .). Lew had said nothing more about it since Wednesday, and she assumed he'd had his little show of indignation and then decided that, after all, she was right. Louis liked to win, and worrying about moral niceties was not the way to win in life. Still, he was impulsive, and that worried her. He just *might* say something about it to the senator that night, which would be disastrous. She decided she had best go talk to him after she got dressed. It was important that everything go smoothly. After all, with South Carolina having voted for secession that afternoon (the news had appeared in the evening paper), a war seemed even more likely – how *could* these ridiculous Americans fight over slavery? – and she knew Louis would run off to enlist the moment the first shot was fired. True, everyone said the war would last only a few months, but still he might get hurt – killed, even! – and she had to prevent that. Happily, she had a plan; but it depended on Senator Cameron.

'*Les émeraudes, madame*,' said Liselotte, holding out a huge cabochon emerald depending from a diamond star. Nicole Louise took it and held it to her ear. Yes, that was better. She screwed it in place, telling herself she looked radiant and nowhere near fifty. Her chalk-white skin was still smooth, though there were fine crow's-feet at the corners of her eyes which had defied her nightly applications of cold cucumbers. But those eyes! Still lustrous, still captivating! Still eyes that missed nothing. . . .

Of course, she had to admit her neck was showing the effects of time's erosion – there wasn't much a woman could do about necks. But her hair was still raven black (aided by the dye she imported from Paris), and how lovely it looked, arranged so carefully by Liselotte in a great roll that swept from behind each ear down below her neck, creating a glistening hoop of silken jet, while above her smooth forehead the carefully combed part bisected the top of her head in the prevailing fashion. Liselotte was a wonder with hair, and she had topped off her masterpiece with the eight diamond stars the beautiful Austrian Empress Elizabeth had made so popular (with women who could afford them): the stars danced and twinkled down the black Niagara, and every time Nicole Louise moved her head, she had the immense satisfaction of knowing her hair would sparkle and people would *notice*.

'We'll wear the emeralds,' she said to Liselotte. 'Give me the other eardrop.'

She picked up her enormous powder puff and lovingly dusted her chest, admiring her big, smooth breasts, letting a little rice powder cuddle cosily into the ravine of her cleavage. Senator Cameron had always admired her breasts, and they would make a useful weapon tonight. Of course, he owed her favours. Louis didn't know it, but the ten thousand dollars Jefferson had paid to get his judgeship hadn't been the only Crandall money to go to politicians. Jefferson had been a regular contributor to the Democrats, the Whigs, and even, at the end of his life, to the new Republicans. True, after he got his judgeship, he never asked for any direct favours, but he thought it prudent to keep friends, and he never felt any moral qualms about it. So Senator Cameron owed her a favour, and tonight she had one to ask: to arrange for Louis a 'safe' commission in case of war, perhaps in Washington or even Philadelphia. She knew she couldn't stop him from enlisting, but she could arrange for him to be kept away from the front. She wouldn't let him know, naturally: he would be furious. But Nicole Louise was used to deception. She even liked it. Now she stood up, straightening her frilled cotton pantalettes.

'Where's Marie?' she said. 'It's time for the hoop.'

Liselotte lumbered out of the dressing room, calling for her twenty-year-old niece. 'Marie? Marie? *Oú est-elle, la stupide?* Marie?' The cuplrit hurried in from the corridor. 'Ah, Marie! *Comme tu es paresseuse! Sotte! Viens maintenant – vite! Madame est pressée!*'

Nicole Louise came into the bedroom with its thick flowered carpet and gilt bed and went to the centre of the room, where a bizarre ritual took place. First, Liselotte attached the big iron cage around her mistress's ample waist (Nicole Louise had what she thought of as a 'majestic' figure). Then the two maids climbed on high stools flanking Madame. Each taking two long poles, they lifted the first of three horsehair crinolines off the floor and held it over Madame's head. Now, as Madame raised her plump arms, they lowered the crinoline down over her head with the poles and let it drop over the cage. This manoeuvre was repeated with the two other overskirts. Then came the magnificent ball gown that had arrived the week before on the Paris packet. Nicole Louise had ordered it in September from M. Worth in Paris. Though he warned her in a letter that crinolines were on their way out – the Empress Eugénie, who had started the fad to promote the sale of more French dress material, had recently just as capriciously banned them from her court – Nicole Louise didn't care. America was so far behind Europe that she would still be in the vanguard. Besides, she knew she would look stunning in the dress. Made of magenta silk, it was festooned with great swags of black fringe. And when the bodice was buttoned in the back, Philadelphia's richest widow looked formidable indeed, her beautiful shoulders bare, her bosom displayed in all its glory, and her skirt almost six feet in diameter, making her look like a mammoth bell.

'*La rivière*,' she ordered, and Liselotte hurried back to the dressing room to fetch the enormous 'river' of diamonds and emeralds that matched the earrings. When this was in place around her neck, Nicole Louise went to the gilt pier-glass between the windows overlooking Rittenhouse Square to inspect the final product as Liselotte and Marie stood behind her, fussing and admiring.

'*Si belle, si belle*,' murmured Marie, who had a homely red face. '*Madame est éblouissante!*'

Dazzling. Yes, she was, though Nicole Louise. Certainly dazzling enough to overwhelm the senator. And now was the time to make sure Louis didn't ruin her battle plan.

She left the bedroom, walked down the corridor, and knocked on his door.

'Come in,' he called, and she opened the door. He was in his bathroom, shaving, his face covered with lather. Now he turned to look out the door at his mother, who had stopped at the foot of his bed.

'You look spectacular,' he said. 'All the women will be green with envy.'

'Nonsense: they'll all say I'm overdressed, the house is too big, my accent's too thick, and my food is too rich. They always do.'

Lew laughed. He adored his mother's perception, if not her affectations.

'Well, you'll give them something to gossip about.'

'I hope I do.' She came up to the bathroom door, her skirt so big she filled the bottom half of the door space with magenta silk. 'Louis, dear,' she said, dropping her voice to a purr, 'I hope you're not going to give me any trouble tonight with Senator Cameron?'

He looked at her from the corner of his eyes as he scraped his lathered neck with his razor.

'What makes you think I would?'

'That letter you found the other day. You were so upset about it – perhaps rightfully so. It was perhaps . . . well, morally untidy of your father, but we all make *some* compromises in life, and I hope you don't hold it against his memory.'

'No, I don't hold it against his memory.'

'Then you won't say anything to the senator?'

He didn't answer for a moment, continuing his shaving. Then: 'No, I won't say anything to the senator.'

She smiled prettily, drinking in with her eyes this splendid creature she had brought into the world.

'Good. I knew I could trust you. Well, I must go down and make sure Eugène has everything ready. When the guests arrive, you and Elizabeth and I will form the reception line inside the door of the salon. It will be a bore, but it can't be helped. I'll have to think, of something pleasant to say to all those hens. . . . Oh, well,' she sighed. 'It's the price one pays for entertaining farmers.'

Lew put his razor on the broad marble basin and wiped the lather off his face.

'Farmers? The Biddles?'

'Well, grandsons of farmers,' she said, matter-of-factly. 'All these Americans are. We de Rocheforts go back to the thirteenth century.'

'When we were farmers. Or was it highway robbers? I forget.'

'It was highway robbers, but successful highway robbers, and as Monsieur de Balzac says, every great fortune starts with a crime. So don't be so tediously egalitarian, Louis: you have noble blood in your veins, and you should be proud of it. Some day, even . . .' She stopped.

'Some day what?' he asked, drying his face with a towel. He knew what was coming. He'd heard it before.

'Well, you know my dream: to return some day to France and buy back my grandfather's estates. We could do it, Louis: we have the money. You love France as much as I. We could take our rightful place in a *real* society, not a society of farmers like these Philadelphians.'

'You forget two things, Mother: I'm marrying one of these Philadelphia farmers. And *I'm* half Philadelphia farmer. I also happen to love this country as much as France, even if we are a bunch of hicks in your opinion. So,' he dropped the towel over the edge of the bathtub, 'I think you'd better forget that dream of yours.'

She looked at him with cool displeasure.

'Perhaps you'll change your mind some day,' she snapped. 'And pick up your towel.' She turned and rustled her way across the bedroom to the door, which she closed quietly behind her.

Lew watched her leave, then picked up the towel. He never felt more American than when he was with his French mother. She had tried all her life to turn him into a Frenchman, and all his life he had fought her, bending over backward to seem more American than his friends. Nevertheless, the ugly, coarse American xenophobia that had haunted Nicole Louise haunted her son as well. Despite his efforts at being super-American, his classmates at Lawrenceville and Princeton had always called him 'Frog', which had been the cause of numerous fights. Lew won the fights, but it did no good: he was still called Frog behind his back. Finally he had started to accept it, though he was still sensitive about it. It couldn't be helped: he *was* half French, and his mother was right: he loved France as much as America. He was proud of his French heritage. He loved the French language, French food, the French style, all of which was so foreign to the rough-hewn American style of the day. He was a sensual man: he loved elegance and all the romantic trappings of lovemaking as well as sex itself. While he was no snob, he had a sneaking fondness for glamour and power. So he knew there was more of his mother in him than he liked to admit, which was why he instinctively fought her every time she tried to dominate him – which was often. It even occurred to him that one reason he was out to 'get' Simon Cameron – and he had glibly lied to Nicole Louise about that – was not only to salvage his father's honour but also to annoy his mother. Worrying about moral fine points was so American, so un-French. Well, he would show her he was an American.

But he knew that his soul was half French. And as he put on his dress shirt and his annoyance at his mother began to simmer down, he told himself for the hundredth time there was no reason to be ashamed of it.

'So we may have a war!' said the fat man with the round red face and the slicked-down black hair. 'Well, well: what do you think of a war, Senator?'

The tall, skinny man sitting beside him in the carriage looked out the window. It had begun to snow, and the flakes flew by as the carriage raced through the streets of Philadelphia toward Rittenhouse Square. Both men were in evening dress, and Senator Simon Cameron – the senior senator from Pennsylvania, one of the foxiest politicians in the country, and a man who had further confused the already confused Republican Presidential Convention the previous summer in Chicago by presenting himself as a favourite-son candidate – was wearing a buffalo coat. Almost as if God had stamped Cameron's character on his face, he had close-set, foxy eyes that had not missed a trick or an opportunity for almost sixty years. A self-made millionaire who had bought his way into the Senate, Cameron was still known as 'The Winnebago Chief' for having tried to steal land claims from the Winnebago Indians twenty years before. His political crony and right-hand man, Ralph Matoon, admired Cameron extravagantly for everything except the 'Winnebago business'. That was Cameron's one great failure, in Matoon's opinion. After all, the senator had been *caught*.

'I think,' said Cameron, 'that a war will offer interesting opportunities.'

Matoon laughed. 'Goddam, Simon, you said a mouthful there! Whew! And with you bein' Secretary of the Treasury? Well, well! It makes a man sort of drool like a pig and get all itchy, just thinkin' about it!'

The senator gave his forty-eight-year-old sidekick a cool look. Cameron admired Ralph Matoon's instinct for the jugular and his slavish loyalty. He admired the fact that, as mayor of Harrisburg, Matoon hounded, hustled, browbeat, and, in extreme cases, blackmailed every politician in Pennsylvania to do exactly what Simon Cameron wanted. What he didn't admire was Matoon's boorishness.

'Ralph, when will you learn to shut your mouth?'

'Well, hell, Simon, it's just you and me. You know I wouldn't say nothing like that in front of anyone *else*. Hell, no.'

'You've got the diplomatic instincts of a bull elephant in heat, and you know it – particularly when you get drunk, which I don't want you to do tonight. This Crandall woman's invited everyone who's anyone in Philadelphia, so keep sober. Understand?'

'You know you can trust me, Simon. I won't pee in the punchbowl, if that's what you're worried about.'

Despite his annoyance, Simon Cameron chuckled. 'You

fat rascal: that would be a pretty sight!' The beaver lap robe started to slip off his knees, and he pulled it up. 'Besides, I haven't got the Treasury yet.'

'You will, you will! Old Abe can't refuse us. Why, hell's bells, if you hadn't delivered the Pennsylvania delegation at the convention last summer, Abe would still be writing wills in Illinois, and he knows it. Goddam farmer! Won't he be a pretty sight in the White House, though? Whew! I don't figure he knows a fork from a spoon. That ape makes *me* look like Prince Albert.'

'I'll grant you he's not much on social polish, but he's a smart horse trader – and not a bad politician, either. That's why I'm worried. He's mad as a wet hen about the deal I made with his boys at the convention. . . .'

'What's a convention without deals? And he got the nomination, didn't he? Don't see him making any offers to give up the Presidency.'

'He hasn't been inaugurated yet.'

'You know what I mean. Anyway, a deal's a deal. You delivered your votes, which got him nominated, now he's got to deliver you the Treasury. That's only fair.'

'Maybe. But I hear he wants Governor Chase. He thinks Chase's character is better than mine.'

'*Have* to be, Simon!' The fat man grinned and winked.

The senator shot him a look. 'Sometimes you go a little too far, Ralph.'

'Hell, Simon, you know I was just kiddin'. Anyways, Chase is such a pissy-assy teetotalin' puritan, he'd make Saint Peter look sinful. I'm tellin' you, Senator, you've got the Treasury in your pocket. Abe owes it to you, and there ain't no way he can wriggle out of it. Now, the question in my mind is: when you get the Treasury, what are you going to do for your oldest friend? Namely, Ralph Matoon?'

'You're certainly not shy, are you?'

Matoon chuckled. 'I didn't get to be mayor of Harrisburg bein' shy.'

'Mm. Well, Your Honour, what would you like?'

'I'd like to be a senator something awful, Simon. I really would. Why, sometimes I wake up in the middle of the night and get all bawly like a baby, I want that Senate seat so much!'

'You cry in the middle of the night because you see what's sleeping next to you.'

'You mean Mildred?' Matoon laughed so hard he choked. 'Well, you got a point there, Simon! You got a definite point there! My wife sure as hell ain't improved with age. Anyways, gettin' serious now for a minute: what *can* you do for me, Simon? I'd sure like to come to Washington. I'd like that awful bad. I figure there's going to be a lot of action in Washington once the war starts.'

'I'll think about it, Ralph.'

'I want you to think real hard, Simon.'

'I will. But let's get *me* the Treasury first, before we start carving up the pie. Here's the Widow Crandall's. You'll like her, Ralph. She's a Frenchie with tits as big as pillows. Shrewd, too. The judge was rich, but I hear she doubled his fortune dabbling in real estate and railroad bonds.'

'Sounds like my kind of woman. Any chance of some action?'

'Keep your pants buttoned, Ralph. Mrs Crandall's got class. Ever hear of it?'

'Oh, somewhere, I think. Say: that's some house! And it looks like a real shindig! Well, well: I'm glad you wrangled me an invite, Senator. Real glad. Something to tell the homefolks about.'

'If you told the homefolks one *tenth* of what you know, you'd be in jail, Ralph.'

'So would you, Simon.'

The fat man winked as he opened the carriage door. Then, removing the lap robe, he stepped out into the snow and took in the scene. A stream of well-dressed people was dammed by the front door, waiting to push into the crowded front hall of the brilliantly lighted mansion, from which the strains of a jolly polka were emanating. Senator Cameron joined him, and the two politicians waited until the footman tending the door squeezed them through. A second footman took their beaver hats and velvet-collared coats. Then Eugène, the butler, took their invitations and announced them to Nicole Louise, who was standing at the door of the main salon with her son and his fiancée.

'Senator Simon Cameron,' intoned Eugène, his French accent rendering Simon 'See-mon'. 'And His Honour, the mayor of Harrisburg, Monsieur Ralph Matoon.'

'The *Honourable* Ralph Matoon,' whispered His Honour.

'His Honour the *Honourable* Ralph Matoon,' corrected Eugène, wrestling with all those H's.

'My dear Simon,' said Nicole Louise, smiling as she held out her hand. 'I'm so delighted you could come.'

'The pleasure is mine, ma'am. *All* mine,' replied the senator, who, though born in poverty and barely educated, had acquired a veneer of suavity from years spent in politicking. 'Your house is beautiful, you are beautiful, and my cup of joy would be running over if it weren't for the distressing news from Charleston.'

'Ah, but we mustn't let those tiresome Southerners spoil our evening. And this is your friend you wrote me about?'

'Yes, Mayor Matoon of Harrisburg.'

Ralph Matoon, aping his boss, grabbed Nicole Louise's hand and brought it to his mouth as his eyes riveted on her breasts and her diamonds – emblematic of the two things closest to his heart.

'I'm honoured, Mrs Crandall, that you would extend your hospitality to a stranger.'

'But any friend of Simon's is a friend of mine,' replied Nicole Louise, somewhat aghast at the mayor of Harrisburg's wheezy adiposity. 'And this is my son, Louis, and his fiancée, Miss Butterfield. . . .'

Matoon was pumping Lew's hand. 'Well, well, a fine-lookin' young man, yessir! My congratulations, sonny.' Lew didn't much like the 'sonny', but he let it pass as Matoon moved on to Elizabeth. 'And lookee here! A beauty!' exclaimed His Honour. 'A rose in pink without the thorns, eh? Well, I wish you both the best.' He had grabbed Elizabeth's right hand to kiss it, but then he noticed the diamond ring on her left hand and hoisted it as well. 'The engagement ring, I'll wager!'

'Yes. Isn't it lovely?'

'A real shiner! Must have set you back a pile, eh, boy?' He lowered his voice, leaning toward Lew. 'Say, I hear you're enrolled in one of them medical-diploma mills. Now, what would a fine young fellow like you be doin' in one of them butcher shops?'

'I sometimes wonder the same thing myself,' replied Lew truthfully.

'I'd hope so! No money in medicine . . . all a bunch of quacks anyways.'

'My father is a doctor,' said Elizabeth, who had taken an instant dislike to His Honour. Matoon turned red.

'Wouldn't you know? Not two minutes in here, and I've stuck my foot in my mouth already!'

'Such a big foot,' smiled Elizabeth coolly. 'And such a big mouth.'

Matoon looked her over. 'Well now, I guess maybe you've got some thorns after all. Anyways, my apologies. And is that champagne I see bein' passed in the next room?'

'It is,' said Nicole Louise. 'Iced and delicious.'

'Then I'll just waltz in and say my howdy-dos to the waiter. You'll pardon me?'

He waddled into the salon as Senator Cameron diplomatically scratched his nose.

'You'll have to overlook a certain country quality in Ralph,' he said. 'He's a bit of a rough diamond, but his heart's as big as his stomach.'

'Oh, I find him rather quaint,' said Nicole Louise. 'We live in such an age of surfaces, it's refreshing to meet someone who says exactly what he thinks.'

'That's Ralph, for certain.'

'How about you, Senator?' said Lew quietly. 'Do you say exactly what you think?'

The senator looked at him.

'I try. Whether I succeed or not is up to the voter.'

'Then you meant it when you said you found the news from Charleston distressing?'

'Of course. Doesn't everyone find it distressing? South Carolina's voted to secede from the Union. It probably means war over this confounded slavery issue.'

'But to the best of my knowledge, you've never made any reference to the slavery issue in any of your public speeches. Consequently, I'd gotten the feeling you weren't particularly interested in it one way or the other.'

Which was tantamount to accusing a Republican of pro-Southern leanings. The man who had earned his niche in American political history by his immortal definition of an honest politician as one who 'when bought, stays bought' stared at the young man.

'Of course I'm interested in it! And I rather resent the implication I'm not.'

'I see. Well, do you regard it as a moral issue or a political issue?'

'It's both!'

Nicole Louise shot her son a glare, then turned on her smile.

'Now, I refuse to hear any politics tonight. Simon, please help yourself to the champagne. And I trust that later on a fading widow may hope that her most distinguished guest might ask her for a waltz?'

The senator returned his eyes to his hostess and smiled.

'You're far from fading, ma'am. A radiant jewel in the crown of this noble city's society!' He looked back at Lew, and the smile vanished. 'It's too bad your son seems to lack your charm. Excuse me.'

He went into the salon, which was packed with Philadelphia's feathered élite, as Nicole Louise whispered to Lew, 'How *could* you have been so rude to him?'

'It was easy.' Lew smiled. 'And a real pleasure.'

His mother started to say something else, but she saw a pride of Biddles come through the door. She rekindled her smile with some difficulty and turned to greet them.

Benjamin Franklin Bramwell took a fresh glass of champagne from a passing footman and stared with loathing at the huge crystal gas chandeliers depending from the twenty-foot ballroom ceiling with its overwrought moulded-plaster medallions and coving. He hated everything about Mrs Crandall's new house – including Mrs Crandall – except the graceful Philadelphia-crafted furniture and the family portraits. But these came from the old house. The new stuff – the heavy red portières, the huge mirrors, the mammoth ballroom's gilt chairs, the potted palms – he couldn't stomach. It was all excessive, and Ben Bramwell hated excess (except in the consumption of wine and champagne). And the buffet! With its giant silver epergnes loaded with fruit, its banked flowers, its gelatined hams and turkeys, its sorbets, its iced caviar, its cookies and cakes – excess. Mrs Crandall was an excessive French snob, and he hated her for it just as, he knew, she hated him for various reasons. Yet he loved her son, his lifelong best friend, as only a homely, pock-marked, clumsy giant of a man can love a golden prince. Not that the love was sexual. Ben Bramwell's tortured sexuality was the cause of much personal agony, but it was not directed toward his own gender. Ben loved Lew almost as an ideal. Lew was everything Ben wished he were and was resigned to never being: handsome, athletic, popular. Everyone loved Lew Crandall. No one loved Ben Bramwell except Lew.

They had grown up sharing a common worry: their partial foreignness. The Bramwells, like the Crandalls, were a well-known Philadelphia family. But Lew's father had married a penniless French girl, and Ben's grandfather, Amos Bramwell, had fallen in love with a beautiful Jewess, Hannah Rosenberg, the daughter of a German immigrant who had made a small fortune in the loan business. Despite Philadelphia's insular dislike of 'outsiders', it differed from other American cities in that it had a history of successful intermarriage between gentiles and Jews. So the marriage had not caused the comment it might have in New York. But still, the grandchild of this marriage was as aware he was one-quarter Jewish as Lew was aware he was half French. Both boys had come to cope in their own ways with what in later life seemed less of a difficulty than it had earlier, but the shared 'problem' had brought them together and formed an important element in their friendship. Lew loved Ben's warmth, his intelligence (though Lew was smart, he knew Ben was smarter, and admired him for it), his compassion for people. He even loved his social maladroitness and his clumsiness, for Ben was a menace in the geegaw-cluttered parlours of Philadelphia and was always bumping into tables or knocking over statuettes. He was also tongue-tied around women, which amused Lew at the same time that it made him sorry for the anguish it caused Ben. They were opposites in so many ways – someone had once called Lew 'Claret' and Ben 'Burgundy', and there was some truth in the comparison – and yet, as so often happens, the opposites attracted. Lew had no secrets from Ben. Ben had only one secret from Lew, a secret he assumed he would carry unshared to his grave.

He was attracted not to women (nor they to him; he was acutely aware of his homeliness) but to girls. Twelve-, thirteen-, and fourteen-year-old girls, barely formed virgins. In the Philadelphia of 1860, he might as well have lusted after brood mares, and the knowledge that he carried this snake of desire inside him caused him to turn to introspection, masturbation, and, lately, alcohol, all of which compounded the misery. Lew had taken him down to Mrs Simpson's, where he had found passing physical relief with the whores. But he assumed he could never enjoy the domestic tranquillity of married life that was so cherished by his world. He would always be an outsider looking in at other people's happiness.

It made him melancholy and in many ways bitter.

If he was not lovable with his moodiness, occasionally sharp tongue, and lack of polish or looks, he was stilll highly admired, and not only for his considerable fortune. He was strong as a bull. Once, two years before, he had single-handedly lifted a heavy overturned wagon and freed the pinioned driver, an exploit that made all the papers. He was admired for his mind, too, for Philadelphia respected intellect, and it was known he was something of a botanical genius. Five years before, his parents had been killed in a train accident, and Ben and his sister had been taken in by their uncle. Then, two years ago, he had bought a farm on the west bank of the Schuylkill and moved out of his uncle's Locust Street house to live by himself. He built a big greenhouse and filled it with plants. Professors at the university who had visited him spoke in awe of the experiments he was carrying out. Just the previous summer, after graduating with Lew from Princeton, he had gone to Austria to look up an Augustinian monk named Gregor Mendel whose experiments on the sweet pea he had read about in an obscure scientific journal. He had returned in September afire with enthusiasm, talking about 'plant heredity'. No one knew what it was all about, but it was generally conceded that whatever he was doing in his greenhouse was 'brilliant'.

Then there was the Underground Railroad. It was known that Ben's farm was a station for runaway slaves, and that his compassion and generosity had sent many slaves farther north with money in their pockets to find jobs in New York, Massachusetts, or even Canada. Philadelphia might have its share of rabid anti-Abolitionists, but the city had a history of antislave sentiment, sprung mainly from the violent objection of the early Quakers to the South's 'peculiar institution' (in fact, one reason the nation's capital had moved to Washington from Philadelphia was that slave-owning senators didn't wish to be subjected to Quaker pressure in Philadelphia). Ben was admired for helping the black fugitives.

So while there was no rush to his side to talk to him as he stood drinking champagne in a corner of the Crandall ballroom, no one in the crowd failed to nod pleasantly as he or she waltzed past. And few commented on the fact that he had come alone to the ball. Ben was considered 'too bright' or 'too eccentric' to have much interest in women, and he made little effort to change their opinion. But he was lonely, and he had made alcohol his friend. Right now, the champagne was getting to him; and as Mr Rawlinson's String Ensemble segued into Weber's 'Invitation to the Dance', the insistent one-two-three of the music and the sight of the swirling waltzers began dispelling the cloud of gloom from his brain. Yes, Mrs Crandall's house was an abomination, but for Lew's sake he would stop thinking dark thoughts about Nicole Louise and try to put on a cheerful face. He was glad for Lew that his best friend was marrying

Elizabeth Butterfield, who was one of the few women in Philadelphia Ben could stand. She had a first-class mind, played the piano beautifully, and, Ben was sure, would make Lew a good wife. That he himself would probably never have a good wife didn't make him envious. For all his faults, Ben Bramwell was not selfish.

He saw Lew making his way around the crowd of waltzers. When Lew spotted him, he came over and grabbed his arm. 'You big baboon,' he said, 'are you going to stand here and scowl all night?'

'Was I scowling?' Ben blinked.

'You weren't laughing. And I have a bone to pick with you.' He lowered his voice. 'Why the hell did you tell your sister about our going to Mrs Simpson's? She told Elizabeth, who threw a fit the other night.'

'Oh.'

'What do you mean, "Oh"?'

'Well, I was drunk. I'm sorry. You know when I get drunk I don't know what I'm saying.'

'Well, don't get drunk tonight. All I need is for you to get on a chair and tell *everyone*. I'm in enough trouble already, and it's going to be worse before the night's over.'

'Why?'

'I've already got a knife stuck in Cameron, but in a while I'm going to push it in all the way, and Mother's going to hit the ceiling. There'll be lots of fireworks, so stand by.' He looked around. 'Have you seen old man Butterfield?'

'He's on the other side of the room with my aunt.'

'I see him. I've got to soft-soap him into letting us move the wedding up. Thanks to you, Elizabeth's afraid I'll want to hold the reception at Mrs Simpson's.'

'Honest to God, Lew, I'm sorry about that. . . .'

Lew grinned and shrugged. 'Spilt milk now. See you later.'

He continued around the room as Ben took another glass of champagne, marvelling at his friend's ability to shrug off the vicissitudes of life. But then, Lew had always been like that. He was subject to occasional brooding moods, but generally he took things as they came, bouncing back when something tripped him up. Ben wished he were like that, but he was subject to one big brooding mood: life.

As the champagne washed down his throat, he began to slip back into the fog of gloom. It was almost like going home.

Dr Butterfield was standing in front of a Rembrandt Peale portrait of Samantha Crandall, Lew's grandmother, who, in her curls and white lace cap, stared stiffly from the canvas, seeming to disapprove of all this French-style gaiety. Ben's aunt, Mrs Clarissa Bramwell, didn't seem too pleased with it either, although when Lew came up to them she smiled and said, 'Such a gala evening your mother is giving, though I must say the food's a bit rich for me. Have you seen Ben?'

'He's over next to the orchestra.'

Mrs Bramwell looked across the packed room and spotted her burly nephew. She lowered her voice. 'Is he drinking?'

'Oh, not much.'

'Now Lew, you always cover up for my nephew, which you shouldn't do. He drinks far too much, and I worry about him. If only we could find him a nice wife to settle him down! Living out on that lonely farm with all those plants . . .' She made a face. 'No wonder the poor boy tipples! It's bizarre!'

'What's bizarre about plants?' asked Dr Butterfield.

'*Living* with them, of course!' exclaimed the white-haired dowager, who had a reputation for expressing herself outspokenly. 'It's not natural!'

'Adam lived with plants,' said Lew.

'And it was an apple that got him in all that trouble! Don't defend Ben, Lew. I realize he's something of a genius, but geniuses need to settle down, just like everyone else. I tried to get him interested in Agatha Cadwalader, but he expressed no interest at all.'

'It would take a real genius to get interested in her.' Lew grinned.

'Well, I'll admit dear Agatha *is* a bit forbidding . . . she has such unfortunate eyes, poor child . . . so *crossed*. . . . Well, I don't know what to do with Ben. Oh dear, there's

Mr Bramwell taking another glass of champagne! You'll have to excuse me . . . sometimes I feel like a policeman in this family!'

She bustled off to corral her husband as Lew turned to his future father-in-law, whose pipe smoke was helping foul the air of the hot room, which already smelled of perfume mixed with sweat from the overheated dancers.

'Sir, I wanted to talk to you about Elizabeth and me,' he began. The doctor cut him off.

'I know. She's already told me you two want to get married next month. You know my feeling about that: you have no business getting married until you get your diploma. If I had my way, you'd wait until your practice was established, but I know I'm not going to get my way, Elizabeth being so headstrong. I still say you should wait till June.'

'By next June we may be at war.'

The doctor took the pipe from his mouth.

'Aye, I thought you'd bring that up, and I won't deny the news looks bad. But Lew, don't you see that's even more of a reason for you to wait? I don't want to sound gloomy, but there *is* a possibility –' He stopped, realizing he wasn't being very tactful.

'You don't want your daughter to be a widow,' said Lew. 'That's a cheery prognosis. But if you'll pardon me for saying this, I think you're being a little selfish.'

'Selfish? How so?'

'If it turns out that I do get killed, I'd like to have had a little time with the woman I love.'

The doctor, looking embarrassed, stuck his pipe back in his mouth.

'I hadn't thought of it that way,' he said gruffly. 'Well, perhaps you're right. Do what you want. I won't stand in your way.'

Lew flashed the smile that he knew was one of his best weapons in life. 'Thank you, sir. And I'm not going to let you change your mind.'

The doctor chuckled. 'You young devil, you could charm pears off the tree.'

'I wish Senator Cameron shared your opinions,' said Lew,

spotting his mother in the next room talking to the gentleman in question. Now's the time, he thought. Everything was going right so far. Old man Butterfield had backed down without too much of a squawk, and now for that moment he had been planning since Wednesday.

Wasn't it some Italian who had said that revenge is something a man of taste likes to drink neat? If that was true, Lew decided, he was a man of taste.

Nicole Louise ushered Senator Cameron into the walnut library and closed the door behind him. She had instructed Eugène to keep guests out of the room because she had wanted to use it to corner the senator. Now she had him. Smiling her most radiant smile, she crossed the room and lifted the stopper of a crystal decanter that was resting on a shelf next to a beautiful set of the Waverley Novels.

'Something special for you and me, Simon,' she said. 'A cognac I guarantee you'll find nowhere else in America. I think you'll agree it's unique.'

She filled two snifters with the amber liquid as the senator watched this beautiful woman with interest. Unlike most of the guests at the ball, he liked the Widow Crandall. He found her accent charming, her house spectacular, her food superb, and, as far as he was concerned, no woman could wear too many jewels: the more the merrier. Simon Cameron had worked hard to make his millions, and he didn't subscribe to the school of whispered wealth.

'One thing about your house surprises me,' he said.

'What's that?'

'There's no portrait of the judge.'

'Ah, but you're wrong.' She handed him the brandy. 'There's a very handsome portrait in the dining room.'

'But isn't the place for a man's portrait in the library of his house?'

'This is *my* house, Simon. I really don't think Jefferson would have liked it. He preferred the traditional brick three-storey bore that's all over Philadelphia. I wanted something new and different, so I built this. And *my* portrait hangs over the fireplace.'

He followed her eyes up to the enormous, slickly painted picture of Nicole Louise standing on some imaginary terrace, wearing a beautiful cinnamon and green dress while behind her a romantic landscape dwindled in perfect perspective to mountains no one had ever seen in Pennsylvania.

'I had that painted by Monsieur Winterhalter five years ago in Paris. Everyone asks if the mountains are supposed to be the Alleghenies, which is of course absurd. But I like the picture. Do you?'

'Very much. I can't say it flatters you, because it doesn't. You're more beautiful than the painting.'

'Dear Simon,' she sighed, 'if we poor women had the vote, you'd certainly be President. As it is, I understand you will be our next Secretary of the Treasury?'

He sniffed the brandy's aroma. 'Mr Lincoln is taking his own good time appointing me, but yes, I think it's safe to say I'll probably get the Treasury post.'

'Then it will almost be a pleasure paying taxes. I emphasize the *almost*.'

'If there's a war, there's some talk in Congress of financing it with an income tax. I don't think you'd find that pleasant to pay.'

'An income tax?' She looked amazed. 'What a grotesque idea! But I'm sure a Treasury secretary with your income would put that scheme right where it belongs: in the trash!'

The senator laughed. 'Let's say I'd try.' He paused to sip the brandy. 'Mmm. You were right. This is excellent stuff. 'Might I ask you something?'

'Please: anything.'

'Why was your son so rude to me this evening?'

She ran her hand lightly over her hair, choosing her approach carefully. 'Louis is very headstrong, you must understand. A few days ago, he came across a letter you had written to Jefferson fifteen years ago. I don't suppose you remember it . . .?'

'I think perhaps I do. Wasn't that about the time your husband got his judgeship?'

'Exactly. As is customary in these cases, there was a

substantial contribution on my husband's part, which you . . . acknowledged in the letter. It . . . well, it upset Louis. He has a rather naïve view of the world, and . . .'

Cameron was staring at her.

'You mean, Jefferson didn't destroy that letter?'

'No. Oh, it was foolish of him, and if I'd known of course *I* would have burned it.'

'Where is it now?'

'Louis has it.'

'I'd like to have it back.'

How interesting, she thought. The existence of the letter had frightened him more than she expected.

'Of course,' she said. 'But first, there is something I wanted to speak to you about, concerning Louis. . . .'

'What?'

She could tell he was tense. 'Since you will be such a powerful man in the new administration, if there is a war, could you possibly arrange for Louis a commission where he would, well, not be close to any fighting? Perhaps something in Washington – or even here in Philadelphia?'

He sipped the brandy, never taking his eyes off her. He rather enjoyed the haggling. Years of politics had made it second nature.

'That would be no problem. As long as he gives me back the letter.'

Again, she smiled. 'Good. Then let me find Louis.' She started toward the door. 'You stay here. I'll have the letter in a few minutes.'

She hurried out of the library to see her son crossing the hall toward her.

'Where's that letter?' she whispered as he joined her. 'I told Simon about it, and he wants it back.'

'*You* told him?'

'Yes! He wanted to know why you were so hostile to him, and I decided it was better to tell the truth. And it *was*. But he wants the letter! Now, where is it?'

'Gone.'

'Gone? Where? What do you mean?'

He opened the library door. 'I was just going to tell the senator.'

'Louis, what have you *done?*'

'Salvaged the family honour.' He smiled, holding the door for his mother. She hesitated nervously, then passed him back into the room, whispering, 'Louis, I warn you: don't do anything you'll regret.'

He said nothing, following her into the room and closing the door. The senator was standing before the fire, holding his brandy, watching them. Nicole Louise hurried across the dark Oriental rug. 'I'm not sure what has happened, but Louis tells me the letter is gone....'

'Gone?' exclaimed the senator suspiciously.

'To Springfield, Illinois,' said Lew. 'Addressed to Mr Lincoln, along with a covering letter, a copy of which I just *happen* to have on me. Would you like to hear it, Senator? It should interest you.'

He pulled a piece of paper from his coat pocket and opened it. The senator's face had gone stony. He said nothing.

'Dear Sir,' [began Lew]. 'May I offer my congratulations on your election to the Presidency? As one who voted for you, I feel I have a certain vested interest in the success of your administration. Consequently, I have been bothered by reports in the papers that you are considering Senator Cameron of Pennsylvania to be your Secretary of the Treasury. Believe me, sir, I realize my opinion can have little weight in your decision. But I feel the appointment of Cameron to a cabinet post would be such a disaster to you and to the country that I am enclosing a letter written to my late father, Judge Jefferson Crandall, some years ago. As you will see by reading it, even then the senator was dealing in patronage to his personal profit. I do not necessarily excuse my father for paying the money which so obviously was necessary for his appointment to the Federal bench; but he has already been judged by the Highest Bench of all. Senator Cameron, on the other hand, is still very much with us. And if the enclosed letter serves in any way to weight your opinion against him, I will feel that my father has been exonerated. Yours most Sincerely etc., etc., Louis Crandall.'

He looked up. 'Did you like it, Senator? The style's a bit lumpy, but I think the content is sensational. Mr Lincoln should get it Monday morning.'

The senator set his snifter on a table and turned to Nicole Louise, whose face was even whiter than usual. He nodded his head and said, 'Madame, I thank you for your hospitality. Under the circumstances, I think you'll understand if I leave now.'

'Simon,' she blurted out, 'I don't know what to say –!'

'Then say nothing.' He started toward the door, then stopped in front of Lew. His expression was cool, but his close-set eyes were hot. Lew stared him down as defiantly as he could, though he was surprised to find himself suddenly nervous. The man's reaction hadn't been the stormy outburst he had expected.

'Young man, I'm sure you think you've done something very clever,' said the senator softly. 'Lots of young men make clever mistakes. But I can assure you, this is one you're not going to be allowed to forget.'

With that, he walked to the tall double doors, opened one of them, and left the room.

The moment the door was closed Nicole Louise turned to her son.

'You fool! You incredible fool! After all that I've done for you – all your father hoped for – all the advantages and education we've lavished on you – you act like an idiot!'

'Oh, Mother, shut up,' he snapped. Now that it was over, he was feeling queasily unsure of his gesture. Maybe he *had* been a fool. There was something in the senator's eyes . . .

She picked up her brandy and finished it in one gulp. Then she set down the glass.

'We'll return to the party and pretend nothing has happened,' she said, crossing the room. 'But I hope you realize you've made a dangerous enemy when you could have had a powerful friend. And *that*, my dear Louis – for all your dithering about family honour – is about the most fatal mistake anyone can make in life.'

She left the room, this time not quietly, but slamming the

door behind her. He stood staring at the fire, feeling deflated and, for the first time in his life, rather frightened.

After a moment, he crumpled the copy of the letter and tossed it into the flames.

4

By two in the morning, when the guests started for home in their carriages, the snow was coming down heavily and Rittenhouse Square was blanketed with almost two inches. In the ballroom the orchestra was packing its instruments as the footmen began dismantling the buffet. Elizabeth ducked in between two of them to take one final piece of cake, which she popped in her mouth. Then she hurried over to Lew, who was leaning against the wall, his hands in his pockets, his face glum. 'I'm stuffed!' exclaimed Elizabeth. 'And I'm talking with my mouth full, and I don't care. Wasn't it a wonderful party?'

'Oh yes, it was grand.'

'Liar. You obviously thought it was some sort of wake. What *did* you do to Senator Cameron?'

He shrugged and forced a smile.

'Something I'm beginning to think wasn't too smart. Say, if you keep gorging like that, you'll get as fat as a pig.'

'Never! I'll always be thin and beautiful so my husband will never look at another woman! Oh Lew, I'm so thrilled! You handled Father magnificently. I think *you* should be a politician.'

'Mmm. Like Simon Cameron. That's just what I want.'

'Are you going to tell me what you said to him?'

'I told him he was a low-life and a thief, and I challenged him to a duel. We meet at dawn under the Liberty Bell, and I chose feather-dusters as weapons.'

She laughed. 'Well, he is a thief, there's no doubt about that. So I hope if you insulted him, you did it right. Do you know I'm the happiest woman in Philadelphia? No – the world!'

'And I'm the happiest man.'

He started to kiss her but saw Mrs Bramwell bustling into the ballroom.

'Lew, come quickly!' she called, waving to him urgently.

They hurried over to her.

'What's wrong?'

'Ben is – oh dear! The poor boy has no control! I *knew* he was drinking too much. . . .'

'Is he drunk?'

'As a lord! He almost fell down the basement stairs – I don't know *what* he was going to the basement for! *Such* a disgrace! Your mother's in a state, and for once, I can't say I blame her! Lew, can you get him in a cab! I don't know if you can get him home – someone said they think the Schuylkill is frozen – but take him *somewhere!* I won't have him in my house in that condition . . . the Lord knows what he might do. . . . Oh dear, such a disgrace!'

'I'll look after him.' He turned to Elizabeth. 'Can you go home with your parents?'

'They've already left. . . .'

'We'll take you home,' said Mrs Bramwell. 'Hurry, Lew, before the poor boy breaks something – or your mother murders him!'

Lew gave his fiancée a quick kiss, then went off, running through the salon into the entrance hall, where two of the footmen were trying to hold up a staggering Ben as Nicole Louise stood by the front door, looking, in fact, quite capable of murder.

'Lew!' slurred Ben, his face breaking into a smile as he saw him. 'Lew, old boy, let's go down Mrs Simpson's! Feel like goin' down there and gettin' relieved – you know what I mean? Takin' all my clothes off and forgettin' this stupid party and this God-awful house!'

'Would you *get* him out of here?' snarled Nicole Louise. 'Drunken oaf! I'll never allow him in this house again!'

Ben stuck his thumb to his nose and gave the Widow Crandall a loud raspberry.

'Fooey on you, you Frog Princess! You know your mother's a Frog Princess, Lew? That's what I always think of when I look at her . . . you'd kiss her and she'd turn into a big green frog! Hm?'

He snorted with laughter, and Nicole Louise swelled.

'I'll turn into a rattlesnake if he's not out of here in ten seconds! Guy! Antoine! *Mettez cet ivrogne à la porte tout de suite! Je ne peux pas supporter cet imbécile!*'

'Buc buc buc buc buc buc buc,' clucked Ben, imitating a chicken. Lew hurried to him and took his arm. 'I've got him,' he said to the footmen, who backed away, relieved to be out of it. 'Easy does it, Ben. Easy does it. . . .'

He started guiding him to the door as the Bramwells and Elizabeth watched from the salon.

'A *perfect* evening ruined by first you and then your friend!' sputtered Nicole Louise.

'Peace,' said Lew. 'All right? Peace.'

'Buc buc buc buc buc,' clucked Ben gaily. Nicole Louise, her eyes blazing, started to slap him. Lew reached up and grabbed her wrist.

'*Don't*,' he said, and he meant it.

Her eyes switched to the son she adored and could have, at that moment, strangled.

'*Louis, tu es aussi insupportable que ton* vilain *ami!*'

And she swept furiously away from the door toward the staircase. Ben blinked as he stared after her.

' "*Vilain*"?' he said. 'Don't that mean "ugly", Lew? Hm? Your mother thinks I'm ugly, doesn't she? Well, *you're* ugly!' he shouted after her, with sudden rage. 'You're an ugly *frog!*'

Nicole Louise stopped on the first step, turned, and gave him a look of contempt. 'You hideous Jew,' she said. Then she continued up the stairs.

Lew literally winced. He looked at his friend, saw his eyes widen slightly, felt him stiffen. Then, to his relief, Ben laughed.

'Your mom doesn't like me, Lew,' he said, shaking his head. 'She really doesn't like me. She never has.'

'Come on, Ben: let's watch our step out here. This snow's slippery. . . .'

'She really doesn't like me! And you know what? I don't like her!' He went into gales of laughter, and Lew barely saved him from diving off the steps onto the sidewalk. 'Whoa, boy – whoa! We don't want to split your skull! All that booze will melt the snow. . . .'

'Buc buc buc buc!' sang Ben, weaving his way down the walk as Lew ran to catch up. 'Buc buc buc buc whee!' He leaned over, scooped up some snow into a ball, then straightened and hurled it at a gaslight. 'Buc buc buc!'

Crash! The ball hit the glass and smashed it.

'Oh God,' moaned Lew, 'the luck of a drunk! No more, Ben – okay? We'll have the cops here. . . .'

'Buc buc buc buc!' Ben quacked, pirouetting to the kerb as Lew frantically hailed a cab. With the help of the cabby, a fat Irishman with a face beet-red from the cold, Lew got the clucking Ben into the hack, then climbed in after him, suddenly realizing he didn't have a coat. 'Do you know the old Stoddard farm on the other side of the river?'

'Aye,' said the cabby, 'but I don't know if the ferry's runnin' this late.'

'We'll wake him up. . . .'

'But the river may be frozen.'

'Then we'll skate across!' roared Lew angrily. 'I've got to get this man home! So *move*!'

'Right you are, guvnor.'

The man scrambled up on his seat and snapped his whip. His blanketed horse, steam shooting from his nostrils, jerked into motion and started thudding through the powdery snow down the street. As a shivering Lew pulled the lap robe over him, he looked out at the house and saw his mother standing in the window of the second-floor bedroom, watching.

'God, what a night!' he muttered, sinking into the seat.

'Buc buc buc,' mumbled Ben, his head on his chest. In a minute, he was snoring.

It took Lew two hours to get Ben home to his farm. The Schuylkill wasn't frozen, but the ferry had shut down for the night, and it took arguments and a five-dollar bribe to convince the ferryman he should get out of bed, get dressed and take the two men across the river. Then Lew had to rent a buggy from the livery stable on the west bank and pile the still-drunken Ben in. All this with the snow continuing to fall, Lew shivering in his dress suit, and his anger at his mother mounting.

Anger can be a purge, and as the buggy bumped through the night, Lew's anger began to rid him of his fears. Yes, perhaps his mother was right: what he had done to Senator Cameron was idiotic, futile, and had made him a powerful enemy. On the other hand, he *had* stuck a knife in the man. The letter to Lincoln had rocked him – who could tell? The letter might even work. Perhaps Mr Lincoln might *not* appoint Cameron to the Treasury, and wouldn't that be sweet? But whether it worked or not, Lew decided he was glad he had done it.

And if the gesture had been aimed at his mother as well as Cameron, so much the better. Yes, Ben was wrong to have gotten drunk and made an ass of himself, and it was Ben who had started the racial mudslinging by telling Nicole Louise she was a Frog. 'Frog' was hardly Lew's favourite epithet, but his mother calling Ben a Jew was somehow worse. American xenophobia was ugly, but French anti-Semitism was uglier. Oh God, he thought, is the whole world prejudiced? Was he going to be a Frog all his life and Ben a Jew? And at the same time he knew the answer was yes, and that both of them would have to come to terms with it. Their world was rent with bigotry – a war was probably going to be fought soon over bigotry – and Lew decided neither he nor Ben could let his life be ruined by being its victims.

The buggy pulled through the white gates of Ben's farm,

and he stopped it in front of the stable. Then he jerked Ben's arm.

'Ben, wake up!'

The big man lifted slowly, and Ben's bloodshot eyes tried to focus.

'Huh?'

'Come on, you big lunk of lead: I've got you home, but I'm sure as hell not going to carry you in.'

'What happened?'

'It's probably just as well you don't remember.'

'Oh God – yes, I *do* remember. Vaguely. Your mother and I had a fight. . . . Oh, Jesus.'

He started moaning. Lew said, 'Look, I'm freezing. Do your moaning inside the house.'

His friend lumbered down from the buggy, almost stumbling in the snow. Lew grabbed him to steady him.

'Are you still drunk?' he said.

'A little. Maybe a lot. Oh God, my head . . . what was in that champagne? Gunpowder?'

'It's called alcohol. Come on.'

Lew helped him through the snow to the front door. The farmhouse had been built in the early years of the century and was a clapboard, unpretentious place set in fifty fertile acres. Ben had done nothing to the house itself, but he had added the greenhouse to the west side, putting in an expensive steam-heating system (running some ducts into the house as his one concession to modernity), and as Lew waited for him to find his door key he noticed that, though the house was dark, a lamp was burning in the greenhouse.

'Is someone home?' he asked.

'Just Jethro.' Jethro was the ex-slave Ben had taken on as his handyman-cook.

'Then do you leave a light burning in the greenhouse?'

'No.' Ben looked, saw, but was too drunk to react. 'Must be a ghost,' he mumbled, unlocking the door and letting himself in the small parlour. Lew said, 'Get a fire going. I'll put the horse in the barn and be right back.' Five minutes later, he returned to the parlour, his teeth chattering. He hurried to the hearth to warm himself, saying, 'You're going to put me up for the night. I'm not going back out in that mess.'

'Oh sure. I appreciate your getting me home. I –' Ben stopped, a look of pain on his face. He put his hand to his forehead. 'Jesus – thump, thump, thump. The trolls are at work, banging away. Oh Christ . . .' He sank into a battered armchair. 'You know, I don't mind your mother calling me a Jew so much. Hell, I'm only a quarter Jewish, and I'm not ashamed of it. No, that's a lie. I *am* sensitive about it, I guess. But it was the "ugly" part that hurt – really hurt. She didn't have to remind me of that, Lew. The "ugly" hurt.'

'Hell, you're too sensitive about your looks, just as I'm too sensitive about being half Frog, and we both ought to start getting over it. Life's too short.'

'I know, but it's easier said than done. God, I feel lousy. Do you want something to eat? Or drink, maybe? Let's have a drink.'

'That's the last thing you need. Do you have any cocoa? I need something hot.'

'Good idea. Jethro?' he yelled. 'Oh hell, no point waking him up. I'll make some.'

He was starting out of the chair just as a frail black man with grizzled white hair came into the room. He was dressed and carrying a lamp.

'Ah thought Ah heerd you, Mistah Ben,' he said. 'You drunk agin?'

Ben snickered. 'Jethro knows all my faults, that's for certain. Yes, I'm drunk again, and Mr Crandall is freezing. Can you make him some hot cocoa? Why are you dressed, anyway?'

'Cause you got some visitors,' said the old man, lowering his voice. 'They showed up 'bout midnight, and Ah stuck 'em in the greenhouse so's they could keep warm. They's a coloured gal and a white man.'

Ben frowned. 'A white man?'

'Yessah. Don't like the looks of him, neither. He say they's from Carolina an' he's takin' the gal to *Noo* York. Say he's broke an' he heerd you loan runaways money. Thass why he's here.'

'But *he's* not a runaway, obviously.'

'No sah. But he wants money. If it wuz *mah* money, Ah wouldn't loan him nuffin'. But knowin' you an' how you throws your money aroun', he'll probably get what he come for.'

'Thanks for that vote of confidence in my investment astuteness. Come on, Lew, let's take a look at them.'

They filed out of the parlour into a low-ceilinged hall that led back to the kitchen. Halfway down the hall, a door had been cut in the wall. Now Ben unbolted the door and opened it, stepping into the greenhouse. What he saw stopped him. Lew pushed his way past him to look.

The greenhouse was large, with a peaked glass ceiling, and filled with rows of wooden tables laden with hundreds of potted plants. Standing in the centre aisle, clutching a dirty shawl around her, was a girl Lew judged was about twelve. Her skin was *café au lait*, and she obviously was a mulatto. Her facial features were an intriguing blend of white and Negro: Lew thought she was one of the most beautiful girls he had ever seen. So, obviously, did Ben, who was staring at her. Standing beside her was a tall, thin man, about forty. He had two days' growth of beard and was wearing beneath his tweed overcoat a rather seedy suit. The man had thin black hair, a sharp nose, and a large mole on his chin. He had kept his hat on his head. Now he took it off, clutched it in front of him with both hands, and came up the aisle.

'Good evening, gentlemen,' he said in a soft voice without a trace of a Southern accent. 'My name's Harvey Winkler. Harvey Winkler from Charleston. Is one of you gentlemen Mr Bramwell?'

'I am,' said Ben.

'Very kind of you, sir, to take us in like this. Very kind. We've had a hard journey . . . very hard.' There was a fawning smarminess about the man's manner that Lew took an instant dislike to. 'You see, sir, I decided that with all the talk of secession in Charleston, I should get my daughter out and up North. For her safety as well as her freedom, you understand. I don't have much money, being a tailor – and that's a very nice cut to your dress suit, sir – but the few dollars I had I used to get this far. . . . Ain't she a lovely little thing, sir?'

He smiled at Ben, who continued to stare. 'What's her name?' he asked.

'Christine. Her mamma was a slave, but she was a beauty. It might have been a folly, but I don't regret it. No sir.' He lowered his soft voice to a whisper. 'Dark meat's the best, sir! Take the word of a man of experience. Dark meat's the best! But then perhaps you gentlemen know what I mean from your own experience? Two fine-looking, well-dressed gentlemen like yourselves – hm?' He snickered and winked lewdly at Lew, who said nothing. 'Anyways,' Winkler went on, 'I need a loan. Fifty dollars should do me. If one or both of you fine gentlemen could see your way to advancing it, I'd be ever so grateful. I've heard of your generosity, Mr Bramwell, but of course, I'd pay you back in time. Once I get settled in New York with Christine, I'd pay you back. With interest. You can trust Harvey Winkler, sir. He's a man of his word.'

'No you're not,' said Ben calmly. 'You're a liar. And this girl's not your daughter.'

Winkler looked pained and bewildered.

'How's that? She's not my daughter? Why, ask her! Christine honey, tell them I'm your daddy.'

'You ain't mah daddy,' she said in a soft voice.

'You goddam bitch!' roared Winkler. 'Tell them the truth!'

'Shut up, Winkler,' snapped Ben. 'What do you take me for, an idiot? You're no more from Charleston than I am.'

'He's from New York,' said Christine. 'He came down south to find girls fo' dee who-houses. He won me in a poker game.'

Winkler swallowed his rage and shrugged. 'Okay, I lied. She ain't my daughter. But I still need some money. How about it, Mr Bramwell?'

Ben took another look at the girl. Then he turned back to Winkler. 'You can stay the rest of the night, but in the morning, get out. I don't loan money to pimps. Come on, Lew: let's go on up. I'm exhausted.' He started toward the door, and Lew followed. Before he left the greenhouse, he took a look back at Winkler and the girl. Winkler was scowling. Lew didn't envy the girl: he had an idea Winkler might beat her for telling the truth. Despite his twitting Senator Cameron for his lack of moral fervour on the slavery issue, Lew was no Abolitionist himself, being not much of a man for causes. He had a conventional disapproval of slavery, like most Northerners of his class, but he didn't believe in going to war over the issue itself: he would fight to preserve the Union, not abolish slavery. But something in the girl's eyes caught his sympathy – or was it the matter-of-fact way she had been won in a poker game? Or was it the menace of Winkler? At any rate, when he and Ben got to the top of the stairs, he whispered to his friend, 'Maybe one of us ought to keep an eye on them. Something tells me Brother Winkler might rough her up for blowing the whistle on him.'

Ben shook his head. 'No, he wouldn't hurt her. She's money in his pocket as long as she's not marked. He can get over a thousand for her in New York. She's gorgeous.'

'But she can't be more than twelve. . . .'

'Twelve can become fourteen awfully quick. Don't worry about them. Get some sleep: you need it.'

Lew hesitated, then shrugged. 'Well, if you say so. Good night.'

He went into the small guest room and lit the bed lamp. Then he sat down on the mattress and removed his snow-soaked shoes and socks. After throwing his jacket over a chair, he took off his collar and tie, then got into bed, not bothering with the rest of his clothes. He turned down the lamp, but he could not get to sleep for a while, exhausted as he was. Ben kept him awake. Ben in the next room, pacing around like a caged lion. He wondered what in God's name was bothering him now, but finally gave up trying to guess. He put the pillow over his head to keep out the noise and fell into a deep sleep.

5

He was awakened by a scream.

He sat up in the bed, trying to get his bearings. Through the small window he could see the sky was just beginning to grow light. Dawn. Who was screaming? And someone yelling downstairs . . . God, what now?

Someone was hurrying up the creaking steps. Then the door burst open. Old Jethro hurried in, dressed in his flannel nightshirt, his legs and feet bare, his wrinkled face frightened.

'Mistah Lew, you better get yo' ass downstairs quick!' he cried. 'Mistah Ben, he didn't go to bed, no *sah*! He got hisself another bottle and got drunk all over agin, then he shag-assed down and got that girl. . . .'

Lew was out of the bed. 'Is that who's screaming?'

'Yessah! Mistah Ben hot after her tail! Oh lordie, it's a *mess!*'

'You mean, he's trying to . . .'

'Thass it! He want to lay that l'il thing! Mistah Ben got a debbil in him. . . . Oh lordie, it's the end of the world! This world and the *next!*'

Lew was out the door, scrambling down the narrow steps in his bare feet, following the noise, wondering why in God's name Ben would attack a girl who could hardly be past puberty . . . at least he *assumed*. . . . Christine was beautiful, but still, a twelve-year-old –! He ran into the greenhouse, where a scene from Bedlam awaited him. The girl was huddling in the corner, her dress half torn off one shoulder, screaming in sheer animal terror as, in front of her, Winkler held off a drunken Ben with a knife.

'Get out of the way!' Ben was yelling. 'Move!'

'If you want her, you pay!' Winkler shouted back. 'She's a virgin and that's worth money!'

'I won't pay your goddam pig-money!' Ben roared, and he lunged at Winkler. Grabbing his knife hand, Ben forced him to drop it as Winkler tried to fight him off. But the alcohol had turned Ben into a juggernaut. He picked Winkler up with both hands and held him over his head. Lew ran toward him, yelling, 'Don't, Ben! For chrissake, don't!' But it was no good. Ben threw Winkler with all his strength at the glass wall. Winkler screamed as he sailed through the shattering glass, landing in the snow outside. Lew grabbed Ben from behind.

'You idiot, you'll kill him!' he cried.

'I want to! I want to kill him!'

'You want to get *hanged?*'

'I don't give a damn!'

He shook Lew off and headed toward Christine, who had stopped screaming and now just gaped. Lew looked around, trying to find something to stop Ben with. He picked up a clay pot, aimed it, then smashed it down on the back of Ben's skull. Ben grunted, staggered and fell into a rubber tree, knocking it over.

Silence, except for the girl who started to whimper.

'Are you all right?' asked Lew, wiping his hands on his pants.

She nodded.

'Sorry about my friend. He, uh, seems to have an eye for girls your age.'

'They's men like that in Charleston,' she said.

'Did you *want* to come north with Winkler?'

'Didn't have no choice.'

Which about summed her situation up. Lew watched her, thinking there was no doubt that she was a beauty, but still. . . . The thought of making love to someone that young disgusted him. He had never dreamed that Ben was a child-molester. It saddened him in a way, but still it didn't make him think the less of his friend. He had classmates at Princeton who had done worse.

He looked through the broken glass at Winkler, who hadn't moved. 'I'd better see if he's alive,' he said, starting toward the door, where Jethro was standing. 'Take her in the kitchen and give her something to eat, Jethro. Calm her down. Then we'll carry Ben up and put him in bed. He's going to have the hangover of the year.'

'Yessah!' agreed Jethro. 'His head gwine look like a balloon!'

Lew left the greenhouse and went down the hall to the kitchen, where he put a pair of boots over his bare feet. Then he threw on a sheepskin coat and went out the kitchen door to walk through the snow to where Winkler was lying on his back, surrounded by shards of glass. His eyes were closed. Lew stopped beside him.

'Winkler?'

He reached out to shake him, but suddenly Winkler grabbed him and pulled him off balance. As Lew fell on top of him, Winkler jammed a six-inch piece of broken glass against his throat.

'Now get this straight, you bastard,' he whispered. 'You're going to do just what I tell you, or your throat's going to need buttons.'

Lew felt the sharp edge of the glass biting his skin. He didn't move.

'We're going to stand up nice and slow,' said Winkler. 'But don't make me nervous. It don't take much to make me nervous.'

Awkwardly, the two men got to their feet, Winkler getting behind Lew, holding the glass dagger to his throat.

'I've been told Mr Bramwell's got a lot of money. A lot of cash he keeps right here on the farm to help the runaways. Now since Mr Bramwell's been so inhospitable to me, I figure he owes me something. So you're going to show me where he keeps his cash.'

'I don't know.'

The glass jammed harder against his throat. 'You're lyin'.'

'I'm not lying! How the hell would *I* know where Ben keeps his money? I didn't even know he keeps cash out here.'

Winkler thought about this. 'Then we'll go in and ask the old nigger. And walk careful, cause if you trip this thing's going right through your windpipe.'

They started moving through the snow toward the kitchen door, Lew wincing with each step as the glass ragged his skin. He was approaching a state of near-manic rage. The scene last night with his mother, then getting Ben out to the farm, then Ben attacking Winkler and the girl and Winkler attacking *him* . . . it was like some crazy nightmare, and he wanted to howl with rage, attack somebody, Ben, Winkler. . . . But he had to *think*. He had no doubt Winkler was ready to carry out his threat.

'I've got to sneeze,' he said, stopping. Winkler didn't say anything for a moment. Then he moved the glass away from his throat.

'All right, go ahead. But don't try any tricks.'

Lew put his finger to his nose, puffing himself up for a mammoth sneeze. His head went back as he turned slightly to the left. Then, suddenly, he flipped over backward, landing on his hands in the snow, then springing backward again, landing on his feet. Winkler blinked with amazement at the display of gymnastics so beautifully executed.

'Put that glass down, you son of a bitch,' Lew roared, 'and get the hell out of here before someone gets killed.'

'You going to make me get out, you goddam monkey?' Winkler roared back, and he lunged at Lew, holding the glass in front of him. Lew scooped up a handful of snow, packed it into a ball, and hurled it in Winkler's face. He did it all in one uninterrupted move, so that Winkler didn't know what hit him. As he reached up to wipe the snow off, Lew grabbed the wrist of the hand holding the piece of glass and twisted it sharply to one side. But Winkler held on. At the same time, he threw his knee up and jammed it into Lew's groin. Lew grunted with pain and sank to his knees, still holding onto the wrist, pulling Winkler down with him so that both men were facing each other on their knees in the snow. Nausea was surging through Lew's middle, but he held on to the wrist. Winkler was wiry. He pushed the glass toward Lew's throat with one hand while the other pounded into his gut, exacerbating the nausea and pain until Lew thought he would vomit.

'You're dead,' Winkler whispered, and Lew felt the edge of the glass on his throat again. Summoning all his strength, he strained against Winkler's arm, but he was panicking. I'm going to die, he thought. He's going to kill me. And for what? Because goddam Ben likes twelve-year-olds. . . . It was absurd, crazy. To die for *that*. . . .

Then he saw Christine come out of the kitchen, carrying a black coal scuttle. She ran through the snow behind Winkler, raised the scuttle, and banged it down on his head. Winkler howled and dropped the glass. Lew let go of his wrists, and the man clutched both hands to his head, rocking with pain. Lew grabbed the piece of glass and staggered to his feet, holding his stomach with his free hand, still so nauseous that the farmhouse swam before his eyes. He saw Jethro standing in the kitchen door, watching, looking terrified. Now the girl raised the scuttle again, but this time Winkler saw her and ducked, rolling in the snow toward Lew as Christine threw the scuttle at him. It missed. Winkler grabbed it and got to his feet as Lew continued holding his guts, fighting off the nausea. Winkler hurled the scuttle at Lew, who also ducked, and the heavy piece of iron crashed through the glass and clanged on the greenhouse floor as Winkler lunged at him again.

Now something happened he would remember the rest of his life. He wasn't thinking clearly, the nausea and violence having muddled his brain, and he reacted instinctively when Winkler grabbed him by jamming the piece of glass into his stomach. He would never forget the gasp of pain, the wince on his face. Lew pulled out the glass, which was dripping blood. The man let him go and clutched both hands to his stomach. Then he stumbled backward a few feet, half turned, and fell on his knees, looking up at Lew with a face full of fear.

'You bastard,' he whispered.

Lew just stood there, holding the bloody piece of glass, staring at the dying man in front of him.

'Get a doctor,' Winkler groaned, doubling over so far his face was almost in the snow. Lew became aware of Jethro hurrying toward them, but still he didn't move. He tried to concentrate his mind. He knew enough about medicine to know a doctor would probably be useless: he had plunged the glass far enough in to lacerate either the stomach or the intestines or both. But still someone had to try to save the man. 'Hitch up the buggy,' he said to Jethro, thinking, I killed a man. He didn't kill me, I killed *him*. Jesus, I killed a man....

'Got to go all the way in town for a doctor,' Jethro mumbled, staring at Winkler.

'Well then, go into town!'

'Yessah.'

Jethro started around the house and Lew tossed the piece of glass into the snow. Then he leaned against a tree as Christine came over to him, her eyes on Winkler. 'Why'd you an' he get in a fight?' she asked softly.

'He wanted Ben's money,' said Lew, forcing the nausea down. 'He's crazy.'

She turned her big eyes on him and said, 'Ah helped you out, didn't Ah? When Ah banged that scuttle on his head?'

Lew nodded weakly.

'You sure did. And I appreciate it.'

'You won't forget Christine helped you?'

'No, I won't forget.' He straightened, having noticed something. Winkler was lying face down in the snow now, and he had stopped moving. Lew stumbled over to him, knelt, and turned him over. Winkler's eyes were open, staring blankly at the sky. Lew didn't need to feel his pulse to know the man was dead, but he did. Then he stood up and yelled, 'Jethro!'

The old man scurried out of the kitchen.

'Yessah?'

'Forget the doctor. He's dead.'

Jethro hurried over and stared down at Winkler's face. Then he started moaning.

'Oh lordie, what we gwine do *now*, Mistah Lew?'

'Tell the police.'

'You crazy, Mistah Lew? We can't do that! No sah! They's gwine string you up and hang you for murder!'

'I didn't murder him, for chrissake! The man attacked me – it was self-defence!'

'Ah knows that, Mistah Lew, but how you gwine prove that? And we can't have policemans runnin' all over this property, askin' all sorts o' questions, findin' out what Mistah Ben done to that l'il girl. . . . No sah, we can't do that!'

Lew closed his eyes in frustration.

'But the whole thing was Ben's fault!' he said. 'I'm not going to cover up a murder just because Ben gets hot for little girls. . . .'

'Ah, Mistah Lew, how come you talk like that? Mistah Ben, he's yo' friend! He thinks the world of you, yessah! You can't do this to him! An' nobody gwine miss this – whass his name? Winkler? Who know Winkler? We take him out to the apple orchard an' bury him, an' no one's ever gwine know he live or die.'

Lew sighed. 'Jethro, we can't do that. . . .'

'Why not? Lots of runaways come troo here. If anybody ever asks any questions, we say, "We know nuffin about it, but mebbe one of them niggers from the South got in a fight wif him an' killed him an' stuck him in the ground, but we don't know nuffin about it. Oh lordie, Mistah Lew, you can't do that to yo' friend. He'd never live down the scandal, no sah!'

Lew felt someone tug his sleeve. He turned to see Christine behind him.

'Ah tell them the truth,' she said. 'Ah tell them Winkler attacked you.'

He looked at her. A twelve-year-old runaway and an aged darkie his witnesses. The brawling in the greenhouse, the broken windows, the drinking, the fighting. . . . It was possible they might not believe him. But even if they did, the papers would have a field day with the story. 'Prominent Philadelphians Involved in Fatal Brawl after Rittenhouse

Square Ball' – he needed little imagination to envision the headline. His mother. Mad as he was at her, this, after the brouhaha with Senator Cameron, would be the final straw. And Elizabeth and her family. And the Bramwells. Philadelphia was a tight little world. It would never let him forget he had killed a man, even if it was convinced it wasn't murder. Who would want to go to a doctor who had killed a man in a drunken brawl?

'Oh my God,' he said wearily. 'I don't know what to do.'

'*Bury* him,' insisted Jethro. 'Come on: Ah helps you dig the hole. Bury him an' forget him.'

Reluctantly, Lew gave in, aware that his future was in the hands of these two Negroes. But first, Christine rummaged through Winkler's pockets until she found what she called her bill of sale, the document proving Winkler was her legal owner. While Lew knew she had no choice, still he was nervous about her carrying it and made her swear not to lose it or show it unless she had to: he didn't want the question of Winkler's whereabouts coming up. Then he and Jethro found a spot several hundred yards from the farmhouse in a clump of apple trees. With considerable difficulty, Lew broke the frozen ground and began digging a grave. It took him an hour. Then, trembling and silent, he wrapped the body in a blanket. He and Jethro carried it to the grave as Christine watched from the house. They dropped it in the hole and Lew began shovelling back the dirt. When the grave was filled, he patted the earth with the shovel, then scooped snow over it. After smoothing the snow with a broom, he went back to the house with Jethro to join Christine in the kitchen.

'Well, it's done,' he said. 'Right or wrong. Where's Ben?'

Christine said he was still asleep in the greenhouse.

'All right, there's no point in his knowing about this. The last thing I want is him getting drunk and telling the world. So we'll keep it a secret between the three of us. Is that agreed?'

'Yessah,' said Jethro. 'But what'm Ah gwine tell Mistah Ben happened to that man?'

'Tell him he and the girl went on to New York.'

'What about me?' asked Christine.

Lew looked at her.

'That's a good question. Obviously, I can't leave you with Ben. That's be like leaving a lamb with a hungry tiger. You'd better come into town with me. I'll think of something.'

For the first time since he had met her, the girl smiled.

Few people would have mistaken Mrs Simpson's three-storey brick house for a brothel, which was the way she had planned it. Situated across the street from the Navy Yard, the source of half her business, the house was neat and, in the summer, boasted pretty red geraniums in its white window boxes. For that matter, few people would have mistaken Mrs Simpson for a madame. Plump and motherly, she was all sweetness and light to her customers (except when they didn't pay, at which point she could become a dragon). One of her favourite customers was Lew ('Such a fine young gentleman,' she always said of him), and thus when he came in her parlour that noon, she put down the 'Home is Where the Heart Is' sampler she was working on, got out of her rocker, and came over to clasp his hand.

'Dear Mr Crandall!' She beamed. Then she spotted the red marks on his throat caused by the glass. 'How did you cut yourself?'

'Shaving. Look, Mrs Simpson: I need your help. I've got a girl outside. I want you to put up for a couple of days. . . .'

'Is she attractive?' she asked, her business instincts aroused.

'Gorgeous. But she's a runaway.'

She made a face. 'Now, Mr Crandall, you know I run a very high-class establishment. No perversions, whips, or mixed couples. . . .'

'I don't want her to *work* for you! Wait: take a look at her. . . .'

He went to the door and signalled out to Christine, who was standing on the sidewalk. When she came in the room, Mrs Simpson said, 'Why she's only a child! And she must be at least half white. . . .'

'Mah father's Mistah Philippe Canrobert from Charleston,' said Christine.

'I know the Canroberts,' said Lew. 'I was at Princeton with one of them.'

'They sound French,' said Mrs Simpson.

'They are. They own a big plantation outside Charleston – rice, I think. Lots of money. Philippe must be the old man. I think he's a drunk.'

'French,' sniffed Mrs Simpson. 'They'll sleep with anything.'

'Thanks,' said Lew.

She cleared her throat. 'Sorry, Mr Crandall. I forgot. But it's a crime the way those Southerners go to bed with the slave women and never think twice about the offspring. . . . What's your name, child?'

'Christine.'

'Can you read or write?'

'No ma'am.'

'What can you do?'

'Clean house and do laundry.'

'Well, I can take her in as a scullery maid, Mr Crandall. She can help around the house. I'll give her room and board for five dollars a week. I take it you are assuming reponsibility for her?'

Lew looked at the girl, who was watching him with an impassive face. He had no choice: she had witnessed the killing. Besides, he felt sorry for her.

'Yes, I guess I am,' he said. 'Do you like it here, Christine? Would you like to stay here?'

She looked around the room, then looked at Mrs Simpson.

'Ain't this a whorehouse?' she asked.

Mrs Simpson stiffened. 'It is an institution of female entertainment,' she said primly.

'Come on, Mrs S.: it's a whorehouse. What's wrong, Christine? If you don't want to stay here, where *do* you want to go?'

'That's where he was taking me in New York – a whorehouse. But if Ah had a choice. . . .'

'You have a choice.'

'Then why can't Ah go to school?'

Lew knew that, after years of struggle, some Negro children had been let into the Philadelphia public schools and that now there were over a thousand enrolled. But the quality of their education wasn't very good. Besides, those children were free, and technically Christine was a fugitive slave, liable to being returned south by men who made a business of returning runaways for the bounty. True, she could prove Winkler was her owner, but where was Winkler? They were both in a dilemma. Then he thought of the Trowbridges. Robert and Edna Trowbridge were a Quaker couple who owned a farm near Germantown. Impassioned Abolitionists, they had recently turned their farm into a private school for black children. He could put Christine in the Trowbridge School, where she would be safe from slave catchers, pay her expenses out of his own pocket, and not only educate her but be able to keep an eye on her. Again, the uncomfortable realization came to him that his life and future were in the hands of Jethro and this girl.

'All right,' he said, 'I know where you can go.' He turned to Mrs Simpson. 'Well, I guess we came to the wrong place. Thanks anyway, Mrs S. Give my love to Irene. Oh, and by the way' – he paused at the door – 'I'm getting married next month, so I won't be seeing much of you from now on.'

Mrs Simpson chuckled. 'Dear Mr Crandall, how naïve you are. We'll be seeing more of you after you're married. *Much* more.'

He gave her a cool look and left the house with Christine. By the end of the day, he had made all the arrangements with the Trowbridges. Wearily, he started back home, dreaming up a plausible excuse for his mother about where he had been. He had no intention of letting Nicole Louise know what had happened at the farm.

A week later, he received the following letter from the President-elect:

Dear Mr Crandall:

Thank you for your interesting letter concerning Senator Cameron. I am taking the information you sent under advisement.

The following story may amuse you; it certainly amused me. I recently had the occasion to ask Mr Thaddeus Stevens of your state his opinion of Senator Cameron's honesty. 'I don't think Cameron would steal a red-hot stove,' Mr Stevens replied. Apparently, this reached Senator Cameron's ears and he demanded an apology. 'Oh well,' Stevens said, 'I apologize. I said Cameron would not steal a red-hot stove. I withdraw that statement.'

Respectfully yours,
A. Lincoln.

6

The Crandall–Butterfield wedding was the social event of the winter. The papers devoted columns to it which the readers, thoroughly fed up with the inactivity of the lame-duck Buchanan administration and the apparent stalemate between Washington and the seceding states, devoured. Lew didn't pay much attention to the columns because he was too busy house-hunting. Nicole Louise had given him as a wedding present one hundred thousand dollars' worth of New York Central stock. He cashed in twenty thousand dollars' worth and bought a charming three-storey house on Locust Street, which Elizabeth fell in love with. The Butterfields, as their wedding gift, furnished the house, sending over Elizabeth's Pleyel piano, among other things. As the wedding approached, everything seemed rosy for the young couple who, like everyone else, tried to forget the war clouds looming over Washington. Lew even tried to forget Winkler, but he couldn't. The seedy pimp's ghost haunted him.

Ben had left for Cleveland two days after the incident. According to Jethro, he had gone to see a botanist about 'breedin' some weeds', but Lew surmised that Ben remembered enough of the drunken evening with his attack on Christine to want to stay out of sight for a while. He returned three weeks later. Lew asked him to be his best man, but Ben declined. He sent a handsome silver tray as a wedding present and made a sheepish appearance at the reception, where he drank nothing but tea. For the rest, he stayed on his farm. Lew wondered if another casualty of that macabre evening had been their friendship.

The wedding went off without a hitch. Elizabeth looked lovely, but Lew felt she was tense. After the reception, they took a train to New York for a week's honeymoon. They checked in at the Metropolitan Hotel at Broadway and Prince Street, a new extravaganza that had cost over a million dollars and boasted not only gas and steam heat but a ventilating system as well. Lew had reserved the bridal suite. After a lobster-and-champagne dinner, during which Elizabeth rattled on so incessantly about the wedding that Lew thought she was letting off nervous steam, they retired to the bedroom. They both felt awkward; Lew told himself to proceed gently. The suite had a small bathroom. Elizabeth went inside to change into her bedclothes. When she came out, wearing a white satin negligée, she stared at her husband who had stripped to his drawers. She tried to think of something to say, but couldn't. She sat on the edge of the bed, staring at the closed curtains over the window, tensely squeezing her hands. She told herself that this was what she wanted, that the experience she had exhausted so much mental energy thinking about was going to be beautiful. The fact was she was terrified. Drawings in anatomy books were one thing: flesh was another.

She felt his hands on her arms, his lips at her ear. He had climbed on the bed behind her.

'I love you,' he whispered. 'Don't be frightened.'

She turned to kiss him. His body was so beautiful that she kept thinking he would be disappointed in her skinniness, her tiny breasts. She tried to relax as he unbuttoned her negligée and eased his hand into her nightgown to feel her breasts. He was kissing her over and over, whispering how happy he was, how he loved her, how wonderful everything was going to be. She lay back on the bed and stared at the ceiling. She was nauseous and was afraid she would throw up. She couldn't understand it: she wanted him mentally, why couldn't she want him physically?

'Lew darling,' she whispered.

'What?'

'I . . . you'll have to excuse me a minute.'

She got up and hurried into the bathroom, closing the door. He sat on the bed, listening to her vomit. Jesus Christ, he thought, I didn't think I was *that* repulsive! What am I doing wrong? After a while, she emerged from the bathroom naked, her face drawn, her thin body white and gangly, the little patch of brown hair puffing at her middle, her fists clenched. She came back to the bed and lay down again, like a prisoner submitting to torture.

'Do you . . . would you rather wait till later?' he said.

'No: I want to do it now.'

'Are you sure?'

'Yes, I'm sure.'

By now, his passion was in danger of ebbing, but determinedly he pulled off his drawers. She raised her head and stared at his penis. 'Well, there it is,' he said, half-heartedly trying to make a joke. She looked at it, half intrigued, half repelled. Then she lay her head back on the pillow and closed her eyes. She stiffened as she felt his nakedness on top of hers, the soft hair on his chest pressing into her skin. He was gentle, loving, and warm; she relaxed somewhat. She actually started to enjoy herself when she felt him go inside her, softly at first, then harder. She stifled a scream at the pain as he thrust through her hymen, then further inside her. She kept telling herself this was nature's way, that it was good and wonderful, that she wanted children by this man she adored, that she was sophisticated and knew about sex, that the musky smell of his body as he humped her was strangely alluring. . . .

When it was all over, he whispered, rather tentatively, 'Did you enjoy it?'

'Oh, yes,' she said. 'It was wonderful.'

She lied. She felt like a filthy animal. The anatomy books had said nothing about that.

2

THE BLACK PRINCE 1848

7

'Miz Julie, de patrol's done caught Big Gabe.'

Julia Devereux Scarborough looked up at Rufus, her dignified, white-haired butler. Miss Julie, as she was known to practically everyone in Talbot County, Maryland – Negro as well as white – was serving mint tea on the veranda of Scarborough Hall to the Reverend Elyot Wainscott and his wife, Emilia, as well as to several other friends and neighbours, so Rufus had whispered the information.

'Where did they put him?' she asked, keeping her voice low, but not whispering. Miss Julie hated whispering. It was not *comme il faut*. Still, she wasn't too eager to have her guests hear about Big Gabe, and Emilia Wainscott – that cat! – was straining her ears.

'In de quarter, mistris.'

'Is he . . . all right?'

'Yes ma'am. Well, one de dogs bit him de ankle, but . . .'

'Dogs?' Miss Julie stiffened in her anger, she forgot about her guests. 'I told Gaines I would *not* tolerate dogs!'

'Ah knows, mistris. But de patrol, dey uses 'em anyways. You knows well as Ah dey all trash.'

Miss Julie was fuming. She turned back to her guests, who were all leaning forward, listening. It was almost comical the way they snapped back when their hostess turned, feigning polite indifference to what they were dying to hear. But Miss Julie was in no mood for comedy.

'Thank you, Rufus,' she said. 'I'll see to it later.'

'Yes'm, Miz Julie.'

Rufus retreated back into the house. Emilia Wainscott sipped her tea.

'Some domestic difficulties, my dear?' she almost purred over the Wedgwood cup Miss Julia's mother had brought with her from her native England. Emilia Wainscott adored everything in Scarborough Hall – it was easily the most beautiful plantation on the Eastern Shore, not to mention the richest, and the furniture, the draperies, the silver, the china, the rugs . . . it was all exquisite. Miss Julie, however, was not so exquisite, in Emilia's estimation. Much too sharp-tongued and cocky, and more a tomboy than a lady. Even now – in her pale yellow dress with the matching bonnet that was so fetchingly feminine – even now there was something hard about her, tough . . . hardly, in Emilia Wainscott's opinion, what a Southern gentlewoman should be like. True, she was beautiful, with the black hair so admired by Southerners because it set off highly prized pale complexions. But then, Miss Julie didn't take care of her complexion the way a lady should. An excellent horsewoman, she failed to protect her skin from the sun, so that it was often burned or even – far worse! – tanned, like a common farmwife's. She had inherited her mother's English prettiness and finely chiselled features, but she was too lanky to conform to Emilia Wainscott's standards of femininity.

But by far the worst thing, in Emilia's opinion, as well as in the opinion of most of the county, was that Miss Julie had also inherited her English mother's Abolitionist proclivities. She loved nothing more than to shock the county gentry with her outspoken criticisms of the 'institution', and since she had taken over the management of Scarborough Hall, it was well known that she had prevented Mr Gaines, her overseer, from inflicting any form of physical punishment on her bondsmen. Everyone assumed that if old Mr Everett, Miss Julie's bedridden father, knew what his daughter was doing, he would have objected strenuously: Everett Scarborough was blissfully untainted by the Abolitionist heresy. But Mr Everett could barely speak; and meanwhile Miss Julie went about her shocking ways, spoiling her slaves and, due to the inevitable gossip that filtered throughout the other slave communities in the county, undoubtedly tainting her neighbour's slaves as well. Miss Julie was highborn, high-handed, and rich enough to get away with almost anything. But Emilia Wainscott would have loved nothing better than to bring her down a peg or two – or even six. Which was why she had been so interested to hear about the runaway, Gabriel.

Miss Julie was well aware of her guests' opinions, and she returned Emilia Wainscott's dislike in hearty kind. She had little but contempt for most of her smug neighbours in Talbot County, and part of her antislavery attitudes were based not only on a genuine dislike of the institution but on a love of scandalizing people like Emilia Wainscott. Now, realizing her guests had overheard Rufus, she decided the better part of valour was frankness.

'We had a runaway,' she said. 'One of the house servants took off last Tuesday, and the patrol's just caught him. But *dogs!* It's perfectly disgraceful using them!'

'Ah, I agree,' said Reverend Elyot Wainscott, who, at forty, made up in social graces what he sorely lacked in evangelical fervour. 'The dogs are sometimes inhumane. . . .'

'I fail to see how a dog could *ever* be humane,' interrupted Miss Julie, who had a particularly low opinion of the Reverend, whom she considered a snob, a hypocrite and a bore, not necessarily in that order. Still, her father insisted she entertain the Wainscotts at least once a month. It was important, said Everett Scarborough, for the planters to support the church so the church would continue to support the planters.

Reverend Wainscott's pale face creased into a cool smile that defied the heat of the August afternoon.

'An unfortunate choice of words on my part,' he said. 'I meant, of course, that the *use* of the dogs can be inhumane.'

'And uneconomical!' interjected Bruce Yarnell, the son of a neighbouring planter and the man most likely to win the hand of Miss Julie – or so thought most of the county. Miss Julie wasn't so sure. 'I mean,' went on Bruce, 'they can chew up the Negroes something awful, and then try and get any work out of them! Much less get your investment back if you try to sell them.'

'Dear Brucie.' Miss Julie smiled. 'Your concern for the Negroes' welfare positively melts my heart.'

'Well, it's true,' he grumped.

'Still,' continued Reverend Wainscott, 'one has to admit that the dogs are the most efficacious method of catching the rascals. I assume Big Gabe is a bad Negro?'

Miss Julie was secretly amused by the Reverend's politely deodorized version of the slave phrase 'b-a-a-ad nigger'. Of course, no one in society used the word nigger. Only servants and trash used that offensive word. Nor, for that matter, was the word slave used, servant being the euphemism preferred by the gentry. 'Slave' and 'nigger' weren't *comme il faut*. Besides, slave was too reflective of the reality of the planters' world, and planters, she knew, were not overly fond of reality. Reality was not *comme il faut* either.

'Gabriel is a very good servant,' she explained. 'By far the most intelligent Negro I've ever known. He's certainly as smart as any one of us.'

She smiled at the shocked looks on their faces. Particularly the shocked look on Bruce. Dear Brucie, she thought. He *is* good-looking, and the best horseman in the country. But he hasn't got a brain in that beautiful head of his. Besides, all he wants is my money.

'Now, Miss Julie!' Brucie laughed nervously. 'Aren't you going a little too far, honey?'

'No. I imagine he can read just as well as you, Brucie. And I *know* he spells better. You can't even spell "cat" right, can you?'

Smile. But the guests were not amused.

'You mean,' sputtered Saint George Tremaine, a cousin as well as another neighbour, 'this man can *read?*'

'Well, of course,' replied Miss Julie casually. 'I taught him. Tea, anyone?'

The remark had the effect of a not-too-small bomb, which Miss Julie knew and relished.

'But Julie, honey, you can't do *that!*' continued Cousin

Saint George, his already-red face getting redder. Cousin Saint George weighed a solid two hundred and fifty pounds, had high blood pressure, and drank. 'Does your daddy know you taught a *Negro* to read?'

Miss Julie shrugged as she popped a teacake in her mouth.

'How do I know?' she lied. 'But if he did, I'm sure he wouldn't care.'

'Now you know he *would*!' said Brucie, who was almost as red in the face as Cousin Saint George. Miss Julie was certainly causing a storm. 'Why, there's a *law* against it!'

'Pooh. There's a law against everything. No one pays any mind to the law, least of all *you*, Brucie.'

'But if you teach them to read,' interjected Reverend Wainscott, 'the Lord only knows *what* they'll read!'

'Maybe the Bible, Reverend?' said Miss Julie, in her sweetest voice.

'Maybe Abolitionist tracts!' snapped Cousin Saint George. 'Do you want them to get *ideas*?'

'Now you listen to me!' It was Miss Julie's turn to snap. 'This is a big plantation with four hundred and fifty servants, and since my father has taken ill, the running of it is up to *me*. While I obviously don't think it's smart to teach field hands to read, or stupid house servants, I *do* think it's important for some of the intelligent ones to be able to read and write so they can be of use to me running this place! I grew up with Gabriel Pembroke, and even though he's of colour, he's almost like a brother to me. I trust him implicitly and would like him one day to run the house accounts, which is what I had in mind when I taught him to read and write. And I don't care who knows it!'

'Julie,' growled her cousin, 'I've listened to your crazy ideas for longer than I like to think, but *this* takes the cake! If you weren't my cousin, I think I'd report you to Sheriff Caldwell.'

'And if you weren't *my* cousin,' retorted Miss Julie, 'I'd tell you to leave my house for being so rude. And my ideas *aren't* so crazy! I say we have to start educating the best of the servants to give them some hope of bettering themselves.

Because if we don't, one day Maryland is going to explode, and it's not going to be pretty. I assume you all remember what happened to Mrs Beecham?'

She looked at the faces of these people she had known all her life and wondered if they believed her. Certainly there was nervousness in the bloodshot eyes of Cousin Saint George. Despite his gruff manner, she knew he was afraid of his slaves – which was one reason he drank. The mention of Mrs Beecham was enough to bring nervousness to anyone's eyes, for that matter. A widow lady who lived in the next county and who had been known for her humane treatment of her slaves, Mrs Beecham only seven months before had had her throat slit by her coachman. True, he had been drunk. True, he was the lover of Mrs Beecham's maid, and it came out in the trial that Mrs Beecham had found out about the liaison and, in her shock, threatened to sell the coachman-lover. But still . . . murder? A collective shudder had run down the county's back. Mistresses and masters couldn't help but look at their trusted servants and mammies with wondering eyes.

'I certainly do remember Mrs Beecham!' said Saint George. 'We all do. And we all know her coachman murdered her *despite* the fact she petted her servants.'

'I haven't "petted" Gabriel,' said Miss Julie, who, despite her enjoyment of the sensation she had caused, was beginning to regret her imprudence in admitting having taught him to read. Talking down the institution of slavery was bad enough. But giving a bondsman the forbidden gift of literacy?

'I'd like to know what you call teaching him to read? If that ain't petting . . .'

'I *trust* him,' reiterated Miss Julie.

'If you trust him so much,' purred Emilia Wainscott, who was enjoying Miss Julie's discomfort, 'and if this Gabriel is so intelligent and good, then why did he run away, honey?'

You cat! thought Miss Julie.

'I don't know, Emilia,' she replied. Then she lifted her teacup. 'But I intend to find out.'

No one missed the determination in her voice. Everyone

in Talbot County knew Miss Julie Scarborough could be *very* determined. Born in 1825, the only child of Everett Scarborough and the beautiful Felicity Devereux of Essex, England, Miss Julie was now, in 1848, twenty-three years old. She was certainly a catch, with Scarborough Hall and over two thousand acres. But not many of the local bucks had the nerve to court her.

She was, they knew, *so* determined.

And yet, as is so often the case, Miss Julie's outward determination concealed an inner uncertainty – an uncertainty about the institution that was the very core of her existence: slavery – or, as she preferred to think of it, bondage, for even Miss Julie wasn't immune to the necessity for an occasional euphemism. Twelve years later, Nicole Louise Crandall might be indifferent to the institution and her son might have, at best, an intellectual distaste for it. But Julie Scarborough lived with it and on it. Slavery shaped her life as much as it shaped the lives of her slaves. Traditionally enough, she considered the slaves of Scarborough Hall as part of her family – her 'black' family – and she viewed herself not so much as their owner (though she was hardly oblivious to the amount of family capital tied up in black skin) as their mother. She took pride in the fact that her bondsmen were the best treated on the Eastern Shore, that her plantation was the best managed and most profitable, and that her converted-from-tobacco wheat fields were the richest. Yet, despite her outspoken criticism of slavery, she was uncertain about the possible alternatives to it. How else could the plantation be run? Who but Negroes would do the work, even for pay? And weren't the Negroes ideally suited to field labour? What could they possibly do otherwise? Could the Negro – childish, uncivilized, 'inferior' as most of them were considered to be, even by Miss Julie – compete with the white man in the labour market even if Maryland had any industry in the first place, which it didn't? It seemed unlikely. Slavery, with all its faults, was an answer not only to the needs of the slaveholder but of the slave as well. Wasn't the slave – as was constantly being pointed out by proslavery apologists – as well off as, if not better off than, the French peasant or the English factory worker or the Irish farmer?

And yet how 'petted' could a slave be? And wasn't ownership of human beings outrageously immoral? Her English mother had thought so. Even though Felicity Scarborough had loved Scarborough Hall, Miss Julie could remember overhearing her mother arguing in her clipped English tones with her father about bondage. The arguments had made Mr Everett apoplectic. He had tried to burn the Abolitionist literature Felicity had had sent to her from England. The arguments had stopped when Felicity died of cholera shortly after Julie's twelfth birthday; but Julie still remembered them. They still raged on in her heart. For a part of her thought like her father, even though intellectually she agreed with her mother. Part of her loved the plantation way of life that was so inextricably married with the 'peculiar institution'. Part of her thought it was wrong and, ultimately, doomed. Like an increasing number of Southerners, Miss Julie's life was not only shaped by slavery, it was agonized by it.

But one thing she was certain of: Gabriel Pembroke had betrayed her trust. And while Miss Julie was notoriously 'soft' on her slaves, she did not like being taken advantage of. Gabriel had taken advantage of her, and she meant to find out why.

He was certainly handsome. Everyone knew he had a white father, and many said it was old Colonel Pembroke himself over in Virginia, from whom Everett Scarborough had bought him as a baby twenty years before, along with his black mother, Sukey. But though there was a certain Caucasian 'refinement' in his features and his skin was brown rather than jet, still his hair was thick and woolly and undeniably African. His forehead was high and noble, his eyes piercing black and intelligent, his jawline strong. He stood six feet tall and was the strongest man on the plantation. As Miss Julie looked at him standing before her in the library of Scarborough Hall, his hands tied behind his back, clad in ragged and filthy Osnaburg cotton trousers and shirt, the same evil and frightening thought suggested itself to her that had occurred so often since the childhood playmates had passed through puberty and separated into their vastly different worlds: If only he were white!

'Untie him,' she said to Tillford Gaines, her white overseer.

'But Miss Julie ...'

'I won't have my servants tied, Mr Gaines! And I thought I told you I wanted no dogs? They might have killed him!'

Gaines was untying Gabriel's knots.

'But they *did* catch him,' he said insinuatingly.

She looked at Gabriel's left ankle. A bandage had been tied around it. How odd, she thought, seeing his big bare feet sunk in the Oriental rug. Her father would have whipped *her* if he knew she had brought a runaway into the Big House. But her father was upstairs in his canopied bed, enfeebled, immobilized, and struck almost dumb by his stroke. She was the mistress of Scarborough Hall now, in fact if not by law. And she wanted Gabriel inside the house. She wanted him to see the beautiful French desk, the chestnut *boiserie*, the Coromandel screen, the silver English sconces, the fine family portraits, the leather-bound books, the silver inkwell. . . . The richness and beauty of Scarborough Hall were part of her authority, the trappings of her divinity. In the quarter, she was mistress. In Scarborough Hall, she knew she was a goddess. Though Miss Julie was, by Talbot County standards, dangerously 'radical' in regard to slavery, she was not immune to the pleasures of divinity. Besides, she knew Gabriel envied the beauty of the fine brick Georgian mansion overlooking Chesapeake Bay. He had always lusted for that beauty: he never said it, but she knew. The sweeping lawns, the boxwood garden that was the finest in Maryland, the ancient oaks, the rose garden, the herb garden, the brick walks . . . he lusted for it. Bringing him in the Big House was pouring salt in the wound. Miss Julie hated the leather lash, but she was Southern enough not to be above using a psychological whip on occasion.

'You may leave us, Mr Gaines.'

'Yes, Miss Julie.'

Gaines left them alone. She was seated in the small sofa in the bay window. He was standing in front of her. Slaves always stood. That was part of the code, another visible manifestation of their inferiority. Gods, kings, and judges sat. Slaves stood.

'Why did you run away?' she said. 'After all I've done for you . . . after all the things I *would* have done for you . . . and you ran away. You betrayed me. Why?'

He looked at her a long time before answering. The look was neither insolent nor, on the other hand, uncaring. It was, she thought, a look that combined a lot of things: sadness, defiance . . . even nostalgia for a charming, if lost, childhood camaraderie. Then he answered. Simply, in his deep voice.

'I want to be free.'

She was smart enough to know that said it all, but her emotions wouldn't let it go at that.

'Free to starve in Philadelphia?'

'Yes, Miss Julie. Free even to starve.'

She lowered her voice.

'I taught you to read and write – the most precious gift anyone can give. . . .'

'No, Miss Julie. The most precious gift is freedom.'

She bit her lip. 'You know the risk I took doing it! Just an hour ago, Mr Yarnell and Mr Tremaine about exploded when I told them. But I did it! And I taught you to talk like a gentleman . . . or *almost* like a gentleman. . . .'

'I don't do no good to talk like a gentleman – even *almost* like a gentleman – unless you're free, Miss Julie.'

'Free, free, free!' she burst out. 'You were free here! At least, you have a good life here. I've taken you out of the fields and put you in the house . . . I've petted you, Gabriel, and you know it! Probably spoiled you rotten. . . .' She took a deep breath. This wasn't going the way she had planned. She was showing her emotions, which was wrong. She was his mistress, his owner. It might be immoral, but she *owned* him. He was her property, like the Coromandel screen.

'What am I going to do with you?' she finally asked.

He remained silent.

'You know what everyone else would do,' she went on.

'They'd tell Gaines to give you a good hundred strokes. Well, maybe I should but I can't, and you know it. You take advantage of my softness, Gabriel . . . and of what we were. How can I whip someone I grew up with? Someone I loved like a brother.' She looked at him. 'I don't want to hurt you. Will you give me your word you won't run away again?'

'I can't do that, Miss Julie.'

'In other words, no matter what I do, it won't make any difference?'

'I won't lie to you, Miss Julie. I aim to be free or dead. One or the other.'

'What if I sell you? I could get fifteen hundred for you easy. Maybe two thousand.'

'Wouldn't want you to sell me, Miss Julie. But you *could* set me free.'

The idea surprised her. Not because she had never considered manumitting some of her servants – she had considered it, but had dismissed it as impractical, at least as long as her father was still alive. But the fact that one of her servants had suggested it surprised her. It was brazen and insolent. It was also rather intriguing.

Gabriel pursued his momentary advantage. 'Lots of planters are doing it, Miss Julie . . .'

'Not lots: *some*.'

'All right, some. You know as well as I that slaves ain't profitable like they used to be – leastways, here in Maryland. Tempt a man with a decent wage instead of drivin' him with a whip, and he'll go out in the fields and work *twice* as hard. Look how the hands all work on Sundays! And why? 'Cause they get paid *money* when they work on their free day.' He lowered his voice to a seductive pitch. 'Why don't you free me, Miss Julie? I loves this place. I loves you and your family. You been good to me – lordie, I knows how good, you don't have to remind me. I don't *want* to run away. You taught me to read and write so I could be a *help* around here instead of just another nigger, and I want to do that. I want to help, earn my way in the world. But I have to do it as a man, Miss Julie, not as a slave. A *man*. Why don't you free me, Miss Julie? You do and you'll never have another moment's trouble from Gabriel Pembroke. For that, I gives you my word of honour.'

She stalled for time as her mind raced. Wasn't this, actually, the answer? Wasn't what he said the truth? Get rid of slavery and she could get rid of all the odious trappings of the institution: the dogs, the chains, the whipping, the cruelty. Replace the collar with the dollar, and wouldn't life at Scarborough Hall become almost idyllic? Or would it? As profitable as the wheat crops were, could they continue to turn a profit if she had to pay for her labour? And what about the capital investment? If she freed one slave – wouldn't the pressure to free all become overwhelming? And to free four hundred and fifty slaves was tantamount to throwing away half a million dollars. A half million!

She couldn't answer him yet. In fact, she couldn't make the decision. As long as her father was alive, he would have to approve it, no matter how feeble he was.

'You're not answerin' me, Miss Julie. Does that mean you're thinkin' 'bout it?'

Again she looked at him. To free him meant recognizing that he was a human being instead of a Coromandel screen. Well, wasn't he?

'I'm thinking about it,' she replied, telling herself to stay evasive, not to get his hopes up. 'But it wouldn't be up to me, it would be up to my father.'

'Then you'll talk to him about it, Miss Julie?'

She squirmed slightly. For all her antislavery convictions, this was putting her to the first real test.

'Perhaps,' she finally said. Then she returned to the attack. 'But don't you *dare* mention this to anyone! If we do free you, there'll be enough trouble with the other hands. I swear, Gabriel, if you breathe a word of this I'll have Mr Gaines give you the whipping you deserve!'

His eyes were bright with excitement.

'I won't say a word, Miss Julie. No ma'am! Not a *word*.'

'You'd better not. Now, go back to the quarter. I'm probably a fool to trust you again after what you've done, but I'll tell Mr Gaines not to lock you up – at least till I decide what to do with you.'

'Thank you, Miss Julie.'

She couldn't help but admire the dignity with which he said that. The other slaves fawned so on their masters. She supposed she couldn't blame them, but still it was annoying, another facet of the institution she despised. But Gabriel didn't fawn. He had dignity, as a man should. Free! A free Gabriel! The thought was growing more alluring and seductive by the moment. If he were free, he would almost – but of course not *quite* – be her equal. It was intellectually seductive to her, but was it also emotionally seductive?

She didn't know. She was afraid even to think about it.

But she was honest enough to confess to herself that if it had been any other bondsman than the imposingly handsome Gabriel Pembroke, she probably wouldn't have given the idea of freeing him even a first thought, much less a second.

Despite her antislavery convictions.

She was nervous about bringing the explosive subject up to her father, but, as it turned out, he brought the subject up to her. As was her custom, at seven-thirty that evening she climbed the graceful curving stair of the main hall to the second floor, followed by Rufus carrying the bed tray holding Mr Everett's simple supper. Then the procession filed down the upstairs hall to the door of the corner room her father had slept in most of his life, ever since the death of *his* father, Adam Scarborough. As she opened her father's door, she reflected on how many memories the walls of the spacious bedroom held. Scarborough Hall had been built in 1768, and four generations of owners had slept in this room, four generations of proud, slave-owning Scarboroughs. And now she – the soon-to-be owner – was entering the room bringing an *idea*. . . .

'How are you, Father?'

She had come to the side of the canopied bed. The evening sun flooded through the west windows of the room, the windows that overlooked the Chesapeake Bay. Her father spent most of his days propped in a wheelchair in front of one of these windows, staring out over the bay. He could barely move, barely talk, but she knew his mind was still active. What did he think of during those interminable sits? The past, surely: his present and future were hardly conducive to pleasant speculation. Then, every evening, his manservant, Bush, would carry him back to his bed, where he would wait for his tray.

He looked up at his only child, his eyes rheumy, his face wickered with wrinkles, his hair wispy and white. Everett Scarborough had been a fine-looking man, even at sixty-five, when he suffered his stroke. Now, two years later, he looked a prime candidate for the grave.

'Passable,' he whispered, his mouth framing the word with difficulty.

'We have a raspberry sorbet for you tonight,' said Miss Julie, standing aside as Rufus set the tray on his lap. 'Peter made it for you because of the heat.' Peter was the Scarboroughs' chef, a man whom Mr Everett had taken with him to Paris in 1837 for a six-month stint with a famous French chef. Peter's natural talent had bloomed under the Frenchman's tutelage. Now he was widely regarded as one of the best cooks south of the Mason-Dixon line. His master had once turned down the staggering offer of four thousand dollars for Peter. Mr Everett appreciated good cooking, even now, after his stroke.

She sat by the bed chattering nervously as Rufus fed her father. He held the wine glass filled with chilled Riesling: Mr Everett was allowed one glass a day, though she often let him have another, contrary to the doctor's order. This evening, she signalled Rufus to refill the glass. Best to put her father in a palmy mood before she mentioned the idea....

The old man's right hand could move slightly. Now he took a folded piece of paper from beneath his sheet and gave it to Rufus, indicating with his eyes that the butler should hand it to Miss Julie. He did so. She unfolded the note. It was written on Beech Grove stationery, Beech Grove being Cousin Saint George's plantation. He had gone home, written the note, and sent it back by one of his servants. She felt queasily nervous as she read:

Dear Everett:

Miss Julie has just conveyed such a shocking piece of information to me that I feel constrained to communicate it to you. As you must know, your man Gabriel has run away and been returned by the slave patrol. Miss Julie informed us that she has taught the man to read and write! Imagine our dismay at this revelation, though your daughter seemed uncaring enough, if not downright willful and proud about it! I need hardly remind you teaching slaves to read is a punishable offense, though I won't deny there are a growing number of foolish slaveholders who have taken to flouting the law under a misguided sense of Christian charity. As much as we all love Miss Julie, I think she must be reprimanded for this foolish and most irresponsible act. Despite your illness, as head of the family it seems to me it is still encumbent upon you to convey to her the danger of her folly.

As ever, respectfully, your cousin,
Saint George

She was furious. What right did her cousin have to meddle? Pompous Saint George with his terror of his own servants. . . .

Her father was watching her. Now she saw his mouth working, trying to form words.

'Wrong,' he finally got out.

She sealed up her anger.

'Rufus,' she said, 'you may remove the tray.'

'Yes'm, Miz Julie.'

She waited till the butler had left the room. Then she pulled her chair closer to the bed.

'Father,' she said in her softest, most wheedling tone, 'I know *why* everyone is afraid to teach the Negroes to read. But Gabriel is different. You *know* he is! I remember how many times you've said he was the smartest Negro you ever knew. . . .'

His mouth was working again, his eyes widening.

'Wrong,' he repeated.

She backed down. There had to be a different tack. 'All right, it's wrong to teach a bondsman to read. Then what if I freed Gabriel?'

Silence. The idea had been let out of its cage. Cousin Saint George had forced it out more abruptly than she might have wished, but it was out. She saw her father swallow with difficulty. The mouth started moving again.

'Wrong to free him. Dangerous.' Then his eyes moved to the bell rope next to the bed. 'Bush.'

She started to say something, then changed her mind and got up to pull the petit-point bell cord. She couldn't excite her father too much for fear of bringing on another stroke. That was what was so damnable about the situation. Her father's illness was what placed her in a position of authority at Scarborough Hall. But, perversely, it was this very illness that prevented her from fighting for what she believed in. *Did* she believe in freeing Gabriel, she wondered as she sat waiting for Bush. Did she believe in it enough to fight her father, her family and neighbours – most of the Eastern Shore? Much as she hated slavery, to reward a runaway with manumission was a monumental step. Could she go through with it? And if she did, might not others begin to question her motives, just as she herself was questioning them? Was her 'folly' a manifestation of something else besides anti-slavery fervour? Something more terrifying? If only Gabriel were white! The thought nibbled at her mind as it had so many times before. But what did *that* mean? If Gabriel were white, what? Was it possible . . .

Bush, the manservant, came in the room.

'Evenin', Miz Julie.'

'Evening, Bush. My father wants to see you.'

'Yes'm.'

Bush shuffled across the room to the bed and bent down. Loyal Bush; strong, faithful Bush. But stupid Bush, she thought. Lazy Bush. She would never consider freeing him. Then why Gabriel?

Bush straightened after listening to his master.

'What does my father want?' asked Miss Julie.

'Massa wants see Massa Gaines,' said Bush as he started shuffling back to the door.

She waited till Bush was gone, then addressed her father.

'What are you going to do?' she asked.

He looked at her, but said nothing. Now she began to realize the enormity of what she had done – or, rather, how appalling it must seem to her father. She cursed her lack of discretion that afternoon. It had been stupid to admit to having taught Gabriel to read: she had left herself wide open to attack. Yet they had all seemed so damnably smug....

She came to the bed and took her father's hand.

'Father,' she said softly, 'please trust me. Perhaps I was wrong with Gabriel... or at least too hasty. But everything's changing, and we have to change too. I love this place as much as you. But perhaps the best way for us to keep it prosperous is to begin to free the servants....'

She felt his hand begin to tremble, and she realized he was trying to pull it away from hers. She tightened her grip.

'Listen to me!' she insisted. 'It may be better to pay them in the long run! We can't seal Scarborough Hall off forever! We're too close to Pennsylvania. . . . Do we want to live in a prison? Don't you realize that by imprisoning the Negroes, we're prisoners too?' Don't go too far, she told herself. Don't go too far too fast. . . . 'It's true! Gabriel's not the first runaway, and he certainly won't be the last! So perhaps the wisest thing would be to work out some system for our people to earn their freedom....'

He was becoming so agitated that she didn't dare continue. Sighing, she let go his hand. It fell to the sheet. Then it was still. He was still, staring at her with eyes full of anger and resentment. She didn't have to guess what he was thinking. Despite his paralysis, his eyes were speaking for him.

Gaines came in the room.

'Evenin', Miss Julie.'

She returned to her chair as the overseer walked to the bed and leaned over to listen to his employer. After a moment, he straightened and smiled slightly at Miss Julie. Gaines never said much, but she knew he disliked her because she wouldn't give him a free hand with the slaves. A free hand meant, of course, a hand holding a whip.

'Your father,' he said, 'wants me to send Big Gabe to Billie Orton for six months.'

'No!' She jumped out of her chair again. 'Father, you can't! That's the wrong way to treat Gabriel – I swear it! Billie Orton will ruin him!'

'Maybe he's already ruined, Miss Julie,' said Gaines. 'Maybe Billie'll fix him up for us. Big Gabe's got a lot of fancy ideas for a nigger....'

'I've told you not to use that loathsome word in my presence!'

'Sorry. For a "servant", then. But Billie's broken fancier boys than Big Gabe. Reckon he'll do a good job on him as well.'

She returned to the bed.

'Father, *please*,' she said. 'My way's the better one – I'm convinced of it. Please let me handle Gabriel. Let me *free* him.'

Her father stared at her. Then, slowly, he shook his pillowed head in a defiant No!

She felt almost sick to her stomach. She knew there was nothing she could do as long as her father was alive. What made her feel sick was that her desire to free Gabriel – to make him her almost equal – was now so intense that for a fleeting moment she had wished her father, whom she adored, were dead.

8

'Ah'm gonna break you, nigger,' said Billie Orton the next afternoon. 'Cause breakin' niggers is my business.'

And he smiled a pleasant smile. He was a pot-bellied gorilla of a man, about forty-five Gabriel figured, with dirty red-gold hair and a freckled sunburned face. He was trash. His son, Junior, who was locking the leg chains on

Gabriel's ankle, was trash: a tall, rawboned twenty-year-old with his father's colouring. Junior picked his nose and stank to high heaven. Billie's wife, Georgina, who was standing under a tree in the farmyard watching the little ceremony, was trash too: skinny trash with a raw face and mouse-coloured, unbrushed hair already streaked with grey. Gabriel had grown up on the finest plantation on the Eastern Shore. Despite his resentment of his bondage, he had long since identified with the Scarboroughs. He considered himself 'quality' even though he was a slave, and he judged the rest of the world by Scarborough standards. Thus, even though he was afraid of the Ortons, he consoled himself by mentally scorning their trashiness, their rundown shack of a farmhouse, their sagging barn, their scruffy-looking fields. The Ortons were trash, but trash, he knew were meaner than quality toward Negroes. And he knew Billie Orton's reputation: he was the meanest trash of all.

'You're gonna work real hard here, nigger.' Billie continued. 'So hard that when we gets done with you, any place else is gonna look like Heaven. That's how the Orton System works. That's why Mr Everett is givin' you to me for free for six months. Cause he knows when you come home again, you're gonna be so grateful you'll burst into tears of joy if he kicks you in the teeth. Ah unnerstan' you're a smart nigger? Know how to read and write. You can answer, boy.'

'Yessir. I can read and write.'

'Uh huh. Talk pretty good too. Don't talk mushie-mouth like a nigger. Well, you'd better learn rule one: around here you don't talk unless we tells you to. Unnerstan'? You can answer, boy.'

'Yessir.'

'Good. Now rule two: we got a system of marks here, just like a school. You do sump'n wrong, you gets a mark. Goes from one to six, and each mark is worth fifty lashes. Can you unnerstan' that? Ah mean, can you count? You can answer, boy.'

'Yessir.'

'What do you think of that, Junior? He can count! We got a real smart nigger here.'

Junior stood up and grinned in Gabriel's face. 'Yeah. Smart.'

'Tell Jake to come here.'

'He still pretty sore, Pa. Don't know if he can move.'

'Well, kick him. An wanna show our smart nigger what he's got to look forward to. *Move!*'

'Yes, Pa.'

Junior headed for a swaybacked log cabin next to the barn. The cabin he had a solid wooden door with a tiny window hole.

'That's your home from now on,' said Billie, spitting on the sun-baked ground. 'Got five boys in there now: you'll make six. Six "students" at the Orton Academy of Higher Learnin'. Very exclusive school.'

He grinned, showing teeth almost black from chewing tobacco. His wife snickered as she brushed away a fly.

A minute later, Gabriel saw Junior leading a Negro out of the cabin. He was young, about Gabriel's age. Like Gabriel, his ankles were chained. Like Gabriel, he wore nothing but a torn pair of Osnaburg trousers. Unlike Gabriel, he was slightly twisted and moved as if each step were excruciating. Junior shoved him, and he almost tripped over his chains.

'Come here, Jake,' called Billie. The slave shuffled up to Orton. Gabriel saw that he was trembling, whether from fear or some sort of fever he didn't know. 'Jake, this is Gabriel, your new classmate. Turn around and show him your back.'

Jake slowly turned. His back was a welter of grey scar tissue, in places as much as an inch thick. Gabriel winced as he looked. He had seen whippings; he had been whipped himself – what slave hadn't? But this was the worst he had ever seen.

'Jake stole a piece of pork three days ago,' said Billie, again spitting on the ground. 'Now, you niggers get meat once a week, which is generous. So we don't cotton to no thievin'. Jake earned five marks for that little business – five out of a possible six. Almost won the whole pot. That's two hunnert and fifty lashes. Was the pork worth two hunnert and fifty lashes, Jake? You can answer, boy.'

'No, massa.'

'You ever gonna steal again?'

'No, massa. Never. Ah swears.'

'What are you, Jake? Describe yourself, boy.'

'Ah's a no-good nigger, massa. Lazy, no-good, wuthless nigger. Lak as not the world'd be better off wifout me.'

'You're a thief too. Say it, boy.'

'Ah's a teef.'

'Now, Jake, you've had three days off. But you're goin' back to work in the morning. You know that, boy?'

'Yes, massa.'

'And how hard you gonna work, boy?'

'Hard 'nuff make massa pleased.'

'That's *mighty* hard, Jake. All right, Junior: take him back.'

'Yes, Pa.'

Junior shoved Jake, who started shuffling back toward the cabin. Gabriel had tears of rage in his eyes. It wasn't so much the physical cruelty as the mental debasement Orton had subjected Jake to that enraged him. Orton had turned Jake into a cringing animal. He'll never do that to *me*, he thought. Never.

Billie was watching him. Now he picked up a stick from the ground and walked over to Gabriel. He touched the end of the stick to Gabriel's right cheek, just below his eye. Gabriel stiffened.

'You cryin', boy?' He turned to his wife. 'You see what Ah see? This nigger's cryin'! Why, he muss have a soul as tender as catfish – assumin' niggers *got* souls, which Ah ain't so sure of. Huh. If yo cries for Jake, boy, what you gonna do for yourself? Hm? We ought to see a whole *river* – that right? You gonna cry us a whole river, boy?' He was walking slowly around him now, poking the stick gently into his chest, his arms, his back, his buttocks. 'Sure is strong, Mrs Orton. He ought to be able to haul a tree. Strong, smart, and he cries for Jake. We got us an interestin' nigger here,

Mrs Orton.' He stopped behind Gabriel and dug the stick into the small of his back, which was glistening with sweat from the broiling sun. He dug the stick in hard and held it.

'Don't move boy,' he whispered. 'Don't you move an inch.'

Gabriel closed his eyes and tensed. The stick hurt, but again it wasn't the pain so much as the humiliation. Why, O God? he thought. Why is this pig of a man doing this to me? Why do you allow it, God? Why do you hate me, why do you hate the black man? WHY??

Then, suddenly, the stick was removed from his back. He heard a swhishing sound, and the stick bit his ear and the side of his head. He howled, cringed, and threw up his hands, covering his head.

'You moved, boy,' he heard Orton say behind him. 'You *moved*.'

Gabriel turned halfway around. A roar of rage was in his throat, but when he saw Orton's smile, he strangled it. That's what he *wants*, you fool! he thought. That's what he wants!

'Gonna hit me, nigger?' said Orton. 'Is that what you're gonna do? You can answer me, boy.'

'No.'

'No, *massa*.'

'No, massa.'

'Ah think you're lyin', boy. Ah think you wanted to hit me. Now tell the truth. We don't like lies around here.'

'Yes, I want to hit you,' he said softly. 'I want to *kill* you.'

The humming of the flies was the only sound. For almost a full minute, Billie Orton stared at him, his grin growing bigger.

'That's more like it,' he finally said. 'You just earned yourself four marks. Junior!'

Junior came hurrying back from the cabin, where he had locked Jake in.

'Yes, Pa.'

'This nigger's just earned hisself four marks for talkin' mean, and movin' and lyin'. So let's get him over to the whippin' ground.'

'Yes, Pa. He sure work fast, don't he?'

Junior was grinning too.

'*Mighty* fast. Fastest nigger in Maryland, Ah reckon. Now boy, walk over toward the barn. Mrs Orton, get the grease ready.'

Georgia nodded and moved toward the house. She seemed only vaguely interested, as if she were so used to cruelty it had become meaningless to her. Or perhaps she tried to hide from it. Gabriel walked toward a patch of bare earth next to the barn. Billie and Junior flanked him. He could see four iron pegs in the dirt, each having a leather manacle attached to it. Beyond the whipping ground, a crude fence enclosed some pigs. Beyond that was a chicken house, and then a field of weeds. Past the field was a forest. He could see three slaves piling logs on an oxcart. There was no driver or overseer; Orton apparently had so terrorized his 'students' he felt no need for a driver. Terror. It lay over the shabby farm like a shroud. Jake was terrorized. Would the Ortons be able to terrorize him, Gabriel?

'Lay down, boy. Face down. Stretch out your arms over your head.' He poked him with the stick. 'Go on now.'

Escape, thought Gabriel. Was it possible? The farm is isolated, and there's only the two of them. Escape, escape, escape. But not yet. Too soon. The patrols are everywhere, and the patrols must watch this place. Perhaps that's why he doesn't need a driver. Too soon. Escape. Philadelphia. Freedom. Follow the North Star to freedom.

Junior punched him in the right kidney.

'Lay down, nigger!' he yelled.

Gabriel sank to his knees. The bare dirt was scorching. Then he lay out and stretched his arms above his head. The earth burned his stomach, his chest, his right cheek. He could smell the heat of the earth. With his left eye, he saw Junior step over him and kneel to fasten the leather manacles on his wrists. The father fastened Gabriel's left ankle, but not the right, since the leg chain prevented his legs from spreading far enough. Then Junior stood up and disappeared from his view.

Gabriel's left eye stared at a distant chicken as he waited.

The first lashes were like streams of scalding water. He

bit the dirt and refused to howl as first Billie, and then Junior, laid into him, the nonwhipper counting out loud. 'Eight . . . nine . . . ten . . .' 'Nineteen, twenty, twenty-one . . . 'Thirty-two, thirty-three, thirty-four . . .' 'Fifty-eight, fifty nine, sixty! Sixty-one . . .'

After about the hundredth, the pain lessened, or rather he became numb; but it was replaced by a dead aching that spread all over his back like a cancer. The aching was worse than the pain because it seemed to penetrate his very bowels. 'Hunnerd and twenty . . . hunnered twenty-one . . . hunnerd twenty-two . . .' Then the scream began in his brain, spreading throughout his head, blasting his ears, his eyes, his nostrils. He didn't know if the scream were real or a product of his ravaged imagination. 'Hunnered fifty-four . . . hunnerd fifty-five . . . hunnered fifty-six . . .'

At a hundred and seventy, he lost consciousness. His last screaming thought was that life was the invention of Satan.

He was taken, unconscious, into the kitchen of the house and laid on the floor. A Negro woman named Sarah washed his back with brine. Then Mrs Orton produced a bucket of grease and smeared it over the raw wounds, after which she applied linen bandages. During this operation, Billie and Junior sat on a bench and drank cider. No one spoke. They just watched.

Gabriel was beginning to stir when they heard a horse galloping up.

'See who that is,' said Orton.

Junior went to the door and looked out. 'Some lady,' he reported. 'She's stoppin' here.'

Orton went to the door, pushing his son aside. Outside, a beautiful woman in a smart riding habit was tying a sleek horse to a tree.

'It's old man Scarborough's daughter,' mumbled Orton. 'Get that nigger out of here.'

Then he left the house and advanced toward Miss Julie. 'Afternoon, ma'am. Mah name's Billie Orton. Do Ah have the pleasure of addressin' Mr Scarborough's daughter?'

'You do, though I'm not sure how much of a pleasure it's going to be. Where's Gabriel?'

'He's out workin' in the forest, miss. We're clearin' some acreage . . . hope to plant it in wheat next year. Course, it won't be like your father's place. . . .'

'Hardly,' Miss Julie looked the fat man over. 'I want you to understand something, Mr Orton. Gabriel was brought here against my wishes. I prize him highly. I'm aware of what you do here, but I'm warning you: if you harm him in any permanent way, I shall bring a legal action against you. Is that perfectly clear?'

'Oh yes, ma'am. And Ah'm in full agreement with you. Wouldn't do for me to harm the Negroes. Why, no master in his right mind would send his slaves to me if Ah ruined them! No, ma'am. But we *do* break them. You won't have no trouble with Gabriel when Ah gets done with him.'

She tapped her riding crop against her skirt.

'I'd like to talk to him. Please fetch him for me.'

Orton hesitated. 'Like Ah said, ma'am, he's in the forest. . . . He won't be back till evenin' . . .'

'You're lying.'

She walked past him toward the house. Orton hurried after her.

'Now, just a minute, miss. You don't own this place! Ah'm a free man. . . .'

'I want to see my Gabriel!'

Orton gave in with a shrug. 'Then you shall see him, ma'am. Junior!' he bellowed. 'Bring him out.' He turned to Miss Julie and smiled. 'The truth is, miss, we just gave him a whippin'. Sort of a welcome gesture, so to speak. Make him feel at home. He's not in very good shape, but he's gonna get lots more in the next six months, so he might as well get used to it. We won't hurt him permanent, so you won't have no cause to hire lawyers. But he's gonna get whipped. *Lots.* That's why your daddy sent him to me, ain't it?'

'Unfortunately . . . yes.'

She saw Junior carry Gabriel out of the kitchen and set him on a stool by the door. He was conscious now. She hurried over to him, removing her gloves. She looked at Junior and said, 'Leave us.'

He moved away. She looked at Gabriel's bandaged back, then at his face, which was covered with sweat.

'I heard what happened,' she said quietly. 'I suppose it's ridiculous for me to say I'm sorry, but I am.'

'I guess you didn't talk your daddy into freeing me, Miss Julie. Either that, or you didn't try much.'

'I tried, Gabriel, I wouldn't blame you if you didn't believe me, but I *did* try. But my father is . . . old-fashioned.'

'Uh huh. So why did you come here, Miss Julie? Your conscience botherin' you?'

Her temper started to flare. How *dare* he talk to her that way? Then it subsided.

'I came here to tell you that when my father passes on, I will free you. That may not be much help to you now, but . . . well, I thought maybe it would be *some* help. And after all, my father's in poor health. It could be soon.'

He nodded his head slowly. 'Could be. Could be five years. Anyway, thank you, Miss Julie. It's decent of you to tell me.'

She felt awkward, even stupid. He was hardly reacting with the heartfelt gratitude she had expected. For some reason she felt she should apologize to him for offering to free him. She felt such pity for him, such helplessness, such dismay at his bitterness. . . .

She reached out and touched his cheek. The action surprised him as much as her. She felt the sweat on his smooth skin. Then she retracted her wet fingers. They looked at each other with mutual confusion.

Then she turned and went back to her horse. She said nothing to the Ortons as she untied the reins. She mounted sidesaddle, turned the horse, and cantered back to the road that led to Scarborough Hall, some ten miles south of the Orton farm.

'Did you see *that?*' muttered Billie Orton to his son.

'Sure was odd,' said Junior. 'Like maybe they was . . .'

Billie looked at Gabriel, sitting on the stool by the kitchen door.

'It's their pricks,' he said. 'Them white bitches all think niggers is hung like bulls.'

'Well, they is, Pa.'

'Shit, what do you know about it? Ain't that sump'n, though? Miss High and Mighty Scarborough and that nigger. Well now, he's even more interestin' than Ah 'spected. Ah figger we're gonna have a lotta fun with this one, Junior. Treat him *real* special. Yessir.'

'Can't harm him though, Pa. We don't want no lawyers, do we? She sounded serious.'

'Well, they's *ways*, Junior. They's ways. When we get done with him, that nigger's gonna wish he never laid a lustful eye on no white woman. In fact,' and he spat on the ground, 'that nigger's gonna wish he's dead.'

The afternoon of 10 September 1848 Miss Julie was driven in her carriage from Scarborough Hall to the Tremaine plantation, Beech Grove. While Beech Grove was not as grand as Scarborough Hall, it was still a beautiful home, approached by a long drive lined with beech trees and oaks. It was a clapboard house, with a graceful front door facing a lawned oval outlined by a short brick wall. Miss Julie climbed out of the carriage and went to the front door, where Thompson, the Tremaines' butler, admitted her to the entrance hall.

'Pleased to see you, Miss Julie,' smiled the butler. 'You haven't paid us a call for a long time. You're lookin' mighty pretty.'

'Why, thank you, Thompson. Is Miss Adelaide in?'

'Yes, miss. She up in her bedroom.'

'Another of her headaches?'

' 'Fraid so.'

'I'll just run up and say hello.'

She hurried up the stairs and went to her cousin's door. Though Miss Julie had still not forgiven Saint George for what she thought of as his interference with her business the month before, his wife, Miss Adelaide, was her closest female relative, and she needed her help. After knocking on the door, she opened it and peered in.

'Adelaide? It's Julie.'

The room was semidark, the shutters having been closed over the windows, but enough light filtered through so that she could see Miss Adelaide sitting in her chaise longue.

'Julie, honey? Why, what brings you here?'

She went in the room and closed the door. It was a fussy room, all chintz and frills and flounces, with pink-and-white striped wallpaper that was almost totally concealed by numerous framed prints depicting scenes from the romantic novels Miss Adelaide devoured by the cart-load. She was wearing a frilly bedjacket with a pink coverlet pulled over her legs. A box of pralines from New Orleans was by her chaise, and a novel rested on her lap. Miss Adelaide was ensconced for the day.

'I had to see you,' said Miss Julie. 'Honestly, it's no wonder you get headaches, the way you read practically in the dark! What's the book?'

'Oh, it's Mrs Fairfield's latest, and *so* wonderful! The heroine is a sweet governess who's engaged to instruct the children of a *very* handsome baronet, Sir . . . what's his name? Oh yes, Sir Hubert. Sir Hubert's first wife died under mysterious circumstances, and his second wife just vanished . . . *he* says she ran off with a Jamaican planter, but it's an obvious lie. *I* think she's the mysterious woman living in the west wing *pretending* to be a Polish countess. . . . Anyway, the heroine – her name is Gwendolyn –'

'I can't stand heroines named Gwendolyn,' interrupted Miss Julie, pulling up a chair. 'And governesses bore me silly. Now are you ready for a surprise?'

'Oh *yes!* The summer's been so tedious. . . .'

'Bruce Yarnell has asked for my hand in marriage, and I've accepted.'

'Oh *Julie!*' Miss Adelaide, who was a plump fifty, trilled. 'Oh, how thrilling! How wonderful! Oh, I'm . . . oh, honey, congratulations! Kiss your old cousin, and pass the pralines!'

Julie laughed as she obeyed. Miss Adelaide hugged her, then popped a praline in her mouth.

'Now tell me *all* about it! Did he get down on his knees? And the ring – oh, let me *see!*'

Julie extended her hand as Miss Adelaide inspected the diamond.

'Well, it's gorgeous. But it's sort of small. . . .'

'Need sharp eyes to see it at all,' replied Miss Julie.

'Well, it's not the size of the stone that counts, honey: it's the sentiment behind it. And I know you two are madly in love. . . .'

'Oh pooh, Adelaide. You've been reading too many syrupy novels. Love has precious little to do with it, and you know it. Brucie's after my money, and I want Brucie because Daddy wants some grandchildren before he dies, and I want him to have them. Brucie's poor as a church-mouse, but he's the best-looking man in the county and he's available. So I said yes.'

'Now Julie, I don't even want to hear you speak that way! I know there's a much more tender sentiment to all this than you'll let on. You just like to shock us all – you always have – trying to be all brains and no heart! Well, I declare: this is *so* exciting! I'm . . . When's the wedding? I *do* hope it's going to be big and gaudy?'

Miss Julie laughed. 'Oh, gaudy as Christmas! And that's why I need you. You'll have to help me and sort of run things, since you're my closest female relative.'

'Oh honey, I'd have been furious if you hadn't asked!'

'You'll have to give up your headaches and your novels, at least till it's over with. It's going to be a lot of work.'

'Weddings aren't work: weddings are fun! Now, who'll we *not* invite? It's so much more fun to start with the ones you're going to cut. . . .' She paused and lowered her voice. 'You *are* in love with Bruce, aren't you? I know how you enjoy talking flippantlike, but I wouldn't want my sweet little cousin to make the *disastrous* mistake of not marrying for love! Marriage is such a sacred institution . . . it mustn't be entered into for frivolous reasons.'

'I'm sure Brucie doesn't think my money is a bit frivolous. And you're sounding like that dreary Reverend Wainscott. I'll get enough treacle from him at the wedding.'

'But it's true, honey! Now be honest: you do love Bruce, don't you? Heavens, he's certainly lovable – outrageously so! He's better-looking than the law allows, the Yarnells are quality even though they're – well, a little strapped financially. . . . Tell me you love him, honey.'

Miss Julie sighed. 'Yes, I love him. I don't think he's got a *seed* of a brain, but I love him.'

Miss Adelaide smiled. 'That's better.' Then softly: 'Theres not someone else?'

Julie threw her sharp look. 'What makes you ask that?'

'Well, you just seem so lukewarmy about Bruce, I couldn't help but wonder. . . .'

Julie laughed as she stood up. 'It's those novels again! No, there's no one else. I'm madly in love with Brucie, he's the light of my life, and we're going to have *scads* of babies. I'm going to ring for Thomas to bring me some tea, then we two have to get to work.' She crossed the room to tug the bell cord. 'I've already sent out invitations for an announcement ball next week. I used Daddy's name, but of course I had to write them myself. . . .'

'I'm sure Cousin Everett is thrilled *speechless*!' Then she gasped and covered her mouth.

Miss Julie gave her a look. 'We'll just forget you said that, honey.'

Jake didn't have a last name. He didn't even know what year he had been born in, though everyone told him he must be about twenty. Jake didn't know who his father was and his mother had died when he was five, shortly after she had been bought by Mr Pingree, a planter near Saint Michael's. Jake had been raised by Aunt Sally, Mr Pingree's ill-tempered cook. Jake knew little about love or affection, but he knew a lot about hate.

He hated Billie Orton as much as he was terrified of him. But in the six weeks since Gabriel had come to the farm, Massa Billie had been almost gentle to his five other 'students' as he subjected Gabriel to a regime of cruelty that had amazed even Jake, who also knew a lot about cruelty. They were whipping Gabriel again right now. Jake and Juba and Tooey and Bones and Quack – Gabriel's five 'classmates' – huddled silently on the dirt floor of their small log cabin and listened to the swish of the hickory.

Finally it was over.

'Don't know how he's *'live*', whispered Quack, a skinny young man who was also from Mr Pingree's. Quack's name was derived from the African word Quaco, which meant a male born on Wednesday. Quack at least knew when he had been born.

'Massa Billie sure mean on him,' agreed Juba. 'Dass de third time dis week dey whup him. An' whaffo? Twarnt *his* fault de mule run wild.'

'Don't make no matter to Massa Billie if de mule sit down, go to sleep. He'd still whup Gabe 'cause he *wants* to whup him.'

'Makes it easier on us,' volunteered Tooey.

The others turned on him.

'What kinda talk is dat?' Jake sounded indignant. 'We all brothuhs, Tooey.'

'Maybe. But Ah's only got fo' mo' weeks in dis place, den mah massa come take me home. An' Ah can tell you, home's gwine look mighty sweet after *dis* hole.'

'Still an' all, don't you be glad Gabe's out dere gettin' skinned alive!'

'Didn't say Ah was *glad.* Jes said it was easier on us.'

'Ah knows why Massa Billie hate Gabe so much,' said Juba. 'Gabe *talk* better'n massa.'

'Yeah, an' he smarter too,' agreed Quack.

'Huh. Don't take much be smarter dan massa,' said Bones. 'He de dumbest white man evah born. He so dumb Ah seen him pee into de wind.'

The others chuckled.

'An' *Junior!*' added Quack. 'Dat boy ain't never so happy as when he pickin' his nose.'

'Lotta nose to pick,' said Juba. 'Ah tinks he done pick his brain one day by mistake an' toss it away, tinkin' it a boogah.'

This sent the others into prolonged snickers. The five of them sat on the dirt floor, their legs chained, rocking back and forth with shared mirth as huge mosquitoes whined through the two tiny, glassless windows – windows that let in precious little air in the blistering summer, but now, on this September evening, were letting in drops of the chill drizzle that was the harbinger of winter's freeze. Often, on the most stifling July nights, they had consoled one another by remarking on how lucky they were to be at Massa Billie's in summer rather than winter. It was, admittedly, not much consolation.

The solid wood door was opened, and Junior pushed Gabriel through. The others made room for him as he stumbled onto his knees.

'Pleasant dreams,' smiled Junior. Then he slammed the door and slid the thick wood bolt into place.

There was still enough evening light so that they could see the bloody stripes on Gabriel's back. The scabs from previous whippings had not had time to solidify, and the new whipping had reopened many of them, making his back resemble a field ploughed by a rampaging maniac. Gabriel knelt for a long time, not moving, burying his face in his tight fists. The others said nothing at first, out of respect for his pain.

Then Jake whispered, 'Can us do sump'n to help, Gabe?'

Slowly, Gabriel removed his fists from his face and looked at them.

'We're going to escape,' he said softly. 'All of us. We're going north, going to get out of this misery.'

The others exchanged nervous looks.

'When?' said Quack.

'As soon as my back's better – that is, if those bastards'll keep off me for a while. . . .'

'You make it sound mighty easy. How we gwine escape?'

'When he sends us into the woods one day, we head north.'

'What 'bout de patrols?'

'We'll travel by night, follow the North Star.'

'De patrols travel by night too.'

'But there's not as many of them. Besides, they can't see at night.'

Tooey shook his head.

'Dey ain't gwine see me, day or night, 'cause Ah'm stayin'

here. Ah only got fo' mo' weeks till mah massa take me home.'

'Then stay. How about you, Quack?'

Quack didn't answer for a moment. Then: 'Ah's feared, Gabe. Ah bin caught twice before. First time massa cat-haul me. Never forget *dat*. Second time, he send me here. Ah's feared, Gabe.'

'What dat "cat-haul" mean?' asked Juba.

'He drag a big tomcat down mah back an' over mah bare bottom, holdin' de cat by his tail. Dat cat was *so* mad, an' he dug into mah back wid his claws till Ah tought Ah go crazy. Don't want to try *dat* again.'

'Juba?' said Gabriel.

He shook his head. 'Only got two months more, Gabe. Ah sticks wid de debbil Ah knows.'

'Bones?'

'Ah stays here.'

'Jake?'

Silence. Then: 'Ah's gwine wif you, Gabe. Ah's gwine north to be free.'

Gabriel put out his right hand. Jake took it with his left and they squeezed each other's hands a moment.

'Let's get some sleep,' suggested Juba.

The six of them curled up in the dirt, slapping desultorily at the clouds of mosquitoes as the rain dripped.

A small cloud scuttled past the full harvest moon that was sailing toward its zenith through a star-sequined sky. A hurricane had bypassed Maryland two days before, bringing in its train glorious weather and brisk breezes, so Miss Julie couldn't have ordered better weather for her announcement ball, and the full moon was romantic icing on the cake. Scarborough Hall blazed with hundreds of candles, while near the slave quarters the hundreds of field hands were gathered around a tent which Miss Julie had put up for the servants. Here, barbecued pork, turkeys and yams were being served along with beer and cider (and Maryland rye whisky, though Miss Julie pretended not to know about that), while two fiddlers sawed wild jigs and reels. The drivers of the dozens of carriages parked in the long drive were there along with the Scarborough people, drinking, eating, clapping time to the music. . . . It was a gay night, for Negro as well as white, and everyone had cause to bless Miss Julie and her impending union with Bruce Yarnell.

Inside the Big House, the gentry of Talbot County were enjoying themselves in a slightly more dignified way, though Rodney Yarnell, Bruce's younger brother, was becoming wildly drunk – to no one's surprise – and Archie Gadsen and Beau Tremaine had spiked the punch in the not overly subtle hope of getting the unmarried females pleasantly and libidinously tipsy. The two parlours were connected by double doors, which had been opened, and the two rooms had been cleared of their furniture and the rugs rolled up to provide a makeshift ballroom. At one end, in front of the big open windows overlooking the moonlight silvered Chesapeake Bay, Fat John, a slave from the Leffingwell plantation and the best fiddler on the Eastern Shore, was leading his four-man slave orchestra. Their owner, Mr Leffingwell, allowed the group to hire out to county balls (in return for half the fee). At the moment they were playing a reel, and twenty couples were 'dancing up a storm', according to Rufus, who was supervising the forty servants who were attending the guests.

'Isn't Miss Julie's dress divine?' said Miss Gladys Rutherford to her slightly bucktoothed sister, Georgianna. The Rutherford girls were sitting this reel out with their despairing mother. It was the third reel that none of the local beaux had seen fit to ask either of the homely sisters to dance, and Mrs Rutherford was in an agony.

'It's gorgeous,' sighed Georgianna.

In fact, Miss Julie looked radiant in a ball gown of topaz silk. The panels of the skirt leaped out from the trim waist, while the bodice was softened by a diaphanous shawl of fawn lace. A huge pink silk rose clasped the shawl at her cleavage, and another rose was pinned in her black hair. Around her neck was a diamond-and-topaz necklace that had belonged to her mother, Felicity, with a matching bracelet on her left wrist. As she danced with Bruce – who, the Rutherford sisters agreed wholeheartedly, was the '*most* elegant and *most* dashing man' they had ever seen – the handsome couple looked as if they had the world at their well-shod, tapping feet.

'Happy?' smiled Bruce to his fiancée.

'Shouldn't I be? All the girls are absolutely puce with envy. I think they'd like to kill me for getting you.'

'You make it sound like you chased me, Miss Julie, when we both know it was the other way around.'

She smiled. 'Maybe *my* way of chasing is pretending the opposite. Land sakes, I've danced my feet off! Can we go out for some air?'

'Why sure, honey.'

He offered his arm as Fat John started another reel, and they made their way through the dancers to one of the open French doors. Outside, Julie led him to a gnarled oak under which was a stone bench. She sat down as he leaned against the oak.

'Look at the moon!' she said. 'Isn't it just romantic as all get out? You feeling romantic, Brucie?'

He took her hand and raised it to his lips. 'I feel romantic every time I even think of you, Miss Julie.'

He kissed her hand. She watched him with almost clinical detachment.

'And just *what* about me makes you feel so romantic every time you think of me?' she asked. 'My soft black hair? Or my big baby-blue eyes? Or my two thousand acres of prime farmland?'

'Now listen!' He released her hand. 'I love you, Miss Julie, and I'm getting sick of all these insinuations you keep making that I'm after your money! Didn't I sign that . . . that thing – what do you call it? – that your daddy's lawyer drew up . . .'

'Our prenuptial agreement.'

'That's it! Didn't I sign that? Which no gentleman would ever *stoop* to sign if he weren't as crazy in love with you as I am. . . . Didn't it say I agree that Scarborough Hall is yours to manage and dispose of as *you* see fit? Didn't I agree never to challenge your ownership legally? Now dammit, Miss

Julie, what belongs to a man's wife by rights should belong to the husband too! But oh no, I signed my husbandly rights away because you made such a fuss over it. . . . So how can you keep on implying I'm after your money? Now, if you don't take it back, I'm going in there and announce to everyone we know that our engagement is *off!* I mean it, now!'

She opened her mother-of-pearl fan and fluttered it languidly.

'Sure would be a funny announcement to make at an announcement ball,' she said. 'But you go ahead, Brucie. I won't stop you.'

A cricket chirped merrily as Bruce fumed.

'Why are you doing this to us?' he finally growled. 'Why are you making our love so *sordid* . . . so financial?'

'Because our love *is* financial.' She stifled a yawn. 'And probably more than a little sordid, too. Oh Brucie, honey, let's not make any mistake about what each of us is after. So many marriages get ruined that way, and honestly, honey, I want our marriage to succeed. I'm not saying you don't love me in your way. But if I were little Miss Julie White Trash with no acres and no servants, would you really love me *quite* so much? Be honest, now.'

'But that's crazy! You *aren't* Miss Julie White Trash, you're Miss Julie Scarborough! And I love Miss Julie Scarborough!'

'Oh, all right. Have it your way. But what *I'm* after is a good lover, which I have no reason to believe you aren't, and a good father to lots of darling little babies. *But* – and this is very important to me, Brucie – Scarborough Hall is *mine*, to run the way *I* want to run it! And I'm not going to tolerate having you or anybody else interfering. You can be the lord of the manor, you can have all the money you want to spend, you can go off and get drunk with your men friends – do anything you want, up to a point. But Brucie, *I* run Scarborough Hall. Is that understood?'

He sighed. 'Miss Julie, this is our engagement party! It seems like you couldn't have picked a worse time to discuss business. . . .'

'You mean our marriage? Funny word you use to describe it.'

'You know what I mean!'

'Yes, I do, and I disagree. It's a perfect time to discuss it. Because if we don't see eye to eye, why then either you . . . or *me* . . . or both of us, for that matter, can waltz inside and call the whole thing off. And wouldn't *that* set the cats to meowing!'

'But I want to dance!'

'In time, Brucie. In time. Meanwhile, there's something else I want to discuss. Now, you know my views on bondage.'

'Good Lord, Miss Julie, the whole county knows them!'

'Exactly. Well, now I think you should know that when I inherit Scarborough Hall, I fully intend to start freeing my servants.'

'*Freeing* them?'

'That's right, Brucie. Freeing them. I won't do it all at once, but over a period of years, probably. I will free them and offer to hire them back to work here for cash money.'

'But . . . you've got over four hundred and fifty slaves! You'd be giving away a fortune!'

'It's my fortune to give away, Brucie. Any objections?'

A distant frog joined the cricket.

'Well, I . . . I think it's crazy! The whole county will be on your neck. . . .'

'I couldn't care less.'

'I . . . *we'd* be thought of as, well, traitors. Yes, traitors! Traitors to our friends and neighbours. . . .'

'Won't bother me, Brucie. Will it bother you? There's still time to back out if it does. I paid for the party, and if it's all a waste, well I still had fun. Want to back out?'

A second cricket joined to convert the duo to a trio.

'No. I disapprove, but no, I don't want to back out. I'm too much in love with you.'

' "Love" again! My goodness, Brucie, you *do* love that word! Anyway, I'm glad we're agreed on that. Now, there's another thing. Remember my servant Gabriel? The one who ran away about six weeks ago, and then my father sent to Billie Orton's?'

'Yes, I remember him.' His tone became guarded.

'Well, my father has promised me anything I want as a wedding present. So I'm going to ask him to give me Gabriel Pembroke. And right after we're married, I'm going to bring him back here from Billie Orton's. And Gabriel is going to be the first of my people I'm going to free.'

'He is?' His tone sounded flat.

'That's right. Then I'm going to hire him back. You see, Mr Gaines is a good overseer, but he and I don't see eye to eye about how to manage the servants. So I'm going to make Gabriel Mr Gaines's assistant. And then in time . . . when I can make my father come around to my way of thinking . . . I'm going to send Mr Gaines packing and make Gabriel the overseer of Scarborough Hall.'

Chirp, chirp, chirp, chirp.

'You'd make a *Negro* your overseer?'

'Why not? Who's better qualified to keep the servants happy and get the best out of them at the same time? Besides, Gabriel's smart as a whip – which means he won't need a real whip. There are quite a few plantations with black overseers, you know.'

'So I've heard. Then you and Gabriel would be working close together?'

'Of course.'

He leaned down and lowered his voice. 'Then what they've been saying is *true!*'

She looked at him. 'What do you mean? Who's been saying what?'

'It's all over the county! Billie Orton's told people how you came to his farm and fawned over that nigger like . . .'

'Like *what?*'

'I can't bring myself to say it!'

'Well, you *better* say it, Bruce Yarnell! What did that pig of a man say about me?'

'That you and Gabriel are lovers!'

She slapped him so hard with the fan that one of the mother-of-pearl ribs broke. Then she was up, running for the Big House. He chased after her, grabbed her arm, and jerked her round.

'Is it true?' he whispered.

'It's a lie! A terrible lie! And I hate you for believing it!'

'Then why do you want him as your overseer? Why do you want to free him? He's a bad nigger, and you know it! He ran away once....'

'Because he wants to be free! And why shouldn't he? Wouldn't *you* want to be free?'

'But I'm not a darkie!'

'You're a *man*, aren't you? Or are you?' She looked at him with contempt. 'I reckon you're not half the man he is.'

'So you *do* love him!'

'Yes, I love him: like a brother. Why shouldn't I? I grew up with him! You fine, dashing white gentlemen get these morbid fancies in your heads every time a white woman looks at a black man. . . . How can we *not* look at them? They're all over the place! They're part of our lives! But that doesn't mean we want them to make love to us. My God, I have half a mind to have you thrown off my property for what you said!'

Bruce Yarnell wasn't the smartest man in Maryland, but he was smart enough to see that his future bride wasn't being honest – either with him or, probably, with herself. Now he put both his hands on her arms and squeezed her flesh.

'You're not telling the truth,' he said softly. 'I see what you have in mind, except maybe you're too afraid to face it yourself.'

'What are you talking about?'

'You say you love him as a brother, but you're either lying or fooling yourself, I don't know which. Because if you free him, he's a man, not a slave. And you want to make him a man because you love him as a man, not a brother.'

Her eyes were wide. 'No!'

He shook her, hard. 'Admit it, Julie! You love him as a *man!*'

Do I? screamed in her mind. Do I love him? Do I want him to touch me, to kiss me, to make love to me? Do I? Oh God, I don't know. . . . Yes! Yes, I *do* love him! I want him, I want my beautiful black prince, my Gabriel of the Sorrows. . . .

'No!' she repeated aloud. 'It's not true.'

He looked into her eyes and saw the truth. He also saw what he had to do. He released her and stepped back. The crickets continued to chirp, oblivious nature continuing to play its billion-year-old role.

'We won't talk about it any more tonight,' he said quietly.

Now she was afraid. Not only of Bruce and the rest of the county, but of herself, of this passion within her she had struggled with for weeks – perhaps even years, as she thought back – and that was becoming stronger by the minute, so strong she couldn't deny it any longer. She was finally admitting to herself she loved Gabriel Pembroke. But the implications of that were so monstrous. . . .

'Bruce, what are you thinking?' For once, Miss Julie was whispering.

His cold grey eyes were a mask to her.

'I'm thinking it's time we went inside and danced and pretended none of this happened out here.'

He crooked his arm, and she put her hand on it.

'Yes, perhaps that's better. . . .'

Gabriel, Gabriel . . . I love him! I love a black man! No, a black prince! Gabriel, my Gabriel, come sing to me, make love to me . . . Gabriel . . .

They started toward the French doors. Bruce looked over his shoulder at the moon. Then he looked at his fiancée, who was suddenly so subdued, so quiet, so . . . frightened?

'Sure has been romantic,' he remarked drily.

She shot him a nervous look, but said nothing.

Gabriel Pembroke was having a dream. He had had variations of the dream many times before, but the subject was always the same, and it terrified him at the same time that it intrigued him. The subject was he and Miss Julie. Sometimes they were children again, playing together in the boxwood garden at Scarborough Hall, their relationship free and untroubled by thoughts of race. Then there were other dreams when they were grown up. Sometimes Miss

Julie would be riding across a field, and he would be riding next to her . . . except he was never quite sure whether it was he on the horse or someone else. Tonight the dream was different. She was sitting in a swing, looking very beautiful in a white dress with a big white hat, and he was pushing her. Except, again, was it he? He wasn't quite sure. Was it he or a white man? He or Mister Bruce? Whoever it was, he was pushing Miss Julie, who went swinging so high her feet almost got caught in the leaves of the big tree the swing hung from. Miss Julie was laughing. . . . And then he – or the man pushing the swing, the invisible man – stopped her. He put his arms around her and kissed her neck. Miss Julie put up no resistance, but she kept laughing. And then he, or the lover, looked up and saw a dead man hanging from another branch of the tree. The dead man was black, and he – or the lover – started to scream as Miss Julie continued laughing. . . .

He felt something cold against his neck and heard a voice say, 'Nigger, get to your feet.'

He woke up with a start and looked up. Two men were standing in the open door of the log cabin. It was still dark, but the setting full moon faintly illuminated them, and he could see they wore canvas bags over their heads with eye-hole slits cut in them. They both carried rifles, and they both stank of whisky. The taller of the two was pressing the end of his rifle against Gabriel's neck.

'What do you want?' he mumbled, still not sure if this weren't a continuation of the dream.

'Ain't you Gabriel Pembroke?'

'Yes . . .'

'We want *you*, nigger. Get up.'

The others were awake now, watching with fright in their eyes.

'Massa Billie gwine be awful mad,' stammered Quack, 'ef'n you steal one of his niggers.'

'That's too bad.'

Gabriel was on his feet. The taller of the two men shoved him out the door. He turned and called back in, 'Jake, if, if I don't come back, get word to Miss Julie!'

'Ah will, Gabe! Ah will!'

'Good-bye. . . .' The two strangers closed the door and slid the bolt over it. Jake heard Gabe yell, 'Follow the North Star!' then silence. The five of them were plunged into darkness again, except for a pale moonbeam slanting through one of the windows.

'Who was *dey?*' whispered Bones.

'How does Ah know?' said Tooey.

'What dey wants wid Gabe?'

'Who knows?'

'Maybe dat Miss Julie done kidnapped him to get him away from Massa Billie.'

'No, dat don't make no sense. Seem to me dey lookin' mighty mean.'

'Dey's gwine kill him,' said Jake softly. 'Dey's gwine kill Gabe for no reason at all. He ain't never gwine get north.'

Follow the North Star! Gabriel's cry rang in his ear. Follow the North Star to freedom!

Jake dragged his chains over to the window and looked up at the night sky. How many times he and Gabe had sat at the window talking about what they would do when they were north and free! How many times had Gabe pointed to the sky at the bright star and whispered, 'See? There it is! The North Star. It's always there, so if we ever get separated, just keep following it and you can't get lost.'

Now Jake looked out the window at the night sky. There it was, the North Star, shining bright. Follow the North Star!

And, suddenly, there were tears in his eyes.

9

Oxford, Maryland, was a small town on the Tred Avon river, an inlet which fed into the Choptank River, which, in turn, at some undefined point became the Chesapeake Bay. Oxford had existed as a town long before Baltimore; in 1694 it had been proclaimed a Port of Entry. It had exported tobacco in the early days and imported, among other things, slaves from Africa and transported convicts from England. It boasted the oldest ferry in America, which connected it with Bellevue, Maryland, across the Tred Avon. Next to the ferry dock stood a handsome inn which had once been the house of Robert Morris, the millionaire who had financed George Washington. On the afternoon following Miss Julie's ball, the heiress of Scarborough Hall rode up to the inn accompanied by Rodney Yarnell. Rodney was just twenty, a strapping young man with thick, curly blond hair. Rodney's blue eyes were still red from the previous night, and he was still hung over. But Miss Julie suspected it wasn't the hangover that was keeping Rodney so quiet.

They tied their horses to the post in front of the inn, then went into the low-ceilinged taproom. There an unusual sight greeted her. The round oak tables had been pushed to the side of the room, creating an empty area in the middle of it. Around this were seated nine men. There was Cousin Saint George. There was Bruce. There was Sheriff Caldwell. There was Dr Harwood, the gentle, white-haired coroner of the county and the Scarborough's family doctor. There was

Reverend Wainscott. There was Saint George's son, twenty-four-year-old Beau; twenty-seven-year-old Arleigh Leffingwell; John Pingree; and Frank Todd. No one else was in the room, which, at two in the afternoon, usually was crowded with drinkers.

Cousin Saint George stood up.

'Afternoon, Miss Julie,' he said. 'We appreciate your coming over.'

'Rodney's been awfully quiet,' she said, 'which for Rodney is peculiar, to say the least. Among the things he *didn't* tell me was that I was being put on trial.'

'This isn't a trial, honey. Rodney, bring up a chair for Miss Julie.'

As Rodney went to fetch a chair, Miss Julie looked at the familiar faces in front of her.

'Looks like a trial to me,' she said. 'All you need's a couple more people, and you'd have a jury.'

'Put the chair in the middle of the room, Rodney.'

Rodney obeyed. They all looked at Miss Julie. She went to the chair and sat down as Rodney took a seat next to Beau Tremaine.

'Billie Orton rode over this morning,' said Miss Julie, 'to tell me that two men kidnapped my Gabriel last night. I assume this has something to do with that?'

'Perhaps,' said Saint George, retaking his seat.

'Was it you, Bruce?' she said, looking at her fiancé. 'Did you kidnap him?'

'Perhaps.'

She began taking off her gloves.

'If you did,' she said, 'I want him back by six o'clock this evening – *unharmed*. Otherwise, you may consider our engagement officially and permanently terminated.'

'Far as I know, Gabriel may be dead,' replied Bruce casually.

'Is he?'

Bruce shrugged. 'How would I know?'

'If he is – if you killed him, Bruce Yarnell, I swear I'll take you to court and charge you with murder!'

Bruce looked at the other men, then back to his fiancée.

'You sure are quick with the lawyers, Miss Julie. The fact is, if Gabriel *was* dead and I had killed him, well, honey, you know you got to *prove* that in court. And I think you also know that no slave can testify in a court of law. So you'd have to find white witnesses to testify they'd seen me kill this man, and – well, Miss Julie, I just think you'd have a lot of trouble finding those witnesses in Talbot County. Don't you agree, gentlemen?'

They nodded and murmured 'Damn right', '*Lot* of trouble.'

Bruce turned back to Miss Julie. 'So I think you'd better cool down and sort of think things over, honey, before you start making a lot of rash statements – know what I mean?'

She slowly tapped her riding crop against the leg of her chair.

'What do you want, Bruce?'

'What do I *want?*' He smiled. 'Why I want to be the husband of the prettiest, sweetest young lady in Maryland – namely you, Miss Julie. Not to mention – as you often point out – the *richest*. You know, honey, it's not nice to go around talking about your money to other folks, accusing them of marrying you for it. . . . It's really not nice. With your upbringing, you ought to know better than that. Why, you know what she did to me?' He turned to the other men. 'She made me sign something called a "prenuptial agreement" stating that I couldn't touch any of her property even after I married her. What do you think of that?'

'I think it's shocking,' stated Saint George flatly. 'Marriage is an institution where husband and wife share and share alike. At least it *should* be.'

'And you *signed* it?' said Rodney increduously.

'I signed it, yes I did, Rodney, because I love Miss Julie and I don't like to think about marriage in such *sordid* terms as money and legal papers and all that. Then, you know what else she told me last night at the ball? And by the way, honey' – he turned to smile at her – 'it was a swell party. It really was.'

'Oh, it was elegant!' agreed Beau Tremaine.

'I'm surprised any of you can remember it,' replied Miss Julie, 'the way you all got stumbling-down drunk.'

'Oh well, you know how it is. Anyway,' continued Bruce, turning back to his companions, 'my fiancée told me last night that as soon as she inherits her property, she's going to start freeing her slaves and paying them cash money to work for her! Now, what do you think of that?'

Saint George looked coldly at Julie.

'We heard about that,' he said. 'As your cousin, I can't believe you'd do such a foolish thing. Why, honey, think about us! What would happen to all our slaves? They're hard enough to handle as it is, but if you started freeing yours they'd get *real* rowdy. So I *know* you don't want to do that, do you?'

She continued tapping her riding crop, looking at them. 'That's why I'm here, isn't it? That's why I'm on trial. So you all can protect your interests.'

'Don't know what you're talking about, honey. There's no "trial".'

'All right,' she said, 'what do you want from me?'

Bruce shook his head. 'There you go, saying "what do we want" again. Well then, let's play a little game. Let's assume that, uh . . . we *have* this Gabriel fellow. Let's assume that one or two of us were crazy enough last night to have gone to the trouble of kidnapping that worthless, uppity nigger. . . .'

'Bruce,' she interrupted icily. 'He's is *not* a "nigger".'

'Hear that, boys? He's not a nigger. Well, he sure looked like one last time I saw him. Anyway, honey, let's assume we have him in a place of incarceration, so to speak, from which he cannot escape. And let's assume we *haven't* killed him, but would dearly love to – for reasons you might be able to guess. Now, the question is, how much does this man mean to you?'

'You know he means a great deal,' she finally said.

'Well, honey, how much is a "great deal"? Would it mean, for instance, your tearing up that prenuptial agreement I signed?'

She stiffened. 'No!'

He shrugged. 'Well, then, not much point playing the game, is there? Course, if we *had* that nigger,' and he winked at Cousin Saint George, 'I wouldn't say he had a long life expectancy, would you?'

'Where *is* he?' she almost shouted. 'What have you done with him?'

'Miss Julie, we don't have him! Honest! We're just playing a game to pass away an idle hour, so to speak. Isn't that right, boys?'

The others murmured agreement. Bruce smiled at her.

'You're so smart, honey, and so quick to tell the rest of us poor boobs how dumb *we* are . . . can't you figure out his is just a game?'

'Fairly high stakes, wouldn't you say?' said Miss Julie. 'A man's life?'

Bruce smiled and shrugged again.

'That means nothing to you, does it?' she went on.

Shrug.

Scarborough Hall, she thought. The control of it meant so much to her. If she tore up the prenuptial agreement, then that control would effectively pass to her husband. Could she do that? And yet, could she let them murder Gabriel? Damn them! she thought. Damn them! They have me checkmated. . . .

'All right,' she said aloud. 'It's a game. So let's say I'd tear up the agreement. Then what would happen to Gabriel? *Assuming* you have him.'

'Well, then he'd be mine, wouldn't he?'

'*Yours?*'

'Mine and yours. When I become your husband, that is. And, of course. Gabriel wouldn't be released from his place of incarceration until you and I got married – which, happily, Reverend Wainscott has volunteered to do for us anytime. Even this afternoon. That right, Reverend?'

He leaned forward to look at the Reverend, who cleared his throat.

'It would be a pleasure, Bruce. Anytime.'

'Of course,' continued Bruce, 'that would sort of cancel

that big wedding we've been planning, but I expect we could have a party anyway.'

'You see, Miss Julie,' said Saint George, 'all of us in the county will feel a lot better about you once you're married to Bruce. Because we know we can trust Bruce, whereas you . . . well, honey, you do have some crazy ideas. When you're Mrs Bruce Yarnell, everything's going to be a lot more comfortable around here.'

'I see,' said Miss Julie. 'And what if I choose *not* to go through with this marriage ceremony that's been so conveniently arranged for me?'

'Well, that's your privilege, naturally,' said Saint George. 'But we think it would be better for you to settle down, honey. You've been displaying some signs of . . . well, mental distress, let's say. Is that what you'd call it, Doctor?'

He leaned forward to look at Dr Harwood who was sitting on the other side of Bruce. The aged doctor was looking nervous.

'Yes . . . or perhaps mental fatigue. . . .'

'I mean, all this talk about freeing your Negroes and your *peculiar* interest in this Gabriel . . . you know what I mean? I think we'd all have to go talk to your daddy about maybe sending you away for a while. . . .'

She stared at them. 'You're not serious?'

Cousin Saint George smiled. 'Oh, I think we are. Aren't we, Doctor?'

Dr Harwood nodded slightly.

'Miss Julie, you know I love you and your family,' he said. 'Why, I even brought you into this world. But . . . they're serious.'

'Of course, none of us likes this ugliness,' continued Saint George. 'We all love you, honey, and Bruce is just crazy about you, as you well know. We want you to be happy. We want you to be our Miss Julie, the mistress of Scarborough Hall – that's the way things *should* be.' He paused, then added coolly, 'But we're serious.'

She could hardly believe this was happening.

'And as far as Gabriel's concerned,' said Bruce, 'well, once we're married, honey, I think we probably should sell him. He has made a *lot* of trouble, you know. And we don't want trouble, do we? We want to be happy.'

'Now, we don't want to *rush* you into anything precipitous,' said Saint George. 'So if you want to think things over, why you go right ahead. We'll wait. We are at *your* disposal, Miss Julie.'

She put her riding crop over her lap, clutching it with both hands, her knuckles white.

'Well, I imagine you're all *real* proud of yourselves, aren't you?' she said. 'You've got the sheriff, who's the law. You've got Reverend Wainscott, Dr Harwood . . . law, religion, medicine, the planting interests . . . you've got just about everybody represented here. All you big men ganging up on a woman – is that what's meant by Southern chivalry?'

'Honey, the way you've been talking lately,' said Saint George, 'if you weren't a woman, you'd most likely be dead.'

'As it is, you're proposing to send me to a lunatic asylum for the rest of my days.' She rose out of the chair. 'Well, I say to all of you: go to hell! This is a country that's supposed to be run by *law*, not this preposterous witch trial out of the Middle Ages!'

Silence. Bruce cleared his throat. 'Uh, Dr Harwood, you were telling me about that incident that happened in Virginia last year . . . that slave they skinned alive? Just how do they do that?'

Dr Harwood was trembling. 'It's . . .' he started to say. 'I couldn't describe it . . . Miss Julie!' He got out of his chair. 'Honey, listen to me. Do what they say! For God's sake, *do* it! It's not so awful, what they're offering you: marry Bruce – be happy. . . .'

'Happy giving up my birthright?' she exclaimed. 'Giving over everything to Bruce?'

'He'll be your husband – he'll love you –'

'But don't you see, I don't love *him!* I love Gabriel Pembroke!'

Dr Harwood winced. 'Miss Julie, you don't mean that. That's some sort of sickness in your mind. . . .'

'It's not a sickness! It's *you* who are sick – all of you! Sick and *stupid!* Because it's your attitudes and stubbornness that are going to ruin everything for all of us!'

Rodney Yarnell and Beau Tremaine had started laughing. Now she turned to them.

'What's so funny?'

'You, Miss Julie!' Rodney wheezed. 'I didn't believe it when they started talking about committing you, but I do now! Why, you must be crazy as a loon! No white lady in her right mind could fall in love with a nigger – much less *admit* it in public. It just ain't natural.'

'And you, Rodney Yarnell, are going to tell me what's "natural"? You're God, I suppose?' She turned to the others. 'Oh, I may be crazy, but I'm not stupid. I know none of you would let me love a black man openly and honestly, so don't worry: nothing will ever happen between me and Gabriel Pembroke. But he's worth *ten* Bruce Yarnells!' She pointed at her fiancé. 'And if you still want to marry me after that remark, it *proves* all you're interested in is my money.'

She walked around the chair and faced them, her hands on the chair back.

'Now gentlemen, you've made your tacky little point. Now you listen to me for a moment. Gabriel Pembroke made me begin to realize how out of step with the rest of the world we are. Maybe it's because I'm a woman and in a sort of bondage myself to you men that helped me see things from *his* point of view. But it's not just that slavery's immoral: any idiot can see that. It's also impractical in the long run, and more trouble than it's worth –'

'Impractical?' interrupted Saint George. 'I'm making more money than ever!'

'But what about the hidden costs, Cousin? Such as, namely, that you're so terrified your slaves are going to murder you just as they murdered Mrs Beecham that you drink yourself into oblivion each night and make life miserable for your poor wife? So Miss Adelaide has to hide from reality by burying herself in trashy novels – how about those *hidden* costs, Cousin? Don't forget Mrs Beecham's slit throat when you figure up your yearly profits and losses.

I say the whole system's rotten, and we could change it ourselves if we had any gumption. Now, I'm a considerable planter on the Eastern Shore. I'm willing to gamble my fortune to prove to all of us that a plantation can be run profitably without slave labour. If I can do it, you can do it. So why aren't you willing to let me risk my money to make the experiment?'

Saint George jumped up and shouted, 'Because we don't *want* to change! We like things the way they are!'

'Even with Mrs Beecham's slit throat?'

'Yes!'

'But some day you may *have* to change! Don't you read the Northern newspapers? The Abolitionists are gathering strength every year! Sone day – ten, twenty, thirty years from now, they're going to *force* us to change. . . .'

'Not if we stick together! We control Congress. . . .'

'For how long? For *ever?* You say *I'm* crazy? Well, if you believe that, I say *you're* crazy!'

Her cousin pointed at her. 'Now you listen to me, Julie Scarborough: you've said *enough*, you hear? Now you either do what we say and marry Bruce and settle down and shut up about your crazy ideas . . . or Dr Harwood is ready to sign the papers committing you to an asylum for the insane. You understand that? You say you love this nigger: well, if you love him, you better do what we say, or his dying screams are going to haunt you to your grave! You understand what I'm saying to you?'

'Oh, stop bullying me!' she cried.

Bruce hurried across the room to her, saying, 'Saint George, take it easy, for God's sake! Honey,' he said to Julie softly, 'this is really for your own good. Believe me! A year from now you'll see we were acting for your own *good.*'

'If sending me to an insane asylum is your idea of my "good", I shudder to think what your idea of my "bad" is.'

'Be reasonable, Julie. You admitted yourself that this . . . this obsession you have with Gabriel is impossible. In time you'll forget him and we'll be happy, honey. I swear. Even if I'm marrying you for your money – which you seem convinced of – I swear I'll make you a good husband.'

She searched his face as she searched her heart. It was impossible to argue with them. Impossible. Impossible to try and change a system that had the weight of a century and a half behind it. She was shouting at deaf men.

'The odd thing is, you probably would,' she finally said. 'Or as good a husband as I'll ever get in the South.' She took a deep breath. 'All right: I see I'm wasting everyone's time trying to make any of you see reason. And since you've given me such a *wide* range of alternatives, I guess I don't have much choice. But first: before I marry you, Bruce Yarnell, I want to see Gabriel Pembroke with my own eyes. I want to see him *alive*.'

He smiled and took both her hands. 'You don't trust me. Well, can't say I blame you. Come on, Rodney. Let's take Miss Julie to see Gabriel. Reverend, you go to the church. We'll be there by and by. Then afterward, we'll have a little champagne and a little loving and start to forget all this unpleasantness.'

He put his arm around his fiancée and kissed her cheek. She didn't respond. She felt drained, dead. She didn't even particularly care any more. They wouldn't listen to her, so why not marry Bruce? Why try and change the world? Maybe the world wasn't even *worth* changing. Maybe she *was* crazy, saying she loved a slave. Maybe they were right, she didn't know.

Gabriel! She would see him once more, then force him out of her life. Gabriel, my black prince! If there were no other people in the world, how she would have loved him! But the world was full of people like Saint George and Bruce. . . .

She looked at Bruce and envisioned a lifetime of being his wife.

'They say,' she remarked, 'that every day a person dies a little. Well, today I think I died a lot.'

And she walked to the door and out of the inn.

Bruce led all of them to Hooper's Mill. Miss Julie, Rodney, Beau, Saint George, Arleigh Leffingwell, John Pingree, Frank Todd. There, at the side of an inlet from the bay called

Peachtree Creek, stood the abandoned gristmill, surrounded by weeds. Of course, she thought, that's where they would take him. I should have thought of it myself.

They dismounted and went to the sagging wooden door. Bruce pushed it open, and its rusty hinges squeaked. 'Bet you haven't been in here since you were kids,' he said to the others. True, they had all used to play there when they were children. The mill was said to be haunted by the ghost of Mr Hooper, who had drunk himself to death thirty years before. Mr Hooper was a miller who had been considered remarkably cruel to his slaves even in an age of remarkable cruelty. Several of them had died from his beatings, but Mr Hooper had always managed to sidestep the lackadaisical law, which was never too eager to prosecute a white man for cruelty to slaves. Mr Hooper had built cells in the basement of his mill where, it was said, he had imprisoned his slaves for weeks on end merely for the pleasure of hearing their cries of hunger, fear, and loneliness. The other whites had not liked Mr Hooper. They said he inflicted punishment not for discipline but, rather, for the pleasure of it. The other whites had snubbed Mr Hooper.

But they had never done anything to stop him.

Now Bruce led the others down the winding stone steps of the mill to the cobwebbed basement, where three low wooden doors were locked by beams in rusted braces.

'Gabriel's in here,' he said, going to the left door. He slid the beam through its braces, then tugged the door slowly open and ducked inside the cell. The others were all looking at Miss Julie, a barely concealed leer on some of their faces. She knew what they were thinking, even without the leers. They were all waiting to hear what she would say to her 'lover'. Probably, she thought, they want to see a real scene. They want to see me throw myself at him, kiss him, weep copious tears, beat my breasts. . . . Well, they're in for a disappointment.

Bruce ducked back out of the cell, his face a study in confusion.

'He's gone!' he said. 'The black bastard escaped!'

'You're lying!' she exclaimed. 'You *did* kill him –'

'Look for yourself!'

He stood aside and she ducked into the tiny room, which was no more than six feet square. An earthen floor, ancient stone walls, a low stone ceiling mossy with dampness. . . . A tiny window just below the ceiling admitted enough light for her to see what had happened. They had chained him to the wall, but where the chains had been embedded in the stone were now gaping holes.

'Goddam,' exclaimed Rodney Yarnell, who had squeezed into the cell behind her. 'He pulled the chains right out of the wall!'

She started to laugh. 'Oh, it's wonderful!' She snickered. 'It's beautiful!' She pointed to the narrow window, which had been smashed. 'He's gone! While you all were ganging up on me, Gabriel took off! Good for you, Gabriel!' she cried at the window. 'Go north! Get out of this lunatic asylum! Take your freedom and run – and God be with you!'

'Let's go!' shouted Rodney, ducking back out of the cell. 'He can't have got far – he's still got on the leg chains. . . .'

She heard them running up the stairs as she leaned against the wall and laughed. The black prince had fooled them all. God be with you, her heart sang. God be with you, my beautiful Gabriel. May your life be a better one than mine.

He had gotten farther than they thought. It wasn't until eleven that night that Rodney Yarnell spotted him going through a wheat field toward a wood, the telltale moonlight illuminating his stooped head. 'There he is!' yelled Rodney to Beau Tremaine. 'You go get Bruce and the others – I'll hold him.' He galloped into the wheat field. On the other side he could now see Gabriel standing, looking back at him. Then he hobbled into the trees. But when Rodney got to the edge of the woods, he had lost him.

He slowed his horse and ducked below the branches, pulling his pistol as he moved cautiously into the woods. Must be hiding in the underbrush, he thought as he strained his eyes to see in the moonlight-dappled darkness. 'Gabriel!' he called. 'Come out on boy! Give yourself up! You'll just make it harder on yourself. . . .' He felt something grab his right foot. He tried to hang on to his saddle, but the force was too sudden and too strong. He went off his horse. He dropped his revolver, bracing for the shock of meeting the ground. He landed on his back, which knocked most of the breath out of him. Then something black was on top of him, a black knee was in his chest and a black fist smashed his chin.

Rodney's world became all black.

Gabriel got up, panting. He threw the horse's rein around a tree trunk. Then he grabbed the pistol, hobbled to a patch of moonlight, and spread his legs as far as the chain would permit. He aimed at the centre of the taut chain and fired. The chain broke.

Now free to run, he sped back to the horse, which was whinnying and bucking from the noise of the shot.

'Whoa, boy.' He soothed it, untying the rein from the tree. 'Everything's going to be all right . . . I *hope!*'

Taking a look at the unconscious Rodney, he got on the horse, then dug the edge of the chain anklets into the horse's side.

'Move your *ass!*' he whispered, and the horse took off through the woods, the broken chains dangling from its rider's wrists and ankles. North! he thought. Follow the North Star! North to freedom!

10

Lester Berkley walked from the back door of his small house in Farwell, Delaware, to his blacksmith shop. It was six in the morning and first light was kindling the east. Lester, who was thirty-one, usually didn't get up this early, but he had thought he heard a noise outside his bedroom window a few minutes before, so he had thrown on a jacket over his nightshirt and gone out to investigate. When he got to the door of his workshop, he saw that the lock had been pulled off the hasp. The lock wasn't all that strong – crime was practically non-existent in tiny Farwell – but Lester knew it hadn't been broken off by a prankster. Lester was a big man, a strong man, and he wasn't afraid of much. Now he kicked the door open.

'Who's there?' he said.

Silence. He stepped inside and picked a hammer off the bench by the door. Then, armed, he lit the kerosene lamp. A Negro was standing against the back wall. He was wearing nothing but torn trousers, but the manacles on his wrists and ankles told the story. He had a gun in his right hand and a file in his left.

'Where'd you get that gun, boy?' said Lester.

The Negro didn't answer.

'Stealin' my file so you can get rid of those chains?'

'Yes,' the Negro said.

Lester started toward him, holding the hammer up. 'Sorry

to disappoint you, boy, but I don't like thieves and I don't like runaways. Now, give me back my file.'

The Negro raised the gun. 'Don't come any closer.'

Lester stopped, looking at the gun. Then he looked at the Negro. 'You're already in big trouble, boy. You don't *dare* shoot a white man.'

'Maybe I'm in so much trouble I don't dare *not* shoot a white man.'

Lester thought about this. 'You ain't gonna fire that gun, boy. It'd wake up half the town. You'd be hanged by nightfall. Now, give me my file and let's not have any trouble.'

'No.'

Lester frowned. 'I don't like to be told no, boy.'

He started toward the black man again. The Negro watched him coming towards him with the hammer. He didn't move.

'Givin' you one more chance, boy,' said Lester. 'Give me my file.'

'No.'

Lester lunged at him, raising the hammer to smash at his skull, certain the 'nigger' would not have the nerve to fire the gun.

The 'nigger' shoved the point of the file into his stomach instead. Lester grunted and fell forward, dropping the hammer and stumbling into Gabriel. Gabriel pushed him off while he pulled out the bloody file. Then, as Lester tumbled onto the floor, Gabriel jumped over him and ran to the door. He took one look back. The blacksmith was getting to his knees, holding his hand to his stomach. I don't think I killed him, thought Gabriel. But if I did, I don't feel guilty before God or no man. Besides, I can't go into Wilmington wearing chains.

He ran out of the shop, then around it to the field in back where he had tied his horse to a tree. He untied him, jumped on, and galloped away, clutching the bloody file in his left hand.

The brigantine *Defiance*, out of Liverpool, was two days out of Wilmington, Delaware, seventy miles off Atlantic

City, New Jersey, in rough seas. Its captain, Thomas Healy, was eating lunch in his cabin when there was a knock on the door.

'Yes?'

Mr Hawkins, the first mate, came in. 'We found a stowaway, Captain,' he said. 'In the hold. A Negro . . . I imagine he's a runaway.'

Captain Healy wiped his mouth with his napkin.

'Second one this year, isn't it? How did you find him?'

'He's seasick, Captain. Breame heard him retching.'

'Charming. Give him a bucket and bring him up.'

'Aye aye, Captain.'

Hawkins left. Captain Healy poured himself a glass of Madeira. What a pleasant place the South must be, he reflected. If they want to keep the slaves, they'd best build a fence around the whole bloody country.

Five minutes later, Hawkins led in the bucket-carrying runaway, who was a sorry sight. His brown face was at least two shades paler than normal, and his expression of profound misery was almost comical. As the ship took a sharp roll to port, the runaway was thrown against the panelled bulkhead.

'Put him in a chair,' ordered the captain. Hawkins helped the man to a chair. He sank into it. Hawkins put the bucket in his lap and pointed at it. 'If you're going to puke, do it there. Understand?'

The Negro looked up sadly and nodded.

'What's your name?' asked the captain.

'Gabriel, sir.'

'And I'm Captain Healy. You're a runaway, I suppose?'

Silence. The captain exchanged looks with his first mate.

'It doesn't matter,' said Captain Healy. 'Have you committed any crimes beside being a slave?'

Gabriel decided it was wiser not to mention the blacksmith. 'No sir.'

The captain took a sip of Madeira. 'Well, Gabriel, you're not the first slave that's sneaked aboard the *Defiance*. Did you know we were an English ship?'

'Yes sir. I saw "Liverpool" on your rear.'

'Our stern, Gabriel. "Rear" is what we're sitting on. So you can read, then?'

'Yes sir.'

'And you even knew Liverpool was in England?'

'Yes sir.'

'Impressive. How'd you learn to read, Gabriel?'

'A lady taught me, sir. A white lady.'

'Was she a lady of quality?'

'Yes sir.'

The Captain said to his mate, 'I'm told most of the poor Southerners can't read. . . .' Just then he heard a gagging noise and looked back at Gabriel. The Negro leaned forward, stuck his head over the bucket, and retched. Captain Healy sighed and put his left hand over his nose, waiting for the eruption to subside. When it was over, he removed his hand.

'You've certainly added to the enjoyment of my lunch,' he remarked.

'I'm sorry, sir.'

'I take it this is your first time at sea?'

'Yes sir. Is it always this way, or does it ever' – he started to gag again, but this time he fought it down – 'stop?'

'One gets used to it, Gabriel. I don't know if you picked us to stow away on because we're English. . . .'

'I did, sir. I thought I'd have a better chance of staying aboard if I was discovered.'

'I see. You're an intelligent fellow, Gabriel. I tell you what: we're headed for New York to deliver a cargo of Cuban sugar. I could put you off at New York, but frankly I wouldn't advise it.'

'I was worried you'd put me off back at Wilmington, sir.'

'I understand, but I wouldn't do that. I have views on slavery, one of which is that it is an abhorrent institution. Now, the trouble with New York is that it is overrun with escaped slaves – like yourself – and also overrun with bounty hunters. The bounty hunters catch the runaways and take them back to the South for a price. So I would suggest you stay aboard when we arrive at New York, and go with us to New Bedford, Massachusetts, instead, which is our next port of call. I know a gentleman there who can help you. He's the publisher of the local newspaper and active in the Abolitionist movement. His name is Anthony van Zandt, and I have a feeling Mr van Zandt is going to be interested in a runaway who can not only read but speak the Queen's English intelligibly – when his head's not in a bucket. So, shall it be New Bedford?'

'Yes sir. And sir, I can't thank you enough. You're the first white man who's ever . . .' He stopped, shut his eyes and groaned, 'Oh my *God.*' Then he plunged his head back in the bucket and let go.

The captain sighed, looked at the wooden overhead, and put his hand over his nose.

'I think you can take him below, Hawkins. Give him some clothes. If he feels any better, bring him back up. I'd like to hear his story.'

'Aye aye, Captain.'

'And open the porthole.'

The portly man with the bushy brown beard finished reading the lengthy letter. Then he put it on his desk, removed his pince-nez, and swivelled around to look at the Negro in the brown checkered suit.

'You're a lucky man to have run into Captain Healy,' said the publisher of the New Bedford *Eagle*.

'Yes sir. Captain Healy was mighty good to me. He even bought me this suit! First suit I've ever owned!'

'And a very handsome suit it is, too, Gabriel. The captain says in his letter you are literate and highly intelligent. He was extremely impressed with you, Gabriel, and now that I've read your story – at least as sketched out by Captain Healy – I'm impressed, too. Would you like a job here on the newspaper? It wouldn't be much at first – a runner – but it pays twelve dollars a week, and there's chance for advancement. You might even become a typesetter some day. Interested?'

Gabriel smiled. 'Mr van Zandt, you don't think I'd *not* be interested? Do you know what it means to be *paid* for a job?'

The publisher nodded. 'Yes, I can imagine. We've helped many runaways in the past five years, Gabriel, and the eagerness with which the vast majority of them have taken to paying jobs is the greatest refutation of slavery I know. Now: you'll have to change your name. A runaway isn't completely safe, even in Massachusetts. I imagine there's a good price on your head, so we don't want to take the chance of having you picked up. You look as if you're a strong man: what would you say to Samson for a last name?'

'Guess Samson's as good as anything. How about Frank Samson?'

Anthony van Zandt sniffed. 'That doesn't have much music, does it? No, I think maybe. . . . Deliverance Samson. In honour of your being delivered out of the South.'

Gabriel cleared his throat. 'Is Deliverance a *name*, Mr van Zandt?'

'Well, no. But it has a moral fervour to it I find appealing.'

'Um . . . excuse me, sir, but I'm not sure I could go all through my life being morally fervent morning, noon, and night. How about Gilbert? Gilbert Samson. That sounds fine to me. I think I could trust a man named Gilbert Samson – even if he were me.'

Mr van Zandt laughed. 'All right: Gilbert it is.' He reached into his coat and pulled out a wallet. 'So, Gilbert, I'm going to give you fifty dollars. That will give you a chance to get on your feet, find a room to rent. . . .'

Gilbert looked at the offered money with amazement. 'Fifty dollars? It'll take me a *long* time to pay that back, sir.'

'But you're not going to pay it back. There's a string attached.'

Gilbert looked at him. 'What's the string?'

'You're coming this Saturday evening to a meeting of the New Bedford Abolition Society and you're going to tell the society members your experiences as a slave.'

Gilbert blinked. 'You mean . . . you want me to get up in front of people and *talk*?'

'Exactly. For which the society will pay you fifty dollars, Here: take the money.' He shoved it into his hand.

'But what'll I say?'

Mr van Zandt leaned back in his chair. 'You'll tell them what you told Captain Healy.' He nodded at the letter. 'You'll tell them about Billie Orton the slave breaker. You'll tell them about Miss Julie –'

'No, not Miss Julie,' Gilbert interrupted. 'I wouldn't want to talk about her. She's a lady. A fine lady.'

'You can use fictitious names, of course. But we want to hear the *horror* of being a slave. The cruelty, the inhumanity. . . .'

'It wasn't "horrible" most of the time,' said Gilbert. 'Just some of the time, toward the end. And the cruelty's not the worst part. The worst part is knowing you're never going to be anything but a slave.'

'Yes, well, bring that in, of course. Yes, that's important. But Captain Healy says you were whipped repeatedly. . . .'

'I was, at Billie Orton's.'

'Well then, concentrate on that. You see, Gilbert, I think you can be very important to our movement. There have been several books written by escaped slaves, and they've sold like hotcakes. The public is eager to know what conditions are *really* like in the South. Now, you're a fine figure of a man, and you speak well. I think in time you might develop into a prime asset for us . . . at least, I'm willing to try you out Saturday night. If it works out, you will not only be helping us slaughter the monster named Slavery – you could also earn yourself some handsome lecture fees.'

Gilbert frowned, thinking about this. 'But isn't that a little dishonest?' he finally said. 'Making money from your own suffering?'

'If there were a scale of dishonesty that went from zero to one thousand, I'd put that at about five – at least in your case. After what this country has done to you, you deserve to get something in return.'

'Well, I'm willing to try. How many people will be there?'

'About six hundred.'

'SIX –! Oh no. Oh, Mr van Zandt, I'd be too scared. . . .'

The following Saturday night, he looked out at the sea of earnest faces that had filled the Temperance Hall and thought he'd faint. He was trembling all over, and sweat was cascading down his ribs.

'Ladies and gentlemen,' he began, and his voice cracked. He tried again. 'Ladies and gentlemen: my name is Gilbert Samson, and up to three weeks ago, I was a slave in Maryland. Mr van Zandt and the other gentlemen of the society have asked me to speak to you, which I'm doing now. And to tell the truth, I'm scared silly!'

There was a ripple of titters that swelled into a roar of laughter and applause. He stared at them, amazed at this phenomenon. They were applauding *him!* They *liked* him!

When the applause died down, he continued, 'The gentlemen of the society have asked me to speak to you about the cruelties of the institution of slavery. They even suggested I take off my jacket and shirt and show you the whip scars on my back. But I declined. You've all heard about the whippings, you've read about them – whipping exists in the South. Exists? It flourishes! But I want to speak to you about something even crueller than whipping. I want to speak to you about the mental debasement of not belonging to the human race. I don't want to show you my scars: I want to take you into my mind.

'For a few minutes this evening, I want to try to make *you* slaves. To make you feel and think like slaves. Look at your hands. How many thousands of times have you done that in your lives? You've looked at your hands and thought: "My hands." But look at your hands now. Go on: take a look.'

He watched the men and women in the audience as they looked down at their hands.

'Now think: "Not *my* hands, but massa's hands." If you think that – if you can think of your own body as belonging not to you but to another human being – then you're beginning to think like a slave.'

He paused for a moment, trying to gauge their reaction. The room was silent except for an occasional cough. But everyone was looking either at his hands or at him. They're interested! he thought. I think they're interested!

Gilbert Samson – born Gabriel Pembroke – was beginning to enjoy himself.

Anthony van Zandt was sitting behind Gilbert on the platform, along with the other officers of the society. Now he leaned over to the vice-chairman sitting next to him and whispered, 'He's a natural! I think we've found ourselves a star.'

The vice-chairman nodded gravely.

3

THE GUNS OF SUMTER 1861

11

While tension between Washington and the South mounted during the winter, Lew Crandall found his interest in his medical studies – which was minimal to begin with – receding further as he watched with fascination the national drama that was unfolding. Whereas his view of the Southern states had formerly been that they were wayward brothers tragically mistaken in their domestic institutions, as state after state seceded and as Southern politicians and spokesmen grew ever more strident in their cries of defiance, Lew began to view the wayward brothers as enemies. The guns of Sumter brought his feelings to the boil. When Brigadier General Beauregard ordered his Confederate troops to shell the island fortress in Charleston harbour on the morning of 12 April 1861, Lew considered the act had made the Southerners outlaws. Despite his misgivings about certain aspects of American life, he loved his country and wanted to fight to preserve it against the rebels. President Lincoln was issuing frantic appeals for the loyal states to raise volunteer regiments, most immediately to march to the protection of the capital city which, surrounded as it was by Virginia and Maryland, was in enemy territory. Lew, as well as Ben Bramwell, wanted to answer the President's call to arms.

But there was a problem.

Two mornings after the fall of Fort Sumter, he slammed out of his new house on Locust Street, literally ran all the way to Rittenhouse Square, tore past Eugène when the butler opened the front door, bounded up the stairs two at a time, and barged into his mother's bedroom, where Nicole Louise was sitting up in her big gilt bed sipping *café au lait* and reading the latest issue of *Godey's Lady's Book*. 'Mother, you've got to talk to Elizabeth!' he roared. '*You* make her act sensibly! I sure as hell can't!'

'Oh, you've had a fight?' said Nicole Louise, instantly interested.

'*A* fight? We've been fighting for two days! She says she doesn't want me to join up – she's afraid I'll get killed. Well, of course I may get killed! So what? I mean, I'm not *eager* to get killed, but I'm not going to sit around dissecting cadavers while everybody else is enlisting to turn a couple of Rebs into cadavers! Even Ben Bramwell's going to . . .'

'Him! With *him* on our side, we haven't got a chance.'

'That's not true. Ben will be a fine soldier, and so will I if I can get Elizabeth to use her head. Washington needs troops! This is a war worth fighting – probably the *only* war I'll ever see – and what does Elizabeth say? That it's more important I stay in school, that the army will need doctors. . . . I hate medicine! It's a big bore! But *she* can't see that! Of all the obstinate, stubborn . . .'

'Louis, calm down. It's only natural Elizabeth should be worried: you've only been married a few months, and –'

'What's that have to do with it?'

'Would you stop shouting?'

'I'm not shouting!'

'Yes you are, and it's hurting my ears. And you *might* say "good morning".'

'Good morning,' he growled.

'That's better. And Elizabeth is also quite reasonable in saying you should stay in school –'

'Well, I won't.'

'Oh, you won't? The fact is, Louis, you are spoiled, you always *have* been spoiled, everything's always been given to you, and now that a war's been given to you, you want to run off and be a hero without thinking of any of your obligations. . . .'

'Whose side are you on? Mine or Elizabeth's?'

She sighed. 'Ring for Liselotte. I'll get dressed and go speak to Elizabeth. And brush your hair. You look like a savage.'

'I feel like a savage! *Are* you on my side?'

'Yes, you know I am.' Feeling wonderfully important, needed, and noticed, she got out of bed to go to her dressing room. At the door she stopped and pointed imperiously at her son. 'You,' she said, 'go read a war book or something. I don't want *you* around while I talk to Elizabeth.' Then she went into the dressing room and closed the door. Actually, his outburst hadn't come as a surprise. Elizabeth had already told her of her nervousness about Lew going to war (that Elizabeth was nervous about something else Nicole Louise also knew. She wasn't sure what it was, but there was trouble in the new marriage, which didn't entirely displease her). Well, it was obvious he wasn't going to stay in medical school, but something had conveniently arrived in the morning mail which had been not only a welcome surprise but provided a handy solution to the problem.

It had been a letter from, of all people, Simon Cameron.

An hour later, Nicole Louise got out of her carriage and walked to the door of the brick house. Her son's house was pleasant, but so typical of Philadelphia: Nicole Louise thought it a bore. She was admitted by Stella, the Irish maid, and she went into the parlour where Elizabeth was practising. When Elizabeth saw her mother-in-law, she got up from the piano. 'How can you sit around playing,' said Nicole Louise as Elizabeth kissed her, 'with your husband running all over town like a madman?'

'I'm trying to calm my nerves,' replied Elizabeth, 'but it's not easy. He told you about our fight?'

'Oh yes. At the top of his lungs. I've come to solve the crisis.' She looked around the neat room with its glass-bowled gas chandelier and rosewood furniture. Pleasant but cheap, she thought sniffishly as she sat down on a brocaded love-seat by the fireplace. Everything looked decidedly cheap: hardly the kind of furniture *her* son should have, but then it had all come from the Butterfields, and what could one expect from them? And dear Elizabeth, while a sweet child in her way, had no flair. Oh, well. Nicole Louise tolerated her daughter-in-law, but not much more. She supposed if Louis *had* to marry an American, Elizabeth was the pick of the crop. But of course he could have had a princess in France, if she could ever have gotten him to go with her to a civilized country. With her money and his looks? A princess or a duchess . . . But what did he have? Elizabeth. Oh, well. At least she was intelligent.

And looking awful, she thought as she examined her. 'My dear,' she said, 'you really must get more sleep. Your face is quite drawn.'

Elizabeth took a deep breath and sat down in a fringed armchair opposite the love-seat. She was wearing a gingham house-dress and knew she looked tired.

'You don't have to remind me, Mother,' she said. 'I have a mirror.'

'Of course.' Unfortunately, she thought. She really is rather plain with that sharp nose, though apparently men find her attractive. 'Anyway, I know all about the fight, and I think I have the solution. Here: read this letter. It came this morning.'

Elizabeth took the letter and read it out loud:

Dear Madame:

Frequently during the past few trying months my thoughts have returned to you and that unfortunate evening at your charming house last December. I say 'unfortunate' because I have so often regretted my rude conduct that night. In my defense, your son threw me off balance by his letter to Mr Lincoln and his hostility toward me. Yet I should not have reacted the way I did. As my temper cooled, I told myself the young man acted perhaps rashly, but not dishonorably by his own lights. Therefore, I have awaited the moment when I would be in a position to redress the wrong I did your family.

That moment is, I think now. You have probably read that Mr Lincoln has honored me with a post in his new Cabinet as Secretary of War. I have not forgotten what you asked of me that evening, to arrange a commission for your son. Perhaps you remember my valued friend, Mayor Matoon of Harrisburg, who accompanied me to your house last December? Heeding his country's call, His Honor has resigned his office, accepted a commission of Brigadier General in the Army, and is joining me in Washington, where he will be in charge of supplying and victualling our troops. He will need an aide-de-camp, and I took the liberty of suggesting your son to him. He is most anxious to talk to Lew again and will be in Philadelphia the 19th when he will pay you a call at 3 P.M. if that is convenient. All arrangements for Lew's commission can be accomplished by me, assuming he is interested in the post. He will, of course, be stationed here in Washington.

I pray, Madame, that whatever differences there have been between us will be forgotten in this hour of national crisis, and that the deep friendship I held for your late husband I will be permitted to continue to hold for his charming widow and brave son.

I am, Madame, yours most sincerely,
Simon Cameron

Elizabeth folded the letter and looked up.

'That's very magnanimous of Senator Cameron,' she said. 'Frankly, I'm a bit surprised.'

'Frankly, so was I. After what Louis did to him – the foolish boy! He *can* behave like an idiot. . . . At any rate, I know how worried you are, but I think you have to realize you can't prevent Louis from doing something in the war, and it strikes me that being aide to a general in Washington would not only be safe for him but something suitably dignified for my son – and your husband,' she added quickly. Elizabeth didn't miss it. 'Do you agree?'

'Yes, I think probably this is as good as anything. Except that Mayor Matoon struck me as being terribly shifty. . . .'

'My dear, he's a politician. What can one expect?'

'I know. Then, I'm not sure Lew will take the job. He's all fired up to see guns shooting. I think secretly he wants to cover himself with glory. . . .'

'Just get him to my house the day after tomorrow. Tell him he's being offered a commission, but don't mention this letter and don't tell him where he'll be going. Perhaps the sight of a genuine general – even if it is that boor, Matoon –

will excite him enough to get him to accept the post, and I can fabricate some story with the general so he won't know the post is coming from Senator Cameron.'

'All right. Perhaps it will work.'

She sat very still, staring at her hands. Nicole Louise watched her a moment, then said, 'My dear, what *is* the matter between you two? I can understand having an argument about Louis going to war, but a two-day battle? That seems rather extreme.'

Elizabeth got up and went to the double doors to slide them shut. Then she turned.

'There *is* trouble,' she said softly.

'Well, that's been obvious for some time. What is it?'

Elizabeth returned to the fireplace and stood before it, her hands fidgeting nervously with a lace kerchief. 'It's something so . . . intimate,' she began.

Nicole Louise's eyes narrowed with interest. 'You mean it has something to do with our baser natures?' she whispered.

Elizabeth nodded. Her mother-in-law stiffened.

'I hope you're not going to tell me my son has not properly performed his husbandly duties?' she snapped.

Elizabeth smiled. 'Hardly,' she said. 'He's performed them too often and too well.'

Nicole Louise relaxed.

'Oh. You had me worried. But "too often"? How is that possible?'

'Mother, you know I adore Lew. I probably love him too much. And I . . . I *want* him . . . you know what I mean.'

'Oh, I do.'

'He's very attractive. Before we were married, I was actually thinking of . . . I mean, I wanted him so much I toyed with the idea of doing something with him *before*.'

'That would not have been wise, my dear, but I understand.'

'You see, he's very amorous. *Very*. And I happen to know he was seeing a woman in South Philadelphia. . . .'

'A prostitute?'

'Yes.'

'I'm afraid that doesn't shock me as much as it should.

I've had some suspicions about Louis's morals these past few years. But prostitutes are a burden we decent women must put up with, Elizabeth. God knows *I* put up with them with his father.'

'You mean, the judge – ?'

'Exactly. Like father, like son.'

'Anyway, I don't think he's going there any more. But what I'm trying to tell you is that I *thought* I would be very good at that part of marriage. It's turned out that I'm not.'

Silence. The two women looked at each other.

'That's unfortunate,' said Nicole Louise.

'Yes, very. And I don't know what to do about it.'

'Well, if you two are not compatible physically, I don't think that's the end of the marriage by any means. And often it takes time, you know. . . .'

'It's just that it's so . . . so animal-ish!' Elizabeth burst out with sudden heat. 'It's nothing like I thought it would be! I thought it would be beautiful and sometimes it *is* . . . but dammit, I'm more of a prude than I thought!'

'One can be *too* genteel. . . .'

'I know, and I'm really *not* genteel! I hate "genteel" people! I don't know what's wrong with me! It's just that Lew wants to do it all the time, and I simply don't have the energy! Oh, I shouldn't be telling you all this, but I have to tell someone, and I'm afraid to tell *my* mother, because she'd faint. It gets on my nerves, I feel I'm being an inadequate wife, and then I get irritable and we fight – and it's not Lew's fault, I suppose. He can't help being the way he is. . . .'

'It would certainly be worse if he were the other way.'

'What do you mean?'

'If he only wanted to do it once a month – or never. There are many men like that, you know.'

'No, I *don't* know. I don't know that much about men or sex, and it's all because of this ridiculous, stupid ignorance we women are kept in! The only reason I had any idea at all what he had beneath his clothes is because I stole a look at my father's medical books! It's so unfair, so rotten, so debasing to us women . . . and now it's ruining my marriage. . . . '

She suddenly sank into the chair, buried her face in her hands, and started sobbing.

'Oh, I'm miserable!' she cried. 'Just miserable. And that's why I fight with him.'

Nicole Louise found herself surprisingly moved. She got up and came over to the daughter-in-law she didn't particularly like and put her arms around her to hold her.

'There, there.' She was soothing. 'I'm sure things will work out. . . .'

'How can they? It makes him furious when I say I don't want to. . . .'

'Have a child, my dear.'

She sniffed. 'I'm trying. It's even possible I am . . . I mean, there are signs.'

Nicole Louise released her and straightened. 'Oh? Have you told him?'

'Not yet, because I'm not certain.'

'Well, keep trying. Have a child and then you'll see that Louis will calm down. If right now he's exhibiting an excess of zeal, it's probably because he wants a son. They *all* want sons.'

'Yes, I think he wants a son. Except he's been so restless lately, I'm not sure what he wants.'

'All men are restless. The best thing for them is to get them settled, give them responsibilities . . . children. And with Louis that steam-engine you've portrayed, that should be no problem.'

'It'll be a problem if he goes to Washington.'

'Oh, but you'll go with him, of course. I'll arrange all that.'

Elizabeth sniffed again, then looked at her mother-in-law. 'Did *you* enjoy it?' she asked quietly.

Nicole Louise smiled. 'Well, yes and no. I enjoyed the romance more, the preliminaries. What it all led up to was . . . well' – she shrugged elegantly – 'what dogs do.'

'But other women seem to like it.'

'Other women,' said Nicole Louise haughtily, 'are less sensitive.'

Elizabeth wiped her nose and said ruefully, 'I wish *I* were less sensitive.'

12

When Lew walked into his mother's library two days later, he was suspicious of the mysterious commission that had so magically appeared out of thin air. He told himself his mother had been manoeuvring again, perhaps with the connivance of Elizabeth. But even though he was suspicious, he wasn't altogether immune to the allure of the idea.

'Here he is!' said Nicole Louise, who was seated in her favourite chair. 'Louis, you remember General Matoon?'

He crossed the room to shake hands with a man whose appearance so belied the role he was to play in Lew's life.

'Of course. How are you, sir? And congratulations on your new commission.'

'Well, well, glad to see you again, son. And thank you. Say, isn't this some gaudy outfit? Look at all that gold! If mayors got uniforms as pretty as this, maybe they'd get more respect – eh?'

And he laughed, his belly shaking like a besashed Santa Claus's. The uniform swirled with arabesques of gold braid up each sleeve. On top of each shoulder, four-inch straps sported his shiny new general's stars. He even had a gold-handled sword that he wasn't yet quite sure how to manoeuvre without knocking something over. Standing in front of the fireplace, the rotund general was a sight, but somehow despite all the gold, hardly an imposing one. Lew was repressing an intense desire to snicker, although at the same time he lusted after a uniform of his own.

'Louis, sit down,' said his mother. 'I've ordered some champagne so we can toast the general's new star – and so dashing you look, my dear general. . . . Please take a seat. . . .'

The general went to a sofa, saying, 'I'm not quite used to this sword yet. I've sat on it about four times already! Well, well, the dangers of war . . .'

He managed to ensconce himself on the sofa without entangling himself. Lew took a chair next to him.

'Now, son, do you know what this is all about?'

'Well, I understand you're with the War Department and you're looking for an aide. . . .'

'Exactly! A big job, Lew, an enormous job! Everything's a mess in Washington. Old Abe's tryin' to get some troops down there to protect the place, but it ain't easy. Your mom tells me you're lookin' for action, son. Well, if you want action, Washington's the place to find it. It's as good as in enemy territory! Maryland's crawlin' with Sesechies, and the state's probably going to go with the Rebs. The smartest thing they can do is take the capital, and don't think Mr Lincoln ain't chewin' his nails worryin' about it! Think of it: the Union fightin' a war with its capital city in enemy territory. I tell you, it makes my skin crawl. So Washington's right on the firing line. We need you, Lew. It's going to be a challenge; a real challenge! I hope you're interested?'

'Does Mr Cameron know you're offering me this commission?'

Matoon laughed. 'Well, the boy's no fool, is he? Your mom and I were going to make up a cock-and-bull story about that, but what's the use, eh? Of course Simon knows. He gave me your name.'

'Why? There's not much love lost between us.'

The general adopted an avuncular tone. 'Now, Lew, Simon feels bad about what happened here that night. Oh sure, he told me all about the letter you shipped off to Abe and how he got hot under the collar. . . . Well, that's water over the dam. And Simon wants to make up with you and your charming mom here. Yes sir! Water over the dam. And just between you and me, Simon *is* a bit of a sly old rogue, eh? No secret is it? Hm? But the point is, we've all got to pull together now to beat these rascal Rebs, eh? So he's willing to let bygones be you know what, and he hopes you feel the same. Now how about it, son? The olive branch is extended: you willing to take it? Hm? You can be a shiny new lieutenant in the U S Army by next week.'

Lew hesitated, then decided. Why not? General Matoon was obviously not America's answer to Alexander the Great, but he seemed jolly enough to work with, and since this whole thing was probably the result of his mother and wife conniving, if he took the commission Elizabeth wouldn't be able to object. Besides, it was rather flattering to think that the Secretary of War – a man he had, after all, insulted – thought enough of him to recommend him for a lieutenancy.

'Yes sir,' he said. 'I'd be proud to accept the commission.'

'Good!' Matoon pulled a small, paper-bound book from his hip pocket. 'Here's the Manual of Army Uniforms, Lew. General Staff uniforms are on page twenty. Aides to generals get a real nice-lookin' outfit – blue with more gold than most, though not as much as mine, eh?' He chuckled as he handed Lew the manual. 'Get yourself some uniforms and a sword, then be in Washington on the first of May. That'll give you chance for a little holiday. . . . When you get there, meet me at Willard's Hotel on Pennsylvania Avenue and Fourteenth Street. That's where I'll be putting up for the time being till I can get me some permanent digs. Washington's going to be crowded, son. It's a hick town anyway. . . . I'll reserve you a room at Willard's, you meet me there, and we'll pitch right in, get this war won, eh?'

Nicole Louise leaned forward. 'What about my daughter-in-law, General? Will Louis be able to take her with him?'

'Not for a while. Later on, after things get settled down a bit and Lew can find himself a place to stay . . . but I wouldn't take her now. I'm leaving Mrs Matoon in Harrisburg. . . . Well, I think things are all settled. Glad it's worked out this way, son.'

Nicole Louise smiled. 'And I'm delighted too. Ah, here's Eugène! We can toast not only you, General, but my son as well.'

Matoon's eyes lit up as he watched the butler pass the silver tray of tulip glasses.

'Splendid idea! Simon always told me you've got the best cellar in the land, and for once the rascal was tellin' the truth!'

When they had all been served, Nicole Louise raised her glass. 'To victory!' She smiled.

'Amen!' chorused the general, guzzling down half his glass in one gulp. 'Ah, delicious. Damned Frenchies may be immoral, but they do have a way with the grape, eh?' Lew smothered a laugh as his mother's eyes bulged. The general whipped off the rest of his champagne, then wheezed out of the sofa. 'Well, I'm off. Got a thousand things to do in Washington. . . . How are you on a horse, Lew?'

'Pretty good, sir,' he replied, getting up also.

'We'll get you a smart mount in Washington, compliments of Uncle Sammie. You'll cut a real figure, son. Can you shoot?'

'Yes sir.'

'Well, that'll be a help. Say, ain't this some rotten business, though? Half the country at the throats of the other half? Brother against brother, and all that? Well well, we'll all have something to tell our grandchildren, won't we? Lew, see you in Washington. Madame, you're as lovely as I remembered. It's been a real pleasure.' He took Nicole Louise's hand to kiss, but got it no further than halfway to his lips before he let out a belch. 'Uh-oh,' he said, looking up sheepishly. 'The bubbly went down too fast, eh? A little gas – hah! A thousand pardons.' He kissed her hand, then picked up his plumed cockaded hat. Lew escorted him into the entrance hall, where he shook his hand.

'Thank you, sir,' he said. 'I hope I don't let you down.' The general fitted his hat on his head.

'I know you won't, Lew. You're going to be a big help. A *big* help.' He smiled at him, then let himself out the door to walk to the waiting hack. Lew closed the door and stood in the hall a moment, thinking. Was he wrong, or had there been a hint of something more in the general's final remark than a friendly platitude? And come to think of it, wasn't

Simon Cameron's apparently genial forgiving of Lew's letter to Lincoln somewhat out of character? Then he told himself he was being petty. The war was too big to let one worry about the petty insults of six months ago – and Lew had to admit that now, in retrospect, his act of bravado did seem petty.

Still, it was odd....

He returned to the library, where his mother was finishing her champagne.

'What a buffoon!' she said as Lew closed the doors.

'As a general, I don't think he's in Napoleon's class,' agreed her son. 'Still, I doubt he's quite the buffoon he makes himself out to be. They say when he was mayor of Harrisburg, he pretty much ran Pennsylvania for Cameron. And while that may not take a lot of brains, it takes *some*.'

'Well, whether he's a fool or not, I'm glad you've taken his offer, and I know you'll make us all proud of you. Why don't you go to New York and have your uniforms cut at Brooks Brothers? Take Elizabeth with you and have a nice holiday, as the general suggested.'

'That's probably a good idea. I've been pretty hard on her the last few days.'

'So she tells me. She also tells me you have been anything but gentle with her in the marital bed.'

Lew looked at her suspiciously. 'What do you mean?'

'Elizabeth has complained that you are making excessive demands of her. You know what I'm talking about. For a husband to impose his baser nature on his wife too frequently is not gentlemanly. I would hate to think that my son is not a gentleman.'

Lew sighed wearily. 'All right, Mother. You've made your point.'

'Elizabeth has faults, but she is sensitive, and you mustn't treat her like one of your fancy women.' He shot her another look. 'Oh yes,' she went on, 'I know all about that. Well, how you conduct yourself outside the home is your affair, but inside the home I don't want you behaving like a peasant. After all, you *are* a de Rochefort, which apparently you keep forgetting.'

He got out of the chair. 'Yes, Mother. Is there anything else? You haven't told me to brush my teeth.'

'Don't be impertinent, Louis. Now come kiss me.'

He came over and leaned down to kiss her. She put her arms around him and hugged him tightly. 'Make me proud of you, Louis, my dearest son,' she whispered. They held each other for a moment, these two who were so much alike and yet so different, and he felt tears on her cheek. He straightened, surprised. He had never seen his mother cry, not even at his father's funeral. Nicole Louise was a rock of strength: she never cried. But she did now. She dabbed her eyes with a handkerchief and forced a smile.

'There: you see? You've made me cry. I suppose you think me a foolish, sentimental old woman.'

'No, of course not.'

She took his hand. 'We've had many fights, haven't we, my dear? And I know what you think of me. That I've tried to make you into something you don't want to be . . . a sort of second-hand Frenchman, and I suppose you're right. But I couldn't help it, Louis. I never much liked this country and it's never liked me. I suppose I tried to get back at it through you.'

'It doesn't matter now, Mother.'

'No, I suppose not. Because now you're a man, and you've left me. Do you know you were the most beautiful child I've ever seen? Oh, of course I'm biased, but you were. Such beautiful golden hair, like an angel's. I've always adored you, Louis. And now you're gone, and I'm alone.' She shrugged. 'For the first time in my life, I feel old.'

He squeezed her hand and kissed her again. Then he left the room without saying anything, because he didn't know what to say.

She not only felt old, for the first time she looked old. His beautiful mother was growing old, and he was going to war. But the discussion about Elizabeth had bothered him, and as he walked home he thought about his wife. He knew she didn't enjoy sex; she submitted to it with resignation. At first he had been hurt, but that had been replaced by irritation. What was wrong with him? Irene and the other whores he had slept with had always given him top marks, why shouldn't his wife? Then he told himself it must be something in her nature, and he shouldn't bother himself that much about it. He loved her as his wife. He supposed it wasn't the end of the world if she wasn't much in bed. He knew that sex, the great guilty secret of his world, wasn't considered that important to a marriage anyway. The important things were domesticity, child-raising, and appearances. Marriage wasn't supposed to be an endless orgy. Well, his wasn't by a long shot. Mrs Simpson had been right: he had already started going back to see Irene (and then, there was Christine. God, she was beautiful, and growing more mature every week. On his weekly visits to the Trowbridge farm – clandestine visits – he had to hold himself in when she ran to kiss him. She was his ward, he her benefactor; he couldn't take advantage of the situation, could he? Or could he?). He had felt guilty about returning to Irene, but this passed as he told himself he couldn't be expected to restrict his sex life to a wife who really didn't enjoy it – even though, lately, she had seemed to be warming up. It caused domestic irritability, but what marriage was perfect? He knew, though, that since Elizabeth was complaining to his mother, he had better bring the 'delicate' subject up and air it.

He let himself into the house. Elizabeth was in the parlour, practising. She was always practising, scales, arpeggios, Chopin, Bach, Beethoven, Liszt, whose ripe music she had a passion for. Now, as she heard her husband, she stopped playing and came over to greet him.

'How did it go with the general?' she asked.

Lew took her in his arms and kissed her.

'You're looking at Lieutenant Crandall.'

'I'm frightened, Lew,' she whispered. 'Tell me you'll be careful.'

'I'm not going to jump in front of bullets, but how careful can you be in a war? Anyway, we're going to New York tomorrow to get my uniforms, so let's put a moratorium on the war. Agreed?'

'Then the fight's over?'

He smiled. 'It's over. And I'm sorry. I guess I've been pretty hard to live with lately. Do you forgive me?'

'Of course I do. And do you forgive me for fighting back?'

'Well, I'll have to think about that. . . .'

'Oh, you're awful! You *have* to forgive me!'

He laughed.

'All right I forgive you.' He hesitated, then said, 'Mother tells me you think I'm sort of a monster in the bedroom.'

'Oh no, I never said that! And I don't think it – honestly!'

'Then what did you say?'

'Just that . . . I think I've disappointed you, and it makes me feel guilty.'

'Well, you haven't disappointed me, and there's absolutely no reason for you to feel guilty about anything.'

'You're lying, but it's sweet of you to lie.'

'I'm not lying. Besides,' and he lowered his voice, 'I think you're beginning to enjoy it a little more than you let on.'

She turned red, but didn't deny it. He took her hand and led her toward a sofa. 'Come here.' He sat down and pulled her onto his lap, putting his arms around her. 'I love you, Elizabeth,' he said. 'I don't know how good a husband I've been so far, but I want to be the best – for you and for our children, when they come. So if there's been some strain between us, it's really been my fault, and you shouldn't blame yourself. You see, it's not only the war. It's the medical school. I think I've made a big mistake going into medicine.'

'You really dislike it, don't you?'

'I don't know, it just seems so futile. The professors know so little. There must be something I can do with my life that can be more fulfilling than medicine. And the problem is, I don't know what it is. Which is why I've been snapping at you lately. Maybe in a way this war will be a good thing, if any war can be "good". Maybe I'll find what I'm looking for. Does that many any sense?'

She kissed him. 'It does. And I hope you find whatever you're searching for, because I want you to be happy more than anything in the world.'

'I *am* happy when I've got you on my lap.' He smiled.

'Although I think you've put on a little weight. Have you been at those chocolates again?'

'Well . . .' She smiled rather sheepishly. 'The truth is, that while I may be a disaster in the bedroom, it . . . seems I'm with child.'

Lew gaped.

'You're joking,' was all he could say.

'No. I saw the doctor this morning. I'm going to be a mother, and you're going to be a father.'

He let out a whoop of joy, then kissed her, then let out another whoop, then kissed her again. She started giggling.

'Stop it, Lew! We don't want to hurt him. . . .'

'How do you know it's a him?'

'Oh, I'm *sure* it's a him. And he's going to be as handsome as his father! Oh Lew . . .' Suddenly she was crying.

'What's this? Why the tears?'

'Because I'm so happy.' She sniffed. 'I love you so much, my darling. You're my whole world. Without you there'd be nothing for me. Promise me you'll take care of yourself?'

He kissed her tears.

'I promise. And I don't want any crying. This is a great day! We're going to have a baby! We should be celebrating. . . . In fact,' he lowered his voice, 'why don't we go upstairs and celebrate properly?'

'But darling it's still the afternoon. . . .'

'I have a theory that that's the best time.'

'Well,' she said, getting off his knees and taking his hand, 'let's go up. I guess I'm going to not reform you, so I'll just have to sink to your level.'

He laughed as he got up. 'Practise the piano less,' he whispered in her ear, 'and practise love more. Practise makes perfect.'

And he nibbled her ear.

I'm going to war, he thought. I'm going to be a father and I'm going to war! It's a great day! A fabulous day!

Gilbert Samson sat on the platform of Corinthian Hall in Rochester, New York, listening to his introduction and thinking about the guns of Sumter.

'Need I introduce you to Gilbert Samson?' Anthony van Zandt was saying to the overflow crowd of Abolitionists. In the thirteen years since Gilbert Samson had escaped from Maryland, Anthony's brown beard had turned snow white (just as fingers of grey were stretching out of Gilbert's scalp). But Gilbert thought nothing had changed the colour of his speaking style. It was still as purple as ever. 'You – his fellow townspeople? Of course not. You and hundreds of thousands of other Americans and Englishmen have heard Mr Samson's inspiring story. . . .' And so has Mr Samson, thought Gilbert. Over and over again until he wondered if it could inspire anything except advanced tedium. In thirteen years, how many lecture halls had he visited? Hundreds, in America and England. And the story? He had told it so often, and had altered it so much, that the wasn't sure what the story was any more. Miss Julie, Scarborough Hall, Jake the slave, Billie Orton the cruel slave breaker, Hooper's Mill, the Great Escape to Freedom that never failed to bring the audiences to tears and the edges of their seats. . . . The reality was so far away and so long ago it was all shadow now. He had trimmed the dull parts, dropping lines and sections that seemed to bore the audience. Then he had begun inventing new details to enliven the narrative. As the whip scars on his back faded with time, the whippings in his lectures became more brutal and electrifying, so that the slave Gabriel Pembroke seemed another person. Which he was. Gabriel was now Gilbert Samson. The slave was now the most famous black man in America: respected, welcomed in the finest homes, courted by the powerful, a hero to the Abolitionists and the free Negroes who read the newspaper he had begun to publish in 1856 (with the financial backing of Anthony van Zandt and other wealthy Abolitionists). *The Freedman's Weekly* was the first newspaper published by and for Negroes. Gilbert Samson had carried out Anthony van Zandt's prediction. Gilbert Samson had become a star.

And now Fort Sumter. War. Would slavery be crushed? They were being terribly cautious about the subject in Washington. And even if it were, what then?

'. . . a man whose newspaper, *The Freedman's Weekly*, published right here in Rochester, is read by thousands of Negro men and women. . . .'

Anthony was winding up his introduction now. Gilbert looked at his plump brown wife, Emma, who was sitting in the third row. Emma had borne him two sons and, just four months before, a daughter. They had a nice home in Rochester. But where were they? Miles above the slave, but still a little below the white man. . . .

'. . . I give you that great fighter for freedom, that great spokesman for his people, that warrior who has dedicated his life to slaying the Monster named Slavery . . . I give you Gilbert Samson!'

The crowd rose to its feet, cheering, applauding. Gilbert rose to his feet, smiling acknowledgement. Yes, they loved him . . . on the lecture platform. His eldest son still couldn't go to the public schools in Rochester.

He went to the lectern, shook Anthony's hand, then faced the audience. It was an ovation. He stood tall and handsome in his well-cut black suit, his crown of greying hair an African glory, and he remembered Gabriel Pembroke. Where was he? But where was Gilbert Samson?

He finally had to raise his hands to still the cheers. The audience sat down. He waited with the sense of timing of the professional performer for that psychologically correct moment to begin. A performer? Gilbert Samson was a star performer, though his critics had called him a 'trained seal' for the Abolitionists.

'The guns of Sumter have spoken,' he began, his richly sonorous voice filling the hall with the resonance of a pipe organ. 'And what have they said? They have said, "Slavery must *die*"!'

Again the audience went wild. They jumped to their feet, jumped up and down, threw their hats in the air . . . it was a circus, an orgy of hate.

Gilbert Samson felt a thrill. He couldn't help but feel a thrill. But *would* slavery die? He wondered. Maybe the old, obvious kind. But wasn't there a new, more subtle variety waiting in the wings? Gilbert had trimmed the dull parts of his story and emphasized the sensational. Admirable or not, it had worked. But what if history did the opposite? Trimmed the sensational and emphasized the dull? Then who would care for the black man?

The audience finally resumed their seats, and Gabriel continued.

'Yes, the guns of Sumter have spoken, but I wonder if the politicians in Washington have heard the message. They talk war, but what kind of war? They talk of preserving the Union, but what about destroying slavery? Why has the Secretary of State, Mr Seward, assured the European powers that slavery will be permitted – *no matter what the outcome of the conflict?*'

A loud booing. Men jumped up and shook their fists, yelling 'Never!' Gilbert waited for silence. Then he lowered his voice.

'But, my friends, you who have been in the vanguard of the antislavery struggle for so many years: I ask you to look into your own hearts as well. For our politicians are, in the long run, only a reflection of ourselves. If slavery does indeed die, I ask you this question: will you ever accept the black man as an equal?'

Silence. An uncomfortable silence.

Gilbert Samson, the star, the professional performer, knew he had just laid an egg.

Robert Elton Trowbridge was in torment.

Forty-two, skinny and sinewy, with a sharp, handsome face, he had the reputation of being a fervent Abolitionist, and his wife, Edna, and he had turned their farm into a school for Negro children. There were twelve of them now, since Mr Crandall had brought the girl named Christine Canrobert out to the Germantown farm five months before. Twelve girls, ranging in age from eight to fourteen. Twelve dancing black princesses in their clean white dresses. Twelve girls who slept in the big attic he and Edna had turned into a dormitory, who took their lessons in the barn he and Edna had turned into a schoolroom. Twelve well-behaved industrious girls.

Girls.

He told himself the evil desire that had tormented him since Christine arrived was a temptation of Satan, and he must thrust it out of his mind. But he couldn't. The girl was too beautiful, and growing too fast. He could swear that in the few months she had been there her breasts had grown fuller, her legs longer (and he had seen her legs often when she played on the swing he had hung in the back yard. They were beautiful legs. She had a beautiful body. How he wanted to caress all of it, her legs, her breasts, her hips, her buttocks, her back . . .)! Lew Crandall had noticed the change too, he thought. He came out once a week to see Christine and pay the Trowbridges; the girl was enraptured with him and never failed to throw her arms around him and kiss him. Robert Trowbridge had noticed lately that young Mr Crandall had begun looking a little nervous about these displays of affection, as if he were thinking those same evil thoughts (which no doubt he was. Robert had an idea Mr Crandall wasn't overly pure, morally, but was he either? He had always thought he was, had always taken pride in his purity, but now? Oh God, pray! Pray to be released from this devil!).

That very morning Mr Crandall had arrived to tell them and Christine that he was going off to war and would be in Washington at Willard's Hotel if they needed to contact him. He had given the Trowbridges a bank draft for five hundred dollars to cover Christine's expenses for the next year. The Trowbridges had praised Christine's academic progress (praise which was not feigned. She was bright – amazingly bright. Already she could read and write and was good at her sums. And Edna had coached her privately, so that now she spoke without that abominable slave accent. *He* had wanted to coach her privately, but for reasons that weren't academic. Oh God, pray!). Christine had gone into near hysterics when she heard her 'Daddy Lew' was going to war (her calling him that had rather embarrassed young Mr Crandall at first, but he had grown used to it. Did Daddy Lew regard this gorgeous girl as a daughter, Robert Trowbridge wondered, even though Crandall always seemed nervously correct around her. God grant that *he* could stay correct!). And then Daddy Lew had returned to Philadelphia, and Christine had been inconsolable. Robert wondered what *her* feelings were. Crandall was good-looking, and he knew the girl knew the facts of life – she had told him so (a delicious moment). Was she in love with Daddy Lew, or did she merely love him as her benefactor? Or was it a mixture of both? (What a wonderful, rich time of life when girls turned into women! Oh, how he wanted to touch her! Shame shame, thrice shame!)

Twelve girls sleeping in the attic above his and Edna's bed. But *one* of them . . .

Pray! he told himself. Pray for strength! Pray to purge this devil from your thoughts!

But he kept thinking of those legs, those buttocks, those lovely, ripe breasts. . . .

4

DEATH GOES ON A PICNIC 1861

13

As Lew Crandall raised the sledgehammer to pound the rail spike, he told himself this was a hell of a way to start a war. He and two dozen men from the New York Seventh Regiment were preparing a section of the Baltimore–Washington rail line that had been torn up by Maryland rebels. On 19 April the Sixth Massachusetts Regiment, the first troops to answer Lincoln's call for men to protect the capital, was transferring from the Philadelphia to the Washington depot in Baltimore when they were attacked by a mob. A riot ensued, shots were fired, people killed. The Sixth got to Washington eventually, but pro-Southern forces in Maryland retaliated by blowing up railroad bridges and destroying sections of the line to prevent any more Union troops going through their state, and the capital was isolated. For six days it waited, tense, frightened, and desperate for news. In New York Lew had read what had happened and, afraid he might not get to Washington by the first of May, he had cut his holiday short and joined the New York Seventh, which was taking a steamer to Annapolis. After kissing Elizabeth good-bye, he climbed aboard the boat, carrying a carpetbag and wearing his handsome new lieutenant's General Staff uniform. The steamer was crowded and hot, and the new uniform soon began to wilt. By the time they reached Annapolis, it was a mass of wrinkles and beginning to have a ripe odour. When they started the march to Washington, repairing the torn-up rails as they proceeded, the uniform gave up, as did Lew. Abandoning all pretensions to military swagger, he and the other men of the Seventh rolled up their tunics and shirts in their bags and, stripped to the waist under the broiling sun, went to work like members of a chain gang. For the well-heeled young bucks of the elite Seventh – as well as for Lew – it was a rude introduction to the glories of war.

Now with the sledgehammer he tapped in the spike, which was being held by Chandler Delanoy, whose father was the rector of fashionable Saint Timothy's in New York. Then, wham! wham! wham! The spike dug into the tie as Lew swung the sledgehammer, sweat flying in all directions. When the spike was in, he wiped his forehead.

'How many more?' He was puffing.

'Too many,' growled Chandler, moving to the next one. 'And I'm hungry. I didn't volunteer to work like an Irishman, but since I am, they can at least feed us.'

'You didn't like that slop they fed us for breakfast?'

'That pig food? I wouldn't wish that on Jeff Davis. Some war.'

And, his head filled with memories of the farewell dinner at the Astor House his father had given on the eve of his departure, Chandler stooped down to position another spike.

'Some war,' agreed Lew, raising the sledgehammer for what seemed like the thousandth time that morning as his back muscles tuned up a symphony of pain.

When, two days later, their train puffed into Washington's new Italian-style depot, they were met by a crowd of cheering Washingtonians. But Lew's back was too sore for him to derive much pleasure from the heroes' welcome. He shook hands with Chandler and the other members of the 'chain gang'. Then, as the Seventh mustered in front of the depot to march to the White House, to be reviewed by the President, Lew carried his carpetbag out of the station and got in a cab. 'Willard's Hotel,' he ordered, and the cab took off.

The city he had finally arrived at was, as General Matoon had said, a hick town. Foreign visitors snubbed it as nothing more than a country village with laughable pretensions. Most Americans looked on it as a sinkpit of iniquity. Most politicians disliked it: they fled from it in the unbearably hot summers, and the more sophisticated considered it a cultural embarrassment. There was no municipal water supply or sewage system. A lot of people thought the smell of the city reflected the quality of its politicians.

Most of the streets were unpaved, and even the city's main thoroughfare – L'Enfant's proud Pennsylvania Avenue – though it had a light cobble paving, had been so rutted by wagon wheels that during wet weather it was a sea of mud. The south side of the avenue was a line of dilapidated buildings, interrupted by the popular Centre Market, a collection of sheds and shacks backing on a smelly canal. But the north side was more pleasant. Here a brick sidewalk passed by the city's principal restaurants, shops, and hotels, offering Washington's only pretence to a cosmopolitan promenade. The hotels were the centre of the city's social life. These big, ugly buildings, mostly new, were brash and overpriced, but their lines of waiting hacks and the bustle of their guests presented an exciting alternative to the rest of the town. As Lew's hack pulled up in front of Willard's, he was surprised to see a number of Negroes lounging in front of it, probably slaves waiting for their masters. He knew the capital was basically a Southern town, but somehow the sight of slaves in the very heart of it was shocking to a Northerner.

He paid the hackman and carried his bag into the hotel lobby, which, with its adjacent bar, was the most popular meeting place in town. Right now it wasn't too full (Lew supposed most of its regulars were out watching the Seventh), though a variety of uniforms was around, and he spotted three colonels and an admiral chatting with a number of attractive women. Lew went to the reception desk and set down his bag.

'My name is Lieutenant Crandall,' he said to the clerk. 'General Matoon has reserved a room for me.'

The clerk checked his reservation book. 'That's not till May first, Lieutenant.'

'I know, but I came in early with the Seventh.'

'Ah!' The clerk smiled. 'Well then, we'll find you a room. How was the trip? We hear you repaired the rails the Rebs tore up.'

'We did. And can I get some liniment? I can hardly move.'

'I'll send some up to your room. We have a vacancy on the fourth floor. Four B. Will you register, please?'

As Lew signed the register, he asked. 'Is the general at the War Department?'

'No sir. He's in the bar.'

Lew looked up. The clerk shrugged, as if to say the general's drinking habits were the way of the Washington world.

'Leave your bag here, Lieutenant,' he said. 'I'll have it sent up to your room. And may I offer the hotel's thanks? It's a great relief to us Washingtonians that you got through. Willard's will take good care of you.'

'Thanks.'

Feeling somewhat better for that, he crossed the lobby and went into the dark-panelled, palm-filled bar, where he spotted the general at the bar with a well-dressed man who had a great halo of white hair and a full white beard.

'Lew!' exclaimed the general. 'There you are! Bet you came in with the Seventh, eh?'

Lew came over to shake hands, totally forgetting he probably should have saluted. 'Yes sir. We had quite a trip.'

'*So* I hear! Those crazy Rebs in Baltimore, tearin' up the rails . . . by God, we oughta roast 'em all in peanut oil! Say, look at that uniform! I like the cut of that!'

'I'm afraid it took a beating on the trip down.'

'Hah! I can imagine! Put you to work, didn't they, son? Well now, this is someone you're going to see a lot of. Lew, meet Bradley Dilbeck. Brad, this here's my new aide, Lieutenant Lew Crandall from Philadelphia. Mr Dilbeck's president of the Dilbeck Bank and Trust company, Lew. He's Mr Moneybags around here, so be nice to him.'

Lew shook the nand of the banker, who said, 'Are you related to the late Judge Crandall?'

'Yes sir. He was my father.'

'Ah. A fine man.'

The general was snapping his fingers at the bartender.

'Bring us three beers, Jerry. You'll have a beer, won't you, Lew?'

'That'd be fine sir. I'm a little thirsty after the trip. . . .'

'I'll bet! And hungry too, I'd say. Bring the boy a sandwich, Jerry. Ham and cheese on rye with plenty of mustard and pickles – that's a specialty here, Lew – and bring me the same, come to think of it. Haven't had a bite since before breakfast. Got to keep the inner man happy, eh? Now Lew, it's a good thing you come along just now because I wanted you to meet Mr Dilbeck. One of your jobs is going to be to take care of my personal expenses – pay my hotel bills, and so forth – and Brad's going to open a savings account for me. I'll give you the money, you stick in in the account, then you pay my bills out of it. It'll be a pain in the ass, but that's one of your jobs as aide, son: to do all the pain-in-the-ass jobs so I can worry about the big stuff – right, Brad?'

'Exactly. If you'll come to the bank in the morning, Lieutenant, I'll open the account personally for you. It will be in your name.'

'*My* name?' asked Lew. 'Why?'

'As a convenience. You'll be making the deposits and withdrawals, not the general, so it will be easier if the account's in your name.'

'Hot damn! Here's the beers!' exclaimed the general. 'Here, son: guzzle a brew and forget your troubles. Doin' my best to forget *mine*. Oh, we're busy as hens in heat already, Lew, buyin' horses for the army, feed for the horses, guns, food, ammo – you name it, the War Department's buyin'! Course, there ain't a goddam red cent in the Treasury – eh, Brad? Hee hee! Old Sammy Chase is scurryin' around trying to get some scratch to pay for this damn-fool war, but he's having his problems, I'll say! Brad and the other bankers is bailin' Uncle Sammie out in the meantime, so let's drink to the banks.'

'Hear hear.' Mr Dilbeck smiled, raising his glass.

'One thing you gotta understand about Washington, Lew is that no one here knows *anything* about runnin' a war. Hell, we don't know our assholes from shotgun shells, do we, Brad?'

'Unfortunately,' said the banker, 'the general's right. Conditions are chaotic, to put it mildly.'

'We're gonna run this war by the seat of our pants,' went on Matoon, 'and our only hope is that Johnny Reb's even dumber than we are, and that's the God's truth, boy. We got to work fast, son! Got to equip an army – hell, got to get an army to equip! – before them Rebs chase us all up to Vermont. What scares the shit out of me is that Jeff Davis knows what a bunch of boobs we are, damn him! Wouldn't surprise me if he didn't send old Beauregard up here with a bunch of peashooters and scare us pissy-ass right out of the city. And here's our sandwiches! Goddam, I sure can work up an appetite jawin'! Now don't you worry 'bout none of this, son: you'll catch on quick. He's a Princeton boy, Brad! A college boy. Speaks Frog, too, so I'm told. How's that? Old Ralph Matoon, who hardly got through eighth grade, and he's got himself an aide that went to Princeton and speaks Frog! Goddam. Only in America, eh? Say something in Frog, Lew. Can't say I've ever heard any.'

Lew racked is brain for something to say.

'Uh . . . "*Allons enfants de la patrie*".'

'Hey, ain't that pretty? What's it mean, boy?'

'It means if I were a betting man, I wouldn't be betting on the North.'

The general and the banker roared with laughter.

'Ain't that the God's truth? Ain't that the God's *truth!*'

Robert Trowbridge stopped the wagon by the pond and got down to tie the horse to a tree. A twenty-acre cornfield surrounded the pond with stately green columns that were already three feet high and that provided a lovely seclusion.

'It's so hot,' said Mr Trowbridge, 'I'm going to take a swim. Dost thou wish to join me, Christine?'

He looked up at his pupil, who was sitting on the wagon seat. She was barefoot, wearing a simple white cotton frock. She was looking at him strangely.

'Would that be decent, Mr Trowbridge?'

'If I say it's decent, it's decent. God brought us into this world naked, didn't he? "So God created man in His own image, in the image of God created He him; male and female created He him." Genesis one twenty-seven.'

A fly buzzed around his sweaty, sunburned forehead, from which the black hair was making a quickening retreat. Christine shifted uncomfortably. She was fiercely hot on this blazing afternoon, and the idea of a swim in the lovely pond was appealing. But with Mr Trowbridge? Mr Trowbridge, who had been acting so *peculiar* lately. . . .

' "And the Lord God made coats of skins and clothed Adam and Eve",' she replied. 'Genesis three twenty-one.'

The flies buzzed. Mr Trowbridge came around the horse and put his hand on Christine's bare ankle. He looked up at her again. She could see his breathing was agitated: she could feel how sweaty his palm was on her brown flesh. She knew what he wanted.

'Thou art beautiful, Christine,' he said softly. 'So beautiful. Thou art a beautiful child, grown into a woman before my eyes. I have watched thee ripen, Christine, like a lovely flower.'

She eyed him coolly, telling herself not to panic.

'Uh huh. I've seen you watching me, Mr Trowbridge. So has your wife.'

He said nothing. His hand crept up her leg under her white cotton skirt. How firm and smooth her flesh was! How he wanted her!

She leaned down to push his hand away. He grabbed her right arm with his other hand and jerked her off the wagon. She grabbed for the back of the seat, but missed.

'Don't!' she screamed.

She fell on top of him. He stumbled backward onto the dirt path, and they both landed in the dust. She tried to roll away from him, but he grabbed her, pinioned her on her back, and then straddled her. He was panting like an animal now. She continued screaming as he grabbed the top of her dress and ripped it open. Then he tore her white undergarment, exposing her small bare breasts, the sight of which drove him to a frenzy. He tore everything off. Then he stared down at her lush loveliness. She stopped screaming and looked at him. The sweat dripped off his red face and fell on her bare belly like wax from a melting candle.

'Thou art the temptation of Satan,' he whispered. He started unbuttoning his pants. 'And I am weak. *So* weak. Thou art sent from Satan to test me, and I have failed the test. I consign my immortal soul to eternal hellfire, but I must have thee. And I *will*.'

He pulled down his pants, and his erect penis bowed up like a pink scimitar. She watched, half terrified, half fascinated, as he grabbed it with his right hand and stroked it three or four times, his head arched back, his eyes closed. He was a dissolving candle now, sweat pouring from his scrawny, sinewy body. Then he eased on top of her. 'Oh Christine, Christine, thou hast bewitched me . . . Christine, Christine . . .'

She felt his hot, sweaty kisses. She was in such a state of shock now she couldn't move. She felt his groping hands exploring her slim body. She felt his wet, hairy skin squishing against her smooth flesh. Then she felt his penis go in her. He started humping, grunting with sweaty lust. She closed her eyes and thought of her golden benefactor, whom she loved and worshipped and missed so desperately now that he had gone to Washington. . . . How she wished it were *he* on top of her!

Tonight, she thought, fighting her panic, I'll run away. I'll find *him*. . . .

And the sperm flooded inside her. And the flies buzzed.

The Secretary of War stood at the tall window of his office and looked through the slats of the closed shutters at the Marine guards three storeys below. It was one of the hottest Julys Simon Cameron could remember in Washington, but his new office in the War Department building just west of the White House was pleasantly cool. And of course, with the Capitol a mess because of the construction of the new dome, it was a blessing to be out of the Senate. In fact, all things considered, it was turning out to be a blessing that he had been given the War Department rather than the Treasury. At first, he had been furious at Abe's tricky treachery, giving the Treasury to Governor Chase of Ohio rather than to him. But now? Well, the opportunities here were staggering.

Mr Bushnell, his secretary, opened the door.

'General Matoon to see you, sir.'

'Show him in.'

Cameron walked over to his enormous desk and sat down. The desk was tidy: Simon Cameron was a tidy man. A small marble bust of Cicero, to give him a patina of scholarship. A small leather Bible for the odour of sanctity. A malachite and silver inkwell from Russia to remind the visitor of his wealth. Behind him a full-length portrait of Andrew Jackson, as a hint of his political connections (he had met Jackson once) as well as to suggest military expertise. On another wall, a large portrait of Empress Eugénie, which the French Emperor had given him five years before when he had made a trip to Europe (which the Senate had paid for). A handsome brass chandelier hung from the tall ceiling, and the office was furnished with a suite of horsehair sofas and chairs. In the cool semidarkness provided by the closed shutters, the Secretary of War's office was imposing.

Matoon came in, and Mr Bushnell closed the door behind him.

'How are you, Simon?' he said, coming to the desk as he mopped his face with a handkerchief. 'Ain't it a bitch of a day?'

'It's bad weather for whales,' said the Secretary of War, eyeing his assistant's waistline. 'You ought to lose some weight Ralph. Fat generals don't look respectable in time of war. The public gets the idea they're eating instead of fighting.'

'Well, they are!' said Matoon, squeezing into a chair. 'All old Fuss and Feathers Scott talks about is his goddam terrapin dinners.'

'General Scott will soon have plenty of time to eat terrapin.'

'You firin' him?'

'The President's looking for a replacement – but don't let that get out. Did you see Whitney?'

'I just finished talkin' to him. He's offered us a thousand horses for the cavalry at a hundred dollars a head.'

'What's the slide?' asked Cameron, picking up a pencil to play with.

'Twenty per cent.'

'Can we do better?'

'Now dammit, Simon, twenty per cent is *good!* We can't afford to get too greedy!'

The Secretary of War thought about this. 'All right. Take it. What about the Wellington deal?'

'We're having trouble there. He won't go above a ten-per-cent slide.'

'Tell him we'll buy the rifles from France.'

'I tried that. He said the Frog rifles ain't no good, and I sort of agree. But he hinted around that if we upped our order he'd up his slide.'

'How many rifles are we talking about so far?'

'A hundred thousand.'

'If we doubled our order, would he double his slide?'

'I sort of think he might.'

'Well, try him. I want to establish twenty per cent as a base. Let me know tomorrow if you can. The President's been pressing me about the rifles. By the way, are you going to the reception Monday night?'

'You don't think I'd turn down all that free White House grub?'

'Are you taking Rosemary?'

'I thought I might. Any objections?'

The Secretary of War leaned over his desk and pointed his pencil at the general.

'Listen, Ralph: I don't care what you do with that red-head in private. But I don't want it getting around Washington that one of my generals has a mistress.'

'*One?*' sputtered Matoon. 'Hell, *all* of 'em do! Except old Fuss and Feathers, and he's too gouty.'

'Nevertheless, keep her out of the White House – understand?'

'All right,' he growled.

'Take Crandall instead.'

'Can't waltz with *him.*' Then he lowered his voice. 'By the way, that little scheme of yours is working out just dandy.'

'Crandall doesn't suspect anything?'

'Naw. Those snot-nose college brats don't know anything about real life. I give him the money, and he trots over to Brad Dilbeck's bank, dumb as a mule. I've got to hand it to you, Simon: you're a fox!'

The Secretary of War leaned back and smiled with satisfaction.

'I told Crandall he'd regret sending that letter to Mr Lincoln,' he said. 'Simon Cameron is a fox with a good memory.'

'You sure are!' agreed the general, hoisting himself out of the chair. 'And I hope you remember your old friend Ralph Matoon when Senator Cadwallader goes to that great caucus in the sky.'

'Don't *you* get too greedy, Ralph.'

'Hell, it's contagious, ain't it?'

And they both laughed.

It was an amateur's war, a fact Ben Bramwell was learning the hard way. The hundreds of men pouring into Washington daily by the first summer of the war knew nothing of military tactics or drilling, and cared less. Farmboys, carpenters, butchers' apprentices, they were fiercely democratic and resented any attempts by the officers to exert military discipline. The officers, on their part, were nervous about trying to enforce their authority and insecure because of their own lack of military know-how. There were only a few hundred professional officers (West Point 'peacocks', as General Matoon called them) and many of these, being from the South, had naturally enough decided to fight for the Confederacy. The rest of the officers were as new to war as their men. But of all the men in Washington, no one was more amateurish, insecure, and generally at a complete loss than Ben Bramwell.

Shortly after the outbreak of hostilities, he had obtained a lieutenant's commission in the Fifth Pennsylvania, and he arrived in Washington three months after Lew. The Fifth under the command of Colonel Archibald T. Raymond, was assigned an open field on the north bank of the Potomac, and there the men pitched their tents and waited for someone to tell them what to do. Colonel Raymond, an intelligent West Pointer, knowing he had an enormous job on his hands turning this mass of raw recruits into something resembling a military machine, quickly set up a training schedule, drill in the morning, firearm and artillery instruction in the afternoon. The men hated it. Lieutenant Bramwell, clumsy in his ill-fitting uniform, hated it as much as his men, particularly since he had learned drill by reading the Army Manual on the way to Washington and was at a loss about how to execute an about-face.

Their second morning in Washington, Lieutenant Bramwell was putting a dozen men through drill as a blazing sun beat down, making everyone thoroughly miserable. The men had been marching for twenty minutes, mostly out of step, Ben marching beside them at the right, out of step with his out-of-step troops, so that no one had the vaguest idea of what was *in* step. Now he shouted, 'By the right flank, march!' and gazed in bewilderment as he saw twelve sweating faces wheel and head directly toward him. 'Oh my God, I mean by the *left* flank – oh hell, stop. I mean, *halt!*' They stopped two inches in front of their lieutenant.

'Mr Bramwell –' began one of them, a red-faced farmer from Greensburg, Pennsylvania, named Hawley.

'*Lieutenant* Bramwell,' corrected Ben, pulling out a handkerchief to wipe his face.

'Yes sir, *Lieutenant* Bramwell. Sir, I had a mule once that didn't know his left from his right till I tied a rag around his left leg. Now, Mr Bramwell –'

'Lieutenant. Oh, to hell with it.'

'Yes sir. Now maybe if you'd tie that kerchief around your right arm, you wouldn't get so messed up.'

Ben scowled at the grinning private, then turned as he heard someone behind him laughing. He saw Lew Crandall under an elm tree. The men started snickering. Ben gave up.

'Fall out,' he ordered. 'Take a ten-minute break. And if you think *I'm* funny, you ought to see yourselves.'

Feeling his dignity somewhat salvaged, he walked over to the tree. He hadn't seen much of Lew since that night the previous December, the night he had only vague memories of. But he remembered enough to know he had caused trouble. The fight with Lew's mother, then the young Negro girl who had so excited him. . . . The next day, he had tried to elicit information from Jethro, but the aged retainer had been strangely close-mouthed, saying only that the girl and Winkler had gone north. But Ben knew he had done something to the girl in his drunkenness, and that Lew had witnessed it, which frightened and shamed him. He had gone to Lew's wedding, but, despite Lew's obvious pleasure at seeing him, he had stayed only a few minutes at the reception. Since then, he had seen nothing of him, and he had assumed his drunken behaviour had shattered the friendship that had meant so much to him. And now, here Lew was, looking as wonderful in his lieutenant's uniform as Ben looked woebegone. Ben said nothing for a moment while Lew tried to control his laughter.

Then Lew said, 'Ben, with you and me in this army, Abe Lincoln better start looking for a job with a split-rail fence company. How are you, you big ape?'

They pumped hands as Ben grinned sheepishly.

'Pretty awful, wasn't it? And to tell the truth, I *don't* know my left from my right and never have. But for the life of me, I can't figure out what that's got to do with fighting a war. Can you?'

'Nope. But if you want to see some *real* incompetence, drop by the War Department. Christ, is that place a mess! Anyway, I saw your name on the list of officers of the Fifth and came right over. Do you want to go to the White House tonight?'

'The White House?' Ben sounded incredulous.

'There's a big do tonight, and I've got an extra invitation.' He lowered his voice. 'My boss decided he'd rather lay Rosemary than meet the new French ambassador, so I'll give you his invitation.'

'Who's Rosemary?'

'Rosemary Fletcher is Matoon's mistress. She owns a

boarding house over on Third Street, and he can't get enough of her. Anyway put on your best duds and meet me at Lafayette Square at eight tonight. I'll get you in. Can you get away?'

'I think so. Colonel Raymond would probably be thrilled to get rid of me permanently, but he'd settle for an evening.'

'Good.' He hesitated, frowning slightly. 'I think I'm in a little trouble, Ben. I could use some advice.'

'What kind of trouble?'

'I'll tell you tonight.' He shook his hand again and smiled. 'It's great to see you, Ben. I've missed you.'

And he walked away to climb on the roan stallion that the Army had provided him. Ben watched him ride off, delighted that their friendship was picking up again and wondering what trouble Lew Crandall, the golden prince of Philadelphia, could possibly have gotten into.

14

'Do you know what a slide is?' Lew asked Ben that night as they stood below the equestrian statue of Andrew Jackson in Lafayette Square, smoking cigars and watching the carriages roll through the gates of the White House in front of them. Heavy thunderstorms late that afternoon had broken the oppressive heat, and the trees in the square were dripping into the puddles. It was humid, but blissfully cool.

'A slide?' said Ben. 'Of course I know. It's what children . . .'

'Not that kind of slide. This slide is a percentage of a deal.

I've heard Matoon use the word a couple of times when he didn't know I was listening. Just this morning, I came into his office when he was talking to a man named Wellington about a big rifle order the War Department's placing. He was talking about the slide when I came in, and he gave me hell later for not knocking.'

'Then what do you think it means?'

'I think it means kickback.'

Ben blew out a cloud of cigar smoke as the crickets chirped and the carriages splashed up the White House drive.

'You think Matoon is taking kickbacks on government orders?'

'I think he and Cameron are squeezing the manufacturers as much as they can. The War Department's placing millions of dollars' worth of orders, and it's all being handled by those two. On the basis of their political reputations alone, I'd bet they couldn't resist the temptation. Putting those two in the War Department is like putting two pigs in a granary.'

Ben tapped his ash. 'If it's true, what are you going to do about it?'

'I'm not sure. That's why I need your advice. I can't *prove* anything yet. And they've set it up so slickly that I think I'm involved in it.'

'You? How?'

'When I got here three months ago, Matoon had me open an account for him at the Dilbeck Bank in *my* name. I thought it was a little odd, but I went along with it. They said it would be more convenient, and in a way it is. The general gave me a thousand dollars to open the account with, and for the first couple of months, that was all I needed to pay his bills. Then three weeks ago, he gave me three thousand dollars to deposit, which surprised me. And last week he gave me three thousand more. Now the questions are, one, where is a general who's not a rich man getting that kind of money? And two, why is he putting that much money in an account that's supposed to be nothing more than petty cash? I certainly don't need anywhere near six thousand dollars to pay his bills.'

'I'm not following you.'

'Don't you get it? I think part of Matoon's kickback money – and maybe part of Cameron's too – is going into this account with *my* name on it! It's a perfect setup. It's all cash transactions, so if anyone starts investigating Matoon, he can say "where's the money"? The money's in my name, and there's no way I can prove Matoon gave it to me.'

'But surely the bank –'

'Brad Dilbeck's in on it. He handles the account personally. He'd back Matoon. On the other hand, if there is no investigation, whenever Matoon wants the money he can tell me to draw it out and turn it over to him. Meanwhile, there's no safer place for the money to sit. He wins either way, and I'm the patsy. So do you see what I mean when I said I was in trouble? If anyone hangs, it's going to be *me*.'

Ben tapped his ash again.

'Well, you may be too suspicious. After all, you're not talking about that much money. . . .'

'Not yet. But what if it keeps growing, like Topsy?'

'Then I think you'd have to tell someone.'

'Who?'

'I don't know. Someone higher up than Cameron, I guess, though he's pretty close to the top.'

'Exactly. And anyone higher than he may not want to listen. Lincoln's so shaky right now, a scandal in the War Department could really hurt him, politically.'

'I see what you mean.'

Ben dropped the cigar in a puddle, and it sizzled out.

'Let me think about it,' he said. 'Meanwhile, I wouldn't do anything. And I sure as hell wouldn't *say* anything.'

'Don't worry. You're the only person I trust in this damned town.'

They started walking toward the White House gate.

'I *could* be wrong,' Lew went on, tossing his cigar away. 'But something tells me I'm not. And I think Matoon's counting on me to be too dumb to catch on.'

'Look, don't think about it tonight. Let's get some fun out of this crazy war. Have you ever been in the White House?'

'No. Matoon steers clear of the place. He likes it at Rosemary's better.'

'The mistress? What's she like?'

'She's a big redhead. I've only seen her a couple of times. She seems pretty smart. What she sees in Fatso is beyond me.'

Ben laughed. 'Maybe he's got hidden charms.'

'They're awfully well hidden.'

'What do you hear from Elizabeth?'

They stepped into the street, heading around the puddles toward the right gate.

'She's four months' pregnant.'

'Hey, I didn't know! Congratulations!'

'Yes, we're very excited. She writes me that everything's fine. Mother took her to the shore for the summer so they'd be cool.'

'Not a bad idea. How's your mother?' This, not so warmly.

'Elizabeth writes that she's getting interested in the Church again. She gave up the Catholic religion when she married Father, but now that she's all alone, I guess she needs it again. Apparently she's met this young priest –'

'Watch out!'

Ben tried to pull him back, but it was too late. An enormous carriage with a coat of arms painted on the door had wheeled past them to rattle through the White House gates. In doing so, it went through a puddle, sending a sheet of muddy water all over Lew.

'Shit!'

As he pulled out a handkerchief to wipe his face, he yelled after the carriage, 'Why don't you watch where you're going?'

A woman stuck her head out the window to look back, but by then the carriage was inside the White House grounds.

'People have no manners in this goddamn town,' growled Lew, wiping off the mud as best he could. 'And it's not cheap getting uniforms clean, either.'

'You're telling me,' agreed Ben. 'Want to forget the reception?'

'Hell no. Let's go. Father Abraham will have to take his noble warriors the way we are – clean or dirty. By the way, they've gotten up a committee of local matrons to dance with the noble warriors, but don't expect much.'

He showed his invitations to the Marine guard, then he and Ben walked through the gates toward the brightly lit Executive Mansion.

'Isn't she absolutely the most gorgeous woman you've ever seen?' said Mrs Helen Turner as she waltzed around the East Room with the young lieutenant in the mud-stained uniform.

'Who's that, ma'am?' said Lew. Mrs Turner, the wife of an Indiana congressman, was one of the committee of matrons, each wearing a blue rosette, who had volunteered to entertain the officers at the reception. Mrs Turner had a flat nasal twang and a receding chin, but she was friendly and having the time of her life, which made her look prettier than she was. Scala's Marine Band was playing a lively waltz, the East Room was festooned with American flags and flags bearing the Imperial, bee-crawling arms of France. Washington's leading caterer, Gautier, had contrived an elegant buffet with pyramids of glazed food, and, after weeks of tension and uncertainty, official Washington was letting itself go having a good time. Even Mr Lincoln was smiling.

'Why, the Baroness de Bow-pree, of course,' said Mrs Turner. 'The new French ambassador's wife. I don't think I'm saying that just right. . . .'

'I think it's "Bow-*pray*",' said Lew.

'Oh, do you speak French?'

'Yes, Ma'am. My mother's French.'

'Isn't that something? I couldn't even say "howdy-do". Anyway, isn't she beautiful?'

'I didn't see her.'

'You didn't? She was in the receiving line. . . .'

'I know, but someone spattered me with mud on the way in, so I thought I'd sort of avoid meeting the President.'

'Well, that's too bad. Oh dear, you *did* get messed, didn't you? Anyway, she's Italian and just radiant! I've never seen anything like *her* in Indianapolis. . . . She has a past, you know.'

'No, I didn't know,' said Lew, becoming a little bored with the subject of the French ambassador's wife.

'Oh yes, She's the daughter of a very noble family from Rome, and she married a count from Milan who turned out to be a drunkard. They say he beat her and was so cruel the poor woman almost went mad, and she had to go to a sanitarium. . . . Isn't that awful? Those Italians! Just like an opera! Poor thing. Anyway, he killed himself in a hunting accident – got what he deserved, if you ask me – and she was married to the baron. Isn't that romantic? Of course, the baron's three times her age.'

'How old is she?'

'I'd say twenty-five or so. All that excitement in a life so short! Of course, she *might* be older . . . it's hard to tell with those foreigners. They're so clever with rouge and powder. . . . I wonder what my husband would say if I used rouge?'

'I'm sure the congressman would say you don't need it, ma'am,' said Lew.

'Why, Lieutenant, aren't you sweet! I wager you're a real heartbreaker. Where are you from?'

'Philadelphia.'

'Such a nice city. And what do you think of Washington?'

'So far not much, ma'am.'

'Me either. And isn't it *hot?* Oh, there's the end of the waltz. You're a very good waltzer, Lieutenant.'

'Not half as good as you, ma'am.'

She laughed. 'You *are* a heartbreaker! Would you like some punch?'

'I'd like some wine, if they have it.'

'I'm sure they do, for the French ambassador. Shall we go look?'

They made their way through the throng to the end of the room, where a white-clothed bar had been set up. Four black footmen were dispensing strawberry punch and chilled white wine to the thirsty crowd, many of whom were looking around for something stronger. 'They do have wine,' said Mrs Turner.

'What can I get you, ma'am?'

'Some punch would be nice. . . . Oh, there she is! Do you want to meet her?'

She pointed to a blonde woman in a blue ball gown whose back was turned to them. She was talking to an attractive young woman with a slightly tipped nose.

'Well . . .'

Mrs Turner grabbed his hand and started leading him around the couples.

'Oh, come on! Something to write to your family about. And she'd love to meet someone who speaks French. . . .' She lowered her voice. 'That's Kate Chase she's talking to, the Secretary of the Treasury's daughter.' They had reached the two women. Mrs Turner let go of Lew's hand. 'How are you, Miss Chase?' she said. 'I wanted you to meet Lieutenant . . .' She turned to Lew.

'Crandall.'

'Yes, Lieutenant Crandall, from Philadelphia. Miss Chase.'

'How do you do?'

'And this is the Baroness de . . . Bow-*pray*.' She got it out rather timidly.

Laura de Beaupré turned to smile at Lew.

'Lieutenant Crandall speaks French,' prompted Mrs Turner. She looked at Lew, who was staring at Laura de Beaupré. 'Um, you *do* speak French, Lieutenant?'

Laura extended her hand.

'So *you're* the one I splashed,' she said in a low voice, looking at his uniform. She spoke in English that had a musical accent that was half-French, half-Italian and, consequently, unique. But Lew barely heard her. He was fascinated by her eyes, which were blue-grey-green. He was fascinated by her hair, which was a soft, Botticelli blonde. By her skin, which was warm pink and unpowdered, contrary to Mrs Turner's allegation. Her mouth, which was thin and yet, somehow, at the same time voluptuous. Her long neck, her full breasts, her magnificent body, dressed in a beautiful blue gown of Egyptian cotton taffeta. Laura de Beaupré was more than beautiful. She was a work of art.

'Lieutenant?'

He woke up. 'Uh . . . yes, I guess I am the one you splashed.' He kissed her hand.

'I am so sorry,' she said. 'I have told Aristide – my husband – that our driver goes much too fast. *Est-ce vrai, monsieur, que vous parlez français?*'

'*Oui, madame la baronne. Ma mère est française.*'

'*Elle doit être fière d'un fils si galant et si beau.*'

'*Madame est trop gentille.*'

Laura turned to Kate Chase and returned to English.

'If all your army is as charming as the Lieutenant, then the South's reputation for gallantry is in danger.' She turned back to Lew. 'I must make up to you for ruining your uniform. My husband is giving a dinner for the Secretary of State a week from tonight. We need an extra man. Could I persuade you to be our extra man?'

'I would be honoured, madame.'

'Good. At the French Legation. At eight o'clock.' She turned to move away, her eyes travelling up his body from his shoes to the top of his blond head. 'And I promise I won't splash you,' she added with a final smile. Then she and Kate Chase moved into the crowd.

'There,' said Mrs Turner. 'Didn't I tell you? Isn't she the most gorgeous woman you've ever seen?'

'Yes,' said Lew, his eyes still on Laura.

'And how lucky for you to have gotten splashed! Now you're going to have dinner at the legation! Well, you *will* have something to write home about. Are you married, Lieutenant?' She waited a moment, then poked her finger in his sleeve. 'Lieutenant?'

He looked at the congressman's wife. 'I'm sorry, Mrs Townsend. . . .'

'Turner.'

'Uh . . . yes. I'm sorry. You were saying?'

'I asked if you are married?'

'Yes, I am.'

Mrs Turner looked across the crowded ballroom at Laura de Beaupré, then back to Lew. She smiled slightly.

'I hope you don't forget you're married, young man.'

He looked back at Laura. 'I hope so too, Ma'am,' he said softly.

And the Marine Band broke into a snappy polka.

Ben Bramwell took a fresh glass of wine from the footman then went to look for Lew. He finally spotted him leaning against the west wall of the East Room, his arms folded across his chest, an odd look on his face.

'There you are!' said Ben, coming up to him. 'Why aren't you dancing?'

'I already have.'

'I got some senator's wife from Michigan. She stepped on my foot, then I stepped on hers, and we finally called a truce. Did you see Father Abraham? He's over there talking with Mr Seward. What a strange bird *he* is! Looks like a parrot.'

'I'm having dinner with Mr Seward.'

'You are? When?'

'A week from Wednesday. Something tells me I've found the man to tell about Cameron and Matoon. Seward doesn't like Cameron. . . .'

'I know. They've been political enemies for years.'

'Right. And Seward's the closest man to the President. So I think Mr Seward's the man to tell.'

Ben drank some wine, thinking about this. Then he nodded.

'Yes, I think you're right. Seward would be perfect. But how'd you get invited to dinner with the Secretary of State? Through Matoon?'

'No. Through a mud puddle. And listen, Ben: don't tell anyone about this. I don't want it getting back to Matoon that I'm meeting Mr Seward.'

'I'll keep quiet – don't worry. This must be a relief to you.'

'It is.' He hesitated, watching Laura de Beaupré waltzing with her tall, lean husband. He wanted to tell Ben what he was thinking, but did he dare trust him? Well, if he trusted him about Matoon . . . 'Ben,' he said aloud.

'What?'

'I've just met somebody I'll never forget.'

Ben finished his wine. 'Who?'

Lew took his eyes off Laura, telling himself to watch out. Ben just *might* say something in a letter to his sister back in Philadelphia. And then it undoubtedly would get to Elizabeth. Elizabeth, whom he loved. Elizabeth, who was carrying his child. He crawled with guilt at the thoughts that were flooding his mind. But he couldn't help himself.

Still, he should be careful with Ben.

'Abraham Lincoln,' he said with a wink.

Ben looked confused. 'Are you drunk?' he asked.

'A little.'

But not with wine he thought. Not with wine.

He got back to Willard's Hotel at a little past one and climbed the four flights to his room. Inside it, he lit the oil lamp, then went over to open the two windows that overlooked Pennsylvania Avenue. His room was small and plainly furnished with a bed, a chair a table with a washbasin and a small armoire. After three months of hotel living he was sick of it. But there wasn't much alternative. Washington was bursting at the seams and housing was almost unavailable. Besides, despite the removal of the immediate threat of the Southerners invading the capital, Virginia was just across the river, and the rumour was that General Lee was massing a formidable army there. Washington was still no place to bring Elizabeth, although she had been barraging him with written pleas to allow her to join him. Elizabeth, four months with child, in this miserable, hot, dangerous city? It was out of the question.

He took off his uniform, threw it over the back of the chair, then sat on the bed. Besides, now there was another reason not to bring Elizabeth to Washington. Or was there? He told himself his fantasies about Laura de Beaupré were ridiculous. What possible interest could the wife of the French ambassador have in a mud-spattered lieutenant, even one who could speak French? True, she *had* invited him to dinner terribly quickly, and he was, after all, her age. . . . Why in God's name, he wondered, would a beauty like that marry a man in his sixties? The Baron de Beaupré looked trim enough, but still his hair was snow white. With all the men in Europe she undoubtedly had had a choice among, why pick a man old enough to be her grandfather?

He got up to put on his bathrobe and slippers. Then, placing his room key in his pocket, he let himself out into the dimly lit corridor, locked the door, and went down the hall to the community bathroom. Here, four tubs and six toilets provided facilities for the men on the fourth floor. (General Matoon, in his suite on the second floor, had a private bath. But then, the government paid for the general. Lew had to pay for his room out of his own pocket.)

He went into the bathroom, which was empty, filled a tub, and climbed in. Laura de Beaupré. Laura. Even the name was lovely! Lew was lonely, and he longed for a woman. Washington was a wild city, grown wilder with the influx of the troops – there were still only a hundred policemen for the entire city – and brothels were springing up like toadstools to service the soldiers. Lew had become an intermittent customer of some of the less grubby establishments, but the best in Washington was sad in comparison to Mrs Simpson's, and the women were, for the most part, dirty and not very appealing. They had been an escape valve, but nothing else. He longed for beauty. He longed for Laura de Beaupré.

Which, he told himself as he climbed out of the tub to dry off, was crazy. The French ambassador might be in his sixties, but he didn't look like a man who would ignore another man paying undue attention to his wife. But still . . . Laura, Laura, Laura. It was insane that one casual meeting could have such a profound effect on him. Insane! He loved Elizabeth. . . .

Then why was he thinking of Laura?

He put on his robe, started out into the hall, and then saw something that stopped him. On the opposite side of the corridor and three doors down, a woman was standing at the door of 4-G. She was tall, in a green dress with a matching green hat, and she had red hair. Even though the hall was dim, he recognized her profile. He stepped back into the bathroom and watched through the almost closed door.

She was talking to Commander Albert Parker, who was

on the staff of Admiral Packenham. Commander Parker had moved into Willard's the month before, and Lew had met him in the hall once or twice. Right now, the commander was wearing nothing but his drawers. The redhead in the green hat whispered something to him, kissed him, then started down the hall to the stairs. Commander Parker went back in his room and closed the door.

What the hell is she doing with *him?* thought Lew. True, she would have left Matoon's suite by midnight – the general rarely kept awake later than that. . . . Then had she come upstairs for another round with Commander Parker? Was Rosemary Fletcher working the entire hotel?

He waited until she had gone downstairs, then returned to his room. There was something distinctly wrong about what he had seen. Apparently, there was more to Rosemary than met the eye – and what met the eye was interesting enough. Rosemary had a rather horsy face and was on the wrong side of thirty, but she was an attractive woman.

By the time he climbed into bed, Lew's mind was filled with women - which was normal. But tonight, there were two new faces in the line-up: Laura de Beaupré's and Rosemary Fletcher's.

Elizabeth Crandall finished writing the letter, then looked out her window at the Atlantic Ocean. It was a grey, windy day in Sea Girt, New Jersey, but the wind hadn't stopped her mother-in-law from taking her customary walk on the beach with Father Dunne. There they were now, almost alone on the long expanse of sand, walking slowly, talking endlessly about the Mystery of God, of Life and Death, of Catholicism . . . as, past them, the surf pounded and roared. Nicole Louise dressed in white, her white veils flying in the wind about her head. Father Dunne, slim and elegant, soft-spoken and sincere, his black cassock flapping about his thin ankles.

It had been a relief to move to the shore from hot Philadelphia, and Elizabeth loved the cottage her mother-in-law had rented. Elizabeth didn't exactly love Nicole Louise: she was too distant, too proudly aloof to love. Still, she had come to care for her. Since becoming pregnant, Elizabeth had noticed a change in her mother-in-law: she had warmed up. Undoubtedly it was because Elizabeth was now carrying a Crandall (or, perhaps more precisely, a de Rochefort). But whatever the reason, Nicole Louise had become thoughtful and even, in her cool way, loving. She had insisted they go to the shore and had made – and paid for – all the arrangements. So Elizabeth had much to thank the beautiful Frenchwoman for.

What she hadn't counted on was Father Dunne. He arrived every Thursday and stayed till Saturday. Of course it was pleasant for the young priest to get away from the Philadelphia heat also, but every week? Elizabeth sniffed a secular motivation in Father Dunne, despite all his talk of God and the Church. If he could lead Philadelphia's richest widow back to Catholicism, it would be no small victory to report to his superiors in the hierarchy. Elizabeth didn't wish to be cynical, but she had the idea Father Dunne's eye was on a cardinal's hat. Wouldn't Nicole Louise de Rochefort Crandall be a big step up to that lofty office?

She moved her eyes away from the beach, picked up the letter, and reread it:

July 8, 1861

My beloved Lew:

How this war drags on, and how I miss you! I know I say that in every letter and you must get tired of it, but oh, my darling, how true it is. You are my whole life.

Well, to the news: the Little Stranger inside me must be a baby giant, because I am putting on weight more rapidly than the doctor expected and am beginning to look like a balloon. And I am *not* eating chocolates! But everything is apparently fine. When he arrives, I will love him – or her – almost as much as I love you. But not *quite*.

Father Dunne is here, as usual. Oh dear, I try to like him. He's really very likeable. He's a most amusing conversationalist, full of funny anecdotes when he's not being sincere. But as I told you, I don't like the way he *works* on your mother. In his defense, I have to admit Nicole Louise seems to thrive on it. I wouldn't be at all surprised if she goes back to the Church before the end of the summer. My only worry is that if she does, she might want the Little Stranger to be raised in the Church, which I would *strongly* object to. So far, though, nothing has been said on that subject – thank heavens!

Dear Professor Schlessing left two days ago, after a week with us – which was so kind of your mother, since the sweet old man can't afford to go to a resort, and of course she really doesn't like him . . . why, I'm not sure, except that he's German, and your mother may have some atavistic French dislike of the Germans (after all, Blucher did turn the tide at Waterloo). Anyway, he had a marvelous time and made me the most astounding offer. It seems his cousin is *concertmeister* in the court orchestra of the Grand Duke of Weimar, in Germany. The Grand Duke, who has just come to the throne, apparently prefers theater to music. As you may know, his late mother, the Grand Duchess Marie Pavlovna, the sister of the former tsar of Russia, was a devotée of music and brought Maestro Liszt to her court, where he has been for many years. Well, now apparently the new Grand Duke has cut back the music budget and M. Liszt feels insulted and has moved to Rome, where I understand he is trying to arrange with the Vatican a papal dispensation, or whatever they call it, so he can marry that Polish princess he has been living with (European morals really are *so* different from ours!). At any rate, Professor Schlessing's cousin says that M. Liszt told him he would very much like to have a pupil from America, as he is interested in our country, and Professor Schlessing asked me if I would be interested in studying with the maestro. Well, needless to say, anyone dreaming of a concert career would leap at the chance to study with the greatest pianist in the world – the cachet of being a Liszt pupil would be, in itself, open the doors of every concert hall in America – but of course I told Professor Schlessing it was out of the question. Now I have you, my darling, and the Little Stranger, and the maestro will just have to find someone else. But it was interesting, don't you think?

I'm glad you're moving out of Willard's, as you've mentioned so often how much you dislike it. But this rooming house on Third Street doesn't sound like much of an improvement. You say the owner, Miss Fletcher, is a 'friend' of General Matoon's? That seems odd. Why would a general with a wife in Harrisburg have an attractive (at least, you called her that) young woman as a 'friend'? I would think the general would be more careful about his reputation, but then perhaps I'm naïve. Thank God I don't have to worry about *you*, my darling – do I? I won't bore you with yet another plea for you know what, but if you have been able to find a room to rent, might not you be able to find a small house for us? Oh, I know you don't think Washington is a fit place for me, particularly in my condition, but how I miss you! How I *long* to see you! How I *wasted* you when I had you! You were right, my darling: I miss *that* too. Never, never will I say again 'I'm too tired.' What a foolish woman I was!

A million kisses from your lonesome wife, who misses you *desperately*.

Elizabeth

She folded the letter and put it in an envelope, which she addressed and sealed. Then she picked up the photograph Lew had had taken in the Washington studio of Matthew Brady. Elizabeth had begged for it, and it had finally arrived a month ago. How handsome he looked in his uniform, standing next to the table! So erect, so strong, so brave! There were tears in her eyes as she kissed the cold glass. Then she put it back on the desk and looked out the window again.

Nicole Louise and Father Dunne were still walking slowly down the windswept beach, talking about God.

15

Corporal Burt Thomson, General Matoon's orderly, disliked Lieutenant Crandall, General Matoon's aide, and his dislike was based on envy. Lieutenant Crandall was handsome; Corporal Thomson's lunar landscape of a face had been chewed up by a virulent acne. Lieutenant Crandall was a college graduate; Corporal Thomson was a graduate of the Manhattan slums. Lieutenant Crandall's father had been a judge; Corporal Thomson's father clerked in a grocery store on Delancey Street. Lieutenant Crandall was a lieutenant; Corporal Thomson was a corporal. To Thomson, Lew Crandall represented everything that was unfair about life in America. Now he looked around the big room on the second floor of the War Department building – the room crammed with dozens of desks for clerks, aides, and secretaries – searching for the man he disliked. He spotted him talking to Sergeant Teasdale, the Army's code expert. Burt Thomson started across the steaming room, weaving around desks manned by sweating clerks.

Lew's official duties were anything but onerous – he spent half his on-duty time fighting boredom – and he had initially struck up a friendship with Sergeant Teasdale to pass the time. But he quickly became interested in Teasdale's work. And Teasdale had become interested in Lew when the latter told him an idea for a code sent him by his wife. Elizabeth had suggested using music as the key to a code. As an example, she had used the second Chopin Étude. To each of the first twenty-six notes of the right hand – a chromatic scale – she had assigned a letter. Thus the first note, A was the letter A. The second note, A♯, was B – et cetera. The encoder would spell out his message using notes. The decoder receiving the notes would go to the key – the étude – and, working in reverse, unscramble the message. Unless the receiver knew the key, Elizabeth reasoned, the code was unbreakable. Sergeant Teasdale had thought this an oversimplification, but the idea of using music as a key had intrigued him, and he had bought a number of scores to toy with the scheme. Right now, he and Lew were checking over a Beethoven sonata when Burt Thomson came up to the desk.

'The general wants to see you,' he said.

'Right.' Lew got up from his chair. 'Be back in a while,' he said to Teasdale.

But Thomson looked at the music spread out on the desk. 'What the hell are you two doing?' he asked.

'Codes!' said Lew melodramatically, enjoying the confusion on Thomson's face. Then he crossed the room, picked up his jacket from the chair of his desk next to the door of Matoon's office, put the jacket on, knocked on the door, and went in. The general was seated at his rolltop desk.

'Ah, Lew,' he said. 'Close the door and take a seat.'

Lew obeyed. The general's office was small and cluttered: unlike Simon Cameron, Ralph Matoon was not a tidy man. Papers were everywhere – rolled-up plans, letters from manufacturers. . . . How Matoon kept everything straight was beyond Lew. In fact, he had a suspicion that the general *didn't* keep everything straight. But Matoon had squelched any attempt to create order out of chaos. He wanted no one touching anything in his office.

Lew pulled up a chair and sat down.

'What's going on at Rosemary's?' said Matoon, lowering his voice as he wiped his fat neck with a handkerchief.

'So far, General, not much. I've only been there two days.'

'Huh. No boy friends?'

Lew shrugged. 'Not that I've seen.'

'Damn her – I *know* she's two-timin' me!' The general looked so anguished that Lew almost felt sorry for him. But not quite. 'Well, the curse of fallin' for a jug-titted redhead at my age,' sighed Matoon. 'I appreciate your movin' to her boarding house, Lew. I hated to ask you, but I have to find out the truth . . . need a pair of eyes in there I can trust, son, and I know I can trust you.'

'It's no hardship, General. I was tired of the hotel anyway, and Rosemary's is cheaper. But so far, there's nothing to report.'

'By God, what if I'm wrong? What if the bitch is bein' true to me? Too much to hope for, eh? Listen, son: take the rest of the day off. Go over to Third Street and hang around . . . see what she does during the day. Oh – and here' – he opened a drawer and pulled out a canvas bag – 'drop this off at the bank on the way. It's two thousand in gold. What have we got in that account now?'

Lew looked at the bag. 'That brings it to a little over seven thousand, General.'

'Good. I'm goin' out and buy a geegaw for Rosemary, so I'll be usin' some of the loot up. Do you think she'd like a gold bracelet?'

'I'm sure she would, sir.' He took the bag and stood up. The general leaned back and once again mopped his neck.

'If I was as skinny and young as you, son, I wouldn't have to buy her love. But dammit, with my belly . . .' He stopped mopping and eyed his aide a moment. 'By the way: I know I can trust *you* with Rosemary. You bein' a gent and a married man . . . I know *you* wouldn't do nothin' dishonourable.'

'Oh no, sir.'

'Well, keep your eyes peeled. I'm on the rack, boy! The rack of doubt! Goddam love – it's a pain in the ass, ain't it? All right – see you tomorrow.'

'Yes sir.'

Lew carried the bag of gold out of the office and closed the door behind him. He had a slight smile on his face. When Matoon had suggested he take a room at Rosemary's, Lew had jumped at the chance to observe the mysterious redhead at close quarters – but not for the reason the general wanted her observed. Lew had his own reasons and his own suspicions about Rosemary. Which was why he hadn't told the general about her visit to Commander Parker's room.

As he left the War Department to head for the Dilbeck Bank, he was also smiling over the lush opportunities the free afternoon provided. It would be a distinct pleasure to double-cross Matoon, who, he was convinced, was so outrageously double-crossing him. Besides, the closer he got to Rosemary, the more he'd find out.

He already had a good idea what it would be.

The heat lay on the city like melting cheese as Lew rode Fate, his stallion, from the Dilbeck Bank to Third Street. The dusty streets were filled with carriages and carts, horses and pedestrians, soldiers and slaves – the heart of the city still pumped, but the heat made its circulation sluggish. Lew knew, from his vantage point in the War Department, that despite all the frantic activity of the government, the North was still woefully unprepared to meet a real military challenge. It was as if the still-new President were unable to master the clumsy bureaucracy he had inherited from the sleepy Buchanan. Or perhaps it was the lack of brilliance on the part of the generals. Or perhaps, simply, it was the heat. Whatever it was, Washington sprawled under the sun like a drugged dog. There was a sense of unreality about it all, as well as a sense of frustration, that gave the sweltering city the feel of a fantasy, the slow motion of a dream. At times Lew repressed the urge to yell to wake everyone up. But tonight, he told himself, at the French Legation, he wouldn't have to yell. He would speak to Mr Seward, and what he would tell him might have the effect of a yell – or even, he hoped, a bombshell.

He galloped down the back alley behind Rosemary's house, then reined in Fate and dismounted behind the stable she owned. It wasn't much of a stable – for that matter, it wasn't much of a house – but there were four stalls, one of which Rosemary kept for her own grey horse. Lew was paying a dollar a week extra for his stall. Now he lead Fate into it, took off his saddle, checked his water bucket and supply of oats, patted his haunch, then walked into the back yard of 114 Third Street.

It was a pleasant yard, surrounded by a picket fence and shaded by an ancient oak. Rosemary was a good gardener, and Lew imagined that in the spring her flowerbeds must have provided a brilliant show of colour. Right now, a few petunias were still fighting the good fight, but the July sun had taken its toll and the roses had given up for the year. The house was a two-storey, white clapboard building in need of a new coat of paint. Rosemary had rented out every room she could. Her tenants were all military personnel (including Chandler Delanoy, the son of the New York rector Lew had met on the way to Washington; to Lew's amusement he had bumped into Chandler one night at one of the new brothels), so he knew the house would be empty.

He went into the kitchen. Rosemary was standing at the

pump sink, an apron around her slim waist, a bandana tied around her red hair, peeling potatoes. She looked at him with surprise.

'What are you doing home?' she said.

'The general gave me the day off.'

'What for?'

'Good behaviour.'

He took off his jacket and put it on a chair. Then he came to the sink and leaned against the wooden counter. She watched him as she continued peeling the potatoes.

'What are you making?' he asked.

'Potato salad. I thought we could eat in the yard tonight. It'll be cooler.'

'Count me out. I have a dinner engagement.'

'Oh? Where?'

'Somewhere.'

She dumped a potato in the pot of water and picked up a new one.

'Aren't you the mysterious one?' she said.

'Not half as mysterious as you.'

'I'm about as mysterious as potato salad.'

'I wouldn't say that. There are a lot of things I'd like to know about you.'

'For instance?'

'Well, have you ever been married?'

'No. This house belonged to my parents, who are dead. I inherited a little income, and I rent out rooms. It's all very dull.'

'It's not *that* dull. There's General Matoon.'

She didn't stop peeling. 'That's right. There's General Matoon.'

'I was wondering how you got to know him?'

'I met him at Willard's.'

'You spend a lot of time there, don't you?'

'Enough.' She tossed the potato in the pot and turned on him. 'Look: what is this? The Inquisition?'

Lew smiled. 'Just trying to get to know you better, that's all.'

'I don't like people prying into my private business.'

'Maybe that's why I'm here. Maybe the general wants me to pry.'

She put down the paring knife and wiped her hands on her apron. 'Why? Doesn't he trust me?'

'Should he?'

She smiled. 'Ralph's too nervous. Do you want any lunch?'

'No thanks. It's too hot.'

'It's not too hot for me,' she said, going to the gaily painted blue bread box. 'It's *never* too hot for Rosemary Fletcher.' She pulled out a loaf of bread and cut two slices. 'So Ralph sent you here to keep an eye on me?' she continued. 'I thought there was something funny about your suddenly moving out of the hotel. But you're not a very good detective, are you?'

'Why?'

'I mean, if you tell me why you're here . . .'

'Oh well, there's no reason why my reports to the general can't be . . . shall we say, "doctored" in your favour?'

She shot him a look. Then she took a ripe tomato from a basket on the counter and began slicing it.

'I'm not *quite* following you, Lieutenant, though I think I'm beginning to get your drift.'

'For instance,' said Lew, casually digging some dirt out from under his thumbnail, 'we're all alone in the house now. And I've been very curious to see your bedroom.'

He looked up and smiled. She placed the tomato slices between the two pieces of bread, then raised the sandwich to her mouth and took a bite. She watched him as she chewed. Then: 'Pretty sure of yourself, aren't you?'

'Let's just say I think an arrangement between you and me would work out just dandy for all parties concerned.'

'And what if I tell Ralph? That wouldn't be so "dandy" for you.'

'Then I'll tell him I saw you at Commander Parker's door last week at one in the morning. Room Four-G? You had on a green dress and the commander had on his drawers. It was a touching scene – romantic as all hell.'

She finished the sandwich, then laughed. 'You're a cool one,' she said, wiping her hands.

'I always get what I want, one way or another.'

'Uh huh.' She hesitated. 'Well: so you want to see my bedroom. Shall we take a tour?'

She walked out of the kitchen. Lew picked up his jacket and followed. So far, he thought, so good.

Her bedroom was across the hall from the kitchen. It was a neat room, with two windows looking out on the back yard. As she went to close the curtains over the windows, Lew looked around. There was a large brass bed with a cheerful white coverlet and big pillows. Above the bed was a framed photograph of Abraham Lincoln with two small American flags tacked above the sombre President. This tickled Lew's fancy. As he pulled off his boots, he said, 'Father Abraham must see some interesting things in here.'

'He sees enough.'

She closed the left-hand curtains, and the room was plunged into a cool penumbra. Then she began taking off her clothes, as did he. They watched each other strip in silence, drinking in each other's nudity. She had a striking body, with breasts that, if they were not 'jugs', in the general's description, were certainly large and beautifully shaped. Her skin was milky white and lightly freckled, her legs long and well shaped, covered with red-gold fuzz, her hips surprisingly wide for such a small waist. There was a lack of self-conscious modesty about her that Lew found extremely erotic. When he came across the room to her, he had a full erection, which she didn't fail to notice.

'You're an improvement over Ralph,' she commented.

'Wouldn't take much.'

He put his arms around her and pulled her into his nakedness. He started kissing her, and she responded warmly. Then he stiffened with surprise as he felt her right hand squeeze his testicles. Not tightly enough to hurt, but enough to be uncomfortable.

'I'm not sure what you're up to, Lieutenant,' she whispered, 'but let's get one thing straight: if the game gets rough, *I* get rough. So don't push me too hard. Understand?'

'Uh . . . I understand. Would you mind letting go?'

She released him. Slowly.

'All right,' she purred. 'Shall we finish the tour?'

She walked over to the bed and lay on her back, watching him. He came over, looking at her relaxed body. She held out her arms, and he eased himself on top.

'Close your eyes, Mr President.' he mumbled. Then he inserted himself into her large vagina, which swallowed him up whole. He began pumping, slowly at first, then more rapidly. Rosemary, he was discovering, was full of surprises. After her warning, he had expected her performance to be mechanical at best. On the contrary, she began writhing and moaning. He felt her hands on the backs of his thighs, where she began massaging him lightly all in the right places, driving him crazy. He came with a great explosion of sweetness. Then, slowly, he pulled out as both of their hearts began to calm down. He leaned down to kiss her breasts.

'I'm beginning to understand,' he said, 'what Matoon sees in you.'

She ran her left hand over his back. 'Let's hope Ralph doesn't see *you* in me. Did you know you have beautiful skin?'

'I haven't given it much thought.'

He moved over to lay beside her, his crooked arm serving as a rest for his head as he watched her.

'Liar. Men always pretend they don't have any interest in their own bodies, but I don't believe it. After all, we only have one body to go through life with, so why shouldn't we be interested in it? I'm interested in my body. I'm fascinated by this little mole next to my navel. See?'

'Yes, it *is* fascinating. And down south a bit is downright intriguing.'

'Mm, I know what you mean.'

'Mind if I ask a question?'

'More Inquisition? What now?'

'Where did you meet Commander Parker?'

He felt her fingers grab his testicles again, this time a little harder. He winced.

'I think we'll have no more questions, Lieutenant,' she said.

He nodded hastily. 'Right, I see your point.'

She released him again, this time a little more slowly. 'You're a very inquisitive young man,' she said. 'Why?'

He turned on his back and stared up at the ceiling, his testicles aching slightly.

'Just a natural curiosity about human nature.'

'Curiosity killed the cat, Lieutenant. I'd hate to see a nice young cat like yourself get killed.'

He looked at her. She was watching him with a slight smile.

He decided that not the least surprising thing about Rosemary Fletcher was that she was dangerous.

On Monday evening, 15 July 1861, Secretary of State William Henry Seward left his house on Lafayette Square and walked across the park to the large house the French government rented from the widow of a wealthy Virginia apple-grower. He was, as usual, alone: Mrs Seward was an invalid who rarely came to Washington, staying in Seward's home town of Auburn, New York, instead. He was, as usual, untidy: his carrot-coloured hair was as messy as his ill-fitting clothes, and his only claim to elegance was his gold-headed walking stick. He was, as usual full of bounce and beans. The second most important man in America was a famous raconteur – even so good a storyteller as Lincoln admitted that Seward was better – and he was going over in his mind several jokes that might amuse the new French ambassador, Aristide de Beaupré. Mr Seward, being a fierce democrat, had little sympathy for the imperial regime of Napoleon III – he thought the nephew of the Great Napoleon was an adventurer with luck, and he regarded all the Bonapartes as a tribe of scoundrels – but it was important for the North to keep France and England out of the war, and he knew the Confederates were doing their best to bring one or both countries into the war on the Southern side. So Mr Seward wouldn't tell any jokes about the Bonapartes, though he knew several good ones. Besides, from what he had seen of M. de Beaupré so far, he liked the man, and, like everyone else in Washington, he was dazzled by his wife. Last, but hardly least, the French Legation had the best chef in town, and Mr Seward appreciated the pleasures of the table. So this tall, chinless, beak-nosed parrot of a man was looking forward to the evening.

He was admitted to the legation by the butler, who led him into an elegant salon where the de Beauprés greeted him. Then, accompanied by his host and hostess, the Secretary of State went around the room, shaking or kissing the hands of the assembled guests, most of whom he knew. There was Baron Stoeckl, the Russian minister, who was one of Seward's closest friends, and his American wife. There was William Howard Russell, the Washington correspondent of the London *Times*. There was also a young lieutenant with blond hair.

'This is Lieutenant Crandall,' said Aristide de Beaupré rather coolly. 'An acquaintance of my wife's. Lieutenant Crandall, the Secretary of State.'

Lew shook hands with the famous statesman and former senator from New York.

'It's an honour to meet you, sir,' he said.

'And it's an honour for me to meet one of our brave lieutenants,' rejoined Seward.

'The lieutenant is aide-de-camp to General Matoon,' de Beaupré went on.

'Ah yes, the fat general. Simon Cameron's friend.' Mr Seward's warmth faded somewhat. He passed by Lew to greet the wife of the Spanish minister. Lew didn't doubt that he had scored low with the Secretary of State because of his connection with Matoon and Cameron. But that couldn't be helped. He told himself that before the evening was over, Mr Seward was going to raise his marks.

The legation's dining room was oval in shape, with tall windows overlooking Lafayette Square. The table was covered with a lace cloth, and the crystal goblets and gold service gleamed in the soft glow of the six-branched Charles X candelabra. Gold-framed portraits of the French emperor and his beautiful wife faced each other on opposite walls, while along the side wall facing the windows was a large copy of David's panting of the coronation of Napoleon I. Laura led the guest of honour into the room, with the ten other guests in tow, Lew bringing up the rear. But, to his surprise, he found that the hostess had seated him to her left, opposite Mr Seward. Mr Seward seemed equally surprised. As the footmen held their chairs, he said to Lew, 'Well, young man, you must have a good deal of pull around here! What's the secret of your success?'

'His secret,' said Laura, 'is that he speaks French and has nice table manners. That's more than sufficient reason to ask him to dinner, but it so happens our carriage spattered him with mud.' She turned and smiled at Lew. 'I had to make up to him for our bad manners . . . in the interests of Franco-American friendship.'

'Mmm, yes of course,' said Mr Seward, sitting down. 'Plus the fact that he's young, and by God, that's the best thing that can be said about anyone. Was the immortal Virgil far from the mark when he said *O mihi praeteritos referat si Jupiter annos?* Of course not, and what I wouldn't give to be young again! Seneca says, "Old age is an incurable disease"; Shakespeare says, "When the age is in, the wit is out". Well, my friends, I am living proof that both those distinguished gentlemen were right on the mark.'

'Perhaps,' said Lew, 'but *nulli desperandum, quamdio spirat.*'

Mr Seward's grey-blue eyes blinked with surprise. Then they lighted with joy.

'Bravo! The cub knows his Latin! Exactly! Well, I'm breathing, aren't I? So you're all stuck with me a while longer. Excellent, Lieutenant. I like you already, and I've always found if I can't like a man within fifteen minutes, I'll never like him. I like you, I might add, *despite* the fact you work for General Matoon.'

Lew was feeling better. The footmen passed the first course, *Délices de nymphe en pithivier*, accompanied by a Château Paneil 1857. Then Mr Seward, who had never let up talking, launched into the topic of the day.

'Well, I'm sure you all heard about Mr Jenkins?'

'Yes, the spy,' said Aristide de Beaupré from the other

end of the table. 'I read about it in the paper. Did he get anything important?'

'Did he! I hope to tell you! He's one of our junior clerks at the State Department . . . a mousy little fellow. I've seen him around, wouldn't think him capable of stealing a joke, much less state secrets. And what did Mr Jenkins do? Why, he was caught red-handed this morning waltzing out of the building with a packet of secret documents tucked in his coat. And where do you suppose Brother Jenkins was headed?'

'Across the river?' said Laura.

'Exactly. He was going to get them over there somehow, but whether he was taking them himself or he has an accomplice we don't know yet. He's being questioned at this very moment, and I imagine Mr Jenkins is not a happy man. There's a powerful lot of spying going on in this town. Well, the fortunes of war, eh, Lieutenant? What does Martial say about fortune?'

'*Fortuna multis dat nimium, nulli satis.*'

'The cub's a wonder!' exclaimed the Secretary of State. 'Exactly. And Mr Jenkins didn't get enough fortune. There may be a noose in his future, I fear. Madame, your chef is *gloria mundi.*'

Laura laughed and said, 'Does anyone here speak English?'

'Wonderful!' said Seward. 'The foreigner's for plain speaking, and the American's showing off his fancy-pants Latin. Absurd, ain't it?'

'Yes,' said Lew, 'but as Saint Augustine said, *Credo quia absurdam.*'

Mr Seward nodded agreement.

'Which just about sums up life, wouldn't you say?'

'You've made a conquest,' said Laura, as she and Lew walked through the French doors into the small garden behind the legation.

'Mr Seward! I certainly tried hard enough. I read that he loves the classics, so I've been boning up on my Latin for the last week.'

'But aren't you clever!'

'I can't afford not to be. I'm in a lot of trouble, and I need Mr Seward's help.'

She sat down on a wrought-iron bench beneath an apple tree. Fitful heat lightning lit up the low-lying sky, while in the distance thunder rumbled over Virginia, heralding the approach of a storm. Gusts of wind turned the leaves of the tree upside down and fluttered Laura's white lace skirt. Lew couldn't take his eyes off her.

'What kind of trouble are you in?' she asked.

'It's nothing that would interest you, madame.'

'How do you know? I obviously am already interested in you, or I wouldn't have given you the second-best seat at the table. For that, you owe me something, Monsieur Lew. And I always collect my debts. So tell me your troubles, my friend.'

He squirmed. 'Well, it's sort of a political secret. . . .'

She laughed. 'So many secrets in Washington! And spies! How intriguing it all is. And I thought America would be so dull. I was wrong, wasn't I?' She smiled at him as her left hand toyed with the single strand of pearls around her neck. 'My husband does not like you, I'm afraid.'

'If I've done anything to offend . . .'

'Ah, you're so polite. You know very well why he doesn't like you. You're young and he's old. *Voilà tout*. Aristide is very jealous, I fear. I probably shouldn't have insisted on having you here tonight, but' – she gave an elegant little shrug – 'I did.'

'I'm glad you did. I . . .'

'You what?'

Don't make a fool of yourself! he thought. 'I'd be lying if I said I didn't find you enchanting.'

She didn't bat an eye. 'I wouldn't want you to lie, Monsieur Lew.'

'I don't suppose you'd allow me to call on you?'

'But that would be risking complications, wouldn't it?'

His heart was beating against his ribs.

'I'm willing to risk it.'

'But the question is, am I?'

The first drops of rain hit the leaves above her. She stood up.

'We must go inside,' she said. She started toward the house. He took her left wrist and stopped her.

'Laura,' he whispered, 'I'm in love with you.'

She studied his face.

'Perhaps,' she said. 'Perhaps you're just lonely. A lonely soldier in a war. Lonely soldiers always think they're falling in love.'

'It's more than that! I . . .'

She put her folded white lace fan against his mouth.

'Say no more,' she whispered. 'I'm honoured. But I'm married, and I respect my husband. I will flirt, but I won't dishonour him. Even with' – she removed the fan – 'a very charming young lieutenant named Lew. Now, come: if we stay out here longer, the others will start talking about us.'

'It seems there's nothing to talk about.'

She hesitated, then smiled. 'Perhaps.'

And she started toward the house. He followed her, even more bewitched than he had been before dinner.

Inside the legation, brandy was being passed. Aristide de Beaupré was talking to Baron Stoeckl and Mr Russell of *The Times* and didn't seem to make much of the fact that his wife and Lew had been in the garden alone, although he did eye them as they came back inside. Laura went to Mr Seward, who was talking to Señor Lopez de Varga, the Spanish minister. 'Excuse me, Mr Seward,' she said. 'But our Latin-speaking lieutenant wants a word with you.'

Seward turned to Lew. 'Of course, young man. What is it?'

'It's rather private . . .'

'Use the library,' said Laura, pointing to a door.

Mr Seward excused himself from Señor Lopez de Varga, then he and Lew went to the door, which Lew opened. Inside, Mr Seward set down his snifter and pulled a leather cigar case from his coat.

'Cigar, Lieutenant? They're Havanas, and the best.'

'Thank you, sir.'

'Cigars are my one vice, beside gabbing. But I always say, if you're going to sin, do it all the way.' He crinkled the cigar by his ear, then clipped its end and lighted it, offering a light to Lew afterwards. Then, wreathed in smoke, he sat down in a leather sofa. 'Now, sir: what can I do for you?'

'Do you trust Mr Cameron?' asked Lew quietly.

Mr Seward's eyes narrowed, whether from suspicion or cigar smoke Lew couldn't tell.

'That's a mightly blunt question for a young lieutenant to ask the Secretary of State, and frankly, sir, I'm not sure I want to answer it.'

'Pardon me, Mr Seward. I know it's not my place to ask it, but I think in a minute you'll agree it's important you answer.'

Seward thought this over a moment. Then he said, 'All right, I'll answer. No, I don't trust Simon Cameron. No one in his right mind would. What of it?'

'Last May, Mr Cameron sent out a letter to the governors of all the states that haven't seceded, authorizing them to raise troops of cavalry with a hundred men in each troop. The letter said the government would supply the firearms, but not the horses or the saddles: Mr Cameron said in the letter that the government was depending on the patriotism of individuals to provide the horses.'

'Young man, you're not telling me anything new. This was all discussed in the Cabinet. I've read the letter.'

'I realize that, sir. But did you know that last week, General Matoon was authorized to buy one thousand team horses from a dealer in Pennsylvania named Sloan? And that he was authorized to pay up to a hundred dollars a horse, when anyone can get a good Percheron for thirty-five dollars if he knows anything about horse trading? Not to mention the fact that draught horses are not exactly cavalry material.'

Seward waved his cigar impatiently. 'Yes, yes, I know all about it. Simon went to the President and told him we'd have to buy horses after all, that he'd gotten word back from the governors that there isn't enough "patriotism" around to get us the horses for free. So the President authorized the purchase of horses and equipment as well as firearms. The Confederates have an advantage over us as far as the cavalry's concerned. Southern boys like to ride. Northern boys like to make money. Consequently, the South has a good cavalry, and all we have is money. You can't ride a dollar into battle, Lieutenant. So we've decided to change dollars into horseflesh. I don't see anything wrong with that.'

'But a hundred dollars for a Percheron – !'

Again, the Secretary gestured impatiently. 'Young man, we can't haggle!' he exclaimed. 'We've got to get a cavalry! What are you trying to tell me, anyway? That Simon's making money off the deal? I'd advise you to choose your words carefully, sir: you're speaking about the Secretary of War.'

Lew cleared his throat. 'I realize that, sir. And I'm not making any accusation – exactly. All I know is that this morning General Matoon gave me two thousand dollars in gold to deposit in an account that's in *my* name in the Dilbeck Bank. The account now has over seven thousand dollars in it. It's supposed to be petty-cash account that I pay some of the general's personal bills out of. So far, in three months, I've paid out a little under twelve hundred dollars.'

Seward sucked on his cigar, his eyes staring at the lieutenant. Lew could almost hear his brain whirring.

'Why,' he finally said, 'is the account in *your* name?'

'Because I was ordered to open it in my name. The general didn't want to be bothered going to the bank himself with the passbook.'

And you have the passbook?'

In reply, Lew pulled the green passbook from his jacket and handed it to the Secretary of State. Seward opened it and looked at the entries.

'Mr Dilbeck is a good friend of General Matoon's,' Lew continued. 'So I've never been able to figure out why he couldn't have opened the account in his name and made an arrangement with the bank that I was to have access to it. Unless there's another reason to have it in my name.'

Seward handed back the passbook. 'I see what you're getting at,' he said. 'Have you told this to anyone else?'

'No sir. Well, that's not exactly true: I told an old friend of mine in the Fifth Pennsylvania.'

Seward got up and walked to the window, where he stood for a while looking out on Lafayette Square. Finally, he said, 'If what you're implying is right, Lieutenant, don't you think it would have occurred to Matoon that sooner or later you might get suspicious and blow the whistle on him? In which case, it's not a very clever scheme.'

'How can I do anything, sir? The money's in my name, all the transactions are cash – if I say anything, all the general has to do is say he's never heard of the account. I'm stuck.'

'Yes, I see. I hadn't thought of that.'

The Secretary of State continued staring out the window. After a while he said, 'Greed. Greed and concupiscence. Those are the two things you can always count on. Here we are in the middle of this century of magnificent achievements fighting a war over something that should have been abolished years ago. And why wasn't it? Greed. Those damned Southern planters are too cheap to pay their workers. And concupiscence. Oh yes, one doesn't like to discuss it in polite company, but there's a definite sexual titillation in owning a human being, and we all know what happens at many of those plantations after dark. But apparently the greed's not all on their side, is it? We may have a nice, stinking scandal right at the top of the Washington heap. And I hardly need add that "*corruptio optimi pessima*". Not that Simon Cameron's the best by a long shot, but if this gets out it could be the worst for this administration. What do you want me to do, Lieutenant?'

'I don't know, sir.'

'Well, it's a tricky situation, and I don't blame you for being nervous. And of course there's no proof of anything, is there? It's all supposition. I have to hand it to Simon or Matoon or whoever thought up having you open that account: it's a damned clever scheme. And what do we do to stop them? Yes, a good question. A good question. I think perhaps I'd better have a chat with the President. Meanwhile, you keep your mouth shut, young man. Maintain a *silentium altum*. Don't let Matoon think you're on to him. Go about your business. I'll get back to you . . . wait: how? Don't want Matoon to know. . . . Ah, our hostess! Perfect! The beautiful Madame de Beaupré – she can be our go-between. I'm liking it better and better! Romance, intrigue, glamour, corruption – well, we'll have a good time at this, won't we?'

'Maybe you will, sir.'

Mr Seward laughed. 'Cheer up, young man. You've done the right thing in coming to me. I'll talk to Mr Lincoln, and I'll tell Madame de Beaupré to ask you back to dinner here next week, at which point I'll tell you what we're doing. I imagine we won't have to twist her arm to issue the invitation? She seems to enjoy your company. Well, well. A thousand Percheron horses. My kingdom for a horse, but my country for a horse deal, eh? Shall we go back and join the others? And remember: not a word to *anyone*.'

Lew got up and followed the Secretary of State out of the room.

When he left the legation at half past midnight, the rain had been thundering down for over an hour and Lafayette Square was a lake. But even though he was soaked two feet from the door, his spirits were dry and soaring. Not only was Mr Seward in his corner – and after weeks of worrying about the situation with Matoon, this came as an incalculable relief – but also Laura had slipped him a note. He had managed to read it before leaving the legation. It was written on official notepaper, and read:

Dear Lew:

You are wildly irresponsible, and I should never see you again. But your words in the garden touched my heart. I am probably a fool to write this, but I want you to know your sentiments are not entirely one-sided.

You have certainly won Mr Seward's heart. He has asked me to invite you back here next Wednesday evening. Aristide is confused, but what can he do? It is the Secretary of State who commands!

Till next Wednesday at 8 –
Laura

He had put the note in his wallet, but its words burned through his soaked shirt into his heart. He was delirious. As he mounted Fate and galloped through the soaked streets of Washington, he couldn't believe that his incredible gamble had paid off, even to *this* extent. 'Your sentiments are not entirely one-sided' – a guarded phrase, true, but could it be interpreted in any way but that she loved him? Of course it couldn't. Laura loved him, and he loved Laura! Thoughts of Elizabeth, thoughts of Aristide pushed into his brain, but he rambunctiously pushed them back. Right now, he was high – higher than he had ever been in his life. Tomorrow, perhaps, the hangover. But tonight, the high!

He was a half block from the corner of Third Street when he saw the grey horse gallop out of the alley. Even in the storm, he recognized the horse as Rosemary's. The rider he didn't recognize at first: it was someone in pants and a jacket, with a wide-brimmed hat tied under the chin. He reined in Fate and watched as the horse galloped towards New York Avenue. A bolt of lightning illuminated the street. Fate whinnied with fright at the thunderclap and reared; Lew held on to prevent being thrown. But the lightning had shown him the rider. From the under back of the rider's hat hung a loose shank of red hair. The rider in men's clothes was Rosemary Fletcher.

He spurred Fate and started in pursuit. He had no idea where she was going, but she was riding so fast it was obviously to somewhere important. Emerging on New York Avenue, he spotted the grey horse several blocks to the west. He followed. At Tenth Street, she turned north, heading for Negro Hill. The streets were deserted, and he wondered at a woman, or a man for that matter, having the nerve to go into the dangerous slum alone at night. He wished he had his pistol.

She never slackened her pace, nor did Lew. He kept a

distance of several blocks and thanked God that the rain helped obscure him, since the mud muffled the sound of Fate's hooves. Rosemary seemed unaware of his presence. She splashed through the puddles, heading into the slum with its dark, squalid shacks. Here, the streets weren't so empty. An occasional slave was wandering aimlessly through the mud; here and there a family would be sitting in front of its house, oblivious to the rain, apparently doing nothing more than taking the night air. Although both horses were galloping, neither seemed to attract much attention.

When they were out of the slum at the edge of the city, it dawned on him why she had taken this route. She was leaving town, and the north slums were unpatrolled. Now she headed into the country, then turned west. The rain continued to pour, and he had trouble keeping it out of his eyes so he could keep her in sight. But although once or twice he thought she looked back, apparently she still wasn't aware she was being followed.

Forty-five minutes after leaving Third Street, she took a road to the southwest. She's headed for the river, he thought.

They were taking back roads which had the disadvantage of being almost impassable because of the rain, but the advantage of being deserted. For an hour he followed her, almost losing her several times, but then managing to spot her again in the distance. Finally, at what he decided must be near three o'clock, he stopped under a tree on a bluff and watched as she spurred her horse into the Potomac. Is she crazy? he thought. The rain had swollen the river, and he didn't think it possible a horse could make it across. He was wrong: Rosemary knew what she was doing. She had picked a ford that was passable despite the rain. Her horse slowly made its way over the slippery rocks, at one point going in up to its neck, but then emerging again, several times almost slipping, but eventually scrambling up the southern bank and heading south into an apple orchard.

He was tired, soaked to the skin, unsure of his ability to make it across the river, and not overly anxious to go into enemy territory alone. But his curiosity got the better of him. Spurring Fate, he made his way down the bank and started across the ford. The horse was nervous and several times balked; Lew dug his heels in and forced him ahead. By some miracle, he made it to the opposite bank. The horse climbed the muddy incline and entered the apple orchard.

Five grey uniforms on five horses suddenly surrounded him.

'Tickle clouds, Yankee,' said one. Lew could barely see their faces in the dark, but he could make out the rifles. He raised his arms.

'Shit,' he said softly.

'What'd you say, Yankee boy?'

'I said "shit",' snapped Lew.

The Rebs howled with laughter.

'You hear that?' cried the first man, who was evidently in command. 'He's mad 'cause we caught him! Well, what'd you think, you asshole? Didn't you think we'd keep a patrol at the one point on this river you can get across? Course, you goddam Yankees are too stupid to watch *us*, but we watch you. Tie his hands behind him, Henry, and I'll take him to the farm. Christ, it's so wet my balls are 'bout to rot and fall off. Jee-sus.'

In short order his hands were tied. Then the leader, who Lew could now see was a captain, took his reins, tied them to his saddle, and started off through the orchard, leaving the others at the river. As Lew bounced along behind him, he marvelled at his own stupidity. At the same time he decided it was a good time to ask some questions.

'Where's Rosemary–?' he yelled at his captor through the rain.

'She went on to the farm. She told us you were following her. You didn't think she didn't spot you, did you? Christ, as a spy, you'd make a good dogcatcher.'

'Is that what she is?'

'That's right, mister. She's the best dogcatcher we got. She caught you, didn't she?'

'I meant, is she a spy?'

'Well, what do you think? She's not over here selling lollipops.'

It was what he had suspected, and now he had proof;

except he wasn't in much of a position to do anything about it. He said nothing for the next fifteen minutes as they trotted through sodden cornfields. Finally, he spotted a light ahead. It was a small frame farmhouse, two storeys high, with a sagging porch in front, surrounded by giant shade trees. There was a large barn in back. The captain dismounted, tied his horse to a rail, untied Lew's reins from his saddle, then came back to his captive.

'Okay, Lieutenant, I'll help you down. You know you're the first Yankee I've caught in this war? Maybe I'll get a medal, what do you think?'

'Could be.'

The captain reached up to steady him as Lew swung his leg over to dismount. Then with all his strength, Lew kicked the captain in the face, catching him on the chin. The man grunted, threw up his arms, and fell back in the mud, where he lay still. Lew swung his leg back over the saddle, almost falling off in the process. Then he dug his heels into Fate's sides. The horse whinnied.

'Shut up, goddam it,' whispered Lew, kicking him again. Now the horse moved, starting off toward the barn. Lew leaned forward, trying to catch the trailing reins in his teeth at the same time that he desperately worked to keep from falling off. It was no good. He saw light spill through the rain as someone opened the front door of the farmhouse. Then shouts.

'Move, move, MOVE!' he urged Fate, but the horse didn't know where to move to, and kept headed for the barn. There was a shot. Fate fell over on his right side, dead, spilling Lew into the mud. He landed on his shoulder and rolled over on his stomach. He thought for a moment he had broken his neck, but he hadn't. His shoulder and neck aching, he got to his knees, mud smearing his face and stomach. Then he saw two men running toward him.

'Don't move if you want to stay alive!' Yelled one of them. They had rifles. Lew didn't move. They grabbed his arms, and pulled him to his feet.

'You son of a bitch, you tryin' to be a hero?' said one of the privates.

'It wasn't much of a try,' replied Lew, looking at Fate.

'Bet your ass it wasn't. Come on.' They shoved him toward the farm, and he put up no resistance. As they neared the front porch, he saw the captain he had kicked getting to his feet, his hand to his jaw. 'You're gonna pay for that,' he mumbled as Lew passed. 'You're gonna *pay*, Yankee boy.'

Lew said nothing. He climbed onto the porch and went in the house. In the small front room were a few wooden chairs and a table with a lamp on it. Seated behind the table were a Confederate major and Rosemary Fletcher. She had taken off the hat, revealing her red hair braided on top of her head, with the telltale shank hanging down the back of her neck. The two privates pushed Lew up to the table. He stood there, smeared with the mud and dripping from the rain, as Rosemary and the major looked at him. Then Rosemary laughed.

'Isn't he handsome?' she said to the major. 'This is the dashing lieutenant I told you about, the Princeton boy from Philadelphia who thinks he's such a ladykiller. He doesn't look much like a Don Juan now, does he?' She added to Lew, 'I told you curiosity would kill the cat.'

'Am I dead?' he said.

'Not quite.'

The major, who was, Lew judged, in his middle thirties, was a big man going to fat. He had brown hair and a rich brown beard. His eyes were as grey as his uniform. He looked intelligent and cold.

'Give the lieutenant a chair,' he said in a soft voice that had a slight Southern accent. A chair was pulled up and Lew sat down.

'My name is Major Albert Desborough,' said the officer. 'I'm attached to the Department of State in Richmond, in charge of military information. Why did you follow Miss Fletcher tonight?'

Lew looked at his quondam bed partner.

'I began to put two and two together,' he said. 'I knew she was sleeping with Matoon. When I found out she was also sleeping with a naval commander, I got the idea there was more to it than just her love of romping around half the beds at Willard's. How much has Matoon told you?'

She smiled. 'A lot more than he realizes.'

'So the picture of Honest Abe over your bed was window dressing? And I suppose the person Jenkins was trying to get the State Department documents to was you?'

'Exactly. And about Lincoln's picture? Well, my people are from Virginia, and I'm loyal to my people before any ridiculous Constitution that gives all the power to the North and tells us Southerners to like it or lump it.'

The two privates mumbled, 'Attagirl,' 'Tell him, Rosemary!' and she looked pleased.

'I don't think we're going to convert Lieutenant Crandall to our side,' said Desborough. 'What I'm interested in is whether he's told Matoon or anyone else of his suspicions about you.'

'I haven't,' said Lew.

'Perhaps, but we have to make sure. Miss Fletcher is a highly effective agent for us, and I don't want to risk having her caught.'

'The lieutenant's playing an interesting game,' said Rosemary. 'I'm not sure whether it's a double one, or maybe even a triple. You'd be surprised where he went to dinner tonight.'

'You followed me?' said Lew.

'Of course. I've been as curious about you as you've been about me. He went to the French Legation for dinner with – among others – the Secretary of State. Now, why would a humble lieutenant get invited to dinner with the Secretary of State when a full-fledged general like Ralph Matoon couldn't get invited even to clean out Mr Seward's chamber-pot?'

'You might be surprised,' remarked Lew.

'Lieutenant, we're in no mood for jokes,' growled the Major.

Be careful, thought, Lew. Be careful....

'So you were waiting for me in the alley?' he said to Rosemary, still avoiding her question.

'That's right. When I saw you coming, I took off. I

figured you'd follow me right into the mousetrap. And haven't we caught us a lovely mouse! Now, what were you doing at the French Legation? And why couldn't you tell me – or Ralph, for that matter – you were going there? What's going on, Lieutenant?'

'It was a social engagement.'

She laughed. 'You don't expect us to believe that?'

He shrugged. 'It's the truth.'

'Miss Fletcher tells me,' said the major, 'that you admitted to her this afternoon that General Matoon sent you to her house to spy on her. What did the general want you to find out?'

'He thinks she's two-timing him. Which she is.'

'Do you expect us to believe you thought Miss Fletcher was a spy, but you didn't tell this information to your immediate superior?'

'You can believe what you want, but I didn't tell him.'

'Why?'

Be careful. . . .

'Private reasons.'

'That is not an acceptable answer, Lieutenant.'

'That's the answer you're getting.'

Silence. Major Desborough tapped his fingers on the table. Then he turned to one of the privates. 'Where's Captain O'Rourke?'

'In the kitchen putting a hot towel on his jaw where this Yankee kicked him,' said one of the privates.

'Tell him to come in.'

The soldier went into the next room to return a moment later with the captain. Now Lew got a good look at him. He was of medium height, powerfully built, with a pock-marked face, curly black hair, and a black moustache. About thirty, he looked like a man you would think twice about before kicking. His jaw had turned blue and was slightly swollen. His forage cap, dark blue with yellow sides and crown, indicated he was a cavalry officer. The yellow numeral five on the front indicated his regiment, the Fifth Virginia. Attached to the back of his cap was a white duck flap called a havelock, named after the British General

Havelock, who had designed it in India to keep the sun off his troops' necks. Lew noticed he had a leather knife sheath attached to his sword belt.

O'Rourke gave the prisoner a look, then said, 'You wanted to see me, Major?'

'Yes, Captain. Miss Fletcher has to start back to Washington and I'm going to Richmond after I get a few hours' sleep. Do you have facilities here to keep this man prisoner for a while?'

'Yes sir. There's a root cellar behind the house. He can't get out of that.'

'Good. Search him first, then put him out there. Under no circumstances is he to get away: is that understood?'

'You don't have to worry about that, Major.'

'I'll be back a week from tonight. By then I'll have made arrangements to dispose of the lieutenant –'

' "Dispose" of me?' interrupted Lew. 'I'm a prisoner of war, aren't I?'

The major gave him a weary look.

'We're not going to kill you, if that's what's worrying you. But we're just getting our prison system set up, and I don't know where they'll want to put you. So for the time being, this is as good a place as any to keep you.' He stood up, unbuckling his sword belt and putting it on the table. 'Captain, you're authorized to interrogate the lieutenant tomorrow. Find out what he was doing at the French Legation, and whether he's told anyone he suspects Miss Fletcher is working for us.'

'You don't have to interrogate me! I already told you I haven't said a word to anyone, mainly because I didn't have any proof. That's why I followed her tonight: to get proof.'

'Which was very brave, Lieutenant, but not very prudent. Find out the truth, O'Rourke. Don't do anything that would permanently harm him.'

Lew sprang out of the chair.

'What the hell is this, the Inquisition? You're not going to let this ape torture me?'

He was grabbed from behind, shoved back down, and held in the chair.

' "Torture" is a strong word, Lieutenant,' said the major. 'Of course we wouldn't permit torture. But you must understand this is war. Captain O'Rourke was formerly chief custodian at an asylum outside Montgomery, Alabama, and he's had a good deal of experience handling rebellious inmates. So I would advise you to cooperate with him.'

'But I'm entitled to my rights!' roared Lew. 'I'm a prisoner of war, not a goddam loonie –'

Something smashed down on the back of his head, and his brain exploded with pain. The last thing he remembered was Rosemary looking at him curiously.

16

When he came to, it was morning. His hands were still tied behind him, and his arms were tingling with a million thorns: the circulation had stopped. His head ached from the blow, and he was filthy from the mud. He was lying on the earth floor of the root cellar, his boots in a puddle. The wood ceiling was still dripping from the rain. The cellar was about five feet square and five feet high. There was a sturdy wooden door with a small window in it. In the distance, a cow was mooing.

Painfully he got to his feet and went to the door to look out, stooping his head to avoid bumping it on the low ceiling. It was a beautiful, fresh morning after the rain. He could see the back of the farmhouse, perhaps fifty feet away. As he reconstructed the past evening, he thought of Ralph Matoon conniving to bilk the government of all he could while at night he made love to Rosemary Fletcher and babbled out military information she took down in her undoubtedly excellent memory. He marvelled at the duplicity of the situation while, at the same time, he told himself he had to keep silent about his own duplicity.

He pushed against the door, but of course it was locked. He sat down on the earth and looked around, trying his best to restore circulation in his arms. The cellar was empty. Wood beams held up the ceiling, and the walls were wood planks which held back the dirt. A week. It occurred to him he might be able to dig his way out.

It was then he realized his wallet had gone. And Matoon's passbook, and Laura de Beaupré's note, and his gold watch. While he had been unconscious, they had taken everything from his pockets. He fought down a surge of panic as he realized how damning the passbook and Laura's note might appear to anyone with imagination enough to connect the two. At the very least, they would arouse suspicion, and certainly Desborough would love nothing better than to find out Lincoln's Secretary of War was involved in a kickback scandal. Such information would be a propaganda victory for the South that could seriously hurt the shaky Lincoln administration. It was possible Mr Seward and the President could handle Matoon and Cameron quietly, but not if the Richmond papers got the word first. He told himself that no matter what, he had to remain silent. It was the 'what' that bothered him. Could he keep his mouth shut if O'Rourke actually applied torture?

An hour passed. At least the cellar was cool. His head began to feel better, but his empty stomach screamed for food. Then he heard voices. Struggling to his feet, he went back to the door to look out. The two privates were walking across the yard toward him.

'Morning,' said one of them as he unlocked the door. 'How'd you sleep, Yankee boy?'

'The bed was a bit lumpy.'

'Uh huh. Cap'n O'Rourke wants to see you. He's got a mean streak, so you'd better tell him what he wants.'

'I hear he used to beat lunatics for a living. Nice bunch of officers you've got. A real classy army.'

'Listen to him, now! Got us a smart lieutenant on our hands. Bet you won't be so smart an hour from now.'

'Bet he'll smart, though,' snickered the other. They opened the door, led him out, and took him to the farmhouse, where, in the front room, O'Rourke was seated at the table drinking coffee. He watched as the soldiers shoved Lew into the chair facing him. Then he said, 'You want some coffee?'

'Will you untie my hands so I can drink it?'

'No. Phil, bring him some coffee. You hold it for him.'

As Phil poured a mugful, Lew looked at his wallet, his watch, the green passbook, and Laura's letter spread out on the table. 'Do I get that stuff back?' he asked.

'In time,' said O'Rourke. 'There were some interesting things on you, Lieutenant. Major Desborough's really fascinated by you. For instance, this note.' He picked up Laura's note. 'Major Desborough says its written by the wife of the French ambassador.'

'That's right,' said Lew. He had rehearsed his cover story in his mind. 'She, Mr Seward, and myself are working on a project together.'

'Uh huh. What kind of project?'

'A benefit concert my wife is going to give in Washington. My wife's a pianist. The proceeds of the concert will go to pay for medical supplies for the Army.'

'I see.'

O'Rourke put down the note and waited while Phil held the mug of coffee to Lew's mouth. When Lew had had a drink, O'Rourke picked up the green passbook.

'This is interesting too,' he said casually. 'This is your savings account, right?'

'That's right.'

'You've been making a lot of deposits lately.'

'Is there a law against making deposits?'

'No, but there's an awful lot of money in this account for a lieutenant. Even a lieutenant who comes from money, which Rosemary tells us you do. Both Rosemary and Major

Desborough think there's something fishy about this bank account.'

Lew shrugged. 'My mother sends me money to pay my bills.'

'You must have lot a of bills.'

'Unfortunately, Captain, I am a fool with money. It melts in my hands. I'd like to reform but, alas, my character is weak. What else would you like to know?'

O'Rourke put down the passbook and opened a drawer in the table. He pulled a cigar from it.

'The truth,' he said, closing the drawer. He struck a match and held it to the end of the cigar.

'I've told you the truth,' said Lew.

'You've told me bullshit.' O'Rourke exhaled, blowing out a cloud of smoke. 'The Secretary of State has time to meet with you and the French ambassador's wife to talk about a benefit concert? Bullshit. A lieutenant keeps close to seven thousand dollars in a savings account to pay his bills? Bullshit. You'd have to be the biggest spender since Nero to need that kind of money. You're lying to me, Lieutenant, and I don't like lies. Ever get burned?' He leaned on the desk, holding up the still-burning match. Lew eyed it. 'We had a way of dealing with our loonies who stole things and wouldn't tell us where they'd hid them. We'd give them a little burn, down where it really hurt. You'd be surprised how sensitive certain parts of the body are, Lieutenant. Now, are you going to to start telling the truth?'

Lew started to sweat. 'I've told you the truth.'

'Bullshit. What are you seeing Seward about?'

'A benefit concert.'

'Bullshit. Where'd all this money in the account come from?'

'I told you. My mother sent it to pay my bills –'

'Phil,' interrupted O'Rourke, standing up and blowing out the match, 'take him in the next room and tie him to the bed. Face up.'

The two privates jerked him to his feet. Don't panic, he told himself. Don't panic. He waited until they had untied his hands. Then, the second he felt the cords off, he swung his right fist at the private named Phil. He caught him on the chin. Phil fell back against the wall, and Lew went for the door. There was a shot, and a bullet hit the door in front of him.

'The next one goes in your skull,' he heard O'Rourke say.

He stopped and turned around. O'Rourke was standing behind the table, holding a smoking revolver.

'Take him in the bedroom,' he repeated.

'You son of a bitch,' said Phil as he grabbed Lew's arm. 'That hurt.'

'The lieutenant's strong,' said O'Rourke. 'We'll see how strong he is with a hot cigar on his balls.'

The dragged him, kicking, into the next room, where there was a wooden bed. They forced him onto it and tied his wrists and ankles to the four posts. Then the two privates stood aside, and O'Rourke came to the side of the bed. He drew on the cigar until its end glowed. Then he leaned down and blew the smoke in Lew's face.

'You going to talk?' he said softly.

Lew spat in his face.

The captain straightened, wiping the spit off with his sleeve. Then he sat on the edge of the bed.

'Hold the cigar,' he said to Phil, giving it to him. O'Rourke began unbuttoning Lew's jacket.

'We'll start on your belly and work down,' he said matter-of-factly.

When the jacket was open, he stared at the lean stomach. Then he held out his right hand. Phil gave him the cigar. O'Rourke touched it to the hair just under the navel. The hair sizzled, and an acrid smell began to permeate the room.

'Have anything to say?' He watched Lew's face.

Silence.

He touched the cigar end to the skin. He held it on the skin for fifteen seconds, shoving it slowly as an even worse stink filled the room. Then he removed it. He looked at the seared, smoking flesh. Then he looked at Lew's face. It was covered with sweat, and he was trembling violently.

'Not as pleasant as having dinner with the French ambassador's wife, is it?' O'Rourke said.

'It's pleasant for you, isn't it?' whispered Lew. The pain had been excruciating. 'Having fun?'

'Fun enough. Going to tell us why you were seeing Seward?'

Tell him! screamed part of his mind. Tell him! Why save Matoon and Cameron! Let the Richmond papers know! Another part of his mind remembered Mr Seward's remark. *Corruptio optimi pessima:* the corruption of the best is the worst. A scandal at the top could jeopardize the whole war effort. But did he care? Was his beloved country worth this pain? Did he care? Tell the sadistic son of a bitch!

'We were playing backgammon.'

'The lieutenant's full of jokes, isn't he? Let's see how he likes this joke.'

He handed the cigar back to Phil, then unbuttoned Lew's fly and pulled down his pants and drawers.

'Nice big balls,' he said. 'Ever smell fried balls?'

The two privates said nothing. They were tense and, to their surprise, frightened. O'Rourke was going further than they had expected. They thought he had been bluffing.

'Give me the cigar, Phil.'

'Cap'n, do you think . . .'

'Give me the goddam cigar!' he roared.

Phil obeyed, his hand trembling. O'Rourke took the cigar and sucked it to hot life. He blew out the smoke.

'Last chance, Lieutenant. It's going to hurt.'

'Go to hell.'

O'Rourke jammed the cigar against the middle of his scrotum. Lew howled, jerking up like an electrified frog, tugging at the ropes. O'Rourke held the cigar. Lew continued to howl.

'Jesus, *stop* it!' yelled Phil, terrified at what he was witnessing.

O'Rourke removed the cigar and stood up, looking at his victim.

'He's passed out,' he said coolly. 'They always do. Take him back to the root cellar.'

He walked out of the room, contentedly puffing the cigar.

Elizabeth Crandall was walking on the beach, a large blue cloak covering her protruding stomach, when she saw Father Dunne hurrying out of the cottage. She stopped to watch. She had never seen Father Dunne hurry. Now he was running toward her. Lew! she thought. Oh my God, something's happened to him! Involuntarily, she pressed her right hand against her stomach, making contact with the child inside her.

'Elizabeth' – the young priest was panting as he came up to her – 'you'd better come up to the house.'

'Is it . . . my husband?'

'We've received a wire from Mrs Crandall's butler. There's word from the War Department. He's disappeared.'

The gentle surf washed over two children sitting in the sand and erased the castle they had started to build.

'Disappeared? What does that mean?'

'No one knows. He's just vanished from Washington.'

'But . . .' She felt a surge of nausea, and she leaned on Father Dunne's arm.

'You'd better come up to the house. Mrs Crandall's taking it rather badly.'

She nodded. Choking back her fear and nausea, she started toward the cottage. Behind her, the two children moved higher up the beach and started rebuilding their castle.

Lew was in agony for three days. He thanked God for the rain, because the cool mud soothed the pain somewhat, but for three days he huddled in the root cellar and suffered. He was terrified that the cigar had sterilized him, for his testicles swelled up to a frightening size. But on the second day they began to return to normal, and on the third the pain finally began to subside, although there was an ugly canker to continue to remind him of Captain O'Rourke. Not that he needed reminding. The sadistic captain was very much in his thoughts.

The afternoon of his torture – despite Major Desborough's demurrer, what else was it? – Phil had come out to the root cellar bearing a cold chicken. As Lew devoured the bird, the private said, 'We ain't gonna let him do that to you again. We told him no man should do that to another man, and we said if he did it again we'd tell the major. I thought he was bluffing!'

'Some bluff.'

'Well, he ain't gonna do it again. I hate Yankees, but I don't even hate *Yankees* that much.'

And Phil had left the root cellar.

Apparently, the privates had frightened O'Rourke, for Lew was left alone. On the third day he began testing the wooden planks to find a rotten spot he could dig away with his nails and perhaps claw his way through the six or seven feet of dirt covering the cellar to freedom. He found a place at the back where the wood was rotten. He picked at it. It gave way without too much difficulty. Once the wood was breached, he was able to splinter off enough of the planking to expose a hole he could squeeze through. He began tunnelling the dirt, carefully spreading his diggings over the floor so his guards would notice nothing suspicious. The digging wasn't as easy as he had hoped: he kept running into rocks that took hours to remove. But he made progress. By the end of the sixth day he had dug far enough to be convinced that in one, or maybe two, nights more he could break through to the surface. Then it should be easy to make his way back to the river under cover of darkness (from what he could see through the window in the door, the farm seemed to be casually guarded), and somehow get across the Potomac and back to Washington. He wondered what Mr Seward and Laura de Beaupré were thinking about his disappearance. He wondered if his wife and mother knew he was in Virginia.

On the sixth night, as he was digging, he heard someone coming toward the cellar. Quickly he backed out of the hole, shoved the planking over it, then spread out on the ground, feigning sleep. A lantern flashed through the window and the voice of Phil said, 'Hey, Yankee, wake up. Rosemary's here and wants to see you.'

He sat up, rubbing his eyes to enhance the illusion he had

been awakened, then accompanied Phil to the farmhouse, where, in the front room, he found Rosemary, again dressed in her male clothes, and Major Desborough seated as before at the table. They gave him a chair, but didn't tie his hands. He didn't sit down. Rather, he came to the table and opened his jacket to reveal the scab below his navel.

'See that, Major? Do you know what it is?'

'It's a cigar burn.'

'Exactly. There's another beauty on a part of my anatomy I won't show, though Rosemary's familiar with it. You may not call that torture, but I sure as hell do.'

'Captain O'Rourke told me what he did. I told him, and I'll tell you, that we deplore that sort of behaviour.'

'Wonderful. I'm deeply moved. But you don't condemn it?'

'Captain O'Rourke has been disciplined. He has been docked a month's pay.'

'Jesus, why bother? Why don't you just slap his wrists?'

'Lieutenant, this is *war!* I agree that O'Rourke went too far, but you're alive and apparently healthy, so sit down and shut up!'

He realized he was getting nowhere and sat down.

'Some interesting things have been happening in Washington,' said Rosemary. 'We've all missed you. Why, Ralph was so upset about your disappearance, he came to my house all in a dither. He said he'd loaned you something valuable, and he wanted to see if you'd left it. I let him search your room, but he didn't find anything. And when I asked him what he was looking for, he said it was a passbook.' She opened the table drawer and held up the green passbook. 'Interesting that he was looking for a passbook that's in *your* name, isn't it? And it's interesting how the deposits keep getting larger as the war progresses. So you see, this fascinating idea occurred to me: that Ralph was giving you *his* money to put in an account bearing *your* name. Now why would Ralph do that? And why would you be seeing the Secretary of State? The joke is, I've been milking Ralph Matoon for information for weeks, but *you* stumbled on the juiciest information of all. No wonder you've been so quiet, Lieutenant.'

'We think,' said Major Desborough, 'that what this means is that Matoon – and probably his boss, Cameron – have been making a lot of money from this war. Isn't that what it means, Lieutenant?'

Lew shrugged. 'I don't know what you're talking about.'

'Oh yes you do,' said Rosemary. 'You see, this puts us in a very interesting position. If the South can expose a major political scandal in Washington, what sort of support is Mr Lincoln going to be able to draw on? What little he has will melt away like ice in the sun.' She smiled. 'And the lieutenant knows it, doesn't he?'

Lew said nothing.

'Crandall,' said Major Desborough, 'we'd be willing to make a deal with you.'

'What kind of deal?'

'If we take you to Richmond and you tell my superiors what you know about General Matoon's finances, we'll take you to a comfortable prison, keep you there for six months, and then exchange you at the first opportunity. Rosemary feels she only has six months more in which she can be of use to us, at which time she's leaving Washington, so it won't matter if we return you then. Would you agree to that?'

'What if I don't?'

'If you don't help us, we'll send you to an extremely uncomfortable prison and make sure you're not exchanged till the end of the war. I'd advise you to consider our offer. When I say an uncomfortable prison . . . well, you've met Captain O'Rourke. There are others like him in the South, just as there are in the North.'

Lew leaned forward. 'Look, I'm no martyr. I don't like prisons, comfortable or otherwise, and I would like very much to get back to Washington. But don't you think I see what you want? You want a Northern officer the Richmond papers can quote to verify a story that will smear the administration. Do you think I'd let you use my name for that? They'd kill me in the North. I'd be a traitor the rest of my life.'

'They may kill you anyway,' said Rosemary. 'You see,

Albert, there's something you don't know about the lieutenant. There's a skeleton in his closet – or should I say a darkie in his woodpile? A very attractive young darkie named Christine, to be exact.'

'What are you talking about?'

'You know. Christine Canrobert. Or at least her white father's name was Canrobert.'

'How did you meet Christine?'

'She's run away from that nice Quaker school you put her in outside Philadelphia.'

'Run away? Why?'

Rosemary smiled. 'Because the nice Quaker schoolmaster raped her.'

Lew sat up. 'I don't believe you!'

'That's what happened. Mr Trowbridge, I think his name is. He raped her beside a pond in a cornfield, she tells me. Very respectable schools you Yankees have. Did he charge extra tuition for rape?'

Lew was stunned. He thought of seemingly pious, scrawny, Mr Trowbridge. Then he thought of Christine's lush beauty. He began to believe it.

'She was terrified, of course,' Rosemary continued. 'And didn't want to stay any longer – can't say I blame her. So she came to Washington looking for her "Daddy Lew", which is what she calls you – charming, isn't it? The poor child was destroyed when I told her you were probably a prisoner of war. Oh dear, it was a touching scene. She broke down and cried and told me how you were so nice to her and that she loves you so much. . . .'

'She *loves* me?'

'That's right. You may have been missing out on something, Lieutenant. Of course, I was very nice to her, and she seems to like me. After a little prompting from me, she told me the whole story. The whole *lurid* story, I might add. How she saved your life when Winkler attacked you? And then how you killed Winkler and rather thoughtlessly neglected telling the police? And how poor Mr Winkler is still out there buried in the apple orchard behind Mr Bramwell's farm? You Yankees have a real flair for the dramatic.'

Silence. The major said, 'What are you getting at, Rosemary?'

'It's simple enough. The Lieutenant is going to cooperate with us whether he wants to or not. Because if he doesn't, it's not just that he'll go to an uncomfortable prison till the end of the war. If he doesn't, I'll notify the Philadelphia police about Mr Winkler's body mouldering in that cold grave. And then, when the war is over, Lieutenant Crandall will come marching home to face a murder charge. That should be an interesting end to a brief but eventful life, wouldn't you think? Of course, if you cooperate with us, Lieutenant, I couldn't care less about Winkler's body. So perhaps you'd better seriously consider joining our side. It is, after all, the winning side.'

'Maybe.' He thought a moment, then said, 'What kind of assurance would I have you'd live up to your end of the bargain?'

'My word,' said Desborough, 'as a Southern officer and gentleman.'

'Excuse me, Major, but I've got two very sore balls that say your word isn't worth a pile of shit.'

The normally unruffled major grew red in the face. 'Why, you young son of a bitch –'

'Albert,' soothed Rosemary, putting her hand on his sleeve. Desborough looked at her and simmered down. 'What kind of assurance would you like, Lieutenant?'

'I'd like to think about it the rest of the night. Can I give you my answer in the morning?'

'That seems fair enough. Is that agreeable, Major?'

'I suppose so. But you'd better think hard, Crandall. About the advantages of helping us, and the disadvantages of not.'

Lew got up. 'Well then, till tomorrow. When are you going back to Washington, Rosemary?'

'In about ten minutes.'

'Is Christine staying with you?'

'No. I've made other arrangements for her.'

'Like what?'

'You'll find out when you agree to help us.'

Lew shrugged. 'Well, I don't see the point in all the secrecy, but if that's the way you want it.' He turned to Phil and the other private, whose name was Tom. 'Shall we return to the bridal suite, boys? This is a swell hotel, but the plumbing leaves something to be desired. So if you don't mind, I'll take a piss before you lock me up. Oh, excuse me' – he grinned at Rosemary – 'I forgot there's a lady present.'

Rosemary stiffened. 'Just because I'm a patriot for the other side,' she said, 'doesn't mean I'm not a lady!'

'Interesting. I've never heard "whore" pronounced "patriot" before.'

And he went out of the room with the two privates.

He wasted no time. The moment Phil and Tom left him, he hurried to the back of the cellar, removed the planking, crawled into the hole, which was stifling, and began clawing at the dirt. It took him a little over an hour – there was less to dig than he had calculated – then he felt a rush of sweet air and saw a star. Removing more dirt, he squeezed his head out and looked around. It was a hot July night and crickets were chirping. Then he heard another noise: a voice. The farmhouse was dark, but two men were standing by the kitchen door, smoking. He waited. After a while, one of the men went inside the house. The other continued smoking, and a puff of breeze brought the smell of cigar smoke over the root cellar. Lew recognized that cigar, of all cigars. The smoker was Captain O'Rourke.

O'Rourke walked toward the barn. Lew carefully wriggled through the hole, then crouched near the root cellar, watching. The captain opened the barn door and went inside. Lew ran across the weeded grass to the open door. He hid behind it and listened. He heard the squeak of a cork and then gulps. Lew grinned slightly: so the captain was a secret drinker. It didn't surprise him. Perhaps he wasn't so secret, but kept his private stock hidden from his men in the barn.

He saw a rusted horseshoe hanging on a nail against the barn door. Quietly, he removed it and held it in his right fist. He waited. He heard the cork squeak back in the bottle, then the rustling of straw. Footsteps. The smell of cigar smoke. O'Rourke came out of the barn, his jacket slung over his shoulder, and started to close the door. Lew was waiting, his hand raised. When he saw O'Rourke's forage cap, he smashed the horseshoe down with all his strength. The captain crumpled to the ground, his still burning cigar dropping next to him.

Lew stooped over his body and removed the bowie knife from its leather sheaf. It was long and sharp. He hesitated a moment, thinking of Winkler, thinking of life and death and war and murder and torture. The man was a sadist, but he was a human being: did he have the right to kill him? But he was in a war. Could he afford to be meticulous? He looked at the cigar, burning on the ground. The cigar.

Grabbing the handle of the knife with both hands, he plunged it into O'Rourke's undershirt. He winced with disgust as the blood spurted up: he had struck the heart. Closing his eyes, he wiggled the knife out. He felt slightly sick. He wiped the knife blade on the grass, then left it on the ground and picked up the body by the armpits. He dragged O'Rourke inside the barn. A horse in one of the stalls snorted, but then was silent. Working quickly, Lew removed O'Rourke's uniform. The grey coat with two gold stripes on the sleeves, the grey suspendered trousers, the shiny new boots of cheap leather. Then he took off his own uniform and rolled it into a ball. He put on O'Rourke's clothes, which were too big. The uniform smelled of sweat, but Lew was no rose. He threw straw over the near-naked body with the dark red hole in the chest.

He checked the stalls, which were mostly empty: there were three horses in the barn and two cows. He chose a black stallion, leading him out of his stall and saddling him. He stuffed his own uniform in a saddlebag and led the horse out of the barn. He picked up O'Rourke's forage cap, which had fallen off when he was hit, and put it on. He picked up the knife and put it in the sheath. O'Rourke's revolver he had also. Then he led the horse into the nearby cornfield. The corn had grown at least half a foot since the night he was captured: he reflected that the South would have a good crop yield, which wouldn't shorten the war. When he was far enough from the farm not to be heard, he mounted the horse and galloped toward the ford.

In the apple orchard next to the Potomac, he was stopped by the patrol. A sergeant came up and saluted.

'Orders from Major Desborough,' said Lew, in his crispest voice. 'I have a dispatch to deliver to one of our agents in Washington.'

Though it was too dark to see the sergeant's face, he knew the man was confused.

'Excuse me, Cap'n,' said the sergeant, who had an Eastern Shore accent, 'but you ain't going over there dressed like *that?* There's a lot of Federals over there. Like a whole goddam army!'

'Of course not. I have a Federal uniform in my saddlebag. As soon as I get across, I'll change.'

'Oh. Well, good luck, Cap'n. If you see Old Abe, take a potshot at him fur me.'

'This is no time for levity, Sergeant. May I pass?'

'Excuse *me*, sir. Sure, go ahead.'

Lew galloped into the river. He hadn't gotten ten feet before the horse slipped on a rock. Into the water he went. As he picked himself up he heard muffled laughs from the south bank. Shit, he thought. After the horse had gotten to its feet, he mounted again and, dripping, made it to the other bank.

When he was far enough from the soldiers, he stopped and changed into his own uniform. It was soaked and a mess, and with his six-day growth of beard, he looked more like a military tramp than the aide to a general. No matter. He tossed O'Rourke's uniform under a bush. Then he mounted the horse and galloped toward Washington. He knew what he had to do: find Ben Bramwell, tell him the truth about what had happened that night last December, then talk him into accompanying him back to Philadelphia to dig up Winkler's body and dispose of it. He had no choice: now that the secret was out, thanks to Christine, his future was in jeopardy. Once the threat of a murder charge was removed, he could go to Mr Seward, deal with Matoon, and arrest Rosemary Fletcher.

He reached Washington at dawn to find the city in turmoil and his plan of action shot to pieces by history.

17

The streets were filled with marching troops, rumbling artillery, carriages, and pedestrians as a great tide of humanity swept through town toward the Long Bridge over the Potomac which led to Arlington, Virginia. Lew, confused by the heavy traffic, stopped his horse and yelled at a Negro woman with a bandanna on her head, 'What's happening?'

She looked at him with surprise.

'What's *happening?* Where you been, mistah? Everyone's gwine out to see dee big fight, dass what's happenin'!'

'What fight?'

'Dee battle! Down by Manassas Junction in Virginee! Dey's gwine be a fight at lass! Gwine whup dem Rebs an' send 'em runnin' to dee South Pole!'

And off she went. Lew plunged back into the traffic, dodging carriages and horses as he made his way to the tentground of the Fifth Pennsylvania. The traffic was sending up clouds of red dust, and the rising sun had already pushed the temperature past eighty. His Brooks Brothers uniform, now a crumpled mess, began to feel like a sticky blanket.

He reached the tentground beside the Potomac to find it empty.

'Where's the Fifth Pennsylvania?' he asked a boy who was searching the field for souvenirs.

'Them? They left a week ago.'

'Where?'

'They went down to Virginia. Everybody's down in Virginia. We're gonna take Richmond – ain't you heard? About time, too.'

Lew sat on his horse, the sweat streaming down his dirty, unshaven face, trying to decide his next move. He could go up to Pennsylvania alone, but with a battle about to erupt, not only were his priorities shifting but he decided he had better make contact with Matoon first to fend off a possible charge of desertion.

He spurred his horse and plunged back into the traffic, heading for Willard's Hotel. He wondered how much he should tell Matoon, and decided that one thing he had to tell him was that his mistress was a spy, if only to stop the flow of information. When he arrived at the hotel, he found the front of it was crowded with people haggling with cab owners, trying to buy transportation to witness the battle. He dismounted and began pushing through the throng to the door. He heard one woman gushing with excitement to a friend about the 'victory ball' that would be held that night at Fairfax Court House. Lew had never heard of Manassas Junction and had only a vague idea where Fairfax Court House was, but he couldn't help but wonder at the confidence of the crowd. Wicker picnic hampers were everywhere, tradesmen were selling wine and food, and it looked more like a great Fourth of July outing than war. He spotted William Howard Russell, the bearded London *Times* correspondent who had been at the dinner at the French Legation, offering a hackman two hundred dollars to take him to the battlesite for the day. The hackman said, 'Hop in!' as Lew pushed his way over.

'Mr Russell . . .'

The correspondent turned. 'Crandall! I heard you were captured.'

'Yes, sir I was. . . .'

'Sorry, young man. Haven't got time to talk. Got to get to Manassas.' He was climbing in the hack.

'What's at Manassas?'

'A railroad and the Confederate Army. I'd advise you to get down there fast if you want to see the end of the war. Drive on!' he yelled at the hackman, thumping his walking stick against the roof. The cab pulled out into the heavy traffic of Pennsylvania Avenue, where the Garibaldi Guards were marching past the hotel singing 'We'll Hang Jeff Davis on a Sour Apple Tree' to the tune of 'John Brown's Body'.

Lew finally made it into the crowded lobby of the hotel, where he pushed his way to the reception desk. There he found the same clerk who had greeted him when he first came to Washington three months before. The clerk was looking haggard, as if he had been up too early and too long.

'Where's General Matoon?' said Lew.

'In his suite, getting ready to go to the battle. . . . What happened to you?'

The clerk was staring at his beard and rumpled uniform. Lew didn't wait to explain, but ran to the stairs and climbed them two at a time till he reached the second floor. He ran down the wide corridor, reached the double doors of the suite, and opened them without knocking. Inside, the general was standing in the middle of the drawing room while Burt Thomson, attached his sword to his side. When Matoon saw Lew, he said, 'Where the hell have you been?'

Lew closed the doors behind him. 'In Virginia. It's too long a story to tell now but, General, you're in trouble. Rosemary Fletcher's a spy.'

The general's face went white.

'A *spy?*'

'Whatever you've told her has gone straight across the river to Major Desborough of the State Department in Richmond. So, General, don't tell her anything else.'

Through the windows came the singing voices of the soldiers below.

'She was also sleeping with Commander Parker two flights up,' continued Lew, 'and maybe some others I don't know about.'

Matoon finally managed to say something. 'Jesus Christ, this puts me in a helluva position . . . are you *sure?*'

'I'm sure.'

'Rosie a *spy*,' he repeated to himself as if trying to digest this. 'Oh my God, what the hell did I tell her?'

'Apparently a lot, sir. She's dangerous, and I'd suggest you have her arrested immediately. She was in Virginia last night, but she should be back at her house by now.'

'Damned right I'll have her arrested! My God, Lew, I'm indebted to you. Listen, son. I'll want to hear the whole story from you, but I think right now you'd better get down to Centerville. I know you're bushed, but we need every man we can get today. Go to General McDowell's headquarters I'll be there later myself. The last word we got is that McDowell's sending his army over some creek called Bull Run, trying to get around the Rebs' left. Don't know if he'll make it. . . . Say, by the way, where the hell's my passbook?'

'Rosemary has it.'

'*She* has it? But . . .'

'General, she thinks you've been taking kickbacks, and that I've been the moneybag man. I told her that was crazy, that you'd never do that sort of thing, but look . . . she's got it in her head, and there was nothing I could do to change her mind.'

Matoon's eyes were bulging.

'Kickbacks?' he whispered, recoiling from the word as if it were a rattlesnake. '*Me?*'

'That's what she thinks, and she has the passbook. I'll see you in Centerville, sir.'

Before the general could say anything further, Lew let himself out and closed the doors, figuring that a fast exit was the better part of valour. Matoon, who was frowning, thought for a moment. Then he snapped, 'Burt, get my hat.'

'Yes sir. Are we going to the War Department?'

'No. We're going to Third Street. Miss Fletcher's been holdin' out on me, Burt. It's time we settled accounts.'

Burt Thomson said nothing as he went to get the general's plumed hat.

Lew pushed his way out of the hotel, then stopped to take another look at the sea of humanity in front of him. Hot, sticky, and dirty as he was, it was a sight he would never forget. The rainbow of different uniforms, the guns, the flags, the horses, the carriages filled with parasol-holding women, congressmen, diplomats, correspondents, all rolling out to Virginia to see the Great Rebellion crushed. Was it really all over, he wondered. Had he spent the most exciting days of the war locked up in a root cellar? Perhaps. But at least he had had his small share of glory: Rosemary was going to pay for her spying. And now it was up to him to make Matoon pay for his graft. As a passing soldier yelled, 'On to Richmond!' Lew remounted his horse and headed for Lafayette Square. He had told Matoon next to nothing: let Matoon hear it all from Rosemary. It soon wouldn't make any difference. He was going to tell Mr Seward everything and let Mr Seward arrest them both – Matoon and Rosemary. And if it came out that he had murdered a man in Philadelphia eight months before, so be it. He would cross that bridge when he got to it and if, necessary, face the charge. After months of stalemate and inactivity, a battle was finally imminent, and Winkler paled in significance compared to Matoon and Rosemary. Perhaps he thought, his personal sacrifice in the war would be his own murder trial, but Matoon and Rosemary must pay. 'On to Richmond, on to Richmond!' A Massachusetts regiment had picked up the cry. 'On to Richmond! We'll hang Jeff Davis on a sour apple tree!' 'On to Richmond!' yelled Lew, now as excited as everyone else. By the time he reached Lafayette Square, he was so eager to get to Centerville he almost begrudged the time he'd have to spend with the Secretary of State.

He dismounted and ran to the front door of Mr Seward's house. He rang the bell, then looked at the White House. The drive was filled with carriages: it was possible Mr Seward would be there. Then he looked across the square at the French Legation. The big coach that had splattered him with mud the night of the White House reception was just pulling away, its uniformed outriders almost ludicrously elegant in the midst of all the dirt, dust and confusion. On top of the lumbering vehicle were strapped two wicker hampers. So Laura was going to Centerville too. . . .

'Yes?'

He turned around to see a wrinkled housekeeper at the door. She gave the bedraggled lieutenant a suspicious look.

'What do you want?'

'Is Mr Seward in? My name's Lieutenant Crandall. He knows me.'

'Mr Seward knows *you?*' She sniffed, looking him over.

'It's important I see him! This is official business. . . . Tell him it's about General Matoon.'

'Mr Seward left for the White House an hour ago,' she said and slammed the door in his face.

He mumbled 'Shit' and ran back to remount his horse. Then he galloped across the square to the White House gate, where he leaned down to say to the Marine guard. 'My name's Lieutenant Crandall . . . I'm General Matoon's aide. It's vitally important I see Mr Seward. Will you let me through?'

The Marine gave a reluctant salute to the ratty, hatless officer on the horse.

'Sir, Mr Seward left for Centerville twenty minutes ago.'

'Jesus,' muttered Lew. 'Thanks.' He turned his horse toward the Long Bridge and began the ride toward Arlington. It was only then he realized the irony: he, a Northern lieutenant, was going into the first major battle of the Civil War armed with the gun of a Confederate captain: a Griswold and Grier six-shot revolver. If he hadn't been so excited and so incredibly hungry, he would have laughed.

General Matoon knew next to nothing about military tactics, but a lifetime of political infighting had taught him to move fast when attacked, and on the morning of 21 July, he was moving as fast as he had in his life. Fifteen minutes after Lew left his suite, the general's carriage pulled up in front of 114 Third Street. Burt Thomson jumped down to open the door for his superior, but the general was already out. 'Wait for me,' he ordered, Then he went up the front porch of the house. It was quiet, and the front door was open for ventilation. Matoon went inside the narrow hall and listened.

Silence. Probably the occupants were on their way to Virginia, along with everyone else. But not Rosemary: she had just come back from Virginia. He pulled his gun and went back to the door of Rosemary's bedroom. Quietly, he tried the door. It was unlocked. He opened it and let himself in.

She was asleep on the bed, dressed in a peach satin camisole, her red hair a cloud on the pillow. Softly, he closed the door. Then he went to the bed and looked at the woman he loved – or at least had lusted for until fifteen minutes before. Even now, she looked tempting. But then he glanced up at the picture of Lincoln over the bed. That did it. He pressed the muzzle of the gun against her forehead. His finger was on the trigger.

She opened her eyes and looked at him. Then the eyes moved to the gun.

'Take that thing away,' she said. 'What's gotten into you – are you drunk again?'

'Sober as I've ever been. You've been playing a double game with me, Rosie. Now you'd better come clean, or your brains is gonna be splattered all over that pillowslip. I mean it.'

'What *are* you talking about?'

'Spyin'! Lew Crandall's spilled the beans, Rosie, and your goose is cooked.'

'Don't be ridiculous. He's a prisoner.'

'Not any more he ain't. I just talked to him, less than a half hour ago, and he told me about you and Major Desborough. That's dirty pool, Rosie. Real dirty. And as nice as I've been to you. By Christ, leave it to a big-titted redhead to be ungrateful.'

'And you believe *him?*'

'I'll believe him before you.'

She was silent a moment. Then she said, 'All right. I'll admit I'm a spy.'

'What did you tell them?'

'For one thing, a week ago I let them know McDowell was moving out of Washington heading for Fairfax Court House and Centerville, preparing for an attack on Beauregard. Which information, my love, you volunteered one night in bed after you'd killed a bottle of bourbon.'

Matoon's face turned cold. 'By Christ, I've got half a mind to kill you right now.'

'I think you'd better listen to me first. You're not in a very good position either, you know. And if you kill me now, you aren't ever going to find the passbook you were looking for – which, believe me, is in a safe place.'

'Lew told me you had it.'

'Oh, he did? He's a cool one, Now take that gun away and let's talk turkey. We have a lot more to gain working together than fighting each other.'

He hesitated, then removed the gun. As she sat up in bed, he pulled up a chair and eased himself into it, keeping the gun pointed at her.

'All right,' he said, 'talk.'

She ran her hand through her red hair.

'In the first place, if you arrest me for spying, it's going to come out at the trial where I got my information, which isn't going to make you look too good. In the second place, the damage is already done, since Beauregard and McDowell are already fighting. And in the third place, if I go on trial, I'm going to tell everything I know about that seven thousand dollars you've deposited in Crandall's name and where it came from.'

His eyes narrowed. 'Lew said you think I've been taking kickbacks. And it's a lie. A dirty, rotten lie.'

She smiled. 'I see Lieutenant Crandall's a few jumps ahead of me. So he told you *I* think you've been taking kickbacks? And what about him? Does *he* think you have?'

'Of course not.'

She gave him a look of disgust. 'You fool. He's known about it all along. And he's been feeding the whole story to the Secretary of State. Here, read this if you don't believe me.'

She reached over to her bed table, opened the drawer, and pulled out the note Laura de Beaupré had written Lew. She handed it to Matoon, who read it.

'Crandall's the one who's playing the double game,' she said. 'And he's the real threat to you, not me. You've got me over a barrel, so I'll shut up. Your problem is to shut *him* up, and I can tell you how to do it'.

He looked up from the note. 'How?'

'He committed a murder in Pennsylvania last year, and I've got an eyewitness to the crime.'

'I don't believe you. *Him* commit a murder? Christ, he went to college!'

'So did Hamlet.' She got out of bed and put on her slippers. 'Now, put that popgun away and don't say anything. Just listen.'

She started toward the window.

'But goddammit, you're a *spy!*' he insisted, his voice a mixture of anger and confusion.

'What do you care? That savings account is what you're interested in, isn't it?' She leaned out the window and called into the back yard, 'Christine? Honey, will you come in here a minute?'

Then she started back to the bed.

'Which brings up another interesting thought.'

Matoon was watching her suspiciously. 'What?'

'If the North wins the war today, there're not going to be any more war contracts, are there?'

'I suppose not.'

She sat on the side of the bed. 'Which means you must have mixed emotions about the outcome of the battle.'

'What are you getting at?'

'You know I'm a spy, I know you're taking kickbacks. Aren't we a natural team? You tell me what the generals are planning, I pass it on to the other side so the South can outmanoeuvre the Federals, and Mr Lincoln has to buy more and more guns and ammunition through the War Department, which means more and more kickbacks for you. We win all around, don't we? That is, as long as Lieutenant Crandall is kept quiet. It's something to think about, isn't it?'

Matoon didn't look uninterested.

'Maybe,' he said, putting the gun in his holster. It was then that Christine came into the room. Rosemary smiled and held out her arms.

'Come here, dear, and meet an old friend of mine, General Matoon. He's Daddy Lew's boss man, and he's doing his best to help get him back for us from the Rebs.'

Matoon watched with interest as the beautiful barefoot girl in the dirty blue dress came across the room. She took Rosemary's hand, then looked uncertainly at the general.

'Do you know where he is?' she asked.

'I've got a pretty good idea,' said Matoon.

'The general's fixing to talk to Mr Lincoln,' said Rosemary, 'and get him to write Jeff Davis personally and ask for Daddy Lew's release. And it's important that Mr Lincoln know what a fine, brave man Daddy Lew is, and how he saved you from Winkler.'

'You're really going to talk to the *President*?' asked Christine, impressed.

'He's an old friend,' said the general unctuously. 'Is it true you saw Daddy Lew kill . . .' He looked at Rosemary uncertainly.

'Winkler,' she prompted.

Christine said nothing.

'Go on, honey,' said Rosemary, squeezing her hand. 'The general needs all the help he can get to help Daddy Lew.'

Christine looked at the uniform, which seemed to reassure her.

'Yes, I saw him,' she said. 'He did it to save himself, and to save me. Winkler was scum.'

Matoon and Rosemary exchanged looks. Then the general smiled. 'Thanks for the help, Christine. I knew Lew was a fine, brave soldier, but I never dreamed he was a fine, brave killer.'

'He's no killer!' she exclaimed. 'I tell you, he did it to save himself!'

'We know, dear,' soothed Rosemary.

'It's true! I won't have no one saying he's a killer! He saved my life and put me into school. . . .'

'We're on *your* side, honey. Honest. Now, give me a kiss, then you go on back outside. No, I tell you what: go into the kitchen and make us some coffee. Will you do that, honey?'

Christine hesitated, eyeing Matoon. Then she nodded. 'All right.'

Rosemary released her hand, and Christine went to the door and opened it. Before she left, she turned to them and said softly, 'Lew Crandall is the finest man I ever met.'

Then she went out and closed the door.

'You didn't have to call him a killer,' whispered Rosemary.

'What else do you call it?'

'Anyway, do you see what I mean! I won't cause the trouble, *he* will. He's going to tell Seward the whole business, if he hasn't already. And that girl's the best weapon you've got to shut him up. She, and that corpse in the apple orchard.'

Matoon scratched his chin.

'No,' he finally said, 'if Crandall's talking to Seward, there's a better way than that to shut him up.'

'How?'

He got up from the chair. 'You'll see, Rosie. You'll see.'

'Then does that mean we're in business?'

He took her hands and pulled her to her feet. Then he put his arms around her. 'Rosie, for a two-timin' bitch, you've got a smart head on your shoulders.'

He kissed her. She purred.

Lew didn't reach Centerville until a little before eleven that morning. The road down to the tiny Virginia town had been jammed with troops, caissons, carriages, ambulances, cavalry . . . the traffic had been so heavy, that often he left the road and took to the fields to make headway. But even the fields were often crawling with soldiers, for many of the men, disregarding their officers' shouts, broke ranks and went into the fields to pick berries. At one point, where a narrow bridge crossed a river, the traffic was stopped for a half hour by a broken wagon axle. Lew, fuming with impatience, found a ford upstream and rode across, heading back to the road to continue south. As the day grew hotter, the excitement of the early morning was replaced by an apathetic grumbling. He heard no more shouts of, 'On to Richmond!' What he heard were complaints about the heat, sore feet, and cheaply made boots. The civilians, who had left Washinton for a larky jaunt to view the great battle, began opening bottles of wine and cider. He saw two couples in an open landau who were drunk. Others read newspapers or novels, or studied maps of Virginia, trying to guess where the action would be. It was a bizarre journey. But Centerville was even stranger.

When he finally arrived, the town was swarming with strolling tourists and milling soldiers, most of whom seemed oblivious to the distant boom of cannons and the smoke rising in the west. The town had a dirt crossroads with a big elm beside it; Lew spotted Chandler Delanoy sitting beneath the tree. He rode over and said, 'What's going on?'

Delanoy looked up. 'Crandall! Where have you –'

'Virginia,' interrupted Lew, truncating the inevitable. 'Where's General McDowell?'

'He left about an hour ago. He took his staff down the Warrenton Turnpike. It's all over.'

'What's all over?'

'The battıe.'

Lew pointed to the smoke on the horizon. 'Then what's that? Those guns don't sound as if it's over to me.'

Delanoy waved a fly from his nose.

'They're just mopping up. They pushed the Rebs back south of the turnpike. General Jackson's formed a line, but I heard about ten minutes ago he can't hold it much longer. Guess we'll all be home soon.'

'Maybe.' Lew looked around. 'Have you seen Mr Seward?'

'He was here, but he went with the general.'

'Where's the Warrenton Turnpike?'

'That way,' He pointed to the west road.

'Don't kill too many Rebs,' said Lew, turning his horse.

'None left to kill,' yawned Delanoy. 'I've seen the elephant, and it's a big bore. If you come to New York, look me up.'

Lew galloped down the Warrenton Turnpike in the direction of the cannonfire, wondering what his reaction to 'seeing the elephant' – which was the slang for seeing one's first battle – would be. The terrain was beautiful – gently rolling hills – but after ten minutes, the grassy fields began to take on a macabre quality. He began seeing bodies sprawled in the grotesque attitudes of death. Flies swarmed over the corpses, and an occasional hawk was circling in the smoky sky, silhouetted motes in the eye of the fierce sun. Death. A few hours before, the bodies had been full of life, like himself. He knew that war meant death, but seeing those silent bodies sprawling to eternity made the abstraction real to him. Who were they? What had they died for? Their deaths suddenly seemed appalling to him. For that matter, he might be one of them.

He rose to the top of a hill and stopped. Before him stretched the battle lines; to the southwest, on a wooded ridge, were the Southern guns and rifles manned by men in grey. To the northeast, the Federal guns manned by men in a variety of colours. The guns belched at each other periodically, sending thunder rumbling over the hills, and the rifles popped. Cannonballs had shattered trees, and the bodies of men and horses were everywhere. Despite the noise and smoke, the 'elephant' seemed static, a stalemate. Where were the dashing charges of cavalry and men? Still, it looked far from over. He decided Chandler Delanoy's information was faulty.

Below him, not far behind the Federal line, he spotted a group of officers standing under a tree. Mounted messengers were galloping between the officers and the line, and Lew decided that that was probably McDowell's headquarters. He started down the hill, heading for the tree. When he was nearer, he saw, standing with the officers, a slightly stooped civilian in a stovepipe hat, carrying a walking stick, and he recognized Mr Seward. He rode up to the tree and dismounted, tying his horse to a bush. A captain standing with the group saw him and came over.

'Who are you?' he said. 'And where's your hat?'

Lew had totally forgotten he had left it in the barn when he put on O'Rourke's uniform.

'I guess I lost it, sir. I'm Lieutenant Crandall, aide to

General Matoon. I'd like a word with Mr Seward. He knows me.' The captain looked him over. Lew added. 'You can tell him I've got important information about General Matoon.'

'Just a minute.'

The captain walked back to Mr Seward and said something to him. The Secretary of State looked at Lew and nodded. Then he said something to the captain, who came back to Lew.

'Mr Seward sends his regards and says for you to come to his office tomorrow morning at ten.'

'But can't I just *talk* to him. . . .'

'Lieutenant, General McDowell is trying to win this battle. He can't be disturbed.'

'I don't want to talk to the general –'

'Lieutenant, you're in the *way*.'

Lew gestured with frustration. 'Then what the hell am I supposed to do? I was sent down here by Matoon. . . .'

'Where is the general?'

'On the way to Centerville.'

'Then go back to Centerville and wait for him.'

The captain returned to the group. It was so ridiculous, Lew wanted to laugh. He possessed explosive information, and he was told to drop by the office in the morning. Still, what to do? Shrugging, he untied his horse, remounted, and started back to Centerville.

Up till now, he had felt no sense of personal danger because the general and his staff had been out of rifle range, and the Southern guns seemed uninterested in or incapable of killing the opposing general and the Secretary of State. But ten minutes after leaving the headquarters, he heard a pop! to his right, then others: pop! pop! pop! He looked to the right to see six men in grey galloping across a ravine toward him. He spurred his horse to a gallop, pulling Captain O'Rourke's Griswold and Grier and turning to fire a shot at the Rebs. Pop! pop! they fired back. Jesus, he thought, they must be crazy breaking through their line. . . . He turned again to fire. They were on the road now, in hot pursuit. He fired two more shots and hit one of the men, who stumbled off his horse. A rifle ball sizzled past his ear, and death almost kissed him. Sweat was flying from him as he turned to fire three more shots. One of his bullets winged another of the men, who dropped his rifle, though he didn't fall off his horse. Then the Rebs stopped, probably deciding he wasn't worth the chase, Lew thought. It was lucky, since he was out of bullets. He put the Griswold and Grier back in his belt, and continued to Centerville. The whole thing made no sense, he thought. Battles probably made little sense, and the grand tactics of generals were more likely than not mostly guesswork and hunches. It was crazy and appalling. The dead bodies were crazy and appalling. By the time he galloped, drenched with sweat, back into Centerville, his horse covered with foam, he had decided that war – even one worth fighting, as this was – was not only crazy and appalling but stupid.

Centerville was now so jam-packed with people that he could barely make his way into town. Carriages were everywhere. He saw a clock on a church steeple to his right: it was half past noon. It was then that he saw a weird sight. In the graveyard beside the church two bewigged footmen were pouring champagne for a man and a woman seated on a carpet spread on the grass beneath a big oak tree. The man Lew didn't recognize, but the woman was Laura de Beaupré, a vision of French chic surrounded by tilting gravestones. She had on a green silk dress, the skirt of which surrounded her like a huge flower, and a wide-brimmed green hat was tied under her chin with a beige ribbon. Behind the church was parked the official coach of the legation with its Napoleonic coat of arms painted on the door. The tableau was so incongruous in this hot Virginia town filled with hot soldiers and tourists that Lew thought, To hell with finding Matoon. Besides, the sight of the food spread on the carpet was driving him slightly crazy. Dismounting, he tied his horse to the hitching post in front of the church and hurried around to the side.

Laura was about to bite into a chicken leg when she saw him.

'Lew!' she exclaimed. '*Mais, c'est incroyable! L'Americain est revenu!* Lew, come here!' She waved at him, then turned to the stocky man on her right, who had just popped a hardboiled egg in his mouth. He was middle-aged, with a broad face that might once have been pleasant but was now jowly and rather dissolute. He had taken off his frock coat and top hat. His shirt, made of the best Egyptian cotton, was beautifully sewn, with exquisite ruffles at the cuffs. On the chest pocket was an embroidered crest, but it was almost invisible: he had dropped a blob of mayonnaise on it. '*Altesse*,' said Laura, '*voici le jeune officier dont je vous ai parlé*.'

'*Ah, le disparu?*'

'*Oui. Nous l'avions supposé capture, mais il est évident que nous avions tort*. Lew, where have you been? You must join us! Aristide stayed in Washington, but the prince wanted to see the battle. . . . Lieutenant Crandall, His Imperial Highness, Prince Bonaparte.'

Lew stared at the cousin of the French emperor, who stared back at the filthy American with ill-concealed scorn. With calculated rudeness, the prince, who was known in Paris as 'Plon-Plon', said nothing. He popped another egg in his mouth.

'Speak in English.' Laura smiled to Lew. 'He doesn't understand a word, and this way we can talk about him. Isn't he disgusting? Sit down. . . .' She gestured to her left. Lew sat cross-legged on the carpet, staring at the bowls of fruit, the bread, the chickens, the cheeses. Laura turned to the prince.

'*Malheureusement, Monsieur Crandall ne parle pas français. Je vous prie de m'excuser, Altesse, je voudrais lui poser des questions*.'

'*Bien sûr, madame. Mais comme il est sale! Suis-je obligé de dejeuner avec cette canaille?*'

She laughed. 'He thinks you're filthy!'

'I am,' said Lew. 'And he's spilled mayonnaise on his shirt.'

'Oh, his manners are terrible, but we have to be nice to him while he's in Washington. He's here to see what Mr Seward's feelings will be if France becomes involved in Mexico. And speaking of Mr Seward . . .'

'I'm seeing him in the morning. Excuse me, Laura, but I'm famished. May I have some chicken?'

'Of course! Help yourself. Guillaume – *de la champagne pour le lieutenant*.'

As the footman filled a glass for him, Lew tore a leg off one of the chickens and started devouring it. The prince stared at him.

'*Dégoûtant!*' he mumbled.

Lew stuffed some bread in his mouth and chewed it blissfully. Then he washed it down with champagne. He smiled. 'Ah, heaven! If you knew what I've been eating for the past week – or more to the point what I *haven't* been eating . . .'

'But where have you been?'

'Buried in Virginia.'

He tore off another leg from the rapidly disappearing chicken and attacked it. The prince's heavy black eyebrows lifted.

'*Salopard!*'

Lew smiled at him, his mouth full of food, and said, between bites, 'I don't like you, Your Highness. You are a fat pig.'

Laura giggled, then turned to the prince. '*Il a dît qu'il n'a jamais connu de prince, et que votre auguste visage fait sur lui une impression inoubliable*.'

The prince looked pleasantly surprised. '*Vraiment?*'

'*Vraiment*.' She turned to Lew. 'He's beginning to like you. Were you captured?'

He started to answer when he heard someone yell, 'Crandall!' He turned to see Burt Thomson on a white horse in the road in front of the churchyard. Thomson was signalling him to join him. Lew sighed and put down the chicken. 'My luck. Excuse me a moment.'

'Hurry back.'

He got up, wiped his mouth on the linen napkin, then went over to Thomson.

'What the hell are you doing?' said Thomson. 'I thought you came down here to fight?'

'I'm waiting for Matoon.'

'Well, he's here, and he sent me to look for you. Think you can tear yourself away from the party?'

'I'll try.'

'You goddam Frogs'd throw a party at a hanging.'

'I would if it were *your* hanging, Burt. Wait a minute.'

He returned to the prince and smiled at him.

'*Altesse*,' he said, '*excusez-moi, mais il semble que la bataille n'est pas terminée après tout. Je vais me battre pour la gloire et la patrie.*'

The prince choked on his champagne at the flawless French. Lew winked at him. Then he took Laura's hand and raised it to his mouth. He kissed it, watching her grey-blue-green eyes.

'I'll love you till the day I die,' he whispered. He squeezed her hand, then released it and walked away. Laura watched him, stunned.

'*Madame, vous m'avez trompé!*' growled Plon-Plon. '*Il parle français couramment!*'

She sighed. '*Il est superbe.*' And she meant it.

'Where's Matoon?' asked Lew after he had mounted.

'Follow me.'

Burt galloped down the Warrenton Turnpike in the direction Lew had come from. Lew followed, yelling, 'Is he with McDowell?'

'You'll see.'

They rode for about a mile, then Burt slowed his horse and pointed to some trees on his right. 'Over there,' he called. He turned his horse and started up a gentle hill toward the trees. Lew followed him, wondering why Matoon was in a woods far from the battlefield. Thomson rode into the woods, with Lew not far behind him. Thomson kept going, riding between the trees, then down the other slope of the hill till he reached a pond. Then he stopped and waited for Lew, who rode up beside him a moment later.

'Is this it?' he asked.

'This is it,' said Burt.

Lew looked around. The woods were deserted.

'But there's no one here.'

'I know.'

Lew turned back to Thomson. He was holding a gun.

'The general has told me to kill you,' said Thomson, 'and it's a real pleasure. I hate your good-looking Frog guts.'

And he fired at his heart, point-blank.

Lieutenant Louis de Rochefort Crandall fell backward off his horse and landed on the ground. The horses whinnied from the noise of the shot. Thomson smacked the haunch of Lew's horse, and it galloped away into the woods. The corporal looked down at the body. The life blood was staining Lew's jacket; his eyes were half open and lifeless; his mouth was hanging half open, and his head was tilted slightly to one side.

Burt Thomson stuck his pistol back in his holster, then spurred his horse and started back up the hill.

He looked pleased with himself.

5

LOVERS AND FRIENDS 1864

18

Letter from Elizabeth Crandall to Benjamin Bramwell, dated 12 April 1864:

Rome

My dear Ben:

Having finally gotten settled in Rome after our trip from Weimar via Paris, I at last have a chance to write you. I feel guilty, because you correspond so regularly and I am, at best, fitful, I fear. But I do treasure your letters from home so much, as they are not only a link to Philadelphia, which I miss, but also a link to the past and the memory of our beloved friend who was so dear to both of us. Oh Ben, you have been so kind to me and little Ward through these troubled years – how can I ever thank you enough? And you with your own troubles! How brave you have been and how proud we are of your fortitude! When I think of the sacrifices you and so many other of our brave boys have made (not to mention the supreme sacrifice of my dearest one), I wonder if I made the right decision coming to Europe to study with the maestro. Was I selfish, Ben? Should I have tried to help by becoming a nurse? And yet I couldn't bring myself to do it. You know the terrible agony I went through after we received the tragic news from Gen. Matoon. I thought the world had come to an end and, as you know, I almost lost little Ward (if that had happened, if my precious living link to my beloved had been taken from me also, I doubt I could have survived!) After that, I couldn't bring myself to work in hospitals, seeing so much suffering and despair. Every wound, every tortured face would have reopened my own wounds, and instead of some poor brave soldier lying there, I know I would have seen my Lew instead, his beautiful face looking up into mine. . . . No, I wasn't strong enough. I had to leave Philadelphia, leave this dreadful, endless war. And yet at times I feel guilty and wonder if, for Lew's sake, I shouldn't return to America and do *something*. But my studies progress so well with M. Liszt I cannot help but think that maybe in the long run I am helping in my own way by being here. Isn't music important too? Isn't culture? On that blessed day when this cruel war finally ends, won't our country need music as well as bandages to heal her bleeding wounds? I don't know. I am torn. In a way, I suppose I am a drifting woman. I have drifted for almost three years now.

We have found a charming home near the Spanish Steps. I am renting the second floor of a house that belongs to a nice American couple who moved here from Boston ten years ago. Their name is Powell, and Mr Powell is working on a book about the Renaissance popes (it must be huge: he's worked on it ten years and is only half done!). Our rooms are clean, light, and airy, and I have rented a Bechstein for practice. The Powells adore little Ward, who is 2½ now, walking, talking (babbling, I should say: he's a real chatterbox) in English, German, and now Italian, which he naturally mixes up so that often he doesn't make much sense. (As for myself, my Italian is nonexistent, but my French, thank heavens, has improved out of necessity. The maestro speaks some English, but prefers French. Nicole Louise's French lessons have paid dividends.) I found a wonderful nurse for Ward named Rosa who teaches him his Italian words. I think it will be good if he grows up being at least bilingual, as his dear father was. Every time I look at him I see Lew. He has his same rich, golden hair and will be as handsome, I think. Sometimes I worry about his not having a father. And yet, who would replace Lew? The thought of remarriage is still too dreadful for me to contemplate – not that anyone has asked, I might add. Still, some day, for Ward's sake, I feel I must consider it. . . .

To bring you up to date: the maestro was restless in Weimar and though the Grand Duke was much more attentive to his resident genius than I had been led to believe, M. Liszt still felt enough was not being done for him and his efforts to bring the 'music of the future' to the public (by the way, the court supported him much more than the stodgy Weimaraners. The townspeople never forgave him for living openly with the Princesse Sayn-Wittgenstein), so he was off again for Rome. I packed up Ward, and, like Gypsies, we followed him (in the first-class carriages, not, like him, second-class. He is somewhat short of funds, to my embarrassment, yet he absolutely refuses to accept payment from any of his pupils. He seems totally uninterested in money now, except to further the music he champions, and when one considers the incredible fortune he made and spent during his performing years – and I have heard estimates as high as 300000 francs a year in the 1830s and 40s – this lack of materialism now seems quite remarkable). In Paris, he kindly invited me to a supper he gave at the Café Anglais, where I met his two charming (and illegitimate) daughters by the Comtesse d'Agoult. Blandine is married to M. Ollivier, a prominent liberal politician in Paris, and Cosima is married to Herr Von Bulow (but I fear is having an *affaire* with Herr Wagner). *He* was there, too – Herr Wagner – and I must say he may be a genius, but he is a loathsome man, horribly conceited and a voracious money-grubber (he kept asking the maestro for loans during the meal! Incredible). Finally, off to Marseilles, then a steamer to Italy and Rome, where apparently we are ensconced for a while.

I have now met the notorious Princesse Carolyne Sayn-Wittgenstein. It was at a soirée the other night at the Palazzo Barberini to which the maestro again kindly invited me (he seems to have taken a fancy to me and gets me invited to all sorts of fascinating places. Since he is by far the most celebrated musician in Europe and has had society at his feet for thirty years, all doors are open to him, so his patronage, if you could call it that, has afforded me a look at the very *crème* of Continental society, both artistic and otherwise, which is not without interest). The maestro played brilliantly, as always, but my eyes were riveted on the Polish princess, whose name and life have been linked with his for almost twenty years. She is certainly not very attractive. If she is immensely wealthy, she is also immense, with a big, square, rather vapid face. She dresses strangely, *à la polonaise* I suppose, and smokes incessant cigars which *stink*. I spoke a few words to her: she strikes me as humorless, surprisingly masculine, and not, I fear, very bright. (In all fairness, the impression may be because her French has a Polish accent, which made it hard for me to understand her). Yet she must have something, for the maestro is devoted to her, and considering the fact that there are few women in Europe he couldn't have if he wanted, the princess must have hidden charms (though I must say the maestro's eyes get a bit glazed when he's with her: whether the cause is boredom or the enormous amounts of cognac and wine he consumes every day, I don't know). He visits her every evening at her place on the Via del Babuino, where she is working on a lengthy exposé of the Roman Church. Considering how badly the Church has treated her, I don't imagine the pope is looking forward to its publication. The princess's husband, Prince Nicolas Sayn-Wittgenstein, the source of all her trouble, died just last month. To everyone's surprise, after all the struggles she went through to divorce him so she could marry the maestro, now there's no talk of a wedding, I assume it's due to M. Liszt's decision to take priestly orders. If he goes through with it, I can't imagine a more worldly abbé; still he seems genuine in his interest in religion. A curious, fascinating man.

He is now 53 and losing his fabulous good looks, but he is still a striking man. The famous lion's-mane of hair is greying, and he's getting warts on his face, but the profile is still there. He has rooms – or rather, a cell – outside Rome at the Madonna del Rosario, but spends most of his time at the sumptuous Villa d'Este in Tivoli. This is where I go for my lessons twice a week, Tuesday and Friday afternoons at two. Though it takes me four hours to get there and four back, the trip is worth the trouble, not only for the lessons but for the villa. It left the Este family at the beginning of the century, when the last of them, Maria Beatrice, died. Her husband was a Hapsburg Archduke. So the place went to the Hapsburgs, who promptly let it fall into a terrible state of decay, including the famous gardens. Fortunately, Cardinal von Hohenlohe, who represents Austrian interests at the Papal Court, fell in love with the place, took a lifetime rental from the Hapsburgs, and poured his considerable fortune into restoring it, so that now it enjoys its former grandeur. Cardinal von Hohenlohe's brother, Prince Constantine von Hohenlohe, is married to the Princesse Carolyne's daughter, Marie, who was devoted to the maestro (he was practically her stepfather), so that's the connection between the maestro and the cardinal. If all these ins and outs strike you as confusing, imagine how they struck *me!* But the interrelations of all these people are rather fascinating.

Now, dear Ben, I must ask of you yet another favor – you who have been so kind! I need your advice on a matter that has recently come up and is extremely confidential (and this may not be pleasant for you, because I know you have never gotten along well with Lew's mother). Nicole Louise has been very generous with me, financially. When my dear father died last year, I inherited a small sum from him; and, as you know, my beloved left me a considerable sum of cash as well as our house, so I have not been pressed, happily. But Nicole Louise has given me numerous gifts of money (unsolicited by me, I might add), which I have accepted for Ward's sake, if not my own. Thus, I really have had no quarrel with her, which makes what I am about to write rather embarrassing, since I know I will sound calculating and mercenary. Yet I *do* have Ward's future to consider.

In short, you know that Nicole Louise has rejoined the Church and that religion has become not only the solace of her later years, but I sometimes feel an escape from her sorrow over the loss of her son. She recently wrote me that she is changing her will. She intends setting up a trust for Ward that will amount to around a million dollars; but the rest of her estate (which, she confided to me, amounts to over five millions – the size of it surprised me, but she says her investments have ballooned because of the war) she is leaving to the Church. Now, certainly, a million dollars is a lot of money, and Ward will never want for anything in his life. But as his mother, I can't help but think he is being somewhat short-changed. After all, he is the *only* Crandall left, and while I certainly don't begrudge the Church's receiving a handsome legacy, I do feel that my darling should receive at least *half* of what would have gone to his father if he had lived. Dear Ben, does that sound unreasonable? Am I being greedy? I don't know what to do, and I have no one to seek advice from except you. Naturally, I cringe from a fight with my mother-in-law (particularly a fight about money, which is the worst kind). But don't I have a duty to try and change her mind? Or is a million more than enough for Ward? I don't know. I have no head for money, which is why I appeal to you for advice. If only my Lew were here . . . but he isn't. So, Ben dear, will you be my surrogate Lew? I hate to burden you, but knowing your sweet disposition and your unfailing kindness in the past, I am taking the risk of trespassing on your good nature.

I will await your next letter anxiously. In the meanwhile, all my love, dear Ben, from your devoted

Elizabeth

Letter from Benjamin Bramwell to Elizabeth Crandall, dated 1 May 1864:

Philadelphia

My dear Elizabeth:

Far from trespassing on my good nature, you do me honor by asking my advice, though, the Lord knows, I am no Solomon. Still, even if it were not for the affection I bear the memory of my dearest friend, I would deem it a pleasure and a privilege to do everything in my power to assist you. Therefore, let me say immediately that I consider it ill advised of you to get into any financial unpleasantness with your mother-in-law. You're right: I don't like her. But putting my feelings aside, if possible, I must tell you that she has changed considerably since you left for Weimar seven months ago. The word is that she is totally under the spell of Father Dunne, and that she has become almost obsessive about religion. I have even heard that she is considering giving her abominable house on Rittenhouse Square to an order of nuns, and then she herself will retreat to a convent to devote the rest of her life to prayer and good works. Whether she does or not, there is no doubt in my mind that any resistance on your part to the settlement of her estate will lead to worse than a squabble; it might endanger what is after all, a handsome settlement on little Ward. Nicole Louise Crandall is *not* a woman to trifle with or cross (as I have learned to my discomfort). Yes, Ward is her flesh and blood, but Ward is far away across the sea and the Church is *here*, all-welcoming and all-comforting. I would say nothing.

Which leads me to a boldness I will perhaps regret, but I hope you will read the following as a *sincere* expression of thoughts that have been building within me for some time now. You know, dear Elizabeth, that my estimation for Lew was as tender as, I believe, any feeling could be between two men. We grew up together, we shared problems in our childhood that created a bond between us that would, I like to believe, have endured all our lives, Alas, the bond was broken on the battlefield of Bull Run. We don't even have a grave or a watch or any memento of him except our memories: he vanished out of our lives. Which is cruel to mention, I know, and yet I do mention it so you will perhaps understand better what I am about to propose. I lost a friend; you lost a husband, Ward a father. You say you can't bear to contemplate remarriage, yet you feel the lack of a father for little Ward. And how right you are, for every child needs a father – it is commonplace to say it, yet it is undoubtedly true.

What I am leading up to in my clumsy way is, could you ever possibly consider giving me the honor of replacing Lew? Oh, dear Elizabeth, I know full well I could never be anything but a surrogate, as you put it. I have no illusions that I could inspire in you anything but a pale reflection of the emotion you held for him, nor would I want you to. I am all too painfully aware of the difference between us. He was handsome and graceful; I am a clumsy brute with very little to offer as far as looks are concerned, and my beauty has hardly been enhanced by the loss of my left leg at Chancellorsville. He was cheerful and fun, I am morose, moody, and, I fear, lacking both the social graces and wit. To lay all my losing cards on the table, there is the fact that I am one-quarter Jewish. And while I am proud of my blood, I know that some people might consider that an obstacle to marriage – though I don't think *you* would. In short, dear Elizabeth, I know I am a poor replacement for him who was everything the world admires.

Yet in my defense, may I humbly point out that my admiration for you is unbounded. That while I will not discomfort you by using the word 'love,' you have always been the one woman I would have liked to marry if I thought I could aspire so high, and your marriage to my dearest friend was a source of great joy to me. While I have no experience as a parent, I feel I would be able to fill a void in Ward's life, and would be overjoyed to do it. To be crassly vulgar for a moment, I do possess a considerable fortune (amounting to several millions) which would be at your disposal, which would go to Ward on my death, and which would make up the difference between his trust and what his grandmother is giving the Church. In short, I offer devotion, service, and my fortune. Pray believe me, I would not dream of offering even that if I did not believe in my heart that he, who meant so much to both of us, would approve. I think Lew would not mind my helping his son and caring for his widow. I even think he might be glad.

Dear Elizabeth, if my proposal offends you, please tell me, and I will never mention the subject again. But if the thoughts of a devoted father to your child and a devoted friend to you holds some appeal, I beg you to consider my offer. To speak for a moment of indelicate matters, I know there is one aspect of marriage for which I could never be an adequate replacement. Nor would I even try unless, of course, you might desire it. Yet, speaking personally, I am a lonely man. I would like a family. In time, perhaps, if it were agreeable to you, I would like to have a child of my own. But if that were never to come to pass, little Ward would more than fill the emptiness in my heart. I would, with your approval, naturally, adopt him.

Have I gone too far? Have I betrayed our friendship, and the memory of him so dear to both of us? I pray not. Please, dear Elizabeth, consider my offer as, if nothing else, heartfelt.

I await, with considerable apprehension, your reply. As always, your devoted

Ben

19

It was sleeting when the cab pulled up in front of the store at Eighth Avenue and Thirty-first Street: it was one of those late-winter, early-spring storms that nodded, Janus-like, at both seasons, unable to make up its mind. The big man in the top hat got out, paid the cabbie, then hurried through the slush to the door with CHEZ ADELE painted in elaborate gold letters on it, a fat gold tail swirling under the words in a terminal flourish. The man let himself in, jangling a bell on the door; then he removed his hat and took off his boots as Madame Adele hurried across the thick red carpet. She was a full-blown woman in her mid-forties, pretty, her hair piled high on her head in a curious sort of bun. She wore a brown dress that was several shades darker than her cocoa-coloured skin. Thin gold earrings dangled from her lobes.

'Mr Samson!' she exclaimed, helping the gentleman with his coat. 'I haven't seen you in months! How are you?'

Gilbert Samson smiled. He liked and admired Madame Adele, who had escaped from New Orleans ten years before to make her way to New York, where she had opened a dress shop and soon become the most fashionable Negro dress designer in the metropolis.

'Well, I'm fine,' he said. 'And you're looking fine too, Adele. Put on some weight, I see.'

'You're not supposed to mention that, Mr Samson. But it's true. I hate the winters up here. The cold and the slush make me feel sad, so I start eating. And then pop! go the buttons on the dress. Oh well, we dig our graves with our teeth.'

'That's the gloomiest thing I've heard all day. I didn't come here for gloom.'

'Of course not. You come here for beautiful dresses for your charming wife in Rochester. And how is she?'

'Well, thank you.'

Madame Adele was hanging the coat upon a brass holder. 'And the children? How are they?'

'Beautiful, spoiled, and growing an inch a month.'

'Good. Would you like a drink? I've got a brandy that will send you right up the chimney.'

'No thanks, Adele. I don't drink.'

She smacked her forehead with the palm of her hand. 'How dumb of me! I read your newspaper, I should know you've become a temperance fighter, as well as a fighter for us coloured people.' She put her hands on her hips and smiled. 'Such a fighter you are,' she said. 'I like men who are fighters . . . strong, handsome men like Gilbert Samson.'

He smiled slightly, not failing to read the signs. 'My wife, Adele. Remember?'

She sighed. 'Huh. Wish I could forget. So, how about a cup of coffee?'

'That'd be fine.'

She went into the rear of the shop, and he sat down on a red plush chair. Everything was red and gold. Big mirrors, a big brass chandelier, a big potted palm in the corner, fringe everywhere. He grinned and shook his head. Madame Adele had hit it big and wasn't afraid to show it. Well, hell, good for her. Let the Negroes make money, let them throw it around: he was all for it. In the last analysis, the only way to real acceptance was to acquire wealth, and now that slavery was legally dead – and what a thrill that night had been fifteen months before when he had been part of the great crowd in the Tremont Temple in Boston, waiting for the first flash over the electric wires of the announcement of the signing of the Emancipation Proclamation! What a cheer went up when the news finally arrived! 1 January 1863: the Black Man's Independence Day. . . . But now that slavery was gone, the fight had to be for the vote and the acquisition of black wealth, and Madame Adele was piling it up. Good for her. And her landlady, too, that stingy old witch, Annie d'Angola. She owned the whole damned block! Wonderful. Let there be a thousand black millionaires, for only then would there be a million black thousand-aires.

Madame Adele bustled back in with a delicate cup of steaming coffee.

'The best New Orleans beans!' she exclaimed. 'Ah, how I miss my New Orleans, though I don't miss the market. The slaves? Gone for ever, and good riddance, huh?'

'Amen.'

'Now: how many dresses do you want? Lots, I hope. Times are hard, and I need the business.'

'You need the business like I need another mortgage. You could buy and sell me ten times, and you know it.'

'Not so!'

'Uh huh. Now, I've got a hundred dollars to spend on my wife, so why don't you show me something pretty? And you know her size and her age, so let's not stretch credibility.'

'I have *just* the thing! Dignified, matronly, and yet *very* à la mode. You sit here and drink your coffee while I go get my mannequins. You'll be so impressed, you'll spend a fortune!'

Off she bustled again. Gilbert chuckled and sipped the coffee. Ten minutes passed. Then Madame Adele reappeared.

'Just like Monsieur Worth in Par-ee,' she announced grandly. 'Chez Adele has the live models to parade her creations! You will see the latest in cut, fabric, ornamentation. . . .'

'You give me this pitch every time, Adele.'

'I know, but it's such a good pitch, it's worth repeating. Here's the first model: Grace, wearing a fantasy in yellow silk.' A tall, thin model appeared in a handsome gown. She walked up to Gilbert Samson, smiled, then turned slowly in front of him as Madame Adele went on: 'Isn't it gorgeous? Perfect for levées or dignified teas. . . . Note the tiny roses *en velours* at the neck . . . aren't they exquisite?'

'Mm. Very nice,' said Gilbert. 'I'm not sure yellow's my wife's colour, but . . . how much?'

'A steal – a *steal* – at one hundred seventy-five dollars.'

He made a face. 'I told you a hundred . . .'

'But for *you*, the great hero of my people, I give it to you for ninety-nine ninety-five. Can you resist that? I lose money, but for you – '

'It's looking better.'

'Don't decide yet. See "Purple Twilight" first. You'll go mad, it's so beautiful. Christine?'

The second model came in wearing a purple velvet dress, the skirt of which draped and pulled back into a giant bow at the back from which the material cascaded down in thick folds to the floor. The bodice was tight, with long sleeves and a swooping neckline. But it wasn't the dress Gilbert Samson was looking at. It was the girl in it. She was, perhaps, eighteen, he couldn't tell for certain. Tall, beautifully formed, with creamy light skin and a most exquisite mouth, nose, and eyes: he had seldom seen anything so perfect. She carried herself proudly, and her big, dark eyes flashed intelligence and spirit. She was a mulatto, he knew, but then he was a mulatto. In the infinitely complex hierarchy of prejudice, he knew there was strong feeling among his people against mulattos – he had encountered it himself – in that they were half-breeds, not pure; but he thought it was, like all prejudice, asinine. The girl possessed the best of both races. He couldn't take his eyes off her as she turned slowly before him, her face a mask, but her eyes showing interest in this celebrated thirty-six-year-old man.

Madame Adele missed nothing. She smiled. 'Charming, wouldn't you say? I mean, the dress.'

'Yes, it's . . . how much?'

'For you, a hundred dollars. I have it in your wife's size.'

'Yes, I think my wife would like that. I'll take it.'

'Good. Christine?'

Christine hesitated before Gilbert. 'Could I meet Mr Samson?' she said softly. 'I'm a great admirer.'

'Of course, honey. Gilbert Samson, this is Christine Canrobert.'

Gilbert rose from the red plush chair and extended his hand. He felt the cool, soft skin of her hand in his. She smiled.

'You're a great man, sir,' she said simply. 'It's an honour to meet you. Excuse me.' And then her hand was gone and she was leaving the room.

Gilbert watched her go. Then he became aware of Madame Adele watching him. He fumbled in his coat for his cheque book.

'A beautiful girl,' he said.

'Isn't she? Do you have a pen?'

'No . . .'

'Here.'

She handed him a pen. He began writing the cheque.

'Could you believe,' she went on casually, 'that a girl that beautiful has suffered?'

'We've all suffered.'

'But with her looks! What a waste! She was in Washington for two years, and she tells me she practically starved. She has a child, you see. A baby. A white man raped her. A Quaker! Can you imagine?'

'A Quaker?'

'And then . . . but if you are interested, you should ask *her* to tell you the story. Are you interested?'

He handed her the cheque, which she waved to dry the ink. He put back the cheque book.

'Well, yes. Yes, I'm interested. I'd like to hear it.'

Again, the slight smile. 'Should I arrange perhaps . . . a supper?'

Gilbert looked her square in the eye and wondered if he should back away before it was too late.

'Perhaps that would be nice. Yes, a supper. I'm free this evening.'

'Then shall we say eight o'clock at Downing's Restaurant? Do you know it?'

'Of course. Number Three Broad Street.'

'I'll see that she's there.'

'Downing's. At eight.'

He felt rather awkward: this wasn't his style. But then, he

wasn't getting any younger, and his appetite for life was still as sharp as it had been when he was a slave – sharper, even.

With Christine, he could sniff magic.

Extracts from the Diary of Private Henry Gaynor of the Eighth Indiana Regiment:

Jan. 20, 1864. Belle Isle, Virginia. Swapped three onions for this account book with a fellow from Michigan this morning. Thought I'd try to keep a diary to fight off boredom and the blues. Is boredom or the cold the worst thing about prisons? Can't tell. This place should take several prizes if anyone was ever dumb enough to hold a Worst Prison Contest. To set the record straight, I was captured last July 3rd at Gettysburg and have been stuck in this stinking island ever since. It – the island – is in the middle of the James River, probably covers ten or twelve acres, and is right across from Richmond. The river between Richmond and the island is about a half mile across, and there's a 'long bridge' at the lower end of the island. There are about six thousand of us here, if you can imagine it, stuck in a big pen enclosed by a ditch. The dirt from the ditch was thrown up on the outside making a breastwork. The ditch is the dead-line: you go in, you get shot. Cheerful, ain't it? About half the prisoners have tents, the rest make do. Yours truly makes do. The prison is under the command of a Lieutenant Bossieux, a young Reb who talks like a Negro. His two assistants, Sergeants Hight and Marks, are bastards, even by Reb standards. We Yanks all hate their guts.

What's there to write about prisons? Good question. Well, first, the hunger. Haven't had a decent meal since my capture, and I must have lost thirty pounds at least. It's lucky I don't have a mirror: I'd probably spook myself. Then there's the dirt. Half the men here stink, and they're the *clean* ones. The other half you wouldn't get near if you could help. Amazing how some people can let themselves become pigs. Then there's the cold. Sleeping outdoors may be a lark in summer, but January? Thank God I have a blanket, which I bought from a man named Barker, or something like that. He died of dysentery a month ago.

Oh yes, there's the loneliness. I've got a bunch of pals here, but we're all lonely. Try to keep cheerful, but it's hard. Wait for news and mail. Talk about nothing but exchange, except we all know in our hearts it isn't going to happen. Still, nice to talk about it. Every once in a while, we curse old Abe for not springing us from this place, but maybe it's not his fault. They say it's Grant who's against exchanging prisoners.

And then there's the graybacks, which is what we call lice. They're everywhere, and it's jolly poking them out of your hair. Whoever wins this damn war, it's the lice who are taking over the world.

Wonderful place, Belle Isle. Lots of Southern charm.

Jan. 29, 1864. About froze to death last night. Literally. Terrible storm. They give us a few sticks of wood for fires, but it doesn't help much. Three of us huddled together through the night for warmth. Bill Hawkins is from Grand Rapids and stinks. Can think of better bed partners, and did. All night. Twenty-four men died yesterday – not unusual. They take them out, wrap them in canvas and throw them in a ditch. Wonder if they keep any records? Wonder if anyone ever tells their relatives or wives? If this stinking war *ever* ends – and sometimes I wonder if it will – I wonder how many thousands of men will rot in their graves and never be identified? Not a nice thought.

They issued some bad pork this morning and it set off a minor riot. Everyone fighting for food like wolves. A man named Starker knocked me down and took my meat. Then I think he felt ashamed and gave me back half. Better than nothing, but I'd rather have all. I've always been strong and never backed out of a fair fight, but the constant hunger has weakened me. Besides, I wouldn't want to take on Starker. He's one of the strongest men in the camp and one of the meanest, they say. A real loner. Still, he did give me back half my meat, so there must be some decency in him. Decency in this place is about as hard to come by as food.

It sleeted most of the day, and I've got a cold. It's a miracle I don't have pneumonia or worse.

Mar. 3, 1864. Rumors of exchange caused some excitement, but I think it's just rumor. They say Grant is against exchanging prisoners because the South needs its men back more than the North, and so would come out ahead in an exchange. That's all very well and good, but General Grant isn't at Belle Isle and *I* am.

Heard a man next to me abusing himself last night. Many here do it, more or less openly, but I don't. Hard not to, though. Other things go on here that disgust me, but apparently doesn't disgust them that do it. I think a lot about Jennifer and tell myself I mustn't do anything I would be ashamed to tell her *if* I ever get home and *if* she hasn't married someone else. She probably thinks I'm dead by now. They say Richmond has gotten sloppy about keeping records, notifying relatives, etc. Judging from the record-keeping at this place, I can well imagine what Richmond's like. Anyway, I've never received any mail, so I don't know if the letters I sent out get to Crawfordsville. Probably not. I guess I'm a dead man, pro tem. Odd feeling.

Thirty-two died today. Almost a record. Guess the Rebs are patting themselves on the back. The bastards.

Mar. 6, 1864. A nice day, springlike. My birthday. I'm nineteen. Happy birthday, Hank. Shit.

Mar. 7, 1864. Starker again. I got in a chuck-a-luck game this morning and won twenty cents Federal, which is worth two dollars Confederate. I knew twenty cents could buy me six nice onions from Jim the Jew – he's the sutler who comes in once a day to sell to them with money. So I headed for the gate to wait for Jim. I passed Starker's tent – he's got a nice setup for himself, one of the best in this place – and he spotted me and stopped me. Where was I going? Like a dummy, I told him. Well, then he gets very chummy and asks me in to his tent to wait. I went in. He's got cans of beans, an actual mattress, lots of wood, some books – a palace. I gaped in awe and asked him how he managed all this luxury. He grinned and said, 'From suckers like you,' at which point he grabbed my arm and jerked it behind me, twisting it till I yelped with pain. 'Give me your money,' he says. Well, I could have kicked myself for telling him I was going to the sutler's. I begged him to let me keep something, told him how hungry I was. 'We're all hungry,' says he, and sticks his hand in my pocket. Out comes the twenty cents, at which point he kicks me out of the tent.

Well, I was so hungry and so mad at myself for being took like that, I sat down on the ground and started to cry. I'm ashamed to admit it but when you're as hungry as I was, you do strange things Out he comes and looks at me scornful-like. Why am I bawling, he wants to know. I looked up at him – he's a big man, six feet at least, and strong as an ox – and sniffed and told him it must be obvious why I'm bawling. 'Because you're a goddam bully,' I said. He scowled, and for a moment I thought he was going to kick me, or worse. Instead he threw my twenty cents on the ground and went back inside his tent.

You can imagine how fast I grabbed the money and got out of there. Bought my onions and had a feast. But I can't figure

Starker out. That's twice he's played the bully and twice he's backed down. Guess he's a little crazy. We're all a little crazy in here. Law of the jungle does it to you, and this place is a jungle, for sure. Jeb Haines told me he heard Starker's been a prisoner since the beginning of the war. If that's true, I guess maybe I don't hold what he done to me against him so much. I've been a prisoner nine months and am ready to call it quits. But three years? My God.

Mar. 9, 1864. Jubilation! They're moving us out! They say to Richmond. Will find out soon.

Mar. 10, 1864. Richmond. We're penned up on the third floor of a building that used to be a tobacco warehouse. It's called the Pemberton building, and it's right opposite Libby prison, which we can see out the windows. Libby's got a bad reputation – supposed to be the worst prison in the South. Hope we're not going there, except it's for officers, so I suppose us peasants will go somewhere else. Everyone sitting around on the floor. Must be five hundred of us in one big room. A lot of griping, nothing new. Can't stick our heads out of the windows or they shoot us. Dead. The Rebs don't kid.

Mar. 12, 1864. Squeezed into a boxcar so tight I can barely write. Going south to a new prison the Rebs just opened. The stench in here frightening. Next to Starker. Asked me why I keep diary. Told him it's come to be my best friend. For some reason, he thinks that's funny. Strange bird.

Mar. 14, 1864. They've let us out of the cars for a breather and to stretch our legs. Thank God! Unimaginable conditions. Everyone crawling with lice, men sick, so cramped in cars it's unbearable. They treat us worse than cattle – they wouldn't do this to cattle. One man pushed a hole through the side of our car last night for air. The guards found out this morning, took him out, and shot him through the head. We yelled at them till they threatened to shoot all of us. Shut us up. Received a pone of cornbread apiece. Day's ration. Can't take much more of this. Even Starker looks beat. He says this is the worst he's been through, and I guess he's been through a lot. Oddly, we've sort of become half-friends on this trip. He don't talk much, but I think he's lonely like everyone else, even though he makes a point of keeping tight to himself. Fine-looking man and keeps himself as neat and clean as is possible, for which I admire him. Told me he comes from Pennsylvania and was captured at First Manassas.

Tried to get exchanged, but it never happened for him. Says he has no family or wife. Got a beard and let his hair grow down to his shouders. Says he got tired of cutting it and shaving. I said I like to shave every morning because it gives me something to do, and if I could get hold of some scissors I'd set me up a barber shop, which is what my father had in Crawfordsville, and make some money. When he heard I knew how to cut hair, he says, 'Why don't we go in business together? I can get you scissors.' 'You can?' says I. 'I can get anything,' says he, and I guess that's true, considering the style of living he had at Belle Isle. So we shook on it. Guards yelling at us to get back in the cars now. Jesus. They won't tell us where they're taking us, but Al Kemp says we're in Georgia. It's sunset.

Mar. 15, 1864. Well, we're in Georgia all right, in a place called Camp Sumter a little ways from a hole-in-the-wall called Anderson, or Andersonville, not sure which. They marched us from the train to the prison, which is big and new and doesn't look too bad, so far. Better than Belle Isle, anyway, and anything is better than the boxcars. I was so cramped I could hardly move. Felt a hundred years old. The prison isn't finished yet. There's a stockade fence around three sides of it. Pine logs twenty feet long, five feet in the ground, fifteen feet above ground. Put up by local slaves, I hear. The pen is a big rectangle, comprising about fifteen acres, and the north side is open because they haven't finished the fence. Two big guns pointing at us there, though, so no one's going to try and saunter out. Pine woods all around us, but inside the pen most of the trees have gone – cut down for the fence. We weren't in the pen two minutes before Starker's off getting wood. He don't waste time, that one. There's about 1600 of us Yankees here now, but not any shelter at all. They expect us to live in the open, like dogs. I guess Starker has different ideas. Guards on the stockade with guns.

Mar. 16, 1864. Starker is a miracle worker! He's got himself a shebang built already on the highest ground in this hole. Can you beat that! He didn't bring anything with him from Belle Isle but his books and beans – they wouldn't let him take his mattress or anything else – but he's back in business again! What's more, he asked me to move in with him! It happened this way. It started raining shortly after we got here yesterday and I was so hungry and beat from the boxcars I just said to hell with it and lay down in the mud to go to sleep. Slept sound enough till I felt someone poking his toe in my side, so I sit up to see it's morning and there's Starker. He asked why I wasn't staking out my territory, and I said it looked like I had. And he said this place was no good: it was too near the swamp, and he figures that swamp's not going to be pleasant to smell pretty soon. There's a stream that goes through the camp from west to east, and each side of it is swampy, about two acres in all. The stream's our water supply, though it's green and slimy and doesn't look very appetizing, needless to say. Plus the fact that they've built wooden privies over it at one point, so that half of it is a sewer, in effect. Well, I told him I hadn't thought of that, I was so tired. Then he pointed to his place, up on top of a rise about one hundred yards from where I was. 'I picked the best spot,' he says. 'Highest place in here. Had to knock out a few teeth to get it, but it's mine now. Want to take a look?' Sure, says I, and got up to follow him. Well, this miracle worker had got himself a shovel and tent poles and two clean blankets. He dug himself a nice rectangle, about four feet deep and six feet long by four feet wide. Then above this he pitched his blanket tent with air-space of about two feet between the ground and the bottom of his 'roof', so there'll be nice ventilation. And he got himself a new mattress (amazing!) and he made a crude stool. He's got two pans, a kettle and a crockery washbasin. He's got a sharp pair of scissors and a *mirror!* 'Jesus Christ,' I said, staring at myself for the first time in months (I've had to shave by the feel-method, which is no fun). 'Where'd you get all this stuff?' He just grinned and said he had his ways. Well, remembering his treatment of me, I have a good idea what his 'ways' are. 'Anyway,' he says, 'we've got everything we need to go in business.' 'I guess we do!' I said, examining the scissors. 'And I'll be your first customer,' says he, pulling the stool out in front of his shebang. 'If you do a good job on me, I'll be our advertisement.' I was staring at some bacon he'd fried for breakfast, and he saw me and told me to help myself. Didn't need any encouragement. He'd made coffee and gave me a cup with *sugar* in it! It was like going to heaven! Feeling fuller than I had in months, I started to work on his hair, which is yellow and thick, has a natural curl – a good head of hair. Then he told me he'd decided to take off his beard, so I cut that all off and then shaved him. By this time, we'd gathered a crowd, and when I was done, Starker stood up and looked in the mirror. 'Hey, you're good!' he said. 'I look halfway human!' Which, in fact, he did. Then he told the crowd that Starker and Gaynor's Tonsorial Emporium was open for business the price was two bits a shave and a dollar for a haircut. '*Federal*,' he added, at which point our prospective customers booed and told us to go to hell, and off they went. He just grinned and said, 'They'll be back. You'll see.' Then he asked me if I wanted to move in with him. Well, I was surprised because he had this reputation as a loner. And I said, 'If you'd like to have me, I sure wouldn't say no to the Grand Hotel.' And he laughed and said that's what we'd call it: the Grand Hotel. So I moved in, which didn't take any time, since I don't have anything to move except this diary. And here I am, living with Starker, who a couple of weeks ago robbed me twice. Life is strange.

20

'You've been making very good progress, my dear,' said Franz Liszt to Elizabeth Crandall as they sat opposite each other in the carriage on the road from Rome to Tivoli. 'I'm proud of you. But your left hand is still not as strong as it should be. You must think of each finger as an individual human being – each as strong and intelligent as the other, and all ten independent. The fourth finger of your left hand is still weak, and you must strengthen it. You've been doing the special exercise I gave you?'

'Yes, Maestro,' said Elizabeth, looking with reverence at the tall, thin man sitting across from her. His greying hair hung straight to his shoulders. His frock coat was slightly frayed – he was no longer the dandy he had been thirty years before, when he took Europe by storm – but he still had an awesome presence. And his hands, folded over each other in his lap – those magic hands, the most famous hands in the world!

'Good. You're very close to a debut, Elizabeth. Very

close. But when that happens, your technique must be so flawless that you can forget it. Let the fingers play the notes, but your soul must play the music. That is the important thing: the soul.'

And the body, he thought, as he looked at the pretty American in her violet dress, a delicate diamond necklace around her throat and diamond drops at her ears. Franz Liszt had thought about Elizabeth's body before.

'You seem distracted tonight, my dear,' he went on. 'I hope you're not nervous about meeting His Eminence? The cardinal is a charming man with an excellent chef.'

'Oh no, I'm not nervous. I'm looking forward to it.'

'But there *is* something on your mind, I think. You see, one gets to know one's pupils intimately. One hears their music, but one must learn to listen to their minds and their hearts as well. I think your heart is sad tonight. Why?'

'Well . . .' She hesitated. 'I received a letter from an old and dear friend of mine in Philadelphia. He's asked me to marry him, and I'm not sure . . . I mean, I'm very fond of him, but I don't love him.'

'I see.'

'And yet he'd be a good husband, and a good father for my son. . . . That's what's forcing me to consider his proposal. I want Ward to have a father.'

'Naturally.'

'And yet . . .'

'You don't love him.'

'I don't love him.'

'Love is not all that important in marriage. From my experience, love – intense, passionate love – only happens outside of marriage. I've been in love many times – too many for my own good – but I've never been married.'

'But I *was* married, Maestro. And I had a love that was . . . very intense and very dear to me.'

She looked out the window at the flat fields they were passing through on the way to the Villa d'Este. As always, when she thought of Lew, she had to fight back the tears. Dear God, she thought, three years and the pain is as great as ever!

'Your husband is dead, my dear,' said the maestro, watching her. 'And we are the living. We must continue to live and love and play music and change with the times, or we become dead. We must not let the dead dominate us.'

She nodded and bit her lip. 'I know. But it's difficult.'

'He must have been a fine man.'

'He was' – she gestured slightly – 'a god. At least, to me. I suppose every woman thinks that of her husband.'

The maestro smiled. 'Very few do, in my acquaintance. At any rate, God has chosen to take him from you, but God does not wish you to stop living.'

'I know you're right. And my mind tells me to accept Ben's proposal. But my heart says no.'

'Perhaps in time your heart will say yes.' He paused, then added, 'I want you to play tonight, my dear. After dinner.'

She was startled. 'But I couldn't – '

'But you must. I command it. The cardinal has an excellent piano, and his guests will be distinguished. It will be good experience for you, and good publicity for your career. Besides, it will help you to stop thinking of the past. The past is gone. Your husband is gone. Live for the present, and for you, the present is music. Give me your hands, Elizabeth.'

She held out her hands. He took them, and she felt his thumbs moving gently over her knuckles, exploring.

'Such fine piano hands,' he murmured. 'They will give the world great music. Tonight, we will put them to work!'

And to her surprise, he raised both of them to his mouth and kissed her fingers. Of course she knew his reputation. Liszt the lecher had scandalized and amused the Continent for decades. Nor had she been unaware that his kindness to her might not conceal another interest. Since moving to Rome, his interest had become more obvious, as if there were something in the Italian air that made everything more amorous and erotic.

But did he intend to try to make love to her? The idea frightened her – the idea was impossible. Not only was there Ward, there was also the maestro's mistress, the Princesse Sayn-Wittgenstein . . . no, the whole thing was out of the question. And yet . . . she had to admit that her reverence for this brilliant, kind, and generous man who was now kissing her fingertips one at a time, slowly, lovingly . . . now she had better start thinking about it. But before she could say anything, he stopped. He released her hands, and she drew them back, putting them in her lap. Neither of them said a word. They sat silently in the twilit gloom of the carriage, bumping and rattling to Tivoli.

Everything was left up in the air. The warm air of an Italian spring.

When the carriage reached Tivoli, it stopped in the small piazza beside the gate to the villa and two uniformed lackeys, holding lanterns, opened the door. Elizabeth stepped down, followed by Liszt, and they were taken by the footmen into the villa grounds. It was too dark to see the famous fountains and gardens below them, and the great fountains were turned off anyway. However, the cardinal had turned on the Hundred Fountains Alley for the entertainment of his guests, and she could hear the gentle splashing of the water below her, which added to the enchantment of the setting.

Inside the villa, they were met by their host, Cardinal von Hohenlohe, an affable, balding man whose red silk paunch advertised his gormandism. 'Maestro!' He smiled, holding out a hand with a sapphire ring.

'Your Eminence.'

Liszt knelt and kissed the hand. Then he stood up and turned to Elizabeth.

'This is my American pupil I've told you about: Mrs Crandall.'

'I am delighted to meet you at last,' said the cardinal, taking her hand and kissing it. 'The maestro has spoken of you in such glowing terms. "His American genius", he calls you. Welcome to the Villa d'Este.'

'You are kind to have invited me, Your Eminence,' she replied, curtsying.

'Shall we go inside? We have some interesting guests tonight, and a *most* interesting menu. It was written – I should say "orchestrated" – by my friend M. Dumas, whose recipes are almost as good as his novels. . . .'

He led them into the main sala of the villa. It was a long room, furnished with heavily carved gilt chairs and sofas. The walls were hung with gold-framed paintings, most of them von Hohenlohe family portraits, though some that had come with the villa were by Renaissance masters. The many candles flickered before the evening breeze that blew in through the tall windows, billowing the white lace curtains. There were around a dozen guests, most of them members of the Roman aristocracy. The cardinal led Elizabeth and the maestro around the room, introducing them, ending up before a couple standing at one of the windows.

'Monsieur le Baron de Beaupé,' said His Eminence, 'who is not from Rome, though his wife is. May I present Madame Crandall, from America?'

Elizabeth curtsied as Aristide de Beaupré kissed her hand.

'Enchanted,' he murmured.

'And Madame la Baronne . . .'

Laura de Beaupré nodded to Elizabeth, looking at her in a curious fashion.

'And I believe you both know Maestro Liszt?'

'Of course. We have met in Paris often,' said Aristide. 'It is a pleasure to see you again, Maestro.'

'And a pleasure to see you. You are looking well. And madame is, as always, lovely beyond words. May I ask what brings you to Rome?'

'My wife's mother,' said Aristide, 'is unfortunately near death. We came to Rome to be with her at the end.'

'I'm sorry to hear it, madame,' said Liszt, drinking in Laura's beauty with never jaded eyes.

'The de Beauprés will be leaving Europe soon,' said the cardinal. 'Louis Napoleon is sending them to Mexico.'

'Ah, a fascinating country, I hear,' said Liszt. 'The Archduke is on his way there now, I believe? With the Archduchess?'

'No longer an Archduke, Maestro,' corrected the cardinal. 'He is now an emperor. Emperor Maximilian of Mexico! It has a nice sound, don't you think? Though I wonder how the Mexicans will like it. But that will be your job, won't it, Aristide? To make sure the Mexicans *do* like it?'

Aristide de Beaupré took a glass of champagne from a tray held by a footman.

'I will be representing the French interests,' he said. 'And of course, our interests in Mexico are great.'

'As are our ambitions,' added Laura.

Her husband gave her a cool look. The cardinal didn't miss it. He turned to Laura. 'Do I detect a note of disapproval in your emperor's policies, madame? Don't you think the French army will bring glory to France by supporting Maximilian's throne?'

'I think the whole adventure is a colossal error,' she replied. 'And I think Louis Napoleon will live to regret it.'

'Laura,' said Aristide icily, 'you forget you are French.'

'On the contrary, Aristide, I am Italian. And when I'm in Rome, I feel free to speak the truth, for a change. Which is so refreshing.' She smiled, then turned to Elizabeth. 'Are you by any chance from Philadelphia, madame?'

Elizabeth, who was sipping the excellent champagne, put her glass down.

'Yes, I am. How did you know?'

'When my husband and I were in Washington, we met a young lieutenant from Philadelphia named Crandall. Would he be any relation?'

Elizabeth didn't answer for a moment.

'He was my husband,' she finally said.

Laura de Beaupré looked at her with astonishment.

'You are Lew Crandall's wife?'

'His widow,' corrected Liszt, watching his pupil's face. 'He was killed three years ago at the first Battle of Bull Run.'

'Yes, I read about it in the papers . . .' Laura turned to Elizabeth. 'I was at the battle. I even saw your husband for a few minutes.'

Elizabeth's face had gone dead white.

'Are you all right?' said Laura, taking her arm.

'Yes,' whispered Elizabeth. 'Perhaps I should sit down. . . .'

Laura and Liszt helped her to a chair. Elizabeth eased into

it. After a moment, she looked up and forced a smile. 'I'll be all right – really. Please don't worry. It's just that . . .'

'I know,' said Laura, pulling a chair next to her and sitting down. 'You poor thing – I shouldn't have mentioned it . . .'

'No, I'm glad you did. I want to hear. I want to hear everything. All I have of him are memories. You see, there's not even a grave.'

'They never found him?'

Elizabeth shook her head.

'No.'

'But then, isn't there a possibility he's a prisoner?'

'None. We've checked all the prisoner lists, but his name is nowhere. The Department of War has listed him as officially dead. We think that he' – she stopped, trying to keep control of herself – 'that he must have been so . . . disfigured . . .' She couldn't go on.

'I understand,' said Laura.

'And you were *there*?'

'Yes. It was a terrible day. The irony is that at noon, when I saw your husband, everyone assumed the North had won. And then, that afternoon, everything turned around . . . I remember that trying to get back to Washington was horrible! It was like a stampede . . . the Northern soldiers just threw down their arms and ran. . . .'

'Not Lew,' said Elizabeth, softly and proudly. 'You say you saw him for a few minutes?'

'Yes. Prince Napoleon and I were having a picnic, and your husband rode by. So I asked him to join us. He was starved, poor thing, and he tore at the chicken. . . .'

'Did he . . . say anything?'

Laura looked at her, remembering what Lew had said. 'I'll love you till the day I die. . . .' How *she* remembered that! And how horrible that that *had* been the day he died. But she could hardly tell the truth to this poor woman, who looked on the verge of collapse. . . .

'He said,' she replied, 'how much he missed his wife.'

Elizabeth closed her eyes, fighting back the tears. Laura put her hand on her arm.

'He was so charming,' she said. 'One of the most charming young men I have ever met.'

Elizabeth nodded, as the tears crept out of the corners of her eyes.

'Elizabeth.'

She looked up. It was the maestro.

'We are called in to dinner.'

She stood up and searched in her purse for a handkerchief.

'Thank you, madame,' she said to Laura. 'You have given me a priceless gift.'

Laura de Beaupré watched Franz Liszt lead Elizabeth Crandall into the dining room of the Villa d'Este, but she was remembering a dashing young lieutenant with blond hair. She was glad she had lied to Elizabeth – the truth would have devastated her. But she wished Lew had lived. Oh, how she wished he had lived!

The story would have been different then.

'Laura?'

It was Aristide, offering her his arm. She took it, and they headed for the dining room.

'Never,' he whispered to her, 'say the emperor is wrong. *Never*.'

Laura looked at her sixty-year-old husband.

'The emperor,' she repeated defiantly, 'is *wrong*.'

And they went into the dining room.

'You played beautifully,' said the maestro after they had climbed in the carriage and started the return trip to Rome.

'I played terribly,' said Elizabeth. She was tired. It was almost midnight, and the evening had been a strain.

'I think I'm a better judge of that than you. Admittedly, your rhythm was a little unsteady at the beginning . . . before attacking Mozart, one must always have the beat firmly in mind. But the clarity of your tone was excellent. The cardinal was *very* impressed, as was I. I really think we must start discussing your debut. It will be in Paris, of course. Conquer Paris and you conquer the world. . . .'

'Oh Maestro, don't lie to me!' she said irritably. 'Please!

I know when I play well, and tonight I was awful. My mind wasn't on the music . . . how could I think of Mozart after meeting that woman? It brought it all back to me . . . all the pain . . . It was like seeing ghosts.'

He leaned forward and took her right hand.

'There *are* no ghosts!' he insisted. 'And you're wrong to let your life be ruined by the past! It's like a curse! You moan and wail like a woman out of a tedious Greek tragedy. . . . Do you think your husband would want you to be like this? From the way you describe him, he must have loved life. He would want you to go on living. He would want you to have a *man*, not a ghost. You need a man, Elizabeth. You've lived alone too long.'

She said nothing, feeling the strength of his hand on hers. Then he released her and sat back.

'Now,' he said, 'let's discuss your debut.'

'Are you serious about that?'

'I'm always serious about music and love, the only two things that count in life. I think you will be a great success. An American, an American woman, an *attractive* American woman – the world will be at your feet. You know, it's such a spectacularly beautiful night, it seems a sin to bring it to a close yet. Are you tired?'

'Yes. Very.'

'Then you need some stimulation. We're nearing the villa of a friend of mine, Prince Cesare Albani. He has a remarkable wine cellar and some even more remarkable antique statues that I guarantee will stimulate you. Would you like to see them?'

'Yes, I suppose so. . . .'

She sounded dubious, but he pretended not to notice as he shouted directions at the driver.

'We won't stay too long, will we?' she asked. 'It's after midnight. . . .'

'We won't stay long.'

He settled back in his seat, and she said nothing more. Soon they arrived at the gates of a villa set in a small park. The gatekeeper admitted them, and they drove up to the entrance of the house. A few windows on the ground floor were lighted, and she could see by the moonlight that the building looked old and distinguished. Liszt got out, said he would see if anyone was up, and went to the door to ring. A servant answered. After saying something to him, Liszt returned to the carriage.

'The prince is awake and is delighted to receive us.'

He helped her out of the carriage, and they went into the house. The servant, who looked sleepy and not very happy about this intrusion, had lit more lamps. Liszt said something to him in Italian, and he scurried away.

'The house has an atrium,' the maestro said, taking her hand to lead her through empty rooms, 'where Cesare has put his statues. They're fascinating. Cesare's great-great-uncle was Cardinal Albani. You've heard of him?'

'No.'

'Then you'll learn something, which is always useful. The cardinal was a great collector of antiquities, and in the middle of the last century he hired the famous Winckelmann as his librarian. You've heard of Winckelmann, of course?'

'I'm afraid not.'

'Dear me, your education has holes. Winckelmann was a Prussian scholar who supervised the excavations at Pompeii and Herculaneum. He brought to light a treasure of ancient art – some of it rather risqué, I might add. But I trust you are not, shall we say, squeamish?'

He used the English word.

'Oh no,' said Elizabeth, thinking, My God, what is he going to show me?

'Good. At any rate, Cardinal Albani managed to acquire some of the choicest pieces, which, when he died, went to his brother, Cesare's great-great-grandfather. Winckelmann, poor man, was later murdered by a stableboy or cook at a hotel in Trieste, I think. Herr Winckelmann must have gotten some evil ideas from the erotic art he uncovered, for apparently he invited the stableboy up to his room, and then . . .' He shrugged. 'Ah, here we are.'

He led her through a door to an open courtyard in the centre of the house. The servant had lit two large lanterns, and she could see that the atrium was planted with lovely bushes and trees. In the centre, a fountain was playing; around it were stone benches. But it was the statues that commanded her attention. They lined the walls of the atrium: tall Roman matrons in togas, their hair frozen in fantastic stone coiffures. Dignified men, many with hands or arms or even heads missing. And then, some not so dignified men. As Liszt led her slowly around the atrium, she gazed in silence, trying not to appear shocked. There was a satyr coupling with a goat. A naked youth on top of a naked girl making stony love in the flickering lantern light. Two women locked in erotic embrace, their mouths planted against each other for eternity.

She turned away.

'I've offended you,' he said softly.

'No, really. Well, perhaps a little.' She turned again to take another look at the lesbians.

'Did they really do that?'

'They still do.'

She looked at the next statue. 'But with a *goat*?'

He laughed. 'Italians are great improvisers. So are Hungarians. Not that you're a goat.'

She felt his arm around her waist. She turned to look into his face, which was so close she could smell the brandy on his breath.

'You're very young,' he whispered, leaning his mouth toward hers. 'And very lovely.'

'Prince Albani . . .'

'He's not here. I lied. He lets me use the house. We can spend the night, if you'd like. Say you'll stay, Elizabeth. Let me be the man to exorcize your ghosts.'

He pressed his mouth against hers, and her mind raced. Was this the *quid pro quo*? He would arrange the debut if she made love with him? Possibly. Probably, even. She knew he had stopped sleeping with the Princesse Carolyne long ago, but there had been many replacements. What if she became the next mistress in the long parade? What if Ward found out? He was too young now, but later, what if someone snickered in front of him and let slip a remark about his mother and Liszt the lecher? What about Ben? She was toying with the idea of accepting his proposal. Would dear, sweet Ben want to marry a woman who had slept with a man twice her age? What about Lew? But Lew was dead, gone for ever, his body turning to dust in some unknown grave, and she had to face that horrible fact. She remembered her wedding night, how disastrously she had performed, how disappointed Lew had been. Perhaps this was an opportunity to improve. She had finally begun to enjoy sex just when Lew vanished out of her life, and since then, nothing. And now, one of the most experienced lovers in Europe was offering her a chance at graduate work. But could she live with herself?

Lew, dear Lew, she thought. But she couldn't be faithful to a ghost for ever.

Liszt moved his mouth away and looked at her rather coolly.

'You don't want to do it,' he said in a flat tone.

She smiled. 'On the contrary: I've been wondering when you'd ask.'

He looked surprised. Then he laughed. 'Americans!' he exclaimed. 'You're wonderful.'

He took her hand and led her through the house to the bedroom.

'How old are you?'

'I just turned sixteen.'

'Really? I thought you were older.'

'The life I've led, you can't waste time looking sixteen.'

Gilbert Samson and Christine Canrobert were seated at a corner table at Downing's Restaurant at 3 Broad Street. Downing's was one of the better Negro restaurants in New York, and Mr Downing, a genial man, was glowing at the presence in his establishment of the distinguished Mr Samson and the beautiful girl in her stylish green-and-white-striped taffeta dress and charming green hat. He had given them a quiet, secluded table, brought Christine a glass of champagne on the house, and recommended the Porterhouse steak, which Gilbert had ordered. Now the two were lost in conversation. Uh huh, thought Mr Downing. Gil

Samson's got a touch of the goat. And why shouldn't he? With that girl, I'll bet Father Abraham himself would sprout horns and a tail.

'Tell me about your life,' said Gilbert, admiring her. He knew Madame Adele had loaned her the dress. Not only good advertisement for her shop, but he knew she would like nothing better than to have one of her mannequins hook Gilbert Samson. Not that the girl appeared out to hook him. She seemed very cool, very mature and self-possessed, and not at all flagrantly seduceable. He wondered what the evening held in store for him.

'I was a slave,' she said. 'I was brought north by a pimp named Winkler who got killed by a white man named Crandall.'

'A drunken brawl?'

'Lew wasn't drunk. That's Mr Crandall. He was the most decent white man I've ever known. And that's why if you hadn't asked me to dinner tonight, I would have asked myself.'

'Why?'

'Because when I saw you in the shop today, it suddenly struck me that you're the one person who might be able to revenge a murder.'

Gilbert's eyes widened.

'A *murder*? Whose?'

'Lew Crandall's.' She smiled. 'I used to call him Daddy Lew. He was very handsome, and I had a terrible crush on him. He put me in a Quaker school outside Philadelphia. That's where I learned to read and write and speak well. That's also where I got my baby.'

'I understand one of the Quakers . . .?'

She nodded. 'He raped me,' she said matter-of-factly. 'I was terrified, so I ran away to Washington to try and find Daddy Lew. Except he'd been captured by the Rebs. He was an aide to General Ralph Matoon. Ever hear of him?'

'Sure. He's just been appointed to the Senate by the Governor of Pennsylvania, an old buddy of his. And he was involved in the War Department scandals at the end of sixty-one – when Simon Cameron got sent to Russia as ambassador to shut him up, or sweep him under the rug, I was never sure which. Probably both. They never pinned anything on Matoon, but I remember thinking at the time he sure smelled guilty.'

'He not only smelled guilty, he *was*.'

'How do you know?'

She leaned forward and lowered her voice.

'When I got to Washington, I went to Willard's Hotel, which was where I thought Lew was staying. They wouldn't let me in, but I got one of the slaves out front to find out if Lew was there, and he told me he'd moved to a boarding house on Third Street owned by a woman named Rosemary Fletcher. The slave said "Miss Rosemary" was well known at the hotel. She spent a lot of time there, and the gossip was that she had lovers, General Matoon included. Well, I went to Third Street, met Miss Rosemary, and found out that Lew had been captured. She was very nice to me, gave me something to eat – I was starved and didn't have any money. Then she said there was a place over the stable in the back yard I could stay in until I figured out what to do, so I accepted. I didn't care if she was a whore: she was nice to me, and I didn't know anyone in Washington.

'Well, she told me how fond she was of Lew and how upset she was that he'd been captured, and pretty soon I told her the whole story, how he'd protected me from a friend of his in Philadelphia, how he got in the fight with Winkler and killed him, and so forth. Then a few days later – it was the morning of the battle of Bull Run – she called me into her bedroom and there was General Matoon. I remember thinking there was something strange about it – not so much that he was in her bedroom in the morning, but that they were both sort of tense, as if there'd been a fight or something. Anyway, she asked me to tell the general the story about Lew and Winkler. She said the general was going to talk to Mr Lincoln to try and get Lew free. I wasn't too happy about telling Matoon, but I figured if he could help Lew, I should help him. So I told him. Then they shooed me out of the room.'

'But what's that got to do with a murder?'

'I'm getting to that. Two mornings later, after that terrible rainy day when all the soldiers came dragging back into town from the battle, I was playing in Rosemary's back yard. The sun had finally come out, and I'd been cooped up above the stable most of the day before, so I was glad to get outside. Well, I heard voices in Rosemary's bedroom – the window was open – and I recognized the general's voice. So I listened. And this is what they said – and I remember the words exactly. The general said, "Well, we don't have to worry about friend Crandall any more. I arranged for him to become one of the Glorious Dead on the battlefield." And Rosemary said, "What do you mean?" And he said, "I had Burt Thomson shoot him. Ain't no better way to shut a man up, is there? The dead don't talk about kickbacks." At which point, she must have seen me or something, because she shut the window.'

She stopped as the waiter served the first course of shrimp gumbo. When the waiter had gone, Gilbert said, 'You're sure he said "kickbacks"?'

'Positive. And I knew what it meant, too.'

'Then Crandall must have found out Matoon was taking kickbacks, and the general arranged to have him killed to shut him up.'

'What else?'

'Why didn't you go to the police?'

'I did. I was scared silly because I realized Matoon had committed murder – or at least ordered a murder – so I ran away. I didn't ever want to see that house again. I wandered around Washington the next two days, crying because Lew was dead – he really was *some* good-looking man – and trying to get up nerve to go to the police. Finally I got the nerve. Well, you can guess what happened. A thirteen-year-old darkie dressed in rags trying to get inside the *Washington* police station? They told me to git, and when I kept pestering them, they got mean. So I gave up.'

'And you've never told anyone since?'

'Who'd listen? Who'd believe? Besides, I had to keep alive. And pretty soon I realized I had a little Quaker baby inside me, which didn't help. I got a job in a laundry and had one helluva time, believe me. But I survived. You know all about survival, Mr Samson, so I don't have to tell you much on that score. Finally, six months ago, I'd had enough of Washington and came to New York with Lew. . . .'

'That's your child?'

'That's my child. You see how much I loved that man: I named my baby after him. I finally got a decent job with Adele and this afternoon I met you. And a little later I thought, "Christine, you dummy: *he's* the man to tell. *He* can do something about it." And then Adele came in the dressing room and said you wanted to take me to dinner. So now, I've told you. Can you do something about it, or is it too late? This all happened three years ago.'

Gilbert chewed the shrimp thoughtfully. 'Well, I don't know. I suppose I could try. . . .'

'Matoon committed *murder*,' said Christine softly, but with so much force Gilbert was startled. 'He murdered a man who was decent and kind to me, who got me in a school – and I don't give a damn if I *did* get raped, which wasn't in the curriculum. The point is, he helped me and he was murdered by that fat bastard, and Matoon shouldn't get away with it. You're an important man, Mr Samson. You know President Lincoln and people will listen to you, even if you are coloured. You've helped all of us, for which we owe you a lot. But you've got a lot of enemies – we all do. Now, what if you went to bat for a *white* man? Oh sure, he's dead. But wouldn't it shut your enemies up if you tried to avenge a *white* man's murder?'

Gilbert looked at her with increased respect.

'You know, you're a very intelligent young lady.'

'And a determined one.'

'So I see.' He hesitated, then added, 'And a very beautiful young lady, too.'

'I know it,' she said bluntly. 'It's the one weapon I've got in this crazy world. And if I've got to use that to get you to go after Matoon . . . well, Mr Samson, with you it would be a pleasure.'

Gilbert looked at her.

'My name's Gilbert.'

'Hello, Gilbert.' She smiled.

He reached out and took her hand. 'You don't have to bribe me,' he said. 'I'm against selling bodies, remember?'

'I'm not selling. I'm giving.'

'Nevertheless, that isn't the way I operate. I'll go after your General Matoon. I'll have to think a bit about how to go about it, but it might be sort of fascinating to pin the scoundrel down. But I'll do it because I like you, not because I want you.'

He released her hand as the waiter removed the shrimp and put down the steaks. As he carved into the juicy, rare Porterhouse, he looked up and added, 'But I *do* want you.'

She said nothing.

He took her to the hotel on Twenty-fourth Street and Eighth Avenue where he had rented a room. During the ride up-town in the cab, he held her hand, but neither of them spoke as their bodies began to become acquainted. When they arrived at the hotel, which was named the North Star (Gilbert liked that) and catered to 'coloureds', he led her into the lobby and received his room key from the night clerk, who gave Christine an admiring inspection. He said nothing, though, except, 'Good evening, Mr Samson.'

They climbed the stairs with their frayed carpeting to the second floor, where they walked down a dim hall to Room 3. Gilbert put the key in the door, saying, 'This isn't the Astor House, but it's clean.'

He went into the room and lit the lamp by the bed. Christine followed him inside, looking around. The place was plainly furnished, with cheap flowered wallpaper. The only object of interest was a large, framed photograph of Gilbert Samson. She pointed at it and laughed.

'You!'

'Me,' he admitted, closing and locking the door.

'Did you hang it?'

He was taking off his wet overcoat. 'Now honey, let's get a few things straight right at the beginning. I'm not the shyest man in America by a long shot, but I don't travel around the country carrying pictures of myself to hang on hotel walls. It so happens the owner of this place not only respects me but has decided to cash in on me by hanging my picture in the expensive rooms. He thinks it gives a little tone to the place. . . .'

'It does.' She was removing her hat and shawl.

'Well, I don't know about that. But the point is, he gives me a discount when I stay here in return for using my face. And with my financial condition, I need all the discounts I can get.' He came over to her and put his hands on her arms. 'Did I tell you you're beautiful?'

'I think so . . . I can't remember.'

'Liar. Well, you are. Beautiful . . .'

He put his mouth against hers, and they kissed a while. Gently, lazily, their mouths becoming acquainted.

'Adele's going to be very unhappy with me,' she whispered, 'if I mess up this dress.'

'Then you better take it off.'

He helped unbutton her. Then he went to a chair in the corner and sat down to remove his shoes as he watched her undress. In the soft light of the oil lamp, her skin looked even lovelier as she stepped out of the green and white dress and then, in a white undergarment, carefully folded the gown over a chair. She turned to look at him, to smile at him. Gilbert Samson remembered a long-ago dream of long-ago Gabriel Pembroke, a young slave's dream of a woman. The dream was standing across the room from him. The dream raised her thin, graceful arms and unpinned her hair, which fell over her shoulders in a soft black cloud. Then the dream reached behind her back to unbutton her undergarment. He watched as she stepped out of it and dropped it on the floor. The dream was naked now, the oil lamp casting its light on her side, warming the splendour of the flesh. She came across the room to him, moving with a natural elegance. Then she was standing in front of him, running her fingers through his thick hair. Gilbert slowly placed his hands on her waist, his eyes drinking in the satin belly, the lovely breasts. He pulled her to him, burying his face in the flesh of her belly, kissing her.

'It's not fair *me* being naked and you with your clothes

on,' she said, loving the feel of his kisses on her skin.

He released her reluctantly and got up to take off his clothes. She watched, admiring his powerful shoulders, his smooth, broad chest, his rippled belly, his slim hips, his muscled thighs and legs.

'You're some hunk of man,' she said.

'You're some hunk of woman.'

They came to each other in the middle of the room, and flesh kissed flesh. Breasts met chest, belly met belly, thighs met thighs. She smelled sweet; he was musky and warm.

'God, you're lovely,' he murmured, kissing her ears, her neck, her throat. Then he got down on his knees, his arms hugging her legs, and kissed his way up and down her thighs, her stomach, finally burying his face in her vagina and kissing it. He wanted to devour her. She stood silently, her hands on his shoulders, her head tilted slightly back, her eyes closed, her mouth slightly open and slightly smiling.

After a while, he stood up. His big penis was gorged with blood, white blood and black blood. She looked at it. Then she put her hand to her mouth and spat in her palm. She spat again until there was a little pool of warm saliva. She reached down and took his penis, slicking it slowly.

'Jesus,' he whispered.

They didn't use the bed. They did it on the floor, in the middle of the room. On the old hooked rug, the knots of which bumped her back slightly. They did it, and it was supremely beautiful, supremely sweet.

The second time, they used the bed.

'Do you want to talk about your wife?'

'Not particularly.'

They were lying next to each other in the bed. It was after love. The lamp was out, the room dark. Outside, the storm, which had dozed during dinner, woke up again and began lashing the windowpanes. Twenty-fourth Street slept.

'Do you love her?' she asked.

'Yes. She's a good woman. A good wife and a good mother. But I don't want to talk about her now. I'm feeling too happy, and I don't want to feel guilty. I'll feel guilty tomorrow.'

She smiled, ran her finger slowly around his nipple, and changed the subject.

'Why are you in New York?'

'Why does anyone come to New York? I'm looking for money.'

'You? Why do you need money?'

'You wouldn't be interested.'

'Try me.'

'All right. It's simple arithmetic. It costs us six cents to print and distribute each copy of the newspaper. We make two cents per copy from advertising, and we sell the paper for five cents. Net profit, one cent. Our circulation is about thirty thousand. That gives us a weekly profit of three hundred dollars, half of which goes to repay the initial investment and interest charges. That leaves me a hundred and fifty dollars a week net profit, which I keep.'

'That's not bad.'

'It's not good. I not only have my personal expenses, but that's the only money I've got to expand the paper. And I've *got* to expand it.'

'Why?'

'Are you really interested in this?'

'I am. Really.'

'Well, *The Freedman's Weekly* was founded by Abolitionists and it thrived on the Abolitionist movement. But now that slavery's been abolished, there's no more movement. I'm a crusader without a crusade. The white Abolitionists don't read my paper any more. They're on to other things, like currency reform and temperance. That's one reason I took up temperance – I not only believe in it, but I've got to beat the drums for something.'

'What about your coloured readers? And what about the coloured vote? You could beat the drums for that.'

'Don't think I'm not. But it doesn't excite the whites like Abolition did. It excites the politicians because they see a new power base, a lot of new votes. But the general public? Slavery was dramatic – hot. Votes for Negroes? Well, yes, they want it. Sort of. A lot of Northern whites are beginning to have second thoughts about us now that we're free and beginning to move into the white labour market. And as far as my Negro readers are concerned, the paper never depended on them. How many Negroes can read? How many Negroes can afford a nickel for a newspaper? So I'm in New York looking for money. Except so far I haven't found any.'

She sat up.

'But you're a very famous man! You shouldn't have to beg!'

'Honey, fame comes and goes. Mine came fast, and now it's going slow. The North is tired of slaves and sick of this war. No one wants to listen to Gilbert Samson any more. I used to bring in a lot of extra money from lecture fees, which is what kept my family going easy. Last year, I made only four hundred dollars. The Emancipation Proclamation set us all free, but it wrecked hell out of my income.'

She ran her hand slowly over his belly.

'If you do raise the money here, what do you plan to do with it?'

'Move the paper from Rochester to Washington. The money's in New York, but the power's in Washington. If I can have a base there, I can try to use the freemen to influence the politicians – fight for the vote, and so on. Men like Thaddeus Stevens – he's for the vote – and Stanton – he's for it, sort of. Stanton's for everything sort of, except his own power, and he's for that all the way. Anyway, if I can operate out of Washington I think I can not only survive but be more useful for our people. God knows, there's still lots to fight for.' He reached his hand over and put it on her cheek. 'Now you know all about me, and I don't know much about you. Do you have a man?'

'Yes. He's a white sailor.'

'He's a lucky white sailor. Where do you live?'

'Well, till I got the job with Adele, I lived over east of the Five Points, which was a *hole*.'

'Were you there during the draft riots last summer?'

'No, thank God. I was still in Washington. I'm not sorry

I missed the riots. But now I've got two rooms down on Thompson Street, in the Village. Want to see them? My sailor's away, and I'd like you to meet my son.'

He rubbed her cheek.

'I'd like to meet him, too.'

'Then how about tomorrow evening at seven? I'll cook you supper. Number two-o-seven Thompson Street, the top floor.'

'I'll be there.'

He pulled her into his arms and kissed her.

'I'm crazy about you, Christine,' he whispered.

She felt his penis growing, pushing against her thigh.

'Gilbert,' she said, 'if I don't get some sleep, Adele's going to have a very doggy-looking mannequin tomorrow.'

'Some dog,' he said as she extricated herself from his arms and turned over on her side. He watched her go to sleep. And the rain whipped against the windowpanes.

He took a cab to Washington Square, then got out to walk the rest of the way. A warm spring day had followed the storm, and well-dressed couples were strolling in the fashionable square. Some of them noticed the handsome Negro in the gaslight, the Negro dressed like a gentleman, and whispered to each other. He was used to it. Whether they recognized him as Gilbert Samson or not, they whispered. A Negro gentleman was a freak.

He walked to Thompson Street, then started south toward number 207. Here, the fashion rapidly vanished, to be replaced by the north-ebbing tide of poverty. Irish, mostly, with pockets of Negroes, flint and steel rubbing together to create sparks of hatred and bigotry. Still, he reflected, Christine was vastly better off here than in the notorious Five Points, the worst section of the city, 'Satan's Kitchen' as it was called, an area near the Bowery that festered with crime, drunkenness, male and female prostitution, the cruellest poverty and unimaginable living conditions. He had heard of twenty Negroes living in a roach- and rat-infested basement. Murder was too common to attract attention. Gangs of toughs carved out their territories and fought each other, and everyone else, to the death. The Dead Rabbits, the Bowery Boys, the Plug Uglies, the Shirt Tails, the True Blue Americans, the O'Connell Guards. The previous July, the gangs had joined the rest of the working class to go on a rampage of violence, protesting the draft. The eruption had turned into a race riot, and dozens of Negroes were hanged from lamp posts, some being slashed with knives as they twisted from their nooses, the rioting women then pouring oil into the knife wounds and setting fire to the corpses. It was indeed lucky, he reflected, that Christine had not been in Five Points then.

He made his way through the crowded street to number 207. It was a four-storey tenement, not dissimilar to the other buildings in the block. A Negro man was sitting on the stoop. When he saw Gilbert Samson, he gaped with recognition and stared.

'Good evening,' said Gilbert as he passed into the narrow hall. The man said nothing. He just stared.

Gilbert climbed to the top floor and knocked on the peeling painted door. After a moment, Christine opened it. He removed his top hat.

'Hello,' he said.

'You're right on time. Come in.'

He came into a small room that smelled of frying pork chops. He looked around as she closed the door. Two clean windows, overlooking Thompson Street, pretty white curtains tacked over them. A bare floor, but a clean one. A sagging bed that she had covered with a handsewn white and yellow quilt. A chair, an oil lamp, a china basin on a stand. A small table in the middle of the room, set for two with wooden plates and tin forks and knives. A highchair in another corner with a two-and-a-half-year-old in it, his skin almost white, his buttoned suit blue. On the walls were tacked cut-out fashion drawings from *Harper's Weekly*, *Godey's Lady's Book*, and other periodicals. Grand white ladies, stiffly posed in grand tinted gowns, somehow not so wildly improbable in these ungrand surroundings as he might have expected.

'I like it,' said Gilbert as she took his hat and coat.

'"It's not the Astor House" – ' she began . . .

'" – but it's clean",' he finished with a grin. 'And this is Lew?'

'That's Lew.'

He went over to the highchair and took the boy out, holding him high.

'Some good-looking boy!' he exclaimed.

'The father wasn't much,' dead-panned Christine, 'but the mother's a knockout.'

'Don't I know it! Does he talk?'

'Not much. It's the white part of him that's slow. The black side's gabby as hell.'

Gilbert laughed and kissed the boy. Then he put him back in his chair and turned back to Christine.

'Is that pork chops I'm smelling?'

'It's not chitlin's. Best pork I could buy. I spent a fortune on it, so you'd better like it.'

'Don't worry. I really like your place.' He looked at her. She had on a simple gingham house dress, not one of Madame Adele's high-fashion concoctions. 'And I really like you. I think I like you better in that thing than Adele's extravaganza.'

'That's because now you know what's underneath.' She winked. 'So you're not so interested in the window dressing.'

'I never was.'

'Don't say that: you'll put Adele out of business – *and* me. Sit down while I get dinner on the table.'

She went into the kitchen. He took the one chair and leaned back, wiggling his finger at Lew. 'I've figured out what to do for your Daddy Lew – what was his last name?'

'Crandall,' she called in from the kitchen.

'That's it. I'm going to Washington next week. I'll get an appointment with Mr Stanton, the Secretary of War. He's a bastard, but I think he's pretty honest. I'll see if he'll let me look through the files. Maybe I can find something on Matoon the investigators overlooked.'

'Do you think Stanton would let you in the files?'

'Don't know, but it's worth a try. Of course, Matoon's a Republican senator now, which doesn't make things easier.

But we'll see.' He looked around the room again. 'What's your sailor's name?'

'Jim. He's a bosun's mate.'

'Do you like him?'

'He's nice when he's sober.'

'I don't drink.'

She appeared in the doorway, holding a pan of steaming noodles.

'What's that mean?'

'What do you think?'

She looked at him, stirring the noodles slowly with a wooden spoon.

An hour later, they were naked in the small bed, the lamp out, he on top, thrusting into her. He came, then slowly relaxed, his mouth on her neck. She ran her cool hands over the small of his back.

'I love you, Christine,' he whispered.

'Bet you say that to all the girls.'

'Haven't been any girls. Just my wife.'

'Am I supposed to believe that?'

'It's true.' He rolled off her and banged his bare buttocks against the horsehair plaster wall.

'God*dam*. This bed's too small.'

'That's what Jim says.'

'I'll buy you a bigger one if you get rid of Jim.'

'Thought you were broke?'

'I can afford a bed.'

She thought about this. 'Are you serious?'

'I'm serious. I love you, Christine. I can't marry you, obviously, but . . . I want you for myself. I had a hard life when I was young. . . .'

'Who didn't?'

'True. But anyway, I'm thirty-six now, and I think I've earned a luxury. You're the luxury I want, Christine. I like your pork chops, I like your flat, I like your baby . . . and I'm *crazy* about you.'

'Mm. You said that last night.'

'I mean it.'

She reached her hand over and put her fingers on his mouth.

'Know something?' she whispered. 'I'm crazy about you, Gilbert Samson.'

21

Extracts from the diary of Private Henry Gaynor:

June 3, 1864. Andersonville. Starker's a strange bird, and hardly the confiding type. I've been living with him almost three months now and still don't know much about him. Oh, I've figured out a few things, and he's told me some. I figured he's educated from the way he talks, and he allowed as how he went to college, though he won't say where. His books tell something. He's got a dozen, including *The Conquest of Peru*, which he loves, and a book in French by a writer named Stendhal. Starker translated the title as *The Charterhouse of Parma*. When I asked him where he learned to read French, he told me he took it in college. Says he traded the book from a Frenchie at Belle Isle for a hairbrush he'd stolen from one of the guards. Funny how he operates, now that he's not operating on me. He must have got shot somewhere along the line, because he's got a scar high up on his chest, but when I asked him about it he just shrugged and said 'Bull Run' like he didn't want to talk about it. He's a cheerful enough fellow (and being cheerful *here* is no mean trick) but sure not one for casual jawing. I get the feeling he's under some threat of danger. Well, we *all* are. But his is a special kind of danger. Wish I knew what it was.

The danger business was sort of pointed out yesterday, when he came running into the shebang, all excited. He deals a lot with

Dyson, the breadwagon driver, who's one of the few that comes in and out of the stockade on a regular basis and has become a sutler on the sly. Well, Starker had just come from Dyson, and he had something wrapped in brown paper. He sits down on the ground and tears off the wrapping while I'm watching. Then he holds up this book like it was the Holy Grail. Except it wasn't a book of words, but a book of music. 'I've been trying to get this for three years,' he says, 'but the goddam Southerners just aren't musical. Dyson got this from Doc Blaine's wife's niece in Marietta, who plays the piano. Cost me three dollars Federal.' 'Three *Federal?*' gasps I. That's a fortune. 'What's worth three Federal?' 'The Chopin études,' he says, flipping through the pages, which were covered with notes. 'You going to give us a recital?' says I, thinking he's gone loonie for sure. Many do in here. 'Ah, Hank my friend,' says he, going for his pencil, 'music hath charms to soothe the savage censor.' Then he sits down Indian-style on the ground and starts writing with the pencil over the notes. Well, I go about my chores – yesterday was laundry day (what a laugh: me and Starker only got three shirts between us, and number three's the spare, waiting for number one or two to die), and while I'm working he's scribbling away. The censors read everything coming in or going out of here, so I figure it's some sort of weird code he's worked out with someone. He works on it for almost two hours. Then finally he gets out a box of Niagara Falls stationery he stole from one of the guards in Belle Isle (he really had a field day with those guards). Now, I've seen stationery before, but know he's never used it. Never writes *anyone*. Well, now he starts writing a letter. Except – and here's the loonie part – it was all musical notes! I looked over his shoulder at this wonder – it was B♭ D F♯, stuff like that – and I said, 'Heat's finally gotten to you, hasn't it?' And he laughed and allowed as how it had. Then he folded the letter and addressed the envelope – in English: I saw that much, though he wouldn't let me see the name, and I sure tried to look – then off he runs to put it in the mail basket. When he comes back, he walks outside, pacing back and forth real nervous, for almost an hour. Strange bird. Wonder what danger he's in.

June 6, 1864. Learned more about Starker. Things have gotten so bad in this hellhole – there's twenty-three thousand Federal prisoners now with more coming each day, and the heat and stench from the swamp is just about more than a person can stand – that yesterday afternoon Starker took off from our shebang and got a bottle of pinetop. 'Come on,' says he when he returned, 'let's get drunk and forget this place for a while.' Well, I was surprised, because although Starker's a fantastic provider by Andersonville standards, he's never gotten any booze since I've known him, and I was under the impression he wasn't a drinking man. But yesterday was different. It rained cats and dogs all morning, then out pops the sun at noon to bake everything into a steamy mess and of course the damned fence keeps out any hope of a breeze, so I decided Starker had a good idea. I'm told people can smell Andersonville twenty miles away, so being right *in* it is no fun. Anyway, we crawled into our shebang to get out of the sun and he passed the bottle. Jesus, that stuff can blow the top of your head off, and I'm not feeling like much today. But it was worth it, because the booze loosened him up and for once he started talking.

Well, we talked about women for a while, which we've done plenty, and he said how hard it was for a man to be penned away from the opposite sex for so long. He apologized for abusing himself every once in a while and said he tried to keep it to a minimum but if he didn't he'd just have wet dreams, and I shrugged and said something dumb like, 'That's life,' which made him laugh. I can remember the day when such talk would have made me turn red to my toes, but in this place you get awful basic awful fast. Then he told me why he asked me to move in with him, which I've often wondered about. He said he was impressed with my keeping a diary. Said he'd been in five Reb prisons since '61, and never yet met a man with the brains to keep a diary, which he said some day would be worth something. I said I wasn't much of a writer, but I agreed it was worth the trouble. Then he said, 'Well, it hasn't worked out bad, has it? You bring in the money from the barbershop and I bring in the supplies.' 'Oh,' says I, 'it's worked out grand.' I didn't mention the fact that I also do all the washing and clean the pans and shave him every day and am a sort of general lackey at the Grand Hotel, but what the hell, I've gotten used to it. Besides, Starker keeps the Raiders away, and the way those bastards are running around this place knocking people's brains out – well, all I can say is, thank God for Starker. But I think another reason he *didn't* mention for asking me to move in is that he doesn't mind having a houseboy. Something tells me Mr Starker likes someone waiting on him. I've often had the feeling he comes from money, not that he's a snob or anything – who could be a snob in here? – but just little things. Like sort of *expecting* me to bring him the coffee. Like I said, it burned me for a while, but I've gotten used to it. And he *does* bring in the groceries.

Anyway, we were both getting pretty high on that mule piss, so I asked him if he'd ever tried to escape from any of the prisons and he laughed and said he was an expert on escape, he'd tried it so much, except he couldn't qualify *too* much as an expert, since he's still here. 'I've dug so many tunnels I feel like a mole,' he said. I asked him what happened when he got caught and he said, 'Oh Christ, the works. One time they put me on a chain gang for three months. Another time I got the stocks and a whipping – the Rebs are crazy about whipping. Guess that's one reason they hate to give up slavery. Let's see: another time I got privy detail for a month. That was charming. Ever clean privies?' I said no. 'Well, it's an experience. Not one I'd recommend, but an experience. What else? Oh yes. The last time I almost made it. That was at a camp in Tennessee. They transferred a bunch of us out there to help lay rail lines. Well, I sure as hell didn't like helping the Rebs, so I managed to break my leg irons with a rock and took off. I *almost* made it. I came *so* close.' 'What happened?' 'The dogs caught me. Bloodhounds. Christ, I felt like Liza crossing the ice. They dragged me back and threw me in a hotbox for a week. It was so hot I thought I'd go crazy. And I told myself if I ever got out of that one alive, I was going to make it through to the end. And I got out. One thing about being a prisoner, it forces you to be tough. Three years ago, if someone had told me what I'd be going through, I would have laughed in his face, and I sure as hell wouldn't have thought I could make it. But I've made it. At least, so far.'

I asked him if he'd come up with a way to escape out of here, and he said his first idea was to try and sit out the end of the war, which can't be too far off, he figures. But things have got so bad here and likely to get worse, that he's been having second thoughts. Lots of men are digging tunnels, but he doesn't put much stock in their chances – have to dig too far to get out. So he wouldn't try a tunnel. But he's putting his mind to work on a way.

Then we jawed a while about the dysentery and the rickets and how the dead-count keeps climbing, which is a big topic of conversation in this hole (the death rate's currently about 120 a day). Then he drank some more and said the whole idea of getting drunk was to forget Andersonville, and let's talk about something else. So I asked him again about the scar on his chest.

Well, for a moment I thought he was going to clam up again. But then he must have changed his mind. 'Well,' he said, 'I guess

I blew all my luck for the rest of my life. The man was standing not more than ten feet away, and he aimed point-blank at my heart. And he missed. I don't know if he was a rotten shot, or something was wrong with his gun, but he missed. The bullet went in just above my collar bone and took off the top of my lung. But he didn't kill me, the bastard.'

I said something like those Rebs couldn't shoot an elephant at three paces, and he said, 'Well, Hank, my boy, believe it or not, he wasn't a Reb.'

'Well then, who was it?' says I, not a little surprised. And his eyes narrowed down and his face went cold, and I can tell you the look on him sent a chill up and down my spine.

'A fat son of a bitch,' says he, 'whom some day I'm going to pay back. And that's what keeps me going.'

All I know is, if Starker ever gets free, the fat gentleman in question better not sleep too sound. I have no doubt but that my friend means business.

Anyway, he explained that a slave came on the battlefield to steal money from the corpses and started working on him. 'I had been unconscious,' he said, 'but I became aware of someone going through my pockets. Well, it so happened he was wasting his time, because I didn't have a wallet or a watch or anything. But I tried to say something and the darkie let out a yip – I must have scared him out of ten years' growth. Then I passed out again, but the slave got me to help, because when I came to I was in a Richmond hospital and a Rebel nurse was looking at me. And she said, "Son, you have no business being alive," and I suppose she was right. Then my lung got infected, and it was one hell of a time before they managed to patch me up.'

'Does the lung work now?'

'Oh yes. The doctor told me the top of it was gone, but it would grow back, and it did. I'm telling you, I blew all my luck. That's why I never got exchanged. That's why I never escaped. I'm still paying off the Luck God.'

'Maybe you're too mean to die,' I said, swigging some more pinetop. He looked at me, sort of amused-like.

'Do you think I'm mean?' says he.

'Well, when I first met you, I thought you were one mean customer. You still are, far as that goes, but at least I'm on your team now.'

'I suppose I'm not exactly a gentleman in this place, but I don't think gentlemen would last too long in Andersonville. But I've never killed anyone in here.'

'I'm glad to hear it,' says I, with a gulp.

Then he leaned forward and got sort of mysterious.

'Don't you think it would be easy to kill in here?' he says.

'I know it would be. The Rebs do it all the time.'

'I'm not talking about the Rebs or the Raiders. But say you were on the outside – up North, even – and you knew there was someone in here you wanted killed. Don't you think it would be easy to send someone through the lines with a Letter of Passage? And he comes down here and pays off one of the guards? Or maybe one of the new prisoners coming in here every day?'

'Pays them off to do what?'

'To come in here and murder! It'd be the simplest thing in the world. That's why I've been a loner all these years. That's why I'm suspicious. Life in here is cheap, Hank. Hell, an onion's worth more.'

He leaned back. I lowered my voice, not knowing why.

'Is somebody out to kill *you?*'

He grinned and said, 'Well, they tried it once. If they knew I was down here, I'm damn sure they'd try it twice – and do a better job of it. Want to pass the pinetop?' At which point, we started singing dumb songs because by now we were pretty sloshed. And I don't remember much more of the afternoon, because pretty soon it was lights out for Yrs. Truly. But I remember what Starker told me. An interesting man.

June 14, 1864. Unbearably hot. The stench of the swamp foul beyond description or imagination. A man killed last night by the sentries. He crawled past the dead-line to try and get some fresh water from the stream. Before the stream enters this hole it's clear. When it leaves, it's a sewer. Sentry shot him through the head.

This morning they brought in six hundred new prisoners. Starker and I watched as the Raiders jumped them – they were hardly through the gate. Poor bastards. The Raiders are mostly toughs from New York who have turned into animals in this place. Well, they jumped the new prisoners – the sentries watching all the while, but not doing anything to stop the brawl, mainly because they're afraid to come inside the stockade – and started beating them, tearing their clothes off, taking whatever they could to barter later on. Horrible to watch. New prisoners so surprised at this reception from their 'comrades in arms' they put up little resistance. I saw one man get his face smashed in. He was stripped naked and left in the mud, where he died about an hour later. Couldn't have been more than twenty or so. It's like a lunatic asylum in here.

Food rations down to almost nothing now. Mostly cornbread that gives you the runs. Even Starker and I are starving. Starker is worried. He says Captain Wirz is either a fool or a madman to allow these conditions. Captain Wirz is the commandant of the prison – most of us call him the 'Dutchman' because he's got a bad German accent, but actually I think he's Swiss. From the few times I've seen him, I'd say he's a madman, not a fool, and mean to boot. Starker says he's a sadist, which I wasn't sure what it meant until he explained. Says he ran into a Reb captain who once tortured him with a lighted cigar (my God!), and Wirz reminds him of that captain. Well, if it's true, Wirz must be the happiest sadist in the world, because this prison is one big torture chamber. Anyway, Starker says by August no one may be alive. Dysentery and rickets taking a dreadful toll. I see men with black gums, their teeth rotting, sores all over them. Hate to think of that happening to me, but it's possible, and my mouth has been sore lately. I think the reason we've both kept our health – if we have, and if being skin and bones can be called 'healthy' – is because of Starker's provisioning. But now the barbershop is doing rotten business, since money is tight. We've cut our prices, but still nothing. Besides, no one cares any more what they look like. Everyone turning into animals. I still try to shave every day or so, and so does Starker, and we both try to wash our clothes at least once a week. But our uniforms are practically rags now.

It's so hot you get to hate the sun. Lice everywhere. Billions of them. Hell must be a letdown after this place.

June 18, 1864. Witnessed a double hanging this morning. Two men went crazy last night and went on a rampage. They knifed a man to death and cut up another badly. They were caught by a bunch of prisoners, Starker one of them, who delivered them to the gates to the Rebs. Starker said he hated doing it, but since the Rebs won't police the inside of the stockade, we prisoners have to start to do something to protect ourselves from the Raiders and maniacs. Anyway, this morning about eight, the gates open and in marches a squad of Rebs armed to the teeth. Well, we all know what that means, because the only time the Rebs come in here is for a hanging or a whipping. The squad was under the command of a Captain Wells, and he marches it over to Punishment Square, the two prisoners in the middle with their hands tied in back. The captain starts checking over the gallows, so we know what to expect. The two prisoners were named Munn and Jackson – Munn a Marine from Vermont, Jackson a big ape of a man from Ohio, I think – and they were yelling that they were innocent and really carrying on. In a way, they *were* innocent. After all, if this place were run like a decent prison instead of a madhouse, they wouldn't have gone loonie. A big crowd gathered to watch, including me and Starker. I've been feeling so weak lately, I haven't been out of the shebang much, but I wanted to see this – guess I'm a ghoul. Captain Wells was satisfied the gallows was working, so he orders the men to bring the prisoners up. And then Jackson, the big ape, let out a howl and broke right through the Rebs, starting to run for the swamp. Great deal of confusion. Jackson goes right in the swamp, up to his neck. Knowing what's in there, he really must have been crazy. He stays in there a few minutes, then starts to back out, as if he knew the game was up. The Rebs caught him and dragged him back to the gallows. He was all slimy and covered with filth, but he was quiet now. They started preparing the nooses, and the crowd shut up, all watching, everyone thinking their own thoughts.

Then, up on the sentry walk, appears Captain Wirz himself. He's a tall, thin man with slight stoop who wears a lot of jewelry – long watchchains, rings, things like that, like some cheap dandy. When we saw him, everyone looks up, glaring at the source of all our misery. Wirz looks back, calm as can be. 'The bastard,' muttered Starker, who was standing next to me. About summed up everyone's thoughts, I'd say.

They hanged Jackson, who kicked a while, then stopped. They cut him down, and then it was Munn's turn. He was a good-looking man in the prime of life, and he stood there, brave enough as they put the noose around his neck. But just before they sprung the trap, he turned and yelled up to the commandant, who was above him, watching, 'Wirz, you suck pigs!'

Well, such a hooting and laughing went up as I've never heard in any theater. And that's what Munn went out of this life hearing because then they dropped him. Sudden silence, as we watched death doing its job. Then the laughter turned to anger. Starker next to me cupped his hands around his mouth and started chanting, 'Wirz! Wirz! Wirz!' Right away, everyone took it up. We all stood there, looking up at the sentry walk, yelling, 'Wirz, Wirz, Wirz!' over and over again – and there must have been at least three thousand there. It was a sound I'll never forget. Wirz watched this a while, then said something to one of this aides, who signaled the sentries. They started firing over our heads, but that didn't stop us. So Wirz whispers something again, and the aide signals the sentries again. And now, they started firing at us – right into the crowd! About three or four men were hit, and the rest of us start running. Pandemonium, people tripping over each other . . . Starker and I reach our shebang, out of breath. Starker furious. 'Munn was right,' he said. 'Wirz sucks pigs.' And I say to that, Amen. Feel sorry for the pig, though.

June 27, 1864. I've had the runs for two days straight. It scares me, because dysentery's the big killer here. I told Starker, but he pooh-poohed it. 'Just lack of decent food,' says he, but I think he was lying again to keep my spirits up, and after all, what causes the dysentery? Lack of decent food. Oh God, if I *do* have it . . . but I'm not going to think that. Starker was gone the entire afternoon to try to find some grub, but he came back an hour ago with nothing but some maggoty beans. He gave them all to me – said he'd already eaten, but that's another lie. I know he's as hungry as I am, and that's *hungry*. I ate a spoonful of the beans and threw them right up. Feeling rotten. Force myself to write but it's hard.

June 29, 1864. Starker talks about women, but never a *woman*, though I've told him all about Jennifer – practically talked him to death about her. But as things have gotten unbearable around here, he's started tossing a lot in his sleep, enough to keep me awake. Last night he was thrashing all over the place, and he started saying a name over and over again. Finally, he shut up. But I figured this was a clue to this mystery man, so this morning I asked him, 'Who's Laura?' Well, he looked sort of dumbfounded. 'What do you mean?' says he. 'Last night you kept saying "Laura" over and over again in your sleep. I figured you must have known a Laura somewhere along the line.' The mystery man clammed up. 'Never knew anyone named Laura,' says he. End of conversation. But he's lying. Something terrible must have happened to him, because the bitterness sweats right out of him at times. Then, at other times, he's cheerful enough. Interesting, baffling man. To my surprise, I've grown fond of him. God knows I ought to, as he's keeping me alive.

July 4, 1864. Happy Fourth of July. Wonder if they're lighting fireworks in Crawfordsville? Seems like another world, now, hardly real, even. Starker asked me if he could read this diary. 'It'd bore you,' I said. 'No it wouldn't,' he says. 'I'd really like to read it. I admire a man who can write.' 'Well,' says I, 'I don't know if you can call this writing. It's just scribbles. But I guess if you want to, go ahead.' I was a little nervous about giving it to him because of the things I've put down about him, but anyway he takes it and starts reading. I watched him, wondering what he'd say. Sometimes he'd sort of smile, as if something I'd written had tickled him. But the rest of the time, old stony-face. Then when he was done, he gave it back to me. 'It's interesting,' he said. 'You ought to keep it and publish it someday.' Well, that secretly tickled me, but I looked properly modest and said, 'What if I never get out?' He didn't say anything. Then he sat back down on the ground, pulling his knees up and putting his arms around them. He's been sitting that way a lot lately, like he's sort of drawing into himself. Of course, it also may be he's trying to kill the hunger pangs. He tells me he's never felt worse in his life, that the hunger gnaws at him day and night and that he's trying to use his will power to shut his stomach up, but that it's hard. I know what he means, except I've got worse than hunger pangs in my stomach. Anyway, after a while he looks up at me and says, 'You said in the diary you liked me. That surrprised me.' 'Why?' 'Well, I'm not very likeable.' 'That's a matter of opinion. You've been decent to me. More than decent, since I've gotten sick.' 'Well,' says he, 'I like you. You're a nice person, Hank, and I won't deny I've been lonely as hell these past three years. It's good to have a friend, and if we ever get out of this place alive, I won't forget you.' I was glad to hear that. 'What do you think our chances are?' says I. 'Of getting out alive? I don't know. I've racked my brain, but I can't figure out how to escape. The place is too damned well guarded. And they say the Rebs are taking a beating from Grant, but that's not doing *us* any good.' Then he fell silent for a while as did I. Not very pleasant conversation. Then he starts up again. 'You know,' he said, 'there's one good thing about this hole, and that's that it makes you really look into yourself. When I was younger, I didn't know myself very well. Oh, I had a lot of ideas about being something important, but it was all sort of vague.' 'I was the same way,' says I. 'Still am, as far as that goes.' 'But you can write,' says he. 'That's a powerful gift. You can do something for the world. I can't write, but I'd like to do something for the world. I used to think the world was a pleasant place, but I sure as hell have changed my mind. It's *rotten*. And some day I'm going to try and do something to change it.' 'Like what?' I asks. He got to his feet and said, 'I don't know yet, but I'm thinking.' Then he looked at me. 'How are you feeling?' 'So-so,' says I. 'Well, I'm going out to see what the pickings are.' And he took off. Strange conversation from a strange man.

I lied to him. Feeling worse all the time. He came back a while ago with some bacon and a black eye. Never saw him get hurt before. Figure the 'shopping' must be getting really tough. He cooked the bacon, took a little hunk for himself, and gave the rest to me. I ate it, but doubt it'll stay in my stomach for long. He sat there, watching me, looking sort of worried.

My gums have been killing me, and I'm getting the dropsy in my ankles and belly. Plus there's a sore on my right leg that scares hell out of me. I think we both know, but aren't saying.

July 7, 1864. Starker and I went to a whipping this morning. Two big social events in Andersonville: hangings and whippings. A society reporter would starve to death in this hole, but then, who wouldn't? The whippee a baker named Dunn from Chicago, I think. He'd been paroled and put to work in the bakery outside the stockade to make the cornbread that's killing everyone. There are about a hundred parolees here, men who can talk fast or bribe the guards or both, and they get prison jobs outside the stockade. Anyway, Dunn escaped from the bakery yesterday. They hunted him with the dogs and found him after four hours. Wirz is proud of his dogs, and guess he has a right to be. The cocky bastard actually announced he'll give any prisoners who want to try a two-hour head start – he'll actually *free* them – if they're willing to take double the punishment if they're caught. It says a lot for Wirz's dogs that no one's volunteered to try the experiment. But how Wirz would love to play cat and mouse with real live humans!

Dunn was caught and this morning he took his punishment. I went to see it because I'm a ghoul and because I feel it's important I get out of the shebang at least once a day, though it's painful for me to walk. The whipping post is next to the gallows in Punishment Square, and a squad of Rebs under Captain Wells marches in with Dunn, who looked terrified. Wiry little man with buck teeth. They took him to the post and tied him up. Big crowd gathered again. Captain Wells announced his punishment for attempted escape: one hundred lashes. One hundred! Jesus! Crowd was muttering, but everyone too weak at this point to do much else but mutter. They tear off Dunn's shirt, then the Rebs stand around, waiting for something. Then Captain Wirz appears on the sentry walk. Should have known he wouldn't miss a whipping. He gives the signal, and the prison whipper steps up. He's Corporal McClanahan, who used to be an overseer on a plantation and so knows his business. He's got a mean-looking whip, and he lays into Dunn. Dunn screams for a while, then shuts up and just moans. Finally, I think he passed out. It made my skin crawl to see a white man whipped like a slave. His back was ribbons of skin and rivers of blood. When it was over, they cut him down, then left him lying in the dirt, face-down. Then the Rebs marched back outside the stockade, happy as larks, the bastards. Some of the prisoners went over to try and help Dunn. Starker was standing next to me, watching. I said, 'Guess it doesn't pay to escape.' 'It doesn't pay to get *caught*,' he says. Then he went to help Dunn.

July 14, 1864. Haven't written in diary for a week because I've been too sick. No doubt about it now: I've got the dysentery *bad*. Wonder if I'll make it?

Starker says he can't scavenge any more because there's nothing left to steal. So he's started selling his things to buy food from the guards. Knows it kills him to do it, but no choice. I'm no help, being too sick to move and it makes me feel rotten. Today he sold his books. Got five dollars Federal for them – a good price. It must have really hurt him, because I know he treasured them. Only one he kept was *The Charterhouse of Parma*, which he said no one wanted because it's in French. He used some of the money to buy bacon, onions, and carrots, and he cooked us a stew, which smelled good. But I couldn't get much down. Funny, I used to do all the cooking and menial stuff, but since I've been sick he's taken it over and never complains. He does everything he can to help me, and has turned into a real Florence Nightingale. When I think of how mean he was when I first met him, it really amazes me. He's turned out to be a true friend. God knows what would have happened to me if it hadn't been for Starker.

My legs are like a skeleton's now except my ankles, which are huge with dropsy. I have, at last count, six sores on my body. They don't give out pus, just a thin fluid.

Afraid to look at a mirror to see my face. Afraid I'll see Death.

July 15, 1864. Starker's got a job in the hospital. He spent some time in a medical school before the war, and Doc Blaine took him on as an orderly. The hospital is outside the stockade and the word is it's filthy beyond description, a way-station to the grave. Prisoners who go there don't return. And everyone knows the orderlies steal everything they can from the sick and treat them almost as bad as the Rebs do. 'How can you do it?' I said when he told me. 'How can you steal from the sick?'

'Godammit, I'm not going to *steal* from them. I'm going to work in the hospital and get us out of here. At least it's outside the stockade, and we've got to get out of here, Hank. We've *got* to! And there's no way we're ever going to escape from *inside* the stockade.'

'But don't they guard the hospital?'

'Of course they do, but I'll think of something.'

'Even if we got out, where could we go? We're in the middle of Georgia, and Wirz has got his dogs.'

'Dammit, I know the questions. It's the *answers* I've got to figure out. But we've *got* to go! It's one in six dying now, and it's getting worse. I sure as hell don't want to be a statistic, and I don't want you to be one, either.'

'I'm closer to a statistic than you,' said I, 'so you'd better count me out.'

'You dummy, that's what gave me the idea! You're so sick they're going to have to take you to the hospital soon. That's how we get *you* out of the stockade. Then at least we'll both be out, and I can work something. Maybe bribe a guard.'

'What with? You've sold everything.'

He sighed. 'Jesus, I don't know. I'll find something.'

And for the first time since I've known this man, he sort of caved in and gave up. He sat down next to me, drew his legs up, put his arms around them, dropped his head down, and sort of died for a while. I just lay there, too weak to be any help. Then after a while he looked up, and I could hardly believe my eyes. Starker was crying!

He was crying for himself, but I think he was crying for me, too. He knows I'm about to die, though he still won't say it, and he *cares.* God bless him for that. Guess no one else in the world cares whether I live or die except me.

He's a true friend, a fine friend, best one I ever had.

Wonder if he can get us out.

22

Despite the fact that he found army drill impossible to master and army routine dull; despite the fact that he found war horrible, if exciting; despite the fact he had lost his left leg, Ben Bramwell had in a curious way enjoyed the war. He had felt a sense of purpose that he had never known in civilian life except in his botany and his work with the underground railroad. He had enjoyed the camaraderie of his fellow officers, and the friendships forged through shared boredom and danger. He had enjoyed the off-duty drinking – he had got drunk more times than he liked to, or could, remember. And though he had not enjoyed killing the Reb who had tried to kill him at Chancellorsville (the Reb had aimed at Ben's stomach and hit his leg. Ben had aimed at the Reb's leg and hit his stomach), when he returned to Philadelphia with his wooden leg he had rather enjoyed being treated by his relatives and friends as a hero, which they insisted on doing no matter how much he tried to convince them he wasn't. The war had given Ben Bramwell a sense of self-confidence he had never known. Though still haunted by his predilection for young girls, he began paying more attention to the eligible women in Philadelphia, determined to find his wife. Unfortunately, the eligible women in Philadelphia were mostly bores, the interesting ones already having been taken or pledged. And then he thought of Elizabeth. Receiving only vague evasions from her on the subject of his proposal, Ben decided to bite the bullet. He wrote her that he was coming to Paris to see her, and on 23 June 1864 he set sail from New York, determined not to return until he had won her hand. During the crossing, he rehearsed his proposal speech, changing it so many times that he finally threw the speech out and decided to let his heart do the talking.

He was looking forward to seeing the new Paris, for Ben, like most of the civilized world, had read with fascination of the transformation of the old medieval city into what travellers and reporters were now calling the most glorious city in the world. Ben had his democratic doubts about the French emperor, Napoleon III. But as he rode from the train station to his hotel and looked at the new, broad boulevards, the hundreds of new office buildings and apartment houses in the ornament-laden, gaudy style a critic had dubbed neo-Gothico-Pompadour-Pompeian-Greco, he had to admit that whatever faults the emperor might have, he had turned Paris into a city of unsurpassed beauty: Imperial Paris was spectacular. And though it lacked the hominess of his beloved Philadelphia, it possessed a glittery magic that only the harshest, most unromantic critic could deny. On this warm early July day, Ben Bramwell was feeling anything but unromantic.

He checked into his hotel, changed his clothes, then ordered a bouquet of roses and a big, heart-shaped box of Paris's best chocolates sent to his room. At noon, armed with all this romantic artillery, he got in another cab, giving the cabman Elizabeth's address. The cab clattered off over the paved boulevards, its horse's hooves echoing in the new Paris sewer system below the street. Soon it reached the Place de l'Étoile, then proceeded west on the new Avenue de l'Impératrice, one of the wide new avenues Napoleon's enemies whispered that he had built so as to facilitate the mowing down of revolutionaries. Finally, it stopped in front of an imposing stone mansion. Ben got out, paid the fare (which was high. Paris was expensive, the exchange rate being five francs to the dollar), then limped to the front door, the roses almost blocking his view. He had grown used to his new leg and with fierce determination had finally managed to walk without a cane. The last thing in the world he wanted was to use a cane in front of Elizabeth.

He found the bell and rang. As he waited, he could hear a piano being played inside the house. The melody was haunting, its major–minor, sweet–sour beauty reminiscent of faded flowers. It was Elizabeth practising, he thought. Ben didn't know much about music, but he enjoyed it. A lifetime of listening to Elizabeth play was an appealing prospect. He had mixed emotions about her seeking a professional career, but if that was what she wanted, he thought he would not stand in her way.

A liveried footman opened the door.

'*Monsieur?*'

Ben had been studying a booklet entitled *The Tourist's Guide to the French Language*. Now he managed to extricate a calling card from his pocket, almost dropping the box of chocolates in the process, and gave it to the footman.

'*Je voudrais* . . . uh, *voir* . . . *Madame Crandall.*'

He was certain the verb 'to see' was wrong, but what the hell.

'*Oui, monsieur. Entrez, s'il vous plaît.*'

He went into the entrance hall, managing to get his top hat off his head without spilling everything. The footman took the hat, then opened two doors and went in the next room. The piano music stopped. A moment later, there was Elizabeth standing in the doors, looking excited and pretty in a yellow dress, her chestnut hair pinned up in a chignon.

'Ben! Dear Ben, you're here! How wonderful to see you . . . that is *if* I could see you behind those roses. . . . Armand – *prenez les fleurs. Et faites dire à Ghislaine que monsieur nous joindra pour le déjeuner*. . . . You will stay for lunch, Ben? I had no idea when you'd arrive. . . .'

'I'd love to stay for lunch,' he said as the footman took the flowers from him. 'I brought you some chocolates . . . I remembered you always liked them.'

He handed her the heart-shaped box.

'Oh dear, the last thing I need! I've put on ten pounds in France. . . .'

'Then I'll take them back.'

'You will not! I'm entitled to my vices. . . . Armand. . . .'

She handed the chocolates to the footman, then smiled at Ben and extended her hands. He took them.

'Dear Ben,' she said. 'And how is Philadelphia?'

'Oh, Philadelphia never changes much. I have a letter from your mother, who's fine. And Debbie told me to tell you she's got a beau.'

Elizabeth laughed. 'She's all of eighteen. Let's go inside. . . .'

'Was that you playing?' he said, accompanying her through the doors into an elegant, high-ceilinged room.

'Yes, the "Funérailles", one of the maestro's compositions. My debut is next week, and I'm working like a slave. The maestro has arranged everything for me, rented the Salle Pleyel. . . . But how wonderful that you'll be here for it!'

'Well, that depends . . .'

'Oh, you *must* stay. I'll need my home-town rooters, even if it's only one. . . . Sit down, Ben. You're looking so well!'

She sat on a sofa, and he moved into a chair beside her. She watched him manoeuvre his wooden leg, but said nothing.

'I've grown used to the leg,' he said.

'So I see. And no cane! Congratulations.'

'That's a new development. But I had to use it on the ship coming over. We ran into a storm, and you can imagine what fun it is to have a wooden leg on a rolling ship. You're looking wonderful, Elizabeth. France must agree with you.'

'It does. I love it, and I adore Paris.'

'Your French sounds good. Not that I'd know.'

'It's improving, but my accent's still wretched. I can't get used to those infernal "r's".'

Ben looked around the room, which was expensively furnished.

'This is certainly grand – a far cry from Philadelphia. Are you renting it?'

'No, it belongs to a family named Mercier. He's a successful banker, and Madame Mercier is a music-lover and a great friend of the maestro's. She very kindly gave me the use of the house while they're at their château. . . . How is Nicole Louise?'

'Deep in the arms of the Church.'

'I did so appreciate your advice about Ward's inheritance. You were absolutely right: it would have been wrong for me to have gotten in a fight with her. I've thanked you a thousand times in my thoughts, but now I can thank you in person. It's been such a relief that I avoided all that unpleasantness.'

'It was just common sense.'

'Common sense is the best kind. I have *no* head for money matters, and of course for Ward's sake. . . . Oh, but you haven't seen him! He's out in the garden. . . .' She got up and started toward one of the French doors that opened onto a garden at the rear of the house. 'Don't get up. I'll bring him in. You won't recognize him, he's grown so! And talking. . . . He probably won't remember you, it's been so long.' She called through the open doors. 'Miss Pritchett? Will you bring Ward inside a moment?' Then she returned to the sofa. 'We've been moving around so much, I finally decided to engage an English nanny for him. He has such an ear for languages – like his father – that he was getting otally confused, learning Germa n, then Italian, and now French. . . . It was all coming o utgoulash, so I thought he should speak English with his nanny and me, and French with the servants.'

'May I ask you something?'

'Of course.'

'Why did you name him after your father? Why not Lew?'

She looked at her hands. 'Lew and I talked about that before . . . he went to Washington. He said he hated "Juniors".' She looked up. '*I* would have named him Lew, but naturally I carried out his father's wish.'

Just then, a beautiful towheaded boy walked in from the garden carrying a black cat in his arms. He was followed by a plump woman in black taffeta.

'*Maman*,' he said, carrying the cat to his mother, '*Ninon essayait de manger un pauvre petit oiseau! Ninon est méchante, n'est-ce pas?*'

Elizabeth smiled at him. 'Cats like to chase birds, darling.'

'*Mais les oiseaux ne l'aiment pas!*' He looked at Ben with big blue eyes. '*Qui est ça?*'

'This is Mr Bramwell, darling. He's from Philadelphia. He was a dear friend of your father's. Go shake his hand. And speak *English*.'

Ward put down the cat, who immediately scurried back out into the garden. Then the boy came over, inspecting Ben with the intense curiosity of a child, and stuck out his hand.

'How do you do? My name's Ward.'

'How do you do, Ward? You're a fine-looking young man.'

'Mamma says I look like my father. Did you know him well?'

'We grew up together.'

'Mamma says he was very brave.'

'He was.'

'Mamma says he was an a-row.'

'A what?'

'"Hero", darling,' corrected his mother.

'Oh yes, hero.'

'Your father *was* a hero.'

'Were you?'

Ben laughed. 'A very clumsy one, if I was, which I wasn't.'

'Mr Bramwell *was*,' said Elizabeth. 'And he was very brave.'

Ward looked at her, then back to Ben. 'When I grow up,' he said, 'I'm going to be a hero and kill all those Rebs who killed my father.'

Ben frowned. 'No,' he said. 'When you grow up, there mustn't be any more killing. And if you're lucky, no more wars.'

'That won't be any fun.'

'Wars aren't fun, Ward. They're anything but.'

Ward thought about this. His mother signalled to Miss Pritchett, who said, 'All right, young man. Shall we go out and lecture Ninon?'

Ward ran back to the door.

'Ninon's bad! Naughty Ninon! Nice to have met you, Mr Bramwell. Mamma, can I have some ice cream for lunch?'

'*May* I. And yes, if you're good.'

'Oh, I'm *very* good. *Je suis un bel ange!*'

And out he went, followed by Miss Pritchett.

'I'm afraid he's anything but an angel,' said Elizabeth. 'I have to be careful not to spoil him, but it's hard for me to say no to him. He knows he's got me wrapped around his finger, which is bad for a child.'

'He needs a father,' said Ben.

Elizabeth looked at him. 'I know.'

Ben shifted uncomfortably in his chair. 'You know, when Lew was a child, his mother used to force him to speak French all the time. It caused him a lot of trouble later on in life, because he was never quite sure whether he was French or American. I'd hate to see that happen to Ward. It's important for a child to have roots.'

'I know, but isn't it also important for a child to know languages?'

'You can always hire translators. You can't hire peace of mind. Lew took a tremendous ragging in school. They used to call him the "Frog". It was his mother's fault.'

'Yes, but Philadelphia is so provincial. They hate anyone who's "different". I don't want my son to be narrow-minded.' She looked rather cross. 'I hope you didn't come all the way across the ocean to lecture me on child-raising?'

'I'm no expert on that. And I think you know why I'm here.'

'Yes, I think I do.'

'You were so evasive in your letters, I thought I'd better come over here and ask in person. I'm . . . not very good at this sort of thing, Elizabeth. To do it right, I should get down on my knees, but getting down on a wooden knee isn't the easiest thing in the world. At any rate, I meant what I said in the letter. I'd be honoured if you would be my wife. I' – he cleared his throat nervously – 'I realize I'm a sad substitute for Lew – '

'Lew is dead,' she interrupted quietly. 'He lives in my

heart and in Ward, but he's dead. His death was the greatest blow I've ever had, as you know. But my friends have convinced me I mustn't live in the past, and they're right.'

'Then . . .' He hesitated. He was being so damned clumsy! He was a nervous wreck. He wished he had a drink. 'May I hope you might want me as a husband?'

She got up and went to the French doors, which she closed. Then she came back to stand beside the sofa.

'The question, Ben, is not whether I want you. The question is whether you want me.'

'But I do! I want you more than anything else in the world!'

'You want the old Elizabeth, the one you grew up with in Philadelphia. But I've changed, Ben. Whether it's for the better or the worse, I don't know, but I'm a different woman. And I must be honest with you.'

He was confused. 'About what?'

'I have a lover.'

He stared at her. 'Might I ask who it is?'

She sat down, amazed at her own coolness. 'It's the maestro.'

'Oh.' *Him?*

'I couldn't very well say this in a letter, which was why I was so evasive. If I'd known you were coming so far, I would have stopped you. But of course, by the time your letter arrived here, it was too late to write. I feel terrible about this, Ben. It's all my fault.'

He was digesting this, to him, amazing information. Elizabeth Butterfield Crandall and Franz Liszt? It was such an incredible combination. . . .

'Do you love him?' he asked.

'No, and he doesn't love me. I admire him extravagantly. And I know this sounds terribly calculating, but having his . . . well, support makes all the difference in the world to my career. That isn't why I became his mistress, but I'd be less than honest if I didn't admit that's why I've stayed his mistress. He opens all the doors. It's that simple. And for a woman trying to make a career? Well, let's just say that Europe is no more eager than America to accept women in the arts – or anywhere else beside the drawing room. Or the bed.'

He could hardly believe what he was hearing. 'You certainly *have* changed!'

'I've had to change to survive. You don't have to say anything, Ben. I know I've embarrassed you . . . I've probably disappointed you, too. I'm sorry. But let me say that I'm deeply honoured by your proposal. And I mean that.'

Ben's mind was whirling.

'Would you give him up?' he blurted out. Now it was her turn to be surprised. 'Would you give him up to marry me? I need you, Elizabeth, and I think you need me. And so does Ward. Will you give him up?'

'But . . .'

'*Now*,' he added. 'Not after the debut.'

'That's out of the question.'

'You're wrong, Elizabeth. Believe me, you're wrong. I don't know that much about music, but I know you can't be a success on someone else's coat-tails. The maestro may have opened the doors, but if you don't have the talent, it won't make any difference in the long run.'

She looked stunned. Then she said, 'Don't you think I know that?'

'Well then?'

She got up and moved around the sofa to go back to the French doors.

'I'm afraid, Ben,' she finally said, looking out the window at Ward chasing Ninon. 'Afraid to do it without his backing. I don't know if I'm good enough.'

'Isn't this the time to find out?'

She stood a long time at the window, thinking about Clara Schumann, music, Ward, the maestro, Lew, Ben. But mostly Ward. Ward was the important one. Then she turned around. Her face was pale.

'If you still want me,' she said, 'I'll give him up.'

A smile came over his face. He got out of the chair and crossed the room to her, limping slightly. When he reached her, he pulled a small black velvet box from his pocket. He opened it and pulled out a diamond ring. She watched as he took her left hand and slipped the ring on her finger.

'You've done me a great honour,' he whispered. Then he took her in his arms and kissed her.

Dear God, she thought, what have I done?

The man who had replaced Simon Cameron as Secretary of War had made some drastic changes in the office on the third floor of the War Department Building. Gone were the malachite inkwell, the bust of Cicero, the portrait of Eugénie. Even Andrew Jackson had been moved to another wall, and now a framed photograph of a sombre Lincoln hung behind the desk of Edwin Stanton. Only the desk remained unchanged, that eternal symbol of the bureaucrat. But Secretary Stanton wasn't behind it. The pudgy, asthmatic man with the mop beard and thin gold glasses was standing in front of one of the many maps that now marched around the room on wooden legs. Maps of all the theatres of war showing the current placement of the almost one million men the North had under arms. Then there were the charts wedged between the maps. Charts showing the cost: two million dollars a day. The deaths: nearing one hundred thousand. The captured: nearing two hundred thousand. The deaths in the Southern prisons (especially Andersonville): nearing thirty thousand. The wounded: nearing a quarter million. There were no frills in the office of the Secretary of War now. Edwin Stanton disliked frills. He was a blunt, many said a cruel, man who had been one of the highest-paid corporation counsels in the country. He was also a man with a morbid fascination with death. As a young man in Ohio, when his sweetheart had died suddenly of cholera, he had become crazed with grief and, convinced she had been buried alive, dug up her grave with his bare hands to inspect her body. When his first child, a baby girl, had died, he disinterred her body two weeks after the burial and kept the metal casket on his bedroom mantel for two years. A strange man, Edwin Stanton, whose fascination with death was in danger of surfeit in this bloodiest of wars.

His secretary, Mr Howe, opened the door.

'Mr Samson, sir.'

'Yes, show him in.'

Stanton returned to his desk, wondering why Gilbert Samson had requested a meeting. Stanton admired Gilbert Samson, but, like so many other former Abolitionists, he had stopped reading his newspaper, *The Freedman's Weekly*. Too many other things to read now.

Gilbert came in the office and went over to shake Stanton's hand.

'Mr Stanton, sir. It's good of you to see me.'

'My honour, sir, though I will ask you to be brief. I have a heavy schedule today.'

'I'm sure you have a heavy schedule every day, Mr Secretary.'

They took their seats, Gilbert in front of the desk, Stanton behind. The Secretary of War pulled out a gold pocket watch, checked the time, then laid it in front of him on the desk. 'Now sir,' he said, 'what can I do for you?'

'Do you know Senator Matoon?'

'I've met him several times. Can't say I know him well.'

'I have a friend who's ready to testify in court that Senator Matoon ordered a murder three years ago, when he was a general.'

Stanton's eyes widened, and his asthmatic wheezing became louder.

'A murder? Of whom?'

'His aide-de-camp, a lieutenant named Crandall. Crandall had information that Matoon was taking kickbacks, and Matoon told his orderly, a Corporal Burt Thomson, to shoot Crandall on the battlefield during the first battle of Bull Run. From the research I've done so far, I've found that Crandall was listed as killed in action, but his body was never found.'

'Not unusual.'

'Oh? But isn't the usual procedure to list such cases as *missing* in action?'

Stanton frowned. 'Yes, as a matter of fact it is.'

'Isn't that suggestive?'

'Yes, but I'm not sure of what.'

'Let's say that Thomson shot Crandall in the face, making

the corpse unrecognizable. He returns to Washington and reports to Matoon. But Matoon is still nervous – he wants Crandall officially dead, not missing. So he jimmies the record a little and lists him dead.'

'You're making a lot of assumptions, sir.'

'Admittedly. But there are other suggestive things. Corporal Thomson was transferred to the west in August of sixty-one and was later killed at Vicksburg.'

'I'll grant you *that's* suggestive. And if you're right about Matoon, Thomson's death was certainly a convenience for him.'

'To say the least. More suggestive facts: when Senator Matoon was the mayor of Harrisburg before the war, he listed his net worth as "not in excess of twenty thousand dollars". His pay as a brigadier general was a hundred and twenty-four dollars a month. Yet he and his new wife have just finished building a mansion on H Street that, according to the papers, cost three hundred thousand dollars. Now, I don't know what that suggests to you, but I know what it suggests to me.'

Silence. The Secretary of War shifted in his chair. The slow, steady wheezing of his asthmatic breath lulled the room like the sound of flies.

'I won't deny,' he said carefully, 'that Senator Matoon's sudden fortune has caused some comment around Capitol Hill, although the senator claims to have invested in a gold mine in Colorado that paid out. . . .'

'Uh huh. Some gold mine.'

'But what do you want from me, Mr Samson? It seems to me you should be telling this to the Attorney General.'

'I intend to, sir. But first I want to get as much information as I can on the case. That's why I'd like your permission to look through the War Department files to see if I can get a better look at Senator Matoon's "gold mine".'

At the word 'files', Stanton's eyes narrowed.

'Well, Mr Samson, naturally I want to be cooperative. But you realize, sir, that all of this has already been aired, and this department took a real drubbing from the press. To start talking about kickbacks again just when the tide of war has started to turn against the South . . . well, I'd like to avoid that if I can.'

'But I don't think you can, Mr Secretary. The Attorney General's going to have to look at the files eventually. To make the murder charge stick, we're going to have to establish the motive, and to do that we're going to have to prove that Matoon was taking kickbacks.'

'Of course, I understand that,' said Stanton impatiently. 'But Matoon has already been investigated, and he was cleared. What makes you think you – or the Attorney General – will have any better luck now, when your job is going to be even harder because Matoon's become a senator? Senators have a lot of power, Mr Samson, and they don't like to be brought to trial. What about this friend of yours? How does he know Matoon ordered the murder?'

'It's a she. A Miss Christine Canrobert.'

'Where does she live?'

'In New York. Number two-o-seven Thompson Street. She heard Matoon admit he ordered the murder to the woman who is now his wife – a Miss Rosemary Fletcher.'

Stanton shrugged. 'As a lawyer who's defended many murder cases, I can tell you I could make mincemeat of your friend in court. It's all hearsay – she says she heard Matoon tell his wife . . . hell, everyone tells all sorts of crazy things to their wives! It doesn't mean it's true just because this Miss Canrobert overheard him say it. Now, if she'd heard him give the order to Thomson – well, that might be different. But she didn't. You don't have a case, sir: believe me. No case. To accuse a senator of murder with *that*? Flimsy.'

'I realize that, Mr Secretary. That's why I want to look through the files.'

Stanton leaned forward and lowered his voice.

'Now you listen to me, Mr Samson. Ralph Matoon was appointed to the Senate when Senator Cadwallader died because Ralph Matoon has powerful friends. Now, sir, your people want the vote, right? But there are a lot of people in this country who don't want to give you the vote, so there's going to be a fight – a big fight – to get the black man enfranchised. Senator Matoon is a Republican. He's a friend of Congressman Stevens, who's the best friend the black man has in Congress. You bring a murder charge against Matoon, and you're going to endanger the enfranchising of the Negro. I mean it, sir! I don't exaggerate! You're too well known, Mr Samson, too well known. You're a symbol of Negro aspirations, if you will! And you're trying to pin a murder on a senator who's on your side? My God, you could wreck everything. Forget it, man. Even if Matoon *did* order that murder – which you'd have a hell of a time proving – it's a long time ago and that lieutenant is nothing but bones now and his actual killer, Thomson, has paid for it, so forget it. It's not worth it. Here's once instance where I say, let sleeping dogs lie.'

Gilbert waited a moment before saying, 'And what about justice, Mr Secretary?'

'Ah yes, justice. Well, what about it? I've been a lawyer over thirty years, and I can tell you from practical experience there's *very* little justice in life, and the little there is is mostly blind luck. Yes, talk about justice. Write editorials about it. A senator commits a murder and gets away with it, and that's unjust. But what about upsetting the delicate balance of political relationships that's going to be needed to enfranchise the Negro – wouldn't that be an injustice? You have to weigh the injustices, sir. Two wrongs *can* make a right. And a right, pushed too far, can turn into a wrong. Forget it, man.'

He picked up his watch and looked at it.

Gilber leaned forward. He was angry. 'Now you listen to *me*, Mr Stanton – and put down that goddam watch, because I'm not leaving till I'm good and ready. I've got a newspaper with a readership of thirty thousand. I've got some important friends. If I start making noise about Matoon in my paper, you and your department are going to be in a *very* uncomfortable position! Now, sir, you talk about my endangering the enfranchising of my people . . . let me tell you, Mr Secretary, I've lived my whole life for the black man. But goddam it, as much as I want the vote, I'm not going to get it at the expense of that word that doesn't seem to mean very much to *you*, sir, and I'm talking about justice: You talk to *me* about how little justice there is in life – my God, do you realize what I was? A slave? Don't you think *I* know? But don't you realize the reason there *is* so little justice is because so few people are willing to fight for that word that you belittle? You, a lawyer? No, sir, I will not forget it! I will not let sleeping dogs lie! I believe that Ralph Matoon committed a murder, and I'm going to make him pay for it! If it besmirches the reputation of the War Department during a war, then so be it! Even if it sets back the cause of the black man, so be it! A right pushed too far is *still* a right!'

The Secretary pounded his desk and yelled, 'By God, Samson, you're a demagogue and an ass! Don't preach that drivel to *me*! Do you forget who I am?'

Gilbert rose to his not inconsiderable height and looked down at the Secretary of War.

'I know who you are, sir. You're one of the best lawyers in the land. Which doesn't say much for the legal profession.'

And he walked out of the office.

Lew Crandall reached down and closed the dead eyes of Hank Gaynor. Hank was lying on his back on the wooden cot in the filthy, pine-built hospital outside the stockade of Andersonville Prison. He was already almost a skeleton, weeks of dysentery and near-starvation having done most of the grave's work before death. He had not been a heavy person anyway, but now Lew guessed he couldn't weigh more than eighty pounds. His face was a near-skull, his brown hair had started to fall out, his eyes were black holes, his mouth was slightly open, revealing his rotted teeth and gums. His ribcage strained at the sore-covered skin, ready to burst through when the skin decomposed – which wouldn't take long. His arms had emaciated down to near-bone.

'Is he dead?' said Sergeant Ellenby, the red-haired, red-faced red-neck from Mississippi who was chief guard of the prison hospital. Sergeant Ellenby had been sitting in his chair at the end of the sixty-foot-long hospital shed, drinking pinetop, when he saw one of his orderlies reach down to close Gaynor's eyes. He had got up and come down the aisle between the rows of cots filled with the sick and the near-dead to see what was going on. Lew noticed he was weaving slightly.

'He's been dead a week,' said Lew, who for three years had gone by the name of Jeremiah Starker. 'It's just official now.'

'Know how old he was?' Sergeant Ellenby looked at the orderly who had been working in the hospital ten days. Starker is no prize himself, he thought. Can't weigh more than a hundred twenty, and he's a big man.

'He was nineteen,' said Lew.

'Shit, not much of a life, was it?'

'Not much of a life.'

'Well, I'll make out the death certificate. You and Babcock'll be the burial detail. Be good exercise for you. Where was he from?'

'Crawfordsville, Indiana.'

'Was he married?'

'He was going to be after the war.'

'Guess they can cancel the wedding. Let me know when you and Babcock are ready. And, nigger, for chrissake get these slopjars clean. This place smells like a privy anyway, no use helping it along.'

Sergeant Ellenby went back to his office and Lew looked down at the private. Hank's death sickened him. He had come to feel great compassion for him as he watched him starve and suffer – even more than he was starving and suffering himself – and he had done everything in his power to save him. But it wasn't enough. Wirz and the war had destroyed Hank as they had almost destroyed Lew. He wondered if he would be next. I'll never forget you, he thought. And he had kept the diary in his pocket. I'll never forget this outrage.

Chester Babcock, a thirty-seven-year-old druggist from Milwaukee, shuffled over. Babcock shuffled from weakness, but he was still strong enough to dig a grave.

'Let's wrap him up,' he said.

The two men folded the sheet over the skeleton, which

was still warm, then carried him down the hospital shed to the door.

'At least he ain't much to carry,' said Ellenby, coming out of his office. He took another swig of the pinetop, then led the burial detail out of the shed.

'Bill,' he yelled to one of the privates on guard, 'get me two shovels. Get sharp ones, for chrissake. Don't want to take all day diggin' no grave in this heat. Then you mind the store while I'm gone. I need some fresh air.'

He walked to a tree where the six sentries who guarded the hospital kept their mounts shaded. He untied his horse, climbed on, then waited while Bill brought two shovels to the two orderlies who were standing by the tin-roofed shed holding the sheet-wrapped corpse. Babcock wore a pair of black trousers that sagged like his emaciated skin, and his shirt was a rag. Lew had grown so thin that he had to hold his ratty trousers up with a rope, and the shirt he had worn for five months was rotting. Shit, thought Ellenby, the goddam Federals may be beating us, but they ain't gonna find much to take home when they reach Andersonville. They're a bunch of goddam ghosts.

'You white niggers ready?' he yelled. 'Let's go.'

His horse started ambling toward the prison burial ground, which was in the pine woods behind the north end of the stockade. The two orderlies followed, carrying the corpse and the shovels.

Sergeant Ellenby looked back to check on them. He grinned and waved his bottle of pinetop.

'My,' he called, 'how the time *do* fly when you're havin' fun.'

Miserable Yankee sons of bitches, he thought. They get what they deserve.

An hour later, as Lew and Babcock began shovelling the loose dirt over the corpse, Sergeant Ellenby finished the pinetop, then threw the empty bottle behind him into the woods. He was sitting on the ground, propped against the trunk of a tree, his revolver in his lap. The two white niggers were ten feet away, shovelling. The slow rhythm of the click of the shovels digging into the dirt, then the soft thud as the dirt landed in the grave, was like a lullaby, and the heat and pinetop had done their work. Lew watched him. Sergeant Ellenby was nodding.

Click, thud. Click, thud. Click, thud.

They worked in the bone-sucking heat.

Click thud. Click, thud. Click . . .

Eight minutes passed. Then Lew stopped. Babcock looked at him, but Lew signalled him to keep digging.

Click, thud.

Lew started toward the Rebel sergeant, whose head had fallen on his shoulder, his eyes closed, his hand loose on the revolver.

Click, thud.

Lew grabbed the handle of the shovel with both hands, tensing his body, summoning up what strength he had left. It was the strength of desperation.

Click, thud.

He was three feet in front of Ellenby. He stopped and slowly brought the sharp shovel back, like a baseball bat, its blade parallel with the ground. His eye was on Ellenby's red neck. The shovel was an executioner's sword.

Click, thud.

'Now, ain't you the sneaky one,' said Ellenby, raising his revolver as he straightened his head and opened his eyes. He grinned. Lew stared at him, shovel poised. 'Put that down, nigger. Go on. Put it down.' Lew obeyed. Sergeant Ellenby got to his feet. 'Thought I'd dozed off, didn't you? You're gonna learn, white nigger, that Jimmie Ellenby can doze and watch at the same time. You're gonna learn the *hard* way. That's an attempted escape. Now, you go back and finish your job. Then we're gonna go have a little talk with Cap'n Wirz.'

Lew went back to the grave, his brain raging. Babcock looked at him, but didn't stop shovelling. Lew filled his lungs with clean air, then went back to work.

Click, thud.

Captain Henry Wirz studied the file card on Jeremiah Starker, then looked up at the ragged prisoner standing in front of his desk, his hands tied behind his back. Sergeant Ellenby stood next to him. Captain Wells was standing beside Wirz's desk, in front of a framed photograph of Jefferson Davis. Wirz spoke, his voice reedy, his English mangled by his Swiss-German accent.

'According to your record, you have made seven unsuccessful attempts to escape in three years, Starker. This is your eighth attempt. You are not a very clever man, are you? And slow to learn, too. Don't you realize that no one can escape from my prison?'

Lew said nothing.

'However, it seems you are a good orderly. Dr Blaine has made a plea that you be kept in the hospital, since he has few men who know anything about medicine. It seems you studied medicine before the war? Is that correct?'

Lew said nothing. Wirz looked at his second-in-command, Captain Wells.

'The prisoner is not very talkative, is he?'

'No sir.'

Wirz looked back at Lew. 'Do you have anything to say before I announce your punishment?'

'You,' said Lew, 'are a murdering son of a bitch. And you'll rot in hell for what you've done here.'

Wirz picked up a pencil and tapped the point on his desk.

'I am growing tired of these insolent attacks on the conduct of my duties as commandant of this prison. The prisoner will be gagged during the punishment, so that we hear no more of this slander. The punishment is one hundred lashes, to be carried out at noon. Captain, you will be in charge of the detail. In deference to Dr Blaine, the prisoner may be returned to the hospital tomorrow. By then, he will realize his escape attempts are a waste of everyone's time. Captain Wells, carry out your orders.'

'Yes sir.'

They took the prisoner out. Captain Wirz continued tapping his pencil.

The tall pine-log gates of the stockade were opened, and he was marched into the foul-smelling place between two columns of armed soldiers. A gag had been tied around his mouth, and his hands were still bound. Only a few prisoners had gathered to watch; punishments had lost their entertainment value through repetition. Besides, it was too hot, and the prisoners were too weak to move from their shebangs. Those that came looked skeletal. Their eyes registered nothing. He was in the land of the dead.

They took him to Punishment Square and tied him to the whipping post. Then Captain Wells read the charge in a bored voice. Lew barely listened. The sun baked down on his hair; sweat streamed down his face. He felt his shirt ripped off his back, and the sun bit his naked shoulders. A mosquito buzzed his wet face, then bit his forehead.

Whish. His body jolted as the whip crashed into his back. He bit the gag. Whish. Slash. Whish. Slash.

When they cut him down to leave him lying in the dirt, face down, his back mangled, his numb mind was barely conscious. Two words repeated over and over in his brain, like muffled drums: escape and revenge. Escape and revenge. Escape and revenge.

Then the drums became silent.

23

The conductor raised his baton, then brought it down, and the lively strains of the Waltz from Gounod's *Faust* filled the huge gold and crimson Salle des Maréchaux of the Tuileries Palace as the Second Empire began to twirl to the favourite tune of its favourite, five-year-old opera. Elizabeth

Crandall Bramwell, looking beautiful in a yellow gown with the sapphire-and-diamond necklace Ben had given her as a wedding present around her throat, stood watching the waltzers from the side of the room and said to her husband of two weeks, 'Isn't it fabulous?'

They had arrived an hour before in their rented *calèche* to find the palace ablaze with light, with huge bonfires burning in the Place du Carrousel to help illuminate the scene. There, at the State Entrance to the palace, they had waited as an endless line of carriages disgorged their elaborately dressed passengers in front of the Pavillon de l'Horloge. Finally, it was their turn. The door had been opened, a pygmy valet in a green silk jacket and white turban had lowered the steps, and a court chamberlain bowed as Mr and Mrs Benjamin Bramwell of Philadelphia stepped out, handing the chamberlain a white envelope with the imperial seal embossed on the flap, inside of which was a cream-coloured invitation to the ball that had been arranged for them by the American ambassador. Then they had entered the palace, gaping at the tall, motionless Cent Gardes – the Praetorian Guard of Louis-Napoleon – in their sky-blue tunics, white breeches, black top boots, their helmets with flowing horsehair manes and their burnished steel breastplates. These men were chosen not for their bravery but for their looks and their height: they had to be at least six feet tall. Cynics scoffed that that was what was wrong with the French army: all looks, no bravery. But cynics were few in this heyday of imperial France.

Two *gardes* stood at either end of each step on the grand staircase, making an impressive tableau as Ben and Elizabeth joined the surging crowd climbing the stairs. They admired the beautiful women in their huge gowns, the men in their uniforms and sashes, their coats pinned with jewelled orders and decorations. Then, at the top of the staircase, the crowd pushed into the Salle du Trône, then on to the Salon d'Apollon, the Salon du Premier Consul – great, high rooms, overdecorated, their walls swirling with gilt, their chandeliers dripping crystal, paintings of the imperial family hanging everywhere, a pantheon of Napoleons. The emperor himself, Prince 'Plon-Plon', the Princesse Mathilde, the young Prince Imperial. But, most spectacular, a huge Winterhalter of the Empress Eugénie, who seemed even more regally beautiful viewed through the rose-coloured, royalty-glamorizing eyes of the Baden-born portraitist than she was in real life.

The new furniture of the palace was gaudily undistinguished, though the old pieces dating from the Bourbon Dynasty were exceptional: the heavy hand of the mid-nineteenth century was everywhere evident, clashing with the taste of the past. Yet even with the ugliness of some of the huge blue vases emblazoned with their gold 'N's' standing on the chunky new mantels, the rock crystal and bronze *doré* bibelots stuffed into the modern vitrines – even with these, the palace and the gardens were still beautiful. Particularly the gardens, which the guests could see through the tall, open windows. They were illuminated by thirty thousand lamps, along with garlands of lights in white glass globes. The trees seemed aflame with Bengal lights, and the fountains and pools were lit with coloured lanterns.

When the crowd reached the hydrangea-banked Salle des Maréchaux, it waited for the arrival of the ambassadors and the imperial family, as ushers in brown and gold, footmen in green and gold and scarlet, and beadles in plumed hats and red baldrics emblazoned with imperial eagles tended to their needs. Finally, the chief usher appeared in the doorway and cried, '*L'Empereur! L'Impératrice!*' The cry was echoed by the beadles, banging their staves on the marble floors. The orchestra struck up the anthem of the Second Empire, 'Partant pour la Syrie', and in strode the unmajestic, pot-bellied, short, wax-moustached, rather ridiculous adventurer who had ridden the whirlwind of history to such incredible success. With him was his tall, swan-necked, copper-haired, serene empress. All eyes riveted on Eugénie. Whatever her faults, no one could deny she looked every inch an empress. She wore a white ballgown swirled with sequin-flecked tulle; across her breast slashed the blue sash of the Garter which Queen Victoria had bestowed on her and the emperor in 1855 when they visited Windsor. Around her throat was the three-strand necklace of faultless diamonds that was supposed to be the finest necklace in Europe. On her head was a magnificent diamond tiara, and on her dress a diamond brooch shaped like a lilac blossom, made for her by Lemonnier, one of the leading Paris jewellers. She had on four jewelled bracelets and wore a twenty-carat diamond ring. But most astounding was the huge Régence diamond, which blazed from yet another brooch on her dress. Yet it was not the diamonds alone that riveted the stares of the onlookers. It was her eyes: large, down-slanting, animated but still rather sad. It was her thin mouth – pretty, but almost cruel. Perhaps, most of all, it was her innate elegance. She looked, and was, incapable of an awkward movement.

'Gorgeous!' whispered Elizabeth as the imperial couple moved past the bowing and curtsying guests, bestowing a personal word or two on everyone.

'Tinsel,' whispered Ben.

Eizabeth laughed.

'But I like tinsel.'

And Ben laughed, too.

Now the emperor and empress were in front of them, and Elizabeth swept into a low curtsy. The chamberlain introduced them, and the emperor shook Ben's hand.

'Americans,' said Louis Napoleon in his excellent English. 'I like Americans. My dentist is an American, you know.'

'I didn't know, Your Majesty,' said Ben.

'Dr Evans is a genius, and the only man in Europe who can keep my miserable teeth happy. If you Americans had given nothing else to the world, you would still be a great nation because of Dr Evans. But haven't I heard of you, madame?' he said, switching his gaze to Elizabeth. 'Aren't you the protégée of Maestro Liszt?'

'Not any more, Your Majesty,' said Elizabeth, glancing at Ben.

'I see.' The emperor was looking her over. 'But you did give your debut recently at the Salle Pleyel?'

'That is correct, Your Majesty.'

'You must come play for us at Compiègne or Saint-Cloud. I've no ear for music, but I have an eye for it.'

He smiled and passed on as Elizabeth went into another curtsy. The empress passed her by, gave her a cold look, then went on without a word. Ben, far from jealous of Napoleon's interest in his wife, was bursting with pride.

'She's jealous!' he whispered to Elizabeth. 'Eugénie's jealous!'

Elizabeth laughed. Despite the unhappy result of her debut two weeks before, she was having the time of her life.

Another guest – a tall, lanky man in his mid-twenties with a pleasant, freckled face and a mop of red hair – had watched the exchange between the emperor and the Americans. Being an American himself, he decided to introduce himself. But he had to wait until the imperial couple had seated themselves on the dais at the end of the room beneath the red velvet canopy embroidered with the imperial gold eagle. Then the chamberlain announced the *quadrille d'honneur*, which traditionally opened state balls. The emperor offered his hand to a foreign princess, and Eugénie took the arm of the ranking foreign prince. After the quadrille, the orchestra broke into the popular Faust Waltz. The young American noticed that the American couple had danced neither the quadrille nor, now, the waltz. He wondered why, and decided now was the time for that introduction. Coming over to the Bramwells, he put his hand out to Ben and said, 'Mind if I say hello? My name's Jefferson Kent, and I don't know many Americans around here.'

He spoke with a slight Midwest twang and had the casual, friendly air of a Westerner.

'How do you do, Mr Kent?' said Ben, shaking his hand. 'I'm Benjamin Bramwell, and this is my wife, Elizabeth.'

Jefferson Kent shook Elizabeth's hand. She liked the looks of this lanky compatriot whose tail coat was a bit shiny at the elbows and a size too small, as if it belonged to someone else.

'We're from Philadelphia,' said Elizabeth. 'Are you here on a visit?'

'No, ma'am. I live here. From Saint Louis originally, but

I work for a private bank here in Paris – the Norton Bank. Do you know of it?'

'I've heard of it,' said Ben. 'Small but very good.'

'Yes sir, that's us. We're on the Place Vendôme. If you need any banking services while you're here, we'd be glad to do business with you. You folks tourists?'

Ben glanced at his wife. 'No, we're living here, for the time being.'

'Well, it's sure nice to see Americans. Say, this is some party, isn't it? Old Nappy does it up brown, doesn't he? I've never been to any of these court shindigs, but I wheedled Mr Norton – he's my boss; he owns the bank – anyway, I got him to get me invited. Thought I might try and pass myself off as a count or something' – he winked – 'but somehow I don't think I've got the goods. Anyway, there sure are a lot of heavy swells here. And say, isn't the empress a looker? You know, my friends say I'm a pretty pushy fellow, and I guess it's the truth because I'm just about ready to act pushy and ask Mrs Bramwell if she'd waltz with me.'

Grin.

Elizabeth looked at Ben. 'Well . . .'

'She'd love to,' said Ben. 'You see, Mr Kent . . .'

'Call me Jeff.'

'All right, Jeff. I lost a leg at Chancellorsville, so needless to say I'm not much of a waltzer. And Elizabeth enjoys waltzing, so it would be a favour to me if you'd do my dancing for me.'

'Well now, that works out swell for both of us, doesn't it?'

'You weren't in the war, Mr Kent?' asked Elizabeth quietly.

His smile never faded. 'Nope. Don't believe in wars. I bought my way out and came to Paris to make some money. I think the war's a big waste of time and money for both sides.'

'Then I'm afraid I'll have to decline your invitation.'

'Oh? You disapprove of me?'

'Frankly, yes. Any American who could doubt the Northern cause is not the kind of American I want as an acquaintance. Ben, dear, it's rather warm in here. Do you think we could find some refreshments in the garden?'

And they moved off, leaving Jefferson Kent standing by himself. He let out a soft whistle. She's a real cool one, he thought. Real cool. But a looker. Oh well . . . win a few, lose a few.

He looked around the room and spotted a pretty blonde in a white dress standing beside a formidable, plumed woman who was probably her mother.

Guess I'll give her a try, he thought, as he started through the crowd toward the blonde.

'You shouldn't have cut the poor fellow,' said Ben, sipping champagne in the Tuileries Gardens.

'Oh, those cowards make me furious,' replied his wife. 'When I think of the sacrifices you made, and he's over here making money and having a good time. . . . It burns me up.'

He leaned against the stone balustrade and looked at his wife, who was bathed in the glow of the Bengal lights. She's so beautiful, he thought. And so intelligent and good. How did I ever win her?

'That's odd,' he said.

'What?'

'You mentioned *my* sacrifice.'

'But not Lew's?' She put her hand on his sleeve. '*You're* my husband now, darling.'

She said it quietly, and he about burst with pride.

'It's been two weeks. No regrets?'

'None. I'm very happy, Ben. Really. Are you?'

'I've never been happier in my life. You don't even have any regrets about the debut?'

She sipped her champagne. 'Oh well, of course I do. When the maestro went back to Rome that morning, I knew what would happen – and it did. None of his fancy friends came, and I played badly. Result? Bad reviews. But I'm certainly not giving up just because I was left in the lurch by my ex-' – she hesitated, then said coolly – '*teacher*.'

'Have you made up your mind what you want to do?'

She turned to him, and her face was suddenly animated. 'Ben, do you like Paris?'

'Well, yes . . .'

'Then couldn't we stay here? I don't want to go back to Philadelphia, at least not yet. There are just too many bad memories there. Couldn't we stay here for a year – or maybe two? We could rent a house and settle down. . . . Ward's happy here, and there are so many good teachers in Paris. Franz Liszt isn't the *only* teacher in the world, even if he is the best. Couldn't we stay, Ben?'

He drained his champagne. 'Well . . .'

'Oh, say yes, darling. Please! You'll be happy here, I promise. And think of the advantages of raising *our* child here.'

He looked at her. '*Ours?* Isn't it a little early?'

She laughed. 'Of course. But Paris is a very romantic city, and it makes me feel *terribly* productive.' She leaned close to him and whispered, 'And you're very wicked here, Ben. I like you wicked.'

'Don't you think I'd be wicked in Philadelphia?'

'You never used to be.'

He smiled, set down his glass, looked around to see if they were being watched, then took her in his arms and kissed her.

'*You* make me wicked, Elizabeth. Not Paris. But if you want to stay, then we'll stay. You know I'll do anything for you. Anything.'

'Oh Ben, thank you!' She kissed him, then toyed with his cravat a moment. 'I'm so glad you came to Paris and swept me off my feet.'

He laughed. 'I didn't sweep you off your feet. I'm not the type.'

'You'd be suprised,' she said tenderly.

Jefferson Kent came out of the ballroom on to the terrace and noticed the American couple kissing in the Tuileries Gardens. He watched a while. He looked interested.

Christine Canrobert left her apartment house on Thompson Street and walked to the kerb. It was eight o'clock on a Saturday morning, and she was going shopping for groceries.

Gilbert was coming for dinner that night, and she was going over the menu in her mind, so she didn't notice the wagon pull out of the alley down the street and head in her direction. It was going unusually fast.

She stepped off the kerb, nodding at Mrs Farley, the fat Irishwoman who lived in the building next door. Mrs Farley was sweeping the sidewalk.

'Morning, Mrs Farley,' said Christine.

Mrs Farley didn't like Negroes, but she had to admit Christine was a sweetie. She turned and smiled. 'Morning, Christine. How's Lew?'

Christine reached up and poked her son, whom she was carrying, papoose-style, in a canvas carrier on her back.

'Lew, honey, say hello to Mrs Farley.'

Lew took his thumb out of his mouth – Christine had yet to break him of that habit, which worried her – and said shyly, 'Hello, Mrs Farley.'

Mrs Farley put her hands on her wide hips and assumed a stern, maternal glare.

'Now, Christine, that child's old enough to walk! You shouldn't carry him around like a load of laundry!'

'But I can't watch him and carry groceries. . . .'

'Watch OUT!' screamed Mrs Farley.

Christine had heard the wagon, but she was close enough to the kerb to feel no danger. Now she turned round. The two galloping horses were no more than five feet from her, their hooves pounding the pavement, their harness bells tolling her death. She screamed, and was starting for the kerb just as something crashed into her.

'Holy Mother of God!' cried Mrs Farley, as she watched the girl and her child fly across the sidewalk to crash into a stone step. 'Murderer!' she screamed at the driver of the wagon as it roared past her. It didn't stop, and she had caught only a fleeting glance of the driver. The wagon was unmarked.

Sobbing, she ran down the sidewalk to Christine and knelt over her. She touched the blood matting her hair, then touched the baby's hand. It was sticking out from under his mother. It was cold.

'Holy Mother of God,' whispered Mrs Farley, crossing herself.

They were both dead.

In October 1863 a wedding had taken place in the White House which the bride, at least, hoped would prove to have historic significance. The bride was the beautiful daughter of the Secretary of the Treasury, Kate Chase. The groom was the skinny, young, alcoholic senator from Rhode Island, William Sprague. Sprague had nothing in his favour except dollars: twenty-five million of them, piled up by his calico mills in Providence. What did it matter if Senator Sprague got falling-down drunk in public? He was the richest man in New England, the election of 1864 was coming up, and Kate Chase had one burning desire: that her father replace Lincoln in the White House. She knew that for that to happen she would need money – lots of it. So, with direct efficiency, she married it.

For months after the wedding, the public couldn't get enough of the fabulous doings of the Spragues. But by 1864 another house was going up not far from the Spragues' mansion that was rivalling even Queen Kate's establishment as a social magnet. It was a house built in flamboyantly gaudy Gothic style, containing forty rooms, a ballroom, a library filled with rare books, the biggest dining room in Washington, a wine cellar lavishly and lovingly stocked, a greenhouse, a carriage house, and quarters for twenty servants. This house was entertaining the cream of Washington, even though it was whispered that the place had been paid for by the millions its owner had piled up during his tenure in the War Department. Still they came, for the junior senator from Pennsylvania was one of the most powerful men in the Republican Party, a bosom crony of *the* most powerful Radical Republican, Representative Thaddeus Stevens.

In the spring of 1864 there could be no doubt that Senator Ralph Matoon and his wife of a year and a half, Rosemary, had arrived in a big way. And one lovely May night, when the Matoons had just seated themselves at their heavy walnut dining-room table to host a dinner for Representative Stevens, the black butler, Henry, bustled into the enormous, palm-filled room with its glass-bowled brass chandelier, hurried to the senator, and whispered in his ear, 'Mistah Gilbert Samson wants to see you, boss, and looks fit to be tied!'

The former general scowled. 'Tell him he'll have to wait till I'm through dinner.'

'He ain't gwine like dat, Senator.'

'I don't give a damn what he likes: tell him to wait!'

'Yes sir.'

Henry hurried out of the room as Senator Matoon smiled down the table at his wife, whom he could barely see through the forest of silver candelabra and jungle of flowers that separated the two. There were eighteen at table, including Senator Herbert Rowlandson, Republican, of New York and his wife; Representative Charles Seymore, Republican, of Pennsylvania and his wife; Senator Penrose Granby, Republican, of Ohio and his wife; Senator Sylvester Carter, Republican, of Massachusetts, and his wife; Representative Harrison Spofford, Republican, of Wisconsin and his wife; and of course the guest of honour, who had never married, and who had come with Secretary of War Stanton and his wife – Representative Thaddeus Stevens, Republican, of Pennsylvania. Stevens was seated at Rosemary's right, and he was admiring the handsome redhead in her green satin gown, matching emeralds around her throat and dangling from her ears. Very grand Rosemary Matoon had become, he thought. Very grand indeed. Now he leaned toward her and indicated her bulging stomach.

'When are you expecting the little rascal?' he asked.

'We think next month.'

'June, eh? What are you going to name him? "Gold mine"?'

The once handsome face crinkled into a leering grin. Rosemary remained unruffled. She was used to Stevens's raspy wit.

'We thought "Patronage" would be nice,' she said with a serene smile.

Thaddeus Stevens chuckled and reached up to make sure his black wig was straight. The clubfooted wizard of Parliamentary manoeuvring liked the Matoons, even though he knew Ralph was twisty as a snake and Rosemary had slept all over Washington. After all, Ralph was the best arm-twister in the business – there was talk of his being the next Senate whip – and Stevens admired arm-twisters. Ralph Matoon knew where all the skeletons were buried, and if he had a few skeletons of his own buried somewhere . . . well, who didn't? Stevens didn't for a minute believe the 'gold mine' story, but he liked the senator's house and the food he served and the wine. Thaddeus Stevens would dine with the Devil if the food was good.

The footmen passed the turtle soup and everyone was dipping in when suddenly the double doors of the room burst open and in strode a black hurricane.

'Matoon!' roared Gilbert Samson, who looked manic. The guests dropped their silver spoons and stared. 'Matoon, you bastard! You killed her! You killed my Christine – my beautiful Christine – !'

And as Rosemary gasped 'My God, he's crazy!' the big black man began to throttle her husband, pushing his face into the turtle soup.

'Stop him!' screamed Rosemary, jumping out of her seat. Matoon was beating the table with his hammy fists as Gilbert, sweat streaming down his face, continued to hold his face in the soup. 'He's killing him! *Do* something!'

The men jumped to their feet, and two burly senators rushed down the table to jump Gilbert, who started roaring, 'Let me go! This man must pay! He killed Christine and her baby! He's a goddam murderer!'

Two footmen joined Senators Rowlandson and Granby, and the four of them managed with much yelling to pull Gilbert off. As Matoon, his face dripping turtle soup, lay back in his chair gasping for breath, the senators and the footmen pinned a raging Gilbert to the carpet, one senator on each leg and a footman on each arm. Gilbert nevertheless continued to rant. 'He killed her! He hired someone to run her and her baby down because she knew he was a murderer – '

'A murderer?' shouted Matoon, jumping up, his anger now sizzling. 'You black bastard, what are you talking about?'

'You know! You and Stanton – Stanton came to you and told you I was trying to get at the files – '

'What files?' cried Matoon, coming over to loom over his supine accuser.

'The War Department files!' Gilbert was trying to push himself upright, but the footmen held him down. 'Do you deny you ordered the murder of Lew Crandall three years ago? Do you deny it?'

'Crandall was killed at Bull Run – '

'But not by the Rebs, sir! He was killed by *you* because he knew you were taking kickbacks – !'

'This is a goddam outrage! I never took a kickback – '

'LIAR!' howled Gilbert, redoubling his fury and his struggling. 'You *lie*, and to cover that lie you killed the *one* person who could prove you lie . . . and don't tell me that wagon just *happened* to run Christine down! Don't tell me, sir, because I'm no fool! I *know* you killed her, and by Christ you'll pay for it – you'll *PAY*!!'

The richly sonorous voice, booming its accusations around the room with such manic rage, froze the spectators, froze Matoon – even froze Rosemary, who knew she was hearing the truth, that the ghost of Lew Crandall was returning, like Banquo, in the guise of Gilbert Samson. But it didn't freeze Thad Stevens. The wily old man, who by now was the only one in the room still seated, realized he had to act.

'Mr Samson,' he said softly, and the quiet tone of his voice commanded attention after all the shouting, 'get control of yourself, sir.'

Gilbert for the first time became aware of Stevens's presence. He stared at the man he knew was the best hope for black enfranchisement. Tears of rage were streaming down his face, but he said nothing as he looked down the long room between the two senators holding his legs and saw Thaddeus Stevens rise slowly from the table. Using his cane, he hobbled toward the spread-eagled Gilbert as the guests stared, silenced and immobilized by Power. Finally, reaching Gilbert's feet, he raised his cane and tapped the arm of one of the senators holding Samson.

'Let him go,' he said.

'But Thad, he's dangerous. . . .'

'I said, let him go!' The voice was louder, harsher.

They obeyed, getting to their feet. Stevens signalled the footmen, who let his arms go.

'Now, sir,' said Stevens, 'stop this ranting and get up.'

Gilbert got to his feet. He was breathing heavily and still trembling with rage and excitement.

'There's nothing you can say to stop me,' he said to Stevens. 'Nothing! I told Stanton Christine's address' – he pointed at the Secretary of War, who was standing behind his chair, transfixed – 'and he went to Matoon. . . .'

'Can you prove this?'

'Of course not! I know it's true, though! And I have an eyewitness to the accident.'

'Can she identify the driver of the wagon?'

Gilbert swallowed hard. 'No.'

'Can you prove Senator Matoon ordered the murder of this . . . what was his name?' He turned to Matoon.

'Lew Crandall,' said Matoon, wiping the soup off his face with a napkin. 'And of course he can't prove it. The whole thing's preposterous!'

'But it's the TRUTH!' roared Gilbert, lunging at Matoon again. Stevens raised his cane and stopped him.

'*Perhaps* it's the truth. But our system of law is based on the assumption of innocence. . . .'

'Your system of law,' said Gilbert contemptuously, 'made me a *slave* for the first twenty years of my life!'

'But you're not a slave now, Mr Samson, thanks to the efforts of the gentlemen in this room *and*, I can say without undue immodesty, thanks to the efforts of myself. And our system of law is about to give your people the vote – thanks again to the efforts of the people in this room. Now, Mr Samson: do you seriously propose challenging our system of law when a bloody war is still being fought for the benefit of *your* people? Fought mainly with white blood, I might add? Do you seriously suggest letting your accusations go out of this room – *even if they're true*?'

Gilbert took a few steps backward and pointed at Matoon. 'Then you admit they're true? You admit he's a murderer and a thief?'

'I admit nothing, sir. But I'm telling you – and I speak with the backing of the Congress of the United States – I'm telling you that if you persist in these accusations, your people will come to hate you. Because *we* are the black man's best hope!'

Silence. Gilbert stared at the tail-coated men and bejewelled women.

'Then,' he said quietly, 'God help the black man.'

He turned and walked out of the room. The guests relaxed somewhat and started mumbling to each other. Stevens waited until he heard Gilbert slam out of the house, then he signalled Matoon to join him.

'It's all a lie, Thad,' whispered Matoon. 'I swear! The man's crazy. . . .'

'Bullshit. Now got the dinner going again, and don't say anything. But after dinner, you and I and Stanton are having a meeting. In *private*. Get it?'

'Yes, Thad.'

'Now go back and sit down. And wipe the soup off your shirt. You're a goddam senator, remember?'

Ralph Matoon hurried back to his chair and smiled at his guests as he mopped his shirt.

'If you thought the soup was exciting,' he chuckled, 'wait till you see what we've got for the main course – eh?'

The guests broke into relieved laughter and went back to their places.

6

WHEN JOHNNIE COMES MARCHING HOME 1865

24

In September 1864 the Confederate prison authorities, made nervous by the publicity in the North about the atrocious conditions in Andersonville Prison – as well as by the impending collapse of the Confederacy – decided to remove most of the Andersonville prisoners who could still walk. One of the prisoners who was transferred was listed as Sergeant J. Starker of the Third Pennsylvania. Starker was taken in a packed boxcar to Savannah, where he was transferred to the military hospital and given a medical examination. The doctor, a humane Georgian named Ryborg, was no more shocked by Starker's physical condition than he was by the other prisoners, but he realized the man was near death. His weight was ninety-eight pounds, he had dysentery and scurvy, his gums were black and inflamed, and he had periods of what the doctor listed in the medical record as 'delirium'. Starker was given a clean bed in a clean tent of the grounds of the crowded hospital, and remedial treatment was begun. Dr Ryborg checked his progress daily, and by October, when the cool weather set in, was pleased to record:

> Patient beginning to take on weight. Inflammation of gums receding, body sores healing. A naturally strong physique is overcoming months of malnutrition and abuse. However, patient still subject to periods of delirium. When rational, seems depressed at times, but morale improving.

By December, as Sherman's troops were nearing Savannah on their march to the sea, Ryborg recorded that Starker's weight was one hundred and thirty-four pounds.

> Still thin, but gaining fast. Body sores completely gone. Teeth still loose, but gums normal. Routine of regular exercise has restored muscle tone and general health. Still suffers periods of depression, but morale greatly improved.

Savannah fell peaceably to General Sherman's troops on 21 December, and the Federal authorities took over the military hospital. Most of the Andersonville survivors were mustered out of the service with back pay. However, no record of a Sergeant J. Starker of the Third Pennsylvania could be found on the rolls, so no back pay could be given. Starker was not the only soldier whose name had been lost, and in recognition of his long imprisonment he was given a new suit of clothes, new shoes, one hundred dollars cash, and a second-class passage back to what he told them was his home town, Philadelphia. On 4 February 1865 Lew Crandall took passage on a ship from Savannah to New York, then travelled by train back to Philadelphia, where he arrived on a blustery winter day. The first thing he did was buy a cheap overcoat and a wide-brimmed black hat, second hand. Then, huddling against the wind, with forty-eight dollars left in his pocket, he started walking toward his house on Locust Street. He wondered if it would be possible to glue together the shattered fragments of his past.

As he trudged through the streets of Philadelphia, the winds of memory blew through his brain. His wife. Did she still love him? After four years, it would be a miracle if she still remembered him. For that matter, did he still love her? He didn't know any more. He was returning to Philadelphia curious, but rather fearful of what he'd find. Besides, he didn't know where else to go.

Philadelphia seemed the same and yet different. He remembered buildings, streets . . . yet it was all out of focus. His family was out of focus. If they knew nothing of him, he knew nothing of them, because he had not dared communicate with them during the interminable years in the Southern prisons. When he had recovered consciousness in the Richmond hospital, he knew he was a marked man. Matoon had ordered him killed; by a miracle he had survived. But Lew Crandall must vanish. If his name appeared on the prisoner lists, might not Matoon see it, arrange his exchange, bring him north again and then kill him twice, the second time doing a better job of it? Or, even simpler, might not Matoon send Burt Thomson south with a Letter of Passage, have him look up Crandall and pay one of the Southern guards to conveniently shoot him through the head? Perhaps while he was 'accidentally' overstepping the dead-line? It sounded improbable, but Lew had seen at first hand how casually the Southern guards treated Northern lives. So he had invented Starker. If Starker were listed or exchanged, who would know or care? Starker was faceless.

As the months rolled by and he didn't get exchanged, he struggled with the question of whether he should try to get word to Elizabeth that he was alive. But that held other dangers. He had quickly figured out the obvious: that Rosemary Fletcher had made some sort of accommodation with Matoon. When he left the general on the morning of First Bull Run, Rosemary had been the enemy – the spy. Yet that afternoon *he*, Lew, had been shot. Who else could have told Matoon that Lew Crandall was more to be feared than Rosemary Fletcher? It must have been Rosemary, and she had connections with the Southern Intelligence. All the mail coming in and out of the prison was censored. If Lew wrote anything to Elizabeth and she started a correspondence, inevitably word would get back to Rosemary and Matoon that Lew Crandall was not dead. Matoon was hardly reluctant to use violence – under the rock of his bumbling, genial façade lay a rattlesnake. Wasn't it possible he might do something to Elizabeth as well as to Lew Crandall? If she knew the truth, she was as much fair game as Lew.

His one chance was to use a code she would recognize, and the musical code she had dreamed up while he was in Washington was made to order. When he finally managed to get his hands on a copy of the Chopin études, three years had already passed, but he thought it was still worth a try. So he had sent her an encoded message: 'DARLING I AM ALIVE IN ANDERSONVILLE THERE IS DANGER DO NOT TRY TO CONTACT ME WILL RETURN AFTER WAR I LOVE YOU LEW.' Of course, there was the risk the censors would spot it as a code, but there was also the possibility they might let it pass. He sent the letter, but had no idea whether she had received it or, if she had, had remembered the code. Meanwhile, he had remained Starker.

It wasn't Starker coming home, though. It was Lew Crandall. He knew the possibilities. Four years a 'widow'? An attractive woman like Elizabeth? It was more likely than not he was going to find a married woman on Locust Street.

He stopped in front of his house and looked at it. It seemed unchanged. He climbed the steps to the front door and rang the bell. Then he saw the brass nameplate on the door. It read PARKER. That was the first jolt.

The door was opened by a young Irish maid, who winced against the wind.

'Yes?'

'I wanted to make some inquiries about the owner. My name is Starker.'

She looked at the thin young man in his cheap coat and crunched hat.

'What do you want to know?'

'May I come in? It's cold out here.'

The maid hesitated. Well, he looked safe, and she was freezing.

'All right, but just for a minute. I'm busy.'

'Won't take much of your time.'

Time, he thought, going into the familiar entrance hall. Four years of *my* time. . . . He looked around, hearing in his memory Elizabeth practising her scales. Parker. Was she Mrs Parker now?

'The owner is away,' said the maid, closing the door with a shiver. 'She lives in Paris.'

'France?' he said, disbelievingly.

'Only Paris *I* know, mister. She's rented this place to the Parkers on a long-term lease.'

Lew looked through the doors into the parlour and caught a glimpse of the rosewood furniture that had been the Butterfields' wedding present.

'Rented furnished?' he asked.

'Yes. What do you want to know for?'

He looked back at her. 'Do you know Mrs Crandall's address in Paris?'

'Who's Mrs Crandall?'

'The owner.'

'Oh yes, that was her old name. Her husband was killed in the war, and she's remarried.'

Silence. Funny duck, she thought. Not bad-looking, though. Sort of peaky.

'What's her new name?'

'Let's see . . . it starts with a "B" . . .'

'Bramwell?' said the stranger softly.

'That's it! Bramwell.'

Odd look on his face, she thought. Like he's just been kicked in the teeth . . . 'Listen, I don't have all day.'

'Yes, I'm going now. Thanks.'

'Thanks for what?'

She opened the door to the cold. He held his hat and went out. Then, before she could close the door, he turned.

'Did she have any children?' he asked.

'Who?'

'Mrs Crandall? I mean, Mrs Bramwell? Did she have a child?'

'How would I know? I never met the woman. Wait a minute. Yes, of course, she must have, because when we rented the house there was a nursery upstairs. All in blue. Quite pretty. The mistress has turned it into a sewing room.'

'Blue?'

'Yes. Must have been a boy. Listen, I'm freezing!'

She closed the door.

Lew walked down to the street. A boy. He had a son . . . no, not his son now. Ben's son now. Ben? Incredible. And yet, perhaps, for the best. . . . He started walking toward Rittenhouse Square. He had left for Washington in April – or was it May? It all seemed so long ago. . . . And Elizabeth was two months pregnant then, wasn't she? Which meant the son must have been born in about . . . November? So he would be – what? A little over three. He would be talking, walking, running, playing . . .

He reached Rittenhouse Square and looked at the familiar Italianate house. How proud his mother had been of it! How proud she had been of him, marching off to war . . . what a laugh. He crossed the square slowly, the wind almost blowing his hat off. He wondered what he would find.

Elizabeth married to Ben! He was still chewing it over. He felt a surge of anger. How long had she stayed in mourning for him? A week? No, that was unfair. He knew Elizabeth. She must have been miserable. He had caused her misery, but Matoon had caused him misery. Was he miserable now, knowing she was Ben's wife? No, not miserable. Too numb for misery. Sad, but Ben would make her a good husband. Perhaps a better one than he. Who would want to be Job's wife? And wasn't he Job?

He climbed the steps to his mother's door and rang the familiar bell. The plaque next to the door read SAINT THERESA ACADEMY. Out of focus. The door was opened by a tall nun. He looked past her into the familiar entrance hall where once Eugène had ruled the domestic roost. Now, from somewhere inside the house, came the ghostly voices of young girls singing hymns.

'Yes?'

'I wanted to speak to someone – '

'This is not a charity,' interrupted the nun, starting to close the door. 'If you need money, contact the diocese.'

'I don't need money, I need information!' he almost shouted, stopping the door.

'About what?' The nun looked suspicious.

'Where's the owner?'

'Of what?'

'This house, of course!'

'The owner's in Rome. He's the pope.'

He stared at her. 'Then where's Mrs Crandall?'

'Why do you want to know?'

'I'm . . . a relative.'

The nun thought for a moment, then opened the door again. 'Come in.'

He hurried in. She closed the door and looked at him with less hostility.

'Then I assume you don't know Mrs Crandall died last spring. She was a blessed lady of sacred memory, and she left this house to the diocese. We have turned it into a school for young ladies. An *exclusive* school, I might add.' She looked at his hat.

He was looking around. Through the open library doors he saw part of the Winterhalter portrait of Nicole Louise, still hanging over the fireplace. And her favourite Voltaire chair. He turned back to the nun.

'What did she die of?'

'A heart seizure. It was quite sudden. Happily, Father Dunne was with her at the end and administered the rites.'

Father Dunne. Yes, he remembered hearing about him. . . .

'Is she buried in the Catholic cemetery?'

'No. In her will she stipulated she wished to be buried next to her husband . . . unfortunately. He was Protestant.'

'Thank you.'

She opened the door. He started out, then changed his mind.

'I assume her grandson inherited the estate?'

'The estate went to the Church.'

'*All* of it?'

The nun thought a moment. 'I believe a trust was left in the grandson's name. He lives in Paris with his mother.'

'Thank you.'

He went out, and the nun closed the door behind him. The wind swept around Rittenhouse Square. That door, he knew, had been closed for ever. But what about Elizabeth? She was *his* wife, not Ben's. His. Maybe he was Job, but he had suffered enough. He wanted his family back, his wife, his son. He could go to Paris and . . .

He started walking.

And what? Reappear in the middle of their lives to claim what was his? But it wasn't his any more. It was Ben's.

Perhaps eventually it could be untangled legally, but what about them? Their happiness? Was it fair to cause them to suffer, to create an incredibly complicated situation? And what if they had a child of their own? What about *that*?

The doors to the past were slamming. Lew Crandall dead would be a sweet memory to his widow. But Lew Crandall, arisen from the dead? She might come to hate him. They all might.

Jesus, he thought, with a shudder. Lew Crandall really *is* dead.

An hour later he leaned down to place a wreath on a grave marked 'Jefferson Shippen Crandall, 1801–1857'. Then he placed a second wreath on the neighbouring grave marked 'Nicole Louise de Rochefort Crandall, 1810–1864'. He stood up and looked down at his past. His mother had died when he had arrived at Andersonville. His proud, beautiful, in some ways impossible mother. Dead. His father, dead. His wife remarried to his best friend. His son unknown. His fortune gone, most of it left to the Church, unrecoverable without years of litigation he couldn't afford. What the pope was given, the pope rarely gave back. . . .

The wind howled around him, blowing off his hat. It danced merrily across the gravestones, laughing at him. He watched it go, but didn't chase it. He put his hands in the pockets of his coat to keep them warm, then he looked back down at the graves.

How much? he thought. How much more, God?

He turned and walked slowly out of the cemetery. He had spent ten dollars on the wreaths. Thirty-seven dollars lay between him and destitution. He thought of his maternal great-grandfather, the Sieur de Rochefort, who had been wiped out by the French Revolution. Three generations later, and he had been wiped out by another kind of revolution. He wondered if, like his grandfather, he could tutor French to rich New York kids. A cheerful prospect.

He walked down the windy streets. The one-time Golden Prince of Philadelphia was a stranger in a hostile city. He bought a newspaper, then went in to a cheap café to buy a cup of coffee. He sat at a table and sipped the hot brew. It was rotten coffee, but it warmed his stomach.

Matoon. He had dreamed of revenge for years, but what could he do? Go to Mr Seward? The dinner date was a little stale now, but it was a possibility. But that meant revealing himself as Lew Crandall, and inevitably word would reach Elizabeth that her first husband was still alive. Besides, what could Mr Seward do now? What could he prove? He had read in the Savannah papers that Rosemary was now Mrs Matoon, so obviously neither of them would testify against the other, and the green passbook was undoubtedly long since gone. That left his word against a powerful senator's that a corporal had *claimed* he had been ordered by Matoon to shoot to kill. It was no good.

Then how to get him? How to repay the fat bastard? If the law was no good, then he had to operate outside the law, and that appealed to Lew. He had learned in prison by necessity how to steal to survive, how to trade, bully, twist arms, cheat, lie . . . but mainly how to steal. He had learned the thrill of circumventing the law. To get Matoon, he would circumvent the law again. Murder? Possible. But murder was too good for him, too easy. And too punishable. After all, he was a senator. There had to be another way, a better, more painful way . . . quieter than murder. . . .

'Ain't this coffee enough to rot your gut?' he heard a raspy voice say.

He became aware of an ageing bum sitting down across from him. Lousy, unshaven, his nose a red roadmap to his wine-soaked soul. He settled himself in the chair, then started spooning sugar into his coffee mug.

'If you put enough sugar in it, it don't taste so evil. Besides, sugar's free. You readin' that paper, sonny, or you gonna use it to line your coat?'

'I'm going to read it.'

'When you're through, don't toss it away. I'll take it. This goddam wind's turnin' my ass blue. New around here?' He slurped the coffee, holding the mug with both hands.

'Sort of.'

'If you're lookin' for a clean bed, try the Ben Franklin

House. Two bits a night, and no cooties. Watch out for the pickpockets, though. They're wicked. Steal you blind.'

'Not much left to steal.'

The bum chuckled. 'Don't need to tell me. I got eyes. You in the war?'

'I was.'

'Looks like it's about over now, don't it? What you plannin' to do?'

'I don't know.'

'Got a gal?'

'*Had* several.'

'Well, I wish you luck, sonny. And when you're done with that paper, don't toss it away.'

He started spooning more sugar in his mug. Lew watched him, then opened the paper. Down, down, down he had slid. From the top to the bottom. His life turned upside down. But he was still young, only twenty-seven. There was a lot of life left, but what to do with it? How to return from the dead without ruining the living? How to repay Matoon? And then what?

His eyes roamed over the newsprint. After years of hearing nothing but rumour, he had been almost totally ignorant of what was happening in the world till he got to Savannah. Now, Lincoln was asking Congress for authority to pay four hundred million dollars to the Southern states as compensation to the ex-slaveholders. Queen Victoria was brooding in Windsor Castle. In Mexico City the Emperor Maximilian and the Empress Carlota had given a ball at Chapultepec Castle in honour of the French ambassador and his wife.

Mexico. There had been talk in the prisons of escaping to Mexico. And then in the hospital at Savannah, as Sherman's army came nearer, the Rebs had started talking about escaping to Mexico to start a new life. The Old South was burning, so try for a new start in a new world. Mexico. Interesting. The Old North was burning, too. A new life . . .

He read on:

The Court wore costumes, an idea suggested by the Emperor, who came dressed as his ancestor, the Hapsburg Emperor Charles

V. The Empress came dressed as Beatrice d'Este. But perhaps the most clever costume was worn by the wife of the representative of Napoleon III, Mme de Beaupré. She came dressed as a shepherdess. . . .

He stopped and reread the sentence. Laura? Laura de Beaupré in Mexico?

'You wouldn't have a nickel, would you?'

He put down the paper. The bum was grinning at him, holding out his hand.

'Or maybe a dime? I know you're down and out, sonny, but if you could spare *something* . . . God will pay you back. Honest.'

Lew got up and pulled fifty cents from his pocket.

'Here's fifty cents,' he said, putting the coins in the bum's hand. 'And don't tell God. He's paid me back enough already.'

He tossed the paper on the table and started for the door. The bum stared at the coins. Then he looked up and yelled, 'Say, thanks! What'd God pay you back *for*?'

'Wish to hell I knew.'

Laura. Mexico. It had a lovely sound. After four mute years, his heart began to sing.

At the door, he stopped, changing his mind. He returned to the table, where the bum was fitting the newspaper into his overcoat. 'Here,' said Lew, pulling the thirty-seven dollars out of his pocket. 'This is all the money I've got in the world. It's yours.' And he put the cash on the table.

'You crazy?' The bum was eyeing the money.

'Could be. That's government money, and after what the government did to me, I don't want it. I'm going to Mexico, and I want to start with a clean slate. Buy yourself a steak and a whore and have a good time. Good luck.'

He started back toward the door. The bum was scooping up the cash. He called after Lew, 'How you gonna get to Mexico if you're broke? How'll you get by?'

Lew looked back. 'I'll get by the same way I got by three years in prison: I'll steal.'

And he walked out of the café.

7

BANDITS
1867

25

On a January morning in 1867 Laura de Beaupré and her Indian maid, Dolores, were riding on the road from Mexico City to Cuernavaca. It was, predictably, a beautiful morning: cool at first, then becoming balmy. The near-perfect climate at Cuernavaca had made the town a favourite of the Emperor Maximilian, who had spent considerable money renovating a villa there, and the de Beauprés had rented a villa for themselves near by, much to Laura's delight. But now she was going to the villa for the last time to pack her belongings. Aristide was waiting in the capital for her to return after closing the villa. Then they were leaving Mexico, returning to Paris via Washington and New York to carry one final appeal from Maximilian to Napoleon III not to withdraw the French troops from Mexico and to continue to support Maximilian's tottering throne. But Aristide knew the journey would be in vain. Napoleon was disgusted with Maximilian's shilly-shallying between being a pleasant tyrant and playing the role of beloved liberal father to the Mexican people. Maximilian was a charming failure, France had spent millions on the ill-fated adventure, the French press was howling, and Napoleon wanted to cut his losses and get out. The Empress Carlota had travelled to Europe the previous fall to demand that Napoleon live up to his pledges of support, but her efforts had ended, literally, in madness: Carlota was confined in her castle, Miramar, outside Trieste. It was rumoured she was totally insane. If Carlota had failed to influence Napoleon, what chance had Aristide de Beaupré? But he would carry the letter, and, after three years in Mexico, the de Beauprés were going home with the French army. They would leave Maximilian to Mexico, and probably to Heaven.

Laura was wearing a blue velvet travelling suit with a charming plumed hat that curved smartly over her head and dipped over her forehead. The outfit had come from Paris, as had the small leather volume of love poems she was reading, and the elegant carriage she was riding in. The six soldiers accompanying the carriage were also French. But though her husband was the French emperor's representative in Mexico, Laura had mixed emotions about going home. She was delighted the French were finally pulling out of the country. She had consistently opposed the French occupation – for that was what it was, no matter what Napoleon called it. Aristide had raged at her for her attitude, but Laura was stubborn. It was wrong, she said. Louis Napoleon was a fool to have become involved, it was all Eugénie's fault – for the beautiful French empress had instigated the adventure in the first place, badgering her vacillating husband into it – and the Mexicans had come to hate the French. Events were bearing out the wisdom of her judgment.

But pleased as she was that the French were leaving, personally she was sad to leave Mexico. She had come to love the country and its people. And, foolish and vague as Maximilian was, she had come to admire him, in an odd way. The former Austrian archduke might be more interested in establishing an elegant court that could compete with the European courts than he was in making the hard decisions of government, but still, he loved Mexico, as she did. He thought Napoleon had betrayed him by pulling the troops out, but Maximilian believed God and the Mexican people had put him on the throne rather than French rifles, and he would not run with the dogs of war. Maximilian would stay in Mexico, galling as that was to the Indian lawyer Benito Juárez, who was leading the Mexican resistance to Maximilian's limp regime. Maximilian refused to abandon his 'people' and his 'duty'. Mad Max maybe, but somehow admirable Max. Laura knew the moment the last French soldier left Veracruz, Maximilian's days were numbered.

So Laura was sad to leave, and this final journey to Cuernavaca was not a happy event, despite the beautiful weather and breathtaking scenery. Laura was trying to lose herself in the elegant poems of Alfred de Musset. She was just relishing a particularly delicious description of love's rapture when Captain Picard, in command of the detachment of French soldiers guarding her, yelled through the carriage window, 'Madame: bandits!'

Laura held on to her hat and poked her head out the window to look back. Behind them, partially obscured by the clouds of dust thrown up by the carriage wheels, she could see what appeared to be several dozen men on horseback chasing them.

'Don't worry, madame!' yelled Picard. 'We're near the garrison. . . .'

Laura pulled her head back in.

'There seem to be a lot of them,' she said to her maid, who looked frightened.

'This road!' wailed Dolores. 'There are always *bandidos*!'

It was then the carriage brakes began screeching.

'What now?' Laura looked out again. 'Why are we stopping?' she called to Picard. The captain pointed ahead. She looked. A hundred feet ahead of them, the road cut through a hill. The cut in the hill was blocked by a dozen more men on horseback.

'Stay inside!' yelled Picard, aiming his rifle at the bandits ahead of them. By now, the carriage had halted. The six soldiers moved their horses close to the vehicle, and waited, the rifles ready.

But so far no one had fired a shot.

Laura pulled back inside. 'Lower the blinds,' she said to Dolores. The Indian obeyed, then began mumbling prayers.

'There's nothing to fear,' said Laura.

'So madame says. . . .'

'Well, maybe there's *something* to fear. But let's not let them see we're frightened.'

She opened her purse and pulled out a small pistol with an engraved ivory handle. She checked to make sure it was loaded, then rubbed her suede glove over the polished barrel. She slipped it under her purse in her lap. Folding her hands over the purse, she waited in the semi-dark. She had carried a gun since she had been in Mexico. The country crawled with *bandidos* and *guerrilleros*; the cities crawled with thieves. Mexico was a paradise for criminals, and neither the Mexican police nor the French army could do much about it.

She heard arguing voices outside, but still no shots.

Then the carriage door opened, and a man climbed inside. He held a revolver, and he looked as if he were enjoying himself. He sat down next to Dolores, who almost swooned, and pointed his revolver at Laura, who was staring at him. He was wearing a black *charro* outfit, which indicated he was a successful bandit. Tight black pants, the seams outlined with white stitching. A loose black vest, or bolero as the Mexicans called it, with no shirt underneath. A black sombrero, which he took off. He was dirty and hadn't shaved for several days. He was lean and tough-looking. His face was extraordinarily good-looking, but no Mexican had ever had a face like that. The blue eyes were drinking her in, roaming up and down her body, insolently stripping her. He looked vaguely familiar.

'Hello, Laura,' he said in English.

Her memory writhed in confusion. She tore her eyes away from him and looked out the open door. The bandits – who were as Mexican as the one opposite her was obviously gringo – had surrounded the carriage. She saw that Captain Picard had dropped his rifle and raised his hands. She looked back at the gringo. His skin was so dark from the sun he might have passed, but that hair? The sun had bleached it almost white.

'I don't expect manners from a bandit,' she said, 'even an English-speaking one. But my name is Madame de Beaupré. I suppose you want my money?'

'Oh no. I want *you*. Señora,' he said to Dolores, switching to Spanish, 'get out of the carriage. Don't worry, you won't be harmed.'

Dolores muttered more prayers, looking at her mistress.

'My maid stays with me,' said Laura, pulling her pistol from under her purse. Lew Crandall looked at it, laughed, twirled his revolver around, grabbed its barrel and offered her the grip.

'Take it,' he said, 'if it'll make you feel better.' Amazed, she took it. He leaned back and crossed his arms over his chest as Laura stared at the two guns in her hands. 'Of course, if you kill me, neither of you will get out of here alive. I've got thirty-five men out there who love to shoot Frenchmen – and women. I've made them swear not to harm either you or the French soldiers – as long as you do what I say. But if you don't? Well, I wouldn't guarantee how long my men would live up to their word. Do you know you're even more beautiful than I remembered? And God knows, I've remembered enough.'

'I suppose this is some ridiculous joke. . . .'

'You don't remember me?'

'Of course not. Where would I have met a bandit?'

'You don't remember me,' he said with mock sadness. 'And I've been looking forward to this historic moment for six years. I even brought you a present.' He reached in the pocket of his vest and pulled out a diamond bracelet. He dangled it a moment, looking at it. 'Isn't it beautiful?' he said, twisting it around. 'French. The French are good at jewellery. Madame de Beaupré, I present you this expensive bauble as a token of my undying esteem. And when a man loves a woman who can't even remember him, I call that undying esteem.'

She put down the guns to take the bracelet.

'*You* stole it!' she exclaimed, looking at it. 'Six months ago, from our house in Mexico City. . . .'

'Seven,' corrected Lew.

'Then you must have my earrings!'

'No, I sold them.' And he snatched the two guns from her lap. She bit her lip, furious at the swindle, but said nothing. He aimed her pistol at her, and his revolver at Dolores. 'Out,' he said. Dolores climbed over him, terrified, saying, 'Don't kill me! Don't kill madame! Oh, *madre de Dios* . . .'

When she had jumped to the ground, Lew yelled out, in Spanish, 'Agustin, let's go!'

Someone slammed the door shut, and the carriage rattled into motion.

He leaned back in the seat, the guns in his lap, and started stripping her with his eyes again.

'Perfection,' he smiled. 'God must have been in a fabulous mood when he dreamed you up.'

She looked him over, thinking the same about him. 'Where are you taking me?' she said.

'My dear lady, you are being raped. I mean it in the classical sense. You are being carried off by force to my palace in the mountains, where I am going to seduce you.'

'Ridiculous. Are you an American?'

'That's right.'

She suddenly blinked. 'You must be El Juero!'

'That's me. El Juero, the blond gringo, the best thief in Mexico City. Specialities: railroad bonds, cash when available, jewels . . . and today, my greatest effort, the brilliant climax to my highly successful criminal career: the French ambassador's wife.'

'You're kidnapping me?'

'Exactly. The ransom note will be delivered to your husband in Mexico City tonight. I'm trying to decide whether your eyes are blue or green or grey. Which are they?'

'They're a mixture of all three,' she snapped. 'And you don't really believe you'll get away with this farce?'

'Farce? The farce was how fast your brave French soldiers gave up when they saw my thirty-five dirty and extremely mean-looking *bandidos*. I picked them for their meanness. I even paid five pesos extra for a man with one eye. There's something about one-eyed bandits that's guaranteed to instil icy terror, don't you think?'

'You must be joking. You sound as if you'd cast a play!'

'That's exactly what I did.' He laughed. 'These aren't my men. I rented them for the day. They work for Diego Sanchez.'

She gasped. 'Do you *know* him?'

'Professionally, not socially. Sanchez is a little bit loco, and much too political for my blood. I keep out of Mexican politics. Hell, I can't even understand them!'

She started to snicker. The snicker grew to a giggle and finally bloomed into a laugh.

'Oh, it's priceless!' She snorted. 'I wouldn't have missed this for the world! To rent a gang of bandits . . . oh, I love it! My husband will be *furious*, but I can't help it. . . .' She pulled a lace handkerchief from her purse and wiped her nose. 'How much ransom are you asking, Señor El Juero?'

'One million American dollars, to be deposited in the Bank of New Orleans.'

She was giggling again.

'One million! Well, you certainly don't think small.'

'Your husband can afford it. I want the money in an American bank because I don't trust the Mexican banks.'

'No one in his right mind would. So you're the famous El Juero! How dashing and romantic . . . slipping into society balls to size up your next victims. . . .'

'Then you've read about me?' he said, with more than a hint of pride.

'But who hasn't? Is that where I've seen you? At a ball? You look terribly familiar. . . .'

'Well, you waltzed with me at a masked ball seven months ago. Do you remember the drunk who claimed to be the younger brother of the Condé de San Cristobal and stepped on your foot?'

'You?'

'Me.' He grinned. 'I was sober as a judge. Ten minutes later, I "wove" away from the ball, rode to your house, climbed through a window – your butler really is extremely careless – and stole your diamonds.' He pointed at the bracelet in her lap. 'It was wonderful dancing with you, Laura. I almost said to hell with the diamonds. But, alas, my greed got the better of me, as usual. Do you know I have almost a quarter million dollars deposited in American banks?'

She was frowning. 'But I never saw your face at the ball, because you were masked. And I *have* seen your face . . . somewhere . . .'

He was suddenly less playful. 'It was six years ago,' he said.

'Six years ago, we were in Washington. . . .'

'Remember the day of the First Battle of Bull Run? We had a picnic together. You and I and that fat Prince Napoleon who had mayonnaise on his shirt.'

Her face turned chalk-white. 'But you're dead!' she whispered.

He leaned forward, took her hands, and kissed them. 'I'm very much alive,' he said. 'And more in love with you than ever.'

As she stared at him, the carriage slowed to a bumpy halt. The door was opened by a grinning Mexican with furious black mustachios and two gold teeth.

'El Juero, we take the horses now,' he said in Spanish, leering at Laura.

'End of the line,' said Lew, getting out of the carriage. Laura watched him. Lew Crandall? Was it possible? But it had to be . . . and that face. Yes, she had never really forgotten that face. . . .

He was standing outside the carriage, extending his hand. She got out, and he helped her to the ground. She looked around. They were in the foothills of the mountains to the east of Cuernavaca – she saw Popocatepetl in the distance – and the bandits were surrounding them. Three horses were tied to a tree. Lew pointed to them and said, 'Over there.' Then he led her toward them as she eyed the bandits nervously.

'Aren't they the most desperate-looking bunch of characters you've ever seen?' he said in English, smiling pleasantly at the bandits.

'They certainly *are*,' and she meant it. Her abductor might be treating it all very lightly, but the faces of the bandits were dead serious. And menacing. 'Are you sure they're safe?'

'About as safe as rattlesnakes. But since I paid them well, and since I'm a member of the same profession – though I pride myself that my operation is slightly more elegant than theirs – they'll let us alone. Tomás: *muchas gracias*,' he yelled to one of them, who was leaning forward on his horse, watching them.

'*De nada,*' said the man. 'El Juero is a friend. El Juero steals from the French. The señora is very beautiful. El Juero has good taste. Too bad she's a Frenchwoman.'

'Well, everyone has faults.'

'To be French is a terrible fault,' said Tomás, turning his horse and digging in his spurs. He galloped down the road. With a great clattering of hooves and snorting of horses, the other bandits followed him. Lew, Laura, and the fiercely mustachioed Mexican who had opened the carriage door watched them.

'Was that Sanchez?' asked Laura.

'Tomás? No. He's Rodriguez, the second-in-command. Charming fellow. They say he roasted a French soldier alive on a spit, but the Mexicans tend to exaggerate.'

'It was no exaggeration. Aristide knew the soldier. And if your idea to kidnap me is so brilliant, don't you think Sanchez might try it himself?'

Lew continued toward the horses. 'He'd like nothing better than to get his hands on you. But he won't.'

'You seem terribly sure of yourself.'

'I am. Sanchez is in Texas, buying second-hand Confederate guns. That's why I could rent his gang. Besides, no one knows where I'm taking you.'

He was helping her on her horse.

'Where *are* you taking me?' she said.

'To my palace in the mountains.' He winked. 'And no one knows where El Juero's palace is except El Juero and Agustin. Agustin, this is Madame de Beaupré.' He had switched to Spanish. The Mexican grinned even more broadly, his gold teeth gleaming in the sun, and he touched his sombrero.

'*La senora es muy hermosa,*' he said. He carried two revolvers. Cartridge belts like those of the bandits crossed his chest, and a dagger was stuck in one of the belts.

'Agustin is my lock expert,' said Lew, getting on his horse. 'There's not a lock or a safe in Mexico he can't open. The two of us are an unbeatable combination.'

Laura shook her head. 'You're insane,' she said.

'But having the time of my life. There's a lot to be said for crime. Plenty of exercise, clean air, thrills – and beautiful women. Shall we go to my palace?'

He dug in his spurs and started up the mountain. Laura looked at Agustin, who was beside her. He pulled out one of his revolvers, pointed it at her, and his gold teeth flashed.

She started up the mountain behind Lew, thinking that if he was insane, he was the world's most attractive lunatic.

They rode for five hours through difficult terrain, some of it seared by dangerous barrancas. At one point, where the trail became extremely narrow, he took her on his own horse, holding her on his lap. She liked the warmth and strength of his body, but when he kissed her ear she gave him a cool look. 'I thought you were a gentleman,' she said.

'Not any more, thank God.'

'You surely wouldn't take advantage of the situation?'

'You want to bet?'

'You're outrageous.'

'I know.'

She said nothing more, trying to maintain her dignity. But her heart was a drumroll.

In the middle of the afternoon, they reached a small plateau with a magnificent view of the valley below. Lew dismounted and came over to her horse. 'Lunch,' he said, helping her down. 'Hungry?'

'I'm starved.'

'Tired?'

'I'm exhausted.'

'But you're having a good time?'

She walked toward a rock to sit down. 'If this is your idea of a good time . . .'

'Don't move.'

His voice was sharp. She turned to see he had pulled out his gun. Now he fired at the rock behind her. She screamed and turned to see a headless rattlesnake writhing on the rock. Then it stopped. Lew came over and threw the snake's body over the edge of the cliff. He put his gun back and said,

'Always look before you sit. Mexican snakes are as mean as Mexican bandits.'

She was trembling. She pushed a lock of her blonde hair that had fallen over her forehead back into place.

'I'm not used to having to worry about snakes,' she said as she started to sit down. She froze in mid-sit and turned to take a second look. No snake. She sat down.

Lew pulled a piece of oilcloth from his saddlebag and unwrapped a plump chicken. 'Concepcion roasted this for us,' he said.

'Who's Concepcion?'

'Agustin's woman. A very pretty Indian girl he fell in love with last month. Agustin's always falling in love.'

'And how about your Indian woman? They say you live with one.'

'I used to. She left me a couple of months ago. She fell in love with Juárez and politics. Love and politics are a bad marriage. Do you like pulque?'

He had pulled a loaf of bread and a corked bottle from the saddlebag. Now he carried the food to Laura, handing her the bottle.

'Pulque?' she made a face. 'I can't stand it. It stinks.'

'Well, up here it's pulque or nothing. Some chicken?'

'I'll have a leg. Here: give me the bread. I'll cut it.'

He gave her the bread and his knife, and she started cutting the loaf on the rock. Behind them Agustin had pulled his own chicken from his saddlebag, plus his own bottle of pulque, and was sitting, cross-legged, on the ground, devouring the bird. Lew pulled a leg off his chicken and gave it to Laura. Then he sat next to her on the rock and started on the other chicken leg.

'You say no one knows where your "palace in the mountains" is,' she said. 'How about your Indian woman who went over to Juárez? Doesn't she know?'

'Nope. I never brought her up. I went to her place instead. That's a nice hat,' he went on, between bites. 'But if you want my advice, I'd throw it away.'

'Throw it away?' she exclaimed. 'I will not! It cost a fortune.'

He shrugged. 'Have it your way. But you're going to be up here a long time, and you're going to get awfully tired of that outfit. Besides, a Paris hat in the mountains is ridiculous.'

'If you'd given me a little warning, I'd have packed some lederhosen.'

He laughed and took the bottle of pulque. He uncorked it, put it to his mouth, tilted his head back, and took a long guzzle.

'Ah,' he said, wiping his mouth with the back of his hand, 'pure fire. Sure you won't try some?'

He held out the bottle. She looked at it dubiously. Then she put down the chicken, took the bottle, and tried a sip. She crinkled her nose.

'I prefer Corton-Charlemagne,' she said, returning the bottle.

'Who doesn't? But admit it's not bad. And admit you're having fun.'

'My dear, befuddled Monsieur Crandall,' she said irritably, 'you seem obsessed with the notion that I'm enjoying myself – why, I have no idea! I was on my way to Cuernavaca to close our villa . . . my husband is waiting in Mexico City to take me back to Paris . . . when suddenly I was abducted – no, "raped!" – by a gringo bandit. . . .'

'Thief,' corrected Lew pleasantly. 'Sanchez is a bandit – or a *guerrillero*. But I'm a thief. There's a difference.'

'Not to me! To me, you're all outlaws. . . .'

'Oh well, yes. You're right there.'

'I certainly am! You make me ride for hours over suicidal mountain trails, you make me lunch with rattlesnakes, with nothing to drink except fermented cactus juice, and you expect me to say I'm having fun!'

'But it's so romantic.' He smiled. 'To be carried off by a thief who has no scruples and who'll stop at nothing to gain his nefarious ends . . . why, Rossini would make a rip-snorting opera out of it.'

'Signor Rossini prefers dining at the Café Anglais in Paris – as do I! And speaking of Paris, it might interest you to know that your wife is living there now.'

'I know.'

'Did you know I ran into her in Rome several years ago? And that the poor woman practically burst into tears when I mentioned I had met you in Washington? I had the discretion not to tell her that you tried to make love to me.'

'I thank you for that.'

'The point is, while you're running around Mexico having "the time of your life" – and I quote – your wife thinks you're dead. I take it that doesn't bother you?'

He looked at her. 'You're taking all the fun out of this,' he said quietly.

'As I told you, it's not fun.'

He shrugged. 'All right. Yes, it bothers me. And of course I want to see my son. Some day perhaps I will. But right now, I'm in Mexico – for a definite purpose. And whether you think it's fun or not – or even ridiculous, as you said earlier – one of the reasons I'm in Mexico is to seduce you.' He stood up and pounded the cork back in the pulque bottle. 'Which I'm going to do. We still have two hours to ride. I think we'd better get started. Leave the rest of the chicken for the snakes.'

He went back to his horse.

They reached the small house at twilight. It was built beside a snow-fed brook near the tree-line; above it loomed a snow-covered mountain. The house was crudely built of rocks and had a wooden roof. There was a stone chimney out of which smoke curled. Beside it was a rock-wall-enclosed chicken yard. About twenty feet away, farther down the mountain stream, was a similar house.

'Welcome to my palace in the mountains,' said Lew, dismounting. 'It's not Fontainebleau, but it's home.'

'It's idyllic,' she said grumpily, getting down from her horse. 'Right out of Rousseau.'

'And since we're getting back to nature, you'll be thrilled to know there's no plumbing. But the stream is the purest water in North America.'

'Probably the coldest, too.'

'You get used to it.'

At which point he scooped her into his arms and picked her up. She held on to her plumed hat.

'*Really*,' she said, 'this is superfluous.'

'All part of the scheme.' He smiled as he started toward the wooden door. 'The Bride of the Mountain should be carried across the threshold of her new home.'

'I have a husband, you know.'

'Who's eighty. . . .'

'Sixty-three.'

'Why did you marry him, anyway? He looks like a cold turkey – an antique cold turkey, at that.'

'Aristide is a kind man and a good husband. We have our disagreements, but I don't intend to dishonour him.'

'Good.' He kicked open the door. 'It wouldn't be any fun if you didn't put up a fight. And here we are.'

He carried her into the one-room cabin and set her down on the earth floor. The scanty furniture in the place was crude: a wooden bed along one wall, its legs strapped to its frame with cowhide thongs. A cheap chest of drawers on top of which was piled a stack of yellowing newspapers. On a wooden pegboard hung an improbable suit of men's evening attire along with a thick sheepskin coat and another *charro* outfit. In the centre of the room stood a wooden table with two wooden stools. In the open hearth a fire was burning. This, and the oil lamp hanging from the wooden ceiling, gave the only illumination. In another corner stood a high-backed iron bathtub. An Indian girl was pouring a kettle of water into the half-full tub. She wore a long skirt, a cotton blouse, and had two silver bracelets on her left arm. Her black hair was pulled back in a bun, and she had a soft, intelligent face. She was looking at Laura as she poured.

'Concepcion, this is Laura,' said Lew, tossing his sombrero on one of the wooden pegs. 'Laura, this is Concepcion, Agustin's woman. I told her to pour you a bath. No plumbing, but a first-class bathtub. It was hell getting it up the mountain, but for you, anything.'

Concepcion emptied the kettle, then returned it to the hearth, where she set it down. She crossed the room to Laura, looked at her, then curtsied.

'Thank you,' said Laura.

'*De nada, senora.*' And Concepcion left the house, closing the door softly behind her.

'She's not exactly verbose, is she?' said Laura.

'Not exactly. You'd better take your bath while the water's hot. I even have some French soap.' He pulled out a drawer in the table, reached in, and extracted a fresh cake of yellow savon. 'Bought it in Mexico City for you.' He tossed it to her. Surprised, she caught it. He went over to the bed and flopped down on it, his hands behind his head. 'If you'll look in the top drawer of the chest, you'll find a towel and a nightshirt, which are for you. Concepcion will take your measurements in the morning and make you some clothes, Indian style. She's not Monsieur Worth, but she tells me she's a genius with the needle.'

She was watching him.

'I assume,' she said, 'that I'm not to be given any privacy?'

'That's right. I want to watch.'

'You do have your gall!' She went to the chest of drawers, angrily yanked open the top one, pulled out the towel and the nightshirt, then slammed it shut.

'I'll bathe in the stream,' she said, going to the door. 'I don't give a damn if it *is* cold!' She opened the door.

'Fine. Just watch out for the snakes.'

She stopped, closed her eyes with frustration, then slammed the door.

'All right,' she said, putting the soap, the towel, and the nightshirt on the table. 'I'll bathe here. And you may watch, if that gives you some sort of adolescent pleasure.'

'There's no pleasure like adolescent pleasure.'

He was grinning. She took off her hat and threw it at him. He caught it, then put it on one of his fingers and started twirling it. She began unbuttoning her jacket.

'And speaking of adolescence,' she said, 'I assume that dress suit on the wall is your costume? Yout put it on when you go into society to rob everyone blind?'

'That's right. I always wanted to be an actor. You wouldn't believe how exciting it is being an actor-thief.'

'It absolutely amazes me how a young man whom I

remember as being *very* charming could have turned into such a lout and a boor.'

'It was the Andersonville Finishing School. It finished my charm.'

She looked at him as she pulled her jacket off.

'You were in Andersonville?' she said, somewhat more softly.

'Yes, and in a lot of other prisons, too.' He put the hat on the floor next to the bed and sat up. 'Four years, all told. And for six years I've been dreaming about this moment. Six long years, Laura, I've dreamed about you. Not my wife. You. And yes, I'm a lout and a boor and a thief and adolescent and probably a little bit ridiculous. But I'm in love with you.' He got to his feet and came across the room to her. He took the jacket from her and put it on the table. Then, gently, he took her hands. 'I suppose I've made a mess of my life,' he said. 'Or life has made a mess of me, I don't know which. My past is gone: my family, my inheritance – everything. My future is there, in those newspapers.' He nodded at the stack on top of the chest of drawers. She looked at them.

'What newspapers?' she asked, curiosity getting the better of her.

'The Washington newspapers. I buy them in Mexico City so I can keep up with the career of a certain senator. Because I'm going back to Washington, Laura. The money I've made stealing, and the million dollars your husband's going to pay me . . . it's all for one purpose: to go back to Washington and pay that bastard back for what he did to me. But that's the future. The present is you.'

He let go her hands, put his arms around her, pulled her to him, and kissed her. At first hard, then more softly. She was amazed at the intensity, the hunger, the pent-up passion that she could feel in that kiss. It seemed to surge out of him like water from a burst dam. And, like water from a burst dam, it was irresistible. But she told herself she *had* to resist. She pushed him back. 'So I'm nothing more than part of your revenge against some senator, whoever he is?'

'Yes,' he whispered. 'Loving you is revenge against all the

ugliness in life. Because you're beautiful, Laura. You're all the beauty I've missed. And I want it. I want you.' He let her go, his eyes never leaving her. 'Now take your bath,' he said, sitting on the table. 'And yes, I'm going to watch. I'm goint to *savour* you. I won't force you to go to bed with me . . . I won't force you to do anything. But' – and he smiled slightly – 'you're going to go to bed with me.'

He reached above him and turned off the oil lamp. Now only the flickering fire illuminated the room with tongues of light. She watched him a moment as he leaned on the table, watching her. Then, uncertainly, she began unbuttoning her skirt. She handed it to him. He took it and put it on the table next to her jacket. He never took his eyes off her. She sat down on one of the stools to remove her shoes.

'Who is the senator?' she asked.

'His name is Matoon.'

He pronounced the name slowly, as if tasting it.

'I've heard of him. He's powerful, isn't he?'

'Very. That's why I need money. Money is power. It takes power to fight power.'

She was rolling down her white silk stockings. 'If you live to destroy someone, you can end up destroying yourself.'

'I won't destroy myself. I plan to do a lot of things with my life. But revenge comes first.'

He watched as she pulled off her stockings, first the right, then the left. Now the firelight licked her smooth, bare legs. She got up from the stool and presented her back to him.

'Will you unbutton me?'

He reached out and began unbuttoning her white linen undergarment, which was beautifully sewn and delicate as a butterfly's wing. He started at the top and worked down, slowly peeling, watching the sweep of her spine and the soft whiteness of her superb skin. Then the last button was open, and he could see the dip of her back just above the gentle curves of her buttocks, with the cleft in the middle. . . . She pulled the undergarment over her head, the white curtain rising over her thighs, then her slim hips, tiny waist, soft shoulders. He drank in the splendour with thirsty eyes. Then she turned to confront him. Her breasts were surprisingly large, ripe melons of snow with large, rosy-brown nipples.

'If you make love to me,' she said, 'there is only one thing I ask. Be gentle. My first husband, Guido, was an animal. He' – she frowned at the memory – 'never made love to me. He *attacked* me.'

'Why?'

'I think he hated women for some reason, and by hurting me he got the hatred out of him.'

'How badly did he hurt you?'

She closed her eyes a moment. Then she opened them. 'He put things inside me that have made me barren. I can never have children.'

He thought what a crime it was that this incredibly lovely woman could not pass her beauty on to the next generation. She went to the tub and put an exploratory toe in.

'One night,' she said, 'he tied me to a chair and put a handkerchief around my mouth. Then he . . .' She stopped as she eased herself into the tub.

'You don't have to tell me.'

'No, maybe it's better to tell. He dipped his second and third fingers in a mixture of wintergreen and acetic acid, then put them inside me.'

'Good God.'

'That was his idea of entertainment. There were other things he put in me, but . . .' She shrugged her naked shoulders. 'He also had a charming habit of exposing himself to the housemaids. It sounds amusing, but actually it was horrible. I finally had to be put in a sanitarium. That's why I married Aristide after Guido died. It was not only that Aristide was rich and I needed the money, but I thought an older man would be gentle.'

'And is he?'

She put her right hand in the water, then passed it slowly over her left arm. 'He is gentle in bed. Out of bed, he's a very cold man. He's only interested in his diplomatic career. Every time I make any remark about politics, he shuts me up. He doesn't want me to think for myself, or be a human being. He just wants me to be a beautiful ornament, like a fancy watch or a sofa. I've never met a man who thought of me as a person. I think for a woman to be attractive is probably in the long run a curse. No one is interested in your mind or your soul, and after all, in twenty years – maybe less – my looks will be gone. Then would you be so much in love with me, my dashing El Juero?'

He didn't answer. She smiled sadly.

'Ah, he doesn't want to look in the future, does he? He only thinks about *now*. Well, maybe that's all any of us think of. Anyway, be gentle to your abductee. Don't be a Guido, and don't be an Aristide. Make it tender and beautiful.' She held out her hand toward him. 'Will you bring me the soap?'

He got up from the table and carried the soap to the tub. He knelt beside the tub, dipped the soap in the water, then worked up a lather. His palm covered with the perfumed suds, he placed it on her heart. He could feel the strong beat. Then he moved it over her right breast, slowly, lovingly slicking the suds over it as his fingers kissed the flesh. She was leaning against the high back, her eyes half closed, watching him as her body hummed with pleasure.

'You need a shave,' she whispered.

He said nothing. His left hand still on her breast, he leaned his face toward hers and started kissing her mouth, her nose, her eyes. She placed her hand on his side, underneath his vest, and began feeling his skin.

'Remember,' she said, softly, 'that day at Bull Run? And you said you'd love me till the day you died? I've always remembered that. I thought you were very dashing. I still do.'

'Stand up,' he whispered.

He got to his feet and helped her to hers. She stood in the tub as he ran his soaped hands all over her body, terminating the journey by softly massaging her vagina. She was in an ecstasy now, levitated, suspended somewhere between the tub and Heaven, a sudsed Venus on a shell of iron. He removed his hand and started taking off his vest. Then his boots, his trousers. She watched, eyes half open, her head slightly back. He wore nothing under the pants but an erection. He took her hands and stepped in the tub. Then he was kissing her, pressing her softness against his golden-haired hardness, transferring the suds to his own body until the two magnificent bodies were a slick unity.

'Waltz with me,' she whispered.

'Here?'

'Yes. Waltz with me here.'

She started humming a slow, lilting waltz as she stepped out of the tub, her nakedness dripping on the earth floor, her wet feet becoming muddy. He stepped out and took her in his arms.

'This is crazy,' he said.

'But beautiful. What could be more beautiful than a naked waltz?'

The two of them began turning slowly to the hummed tune, his arms hugging her, his mouth kissing her, their feet becoming black. They slowly moved around the table, he guiding her toward the bed. She saw where they were headed.

'No,' she whispered. 'I want to do it on the ground.'

'But we're soaked . . . we'll get filthy. . . .'

She smiled into his blue eyes. 'I want to be filthy. I want to roll in the mud with my beautiful Lew.'

She knelt slowly down, kissing her way down his chest, over the ridges of his muscled stomach, then kissing the crown of his penis. She stretched on her back on the warm earth and looked up at him.

'I'm glad you kidnapped me.' She smiled. She reached up her left hand. He took it, then knelt over her, straddling her, his hands pressing both of hers in the earth on either side of her golden-aureoled head.

'Six years,' was all he said.

Then he lowered himself onto and into her. She felt his enormous penis going into her and she moaned with pleasure. Then, slowly, he began thrusting. Slowly, the sweetness began rising up the volcano. When they both erupted, they were both covered with mud.

'Golden fireworks,' she whispered, her eyes closed, her mouth smiling. 'It was beautiful.'

And she ran her fingers lovingly through his hair.

'Are there really snakes in the stream?' she asked. It was

a half hour later. They had made love a second time on the floor, rolling around, laughing, until the place looked like a sty.

He sat up, then leaned over to lick her left nipple.

'Of course not. We're too high up. I just wanted you in here.' And he licked.

'Then let's go wash the mud off in the cleanest water in North America.'

'It's cold out.'

'That doesn't matter. We can't get in bed like this. Come on.'

She got up, took the towel off the table, and went to the door to open it. It was a beautiful evening, with a half moon rising over the mountain, but the temperature was in the forties.

'It's a little colder than I thought,' she said, shivering.

He took the sheepskin coat from the wall peg and put it around her shoulders.

'Wear this.'

'But I'll get it muddy. . . .'

'It won't hurt. The sheep got muddy, didn't he?'

He went to the bed and jerked off the top blanket, which he threw around himself. Then he returned to the door. 'Let's go,' he said, slapping her bottom. 'Last one in washes dishes after supper.' The two ran out of the house down through the trees to the stream, which sparkled in the moonlight. A rough stone dam had been constructed, forming a small pool in front of the house.

'It looks icy.' She gulped.

'It is. You like my dam?' He pointed.

'Did you build it?'

'That's right. And the two houses. Total cost, three hundred pesos and a lot of sweat. The pool's deep enough to dive.'

'Dive? I'll go in an inch at a time, thank you.'

'It's worse that way. One final kiss before we turn to ice.'

He kissed her again, long and lovingly, hugging her to his warmth.

'Laura,' he whispered. 'God, even your name is beautiful!

Stay here with me . . . I'll forget Washington. I'll even forget the ransom. To hell with Aristide – let him keep his million if I can keep you. We could have a wonderful life here . . . I mean it. It's beautiful up here. . . .'

'Yes, it is. . . .'

'The only thing that's been missing is you. Will you stay with me?'

'Darling, we have to be practical. . . .'

'People always say that, but why? What's being practical worth when you have happiness? I've learned the hard way to seize happiness when you find it and hold on to it with all your strength, because someone will try to take it away. . . . I'm happy tonight, Laura. Happier than I've ever been in my life. Oh God, I love you! I wish I could write you a sonnet, or a great symphony – I wish I could make the moon explode and the stars shoot all over the sky, spelling out "I love Laura!"'

'You just love me tonight. It's a magic night, but it's just . . . tonight.'

'No,' he said tenderly. 'I'd love you twenty years from now. A *hundred* years. And it's not just your looks, though God knows I love them. It's you.'

'What do you know about me?'

'That you've been hurt. I've been hurt. Maybe it's only when life has kicked you around that you can *really* love. I loved you the first moment I saw you – it was the great cliché: I fell in love at first sight. But that was a schoolboy crush. Now I want to spend the rest of my life with you. I'll do anything you want, take you anywhere you want to go . . . just never leave me. Say you'll never leave me.'

'I can't make any promises. I have to think. . . .'

'Think with your body. Think with your heart.'

'Oh my darling Lew, the problem is I have to think with my brain.'

'But you love me? Say you love me.'

She smiled. 'Of course I love you. How could I not love you? Do you think you're the only one who fell in love at first sight? I took one look at you and thought, "My God, that's the most gorgeous man I've ever seen." And here I am, in your arms, freezing to death on a mountain in Mexico.'

'And in love?'

'Yes, you foolish, adorable, mad creature. Desperately in love. And God knows what's going to happen to me.'

He kissed her again. Then he released her, threw off his blanket and towel, turned, and dived into the pool. She watched his slim body bow, then knife the water and disappear, only to surface a moment later near the dam.

'Is it as cold as it looks?' she called.

'It's toasty! A steam bath! Come on: you'll love it.'

He started swimming toward her with strong strokes.

She put a foot in, groaned, then forced herself to jump. When she surfaced, she sputtered.

'Oh my God, it's like the Antarctic!'

'Think how warm it will be when we go back to the fire . . . and I'll cook you some tamales. My tamales are fantastic! And we can drink pulque and make love twenty-seven times.'

She giggled. 'Why twenty-seven?'

'Once for every year of my life.'

'So that's how old you are, El Juero?' said a voice in accented English. They both turned to look at the bank. Six men on horses were emerging from the trees, coming to the pool. Their rifles, gleaming in the moonlight, were aimed at the swimmers. 'You've had a busy life for one so young,' continued the voice, which belonged to a thin man with a short black beard.

Lew grabbed Laura's hand under the water.

'Don't say anything,' he whispered. 'That's right, Sanchez. It's been a very busy life. I thought you were in Texas?'

'I came back early, my gringo friend. Because I was told about your daring exploit, your plan to kidnap Madame de Beaupré.'

'Tomás told you.'

'No, no. I knew about the scheme last month. Madame de Beaupré, will you be so kind as to leave the pool and get dressed? We're all very eager to see the French lady emerge from the water. *Very* eager.'

'I think we'd rather stay in the water,' said Lew. 'Why don't you join us for a swim?'

Diego Sanchez laughed. 'That's a very funny joke, El Juero. Yes, we jump in and swim with you. Very funny. Except the joke's on you, my friend. You've kidnapped the wife of the French ambassador, for which I, Diego Sanchez, thank you. Unfortunately for you, I, Diego Sanchez, intend to collect the ransom. Now, out of the water. Both of you. It's a long way back down the mountain.'

'Lew,' whispered Laura, 'how did he know . . .'

'I don't know. Do what he says.'

They swam to the edge of the pool and climbed out, shivering in the cold night air. Sanchez looked Laura over.

'The French woman,' he said slowly, 'is as beautiful as I've been told. It's a pity to cover such beauty, but we don't want our guests to catch pneumonia. Concepcion, give them their towels and coats. Then take Madame de Beaupré to the house and help her get dressed.'

The Indian girl stepped out of the shadows of the trees and picked up the towels. She threw one to Lew, then handed the other to Laura.

'You,' said Lew softly. 'Why?'

Concepcion picked up the sheepskin coat and put it around Laura's shoulders.

'You gringos steal from Mexico,' she said. 'The French steal from Mexico. It is time the stealing stopped. Mexico for the Mexicans!'

'Mexico for Mexicans!' repeated the men on horseback, softly but earnestly.

'So,' said Lew, 'Agustin got a political woman, the same as I did. And where is he?'

'Your partner,' said Sanchez, 'has been executed in the name of the Mexican Revolution.'

'Why, you son of a bitch . . .'

'Ah-ah, my friend. We don't want to execute a gringo, but we could be talked into it.'

'What did Agustin do to you?' Lew raged.

'He stood in my way.'

'Dolores,' said Laura fearfully. 'And my sentries . . .'

'The French dogs, madame, are now in French Heaven gnawing bones from God's table. Your maid I let go.'

'But I had a bargain with Rodriguez!' exclaimed Lew. 'The French soldiers were to be let go – '

'Rodrigeuz changed his mind. Concepcion, take Madame de Beaupré to the house.'

The Indian girl gave Laura a push, and they started toward the house. Lew bottled his rage at Sanchez's betrayal. He had been tricked, but it was too late to regret his foolishness. He had to think, to act. . . .

'Maybe I'm a gringo,' he said, looking up at the thirty-six-year-old son of a Veracruz importer. 'But my gringo dollars are good. How much do you want for Madame de Beaupré?'

Sanchez leaned over and casually placed the point of his rifle under Lew's chin.

'How much are you offering?'

'I've got a quarter million dollars in two New Orleans banks. It's yours if you let her go unharmed.'

'Mm. A quarter million. Concepcion told me you and Agustin were doing good business, but I didn't realize it was that good.'

'Then do we have a deal?'

Lew moved his head, trying to avoid the rifle muzzle that was nudging his throat.

'El Juero is not political, which is a pity,' said Sanchez. 'He thinks I want money for the French bitch. I don't want money: I want the French out of Mexico.'

'And they're leaving.'

'But not fast enough. When the last French soldier has boarded the last French ship at Veracruz, then de Beaupré will get his wife back. Meanwhile, she is my prisoner. As are you, my friend.'

He removed the rifle.

'For how long?' asked Lew.

Sanchez burst into laughter. 'Until you give me your quarter million, of course! Bring them to the camp,' he ordered. Then he spurred his horse and galloped back into the trees.

Lew started toward the stone house where, a half-hour before, he had held the world in his arms. Now, once again, his arms were empty. He felt sick, and his heart and mind and body raged at God.

26

Ben Bramwell climbed the mahogany stairway of the house he had rented on the rue la Pérouse, then made his way down the carpeted hall toward the nursery in the rear that overlooked the snow-blanketed garden. The house had been built six years before by a real-estate speculator. It was designed in the French Renaissance style, and its stone façade was a fantasy of arched windows, tourelles, spires, all surmounted by a peaked slate roof bristling with two elaborate brick chimneys. The speculator had become carried away by his fantasy and poured hundreds of thousands of francs into the four-storey house, installing modern plumbing, dumb-waiters, gaslights, call boards, and a basement kitchen with all the modern conveniences, including a cavernous Rumford stove. As was not unusual in the speculation-mad Paris of Louis Napoleon, the builder had been in his new house less than two years when the stock market dipped, wiping out his real-estate millions in less than a week. The builder was forced to rent out his Renaissance fantasy, and the renter had been the wealthy Philadelphian Mr Bramwell, who took the place on a five-year lease at a rent of one hundred thousand francs per annum. The Bramwells had lived in the house three years now. But the happiness Ben had thought he would find in the high-ceilinged rooms of 6 rue la Pérousse was proving to be elusive.

He opened the nursery door and went in. Elizabeth had papered the big room with a delightful fantasy of bedtime-stoıy characters: Puss in Boots, Mother Goose, the Ugly Duckling, Cinderella, the Country Mouse and the City Mouse all romped around the walls against a rainbow of bright colours. There was a big doll's house on the floor which Pauline, Ben and Elizabeth's two-year-old daughter, was sitting in front of. And two regiments of gaily painted toy soldiers were bivouacked around the carpet battlefield, with General Ward, who was now six, standing in the middle of the enemy lines directing a charge of wooden cavalry from Bavaria.

'*À la gauche!*' he was yelling. '*Tirez! Tirez, mes braves! Boom, boom, boom! Tuez les chiens!*' He saw his stepfather in the door, tall, decked out in his evening clothes. 'Oh – *bon soir, papa.*' He ran over to hug him. '*Pauline a cassée un de mes soldats, mais je lui ai pardonné, comme tu me l'avais demandé.*'

'That's good, Ward. You have to be gentle with your sister, because you're older. And speak *English.*'

Ward sighed. 'I'm sorry.'

Pauline had gotten to her feet and was toddling over to her father, her arms outstretched.

'*Papa, papa,*' she cried. '*Ward a tiré mes cheveux! C'est un monstre!*'

She pushed her disgusted half-brother aside, and Ben picked her up to kiss her.

'Ward's not a monster,' he said. 'Are you, Ward? Did you pull your sister's hair?'

'Well, I didn't pull hard.'

'He did too! He's a *monstre*!'

'Mon-*ster*,' corrected her father.

'Monster.'

Ben kissed her again, then set her down.

'You two be good and don't give Miss Pritchett any trouble this week. Or your mother. I have to go to Vienna. . . .'

'*Again?*' sighed Ward.

'Yes, again. I'll be back a week from Friday, then I'll take both of you . . . well, where do you want to go?'

'The zoo!' said Ward. 'I want to go see the elephants.'

'And the mee-monks,' said Pauline, who was a chubby little girl with brown hair and pretty blue eyes.

'That what?' smiled her father.

'The mee-monks.'

'She means "chipmunks",' said Ward with a superior sniff. 'She gets words all mixed up.'

'You get languages mixed up.' Ben smiled at his daughter again. 'All right, we'll go to the zoo and see the mee-monks. How's that?'

Both children clapped their hands. Ben kissed them both again, then said, 'Good night. And be good.' He left the nursery, closed the door, and walked down the hall toward the front of the house, opening the door to the master bedroom. It was warm in the big room, the two tall windows of which overlooked the gaslit rue la Pérouse. A fire burned in the hearth; above the round-topped mantel, which was heavily carved with bunches of marble grapes, hung a tall gilt mirror Ben didn't like. They had rented the house furnished, and the speculator's taste ran to the gaudy. The big bed was someone's idea of a bed for Francis I: the headboard had as many carved towers and spires as the façade of the house, and had been splashed with gilt to compound the error. As if the speculator had run out of either nerve or money or both, the rest of the furniture was contemporary: chintz chairs and a long chintz chaise, behind which stood a tall floor lamp, the shade heavily fringed.

Ben crossed the room to the dressing room, where Elizabeth was sitting in front of her vanity, brushing her hair. She had on a dressing robe, and had just finished her bath in the adjoining bathroom.

'Oh hello, darling,' she said. 'I'll be ready in twenty minutes.'

'Plenty of time,' said Ben, leaning over to kiss her. Then he sat down in a reproduction Louis XV chair (reproductions of eighteenth-century furniture had become the rage after Eugénie had discovered a warehouse full of palace furniture that had been forgotten for seventy years). 'Mind if I smoke?' he said.

'Well, you know I hate the smell, but go ahead if you must.'

He pulled out a cigar, clipped the end, then lit it. Elizabeth continued brushing her hair, wrinkling her nose at the smell.

'If I smell like a cigar the opera, it will be your fault,' she said.

'I realize that.' He puffed again, watching his wife. 'Elizabeth,' he finally said, 'we've been in Paris too long. I want to go home.'

She stopped brushing for a moment, looking at his reflection in the mirror. Then she continued.

'Oh? Just like that?'

'Just like that. Three years is enough.'

'But we still have two years on the lease of this house. . . .'

'That can be negotiated.'

'I see. And exactly when are you planning to return to Philadelphia?'

'We'll wait till the end of the school year. We'll go home in June.'

'I take it this is an ultimatum? I mean, you're not *discussing* this with me. You're *telling* me.'

'There's nothing to discuss. We're Americans, and we should live in America. The children don't know what they are. Pauline's getting as bad as Ward, speaking French when I'm not around forcing her to speak English. . . .'

'French is a perfectly respectable language, you know.'

'So is English. And I want *my* daughter to speak English.'

She put down her silver brush and turned to face her husband.

'All right. I've known this has been coming for some time now. You don't like it here, which is perfectly legitimate. . . .'

'It's not that I don't *like* it. Paris is a marvellous city, in its way. But I'm a Philadelphian! I don't feel at home here! The French will never accept me as one of them, nor should they. I'm *not* one of them. I can barely speak the language after three years! I feel like a permanent tourist! I want to go home.'

'To what?' asked Elizabeth. 'What do we have in Philadelphia? Both our parents are dead, your sister's married, mine will be soon . . . we hardly know anyone any more. . . . Besides, Ben, admit it: Philadelphia is a provincial town in a provincial country. Paris is the centre of the world! And if you'd *try* . . . I mean, heaven knows we have the entrée to the best circles in society, thanks to Princesse Mathilde. She *likes* me, Ben. And she'd like you, if you'd make an effort – *and* not drink!'

Ben sucked on the cigar. 'The Princesse Mathilde is an intellectual snob,' he said, 'who has taken you up because she likes to champion musicians who need her support.'

Elizabeth frowned.' That's very cruel, Ben. I don't *need* her.'

Ben leaned forward. 'Elizabeth, face facts. Now, I don't want to be cruel, but you're not being realistic about yourself. You don't have the talent to become Clara Schumann. First it was Liszt, now it's the emperor's cousin . . . the fact is, it's been three years and you still don't have a manager, you have yet to give another recital . . . all you do is go to boring parties and butter up the people in society, hoping they'll give you the success you can't give yourself. And it's wrong! They can't do it! And meanwhile, your family sits around day after day letting their roots rot. And their roots are *American*.'

She turned back to the vanity, put her face in her hands, and burst into tears. Ben closed his eyes wearily.

'Elizabeth . . .'

'Go away!' she sobbed. 'I've never known you to be so cruel, so callous . . . God knows, I've tried to be a good wife and mother, but there *are* other things!' She turned back to him, her eyes red but flashing. 'I refuse to be just a housewife and a mother!'

'*Just?*'

'Yes, *just*. I love you and I adore my children, but *I* have a life to lead too! Music is important to me. You say I butter up society – all right, I'll admit I do! But do you realize how hard it is for a woman. . . .'

'You've used that excuse! You've used it to death! How about how hard it is for a woman with a second-rate talent?'

She closed her eyes and clenched her fists. 'That is the cruellest thing you've ever said to me, and I'll never forget it.'

'The truth is cruel.'

She said nothing for a moment, trying to control her shock, her rage. Then she opened her eyes.

'All right,' she said. 'We'll go back to Philadelphia. We'll throw away my career, we'll throw away the stimulation of an exciting city . . . we'll throw away the Princesse Mathilde. And *you'll* throw away the bottle!'

He stubbed out the cigar. 'That has nothing to do with it.'

'Oh? Do you realize how many nights you've been drunk this year – and it's only the twentieth of January? Twenty times, Ben! You're drunk every night – and that's the cruel truth about *you*. Is it any wonder I prefer the society of Princesse Mathilde? Of writers, artists . . . people who are interested in life, instead of escaping from it by diving into the bottle?'

He got up. 'Did it ever occur to you why I'm escaping?'

'Oh, blame it on me.'

'Yes, I'll blame it on you! I'm escaping a wife who's turned into a social butterfly and a *snob*! My God, I thought I'd married Lew Crandall's widow. It's turned out I married his goddam mother!'

'Perhaps,' she said softly, 'what you wanted was Lew Crandall.'

His face turned red as he stared at her.

'How dare you make such a disgusting insinuation?' he whispered. 'He was my friend. How dare you say that?'

'Then why don't you make love to me any more?'

'Because it is difficult,' he said, biting each word, 'making love to a woman who is always at a goddam *party*!'

'You make love to the bottle every night!'

'The bottle makes love to *me* – unlike you!' He went to the door of the bedroom. 'You can go to the goddam opera by yourself. . . .'

'Ben!'

'The opera's a bore anyway.'

'Where are you going?'

'To Vienna. I was going in the morning, but now I think I'll take the night train.'

'Those stupid *plants* again, I suppose?'

'Those stupid plants. And you know the wonderful thing about those stupid plants? They never go to parties! Good-bye, Elizabeth. I'll be back a week from tomorrow.'

He left the room. She jumped up and ran to the door.

'Ben,' she called, 'I'm sorry. Please . . . don't go. Stay with me. I didn't mean that about Lew . . . it was a horrible thing to say, and I hate myself. Please stay . . . I love you, Ben, and I want you to love me.'

He was at the bedroom door. Now he opened it and looked at her.

'I'll love you,' he said, 'when you tell me you're ready to go back to Philadelphia.'

He went into the hall and closed the door.

She took a deep breath. Oh God, she thought, what is happening to us? She went back to sit at the vanity and lean her forehead on her hand, staring at her reflection. Philadelphia. She couldn't go back. Paris was her home, she loved it . . . damn him! Why couldn't *he* love it? And it wasn't true what he had said, was it? That her talent was second-rate? The Princesse Mathilde told her she was the best woman pianist in Paris . . .

She straightened, her face turning white. The Princesse Mathilde! She was playing there tomorrow night! Oh my God, and Ben wouldn't be there . . . what could she tell the princess?

Then she relaxed. No, it was better this way. Let Ben go to Vienna and talk to that idiot monk, Mendel, about idiot pea plants, or whatever they were. If he came to the Princesse Mathilde's, all he'd do would get drunk and make a fool of himself. . . .

It was better this way. She would show him. The Crown Prince of Sweden would be there tomorrow night, and she would play beautifully for royalty.

Second-rate talent indeed! She'd show him. And if she finally became the toast of Paris, well, then he could hardly take her back to Philadelphia, could he?

She smiled at her reflection. Wipe your eyes, you ninny! she thought. Wipe your eyes and go to the opera, even if you have to go alone.

They say the emperor will be there tonight. . . .

Princesse Mathilde Bonaparte laid her hand on the wrist of Crown Prince Oscar of Sweden, who was sitting at her right at the table. They were in the flower-and-palm-filled dining room of her mansion on the rue de Courcelles, not far from the Arc de Triomphe, which had been built sixty years before by the princess's uncle, Napoleon le Grand, and which had been made the centre of a star of wide boulevards by her cousin, Napoleon le Petit.

'Did you have enough to eat, Your Highness?' she asked, and the tall, blond Swedish prince in his white uniform laughed.

'I think you underfed us, Mathilde.'

The whole table smiled, because the meal had been spectacular, and Elizabeth Bramwell intended to keep the menu card as a souvenir. It read:

Hors-d'Oeuvre
Oeufs de vanneau, poularde, caviar.
Potage tortue à la Charles VI.

Relevés
Carpe du Rhin à la Chambord.
Baron de mouton à l'Anglaise.

Entrées
Filets de faisan à la Metternich.
Filets de poularde à la Mazarin.
Croustades à l'Impératrice.
Filets de sterlet et crevettes Bagration.
Punch à la romaine et sorbets crème d'Alast.

Rôtis
Dindonneaux nouveaux. Ortolans.
Salade princesse. Romaine.

Entremets
Petits pois de Paris. Truffes en rocher.
Petits soufflés Lavallière. Bombe royale.

Desserts
Fraises, pêches, raisins, reines-Claude,
fromage de la Croix de Fer.

Vins
Madère retour de l'Inde. Château d'Yquem 1847.
Mouton Rothschild 1847. Château-Lafite 1848.
Romanée gêlée 1858. Johanisberg Metternich 1837.
Tokai 1824. Roederer et Pommery.

Enough to kill a horse, Elizabeth thought, though it had all been succulently cooked and magnificently displayed: the Princesse Mathilde's chef was one of the best in Paris. And how beautifully it had been served by the dark-blue-liveried footmen! And how stunning was the big, Roman-style dining room with its square skylight through which dropped a gleaming brass chandelier, its tall columns with their Ionic capitals, the ivy that crawled up the columns and over the walls, the banks of beautiful flowers, the rich red and blue Oriental rug over the marble floor! The Princesse Mathilde had great style, and to be invited to her house meant not only that one had arrived in Paris society but that one was in for a splendid evening as well. The emperor's cousin was a handsome, imposing woman. She was also staggeringly rich, having married Prince Demidoff, one of the richest men in Russia. She was separated from Demidoff now, but, thanks to the intervention of her relative the tsar, she had separated Demidoff from a considerable hunk of his fortune, so she could afford to entertain in the grand style. If she was, as Ben said, something of an intellectual snob, she was also quite intelligent and artistically talented. That evening, for example, Elizabeth had been seated between that apostle of Art for Art's sake, the bearded poet, playwright, and critic Théophile Gautier (who had been pleasant, brilliant, and oddly fascinated by women's clothes) and the young novelist Jules de Goncourt, whom she had found handsome and witty but always deferent to his older brother,

Edmond, across the table (who, in turn, kept deferring back to Jules).

Elizabeth was the only musician present. When the Princesse Mathilde had decided to 'take her up', Elizabeth had acquired a formidable champion who made sure there were no other pianists around to deflect from Elizabeth's glory. But the novelist Daniel Stern was there; and of course everyone knew that she (for Daniel Stern was her pen name) was really the Comtesse Marie d'Agoult, who for years had been the mistress of Liszt and the mother of his children; and so music was represented, in a way, by her also. Elizabeth had rather nervously steered clear of the countess during the evening. Her *affaire* with Liszt was a thing of the past, but she was a little wary of the countess, who, it was said, had a vicious tongue. If she knew Elizabeth had at one time slept with her former lover (and Elizabeth didn't think she knew, but still . . .) she might become scathing. And even though the countess was now sixty-one, people said she knew everything. So best to keep a safe distance.

The Princesse Mathilde did not believe in the custom of leaving the men alone for cigars and port – why should she miss all the fun? – and so now, when she rose, everyone passed from the dining room to the salon. Here, more splendour: handsome malachite and alabaster globed lamps, green velvet portières, a black teakwood screen in one corner, rich rugs, a fire in the marble fireplace flanked by huge Chinese vases out of the mouths of which sprang soft palms. . . . As the footmen passed coffee and cognac, the guests seated themselves. Then the Princesse Mathilde moved to the side of a huge piano with fat, carved legs. Her heavy-set figure blazed with diamonds almost as good as the empress's, and white feathers soared from her elaborate coiffure: she looked as regal as she actually was, for she was related by blood and marriage to half the royal houses of Europe. She signalled for silence and said, 'I have asked Mrs Bramwell to play for us. As most of you have heard me speak of this lovely young American who has won my heart, I shall make no further introduction except to say that she is an accomplished artist and dear friend. Elizabeth?'

She smiled and extended her hand as Elizabeth made her way through the chairs. Elizabeth curtsied to the princess and said, 'Thank you, Your Highness.' Then she turned to the guests. She was nervous as she faced the cream of Paris society, both social and artistic. She told herself to keep calm. The piece she had selected to play was technically simple, well within her control. 'I will play the Schubert Impromptu in E flat,' she said. She seated herself at the keyboard, removed her rings, and placed them on the piano. Then she rubbed her fingers for a moment, studying the keyboard as the rattling of coffee cups subsided. Silence. Control, she thought. Control.

She began the music tenderly. The lovely melody gushed out of the piano strings like a mountain spring.

She finished the piece to muffled applause. She had had a memory lapse halfway through and had been forced to fake a segue, but she thought that only a professional would have noticed . . . and they seemed to like it, didn't they? She curtsied to the guests, as the Princesse Mathilde joined her.

'Lovely, my dear,' she said. 'Could we possibly coax you into an encore?'

'Well . . .'

'Yes, encore! Encore!' cried Théophile Gautier, who had taken a liking to his pretty dinner partner.

Elizabeth took a deep breath. She would have to try something more difficult, technically. . . .

'The "Aufschwung" from Schumann's "Fantasiestücke",' she announced. She returned to the piano, thinking, Oh my God, can I get through it? Her hands were trembling and sweating as she attacked the tension-filled opening. She started too fast and had to slow down at the more difficult parts, but she got through it without a memory lapse and not too many technical errors. Still, as she curtsied again to the applause, Ben's remark was haunting her. Second-rate talent. Second-rate. That performance would have been booed out of the Salle Pleyel. . . .

Still, the guests, prompted by the Princesse Mathilde's patronage, flocked around her. A minor German princeling, who was being alternately bullied and cajoled by Bismarck to ally his tiny state with Prussia, gushed, 'I have never heard such playing – never! And from a woman – remarkable!' Lady Duffield, an Englishwoman who was having an *affaire* with Paris and a Paris stockbroker, said, 'But my dear, such noble purity of tone! Such sensitivity! You must come to London and play!' The Comtesse d'Agoult insinuated her way through the crowd to Elizabeth's side. 'Do you ever play any of the maestro's compositions?' she purred, and Elizabeth tensed.

'I have, of course . . .'

'But surely a Liszt pupil – and *friend*, I hear – would play Liszt compositions at every opportunity?'

Marie d'Agoult's smile was all witchery and bitchery. Elizabeth forced herself to remain cool.

'No one appreciates the maestro's music more than myself, madame. If I hesitate to include his compositions in my repertoire, it's only because of their extreme technical difficulty.'

'But I'm told you used to play the maestro with admirable expertise. I mean, of course, used to play the maestro's *music*. . . .'

Elizabeth was saved by the Princesse Mathilde, who took her protégée's arm and said, shooting darts at the countess, 'Marie used to "play" Maestro Liszt as a full-time career. But unfortunately, she hit a few wrong notes – didn't you, my dear? And she can't quite forgive anyone else who plays better.'

The Comptesse d'Agoult bit her tongue, since everyone knew her jealousy and ego had long since sent her lover Liszt into the fat arms of the Princess Sayn-Wittgenstein. The Princesse Mathilde steered Elizabeth away to a neutral corner. 'Don't mind Marie,' she whispered. 'She's like an ageing cobra to any woman who has known the maestro . . . just ignore her. And your music was magnificent! Such a triumph!'

'Thank you, Your Highness. However, I did make some mistakes. . . .'

'Pooh. Who cares about wrong notes? It's the soul that's important, and your music, my dear, has soul.'

Liszt had also said it was the soul that was important, but he had warned that technique had to be flawless before the soul could come out. . . . And her technique, she knew, was hardly flawless. Second-rate? The truth was cruel. . . .

She saw the princess's butler making his way to her. He was holding a silver salver with a calling card on it.

'Madame,' he said, 'there is a gentleman to see you. A Mr Kent.'

'Who?'

She took the card from the tray. It read:

Jefferson Kent, Esq.
Land development
23 Blvd. du Montparnasse

'The gentleman says it's urgent,' the butler added.

Having no idea who Jefferson Kent was, Elizabeth followed the servant out of the room to the entrance hall. There, a tall young man in evening clothes was standing, holding his silk hat. When she saw his freckled face and red hair, she remembered. The American from Saint Louis who had asked her to waltz at the Tuileries ball three years before. The young American who didn't believe in wars. Coming up to him, she said, 'I thought I made it clear to you three years ago that there are certain kinds of Americans I prefer not to know.'

He grinned that broad, friendly grin.

'You sure have a way of making a fellow feel welcome,' he said.

She backed down. 'I'm sorry. I didn't mean to be rude. You wanted to see me about something urgent?'

'Yes ma'am. I just left your husband, and – '

'My husband? He's in Vienna.'

'Mr Bramwell's in Paris. I just left a big party where he – '

'Is this a joke?' she interrupted.

'If you'd let me finish a sentence, you'd see it isn't. He's at the Hôtel Païva, and he's really tied one on. Excuse me, ma'am, but I wouldn't tell you this if it weren't an emergency. The fact is, your husband's loaded to the gills, and he's made a crazy bet that I'm afraid might cost him his life. That's why I thought I'd better come get you. . . .'

'What has he done?' she asked, now alarmed.

'He's bet ten thousand francs that he's got the nerve to fire a gun at his head with only *one* chamber empty. And I think he's just about drunk enough to do it.'

She went pale. 'Oh my God . . .'

She hurriedly called for her furs, then followed the American into the snow, where he had a cab waiting. Ben, Ben . . . why had he sneaked back into Paris without telling her? Perhaps he had never left Paris. . . . And what was he doing at the notorious La Païva's, making crazy, suicidal bets?

She climbed in the cab, and Jefferson Kent followed her. 'L'Hôtel Païva,' he told the cabman. 'On the Champs Elysées.'

'Oh, I know where *that* is,' chuckled the cabbie, cracking his whip. The carriage jerked into motion.

'How did you know where I was?' asked Elizabeth, trying to keep as calm as possible.

'I read in the paper about the dinner party the Princesse Mathilde was giving and saw your name on the guest list. You're travelling in some pretty fancy company, Mrs Bramwell.'

She was in no mood to discuss her social triumphs.

'I can't *believe* Ben would come back to Paris without letting me know,' she said, more to herself than to her companion. 'I just can't believe it! And what's he doing at La Païva's? That terrible woman . . .'

'Oh, she's not so bad when you get to know her,' said Jefferson Kent. 'And she throws wild parties.'

'So I hear. But I wouldn't think it's a very good place for a young banker to be, either.'

'I'm out of banking.' He smiled. 'I got caught with my hand in the till.'

'You *what*?'

'Well, let's say the books didn't quite balance out so well. A hundred pounds seemed to have floated away, and old man Norton got it in his head I'd taken them. Well, he didn't prosecute, but he didn't exactly retire me on a pension, either.'

'Well? Did you?'

'Did I what?'

'Take the hundred pounds?'

'Of course I took them. I'd lost a lot of money on the horses, and I needed to pay off my debts. I asked Mr Norton to loan it to me, but he wouldn't so I took the money from the bank. Sort of an unguaranteed loan, you might say. That's what banks are for, aren't they? Of course, I meant to pay it back – with interest! Yes ma'am, I would have paid the full interest. But he caught me before I could get the cash together, and Mr Norton just didn't quite look at the whole thing my way. So now I'm out of banking and into land development.'

'Remind me not to buy land from you,' she said drily.

He laughed. 'I'm no more of a crook than the rest of them, and at least I'm honest about my shortcomings. Now, it would appear your husband's not been *quite* so honest with you.'

She frowned. 'Please, Mr Kent. I appreciate your coming for me, but I'd prefer not to discuss my husband with you.'

'Well, I think you'd better. And call me Jeff. You see, there are quite a few disreputable types at this party, and one of them is a little gal you'd better get to know.'

'What do you mean?'

'She's a singer – or an actress – or maybe both, I'm not sure. Her name's Zaza.'

'What a cheap name. Why should I want to know her?'

'Because Zaza is your husband's mistress.'

She stiffened. 'You *really* are incredible! My husband has no mistress. . . .'

'Want to bet?'

She closed her eyes, tight. 'No,' she whispered.

'Why do you think he didn't tell you he's in Paris?'

Of course. The trips to Vienna to work with Gregor Mendel. How blind she'd been!

'What . . .' She stopped. Her hands were trembling. 'What is she like?'

'Oh, she's young. About fifteen, I'd say. And sort of crazy. I don't know her too well. I hear it's been going on a couple of months.'

'Is he . . . does he love her?'

He shrugged.

'Well now, Mrs Bramwell, how would I know? Tonight's the first time I've seen your husband in three years. But I'm told he pays her rent and buys her clothes and jewels, so he might as well love her. If he doesn't, he's getting robbed.' He saw in the light of a street lamp the tears in her eyes. 'I'm sorry,' he said sympathetically. 'I guess I shouldn't have told you so bluntly, but I figured you were going to meet Zaza anyway, so it's better you come prepared . . . with your guns loaded, so to speak.'

She pulled a handkerchief from her purse to wipe her eyes. 'I don't know if I have any guns,' she said sadly.

'Haven't you got some kids?'

She nodded. 'Two. A son from my first marriage, and a daughter by Ben.'

'Well, kids are guns. Anyway, don't get too upset about it. Hell, this is Paris. And in Paris, everybody does it!'

He grinned. She sighed.

'Apparently, you're much wiser than I, Mr Kent.'

'Oh, I get around.'

Grin.

The respectable bourgeois wives of Paris called them *les mangeuses* – 'the eaters', or more accurately, 'the gobblers', since they gobbled up their husbands' fortunes. They were also called *les grandes horizontales*, which summed them up nicely: they were certainly grand, and during their income-producing hours, they were certainly horizontal. They were the glory – or the curse, depending on one's point of view – of the Second Empire: the infamous courtesans. Parasites of a money-loving, luxurious, immoral age, encouraged (or certainly not discouraged) by a womanizing emperor who ran a lax court, they thrived in Paris, elevating pleasure to the level of art and prostitution to the level of big business. In 1855 Dumas *fils* had written a play about them called *Le Demi-Monde*, and a new word entered the language that perfectly described their world. Not in society, they still were not entirely out of it. No respectable woman would receive them, but the respectable women aped and envied these glorious creatures who paraded their looks, their fabulous clothes and jewels, their fine carriages in the Bois de Boulogne every noon. The new French middle class, rich and riding the crest of the Industrial Revolution, found itself following the lead of whores, for the demi-monde set the tone of society. Elizabeth knew about them, of course: everyone did. She knew that many of her dinner partners at the Princesse Mathilde's that evening commuted easily between the two worlds. Théophile Gautier – fat, bearded, and brilliant – had been the lover of Madame Sabatier (where he and half of Bohemian Paris smoked hashish) as well as La Païva, Cora Pearl, and others. Even the Tweedledum-Tweedledee de Goncourt brothers went to La Païva's. Cora Pearl, the English transplant, was then at the height of her dizzy career. Prince Plon-Plon had fallen madly in love with her. Giving her twelve thousand francs a month, he installed her in two town houses, 101 rue de Chaillot and 6 rue des Bassins. She had a million francs' worth of jewels, and her initials were inlaid in the bottom of her bathtub in solid gold.

So the courtesans were rich, envied, and, in their half way, accepted. But none was so rich as Thérèse Lachmann, the Marquise de Païva, to whose incredible house on the Champs Elysées Elizabeth was hurrying. Born in the Moscow ghetto in 1819, Thérèse was the daughter of a weaver. When she was seventeen, she married a consumptive tailor; but she soon decided she'd had enough of poverty, and, abandoning her husband and son, she made her way to Paris. She wasn't particularly beautiful, but she had an exotic sensuality that attracted men, and soon she began to sleep her way up the ladder. Her first real triumph was to ensnare the heart of a minor Portuguese diplomat, the Marquis de Païva. He married her. The morning after the wedding night, she coolly told him that she had married him only for his title, she had paid him off in bed, and now he should go back to Portugal and not bother her any more.

Incredibly, he did as he was told.

Thérèse worshipped money, and now, being a straightforward type, she set her cap for the richest man in Europe. She got him. He was Count Henckel von Donnersmarck, a big blond Siegfried who owned coal, iron, zinc, and copper mines in Silesia, vast estates and industrial interests that made him, if not the richest man in Europe, easily the richest man in Germany. Whatever initial resistance Henckel had had to Thérèse's charms soon crumbled, and he became her lover, telling her, 'I have three million a year. Let's share it.' She needed little urging.

Financed by her new lover, she bought property on the Champs Elysées and began building a mansion that fast became one of the legends of Paris. And it was in front of this flamboyant building that Elizabeth and Jefferson Kent pulled up that snowy night in January 1867.

Despite her concern for her husband, Elizabeth couldn't help feeling a twinge of nervousness as Jefferson rang the bell. To enter the Hôtel Païva was, for a respectable woman, like entering Hell. But it had to be done. And just as the footman opened the door, she heard a shot.

'We're too late!' she cried, and, pushing her way past the fat servant, she hurried inside the house. She had a fleeting impression of incredible luxury: a twisting staircase made entirely of onyx illuminated by a sculpted bronze chandelier (the staircase alone had cost a million francs, its money-mad owner boasted). Then into the spectacular grand salon, which blazed with gilt, its overly ornate walls hung with crimson silk, its huge red marble fireplace sporting two carved half-naked goddesses lounging on the mantel, its magnificent ceiling dominated by an oval vault where the artist Baudry had painted a muscular Day chasing a voluptuous Night, mythology providing the excuse for displaying as much naked flesh as possible. But Elizabeth was only vaguely aware of all this celebration of sensuality because her eyes were riveted on her husband. Ben, bleary-eyed drunk, was standing in front of the fire, holding a revolver to his head while a dozen well-dressed guests sat watching him with ghoulish fascination.

'Ben, don't!' she blurted out.

He saw his wife, and a look of drunken confusion came over his face.

'Elizabeth . . . ?'

She told herself she mustn't jar him into squeezing the trigger. As coolly as she could, she came toward him, holding out her trembling hands.

'Ben, I love you,' she said in a calm tone. 'I want you home. Pauline and Ward want their father. Now, darling: give me that gun. Please.'

He didn't move.

'But there's a bet,' he slurred. 'I just fired the gun out the window to empty the chamber, and now we've spun it round and round and who knows which one's empty now? Isn't that exciting? It's a bet!'

She knew that when he was drunk he became a child. She would have to treat him like a child.

'Yes, it's very exciting, darling, but shouldn't we have a drink first?'

'Already had a drink! Had about two million of them. Hope you're not going to lecture me?'

'Of course not, but I'd like a glass of champagne, and I know you would, too.' Without taking her eyes off the revolver, she snapped her fingers at a lackey and ordered, 'Two champagnes.'

The others in the room were watching the drama in silence. Now the hostess, the forty-seven-year-old Marquise de Païva, who was sitting by the fire, signalled the footman to comply. Hastily, the glasses were brought on a silver salver. Elizabeth took one. 'Give my husband the other,' she said quietly. The footman took the tray to Ben, who looked at the tall glass filled with amber Perrier-Jouët.

'It's delicious,' prompted Elizabeth, taking a sip. 'So cool and dry. Shall we have a toast, darling?'

Slowly Ben lowered the gun, his eyes on the glass. Placing

the revolver on a table, he reached his hand out for the champagne.

'That's cheating.'

Elizabeth looked in the direction of the soft, husky voice and saw a dark-haired child in a Gypsy skirt and blouse going to the table. She was barefoot, and her brown hair was unbrushed, springing from her head like an aureole. Elizabeth thought there was something affected in her appearance, something too self-consciously Bohemain. Still, she was striking: she had what in the theatre was called presence. Her face was odd. Oval, with enormous green eyes and a small, slightly poutish mouth. She wore no make-up or jewellery. She gave Elizabeth a cool look, then picked up the revolver.

'A bet's a bet,' she said. 'And if Benjie won't do it, I will.'

Casually she raised the gun, pointed it above her right ear, and pulled the trigger. As Elizabeth screamed, the gun went off. But instead of the girl falling dead, she merely smiled and tossed the smoking revolver on a brocade sofa.

'Blanks,' she said. 'You don't think I'd let Benjie kill himself? Who'd pay my rent?'

The room burst into laughter and applause. Elizabeth put her hand to her head: she was suddenly dizzy. The gilt, the crimson silk, the rock-crystal chandeliers, the mythological ceiling – all started swirling in a giant whirlpool of colour.

She felt herself falling to the floor.

'Drink this.'

She opened her eyes to see the sharp-chinned face of the Marquise de Païva watching her. A scarlet gash of a mouth, with a large mole below it, on the right side of that shovel of a chin. Skin dead-white from *poudre de riz*. Large brown eyes snapping with intelligence. Dyed red hair. Diamond and pearl eardrops and a matching necklace worth thousands. A bright green satin dress swathed in softening tulle. She was standing next to the bed holding out a glass of cognac. Elizabeth sat up, looking around as she tried to get her bearings. Then she remembered: the gun, the shot, the shock. Ben. She took the brandy and sipped it.

'Feel better?' asked La Païva, whose French was heavily accented.

'Yes, thank you. Where's my husband?'

'Zaza took him home.'

'To *my* home?' she asked, in shocked tones.

La Païva chuckled. 'Hardly. To *her* home. The apartment he rents for her on the rue des Acacias. It's very chic, I'm told. The cute American – what's his name? Jeff? – told me you didn't know about her.'

'No. I suppose it's stupid of me.'

'Very stupid. She's a vicious little minx, that Zaza, and your husband's crazy for her. I don't envy you.'

'But she seems a child. . . .'

'She isn't. She just looks it. There are men who like little girls. Your husband is one of them. You didn't know?'

'No . . .'

'You Americans are curiously unobservant.'

Could that be it? The reason for the drinking? The reason he didn't make love to her any more? She had been certain it wasn't other women, because Ben never showed any interest in other women. Then, when she heard whispered stories about the homosexuality that was rife in Paris, she had begun to wonder if it were men. The emperor's handsome young cousin, the Duc de Mouchy, whose hobby everyone knew was chasing handsome guardsmen, had recently been arrested for dancing naked for the amusement of the troops at the Pepinière barracks. Was Ben another Duc de Mouchy? had run through her mind. And now she knew the answer. Not men, but young girls. Nubile girls in their teens. What a blind fool she had been.

'You like my bedroom?' she heard La Païva ask.

She looked around. The bedroom was as ornate as the grand salon below it. It overlooked the Champs Elysées, and the ceiling was a pseudo-Gothic nightmare of gold and red paint and down-hanging knobs of wood presumably intended to give the room the feeling of a chapel. Perhaps it was a chapel: a chapel of love. She was sitting on a quilted, satin-covered bed that was one of the strangest things she had ever seen. Enormous, carved out of mahogany, it was a swan-pulled barge of love, the headboard consisting of a life-sized carved naked mermaid holding the swans' reins with her left hand while her polished right hand was raised in a wave, as if signalling her lover on the shore – or, perhaps, keeping score?

'Well, it's different,' said Elizabeth.

The marquise laughed. 'Oh, it's that. And my bed! One of the wonders of the civilized world! It weighs a ton and a half. Isn't it marvellously vulgar? I like vulgarity. So do my clients. When Herr Wagner slept in it, he told me it reminded him of the swan boat in *Lohengrin*. I didn't tell him that that was what had given me the idea. It cost a hundred thousand francs, but I always say one can't spend too much on one's office. Would you like to see my bathroom?'

Elizabeth was surprised at her own curiosity. Here she was, on the most wicked bed in Paris, talking to the most wicked woman in Paris, and there was no doubt in her mind that she should get out of the house as quickly as possible. But she couldn't resist.

'Well . . . may I?'

'Of course. Come.'

The marquise held out her jewelled hand, and Elizabeth took it, getting off the bed. She followed La Païva through an adjacent dressing room to the door of the bath. 'We just finished the house,' La Païva was saying. 'It took ten years to build, but it was worth it, don't you think? Théo Gautier – that goat! – said last month everything in the house has been laid except the pavement.' She winked. 'Well, now even *that's* been laid. Here's the bath. Isn't it delicious?'

She depressed the silver door handle and pushed the door open to the Arabian Nights. The ceiling was a Moorish fantasy, the walls onyx and marble, the bath and lavatory solid onyx. The bath was lined with silvered bronze, with gilt fleur-de-lis engraved on it. The three sculpted gilt taps were set with rubies, opals, and turquoises.

'Do you like it?' asked La Païva, watching her young guest with interest as Elizabeth gaped.

'I don't know if one *likes* something like this,' mumbled Elizabeth.

'You're probably right. But one *respects* it, because of what it cost. Twenty years ago, I spent a cold night huddling in the door of the house that used to stand here. I didn't have a sou. Now I'm worth millions, and I did it all with my body. That's to be respected, don't you think? Henckel draws millions out of his Silesian mines, and I draw millions out of Henckel. It's an interesting cycle of nature. I assume you don't approve?'

Elizabeth looked at her sharp, powdered face. 'Of course I don't approve. How could I? But I'll admit I'm rather impressed.'

La Païva smiled. 'Good. And I'm rather impressed with you. Most "respectable" wives would never be honest enough to admit they were impressed. Or are you respectable? You're very attractive. Do you have lovers?'

Elizabeth blushed slightly, thinking of the maestro. 'I've had one,' she said quietly. 'But that was a long time ago. So I suppose I'm not all that respectable.'

'Bravo: you score again. How many wives will admit to even one lover? I like you more and more. Perhaps we can become friends, my dear.'

'I don't think so.'

The marquise shrugged. 'Well, at least not enemies. Perhaps I can help you with Zaza. Believe me, you'll need help. She's a sharp one, and she's on the make. And if there's anyone who knows sharp tarts on the make, it's me. I've been one all my life.'

Elizabeth studied her with curiosity. 'You feel no guilt at all, do you?' she asked.

'Guilt? Why should I feel guilty? I'm proud of my life! I've only done what most women would do if they had the looks and the guts. Frankly, it's been fun. Men rule the world, but the demi-monde rules men. The revenge of Eve, my dear. The revenge of Eve. Shall we go downstairs?'

Elizabeth followed her out of the bathroom as La Païva continued, 'You've got guts. I saw that in the way you handled your husband downstairs. It was clever of you to offer him champagne – the one thing that would stop him from pulling that trigger! You realize the others didn't know

Zaza had put blanks in the pistol? They were actually hoping to see a man blow his brains out. What ghouls! Paris has become so jaded, the only thing left that interests anyone is violence and death. France is decadent. If you want good advice, don't buy French bonds, my dear. Henckel says the Empire won't last the decade, and he should know. I suppose, though, it's fun while it lasts.'

'But *you* knew they were blanks?'

'Of course. You don't think I'd let a man blow his brains out in my salon? It would ruin the rugs.'

Elizabeth shuddered slightly, then went out into the small hall.

'Do you want to know about Zaza?' said the marquise, taking her arm as they started down the spiral onyx stair.

'Very much. What's her last name?'

'Which one? She's used a dozen, at least. Right now, she's calling herself Zaza d'Antibes, but that's a phony. Her real name is Sévérine Dulong and her father is a chimney sweep in Orléans – at least, that's what I've heard. Her mother? Who knows? Zaza came to Paris when she was eleven and she's been in the streets ever since. That was five years ago.'

'Then she's sixteen?'

'Yes, going on forty. She's clever, crude, and will do anything for money. I won't insult alley cats by comparing her morals to theirs. The fact is, she doesn't have any morals. She's brave: I'll give her that. She boasts that she's never cried and never known fear, and I can believe it.'

'Do you know where my husband met her?'

The marquise shrugged. 'Who knows? At the Café Anglais? The Closerie des Lilas? The Bal Mabille? The Passage de l'Opéra? It could have been a hundred places. Paris is one huge tryst. Ah: here's Jeff. What a strange name, but I love his hair, don't you? It's a natural red, unlike mine. It's so hard to find anything natural in Paris these days. But then, nature can be a bore. . . .'

They had reached the bottom of the staircase, where Jefferson Kent was waiting.

'You're looking better,' he said to Elizabeth.

'I am, thanks.'

'Want me to take you home?'

'Yes, that would be nice.' She turned to La Païva and squeezed her hand. 'You've been very kind,' she said. 'Thank you. I appreciate it. Perhaps I can repay you some day.'

'Perhaps.' The courtesan smiled. 'But if not, it doesn't matter. I like you. I'm on your side . . . which is odd. I'm never on the side of the wives. But Zaza is a bit much, even for me. Or perhaps I'm mellowing with age. At any rate, if you need me . . .'

'I'll remember.'

The majordomo held her furs, then she and Jeff went out into the night.

'She's an interesting woman,' said Elizabeth as her partner signalled a cab.

'She's a corker. But don't be fooled. Her heart's made out of the same stuff as the bathtub. I wouldn't trust her farther than I can spit.'

It occurred to Elizabeth that a self-confessed embezzler was hardly an expert on trust, but she didn't say anything. After they had got in the cab and Elizabeth had told the cabbie her address, Jeff said, 'So, what did you think of Zaza?'

'What do you expect I thought? I detest her.'

The young man reached over, took her gloved hand, and squeezed it. She looked at him with surprise as he said, 'Well, things could be worse. She might not have put blanks in the pistol.'

'That's a cheerful thought. And I'd prefer your not holding my hand, Mr Kent.'

He didn't let go. 'Now, you've really got to try harder to like me, you know. I'm really an immensely likeable person.'

'You're immensely self-confident, if nothing else. The hand, Mr Kent.'

'Most women find me irresistible. They just take one look at me and swoon dead away.'

'I'm sure. The hand, please.'

'Tell you what: why don't we stop somewhere and have a glass of wine? It's cold and . . .'

'Mr Kent, I am tired, terribly upset about what's happened, and I'm definitely not in the mood for a seduction.'

'Call me Jeff.'

She sighed. 'All right, Jeff. Now please let my hand go and try to behave like a gentleman. I do appreciate what you've done for me, but I can assure you your looks don't make me swoon. I'm not the swooning type, in spite of what happened in there.'

He let her hand go but retained his cheerfulness. She wondered if it were possible to insult him.

'You know, you really ought to do something about your husband,' he went on. 'He drinks too much. Take him to a temperance rally.'

'Thanks for the suggestion.'

'Wait a minute – I've got a better idea! I know a girl – and say, she's a looker! – anyway, her father is a sort of faith healer, and Marie – that's the girl – she told me that her father's done wonders with drunks.'

'My husband isn't a "drunk", Mr Kent.'

'There you go again, getting formal. . . . It's Jeff, remember? And what is he if he isn't a drunk?'

She tried to curb her temper. 'He . . . he occasionally drinks too much, I'll admit.'

'Uh huh. Anyway, you ought to take him to this man. His name's Professor Brandini – he's Italian, in case you couldn't guess – and he lives out in Neuilly. Want me to set up an appointment for you?'

'My husband doesn't believe in faith healers.'

'What does that matter if he can help him? You see, he's also a mesmerist, and Marie says sometimes he puts people under a spell and then sort of draws whatever it is that's bothering them right out of their minds! Isn't that fantastic?'

'Are you serious?'

'Sure. I'm always serious. Well, almost always. Why don't *you* see the professor first? That way, you can talk to him and get an idea whether you think he can help your husband. Wouldn't cost you anything, and who knows? He might be just what your husband needs.'

She thought about this. 'Well . . .'

'I'll make an appointment for next Tuesday morning. Will you be free then?'

'I didn't say yes . . .'

'Tuesday at ten. I'll come pick you up and take you out myself.'

'You know, you really are *extremely* pushy.'

He grinned. 'I know. But you're getting to like me, aren't you?'

She started to say something, then, despite herself, she laughed. 'Incredibly enough, I am. And don't ask me why, because I usually loathe pushy people.'

'It's my irresistible charm. And here we are. Say: this is some swell house! Must cost your husband a bundle! What's he do?'

'He's a botanist.'

'Is that a job?'

'No, of course not. My husband has independent means.'

'Think he'd be interested in buying some real estate?'

'No.'

'Oh well, worth a try, wasn't it?' He hopped out of the cab, then helped her down. 'By the way, I don't suppose you could loan me fifty francs? I'm flat broke, and I don't think the cabbie's going to be very happy when he finds out. I'll pay you back Tuesday.'

She looked at him curiously. 'You mean you have *no* money?'

He smiled cheerfully. 'Nope. I'm bust-o. I've got a client coming around in the morning who owes me a bundle, but until then . . .'

He spread his hands. She reached in her purse and took out fifty francs, which she gave him.

'Thanks a lot – this really helps. Well, it's been swell being with you, Elizabeth. Do you think we know each other well enough to kiss?'

'No.'

He laughed. 'Well, it was worth a try, wasn't it? Okay, let's shake. Good night. I'll see you next Tuesday. And don't worry about your husband: I'm sure the professor can fix him up. *À bientôt*, as the Frogs say.' He blew her a kiss and climbed back in the cab, which rattled off. She let herself in the house, shaking her head in wonderment at his brashness and appalling lack of manners. Yet she had to admit there *was* something likeable about him. And while it was probably a waste of time to see this Professor Brandini, still, if he *could* help Ben . . .

And then the full impact of the evening hit her. Ben and that repulsive Zaza. Maybe the answer was to give Ben what he wanted and return to Philadelphia. That would be the quickest way to get Zaza out of his life. But apparently Ben wanted something else beside Philadelphia. He wanted young girls, and there were plenty of young girls in Pennsylvania, so perhaps returning home wasn't the answer. Then what was? How to fight Zaza? And she did intend to fight her. She wasn't going to accept a 'Continental' situation. She wanted her husband to herself, with all his faults. How galling to think that, at that very moment. Ben was probably in Zaza's bed, while she would sleep alone, as she had for so many nights now . . . !

She started up the stairway, noting the time as she passed the French clock on the wall bracket. Ten past one. She would have to write the Princesse Mathilde a note in the morning, explaining her abrupt disappearance from the party . . . but how to explain it? 'My dear Princesse: I had to leave your party to go to the Hôtel Païva to stop my husband from blowing his brains out'? Hardly. She would have to start lying, and Elizabeth hated lies. That was perhaps the worst of it: the lies, the deceit, the loss of trust. . . . Oh Ben, how could you? How could you be such an idiot as to involve yourself with that slut?

She reached the upstairs hall and started down it. Was it her fault? He had called her a snob . . . had she driven him from her bed to Zaza's? Perhaps, she didn't know. But then, what to do about it? She reached the nursery, opened the door, and went inside. She lit a lamp and then picked it up, stepping over the toy soldiers as she went to the door to Ward's room. She opened it quietly and looked in. Tiptoeing, she went to his bed and looked at him. How angelic he looked with his golden curls! . . . She kissed his forehead, then returned to the nursery and closed the door. After crossing the room, she opened the door to Pauline's room. Miss Pritchett slept there also, and Elizabeth could hear the English nanny gently snoring as she went to the small bed and looked at her daughter. How Ben adored this child! And how was it possible that he could betray his family by . . .

She leaned down and kissed Pauline, then tiptoed out of the room through the nursery to the hall. Men. There was a streak of the animal in all of them.

She went to her bedroom and turned up the lights. Was it possible this marriage, for which she had held such high hopes, was doomed to failure? Oh God, I hope not, she thought. After what happened to her first husband . . .

Lew! On an impulse, she went to her chiffonier and pulled out the bottom drawer. She reached under the quilted bags holding her lingerie and felt for the photograph. She found it and pulled it out. She stared at the handsome young lieutenant smiling so confidently at Matthew Brady's camera who until now had been embalmed in a wooden frame, hidden from her perhaps sensitive husband under her underwear. Perhaps she had been wrong to hide the photograph. She had thought it would hurt Ben's feelings, but to hell with Ben's feelings! Maybe what he needed was the image of his old friend. Perhaps that would remind him of his responsibilities to his old friend's widow (and not Lew's mother)! What a rotten remark that had been!

Defiantly, she went to her bed table and set the picture under the lamp. Lew. Then she picked it up again. There were tears in her eyes as she kissed the cold glass. The past, dead, gone for ever. She put the photo back on the table, and her heart ached. Every time she took out the picture, it was like falling in love with him all over again.

27

The sugar plantation of Don Francisco Pérez Salazar Jesús Gonzaga y Hernandez, the fourth Marqués de Veracruz, lay in the rich Morelos Valley, near Taxco. This was the *tierra caliente*, or 'hot country', which was tropical in the summer and pleasant in the winter, excellent growing conditions for sugar cane as well as coffee and oranges. The plantation's extensive canefields produced bumper crops, and the sugar was refined in wooden sheds not far from the stucco walls of the hacienda. Over two hundred peons were employed on the estate, and, thanks to the marqués's enlightened views, they were better paid than most field-workers in Mexico and were considered enviable. The marqués had even built an infirmary for them and staffed it with an English doctor.

The hacienda itself was a large square built around a courtyard, the north side of which was a high wall pierced by heavy wooden gates. The main house formed the south side of the square, the kitchens and laundry rooms the west side, and the east arm contained guest quarters. On the northeast corner of the square was the small private chapel, the bell tower of which dominated the entire compound. It was one of the highest man-made structures in the valley, soaring seventy feet in the air, and its huge bell was visible from the ground, hanging just below the tile roof, open on all four sides to enable its ring to be heard all over the plantation.

Unlike most haciendas, the Marqués de Veracruz's had a formal dining room. But, like most *hacendados*, he followed the custom of taking family meals in various parts of the house, depending on the weather or the whim. On this January afternoon he, his sister, and his daughter were lunching in the lovely, plant-hanging loggia that ran along the south side of the courtyard.

'I find it incredible that you are actually permitting Ysabel to proceed with this bizarre project!' said Doña Ana, the maiden sister of the marqués. Tia Ana, as she was familiarly known in the family, was a stiff, white-haired, black-laced aristocrat who, since the death of her sister-in-law ten years before, had doubled as surrogate mother and *duena* for her twenty-year-old niece, Ysabel Felicidad Teresa Alicia Gonzaga y Hernandez, Don Francisco's only child. Ysabel was seated opposite her aunt at the wrought-iron table and was trying to ignore Tia Ana's thunderous glares.

'Ana,' said Don Francisco patiently, 'it's not as if Ysabel were conducting experiments in black magic. All she wants to do is set up a schoolroom in the chapel for the children. . . .'

'The chapel is a holy place!' said Tia Ana. 'To let those dirty children inside to teach them to read is a sacrilege! Father Gaspardo has been derelict in his duty to permit it.'

'If Father Gaspardo taught the children himself,' said Ysabel, 'I wouldn't have to do it for him.'

She was a soft-spoken girl who had inherited her intelligence and determination from her father. Unfortunately, she had also inherited Don Francisco's tendency toward overweight: she was thirty pounds too heavy, and a potentially pretty face was puffed into jowliness, which was not helped by thick black eyebrows that needed plucking. Her dark eyes and white skin, however, were arresting and testified to the Spanish blood that flowed in her veins. Ysabel might not be a beauty, but her bloodlines were the best in Mexico. Since her father was one of the largest landowners in the country (having inherited vast tracts of land from his great-grandfather, the fifty-second viceroy of Mexico, the Condé de Revillagigedo) as well as the owner of silver and gold mines and the promoter of Mexico's first railroad, Ysabel was also in the enviable position of being one of Mexico's richest heiresses. However, she was guarded by that dragon, her aunt, like the Ring of the Niebelungen. The few suitors who so far had had the nerve to try for the ring of gold had been withered by Tia Ana's scrutiny. They had slunk back to Mexico City, licking their wounds. 'Fortune hunters,' Tia Ana had labelled them, and Ysabel was smart enough to know that her aunt was probably right. On the other hand, Ysabel was also smart enough to know that her fortune would inevitably be a factor to be considered by any potential husband. And since she was anything but immune to the attractions of the opposite sex (though she was confused by the strange stirrings inside her that those attractions kindled) and did not want to die an old maid like Tia Ana, she had begun to rebel against her aunt's overzealous protection. Part of her rebellion had taken the form of the project under discussion.

'It is the Church's duty,' said Tia Ana, waving away the white-jacketed Indian footman offering a second helping of *frijoles*, 'to save the peons' souls, not teach them to read.'

'Then why is the Church charging them money to perform the holy rites?' countered Ysabel, who loved a good fight. 'And why is illiteracy rampant?'

'Why does a fieldworker need to know how to read or write?'

'Because maybe he could be a better fieldworker! Or a happier one! Tia Ana, Mexico is being torn apart. The people want something better than they have, and I don't blame them! The least we can do is give our children some schooling, and the least *I* can do is teach them.'

'A revolutionary!' said Tia Ana, her narrow face a study in genteel horror. 'The next thing you'll want is to join up with Juarez or Sanchez and burn the haciendas!'

Don Francisco declined a second helping of his beloved *frijoles* – he was trying to control his rampant waistline – then changed his mind and signalled for seconds.

'Ana,' he said, 'Ysabel is right.'

'You always side with the child! She's spoiled and wilful.

No lady of her station in life should be doing anything more active than needlework.'

'Tia Ana,' said Ysabel, fighting down her anger, 'I *hate* needlework!'

'Shocking.'

'And I do not intend to waste my life like every other girl my age making fancy pillowslips! I'm the last one to want to burn haciendas, but Mexico is changing, and I intend to change with it!'

'The change in Mexico,' said her aunt, 'is anti-Church and anti-*us*. You'll think about that, young lady, when you teach your peons to read revolutionary literature.'

'Ana,' said her brother, 'the Church refuses to move with the times, which is why the country has turned against it. The landowners must learn a lesson from this, or we'll end up like the Church – the enemies of the people.'

'Exactly!' agreed Ysabel. 'And if the people are against us, no walls are going to keep us safe.'

Tia Ana put down her napkin. 'I have never heard such twaddle. The people are *ours*. We pay them, we feed them – where would they be without us?'

'A lot of them seem to think,' said her 235-pound brother, 'they'd be a lot better off without us.'

'Ridiculous,' said his sister, getting up from the table. 'I will take my coffee in my bedroom,' she said to the footman. Then she turned back to her niece. 'I wonder what your mother would say if she heard you speaking this way.'

'Tia Ana' – and Ysabel smiled – 'I think Mother would say "Bravo!"'

'Bizarre.' Her aunt sniffed. Then she went inside the house.

Don Francisco waited until his sister was out of earshot. Then he turned to his daughter, who was seated to his left.

'Don't worry,' he said. 'I'm on your side.'

Ysabel smiled at her father, whom she adored. 'Thank you, Father.' She lowered her voice. 'Do you think some day we might even get her to leave me alone when the young gentlemen pay me a call?'

Her good-natured father tried to look stern, but he couldn't quite manage it.

'That would be difficult. But . . . perhaps. For a few minutes, anyway.'

'I think I could make a favourable impression, if I were given a chance. But every time I say anything, Tia Ana just glares at me.' And she made a glare-face, imitating her aunt.

Her father sighed. 'I know. I don't envy you, Ysabel. But we'll get you a husband, don't worry.'

Ysabel looked down at her hands. 'I know I'm no beauty,' she said quietly. Then she looked up rather defiantly. 'But I'll make someone a good wife.'

He smiled and took her hand.

'I know you will,' he said.

The problem is, he thought, who?

After lunch, Ysabel walked across the courtyard toward the chapel. The courtyard was a pleasant area with its dozens of clay-potted geraniums and its shade trees, under which several of the men her father employed to guard the estate were dozing, rifles across their laps. Don Francisco had a small private army of fifty men who patrolled the fields to guard agains crop-burning *insurgentes* and guarded the house itself against attack by the bandits and guerrillas that infested the valley. The estate was better guarded than most. But with the French pulling out of Mexico, conditions had become even more chaotic, and the inhabitants of the hacienda had reason to thank the foresight of Don Francisco's grandfather, who had built the high wall to the north fifty years before, when Mexico had thrown off the centuries-old rule of Spain and the Mexican Revolution had begun its long struggle. All the windows of the house facing the outside were heavily grilled, and the doors were three inches thick. In a sea of lawlessness, the hacienda was an island of security.

Ysabel pushed open the heavy door of the chapel and went inside, closing the door behind her. She loved the small chapel. It was always cool, always peaceful, a place of refuge. Its peaked, beamed ceiling soared forty feet above the clean stone floor. At one end was a wooden gallery, which boasted a small pipe organ, its organ case a fantasy with gilt cherubs swirling around tin pipes. Opposite the gallery was the sanctuary, with its red Vigil Light hanging above the altar, indicating the presence of the Host. The chapel was private, for the family of the marqués and his domestic retainers; but it was a working chapel.

Ysabel genuflected and crossed herself before the altar bearing its beautiful gold monstrance. Then she got up, walked past the bank of votive candles honouring Saint Teresa, and opened a door that led to the small robing room to the side of the sanctuary. Here, on a table, were piled the three dozen Spanish grammar books she had badgered her father into ordering for her from Madrid. Don Francisco had at first been dubious about Ysabel's idea of starting a classroom for the hacienda's children, but she had won him over, and the books had finally arrived the day before, precipitating the storm of protest from Tia Ana.

Ysabel picked up one of the books and opened it. She had no training as a teacher and was nervous about how she would go about drumming literacy into the heads of the children. But she was determined. Her first class would start the following Monday morning. And though the Indian and Mestizo workers had expressed a certain understandable reluctance about sending their children to Ysabel's school – after all, it was 'new' – she had enrolled twenty-eight pupils. Now she had to figure out how to start.

It was then that she heard the explosion.

A loud BOOM shook the chapel, and she heard shouts, screams, and rifle shots. Dropping the grammar book, she ran back into the chapel. The noise outside was deafening; through the courtyard windows she could see billowing smoke. After grabbing a stool from the sanctuary, she ran to one of the windows, placed the stool on the floor, then climbed on it to look out.

The courtyard was filled with smoke and shouting *guerrilleros*, their horses trampling the flowerpots. The men were firing into the air, but she could see the dead bodies of her father's guards sprawled on the ground beneath the trees, and she knew that the *guerrilleros* had been the first to fire into hearts and heads. Some of them were riding their horses into the loggia where she had just eaten with her father and aunt. More were pouring through the great gates, which had been shattered by an explosion of some sort: what was left of the gates was sagging on the giant iron hinges. It was chaos. Chaos and death had imploded into the island of security.

She was panicked, but she told herself to use her head. She climbed down from the stool and looked around the chapel. Was there any point in hiding? she thought. But then, was there any point in *not* hiding? If she left the chapel, she would probably be shot on sight. She was no help to her father dead, but conceivably she might be some help alive. But where could she hide?

The organ. The baroque organ in the gallery with its swirling cherubs. She ran to the end of the chapel and hurried up the narrow spiral staircase that led to the gallery. When she reached the top, she took another quick look out the gallery window. She was above the wall now, and she could see on a distant ridge before the hacienda an artillery gun. Artillery? In the Morelos Valley? It was like a war! She looked back down into the courtyard. She saw four of the *guerrilleros* carrying a heavy, odd-looking gun toward the chapel door. She had never seen anything remotely like that gun, with its cylindrical barrel consisting of six separate smaller barrels connected in a circle. But she didn't have time to inspect it at leisure. They were coming inside the chapel! After taking one last look through the window – and she saw at least fifty more horsemen *outside* the hacienda – it was an invasion! – she ran to the organ. It was possible, she knew, to climb inside the organ case. There was an area behind the pipes with room enough for a repairman to work on the pipes. Now she opened the small door at the side of the case and squeezed through, wishing not for the first time in her life that she were thirty pounds thinner. She closed the door behind her and squeezed through the workings of the organ until she found the space behind the pipes. She was able to stand up, but the space was confining and the musty air stifling. Still, she found a chink between two pipes that enabled her to see out, giving her an excellent view of the chapel below, while at the same time she was sure no one could see her. So no matter how uncomfortable and stifling her hiding place, it had its advantages.

The noise outside was dying down now, and she saw the chapel door swing in. The four *guerrilleros* carried the odd gun inside. Judging from the way they were straining under the load, it must have been heavy. Behind them, another man was carrying a steel tripod while yet two others were bearing a heavy wooden chest. She knew next to nothing about guns, but she assumed the chest contained the ammunition.

'Where's the tower door?' one of the men said.

'Must be over there,' said another, nodding his head at the wooden door in the north-east corner of the chapel, below the gallery. The men started lugging their burden across the stone floor.

'Jesus, this thing is heavy,' grunted one.

'And the tower's high. Wish Sanchez had to help us carry this thing up.'

'Sanchez doesn't *work*. Sanchez just gives orders.'

The men disappeared from her view as they went under the gallery. But she heard the hinges of the tower door squeak and listened to the grumbling of the men as they started up the winding stone stairs.

There were over a hundred steps, she knew. It would be a back-breaking climb. She wondered what magic this strange gun possessed to make it worth while to carry it up a hundred steps.

The chapel was empty again. She began to consider the possibility of getting out of it – perhaps that night – going through the exploded gates, and finding help from the outside. But then two more *guerrilleros* came into the chapel, pushing a man in front of them. He was a gringo, judging from his hair, and his hands were tied behind his back. The two *guerrilleros* closed the chapel door, then pointed to the centre of the room.

'There's your new home, El Juero,' said one of them in

English, which Ysabel could understand if not speak too well. Now she saw that the guard was also a gringo. 'Might as well start warming up the floor. You're going to be here a long time.'

The man whose hands were tied said nothing. He went to the centre of the chapel and sat down on the stone floor. The two guards sat on the floor also, although next to the wall so they could lean their backs against it. The gringo guard pulled out a cigarette and lit it. The other yawned.

'Where have they taken Laura?' the gringo said softly.

'Sanchez wants to talk to her again,' said the guard. 'Don't worry: she's safe.'

Ysabel watched it all through the chink in the organ pipes, wondering what was going on and what was happening to her father and Tia Ana.

Having been raised by well-to-do parents and educated in Paris, Diego Sanchez had a taste for the finer things in life – which meant French in his mind – that conflicted with his passionate hatred of the French. As he waited in the library of the Marqués de Veracruz, he passed his time examining the excellent Louis XV leather-topped desk, marvelling at the workmanship while at the same time loathing the workman's homeland. Then there were the fine collection of Chinese export dishes in the French vitrine, the four Goya prints in the French frames, and the superb collection of books in the French-panelled shelves. France was inescapable in Mexico.

He went to the shelves and pulled out a calf-bound copy of *Don Quixote*, illustrated by the French artist Doré. The cover was imprinted with the coat of arms of the Gonzaga y Hernandez family. Beautiful. He replaced *Don Quixote* and looked at the other spines. The *Dialogues* of Plato. The *Decameron*. A history of the viceroys of Mexico. The works of Shakespeare, translated into Spanish.

It was then that he heard the sharp BANG! outside. He went to the window behind the desk and looked out. Through the arches of the loggia he could see Tomás and Carlos in the courtyard. They had hauled the marqués's safe outside and blown the door off with gunpowder. As the smoke cleared, Tomás reached inside.

Sanchez went to the desk and sat down. He was slim, balding, with a sharp-featured, bearded face that might have been pleasant except for its cold, intelligent eyes. He wore leather pants and a cotton shirt crossed by cartridge belts. He spoke French fluently and some English. At the Sorbonne, he had won prizes in philosophy and history and had fallen in love with the writings of Louis Auguste Blanqui and other French radical thinkers. He had returned to Mexico armed with radical French thought and determined to profit from the chaos his country was in. To him the answer to Mexico's problems was not the vaguely American-style democracy promised by the Indian Juárez, but a violent social upheaval led by the pure-blooded Creole, or white Mexican, Diego Sanchez. To Sanchez, the road to power was paved with blood and guns – guns like his new ten-pound Parrot field gun, which he had brought down from Texas. The Parrott had made mincemeat of the hacienda's gates.

Tomás Rodriguez came into the library carrying two steel lock boxes.

'Anything interesting?' asked Sanchez.

'A lot. Shall I put them on the desk?'

'Wait a minute' – Sanchez opened a newspaper to spread over the hand-tooled leather – 'no use scratching the leather. . . .'

Tomás placed the lockboxes on the paper. The lids had been pried loose, and now Sanchez opened the top one. He pulled out a stack of bonds and looked them over.

'Mexican Railroad bonds,' he said. 'Face value, one million gold pesos. Actual value, maybe fifty thousand.'

'They may be worth more later,' said Tomás.

'True.' Sanchez put the bonds to one side and pulled out a pile of bank notes. 'One hundred thousand pesos, issued by the Bank of Mexico. Worth shit.' He tossed them on the floor. 'Ah: *here's* something.' He pulled out another pile of bank notes and flipped through them. 'Five thousand pounds sterling. Now we're hitting pay dirt.'

He put the pounds sterling and the railroad bonds back in their box, then moved the remaining lockbox to one side and opened it. He whistled.

'Here we go! Two fifty-thousand-dollar United States Treasury bonds! So our friend Don Francisco invested in the winning side. Smart man. Plus' – he pulled out a bound stack of bank notes – 'about forty thousand dollars in American currency.'

He replaced the money and closed the lid. Then he smiled at Tomás.

'And this,' he said, 'is only scratching the surface. Tomás, I think we've done good work today. What's the count on Don Francisco's guards?'

'Nineteen dead, six wounded.'

'And the rest?'

Thommaso grinned. 'Ricardo is "talking" to them.'

'Good. I imagine they'll see the advantage in joining our side. Take these lockboxes . . . put them in the cellar with a guard . . . then send in Don Francisco.'

'Yes, my captain.'

Tomás picked up the boxes and headed for the door as Sanchez leaned back in his chair and studied the arched stucco ceiling of the library. How easy it all was, in the last analysis. All it took was men, guns, and the element of surprise, and the world's riches dropped into one's lap.

'How about the Gatling gun?' he asked, as Tomás opened the door.

'They took it to the top of the tower.'

'Good.'

Tomás left the room. Sanchez put his hands behind his head and his boots up on the desk, being careful to place them on the newspaper. Then he studied his dusty toes. Juárez, that bloody little Indian. The peons loved Juárez, but Juárez didn't have a Gatling gun and he, Diego Sanchez, did. How lucky to have run into that arms dealer in Texas who had had six of them, second hand, war surplus from the Union Army! He had been able to buy only one at the price of $850, but now, with Don Francisco's hoard of cash, he could send back to Texas to buy the other five. Six

Gatling guns, each able to fire two hundred rounds a minute! They were worth six regiments! Juárez might be closing in on Maximilian, but Diego Sanchez was closing in on Juárez.

The library door opened and Tomás brought in Don Francisco. The fat *hacendado* in his rumpled white suit looked in a state of shock, his greying mustachios drooping sadly.

'Ah, Don Francisco,' said Sanchez, pointing to a gilt armchair. 'Tomás, pull up that chair for our guest.'

Tomás carried the elaborate chair to the desk. Don Francisco sat down as Sanchez pulled out his revolver and placed it on the desk. 'Where is your daughter?' he said.

'My daughter?'

'Your servants tell us your daughter is here. Or was here. We can't find her.'

Don Francisco, despite his shock, was thinking. 'Then she must have left the hacienda when she heard you attack the gates.'

'We've sent out search parties.' Sanchez looked at Tomás. 'Keep looking for her. I want her back *here*, at the hacienda.'

'Yes, my captain.'

'And lock the old prune in her room. If she keeps on screaming, tie a gag around her mouth.'

'Yes, my captain.'

Tomás left the room, and Sanchez turned to Don Francisco.

'Is the old woman your sister?'

'Yes.'

'She's enough to drive a man crazy.'

'I agree.'

Sanchez chuckled. 'What's your full name?'

'Don Francisco Pérez Salazar Jesús Gonzaga y Hernandez.'

'Very nice. Very florid. I like florid names. Your age?'

'Sixty-one.'

'You are the fourth Marqués de Veracruz, a title bestowed on your family by the King of Spain?'

'Yes. He bestowed it on my great-grandfather, the fifty-second viceroy.'

'Along with half of Mexico?'

Don Francisco said nothing. Sanchez removed his boots from the desk and sat up.

'Well, not *half*,' he said. 'But a lot. You are a rich man, Don Francisco. Too rich. You have exploited the people of Mexico – '

'Exploited?' interrupted Don Francisco. 'I have treated my people fairly! I have paid them well, I have set up an infirmary to give the sick medical treatment – '

Sanchez waved his hand. 'Yes, yes, I've heard all about that. You are an enlightened man, Don Francisco. An enlightened despot. The fact is, *you* own the land. *You* reap the profits. Well, my friend, that's all coming to an end. Today, this hacienda has been expropriated in the name of the Mexican people.'

'You mean in the name of Diego Sanchez!'

Sanchez shrugged. '*I* am the Mexican people. I have been given a mandate to lead them. Mind you, I have nothing against you personally, Don Francisco. In fact, I rather admire you personally. You have excellent taste in furniture and books . . . plus you are, like me, a Creole. We are of the pure Spanish blood, and unfortunately certain elements in this country – namely Señor Juárez – represent impure blood. But I'm afraid you are a symbol. You are the richest man in the country, one of the greatest landowners. . . . That's very bad, Don Francisco. Very bad. Consequently, painful as this is to me, I have no choice but to make an example of you. I must commit a symbolic act, so to speak, to prove to the Mexican people that I represent their best hope against the oppressing landowner class. Therefore, I must pass sentence on you, Don Francisco. For your crimes against the nation, you will be executed before a firing squad tomorrow morning at eight.' He looked at him. The older man's red face had turned pale pink. 'Do you have anything to say?'

Don Francisco looked baffled. 'What can I say? You have the guns!'

'You have an admirably clear view of the situation.'

'But I don't believe this . . . this "symbolic act". To execute the one landholder who has treated his people fairly? This won't do you any good, Sanchez. Kill me if you want, but the people will call you a butcher.'

Sanchez picked up a delicately carved silver letter opener and played with it.

'Of course,' he said, 'there may be an alternative. If you would be willing to donate a large portion of your non-agricultural holdings to the Mexican people as a gesture of goodwill, perhaps the people, in their gratitude, would spare your life.'

Don Francisco stared at the thin young man sitting at his desk. 'How much?' he said.

'Oh . . . half your silver and gold mines?'

'I see. I take it that the Mexican "people" are – again – you?'

'Precisely. The country is in chaos, Don Francisco. I offer the Mexican people order and social justice. In times of upheaval, the strong man is given a mandate to lead his people. I have been given that mandate.'

'By whom?'

'By myself. Why don't you think my offer over, my friend? There's no hurry. We have time. Think it over. I'll see you again at – oh, seven o'clock this evening. You may go now. Tomás!' he called.

His second-in-command opened the door.

'Take Don Francisco out. Treat him well. Give him whatever he wants except his freedom. Then send in the Frenchwoman.'

Don Francisco got to his feet. 'What are you doing with Madame de Beaupré?' he asked.

'We kidnapped her two nights ago,' said Sanchez casually.

'In the name of the Mexican people?'

Sanchez aimed at the panelled wall opposite him, then flipped the silver letter-opener across the room. Its blade went into the panelling.

'In the name of the Mexican people.' Sanchez smiled, leaning back and putting his boots up on the desk again.

Lew's gringo guard was named Billie Hopkins, and he was one of the hundreds of ex-Confederate soldiers who had made their way to Texas at the end of the war, crossed the Rio Grande, and become soldiers of fortune in Mexico. Now he lit another cigarette and looked at the notorious El Juero sitting in the middle of the chapel, his hands tied behind his back. El Juero hadn't said much for the last few days.

'Ever rob this Don Francisco fellow, El Juero?' asked Billie, tossing his match on the floor.

'Once.'

Billie chuckled. 'Goddam, you really got around, didn't you? What'd you get?'

'Two thousand pounds sterling. Don Francisco likes cash and doesn't trust banks. It's cost him a lot over the years.'

'Hell, Sanchez says he's so rich he won't miss it. Did you rob him here? In this place?'

'No. He's got a big spread in Mexico City.'

'Goddam. So you just climb through windows and take the pickin's? Pretty nice life.'

'It was fun while it lasted. Why does Sanchez keep talking to Laura?'

'Your girl friend? I don't know. Say, that's some swell piece of ass! You had a real nice set-up goin' for you till we showed up, didn't you? Bare-ass swimmin' in the moonlight? Say, I could sure use some of that.'

'You make it all sound very romantic.'

'Oh well' – Billie took a drag on the cigarette – 'it's what you get in the end that counts, ain't it? That's what we used to say in the late, lamented Confederate Army, and look what we got in the end. Shit.'

Lew looked at the wooden door under the chapel gallery.

'What did they take through that door?' he asked. 'When they came out, they looked half dead.'

'No wonder. They was carryin' a Gatling gun to the top of the bell tower. Weighs a ton. Ever see one of them things?'

'I've heard about them. You crank them, don't you?'

'That's right. They spit out bullets like hogs lettin' farts. Sanchez bought this one up in Texas. Union surplus. Shit, if the South had had a couple of *them*, we'd-a won the war.'

'What's he going to do with it up in the tower?'

'Stand guard, of course. Damned tower's seventy foot high. Anyone tries to attack us, rat-tat-tat-tat – we'll mow 'em down. That's why Sanchez decided to take this place. It's built like a brick shithouse. This'll be our headquarters till we march on Mexico City.'

Lew turned back to look at him. 'Sanchez doesn't really think he can take the capital?'

'Why not? Soon as the Frenchies clear out, there's no one left but Juárez.'

'Juárez has a lot of men.'

'So have we, and we're recruitin' more every day. *And*' – he pointed his finger to the roof – 'we got the Gatling gun.' He grinned as he stood up to stub out his cigarette. 'Old Billie Hopkins was on the losin' side last time. But *this* time, looks like he's picked a winner. And there's gonna be a lot of loot.'

He stretched and yawned. Something in the gallery crashed. The other guard looked up, as did Billie.

'What's that?' he whispered in Spanish, picking up his rifle.

'Something up there,' said the other guard. 'Near the organ. . . .'

'You stay here and watch El Juero. I'll go take a look.'

He hurried to the rear of the chapel and went up the spiral stair. Reaching the top, he looked around. Nothing but wooden benches and the organ. Holding his rifle with both hands, he started toward the organ, moving quietly. Silence.

Then, suddenly, a mouse ran out from under the organ bench and scurried to a hole under one of the pews.

Billie Hopkins laughed. 'Goddam *mouse*!' he called down. 'Must of knocked something over.'

He went back to the stairs and started down.

Ysabel, frozen behind the organ pipes, thought her heart had never beaten so fast in her life. First the mouse, which had caused her to jump, making the noise. Then the guard. . . .

Tomás opened the door to the library to admit Laura de Beaupré, who looked exhausted after the strain of the past two days.

'Guess what Carlos found in the cellar?' said Tomás. He pulled a bottle of Bordeaux from under his arm and held it up.

Sanchez got to his feet. Taking his revolver, he came to the door and took the bottle to examine the label.

'Château Lafite,' he said. 'Eighteen forty-eight. I might have known Don Francisco would have the best. Madame, would you join me in a glass of French wine?'

Laura looked at him dully. She nodded. Then she went over to the chair in front of the desk.

'Why not?' she said, sitting down. Her blue velvet suit was dusty, and the left sleeve had been torn.

'Get two glasses and open the bottle,' ordered Sanchez. Tomás nodded and closed the door.

'Wine, furniture, and philosophy are the best products of France,' said Sanchez, returning to the desk. 'Colonialism is your worst product. I love your wine and philosophy, but I hate your colonialism.' He leaned against the desk. 'Ah, but I'm ungallant. I should have mentioned French *women*.'

'I'm Italian,' she said listlessly.

'But married to the French ambassador. I've been so preoccupied I haven't had a chance to continue our interesting discussion of the other afternoon. The one where you told me your husband was planning to take Maximilian's final appeal to Louis Napoleon.'

'What more is there to discuss?'

'There was one point that intrigued me. You mentioned that you weren't going directly to Paris, but rather that you were stopping at Washington *en route*. Why Washington?'

'My husband is to see the Secretary of State.'

'Mr Seward? Why?'

'I have no idea.'

Sanchez smiled. 'Come now, madame. A woman as beautiful as you must hear all sorts of things from your husband' – he leaned near her – 'as he lies next to you in bed.'

Her eyes widened slightly. 'I hear his snores, señor.'

'Your husband sleeps? I wouldn't fall asleep next to you.'

'How fascinating,' she said, stifling a yawn. 'However, if I were unlucky enough to find myself in bed next to you, I think I would either fall asleep from boredom or' – and she smiled prettily – 'faint with repulsion.'

Sanchez ran his finger over his thin lips.

'French bitch,' he said softly.

'Italian,' she corrected.

Tomás opened the door. He carried a tray with a bottle and two glasses to the desk and set it down. Then he shot the two a look and left the room. Sanchez stood up, went around the desk, and poured some wine into one of the glasses. He sniffed it, then tasted it.

'Excellent.'

He filled the two glasses, then brought them around the desk, handing one to Laura. She took it. He leaned on the desk and raised his glass.

'To the Mexican people,' he said.

'I'll drink to that,' she replied, and she did. 'Where did you acquire your taste for French wine and philosophy?' she went on.

'At the Sorbonne. I studied there four years.'

'So your parents have money?'

'My father is a Veracruz exporter.'

'He must find it amusing that his son rides around the countryside killing people, blowing up haciendas – '

'My father is a bourgeois,' he interrupted. 'I learned at the Sorbonne that the bourgeoisie is the greatest enemy of mankind – at least, in Europe. Here, there is no middle class to speak of. Here, the landowners are the enemy – like Don Francisco. And, of course, you French colonialists.' He drained his glass, then picked up the bottle to refill it.

'Good wine should be sipped,' said Laura.

He set the bottle down. 'That's a rule for people with patience. I don't have much patience. I like to get drunk fast, and I like to find out information fast. Madame, I'm a busy man. I want to know why your husband wishes to see Mr Seward.'

'Why do you want to know?'

'Because I have the feeling the French are making one final attempt to keep the Americans out of Mexico. That will be useful information to tell the Mexican people – proof of the perfidy of the French, as if they needed proof. Still, I want to know.'

She sipped her wine, eyeing him. 'I have no idea.'

He drained the second glass, then set it on the desk. He got up and came around her chair. She didn't move as she felt his hands on her shoulders.

'I'll give you one more chance,' he said softly.

The hands moved down to her breasts. She looked at them. They were thin, delicate hands, covered with fine black hair. Fingers of fear started squeezing her brain. Did she have the right to betray Aristide? And yet she violently disagreed with Aristide. . . .

'My husband,' she said, 'intends to offer Mr Seward a deal.'

'What's the deal?'

'If the Americans will allow the French to stay in Mexico . . .' She hesitated. Could she do this? It was tantamount to treason! And yet Sanchez was dangerous. She knew what was in his mind. Violence was in his mind. Violence to her.

'Yes? If the Americans will allow the French to stay in Mexico?'

'The French will cede Baja California and Sonora to the United States.'

She felt the hands squeeze her breasts. Just as the pain became intense, he abruptly released her. He walked around the chair. 'My God, I knew the French were cynics, but this . . .' He was speaking softly, almost to himself, as he paced around the room. 'Sonora and Baja California – with all the mineral deposits in Sonora. . . . Why not throw in Chihuahua for good measure? And the Yucatán? Why not just give them the whole damned country? Incredible. Absolutely incredible. And Seward might accept it! Oh yes, one can't rule that out. . . .' He stopped his pacing and turned on Laura. 'You pigs! You'd give away a tenth of the country just so the French can stay to suck us dry. You vampires!'

He grabbed the bottle of Château Lafite and threw it with all this strength through the window. It crashed through the glass and smashed against one of the stucco pillars of the loggia.

Laura stiffened upright. 'I don't defend the policies of my husband's government,' she said, trying to keep calm. 'In fact, I've fought them all along.'

'How convenient for you.' He sneered. 'You can deplore your husband's politics while you enjoy his income. If you really felt he was wrong, why didn't you leave him?'

'He's my husband. . . .'

'Your sense of wifely duty didn't seem to stop you from swimming in the nude with our gringo friend the other night?'

He was coming closer to her.

'I've told you what you want to know,' she said. 'May I go now?'

'No.'

His tone was sharp. Watch out, she told herself. He's a rattlesnake. . . .

He leaned on the arms of her chair, his face close to hers. She could smell the wine on his breath.

'How many other men have you fucked?' he whispered. 'The whole French army?'

She slapped him. He grabbed her wrist and jerked it down over the arm of the chair, forcing her to twist to the right.

'You're hurting me. . . .'

'Good.'

With his free hand he was unbuttoning her jacket.

'Don't do this,' she whispered, terrified.

'The French have raped Mexico. Why shouldn't I rape you?'

Now her jacket was open. She felt his hand go under her linen camisole and cup her breast. She twisted her head around and bit his hand with all her strength. He roared with rage and tore his hand away.

'French bitch!' he howled, hitting her so hard in the face her chair toppled over to the side. She sprawled on the floor, sobbing. She saw him come at her, and she tried to crawl away, but it was useless. 'French bitch!' he kept yelling over and over as he grabbed her clothes and tore them off her like an animal. He ripped at the skirt till it tore in half. Then, throwing the pieces across the room, he reached down with both hands, grabbed her undergarment, and ripped it apart. She tried to cover herself, but it was like spitting at a whirlwind. He had gone crazy. She closed her eyes, gasping for breath. Then she felt him on top of her. One hand held her throat, while the other opened his fly. She felt something hot and rubbery hit the soft skin of her belly.

'French bitch,' he whispered. 'Excuse me: Italian. *This* is for the Mexican people!'

And he rammed into her.

She started screaming in Italian, 'Guido, no! Please don't, Guido! Oh mother of God, you're hurting me! Guido, *no*! *Please!*'

Sanchez thought she was a little crazy, but he didn't stop.

'*Guido, basta! Basta, Guido! Per piacere* – BASTA!'

8

CAN-CAN
1867

28

Zaza d'Antibes stepped out on the stage of the Théâtre du Vaudeville and confronted the apathetic audience. They hadn't come to see her, she knew. They had come to see the star, Léonide Leblanc, whose flagrantly loose morals had earned her the title of Mademoiselle Maximum and about whom some wit had said, 'If you put her on top of Mont Blanc, she would still be accessible.' Zaza didn't care. After tonight, they would come to see *her*. She would be the star. A slight surge of nervousness assaulted her as the orchestra struck up the introduction of her song – even Zaza got stage fright. She looked out over the gaslights at the horseshoe-shaped house with its immense and dirty crystal chandelier. The 'swells' in the boxes, studying her face and breasts with ivory opera glasses. Three tiers above them, 'Paradise', or the peanut gallery, jammed with the raucous Paris *canaille*, mostly men and boys in billed caps, some dangerously perched on the railing, their legs dangling in mid-air. If Paradise didn't like you, you were dead; but she would make it like her. She fought down her nervousness and began singing the ditty her friend, the absinthe-drinking composer Georges Ricard, had written for her. It was called 'Sévérine' (after her real name) and the lyric went:

> Sévérine, Sévérine . . .
> Of love in Paris she is the queen!
> Not so clean, slightly mean.

Still, cold men
And old men
She makes feel seventeen!

Her smooth thighs evoke sighs:
They say paradise lies somewhere in between. . . .
She's a chick who is quick,
She's one hell of a trick –
She's Sévérine!

The tune was catchy, and the audience laughed at the bawdy lyric. When she repeated it in a higher key, belting the song at full voice, she slowly started raising her green skirt, timing it so that when she reached the penultimate line – 'She's one hell of a trick' – her shapely legs were in full view. Paradise loved it. So did the boxes.

The skirt dropped, Zaza winked, and the curtain fell.

The crowd went crazy. Zaza was right: that night, she was a star.

They gave her a dozen curtain calls. Finally, the stage manager signalled the orchestra to start the can-can music, and six can-can girls came on stage, screaming and squealing as they went through their orgiastic paces. Zaza, flushed with triumph, made her way through congratulating stage-hands to her tiny dressing room, which was hardly more than a large closet. There, a muscular man in leotards was waiting for her. He was bare-chested and handsome – which he knew. His name was Gustave Sully-Flandrin, and he was a tightrope walker by profession. He opened his arms. Zaza came to him and he kissed her.

'A triumph!' he exclaimed. 'You're a success. I'm jealous.'

'Good,' said Zaza. 'I want all the world to be jealous of me.'

'They will be. By tomorrow, half the singers in Paris will want to slit your throat.'

'And the other half?'

'They'll be slitting their own throats. Are you coming with me to the Bal Mabille?'

'Are you paying or am I?'

'Slut. Have I ever stuck you with the bill?'

She laughed as she went to her junk-covered dressing table.

'Have you ever *not*? Anyway, I can't go. Benjie's rented the Grand Seize for me.'

'Oh, the Grand Seize. Very impressive!'

'Isn't it?'

She smeared cold cream on her face.

'Benjie – that drunken oaf.' Sully-Flandrin sniffed. 'What do you see in him besides his money?'

'Isn't that enough? And what do I see in you besides your muscles? It's certainly not your subtle wit. Besides, Benjie's rather nice, in his dull way. I like him.'

Sully-Flandrin came up behind her and kissed her neck as his big hands reached around to squeeze her little breasts.

'Benjie doesn't please you in bed like *I* do,' he mumbled in her ear. 'And I bet you don't do for him what you do for me. Or do you?'

She started to answer when she saw something in her mirror. She pushed the acrobat away and turned to stare at the woman standing in the door. She was wrapped in a gorgeous sable, and her face, with its sharp nose, was frosty. Sully-Flandrin also looked at the stranger, who said to Zaza, 'Might I speak to you a moment – alone?'

Zaza said to Sully-Flandrin, 'Scram.'

The acrobat looked annoyed. 'You might introduce me.' He sniffed.

'All right. This is Benjie's wife.'

Sully-Flandrin blinked. 'Oh.' Gulp. 'Well then . . . excuse me. Uh . . . glad to have met you, Madame Benjie.'

And he squeezed past her out the door. When he was gone, Zaza turned back to her mirror and continued removing her make-up.

'Did you see the show?' she asked.

'Yes.'

'How did you like my song?'

'It was lewd. Like you.'

Zaza smiled. 'Benjie likes me lewd. He's really a terribly sensual man – or did you know?'

Elizabeth came up behind her, looking over her shoulder at her mirror reflection. 'How much?' she asked.

'How much what?'

'How much money do you want to leave my husband alone?'

Zaza laughed. 'Really. You don't think you can buy me off?'

'Why not? You're for sale.'

'Perhaps. But you don't have enough money to buy me.'

'Twenty thousand francs?'

Zaza's eyes darted from her own reflection up to the reflected face of the woman behind her.

'Are you serious?'

Elizabeth reached in her purse and pulled out a folded wad of thousand-franc notes, which she tossed on the dressing table. Zaza picked them up and quickly counted.

'I thought you said twenty thousand?' she asked. 'There's only ten thousand here.'

'If, in six months' time, you've lived up to your bargain, I'll give you the rest.'

'You don't trust me?'

'Should I?'

'Should I trust you? Oh well.' She smiled. 'I see you Yankees are as shrewd with your money as I've heard. At least you're a lot shrewder than your husband. All right, Madame Benjie, you've got a deal. I was getting bored with Benjie anyway. But I'll warn you: he's not going to be happy about this. And how do I keep him out of my flat?'

'Change your lock.'

'Well, that's crude, but I suppose it's as good a way as any. What about tonight?'

'What about it?'

'He's rented the Grand Seize at the Café Anglais. He's waiting for me there now.'

'I'll go instead.'

Zaza turned and grinned at her. 'You Americans are funny,' she said. 'You don't really think he's going to love you for doing this? If anything, he'll hate you.'

'What would you suggest doing?'

Zaza shrugged. 'Living with the situation. That's what everyone else does.'

'I'm not everyone else. So we have a deal?'

'We have a deal.'

Elizabeth looked at her a moment.

'If I weren't a lady,' she said, 'I'd spit in your face.'

'If you weren't a lady' – and Zaza smiled – 'your husband wouldn't need a mistress.'

Elizabeth spat in her face. Then she walked out of the room. Zaza didn't move for a moment. Then she turned back to the mirror and wiped the spittle off.

She folded the money and stuffed it in her bosom.

Of all the Paris restaurants, the most famous was the Café Anglais, where the great chef Adolphe Dugléré created the best food in the world. In its cellars were two hundred thousand bottles of wine, and a small railroad ran from table to table to bring in its miniature cars the endless bottles of Château Lafite and Château Margaux to M. Dugléré's happy customers. Rossini, whose passion for food equalled his talent for composing operas, had dubbed Dugléré 'the Mozart of French cooking', and the master chef's worth was reflected by his salary of twenty-five thousand francs, which was a small fortune (as Elizabeth was painfully aware). His customers included the viceroy of Egypt's brother, Mustapha Pasha; the Prince of Orange; Prince Galitzine; Prince Paskevitch; the Russian millionaire M. de Kouqueleff; the socialite Arsène Houssaye; and the *boulevardiers* Gustave Claudin and Aurélien Scholl. He also skimmed the cream of the demi-monde: Dugléré invented Potatoes Anna for Anna Deslions, one of the emperor's mistresses.

The Café Anglais, like all fashionable restaurants, had a series of private rooms which were available for dinner and lovemaking. Each had a different entrance, a different staircase, a different bell, different furniture, and different prices: each was absurdly expensive. Of all the rooms, Number 16 – the Grand Seize – was the most famous, and probably the most notorious, room in Europe. It was nobly proportioned and decorated in lavish Turkish style: there were pierced brass tables, huge red-plush divans, potted palms, draperies on the walls to give a tentlike effect, oil lamps with coloured glass shades, thick carpets, a Pleyel piano, and a huge vase shaped like the Sphinx and filled with orchids. It was a nightmare of a room, but Ben Bramwell loved it despite its garishness. And at eleven-thirty that evening he was sitting on one of the divans discussing the menu with Dugléré as a white-gloved waiter opened a bottle of Dom Pérignon.

'We have some beautiful char,' said the chef. '*Exquisite* char.'

'No, no, I don't like char. Neither does Zaza. She was brilliant tonight – brilliant! Brought the house down. We have to have something special for her. . . .'

'Ortolans, perhaps?'

'Perfect. She loves ortolans, particularly the way you do them. And then an *entrecôte* – Zaza loves steak. She says it gives her something to dig her teeth into. Have you ever seen her teeth? They're the prettiest teeth in Paris . . . Oh my God.'

The chef, startled by the look on Ben's face, turned to see Elizabeth come in the room. Ben rose to his feet as the waiter looked at Dugléré and shrugged with bewilderment.

'Uh . . . Adolphe,' said Ben, almost choking. 'This is my wife. Elizabeth, may I present Monsieur Dugléré, the greatest chef in France.'

Elizabeth smiled and extended her hand, which Dugléré nervously kissed.

'I've had the honour of eating Monsieur Dugléré's food several times,' she said. 'One unforgettable evening with Monsieur Liszt and Herr Wagner . . .'

'Of course,' murmured Dugléré. 'I remember. . . .'

'Though we weren't in the Grand Seize,' she added rather drily. Then she smiled at her husband. 'How thoughtful of you, Ben, to prepare this little surprise for me. I've always wanted to see this room' – she looked around – 'it's so subtly decorated. I don't imagine too many wives ever are brought here. . . .' Again she smiled at the chef, who was trying to look unruffled. 'Has my husband already ordered dinner?'

'We were just discussing the menu. . . .'

'Good. I'm famished. Whatever dear Ben wants will be fine with me. He's developed into such a connoisseur of food *and* wine . . . but then, he's had excellent instruction, hasn't he? Would someone help me with my furs?'

Both Dugléré and the waiter jumped. The waiter took her sables as she removed her long white gloves. She was wearing a magnificent emerald-coloured dress, and her naked shoulders were powdered. Her diamond necklace caught the coloured lights from the glass lampshades and sparkled blue, red, green, and yellow fire. She looked her best, and she knew it. She *had* to look her best.

The men were struck dumb with embarrassment.

'Is something the matter?' she smiled.

'Everything's the matter,' said Ben. 'Adolphe, will you excuse us? I think my wife and I have something private to discuss.'

The chef bowed his way quickly out of the room, signalling the waiter to follow. When the door was closed, Ben turned to his wife.

'What's this all about?' he said quietly.

'It's about our marriage,' she replied. 'It's about your drinking and Zaza. It's about lies and deceit. It's about our children and you and me. I know you're expecting Zaza, but she's not coming.'

'Why?'

'Because I bought her off.'

'You *what* – ?'

'I took every cent I have in my Paris account – ten thousand francs – and gave it to her to stay away from you. I invested a lot to save our marriage, because I had no other way to fight her. I love you, Ben. I know I have faults – many faults, so I'm not saying this is all your fault and that I'm blameless. She says you'll hate me for this, and maybe you will, I don't know. But I had to take the gamble, because' – she hesitated – 'because I love you and I need you. And I think you need me. Do you hate me for doing this?'

He sank into a chair and said nothing for a moment, staring at his patent-leather pumps. Then he looked up.

'Of course I don't hate you,' he said. 'But, you see, I . . . I *want* her. I can't help myself. I know what I'm doing to you and the children is rotten, but it doesn't matter: I have to have her. I have to . . . to touch her. To hold her. It's like a disease, or something. I can't help myself.'

She came to him and held his head against her bosom. 'Then *I'll* help you,' she said. 'I want to help you. That's what wives are for. And you were probably right about me. I guess I have turned into a snob and a social butterfly. . . . Well, that's all over now. I've faced the truth about myself, and you're right: I am a second-rate talent. It's not pleasant to admit, but I'm admitting it. And if you want, we'll go back to Philadelphia.'

He looked up at her. There were tears in his eyes. 'You're so good, Elizabeth,' he whispered. 'I feel so ashamed. . . .'

'There's nothing to be ashamed of, darling. Will you come home with me – now? We want you home so much.'

He stood up, took her in his arms, and kissed her. 'What a mess of a husband I've turned out to be.'

She put her hand on his cheek. 'You're a wonderful husband, which is why I'm fighting for you. I've lost one husband who was precious to me. I don't want to lose two.'

He took her hand and kissed the palm.

The door opened, and Zaza walked in. When she saw them, she laughed.

'How touching,' she said, throwing her coat on a chair. 'Domestic virtue triumphs, and vice is defeated by true love! Except that vice is hungry and wants her dinner. Benjie, how about some bubbly?'

She went to the wine cooler, pulled the bottle from the ice, and filled a glass. Then she turned and raised the glass to Elizabeth.

'To Franco-American relations!' She grinned, then drained half the glass.

'We made a deal,' said Elizabeth. 'I *paid* you. . . .'

Zaza pulled the money out of her bosom and tossed it on the floor.

'I changed my mind,' she said as she came up to Ben. 'I decided I loved my Benjie too much to be bought off by his nasty, mean old wife. I'd miss my Benjie . . . wouldn't my Benjie miss his Zaza? Hm?'

She put her hand inside his coat and rubbed his chest as she held the champagne glass to his mouth. Ben didn't move.

'Get away,' he finally whispered. 'Get away from me.'

She watched his eyes a moment, then went over to one of the divans and flopped down on it.

'Oh well, I see vice is defeated after all. Too bad for vice, but something tells me it will survive. . . . Are you two lovebirds going home to kiss the kiddies good night? That should be a tender scene. And then Benjie takes Lizzie upstairs and tucks her in bed? And then what? A night of mad passion? Does Lizzie do for you what I do, Benjie? Hm? You know, that little trick I introduced you to and you've grown to like so much? Bet she doesn't. Bet she thinks it's dirty.'

She looked over and winked. Ben's face was scarlet. Elizabeth looked confused.

'What does she mean?'

Zaza giggled. 'Oh, you don't want to know. You're too much of a "lai-dy". But Benjie's gone French all the way.'

Elizabeth picked up her furs. 'I'm leaving, darling,' she said. 'Are you coming with me?'

'Go on, Benjie. Go home with little wifey. But if you don't mind, I'm staying for dinner. A girl doesn't get invited to the Grand Seize *that* often – it would be a shame to pass it up. Oh, and Liz, darling: don't forget your ten thousand francs. It's a lot of loot to leave on the floor.'

'Are you coming, Ben?' repeated Elizabeth softly.

He was staring at Zaza. 'I . . . I'll be home in a while,' he said. 'I have to pay Adolphe.'

'Pay him now. I'll wait.'

'No, please. Go home. I'll be there in an hour.'

Now the tears were in Elizabeth's eyes. She knelt to pick up the money. When she straightened, she looked at her husband.

'I'll wait for you,' was all that she said. Then she left the room.

During the interminable drive home, she sat in the *daumont* and cried. She knew she had lost.

Just how much she had lost she was to find out the next morning. At eight o'clock she was wakened by her maid, Henriette, who opened the curtains and said, 'Madame, there's a man downstairs who has come for the master's clothes.'

Elizabeth sat up. 'His clothes?'

'Yes. And there's a note for you.'

She handed her an envelope. Elizabeth opened it and read:

Elizabeth: Zaza has told me what you did to her last night. I can understand your feelings toward her, but spitting in the face of a girl who has had nothing all her life, who has had to struggle against appalling poverty and wretched conditions, exhibits a lack of sensitivity on your part that surprises me. We who have been given much must always display charity to those less fortunate than ourselves.

I love her. I love her with all my heart and soul – I know that now, after what happened last night. When forced to choose between you and her, I could not bring myself to remove from my life the one thing that makes my life worth living. I suppose I am drunk with her, but if I am, I never want to sober up. I am of course aware of the unhappy position this places you and the children in. While I do not shrink from the blame, I will say that your forcing the issue last night was perhaps unwise. After all, before we could at least keep up the appearance of a happy marriage. How many other marriages are managed the same way! But now, since you force me to choose, I choose Zaza.

I am moving into our flat on the rue des Acacias. I will of course continue to pay your rent and the household expenses; but maintaining two establishments forces me to be somewhat less generous with you than I would like. Therefore, I am instructing my lawyers to forward to you the first of each month a draft for one thousand francs as pocket money. While this may not allow you to lead a lavish life, certainly it will allow a comfortable one.

I am sorry it has come to this. Don't think too harshly of me. I have never known such bliss as when I am with her.

Ben

She was stunned. How easily the rug was pulled out from under her life!

'Will there be a reply, madame?' asked Henriette.

'Oh, there's a reply, but it's unprintable. Help the man pack up my husband's things.'

'Then the master is moving out?' asked the maid, unable to conceal her raging curiosity.

'The master is moving out.'

She couldn't eat breakfast. She sat in the morning room off her bedroom staring at her croissant, spooning her *café au lait*. Abandoned. Left high and dry. As simple as that. And Ben! Shaking his finger at her for being 'insensitive' about Zaza's wretched childhood. . . . Clever little minx, she obviously plays on his pity, telling him sad stories of how terrible life has been to her. . . .

Her mood shifted violently from bitterness to despair. And the children! How easily he cut them out of his life! After all his promises to love and protect Ward, after all the love he seemed to have foı Pauline . . . gone. All blown away by a breeze named Zaza. . . .

She thought about money. Ward was well off, thanks to his grandmother's trust fund, but Pauline? Would she inherit nothing from her father? Would Ben throw away his fortune on that slut? Obviously, the reason she had changed her mind about the twenty thousand francs was that she had decided she could eventually milk Ben for more. Which she undoubtedly would, since he was so 'drunk' with her. . . .

She was afraid. Helpless and afraid. Divorce was out of the question. The stigma was too great, even in casual France. The notoriety could blight the children's lives. . . . Even the Princesse Mathilde hadn't been able to get a divorce, and if the emperor's cousin couldn't, how could she? And then there had been the Princesse Sayn-Wittgenstein, who had spent twenty years and a fortune trying to get a divorce so she could marry Liszt, only to fail at the end. No, divorce was out. Then what *could* she do? Whom could she turn to?

Antoine, the butler, came in the room. 'Madame, there is

a Mr Kent to see you. He says he has an appointment.'

She had completely forgotten. The Italian professor, the faith healer, or whatever he was. . . . Her first instinct was to have Antoine send him away. But then she changed her mind. It was a slim chance, but it was a chance, and her hand held no trumps.

'Tell Mr Kent I'll be down in ten minutes.'

'By the way,' said Jefferson Kent a half-hour later as he sat beside her in the *daumont* driving out to Neuilly, 'here's that fifty francs I borrowed from you last week. Bet you thought you'd never see that again, didn't you?'

He pulled a wallet from his coat and took out five ten-franc notes, which he gave her.

'As a matter of fact,' she said, 'you're right.'

'Ah, but you see you don't realize how crafty old Jeff is. I didn't need money that night. I had over a hundred francs on me.'

'Then why in heaven's name did you borrow fifty from me?'

'Because I always borrow money from people when I first meet them. That way, they assume I'm a deadbeat. Then when I pay them back, they're so surprised they begin to think, "Good lord, is it possible this scoundrel has some character after all?" Isn't that what you're thinking now? Be honest.'

She laughed. 'All right, you win. I *am* thinking you may have some character after all. A lot more character,' she added drily, 'than certain other people I can think of.'

'Like who?'

She hesitated, unsure whether to tell him. Then she decided. Why not? Whom else did she have to turn to? And this improbable redhead from Saint Louis was at least *there*. . . .

'My husband. He's moved out.'

'I see. And moved in with Zaza?'

'Yes.'

'It doesn't surprise me.'

'Well, it did me.'

'Did you read the morning papers?'

'No.'

'The critics went crazy about her. She's the toast of the town.'

Elizabeth stared out the window. 'Well,' she sighed, 'she obviously has something I don't.'

She felt his hand on hers. She looked at him, started to say something, then changed her mind.

Why not? She needed to have her hand held. And he really was rather attractive, in his brash way. . . .

Professor Brandini's suburban villa was surrounded by a wrought-iron fence and almost hidden from the road by tall pines on which the snow was melting because of an unseasonably warm sun. The carriage pulled through the gate and drove up the short, winding gravel drive to the front door of the stone house, which looked as if it had seen better days. Jeff helped her out and rang the bell. A moment later, the wrought-iron-and-glass door was opened by a pretty girl in a black dress. When she saw Jeff, she smiled.

'Good morning,' she said, her French having a heavy Italian lilt so that *bonjour* sounded more like *Bon giorno.* 'Father's expecting you.'

'This is Mrs Bramwell,' he said, following Elizabeth into a small hall. 'And this is Marie Brandini.'

'How do you do?'

The girl took their coats, then said, 'Father's in his study. If you'll follow me, please?'

'Are you coming with me?' Elizabeth asked Jeff.

'No, I'll wait here. You talk to him alone.'

Rather uncertainly, she followed Marie down a narrow hall to a door, which she opened.

'It's Madame Bramwell,' she called in. Then she held the door for Elizabeth, who went into the small study. Her first sensation was of the musty smell of books, and the room was filled with them: on tables, chairs, stacked on the floor. On top of one stack was curled a white cat, which looked at her sleepily. The room had an alcove, framed by brown velvet curtains. In the alcove was a desk behind which was seated a man. He was bald, in his fifties, and rather small, with a pleasant face and brown eyes peering through gold-rimmed pince-nez. He stood up and came around the desk, removing his pince-nez. He was wearing a blue velvet smoking jacket with gold frogs, and she noticed that his trousers were unpressed.

'Madame Bramwell? I'm Professor Mario Brandini.'

He kissed her hand, then lifted yet another pile of books from a leather chair in front of the desk, blew some dust from the chair back, and motioned to her to sit down.

'You'll excuse my messy office,' he said. 'My daughter is a good housekeeper, but I won't let her in here. Tidy rooms are like tidy minds: they bore me. Give me a mess any day.'

Elizabeth sat down. 'Is your mind a mess?' she asked.

He laughed as he returned to his tilting desk chair. 'Definitely. One of the messiest minds in Paris. My mind is a junk shop filled with all sorts of information. People come to browse through my mental flea market, and surprisingly often they find something that can be of help to them. That is my profession, madame: helping people. And young Jefferson tells me perhaps I can help you. Your husband drinks?'

'Yes. But it's more than that. He also has left me.'

'Ah. My condolences, but these things happen – how frequently, the newspapers remind us all too often. Do you mind if I ask a few questions of a personal nature? I know it will seem that I am prying, but the more I know, the better the position I will be in to help you.'

'I understand.'

He tilted back in his chair. 'I am told your husband is involved with a singer?'

'Yes. Her name is Zaza d'Antibes.'

'Unfortunate creatures, these theatre people. . . . But isn't she the one who made such a success last night at the Théâtre du Vaudeville?'

'That's the one. This morning I received a note from my husband informing me he's moved in with her.'

He shook his head. 'A tragedy. Marriage is a difficult institution under the best of circumstances, but our swift modern society is subjecting it to many pressures. I need hardly inform you that the modern Parisian is inclined to view marriage as an exercise in hypocrisy – '

'That's the problem,' she interrupted. 'I hate deceit and hypocrisy. If I had closed my eyes to Zaza, my husband probably wouldn't have left me. But what kind of a marriage is that? And then there are the children to consider. I don't wish them brought up in a . . . an immoral atmosphere.'

'Of course. I understand. Still, it is a difficult situation. . . . Might I inquire, madame – and I realize this is indelicate – was the physical side of your marriage entirely satisfactory?'

She stiffened. 'I'm not sure I wish to discuss that, Professor.'

'Madame Bramwell, I fully realize this is a subject of the utmost privacy. But if I am to help you . . .' He spread his hands.

'I will say,' she replied after a moment, 'that my husband's . . . ardour has diminished somewhat lately. Apparently, he is interested in less mature women.'

'Girls?'

She shifted uncomfortably. 'Yes.'

'I see. Might I inquire about your financial situation?'

'My dear Professor, I really fail to see what *that* has to do with anything – !'

'Madame Bramwell, whether we like to admit it or not – and few of us do – two of the most powerful forces in our lives are the urge to reproduce and money, not necessarily in that order. We may pretend we are motivated by higher, more spiritual interests – and I certainly don't deny the role of religion and mysticism in our lives – but for most of us – '

Again she interrupted. 'My husband is quite wealthy,' she said shortly.

'Do you have a source of income other than your husband?'

'Yes. There is a trust fund – a quite considerable one – that was left to my son by my first husband's mother. I am the executrix of the trust and have the usufruct of the income until my son reaches maturity.'

'So we can assume there is no financial problem?'

'That is correct. Though what any of this has to do with my husband's drinking is quite beyond me.'

'Perhaps it has nothing, perhaps it has everything. Only time can tell. Now, madame, if you would be so kind as to tell me the details of your husband's drinking habits. When he began drinking heavily, how much he drinks, et cetera.'

She told him. For the next twenty minutes she told as much as she could remember about Ben and the bottle. He listened attentively and took occasional notes. She found, rather to her surprise, that the telling in itself seemed to ease her hurt. When she was finished, she felt better. Why, she wasn't sure.

The professor cleared his throat. 'What I would like to do is think everything you've told me over – let the facts simmer in my head, so to speak. Would it be possible for you to come back tomorrow at the same time?'

'Well . . . yes, I suppose so.'

The professor stood up. 'Good. I think in the morning I may be able to make some concrete suggestions that may be of value to you.'

'Since you've been so blunt, Professor, may I be also? Is there a fee for your advice?'

'If I can be of assistance to you, then we can discuss fees,' he said, coming around the desk. 'In the meantime, try to get some rest. You've had a shock, and the brain needs rest to recuperate, just as the body does.'

He escorted her to the door and followed her down the hall to the entrance.

Jeff came out of the overfurnished parlour and said, 'How did it go?'

'Well, I'm not sure,' said Elizabeth, looking at the professor.

'We made a beginning,' said the older man. 'Perhaps we made more progress than either of us knows.'

'Good,' said Jeff. 'I'll get our coats.'

The professor showed them to the door. As Elizabeth walked to the waiting carriage, the professor mumbled in Jeff's ear, 'There's a trust fund. A big one.'

'I told you there's money there.'

'Bring her back tomorrow. She's hooked.'

Jeff climbed in the carriage after Elizabeth and closed the door. As the professor watched, the *daumont* rattled down the drive and through the gates.

He went back in the house, a smile on his face.

29

At quarter to eight in the evening, the door to the private chapel of the Marqués de Veracruz opened, and Diego Sanchez strode in. The chapel lights had been lit, and the circular iron chandelier filled the room with pale candle light that cast the *guerrillero*'s face into sharp chiaroscuro.

'El Juero,' he said to Lew, who was still sitting on the floor, his hands tied behind him, 'your friend Madame de Beaupré seems to be a little confused. She keeps calling me Guido. Maybe you can straighten her out.'

Laura was pushed through the door by Tomás Rodrigeuz. When Lew saw her, he winced. Her golden hair was a mess, hanging over her shoulders. Her face was dirty, and there was a cut on her right cheek. She was barefoot and had on an Indian skirt and blouse. Her hands were tied behind her, and she had been crying.

'You son of a bitch,' said Lew softly. 'What have you done to her?'

'Ask her,' said Sanchez. He turned to Tomás. 'Bring in Don Francisco.'

Tomás went out again as Laura sat down on the floor next to Lew.

'The two lovers are reunited.' Sanchez smiled. 'You know,

El Juero, I should thank you. You gave me the idea to kidnap Madame de Beaupré. You even did it for me. I've been trying to decide how best to reward you, and I think I've come up with the answer. Have you changed your mind about writing your bank in New Orleans?'

'I told you I'll write my bank when you free Laura.'

'Then we're nowhere, are we? Still, I owe you something.' Tomás reappeared with Don Francisco, whose hands were also tied. 'It seems,' continued Sanchez, 'that since Don Francisco and I have made an amicable settlement of our differences, my firing squad has no one to fire at in the morning. So I thought you'd enjoy giving them some target practice. That is, if you still refuse to write your bank. Would you enjoy being target at target practice?'

Lew said nothing.

'Madame de Beaupré would enjoy watching, wouldn't she?'

Laura looked at Lew. 'Write the letter,' she said.

'Yes, write it,' echoed Don Francisco. 'He's not bluffing.'

Lew said nothing.

'Well, think it over, El Juero. You have till eight in the morning. If you change your mind, I'm open to negotiation.' Sanchez started toward the door, saying to Billie Hopkins, 'You two get relieved at eight. Tell your relief to guard them well.'

'Right, Captain,' said Billie.

Sanchez and Tomás went out, closing the door behind them. Don Francisco sat on the floor near Laura and Lew.

'This is all my fault,' said Lew.

'I don't know who you are, my friend,' said Don Francisco, 'but don't blame yourself. Sanchez would have come here anyway.'

'But Laura wouldn't be here.' He was looking at her. 'What did he do to you?'

She frowned and shook her head slightly. He knew. He felt sick.

Don Francisco said to the Mexican guard, 'Can't you untie our hands for the night? We can't sleep like this.'

'Then stay awake.'

Don Francisco sighed. He turned to Lew. 'Who are you?' he said.

'My name's Lew Crandall. I'm an American.'

'I don't know how Sanchez got you, but believe me, write the letter he wants. It's not worth your life. I gave him what he wanted from me. I pray God he leaves me and my people alone, but I don't know if I can trust him.' He looked at the guards, then lowered his voice to a whisper. 'We have one hope: I think my daughter escaped.'

'How?'

'I don't know, but Sanchez doesn't know where she is. She was here in the chapel when they attacked. I think she must have gotten out, some way. . . .'

'Some men searched in here a couple of hours ago. They must have been looking for her. . . .'

'No whispering!' barked the guard.

Don Francisco glared at him, then shut up. Lew thought a while. Once, he looked up at the gallery. Then he said to Billie Hopkins, 'The stone floor is cold. Can't we go up in the gallery and lie down on the benches?'

Billie Hopkins thought about this.

'Come on,' said Lew. 'You can watch us up there as easily as down here.'

Billie shrugged. 'All right.'

Lew got to his feet. 'Let's go,' he said to the others.

'I'm too tired,' said Laura. 'I'll stay here.'

'The floor's cold – believe me. I've been sitting on it half the day.'

'I don't care.'

'Don Francisco?'

The older man shook his head. 'What's the difference between stone and wood?'

'Have it your way.'

Lew walked to the rear of the chapel and climbed the stairs. The gallery was shadowy, but the chapel's chandelier bathed it in soft light. He made his way to the organ and sat down on one of the pew benches. Billie Hopkins was watching him. Lew spotted something on the floor, beneath the organ pedals.

The light from the chandelier was gleaming on a small puddle of yellow water.

Despite his rage at himself and at Sanchez for what had happened to Laura, Lew couldn't help but smile. No mouse had ever made a puddle that big.

He stretched out on his back on the bench, feeling rather pleased.

He had found Don Francisco's daughter.

He waited until the guard was changed. Then he waited another hour. He sat up to look downstairs. Laura and Don Francisco were asleep on the floor, but one of the guards was smoking. He lay back down.

He waited another hour. It dragged interminably. Then he sat up and looked again. The guards were silent and not smoking. He couldn't tell if they were asleep, but he decided it was worth the chance.

He lay his back down on the hard bench and stared at the ceiling. His head was less than a foot from the pipe organ.

'Are you Don Francisco's daughter?' he whispered in Spanish.

A long silence. Then: 'Yes.'

'My name is Lew. Are you all right?'

'I'm scared, and I'm hungry.'

'So am I. Can you get out of there without making any noise?'

'I think so. I can see the guards through the pipes.'

'Let's wait a few hours. Let them go to sleep.'

'All right.'

A long silence. Then, from the organ pipes: 'Did you really rob our house?'

'Yes. I'm sorry.'

'My father was terribly angry.'

'I can imagine.'

'Are you going to give Sanchez your money?'

'Not if I can help it. A lot depends on you. You wouldn't have a knife?'

'No.'

Shit, he thought.

'But one of the organ pipes in here is loose.'

He looked at the tall pipes above him. 'One of the big ones?'

'No, a little one. Its edge is sharp.'

'Can you bring it out?'

'Yes.'

'All right. Wait.'

He closed his eyes and smiled. An organ pipe! It was wonderful.

He wondered what Don Francisco's daughter looked like.

It wasn't until after five in the morning that he heard the soft snores of the guards mingling with Don Francisco's rich rumbles.

'Are you awake?' he whispered to the organ.

'Yes.'

'Let's try it.'

He continued to lie on the bench, tense, waiting. He could hear movements inside the organ case beside him. He prayed she wouldn't hit something. Then, after what seemed hours, he heard a soft click. He turned his head and looked behind him. A recessed door in the side of the case was slowly opening. He saw a plump girl in black stoop, then crawl out. In her right hand was a thin organ pipe, about a foot long.

He signalled her to keep down. Then he turned on his side, presenting his tied hands to her. After a moment, he felt something cold in his right hand. He grasped the organ pipe.

'I think I can untie the knots,' he heard her whisper.

It took her several minutes, but then he felt the ropes loosen. He brought his hands around. His arms were stiff, and his wrists sore, but he was free.

Watching the guards, he sat up.

'Wait here,' he whispered.

He crouched below the gallery's solid wood rail and crawled to the stairs, the pipe in his hand. Then he got to his feet. The stairs creaked, but he had no choice. He started down slowly, testing each step before putting his weight on it. Once, a step creaked. He froze and listened.

The snores continued.

When he reached the bottom, he looked at the guards. One was leaning against the wall, his head back, his sombrero on the floor beside him, his rifle on his lap. The other, beside him, had his sombrero on. He had drawn his legs up, his arms around them, and his head was leaning forward.

Lew put the organ pipe behind his back and started down the wall toward the guards.

He was within four feet of the first one when the man's eyes opened. Lew froze. The guard yawned, then pulled a cigarillo out of his shirt pocket. He put it in his mouth and searched for a match. Finding one, he scratched it on the stone floor and lighted the cigarillo. He was exhaling when Lew rushed him and smashed the organ pipe down on his head with all his strength, hitting the skull so hard the pipe bent. The guard grunted. Lew grabbed his rifle by the muzzle end, stepped over him, and swung the butt of the rifle. It crashed down on the second guard's sombrero.

Lew pulled the man's knife from his sheath and slit his throat. Then he went to the first guard, who was sprawled on his side, semi-conscious. Lew plunged the knife into the man's heart.

He stepped back, wiping the knife blade on his pants. Then he went to Laura, who was asleep on the floor.

He knelt behind her and began cutting her ropes with the knife. When she woke up, he went 'Ssh.' He cut through the ropes, freeing her. She sat up, looking at him. Then she looked at the guards and winced. He gave her the knife.

'Free Don Francisco,' he whispered. 'Then lock the chapel door. I'm going to the tower.'

'Why?'

'The Gatling gun.'

He took the other guard's rifle from his dead hands and gave it to her.

'Don't be afraid to use it,' he said.

'I won't.'

She put the rifle on the floor, then came to him. He took her in his arms and kissed her.

'I'll never forgive myself for what happened,' he whispered.

'He was like Guido. Oh God, I was so afraid . . . and I wanted you.'

'A lot of help I was.'

'Oh Lew' – and there were tears in her eyes as she looked at him – 'I'm so sick of ugliness. I'm so tired of cruelty. Do you really love me?'

'I adore you.'

'Then take me away somewhere . . . anywhere . . . some place where people don't hurt each other. Take me away and be gentle to me, as you were the other night. Will you do that?'

'Yes. But I'm going to have to be a little ungentle to get us out of here.'

He kissed her again, then released her and ran across the chapel to the door under the gallery. He saw Ysabel at the foot of the spiral stairs. He pointed at Laura. 'Help her,' he whispered. She nodded. Then he slowly opened the tower door and went inside, carrying the rifle.

It was dark, but the pale pink of dawn was coming through an occasional window, so he could see enough. He started up the stone steps, moving quietly. It was a long climb, and twice he stopped to catch his breath. Finally, near the top of the spiral, he stopped again and listened. Silence. He looked at the rifle he had taken from the guard. It was a Spencer carbine, one that Sanchez had bought from the American arms dealer. Thirty-two calibre, it weighed eight and a quarter pounds and was thirty-nine inches long, but its best feature was that it was a seven-shot repeater, fully loaded. This was an advantage, but not if the men at the top of the tower turned the Gatling gun on him. Death was at the top of the stairs. But so was the best weapon in the world to turn on Sanchez.

He started up. Softly, slowly. At the final turn, he stopped again. He strained to hear above the pounding of his heart. Silence except for the sigh of the dawn breeze flowing through the open belfry. He peered around the curved stone wall. A big bell hanging from a beam. Beneath it, the Gatling gun on its tripod with an open case of ammunition beside it. Three Mexicans, two asleep on the floor, one leaning against the corner wall watching the sun come up through the tower opening, his back to Lew.

He climbed the last three steps and aimed his rifle at the man.

'Turn around with your hands up,' he said in soft Spanish. The man turned, grunted an oath, and reached for his rifle. Lew fired. The man stumbled backward and stepped off the tower, his scream piercing the air until he hit the ground seventy feet below. Now the two others were awake, staring at Lew's rifle.

'Don't sh-shoot,' stammered one of them.

'Get up.'

They obeyed, their hands raised, their faces frightened.

'Push your rifles to me with your feet.'

They obeyed.

'Now give me your cartridge belts. Fast.'

Fumbling, they took them off.

'Put them on the floor.'

They obeyed.

He came over to the Gatling gun.

'How do you work this?'

The first man pulled a long steel clip of bullets from the ammunition case.

'You put this in here,' he said, sticking the clip in a slot on top of the gun, his hands trembling. 'Then you crank.' He pointed at the wood-handled crank on back of the gun.

'All right, go down to the chapel. And send Don Francisco up.'

'Yes, thank you . . . Yes . . .'

They were backing to the stairs. Then they turned and ran, scrambling down the stone stairs. Lew grabbed the bell's clapper rope and swung. The iron ball hit the bell's side, and its thunderous voice bellowed. Again and again he swung, his eardrums almost bursting as the bell sang the hacienda awake. He could see men piling into the courtyard below, rubbing their eyes as they looked up at the noise. He stopped ringing, grabbed the Gatling gun, and turned it. He shot a brief burst, the rat-tat-tat shrilling in the dawn and sending the men diving for cover. But he had aimed above the roof-line.

He went to the edge of the tower, cupped his hands around his mouth, and yelled, 'Sanchez!'

The name echoed.

'Sanchez, come out! This is El Juero! I have the Gatling gun! Come *out*!'

He turned to see Don Francisco at the top of the steps.

'Take those rifles back down. Take position at the chapel window. Don't shoot unless we're attacked, which I hope we won't be. If the Mexicans give you trouble, kill them.'

Don Francisco picked up the rifles. 'My daughter says you're El Juero.'

'That's right.'

'You stole two thousand pounds from me. . . .'

'You're getting ten thousand pounds' worth of protection now, so you've got a bargain.'

'What are you going to do?'

'Get rid of Sanchez – one way or another. He may have us penned up in the chapel, but with the Gatling gun I've got him penned up in the hacienda. So one of us is going to have to give, and it's not going to be me.'

He saw Sanchez walk out of the house. He came to the centre of the courtyard and looked up at the tower.

'Get downstairs!' Lew barked to Don Francisco. The older man hastened to obey, taking the rifles and the cartridge belts with him.

For a moment, Lew and Sanchez stared at each other. Then Sanchez shouted, 'I'll give you five minutes to surrender.'

'And if I don't?'

'We'll attack the chapel. There won't be any survivors. I've got a hundred men.'

'I've got the Gatling gun. Now you listen to *me*, you raping bastard. I'll give you ten minutes to get your men out of the hacienda. If you leave under a white flag, I won't shoot this thing. But if you fire *one* shot, I'll start firing, and you've got no cover, inside or outside the walls. So it's up to you.'

Sanchez looked up for a while. Then he shouted, 'Go to hell.'

He turned and walked back inside the house. Silence. Lew looked to the rear of the compound, where, through an occasional break in the trees, he could see horses. The army was camped there. If Sanchez attacked the chapel tower, he would probably come around the east side, attacking from the north and east. The worst would be if he sent men into the courtyard also, attacking from all sides. Even then, he counted on the immense superiority of the Gatling gun's firepower, even if it meant spraying the fire in a three-hundred-and-sixty-degree arc.

He heard whooping and shots. He saw the horses emerging from the trees, galloping down the east wall of the compound, their riders aiming their rifles at the top of the tower. There were about a dozen of them. Lew grabbed the Gatling gun, swung it around, and started cranking. Rat-tat-tat-tat. Rat-tat-tat-tat. The bullets sprayed down, a scythe harvesting a wheatfield of death. Men pitched off their horses as the horses stumbled to their knees.

Then the gun jammed.

'Shit!' He roared.

He pushed at the crank, but it wouldn't move. He looked below him. One rider was still alive, and he was galloping across the fields in front of the hacienda toward the ridge. The Parrott ten-pounder! The field gun they had used to blast the gates. Of course. That would be what Sanchez would think of, and the rider was going to tell the gun crew to fire at the bell tower . . . SHIT!!!

Sweat was streaming down his face. He grabbed the verticle ammunition clip and shook it. Jammed, and it had jammed the gun. He tore at it with all his strength, but it wouldn't move. He grabbed another clip from the crate and, using it as a hammer, swung at the clip in the gun.

He heard shots. He looked down. They were pouring out of the loggia of the house. They were pouring out of the orchards. A flood of horses, men, and rifles, converging on the chapel, all firing at the top of the tower. A hail of bullets pinged off the big bell, ricocheting crazily. The bell provided a sort of huge helmet, since the gun was directly under it. But if a bullet went *inside* the bell . . .

He grabbed the ammunition clip and yanked. It came loose. Throwing the thing over the side, he inserted a new clip, swung the gun towards the courtyard, and started cranking. Rat-tat-tat-tat. Rat-tat-tat-tat. The Gatling gun spat death. Men and horses died, their carcasses piling up confusion and terror. Lew swung the gun around and began firing outside the compound to the north and east. Ping, ping . . . bullets kept hitting the bell, causing it to hum eerily. . . .

And then, a distant BOOM! He looked around at the ridge. Smoke was rising above the Parrott. Something crashed into the roof of the tower above him, and the whole structure shook. He saw the big bell dancing crazily. He grabbed the gun, then tugged it toward the stair door. Then he started back for the ammunition crate. Too late. With a resounding crash, the bell fell to the floor, landing on its rim, missing the crate literally by inches. It fell on its side, teetered precariously on the edge for a moment, then plunged into the courtyard. He heard screams, then silence.

He pushed the gun back into the centre, stuck in a new clip, and started cranking again, firing outside the hacienda. Without the bell as a protective helmet, he was more exposed; but by now there were only a half dozen men still outside the compound, and he sprayed them into the next world. The ground was a charnel house. He wondered how many he had killed. He turned back to the courtyard just as another distant BOOM resounded from the ridge. For some reason, he remembered Bull Run, so long ago. He had missed a battle then, but he was getting it now in spades. The cannonball crashed into the loggia. Their aim was off.

Now a new surge of horses poured into the courtyard. Rat-tat-tat-tat. Rat-tat-tat-tat. He cranked the wheel until he thought his arm would drop off. Then an explosion rocked the tower, and it wasn't from the Parrott gun. A cloud of smoke rose up from the chapel door.

'Laura!' he yelled. Christ, a bomb! They had made a bomb and thrown it at the door! He cranked, spraying the courtyard. He had to keep them from getting inside, where Laura was. . . . Screams, shots, the neighing of terrified horses. He couldn't see what he was firing at, but he cranked the wheel. Then the clip ran out.

He pulled out the empty one, grabbed a new one, and shoved it back in. He looked below to see whom to fire at.

Silence.

He looked the other way, outside the hacienda. Dead men, dead horses. The slaughter machine had taken its grim, mechanical toll. An incredible scene: at least fifty dead, perhaps more.

And, suddenly, it was all over. Suddenly, they started riding away, fleeing the tower of death. Whooping, occasionally turning to take a final shot at the tower, they headed for the horizon.

The gun was smoking, red-hot. He stood up, sweat pouring from him. He was too exhausted, his brain too jangled from the gun's recoil, to know whether they were giving up.

He looked at the ridge where the field gun stood. He saw four horses riding away from it. If they were abandoning the field gun, then they must be giving up. The field gun was their best bet.

The hacienda was eerily silent. He walked to the edge overlooking the courtyard and looked down. And then he saw why he had won.

Below him, his bearded face staring up at the morning sky, was Diego Sanchez. The bell had landed on him, nearly cutting him in half.

He turned to see Don Francisco leaning against the wall at the top of the stairs. He looked exhausted.

'They've gone,' he said.

'Did they get in the chapel?'

'No, but . . .'

'But what?'

'When they threw the bomb at the door . . . Madame de Beaupré was near. . . .'

He felt as if he were moving in a dream. Afterwards, he remembered running down the twisting stair, the ancient stones whirling like a crazy carrousel. And then he was in the chapel, staring at the still-smoking rubble that had once been the door. Ysabel, her face soot-black, her dress torn, stopped him.

'Don't look,' she said.

He saw the golden hair beneath a smouldering beam. They told him afterwards he went mad. They told him they couldn't stop him as he tried to uncover her corpse. They said he was crying and raging. They told him he kept howling that she was too beautiful to die, that all the beauty in his life had been taken from him, but *she* couldn't be taken from him, too. When he saw her face, half burned off, they said he ran out into the courtyard, found Sanchez's corpse, and began beating its head with a wooden plank. When they finally managed to pull him off, they said he was crying like a child, mumbling over and over two names: Laura and Matoon.

He hardly remembered any of it. All he knew was that the one woman he had loved deeply in his soul was dead.

He felt cursed.

30

Elizabeth Bramwell struck a chord on her piano. Then she removed her hand from the keyboard and reclosed the cover. Every once in a while she would play something, but her heart had gone out of it. If she couldn't be Clara Schumann, why play at all? Oh perhaps later on in life, she might take it up again, but now it hurt too much to play. Every note was a reminder of her failure.

'Madame?'

She turned to see Antoine, her butler, standing in the door of the salon.

'Yes, Antoine?'

'There's someone to see you.'

'Who?'

'It's . . .'

He couldn't bring himself to say it. Instead, he brought her a silver tray with a calling card on it. She read the card and laughed.

'The Marquise de Païva?'

'Yes, madame. She's . . . she's *here*.' He looked ready to faint.

'For heaven's sake, Antoine, the marquise won't bite. Besides, she's an acquaintance of mine.'

'She is?'

'Yes, and I rather like her. So show her in. And be polite to her.'

'Very well, madame. If you say so.'

Looking as if the end of the world had come, he hurried out of the room. A moment later he announced the guest, and La Païva swept in. She was dressed to the nines in the latest style. Crinolines had long since softened, but the skirts were still large, and La Païva's brilliant yellow skirt trimmed with black lace filled the door. Above it she wore a tight-fitting black jacket, and on her head perched a feathered toque. A yellow shawl was around her, and her arms jangled with flexible gold bracelets, called *jarretières*, which had taken the fashion world by storm. On her bosom was a huge cameo surrounded by diamonds. When she removed her yellow gloves, the first thing she did was pull a big diamond ring from her fringed purse and shove it onto her finger.

'There,' she said. 'I feel better. I always feel naked without a diamond or two. How are you, my dear? Your butler looked apoplectic when he saw me. Tell him you can disinfect the house after I leave.'

'Don't be silly. And I'm delighted to see you. Will you take tea?'

'Well, I *could.* But I'd prefer something stronger.'

'A cognac?'

'Delicious. Make it a double. Mind if I sit down? What a charming house! So understated! I sometimes think I overdid the décor of my place, but then everyone *expects* a whore's house to be overdone, and I hate to disappoint my public. It's a breathtaking day! Why are you cooped up in here when you could be riding in the Bois with the rest of the girls? Business is booming today – absolutely booming! I saw that new Spanish girl in town – what's her name? I can't remember . . . anyway, she's a knockout but dumb as a gourd, so everyone's laughing at her. Still, I saw her turn down two stockbrokers in ten minutes because she had a lunch date with a judge, and that's what *I* call good business.'

Elizabeth rang for Antoine.

'Well, you know, I'm *not* one of the girls.'

La Païva laughed. 'No, of course not. I know that. But even decent women ride in the Bois. So: How's life been treating you, my dear? You don't have to tell me about your husband and Zaza. It's been all over town for months. Well, you can't say I didn't warn you.'

'You warned me.' The butler appeared, shooting nervous looks at La Païva, who was lighting a cigarillo. 'Antoine, a double cognac for Madame la Marquise. Get the good cognac in the cellar. And tea for me.'

He bowed out.

'You don't have to get the good stuff for me,' said La Païva breezily. 'I'll drink rotgut.'

'But I want to give you the good stuff.' Elizabeth smiled, sitting opposite her. 'You were so kind to me that night, it's the least I can do. It'll take a little longer for Antoine to bring it up, but it's worth the wait. One good thing about Ben was that he bought the best when it came to wine.'

'Yes, I know.'

La Païva blew out a cloud of smoke and eyed the American.

'You're a fool, you know,' she said quietly.

Elizabeth shrugged. 'What could I do? He left me. I tried to bribe Zaza to stay away from him, but it just made things worse.'

'Oh, I'm not talking about Zaza. I'm talking about this self-styled Professor Brandini. That's why I came: to tell you you're being sucked in by crooks and apparently you're too blind to see it. Americans!' She shook her head.

'What do you mean, "crooks"?' said Elizabeth defiantly. 'Professor Brandini has been wonderful to me! Why, if it hadn't been for him these past two months, I think I would have lost my mind! He's a wonderful, kind, *wise* man who's been a tremendous help to me. . . .'

'Oh, I know. Let's see: you go to his place in Neuilly two or three times a week – correct? And he talks to you, except that *you* actually do most of the talking. You tell him all your troubles, and he listens *so* sympathetically. . . .'

'Well, he does! And it's very soothing.'

'Yes, I know at least a dozen other women in town who find him equally "soothing". And how much do you pay him for this mental massage?'

Elizabeth smiled. 'Nothing. He hasn't asked for a sou. I've tried to pay him, but he won't accept it. So you see, madame, I think you're being a little too cynical. Nor am I so gullible as to be taken in by a confidence man.'

'Perhaps,' La Païva said sceptically. 'I'll admit it surprises me he hasn't asked for money. Usually, after a week or two, the professor becomes amazingly payable.'

'What have you heard about him?'

'Oh, my dear, Professor Brandini is well known . . . *well* known. His *spécialité* is soothing the frazzled nerves of wives whose husbands have strayed – rich wives, I might add – and in Paris that gives him a wide field to operate in, needless to say. He milks them for thousands. And when I heard the other night that *you* had fallen for it, I decided to come here and set you straight.'

'But you see, there's nothing to set straight. I don't know

. . . perhaps he *has* taken money from other women. But he certainly hasn't from me. And he's been extremely helpful. So while I appreciate your concern, there's really nothing to be concerned about. At least in his dealings with me, Professor Brandini has been the soul of integrity.'

La Païva tapped her cigarillo ash in a potted palm.

'Then there's something I'm missing,' she said thoughtfully. 'Call me a cynic, but I can't believe there's not an angle somewhere. . . .'

'An angle?' said a voice at the door. 'An angle to what?'

La Païva turned to see Jefferson Kent in the door. He looked distinguished and handsome – much more distinguished than the last time she had seen him. He was wearing a well-cut three-piece tweed suit *à l'anglais* that was the latest rage for town, and La Païva's practised eye knew it had come from an expensive tailor. He took off his grey top hat, casually tossed it on a chair, came to Elizabeth, and kissed her hand. La Païva didn't miss a thing.

'How are you?' He smiled at Elizabeth, who smiled back.

'Oh, a little tired. You remember Madame la Marquise, of course? She dropped by to warn me about the professor. She thinks he's a sort of confidence man. Isn't that amusing?'

Jefferson straightened. 'I'm sure some people would say he is, but I think we know better, don't we?' He turned to La Païva. 'I'm sure some people would say *I'm* a sort of confidence man, for that matter. And I am. You have to gain people's confidence when you ask them to invest in you.'

La Païva looked him over.

'How right you are. And have you asked Madame Bramwell to invest in you?'

Jefferson laughed as he sprawled in a chair next to his hostess. 'Oh no. I'm too smart for that. Elizabeth's *very* careful with her money – as she should be. Besides,' and he reached over to take her hand, 'our relationship is based on something too pure to soil with money.'

'Oh? How fascinating. And what is this "pure" relationship based on?'

Jefferson looked at her. 'Trust. Friendship. And love.'

Elizabeth looked embarrassed, but she didn't remove her hand from Jeff's.

'Aha. So you two are in love?' asked the marquise.

'Very deeply.'

'You see, Jefferson has been so kind,' said Elizabeth, rather defensively. 'After my husband left me, I was so . . . so at a loss. . . .'

'And Jefferson was a compass, so to speak? Jefferson and Professor Brandini?'

'Yes, that's it.' She smiled warmly at the young American. 'A compass. And a dear, true friend.'

La Païva laughed as she stubbed out her cigarillo and stood up.

'You Americans are full of surprises,' she said, pulling off her diamond ring and returning it to her purse. 'Well, I can see my advice isn't needed here. You have someone much more worldly-wise than I to guide you through life's treacherous shoals, my dear. By the way, Jefferson, is what I hear true? That you're developing a de luxe seaside hotel at Deauville?'

'That's right. It's going to be the fanciest resort in Europe. A casino, bathing facilities, the best food outside Paris . . . oh, it's going to be something!'

'It really is terribly exciting,' said Elizabeth. 'Jeff's been working on it for months, and he's almost completed the financing. You should see the architectural studies! It's so beautiful . . . all white, with lovely wide verandas and marvellous towers. . . . And then he's going to build private villas near the hotel to sell to individuals. . . .'

'Only the best people,' Jeff added. 'The *very* best.'

'Dear me,' said La Païva, drawing on her gloves. 'I'm afraid that lets *me* out. You'd hardly want an old tart like me around, would you? Scaring off the duchesses – if not the dukes.' She winked. 'Well, I shan't waste any more of your time, my dear. I'm sure you have *so* much to discuss with Jefferson.'

'But your cognac – '

'Some other time, thank you. No need to show me out, I know the way.'

Jefferson was on his feet. 'But I insist.'

He took her to the front door and opened it, not failing to check out visually the elegant landau waiting at the kerb. La Païva said in a soft voice, 'Congratulations, my friend. That's a nice little racket you've got going for you.'

Jeff's smile didn't fade.

'There's no "racket". You're really too suspicious, you know.'

'Oh, come now. Don't try to fool an old professional like me. So you haven't asked her to invest in your hotel scheme yet?'

'That's right. Nor will I.'

'Oh yes you will, Jefferson. When the time is ripe – which looks as if it should be soon. You know, you and the professor are a very smooth team. He massages the mind, and you massage the body – so to speak. I suppose you give him a cut?'

'Nope. We're just friends.'

'Charming. But does she have enough money to make all this worth while?'

'Of course not. I tell you, Elizabeth and I are in love.'

She laughed. 'That's a good one. Well, I wish her luck. With you, she'll need it.'

She started out the door, then stopped and looked back at him.

'Of course,' she said, 'how stupid of me. The first husband – the one killed in the American war. I've heard he was very rich, and *she* must have gotten it!'

'The son got it.' Jefferson smiled. 'And it's all tied up in a trust. *Au revoir*, madame.'

And the door clicked shut.

Don Francisco finished inspecting the repair work being done on the gates of the north wall and the top of the bell tower. Then he walked to the east wing of the hacienda, beyond which, a month before, Diego Sanchez's men had charged out of the orchards, firing at the Gatling gun. The man who fired back at them had developed what Dr Drake, Don Francisco's English doctor, had called brain fever for want of a better term. Then the brain fever had developed into body fever, which became pneumonia with a touch of malaria. El Juero had been seriously ill, and Don Francisco wanted to check on the condition of the man who had saved him his fortune. He knocked at one of the doors in the east wing. His daughter answered, coming out into the loggia and closing the door behind her. 'Father, you're back!' And she kissed him. She lowered her voice. 'How did it go in Mexico City?'

'It's all arranged. It cost me plenty, but he's worth it. How is he?'

Ysabel was wearing a new white dress that her maid had sewn for her. The dress was a full size smaller. Ysabel was dieting.

'Well, his fever's gone,' she said. 'Dr Drake says the pneumonia is over, and the malaria has died down. But . . .' She touched the side of her head and shrugged.

'Is he still raving?'

'Oh no. He hasn't had any delirium for a week. But he just doesn't talk. I mean, he *talks*, but . . .'

'I know. I want to see him. You wait out here.'

She nodded as her father opened the door to the guest room and went inside. It was a pleasant room with white walls and handsome Mexican furniture. A heavy Mexican chest stood at the foot of the bed, and the two barred windows, through which sunshine poured, were decorated with bright yellow curtains.

'How are you?' said Don Francisco, pulling a chair over beside the bed. Lew was sitting up. His tan had long since faded and he had lost weight, but physically he seemed all right. It was, as Ysabel had said, the mind that was sick. His eyes were listless.

'Better,' he said. 'Ysabel says you've been in Mexico City?'

'Yes, and I have good news for El Juero. Through the judicious application of cash payments – in other words, bribes, and in American dollars, I might add – I have arranged for El Juero's name to be expunged from the police records. Your criminal career, my friend, is at an end.'

Lew nodded slightly. 'Thanks.'

Don Francisco grinned. 'You rascal, how many thieves get let off by the very man they robbed? I'm a veritable saint! And look at you: you don't even care.'

'No, I care. You've been very kind to me, Don Francisco. And so has Ysabel.'

'Have you thought about the future? The doctor says you're well now. . . .'

Lew didn't answer.

'My friend,' said Don Francisco softly, 'I understand how you feel. But she's dead, and you have much to live for.'

'What?'

'Matoon, if nothing else.'

Lew shrugged. Don Francisco stood up and went to one of the windows. Putting his hands behind his back, he stared out at the orange trees. Then he said, 'Do you have any interest in railroads?'

'Not particularly.'

'Well, I do. I've been working for several years putting together the financing for a railroad connecting Mexico City with Guadalupe, then going on up to Laredo on the Texas border. I have the money now, and I think when things settle down politically – perhaps in six months or so – we can start construction. You realize the enormous potential of such a railroad? It would mean access to the markets of the United States for Mexican cotton, fruit, minerals . . . it would mean *dollars*, which Mexico desperately needs. Of course, there will be all sorts of difficulties involved in the construction, not the least of which will be the *bandidos*. But I need hardly tell you about *bandidos*, need I?' He chuckled. 'Since you were one yourself.'

'I was a thief. There's a difference.'

'Ah yes, of course. Anyway, once the railroad is built, I want to try to connect it to an American line that will continue from Laredo to San Antonio, then perhaps to Saint Louis. I'm negotiating with representatives of an American company now, and I have offered an extremely good price for a position in the ownership. You can of course see the advantage of the Mexican line and the American line being – shall I say, related?'

Lew poured himself a glass of water from the earthen pitcher Ysabel had placed on his bed table. 'I suppose.'

'Shipping rates could be adjusted to the benefit of both sides of the border. Naturally, there will be difficulties here, too. In time, I would need a representative in Washington to deal with the Congress. There will be customs problems and so forth. . . .'

He turned to look at the young American. He was sitting in the bed, staring at the glass of water on his hand. Then Don Francisco returned his gaze to the orange trees outside the window.

'At any rate, I need a man. A very unusually qualified man, I might add, to supervise the entire operation. First, to supervise the construction of the Mexican line. Then, later, to deal with the Americans. I need a man with courage and inventiveness. I need a man with balls. I need a man who can deal with the *bandidos* as you dealt with Diego Sanchez – not that I'm thinking of you, mind you! I know you're not interested. . . . I need a man who can speak English and Spanish. I need a man who knows Americans as well as he knows Mexicans. Well, I could go on, but, as you can see, such a man is not going to be easy to find. Certainly, there are few qualified Mexicans. The Mexicans with any resourcefulness have all turned into *bandidos* or are trying to become generals. They don't see the potential in business – nor do they see the need for it, unfortunately. So I will have to pay this man an enormous salary. A fantastic salary! It makes me shudder to think of what I'll have to pay.'

He shot a look at Lew, who was still fiddling with the glass. Silence.

'I would have to pay,' Don Francisco went on, 'oh . . . probably twenty-five thousand American dollars a year.'

He looked at Lew. Silence.

'Maybe even *thirty*-five thousand.'

Silence. Lew set the glass back on the table. Then he looked at Don Francisco. 'Make it fifty thousand,' he said, 'and ten per cent of the stock, and you've got a deal.'

'You're a *thief*!' exploded Don Francisco.

For the first time in a month, Lew smiled. 'I know. I've

already robbed you, remember? This time, it'll be legal.'

Don Francisco, red in the face, bit his lip. Then he laughed and held out his hand. Lew shook it, and they both laughed.

The coffin was lowered into the grave, and the priest sprinkled it with holy water as he repeated the prayers for the dead. The party of black-clad mourners watched. They were mostly women, well-dressed women, their faces veiled in black. Then it was over. The mourners started back to their carriages. It was a beautiful May day, and the tombs at the cemetery of Père Lachaise had been washed comparatively clean by a rain the night before.

'He was a good man,' said Jefferson Kent, who looked handsome in his well-cut black suit and top hat. 'He'll be missed.'

'By me, particularly,' said Elizabeth, looking at the tomb of Frédéric Chopin, which they were passing. 'He was a true friend.'

'Cancer. And no one even knew he had it until the end. Such bravery.'

'Oh Jeff, I don't want to talk about it.'

'I'm sorry, darling.'

They reached Elizabeth's *daumont*. Gustave, her husky coachman, an ex-cobbler from the Paris slum of Belleville, which was not far from the cemetery, held the door, touching the brim of his top hat.

'Home, Gustave,' she said, climbing in. Jeff followed her. Gustave closed the door, and Jeff took Elizabeth's black-gloved hand. Gustave climbed to the driver's seat, untied the reins, shook them, and the carriage jerked into motion.

Elizabeth looked out the window at the passing tombs. She was trying not to cry, but the unexpected death of Professor Brandini had shaken her more than she would have thought. She turned to Jeff and forced a smile.

'Professor Brandini dead,' she said. 'Ben taken off with Zaza. Now all I have is you.'

He lifted her veil and kissed her on the mouth.

'We have each other,' he said.

'Oh Jeff, I'm feeling terribly depressed. I don't know why, but I am. I suppose it's the funeral. . . .'

'Why don't we go to my place?'

She thought about this. Then she smiled slightly and nodded her head.

Jeff opened the small door in the roof with his cane. 'Gustave,' he called up, 'take us to my place instead.'

Gustave smiled to himself. As the carriage rolled out of the cemetery, he headed for the Boulevard du Montparnasse.

She felt wonderful after love, as she always did with Jeff.

He had a handsome, muscled body with milky skin. In many ways it reminded her of Lew's body, except the hair on the legs and chest and arms was red-gold instead of gold. She watched him from the bed as he walked across his one-room flat with its skylight to turn on the kettle on the gas ring.

'Tea?' he said, lighting a cigarette.

'That would be nice.'

At first, she had been shocked, as well as intrigued, by the totally unselfconscious way he walked around his flat completely naked. But she had quickly grown to like it. She liked being naked, too.

'You know,' she said, 'on my first wedding night – more years ago than I like to remember – I was so frightened when I saw my husband, I actually got sick.'

'Really?' He waved out the match and put it in the butt-piled ash tray. Jeff Kent was a dapper dresser in public, but his flat was a mess.

'Yes. It seems so funny now. Now, I enjoy watching you. I suppose I've become a total sensualist. Isn't that awful?'

'Oh, I don't know. What's wrong with bodies? God made 'em. I enjoy watching you.'

'You do?' She purred.

'Of course.'

He flopped down in the sagging armchair and put his feet up on the torn ottoman. He exhaled, watching the smoke drift up through the tilted skylight. Then he looked at her.

'Elizabeth, you may have to do without me for a while.'

She sat up in the bed. 'Why? What's wrong?'

'Oh, it's business. And you know our rule: never talk about money.'

'But . . . where are you going?'

'London first. And if I don't have any luck there, I may have to go to New York.'

'New York? That could be several months. . . .'

'It may be half a year. I have to raise a lot of money.'

'How much?'

'You know our rule.'

'Oh, bother the rule! What's wrong? Is it the hotel?'

'Yes, it's the hotel.'

'Has one of your investors – ?'

'Lemaître. He's pulled out.'

'But why?'

'Oh, he's worried about Bismarck. He thinks Prussia is going to pick a fight with France soon, and he says Prussia will win and then France is going to go in the bucket, so he's putting his cash in Swiss banks rather than French beach resorts. I told him he was a fool, but he won't budge. So if I can't raise the equivalent of his investment, the whole thing's kaput because the other investors will pull out. They're already crying. And, of course, Bismarck *isn't* making it easier to raise money. . . . There's the kettle. . . .'

He got up and went to the whistling kettle. Turning off the gas, he poured the boiling water in the teapot. She watched his strong legs, his muscular buttocks . . .

'How much did Lemaître invest?'

'Three hundred thousand francs.'

'Oh my God! Sixty thousand dollars? I couldn't afford that.'

He turned to look across the room at the rumpled bed. 'Now listen: I've told you I never will ask you for money, and I don't want you to offer it. You know what people say about men like me – look what La Païva said! They all think I'm after your money, which is why I have to be so goddam particular about *not* touching your money. The moment I do, you're going to become suspicious of me. And no hotel is worth ruining what we have between us. Sugar?'

'Yes, please. And Jeff, you're too sensitive about money! If two people love each other the way we do, they have to *share*. Love is a two-way thing. I can't just take from you all the time . . . take your love, your friendship, your companionship – all of which are precious to me – and not give something back in return!'

'You *do* give back.'

'You know what I mean. . . . If you were my husband, I'd give you the money, wouldn't I? But since you can't be my husband. . . .'

'No!' He almost, but not quite, shouted. 'Now dammit, Elizabeth, shut up! I should never have said anything in the first place! End of discussion. Period.'

She was silent as he carried the two cups of tea to the bed. He gave her one, then kissed her nose.

'Don't you see,' he whispered, leaning over her, his free hand on the wall, 'you're just making it harder for me? Don't you think I *want* to ask? I'm human. It would be a lot easier for me to ask you than to ask a bunch of steel-plated London bankers who are going to say, "But you have no *assets*, Mr Kent." My God, assets! What do they think *brains* are? Imagination? Energy? The ability to get a project this big off the ground? But oh no: all they want to see is how much money I have in the bank, which is zero. So don't tempt me, Elizabeth. I'm going through hell as it is.'

He climbed into the bed next to her, leaned against pillowslips that hadn't been changed in a month, and stirred his tea.

'Well,' she said, 'I think you're wrong, but . . . Besides, I don't have sixty thousand dollars anyway, so the whole thing's academic. . . .'

'There's Ward's trust fund,' he said quietly.

She looked at him. 'But I can't touch that. I'm just the executrix.'

'You wouldn't touch it. But you could use it as collateral for a loan.'

She took her head. 'No, the bank doesn't allow that.'

'The *Philadelphia* bank doesn't. But French banking laws are different. If you transferred it here to Paris, any bank would make a loan. After all, the trust is a million dollars, which is a lot of money.'

He sipped his tea.

'I suppose so,' she said slowly. 'But the money isn't really mine. . . .'

'Whose is it?'

'Well, it's Ward's. It's Crandall money.'

'Isn't Ward you?' He put the cup on the floor and turned on his side, facing her, putting his red-haired hand on her breast. 'Darling, *you* brought this up, not me. And God knows I wouldn't pursue it if I didn't know the hotel is a solid-gold investment that's going to make millions for everybody involved. So why let the opportunity go out o the family? And let's be honest: I'm your family now. Ben sure as hell isn't. Why let the opportunity to double your money – triple it, even – go to some pie-faced banker who's too rich already? Why not let Ward benefit? And you? And me?'

She was suddenly cool. 'I'll have to think about it.'

He removed his hand from her breast and sank back into the pillows.

'See?' he sighed. 'I did it. Goddam, I did the *one* thing I swore I'd never do! Shit!'

He got out of the bed and went to the two dirty glass doors that opened onto the narrow rooftop terrace. Flinging them open, he went out and leaned on the chest-high cut in the mansard roof to stare out over the Boulevard du Montparnasse. After a moment, she got out of bed, threw his cigarette-burned Japanese robe around her shoulders, and went out to join him.

'Darling,' she said, 'you're naked. . . .'

'Who cares?'

'The neighbours . . .'

'They've seen it all before. I knew it would happen. I *knew* it! You're suspicious.'

She put her hand on his arm.

'No I'm not, darling. Really. It's just that . . . well, it's *not* my money.'

He turned to her and smiled. 'I know. It was a crazy idea

anyway. Listen: let's get dressed and go to Magny's for lunch. On *me*.'

'But Magny's is so expensive. . . .'

'Money, my darling Elizabeth, is what I do *not* want to talk about.'

He took her chin and kissed her. 'Then afterward you can come back here and help me pack. You know I don't know where anything is in this pigsty.'

He went back through the doors to look for his underwear. She watched sadly.

'When will you be leaving?' she called in.

'The sooner the better. Tomorrow, if I can book passage.'

She stood by herself on the tiny terrace of the messy one-room flat she had come to love and watched the clever, good-looking young man she had come to love pull his pants on.

'Jeff?' she said.

'What?'

'Would you help me write the letter to the bank?'

He was buttoning his fly. Now he stopped to turn and look at her.

9

THE DEAD ARISE 1870

31

One September morning in 1870, Rosemary Matoon, who was opening the mail at her breakfast table, looked up at her husband and asked, 'Who's Peter Fraser?'

Senator Ralph Matoon put down the one piece of dry toast his doctor allowed him for breakfast.

'Why do you ask?'

Rosemary held up an engraved invitation.

'We've been invited to a ball at his plantation in Virginia. It sounds terribly grand.'

'He told me he was inviting us. Let me see.'

'So you know him?' She handed him the invitation.

'Sure. Met him last month when we elected him to the board of the Saint Louis–Denver.'

They were in the conservatory of their Washington mansion, surrounded by a forest of plants and palms that were Rosemary's passion. Since they had built their gaudy house seven years previously, Rosemary had become an accomplished gardener. So accomplished, in fact, that at the prompting of her friends, the former Confederate spy had written a small book entitled *The Green Thumb; or, Mrs Matoon's Handbook on the Care and Feeding of Houseplants, With Useful Hints as to their Propagation*. She had had it printed privately, and it enjoyed a surprising vogue among the housewives of the capital.

Her husband examined the invitation, which read:

Mr. and Mrs. Peter T. Fraser
Request the Honor of the Presence of
Senator and Mrs. Ralph A. Matoon
at a Ball
Celebrating the Opening of West Wind
Alexandria, Virginia
Saturday, the 22nd of September, 1870 RSVP
Eight O'Clock Decorations

The senator handed back the invitation.

'I'll tell you who he is, Rosie. He's the president of the Mexico–Rio Grande Railroad, president of the Laredo–San Antonio Railroad, president of the Sonora Mining Company, owner of the biggest newspaper in Mexico City . . . let's see, what else? He's bought a pile of stock in our railroad, the Saint Louis–Denver, and we're talking about a merger . . . that's one reason we elected him to the board. . . .'

Rosemary refilled her coffee cup from a swirled silver coffeepot.

'I take it he's rich?'

'Rich?' Her husband laughed. 'He's worth millions. Millions! He's Croesus! And last year, he bought up an old plantation on the Potomac outside Alexandria – place had been burned down by slaves during the war – and poured a fortune into fixing it up. Sent his wife over to Europe to buy up chandeliers and geegaws – hell, it's supposed to be a real showplace. Well, well, so we're going to West Wind. Sure like to see it. Strange fellow.'

'What do you mean?'

'Well, he don't say too much . . . keeps to himself. But those eyes! My God, they go right through you! Sort of spooky.'

'What's he look like?'

'Oh, nice-looking man. About thirty, I'd say. Brown hair and beard. . . . He's an American, but he's got Mexican citizenship now. He should! Practically owns the whole damn country. He and his father-in-law own most of the mineral rights to Sonora. I've seen some private reports made by the Bureau of Mines back in forty-eight during the Mexican War, and Sonora's supposed to be sitting on another Sutter's Mill. Wouldn't mind getting a piece of *that.*'

'Who's his father-in-law?'

Matoon leaned on the table, his small eyes glittering. 'The Markwiss de Veracrooze, who's the richest man in Mexico. Oh, this Fraser's smart, I tell you. Married the richest heiress in Mexico! The story is, he saved the mar-kwiss . . .'

'"Mar-qués," dear. Mar-kee in French, mar-kays in Spanish.'

'Well, hell, I'm speaking English. Anyway, he saved the mar*kays* and his daughter from some bandit raid on their hacienda – that was three or four years ago. You know those damn Mexiques, always riding around shooting each other into Swiss cheese . . . worse than the goddam Texans. Anyway, Fraser saved the family's skin – I heard he got a Gatling gun up in a tower and mowed 'em down. By God, that must have been something to see! And the markays was so grateful, he offered him a job supervising the building of the Mexico–Rio Grande. And Fraser did such a slam-bang job of that, chasing *bandidos* all over Mexico and what have you, that pretty soon the old boy said "Son, take my daughter too." So Fraser – who's supposed to be slick with the ladies – ups and marries the old boy's daughter! Gets the whole shebang! Ain't that something? Can I have some more toast?'

'No. You know you have to lose weight.'

'Doctors!' snorted the senator. 'What do they know? If they was smart, they'd be rich.'

'Well, you're rich and you're too fat, so forget the toast. So the wife's Mexican, but Fraser's American.'

'Right. Got a passel of kids, too. And the Marqués gave his daughter for her wedding present a thirty-carat diamond called the Star of Mexico. Thirty carats! Whew! I'd like to see that! Maybe she'll wear it at the party.'

'Isn't West Wind a strange name for a house?'

'Well, there's a story behind that, too. They say he named the place West Wind because no one knows where the west wind comes from – except the west. And all anyone knows about Pete Fraser is that he comes from the west. Originally, I mean.'

'You mean he won't tell anyone, or no one knows?'

'Both. He won't tell, and no one knows. A man of mystery except for the bank account. No mystery there! Richer than God. There ain't nothing better than rich, is there, Rosie? Unless it's richer, eh? Well, well: you'll wear some of your own diamonds. We'll show the Frasers the Matoons have been doing all right for themselves. I told Fraser about our jewel collection. Said he'd like to see it –'

'Miss Rosemary!' A voice from the door interrupted. The senator turned to see his butler, Henry.

'What's wrong?'

'Miss Rosemary, you better come quick! Master Charles just fell again. . . .'

'Oh God . . .'

Rosemary threw down her napkin and got up from the table, following her butler out of the conservatory. 'Is he hurt?'

'Got a bad bump on his forehead. Selina's fixing him. . . .'

'But wasn't she *watching*?'

She was hurrying into the entrance hall. Now she started up the great staircase. Henry puffing behind her.

'Yes ma'am, but she can't watch him twenty-four hours a day!'

'That's what she's paid for. . . .'

'Now Miss Rosemary, ma'am, that's not fair! You know Selina loves that boy. . . .'

'I know. I'm sorry.'

She reached the top of the stairs and ran down the wide upstairs hall till she reached her son's playroom. She opened the door to see Selina Jones, Henry's wife, standing beside a chair applying hot towels to the forehead of Charles Fletcher Matoon, Rosemary's six-year-old son. Miss Richardson, the governess, was kneeling on the other side of the chair, holding the boy's hand. When she saw her employer, she stood up.

'I think he's all right, Mrs Matoon. . . .'

'What happened?' Rosemary was hurrying across the room.

'There were some toys on the floor, and he tripped. . . .'

'Why didn't you pick them up?' snapped Rosemary. She put her arms around her son and kissed the top of his head. 'Are you all right, darling?' she said. 'Does it hurt?'

Charles Matoon looked up in the direction of his mother's voice.

'I'm all right, mamma,' he said.

Charles Matoon had never seen his mother or his father. Charles Matoon had been born blind.

The night of 22 September 1870 was a memorable one in the annals of Washington party-giving. God had provided an almost perfect evening for the Frasers: it was crisply cool, and the sunset was a brilliant pink. But the guests were more interested in West Wind than the western sky. And as the elegant carriages pulled through the wrought-iron gates and started down the long gravel drive lined with magnificent oaks, some of the guests couldn't resist sticking their heads out the carriage windows to gape at the columned white mansion looming in the distance. 'Goddam,' muttered Ralph Matoon, 'that's some big house! Looks even bigger than ours.' He sat back in his seat and sniffed with envy. Rosemary, whose mind was on other things, said distractedly, 'Don't worry, dear. Now people can talk about somebody else being showy.'

The senator looked at his wife. She was wearing a turquoise and diamond necklace he had given her for her fortieth birthday three months previously. Her red hair was braided in a circle on top of her head, and a small diamond tiara perched in its braided nest like a blazing bird. She had on a white silk gown trimmed with mink, and the fur swooped around her shoulders, framing her magnificent breasts. A sable cape was folded in her lap. 'Well,' he said, 'nobody will show *you* up, Rosie. You look a picture.'

'Thanks, Ralph.'

The carriage had stopped, waiting for the ones in front to discharge their passengers.

'What's wrong?' he said. 'You look off your feed.'

'Oh, it's that Miss Richardson. I think I'm going to have to fire her.'

'Not another! My God, the governesses come and go. . . . What's wrong with her?'

She sighed. 'Charles fell again this afternoon. That's twice in less than three weeks. She's just not watching him!'

'Rosie, the boy is blind! He's going to be falling over things the rest of his life! You can't blame the governesses. . . .'

'Then who *do* I blame?'

She had turned on him, angry. He knew enough not to push.

'Fire her,' he sighed. 'Except you brood too much about him. Charlie's going to be all right.'

'When? He'll never see – *never*! He'll never see a tree, or the sky, or a flower. . . .'

Tears came to her eyes. He took her hand and patted it.

'Come on, Rosie. There's no use in crying. You've cried before. . . .'

'And I'll cry again!' She sniffed, pulling her hand away to search for a handkerchief in her purse. 'Every time I look at him, it just kills me. And it's our fault.'

The senator rolled his eyes. 'Good God, you're not going to start *that* one again –!'

'Well it *is*!' she whispered angrily. 'Do you think it just happened that our child was born blind? Don't you think God had something to do with it? We're *paying*, Ralph. But not as much as Charles is paying.'

'My God,' he mumbled in a disgusted tone.

'Well, it's true. Nothing is gotten in this life without a price. And the price for our money is Charles's sight.'

'Ridiculous.'

'You say so, but I'm right.'

'Good God, get you women near a Bible, and the whole world turns into a big scale! I shortchanged a shoe salesman last week, so God gives me a cold this week to pay me back. . . .'

She looked at her fat husband. 'We did a lot more than shortchange a shoe salesman,' she said softly.

He shook his head and looked out the window. 'Wish this

damn line would *move*,' he grumbled. 'I'm dying to see this place. . . .'

'You don't care, do you?'

He turned on his wife. 'Care? Of course I care! Charlie's my son! And it's rotten that he's blind, but he'll have the best of everything all his life, so it could be worse for him.'

'I'd rather be poor with sight than blind and rich.'

'Oh sure. Well, Rosie, with all your Bible-thumpin', I don't see you trading in your sables for a hair shirt.'

She looked morosely out the window. It was true. For all the guilt she had felt since the birth of her son, she couldn't give anything up. . . .

'We're moving at last! I hear half the diplomatic corps's here tonight, plus a good hunk of Congress. . . . Look at them columns! My God, Pete Fraser has *some* place!'

The Marquis de Noailles, the French ambassador, was there with the Marquise. The Secretary of State, Mr Hamilton Fish, was there with Mrs Fish. Kate Chase Sprague, still the queen of Washington society, was there, though her husband, the senator, had stayed home 'with a cold'. Mrs 'Puss' Belknap came with her husband, the Secretary of War. Senator Herbert Rowlandson, Republican, of New York and his wife. Representative Charles Seymore, Republican, of Pennsylvania and his wife. Senator Penrose Granby, Republican, of Ohio and his wife. Senator Sylvester Carter, Republican, of Massachusetts and his wife. Representative Harrison Spofford, Republican, of Wisconsin and his wife. Over one hundred people were passing up onto the columned veranda, through the door framed by a graceful fan window and sidelights, into the enormous white marble entrance hall with its spectacular chandelier and sweeping curved staircase lined with stately portraits of the Marqués de Veracruz's ancestors. Flowers were everywhere, liveried servants . . . the wide-skirted women in their jewels and the tail-coated men might have been dressed in the height of Grant Era style, but the setting was, with its gleaming antiques, pure eighteenth century. Money had blotted out the ugly Reconstruction Era and reconstructed a more charming and graceful age.

Rosemary Matoon, for all her moroseness, was dazzled. 'It *does* take your breath away,' she said to her husband as they waited to go through the receiving line. She looked above her at the fifty-light crystal chandelier that hung from the ceiling two storeys above and around which the wide stair curled like a lemon peel. 'The chandelier alone must have cost a fortune.'

'Sir Edward and Lady Thornton!' announced the major domo, and the English minister and his wife moved past the hostess and host.

'Señor and Señora Potesdad!'

The Spanish minister and his wife passed by.

'Senator Carl Schurz of Missouri and Mrs Schurz . . . Señor and Señora Flores . . . Senator Ralph Matoon of Pennsylvania and Mrs Matoon . . .'

Rosemary saw an attractive young woman in a taupe taffeta gown who had starved herself down to a gracefully plump hundred and thirty pounds and put herself in the hands of a clever French maid named Ghislaine. Ghislaine had plucked Ysabel's thick brows to thin arches, dressed her black hair in a flatteringly simple coiffure, and been smart enough to let her beautiful skin alone. The result was that Ysabel had blossomed into, if not a beauty, definitely a woman men would look at twice. She carried herself well: Rosemary was impressed. She was also impressed, if not dazzled, by the diamond and ruby tiara with matching eardrops, necklace, and bracelet. But what made her eyes bulge was the enormous blue-white diamond on Ysabel's left hand. Rosemary supposed this was the thirty-carat spectacular named the Star of Mexico.

'Welcome to West Wind, Mrs Matoon,' Ysabel said in lightly accented English.

'You were so kind to invite us,' replied Rosemary, wondering why the young woman was looking at her so strangely. 'And your house is beautiful. I understand you decorated it yourself?'

'Oh no. The entire thing was done by a very talented

Englishman – Mr Tewesbury, who worked with Sir Joseph Paxton. He did everything, inside and out. The credit goes to him.'

'Then Mr Tewesbury is a very gifted man.'

And she moved on to her host.

'We're honoured to welcome you to West Wind.' Peter Fraser smiled, and then this man with his trimmed brown beard and thick brown hair raised her hand to his lips.

'I was just complimenting your wife on your house, Mr Fraser. It's breathtaking.'

'Thank you.'

Then his blue eyes were staring into hers and she felt oddly cold. She remembered her husband's remark that Peter Fraser's eyes went right through a person. True, but there was something else in those eyes: something unnerving, something familiar, something haunting, something rather frightening. . . .

He let her hand go and turned to the next guest, and she and Ralph went into the drawing room.

'Did you see that diamond?' he whispered. 'Rock's as big as Pike's Peak! Whew!'

'She's quite lovely,' said Rosemary, smiling at Senator Granby's wife. 'And speaks English well.'

'Don't she? He told me she hired a tutor in Mexico City. What did you think of him?'

'Well, you're right. He does look right through you. Odd . . .'

'What?'

'I could swear I'd seen him before.'

'Well, I doubt that. There's Charlie Seymore and Bonita. Let's go say hello. Goddam, that Bonita's gettin' homelier every day!'

As they made their way through the crowd to Representative Seymour, Rosemary turned back to look at her host again. He was looking at her. Again, she felt cold, as if a chill wind had swept through the elegant room. Then Peter Fraser turned to shake hands with the vice-president.

Those blue eyes. . . . Where had she seen them before?

The original plantation had had no ballroom, so Mr Tewesbury had built an extension onto the river side of the house, pushing the original building out another thirty feet to provide a graceful room with arched windows overlooking the river below. Gold ballroom chairs lined the white walls, which were hung with a fine Vandyke court portrait, a van Ruysdael landscape, and, at one end of the room, an enormous Zoffany portrait of the family of the third Earl Stanhope. It was beneath the Stanhope clan that Mr Fontaine's string ensemble was standing, the conductor's baton poised rather nervously as he looked at the unfamiliar score. Then he brought the baton down to the slow, swinging beat of 'La Paloma'. Peter Fraser led his wife onto the dance floor, and the couple began a *habanera*, a dance Ysabel preferred to the more fashionable waltz. The guests remained off the floor, most of them not knowing the dance. But even those who did, such as the Floreses from Ecuador, decided to let the young couple have the floor to themselves. It was, after all, the first time anyone had danced in the room.

Ysabel raised her hands over her head and began clicking her castanets as she danced around her husband.

'Having fun?' said Peter Fraser in Spanish.

'No,' she replied. 'But I suppose you are?'

'Well, I think the party's a great success.'

'For Peter Fraser, whoever *he* is.'

Clickety-click went the castanets.

'What do you think of the Matoons?'

'I don't think they're worth going to all this trouble for.'

'That's one thing we disagree on.'

'Oh, there are *lots* of things we disagree on! For instance, this ridiculous idea of using a false name.'

She put her hands behind her back, still clicking the castanets, and tossed her head back as her feet beat the floor to the sensual rhythm. Now he circled her, saying, 'Your father thought it was an excellent idea.'

'That doesn't mean *I* do.'

'Ysabel, shall we have a fight right here on the dance floor with half of Washington watching?'

'I wouldn't know whom I was fighting – my husband, or

this stranger named Peter Fraser! The man I fell in love with had beautiful blond hair. I happen to detest brown hair.'

'It's the best dye on the market.'

'Well, I hate it.'

Clickety-click-click, clickety-click-click . . .

He smiled. 'I love you when you're angry.'

'Then you're in for a very loving time, because until this cheap charade is over . . .'

'Smile. Everyone's watching.'

'I *am* smiling!' Now they were both circling each other. 'And if you really loved me, you'd tell them who you are.'

'That will happen in time.'

'And just *what* are you going to do to him, anyway?'

'That's my secret.'

'Oh, damn you!'

Clickety-click-click . . .

'Smile.'

'*Madre de Dios!*'

The *habanera* come to a close, and the crowd applauded their host and hostess, who smiled back.

Then Mr Fontaine began a waltz, and the polished parquet floor rapidly filled with swirling couples.

During a lull in the music, Rosemary Matoon joined the women who had surrounded Ysabel Fraser. Madame Catacazy, the statuesque wife of the Russian minister, was saying, 'We want to know *all* about your husband. Everyone says he's very mysterious.'

'Yes,' chorused Mrs Granby. 'Someone told me he's from California, and someone else said he was born in Vermont. Either your husband is terribly absent-minded, or his parents were terribly peripatetic.'

Ysabel laughed. 'Well, the truth is about halfway in between. Peter was born in Chicago.'

'And how did he come to be in Mexico?'

'My husband does not believe in violence. So when your war broke out, he went to Mexico to avoid becoming involved. That's where my father met him. He came to our hacienda looking for work, and my father hired him. It was the most fortunate thing my father has ever done, because my husband saved our lives.'

'Yes,' said Madame Catacazy, 'I heard about the Gatling gun. For a man who doesn't believe in violence, you husband seems to have overcome his scruples in a rather spectacular fashion.'

Ysabel gave her a cool look.

'My husband only did what was necessary to save us.'

'But he couldn't save poor Laura de Beaupré. Wasn't she there at the time?'

'Unfortunately, yes.'

Rosemary Matoon frowned. Laura de Beaupré? She remembered that note so many years ago in a Virginia farmhouse . . . that note written by Laura de Beaupré to Lew Crandall. . . .

'We hear you have three adorable children,' said Mrs Granby.

'Yes, twin boys, and then, just six months ago, we had a daughter. Would you like to see them?'

'Well, they're probably asleep . . .'

'Oh, nothing wakes them up. Besides, I want to show them off. Come: we'll go upstairs. . . .'

She led the ladies through the crowd to the entrance hall, then up the curved staircase. Rosemary followed. Lew Crandall . . . those blue eyes. . . . No, that was absurd. But it was a strange coincidence. . . .

At the top of the stairs, Ysabel led them down the hall to the end, where she opened a door.

'Micaela,' she whispered to an Indian woman, 'the ladies want to see the children.'

Micaela curtsied and held the door as Ysabel led the others into a nursery which was dimly illuminated by an oil lamp. Now Ysabel turned the lamp higher and took the women to a big bed where two towheaded two-year-olds were asleep.

'The one on the left is Francis,' whispered Ysabel. 'And the other is Lewis.'

'They're adorable!' said Mrs Granby.

'Where did the blond hair come from?' asked Rosemary Matoon.

'My husband. He was blond when he was a child. And over here is Alicia. . . .'

She took them to the other side of the room where, in a crib, a baby girl had just woken up and begun crying. Ysabel picked her out of the crib and held her in her arms, patting her back.

'Oh, we woke you up, poor thing,' she said. 'And now you're hungry!' She kissed her, then gently returned her to the crib.

'Is the Indian woman nursing her?' asked Madame Catacazy.

'*I'm* nursing her,' said Ysabel.

'But my dear, it will ruin your figure!'

'My children get *my* milk, madame. And I suffered through too many hunger pangs to get my figure to what it is now to let it go to ruin again. Thank you, Micaela. Good night.'

She ushered the ladies out of the room. Then she saw Rosemary Matoon standing at the foot of the bed, looking at the twins. 'Mrs Matoon?' she said.

Rosemary joined her at the door. 'They're so beautiful,' she said. 'You must be very proud.'

'Any mother is proud of her children,' said Ysabel, leading her back out into the hall. 'But of course I think mine are the best in the world.'

'Yes, I think my son is the best in the world.'

They started down the hall towards the other women.

'Oh, you have a son? How old is he?'

'Six. His name is Charles. Charles Matoon.'

'I'd love to meet him some day.'

'Yes, I'd like you to. He's' – she hesitated – 'he's blind.'

Ysabel looked at her.

'Oh, I'm sorry,' she said. 'Was it an accident?'

'No, he was born that way. God made him blind.'

'How . . .' she started to say 'horrible', then changed her mind. Rosemary caught it. She smiled slightly.

'Yes, one doesn't quite know what to say, does one? How sad, how terrible, how unfortunate. . . . All of them are true, and none of them helps.'

They joined the other women, and they started down the stairs. Below them, a new waltz was beginning. Ysabel watched Rosemary Matoon and felt a surge of pity for the handsome redhead.

Ralph Matoon's intake of alcohol had been severely curtailed by his doctor, but he would be damned if he'd pass up the excellent cognac being served by Peter Fraser. So he had taken a snifter to the terrace outside the ballroom and was enjoying the moonlit view and a cigar when he heard a voice behind him say, 'Having a good time, Senator?'

He turned to see his host.

'Yes sir, I am. A wonderful time!' he exclaimed. 'I love your house, your wife's a Latin beauty – say, I liked that dance you two did. What's it called?'

'The *habanera*. It originated in Havana, but it's very popular in Mexico.'

'Well, you two danced it like real Mexiques.'

'My wife *is* a real "Mexique". By the way, that word isn't appreciated in Mexico.'

'Oh . . . sorry. Anyway, it's some party. And say, Pete – I hope I can call you Pete? And my name's plain old Ralph. Can't stand a lot of formality – anyway, as something of a connoisseur of gemstones, I have to tell you that diamond your wife's sportin' is a knockout. Whew! Beautiful colour, beautiful cut . . . well, I wish I had that in my collection.'

'Thank you. And I hope I can see your collection soon. I hear it's got some interesting things.'

'Well, I don't like to brag, but I think you'd have to go to New York to find anything better. Rosie and I will have to invite you and your wife over soon to see it.'

'How about tomorrow?' said Peter Fraser, lighting a cigar.

Matoon looked at the face illuminated by the match.

'Well, I was thinking more like next week, maybe. . . .'

'Tomorrow morning at ten, perhaps?' Fraser threw the match over the stone balustrade onto the grass. 'You see,

Ralph, I'd like to discuss some business with you. Business that will be mutually advantageous, I believe. And I'd rather not be seen at your office in the Capitol.'

Matoon raised the snifter and sipped the brandy.

'Uh huh,' he said. 'Well, I'm beginning to see what you mean. In that case, tomorrow at ten will be fine.'

'You may have noticed I took the liberty of inviting tonight what the newspapers call the "Matoon Gang". Messieurs Rowlandson, Granby, Seymore, and so on.'

Matoon chuckled.

'Oh, I noticed! But you mustn't believe those rascal reporters. Nothing makes them happier than hanging labels on senators – unless it's hanging senators. We're no "gang". Just a bunch of like-minded Republicans doing our best to put through legislation that will benefit the country.'

'I see. Then perhaps I misjudged you. Perhaps you're not the senator I want to see.'

Matoon lowered his voice.

'Well now, Pete, don't get me wrong. We're patriotic, but we look after our friends, too. Yes sir. I can guarantee you that the senator you want to talk to is Ralph Matoon.'

'Then I'll see you in the morning. And I'll look forward to seeing your jewel collection. By the way, I assume you have a safe?'

'Of course.'

Fraser inhaled on his cigar, and the ash glowed red.

'Good,' he said, blowing out the smoke. 'I'll bring you something that should be kept in a safe.'

He walked away. Ralph Matoon smiled as he finished his brandy. So Mr Fraser was interested in a little deal-making. Well, well. The evening was turning out better than he had expected.

Ysabel put on her nightgown as Ghislaine carefully hung her ball gown in the large cedar closet that had been one of the many architectural innovations Mr Tewesbury had introduced to West Wind.

'Madame was very beautiful tonight,' said the thin Frenchwoman.

'Thank you, Ghislaine,' said Ysabel, sitting down on the edge of her canopied bed. 'Madame is also very tired.'

'But such a success! The guests all had such a good time.'

'Yes, I think it was a success.'

'Will there be anything else, madame?'

'No, Ghislaine. Thank you. And good night.'

'Good night.'

Ghislaine curtsied, then left the bedroom. Ysabel rubbed her bare feet, then stretched out on the bed. She was tired, but she wouldn't go to sleep yet. She had to talk to her husband, had to try and stop him from this insane course of revenge before . . . before what? She didn't know. But the gala evening had been anything but gala for the hostess. She had veered between irritability and anxiety, and now she felt crushed with depression.

The door opened, and Lew Crandall came in the room.

'Well, the last of them is gone,' he said. 'And good riddance. This party-giving is hard work.'

He took off his tail coat and out it over the back of a chair. Then he sat down to remove his shoes.

'Are you still damning me?' he said.

'I don't know.'

'Can't you make up your mind?'

She sat up.

'Oh Lew, please give this idea up before it's too late. *Please.*'

'It's already too late.'

'But it isn't! I know what this man has done to you – I know how you feel. But darling, he's already been paid back!'

'Oh? How?'

'His son is blind. She told me tonight – what's her name?'

'Rosemary.' He stood to take the shoes to his closet. 'Rosemary Fletcher, ex-spy, ex-lady around town, ex-woman who thought it amusing when a Southern captain burned me with a cigar. And I know her son is blind. What's that have to do with it?'

'Everything! Let God be the avenger, not you.'

'And how about the thousands of soldiers who died

because of the information Rosemary took across the Potomac? Is God going to avenge them, too? Not to mention the shoddy uniforms, sway-backed horses, and rotten rifles Matoon ordered while he was in the War Department, raking off his twenty per cent? How many soldiers died because of a malfunctioning rifle? Is God avenging them, too? That's leaving a lot to God. If you ask me, a blind son isn't enough. If you ask me, so far Matoon's gotten off cheap.'

He took off his trousers, then went in the bathroom. Ysabel rubbed her forehead. Everything he said was true, but still she felt in her heart he was wrong. But how to convince him?

He came out of the bathroom in his nightshirt and started lowering the gaslights.

'Is there nothing I can say to stop you?' she asked.

'Ysabel, we have a good marriage, and I owe a lot to you and your father. I realize this is unpleasant for you, I realize this "cheap charade", as you call it, is putting you to a lot of inconvenience . . . but the answer is *no*. There's nothing you can say to stop me. Matoon is going to be destroyed, one way or another.'

'But this is so petty of you!'

He turned, 'Petty? After what he's done to me? After Andersonville? He cost me everything! My family, my inheritance – everything! Even my name!' He came to the bed and opened his nightshirt. 'And how about that scar?' he said, pointing to his upper chest. 'A bullet went in there that was fired by Matoon – by proxy, I'll admit. That bullet was aimed at my heart. You may think it petty of me, but I can assure you being fired at point-blank is a not a petty experience.'

She took a deep breath. 'Yes, I know. And my father has told me to stay out of this. "A debt of honour", he calls it. But I just can't see any honour in destroying a man – I don't care *what* he's done!'

Lew sat on the bed next to her and took her hand.

'If it were just me,' he said, 'I might agree with you – or at least listen to you. If all this were in the past, I might listen to you. But Matoon is *still* getting away with murder! He and his cronies in Congress – the "Matoon Gang": you met them tonight – are into God knows how many crooked deals, and no one will stop them, because they're so powerful! President Grant won't lift a finger. All he's interested in is his horses. And everyone else is either paid off or too afraid to take them on. Well, I'm not paid off, and I'm not afraid. And I'm going to *get* Matoon. I'd rather do it with your good wishes. But I'm going to do it – with or without them.'

'It will be without them.'

'I'm sorry to hear that.'

He let her hand go and got up to finish turning off the lights. She watched him. After a moment she said, 'Lew, do you love me?'

'What kind of a question is that? Of course I love you.'

'You didn't love me when you married me. My father badgered you into it. And my money didn't leave you entirely . . . shall we say "uninterested", did it?'

He turned off the last light and stood in the dark.

'No,' he said. 'I told you that at the time. But I'm a little bit leery of love after thirty-two years. At least the love everyone talks about. I was in love that way once, and it cost Laura de Beaupré her life. You should consider yourself lucky that I didn't talk about shooting stars and exploding moons when I proposed to you. At least you're alive.'

'But the moon exploded for me. It still does every time you touch me.'

He went back to the bed and climbed in. Then he took her in his arms.

'Ysabel,' he said, 'I love you. You're my wife. I love our children, I love our life together. I'm happy with you. I don't care about exploding moons any more. I've had enough explosions in my life.'

She ran her finger over the scar on his chest.

'You really do love me?'

'Why is it no woman believes a man when he tells her the truth? Yes, I really do love you.'

'But not the way you loved Laura?'

'No, not the way I loved Laura. And Laura is dead.'

She put her head on his chest, and he felt the tear drop on his skin.

'Maybe some day,' she said, 'you'll love me the way you loved her.'

'But I don't *want* that!' he said tensely. 'And neither should you! That was crazy – wild . . . and destructive. What we have is better. What we have is solid.'

'Lew?' she whispered. 'Or should I say Peter?'

'What?'

'The moon is exploding.'

'Then no more fights about Matoon?'

A long silence.

'I still think you're wrong,' she finally said. 'But all right: no more fights.'

'And no more worrying about whether I love you the way I loved Laura?'

She sighed.

'All right. No more worrying about Laura.'

He raised her up and kissed her, slipping his hand inside her nightgown.

'Then,' he whispered, 'let's shoot the moon.'

She told herself she was wrong to give in, wrong not to make more of an issue about Matoon. But what could she do? Continue to fight? Take the children back to Mexico? Throw things at him? She loved him, even though she knew she had been his second choice, a choice based more on calculation that passion. Well, she had made her bed and now she would have to lie in it.

The wonderful thing – or, she sometimes thought, perhaps the tragic thing – was that she loved the bed so much.

32

The next morning at five minutes before ten, Lew's carriage pulled into the drive of the Matoon mansion. Halfway up the drive, Lew told Arturo, his Mexican coachman, to stop a minute. He looked out the window at the sandstone house in front of him, surrounded by rhododendron bushes. It bristled with wrought-iron weathervanes, ornamental railings, and chimneys. The wisteria-covered porte-cochère, which jutted out from the front door like a sore carbuncle, was even crenellated. Ivy was climbing the walls as if nature were valiantly striving to throw a discrete veil over this architectural monstrosity.

Lew took it all in, then signalled Arturo to drive on. The carriage stopped, and Lew got out to go to the etched glass doors and ring the bell. Henry, the butler, answered.

'Yes sir?'

'Mr Fraser to see the senator.'

'Yes sir, Mr Fraser. You're expected.'

He went into the entrance hall, giving his hat to Henry. A tile floor with a Moorish design; dark panelled walls with an imperial full-length portrait of the senator standing in front of a Corinthian column holding a rolled piece of legislation in his right hand (Lew fought back a laugh); a broad staircase dominated by bronze nymphs on either side holding glass-flame torches in their raised arms.

'The senator is upstairs in his office, sir. If you'll follow me?'

Henry led him up the stairs, then down the hall to a door. He knocked.

'Yes?'

Henry opened the door.

'Mr Fraser, Senator.'

'Show him in.'

Lew went in the room. Matoon was sitting at his ornate desk in front of two windows overlooking the crenellated porte-cochère. Now the senator got up and came around to shake his hand.

'How are you this morning, Pete? A little whipped after your party?'

'Oh no.'

'Well, it was some show. Rosie and I had a swell time – swell! Would you like some coffee?'

'No thanks.'

The senator signalled his butler, who silently withdrew. Then Matoon indicated a leather chair before the desk.

'Take a seat, Pete.'

Lew sat down, looking around the room, which was lined with recessed bookshelves reaching almost to the ceiling. Most of the shelves held ominous legal and legislative tomes that looked seldom used, judging from the light dust on some of them. A few shelves contained personal mementos of the senator's career: a miniature of Rosemary, a lump of anthracite coal from a mine he had opened in Pennsylvania, a gavel presented to him when he chaired a state Republican convention, a Civil War medal. Hung over the books were a half-dozen framed political cartoons of the senator, one by Thomas Nast. The cartoons were a bestiary: Matoon as a vulture, Matoon as a hog, Matoon as a boa constrictor...

The senator went around his desk, gesturing at the cartoons.

'That's my rogue's gallery, Pete, the rogue being your humble servant. By God, I love those cartoonists! And do they have a field day with me! I see myself as a lion of the legislature, but obviously Mr Nast and the other pen pushers see me different, eh? Now, sir: you said you wanted to talk business.'

Lew turned back to the fat man seated behind the desk, his hairy hands folded in front of him.

'It's pretty simple, Ralph,' he said. 'We figure our railroad from Mexico City to the Rio Grande will be finished in six months – barring any accidents. Now as you know, I'm also president of the Laredo–San Antonio Railroad, which we're just getting started. When the two lines join at the border, we'll be able to ship goods from Mexico City straight through to San Antonio, then hook up to the Saint Louis line and have a clear shot at Chicago and New York. However, we realize we're going to run into problems at the border, and we want someone in Congress to represent our interests and smooth those problems out for us. It occurred to me you'd be just the man for us.'

Matoon nodded.

'Possibly,' he said.

Lew pulled an envelope from his coat and handed it across the desk.

'I think you'll be interested in what's in the envelope.'

Matoon opened it and pulled out five pieces of engraved bond paper. He examined them, his eyes widening. Then he looked up.

'Five thousand Class A shares in the Sonora Mining Company!' he said, with soft excitement. 'Why Pete, I'm flabbergasted! This is extremely generous, sir! Extremely! By God, I hear Sonora is a potential El Dorado!'

'We think so I'd uh . . . put that in your safe.'

He indicated the six-foot-high steel safe that was recessed in the north wall of the room. Matoon got up.

'Don't you worry! Into the safe she goes! Well sir, needless to say, you have your man in Congress. And by God, you'll see that Ralph Matoon earns his pay.'

'Then we have a deal?' said Lew, getting up also.

Matoon came around the desk, his hand extended. 'We have more than a deal, Pete. We have a partnership.'

They shook.

'Good. From time to time, I'll be letting you know what it is we'd like you to work on for us.'

'Certainly. Any time. The Senate doors are open to you, Pete.'

'I think I'll steer clear of the Senate.'

Matoon chuckled as he went to the safe. 'I see what you mean. But don't get too nervous. We're servants of the public, sir, and the business interests of this country – and Mexico, now! – are the public we serve.'

He leaned over the safe, which stood on four short legs, and began turning the dial.

'This is a new wrinkle,' he said. 'Ever see one of these combination safes before? I just bought this one six months ago . . . beats hell out of the old key-safes.'

Lew stood by the chair, watching. Eighteen right. Thirty-eight left. Four right. Eighteen, thirty-eight, four. Easy to remember, he thought. Eighteen thirty-eight was the year I was born.

'It looks pretty formidable,' he said aloud.

'It is. Double-layered eight-inch tempered steel. No thief will break into this beauty, Pete. It's made by the Chubb people in London, and they're the best in the business.'

He depressed the handle and opened the thick door. The safe bulged with documents, folders, envelopes. Matoon put the envelope on the top shelf.

'Nevertheless,' said Lew, 'I assume you keep watch-dogs?'

'No. Don't need 'em, and dog fur makes Rosie sneeze. Now that you're here, let me show you something that'll make your eyeballs pop.'

He pulled one of a number of handsome wooden boxes from the bottom of the safe and carried it to Lew.

'Take a look at these beauties,' he said. 'My collection of carved emeralds.'

He unhooked the box and raised the lid. Inside, set in white velvet, were over two dozen emeralds of varying size and cut. 'Ain't they pretty?' He was holding the box for his guest's perusal. 'They came from all over the world, but mostly India. Them fakirs carve prayers on 'em. Go on: pick one up. Look at it close. You can see the carving. Remarkable what those niggers can do.'

Lew picked one of the cabochon emeralds out of the box and looked at the delicate engraving.

'Beautiful,' he said. He put the gem back in the box.

'Ain't they? I tell you, Pete, I love these little rocks more than I can put in words. I love their colour. Sit in here and stare at them for hours on end. Let me show you my diamonds. . . .'

Matoon closed the box and returned to the safe.

'I've got white diamonds, pink ones, yellow ones, brown . . . all colours. . . .'

'Listen, Ralph, I've got an appointment in a half hour, so I won't be able to do justice to your collection today. When you have Ysabel and me over for dinner, we'll have the time to get a good look. I'd love her to see them, anyway.'

Matoon looked disappointed.

'Well . . . I guess you're right.' He brightened. 'I'll tell Rosie to fix a night next week.' He closed the safe door and twirled the dial. 'Say, we've got a cook who can do miracles with mutton. You like mutton?'

'Love it.'

Matoon guided him to the door. 'Well sir, we'll cook you the best Southdown mutton chops in the United States and points west. It's been a real pleasure doing business with you. A real pleasure.'

They shook hands. Matoon opened the door, and they went into the hallway, heading for the stairs.

'You know,' said Matoon, 'when I first met you, I had a funny feeling you didn't like me. Well, that just shows how wrong a man can be, eh?'

Lew smiled slightly.

'I was just sizing you up, Ralph. You turned out to be everything I expected. And then some.'

'Well well, never show all your cards at once, eh? You a gambling man? Me and some of the boys in the Senate got us a red-hot poker game going Thursday nights. We'd love you to sit in – get some fresh money in the pot.'

'I never gamble, Ralph. I only like sure things. You're a sure thing.'

'Hah! You're right there! Solid Ralph Matoon.'

They were halfway down the stairs when Lew pulled his pocket watch to check the time. Then he stopped.

'Something wrong?' asked Matoon.

Lew held up the end of the watch chain. No watch.

'My damned watch must have fallen off. The chain link's loose . . . it must be on the floor in your office. I'll go back and take a look.'

Matoon waited on the stair as the well-dressed millionaire hurried up to the hallway, then went back to the office. Lew let himself in, closed the door, ran to the two windows overlooking the porte-cochère, and unlocked both of them. Then he returned to the door, went out to the hall, and pulled his watch from his coat pocket. Rejoining Matoon on the stairs, he held the watch up in his hand.

'It was under my chair,' he said.

'Well, I am glad you found it,' said Matoon.

And they continued down the stairs.

At four o'clock that afternoon, he kissed Ysabel good-bye, hugged the twins, then left West Wind for a two-day business trip to New York. He climbed in his carriage. Arturo put his valise on the luggage rack, then climbed in the driver's seat and flicked his whip. The four matched bays came to life, and the carriage rolled down the long drive. Ysabel stood on the columned veranda, waving. Then, when the carriage reached the distant gate, she took the twins back in the house to give them some tea and cake.

An hour later, the carriage pulled up in front of the Metropole Hotel on Pennsylvania Avenue. Arturo jumped down to open the door for his employer. Lew climbed out. Arturo handed his valise to the porter. Then Lew said to Arturo in Spanish, 'Eleven-thirty tonight.'

Arturo nodded.

Lew walked into the second-class hotel. He went to the desk and the clerk nodded.

'Good afternoon, Mr Jardine. Do you want your room key?'

'Yes, please. And would you send someone up at eight

this evening to wake me? I'm going to take a nap.'

'Yes sir. Eight o'clock.'

Lew took the key to Room 2-G, then tipped the porter and carried his valise himself up the stairs to the second floor. He walked to his room, which was at the rear of the hotel overlooking an alley. After letting himself in he locked the door and put his valise in the armoire. He checked the black canvas bag he had placed in the armoire the day before: everything was there. He looked at the black canvas, rubber-soled shoes, the black trousers, the black sweater. Then he closed the armoire doors and stripped to his shorts. He pulled the curtains over the windows looking onto a fire escape, lay down on the bed, and went to sleep.

At eight that evening, he was wakened by a knock.

'Mr Jardine? It's eight o'clock.'

Lew sat up, rubbing his eyes. Then he went to the door and opened it. 'Can you bring me some supper?'

'Yes sir.'

'A ham sandwich and a bottle of white wine. Chablis, if you have it.'

'Yes sir.'

Lew closed the door and yawned.

He looked at his watch: eleven. He put the watch on a table and took the black trousers out of the armoire. He put them on, then the black shoes and the black sweater. He put the canvas bag with its two long handles on the floor by one of the windows. He put his watch in his pocket, then turned off the gaslight, opened the curtains, opened the window, and looked down at the alley. He waited. At eleven-thirty, a one-horse buggy pulled into the alley. Lew picked up the bag, stepped out of the window onto the fire escape, and climbed down, jumping the last few feet to the dirt. Then he climbed in the buggy beside Arturo.

'Right on time,' he said. 'Good. Let's go.'

Arturo flicked his whip, and the horse trotted to the end of the alley and turned into the street.

At twelve-forty, the buggy pulled up to the gate of West Wind.

'I shouldn't be more than a half hour,' said Lew, climbing out.

'I'll wait.'

He let himself through the wrought-iron gates of his estate and jogged down the long drive toward the dark mansion. When he reached the house, he ran around to one side and looked up at the second-floor window of his bathroom. He set down the bag and pulled out a slim rope. After uncoiling it, he tied a wide slipknot in one end. Then, standing back from the house, he started twirling the lasso. After a moment, he threw it with all his strength. The rope flew up in the air and landed on the roof, missing the brick chimney.

El Juero's out of practice, he thought, retrieving the rope. He tried again; again, he missed. The third time, however, the noose ringed the chimney. He pulled the slipknot tight, then picked up the canvas bag and hung it around his neck, dangling it down his right side. He grabbed the rope with both hands and started climbing. He went up swiftly, hand over hand, until he was swinging gently outside his bathroom window. He wrapped the rope around his right foot to rest his weight, brought the bag round, and reached in with his free hand. After a moment's search, he found the rubber suction cup. He stuck it on the glass over the lock. Then he pulled a glass cutter from the bag and silently cut an arc around the suction cup.

After returning the glass cutter to his bag, he gently pulled the suction cup. The cut-glass section came out. He put it in his bag and reached in to unlock the window. Then he pushed the bottom section up. It moved easily, because he had soaped it the day before. He climbed into his bathroom, letting the rope swing free.

He listened for a moment. The bathroom door was shut. He knew Ysabel would be asleep, and he knew she was a sound sleeper. Now he pulled a small bull's-eye lantern from his bag, lit the wick, and played its beam around the large bathroom. It stopped on an English sporting print between the big marble washbasin and the claw-foot tub. He went to the print and took it off the wall.

Behind it was a safe. It was a key-safe. Now he pulled a twirl from his bag and inserted it in the keyhole. This was no ordinary twirl, or picklock. It had been designed by Agustin himself, the master Mexican lockpicker, and El Juero had watched him use it on numerous safes in the mansions of Mexico City. Besides, El Juero had the advantage of picking the lock of his own safe, and he had spent several hours the day before taking the lock apart to study it. He knew where to put the twirl.

In less than a minute, he had opened the safe. The police would know the lock had been picked: that was important (else he would have used his own key). Now Lew reached in and pulled out a black box. He opened it and shone his bull's-eye on the Star of Mexico. The diamond blazed like a solar eruption in the light.

He closed the box, stuck it in his pocket; then shut the safe door and went back to the window. After crawling out, he grabbed the rope and swiftly made his way to the ground, jumping the last few feet.

He looked up at the open window, smiling.

Then he ran back to the driveway.

When he reached Arturo, he had been gone twenty-six minutes.

At two-forty-three in the morning, Arturo stopped the buggy under a tree a block from the Matoon mansion. A gaslight down the street dimly illuminated the beginning of the ornamental wrought-iron fence that surrounded the property.

'I don't know how long I'll be,' said Lew. 'But for God's sake, don't give up on me.'

Arturo, a man in his thirties, shook his head.

'I'll wait, señor. Don't worry.'

Lew squeezed his arm.

'Good.'

Taking his canvas bag, he jumped down from the buggy and hurried into the shadow of the tree. The street was deserted. He ran into the yard of the neighbouring house, easily jumped the wrought-iron fence, then hurried across the lawn to the crenellated porte-cochère of the dark house. He had another rope, but he tested the wisteria vine first. It was thick and seemed strong. He decided to try it. He began climbing.

The vine held. Once on the roof of the porte-cochère, he went to the windows of Matoon's office and slowly raised the left one. Fortunately, no one had checked the windows since he unlocked them that morning. He stepped into the office, pulled his bull's-eye lantern from his bag, and lit it. He played the beam on the heavy Chubb safe.

He went to it, knelt down, and twirled the dial. Eighteen right. Thirty-eight left. Four right. He heard the tumblers click. He depressed the handle and opened the safe.

He pulled out a stuffed envelope from the top shelf and started through the papers. Correspondence. He couldn't read it all, but his eyes darted over the letters, looking for information. Letters from constituents, mostly. Nothing of particular interest. He put the contents back in the envelope, replaced it, and pulled out another.

This seemed no more promising at first. Mostly old correspondence. He had started to return the envelope when he noticed a letter dated 1862. It was on stationery marked Kemp Armaments Company, Inc., and was from Mr Kemp himself. He skimmed the letter. It was something about an order of hand grenades. The tone of the letter struck him as suggestive. One phrase read 'the difference between our bid and the Government price'.

It was then he heard the door open.

He looked up to see a six-year-old boy standing in the doorway. He was wearing a nightgown. Lew started to close the lantern when he realized he didn't have to. The boy was blind.

Lew froze, staring at the boy, whose sightless eyes were blanks in his face. His ears, though, thought Lew. His ears compensate for his eyes. He must have heard me. Is he hearing me now? Jesus Christ . . .

Charles Matoon didn't move. He just listened. He listened

for a full minute as Lew, kneeling in front of the open safe. stared at him, afraid to breathe, afraid the boy's bat ears would hear his heartbeat.

Then the boy backed into the hall, closing the door.

Lew stuffed the papers back in the safe. As quietly as he could, he closed the safe door and twirled the lock. Then he pulled the Star of Mexico from his bag. He took it from its box, pulled a piece of cotton bandage from his bag, and wrapped the big diamond in the cotton. Taking a bottle of glue from his bag, he poured glue over the bandage, working as fast as he could. When the cotton was impregnated, he reached under the safe and pressed it against the safe bottom. He held it there until he thought the glue had bonded. Then he put out the lantern. He grabbed his bag, hurried back to the window, and let himself out onto the roof of the porte-cochère. He closed the window, then went to the edge of the roof, grabbed the vine, and rapidly made his way back to the ground. He ran for the buggy.

Breaking into his own house had been a lark, but the sight of the Matoon child staring at him with those blind eyes had turned his blood to ice. When he reached the buggy, he was drenched with sweat.

'Move it: *fast*. Back to the hotel.' He snapped the order as he climbed in the buggy. Arturo cracked the whip and the horse broke into a frightened gallop, heading down the street towards the Metropole.

'What happened?'

'The boy must have heard me. He's blind – the son. He came in the room – scared the shit out of me. My God, those eyes!'

Ralph Matoon was awakened by a hand on his face. He jerked around in bed.

'Who's that?'

'It's Charlie.'

'Jesus Christ, son, you scared me – what's wrong?'

'There's someone in the house.'

'Huh?'

'I heard him open the window to your office. He's gone now. I heard the buggy go down the street.'

Rosemary was sitting up.

'What is it?' she said.

'Charlie says someone was in the house. Turn on the light.'

As Rosemary lit the bedlamp, the senator heaved his bulk out of his bed.

'The office, you say?'

'Yes sir. I went to the door and opened it. He was in the room. I could hear him breathing.'

'Oh darling,' exclaimed Rosemary, throwing on a peignoir, 'he might have hurt you!'

'But he didn't.'

'It's the jewels,' mumbled Matoon. 'He must have been after the collection . . . goddam . . .'

He hurried to the door, then went out into the hallway, pausing to turn on the gas sconce. Rosemary and her son joined him, Rosemary carrying the lamp.

'Come on. . . .'

They ran down the corridor to the senator's office, which was next to his son's bedroom. Matoon opened the door and went in, waiting for Rosemary and the lamp. He looked around.

'Nothing's out of place. . . .' He went to the safe, twirled the dial, opened the door, and looked in. 'Bring that lamp over here, Rosie.'

She did. Quickly, he pulled out the boxes of his jewel collection and opened them one by one to inspect them. When he was finished, he looked at his son.

'There's nothing missing,' he said. 'You sure you didn't dream all this, son?'

Charles Matoon was standing by the door. Now he pointed at the windows.

'I heard the window open,' he said. 'And I heard him breathing.'

Matoon went to the window.

'They're unlocked,' he said. 'Goddamit, Rosie, will you tell Henry to check these things?'

He locked the windows, then turned to his wife.

'Well?' she said. 'What do you think?'

The senator sniffed. 'I don't know.'

'You know Charles hears things we don't. And the windows *were* unlocked.'

The senator headed for the door. 'Come on, let's go back to bed. If someone was here, he sure as hell didn't get anything. No one could open that safe. And Charlie, next time you think you hear somone –'

'I didn't *think* I heard him. I *heard* him.'

'All right, you heard him. But come to your father first, understand?'

'Yes sir.'

'Now go to bed.'

'I'll take him.'

Rosemary led her son back to his room as Matoon returned to the master bedroom. When Rosemary rejoined him, he was sitting on the edge of the bed.

'That was strange,' she said, closing the door.

'Yes it was.'

'You know Charles doesn't make things up.'

'I know. I think maybe he's right. Maybe someone *was* here.'

Rosemary put the lamp back on the table and got in bed.

'Wasn't Peter Fraser here this morning?' she asked.

'Yes.'

'And wasn't he in your office?'

'Of course. I told you about the Sonora stock.'

He put his feet under the covers.

'Mightn't he have unlocked the windows?'

The senator looked at his wife.

'Are you crazy? Why would he do that?'

'So someone he hired could climb through them later on, of course. Or maybe so *he* could climb through them.'

Matoon shook his head.

'Of all the dumb . . . why should he want to rob me? He just gave me a fortune in mining stock! Use your head, Rosie.'

'I am.'

He turned his back to her and sank his head in the pillow,

closing his eyes. 'Turn out the light and let's get some sleep. I've got a big day tomorrow.'

'Ralph,' she said quietly, 'I think I know who Peter Fraser is.'

'What do you mean, who he is? He's Peter Fraser.'

'Maybe. Remember I told you last night I'd seen him before? I've been thinking about it all day. That face and those eyes – they've been haunting me. And I think I know who he is. He's Lew Crandall.'

The senator's eyes blinked open.

'Huh?'

'He's Lew Crandall.'

'My God, you *are* crazy. Lew Crandall's been dead ten years.'

'How do we know?'

'Because I told Burt Thomson to shoot him, that's how we know. And Burt came back and told me he shot him through the heart, point-blank. Now go to sleep before I have you committed. Lew Crandall? My God.'

'Ralph, Lew Crandall was an extremely good-looking man with a face a woman doesn't easily forget. This Peter Fraser has the same face! Oh, he's grown a beard and dyed his hair brown – although he isn't as clever as he thinks, because the hair on his hands is still blond: I noticed. And his twin boys? They're towheads, and one of them is named Lewis. . . .'

'So what?'

'Plus: Laura de Beaupré was killed at his wife's hacienda. And there was something going on between her and Crandall. Now that just *might* be coincidence. . . .'

'I'll tell you what is: ancient history. I don't know what you're talking about.'

'I'm talking about a bomb!' she insisted. 'If I'm right and he *is* Lew Crandall, he knows enough to blow both of us off the face of the earth – so you listen to me! And I'm not crazy.'

Matoon sat up and looked at his wife with sleepy eyes.

'Rosie, the dead don't come back.'

'And I'm saying we don't know he was killed! Thomson might have lied to you –'

'Why?'

'I don't know! Or maybe he missed –'

'Point-blank? Come on.'

She was frowning. 'I know I'm right,' she said quietly. 'I know it. And he's come back to punish us, Ralph. God has sent him to punish us.'

'I thought God had already punished us with Charlie's eyes? You're runnin' God ragged, Rosie. And I mean it, now: you *are* sounding like a loonie. Now put that light out and shut up. I've got a caucus at eleven in the morning, and I need my sleep to face those goddam windbags.'

He turned over on his side again and shut his eyes.

'I'll prove it,' she said. 'Somehow, I'll prove it.'

'When you prove to me Lew Crandall's alive . . .' He stopped and opened his eyes again. 'Jesus Christ, the watch!'

'What watch?'

He turned over to look at his wife. 'Pete Fraser's watch! After we left my office this morning, he was halfway downstairs when he said his watch was gone. So he went back to get it.'

'That's when he could have unlocked the windows!'

'Yes, except' – Matoon's eyes were narrowing – 'why? What does he want? Something in the safe? But even if he got into it, nothing's missing . . . the jewels are all there. . . .'

'Why would a man worth millions be interested in jewels? But Lew Crandall would want something in that safe.'

'What?'

'Information.'

Matoon's eyes were darting nervously about, as if he were seeing ghosts closing in on him. 'Oh hell, this is crazy! *Crazy!* Now go to sleep, goddammit! You're turning me into a nervous wreck! Jesus! Lew Crandall . . . and Pete Fraser's my *friend!*'

For the last time, he turned on his side and shut his eyes. But he didn't fall asleep again. The ghosts haunted him until dawn.

33

Flora Marshall pushed open the sagging door of the bedroom and went to the plank bed. Her lover was sprawled on it, one arm off the bed, his head off the pillow. He hadn't undressed, but his feet were bare. His dirty white shirt was half open, and his black trousers were torn on the left knee where he had fallen down two nights before. On the plank floor beneath the bed stood an almost empty bottle of rye whisky.

Flora Marshall was a tall woman in her early forties. She had light chocolate skin and handsome features. A blue bandana was on her head, and she wore a clean white apron over her blue homespun skirt and yellow blouse. She shook her head as she looked at her lover, who was snoring. Now she leaned over and shook his arm.

'You! Gilbert! Wake up, honey. There'a a man to see you.'

Snore.

'Lordie, this man sleep like a log. A log filled with likker. . . . Gilbert, you wake *up*, you hear? Come on, now. Wake *up*.'

She was shaking him hard. Gilbert Samson opened his eyes.

'What you doing, woman?' he mumbled. 'Leave me alone.'

'Gilbert, there's a man to see you. A white man, name of Peter Fraser. Now he's a gentleman, and I don't want him to see you lookin' like you just danced out of a whisky bottle like the tooth fairy on a binge, you hear? So you get up and wash your face and drink something *non* alcoholic, 'cause your breath's enough to make strong men weep! You hear?'

Gilbert Samson was sitting up, holding his head with both hands.

'You know something, Flora? You got a big mouth.'

'Uh *huh*. And I got a big heart to put up with a drunk like you. Now, you pull yourself together. Mr Fraser is waiting for you in what we laughingly call our parlour.'

'Who's Mr Fraser?'

She lowered her voice.

'If you'd ever read anything beside the labels on whisky bottles, you'd know he's the "Man of Mystery from Mexico". Mmmm-*mm*! Do I like the sound of that! That's what they call him in the newspapers. He's the one they stole that big diamond from the other day. The Star of Mexico? Mmmm-*mm*! Do I like the sound of *that*!'

Gilbert was looking at her in utter confusion. 'Does he think *we* got the Star of Mexico?'

Flora Marshall laughed. 'Oh sure, honey. Now let me see: where *did* I put it? Oh yes, I loaned it to Maybelle Peterson, who's going to wear it to the Church social. . . .' She scowled and put her hands on her ample hips. 'Are you dumb, or something? He wants to see *you*. Why, I don't know. Now pull yourself together and get on out there.' She went back to the door, then turned and lowered her voice. 'Wait till you see his carriage! It's *something*. Half of Nigger Hill's outside the house looking at it. Mmm-*mm*!'

And she went out.

Gilbert Samson's head was splitting. Now he reached down, groping for the bottle. When his hand found it, it brought it up to his mouth. He tilted his head and took a long guzzle. He shuddered as the stuff hit his stomach. The one-time temperance advocate had started drinking six years before, after closing his newspaper. The alcohol had not yet broken his health – he was still strong, and looked younger than his forty-two years despite his grey hair – but it had broken what was left of his spirit. Gilbert Samson drank because he didn't give a damn any more. He drank because he didn't know what else to do.

He got to his feet and tried to cross the tiny room to the paint-peeled door, but halfway there he felt a surge of nausea. He doubled over, holding his stomach, as the pain bit his intestines. Then the pain eased. Gilbert Samson didn't know it, but the whisky was giving him a first-class ulcer.

Now he made it to the door. The house – or shack – was in the north slums of Washington. It had four rooms and was divided by a narrow hall. Gilbert rented it from a white man named Brill for twenty dollars a month. Gilbert was a month in arrears. Now he went down the hall to the kitchen. He went to the pump sink and filled the tin basin with water. Then he stuck his face in the water, holding it there for as long as he could. When he brought it out, water dripping all over him, he felt a little better. He took the ratty towel from the rack and wiped his face and neck.

Then the pain hit again.

'Flora!' he yelled, leaning against the sink as he held his gut. 'Flora!'

She came running in. 'Your stomach?'

He nodded. 'Get me some whisky. . . .'

'Now you get sober!' she hissed. 'That man just told me he's going to offer you a *job* – why, I don't know, must be crazy – so you get sober!'

He closed his eyes. 'Get me the goddam *whisky*!' he bellowed.

'Gilbert, you're a *fool*!'

She opened the broom closet beside the door and took a bottle from the floor. She brought it to him. He grabbed it, uncorked it, and put it to his mouth. She watched as he drank. She watched with sadness.

'Honey,' she said, 'that stuff's going to do nothing but kill you. Why do you want to die?'

He took the bottle from his mouth and wiped his lips with his sleeve. 'Why do I want to live?' he said matter-of-factly.

He recorked the bottle and stuck it in his hip pocket.

Then he started across the kitchen. Halfway to the hall, he had to steady himself by leaning for a moment on the wooden table. But he made it to the hallway. Flora followed him, shaking her head.

Gilbert Samson leaned against the frame of the parlour door and looked at the man in the well-cut grey suit. The man had a trimmed brown beard. He was sitting in the rocking chair that was one of the four pieces of furniture in the small, airless room. Now he stood up.

'Gilbert Samson?' he said.

'That's right.'

'My name is Peter Fraser.' He came over, his hand extended. 'I think we have something in common.'

Gilbert looked at the extended hand. 'What?'

'We've both been ruined by Ralph Matoon.'

Gilbert didn't shake the hand. He looked Lew up and down. 'Wouldn't mind being ruined like you, Mr Fraser.'

He came into the room and sat down on the sagging horsehair sofa. Lew stuck his hands in his pockets. He looked at the once famous Negro.

'I understand you drink?' he said.

Gilbert shot him a look.

'He's a sometimey drunk,' said Flora, who was standing in the doorway, her arms crossed. 'Sometimes he stays sober a whole week at a time. Won't touch the stuff. Sometimes he stays drunk a whole week at a time. Won't touch nothing *but*. You hit the wrong sometime, Mr Fraser.'

Lew said to her, 'Maybe some coffee . . .?'

'Gilbert, honey, will you drink some coffee?'

Gilbert shook his head. She shrugged helplessly.

Lew walked across the squeaking plank floor, then leaned his back against the wall, his hands still in his pockets, watching Gilbert Samson, who was watching his toes.

'Mr Samson, I know a lot about you,' he said. 'I hired private detectives to tell me all about you, and the detectives weren't cheap. I want to check out how good their information was . . . see if I got my money's worth.'

'I'm listening.'

'Six years ago, you accused Senator Ralph Matoon of

murdering a girl named Christine Canrobert. Is that right?'

'That's right.'

'Shortly afterward, your newspaper went bankrupt. You accused Senator Matoon and several of his cronies in the Senate of pressuring your advertisers to take their business away from your paper, which they did. You claimed this was Matoon's way of shutting you up about the Canrobert girl. How am I doing?'

'So far, you're getting your money's worth from the detectives.'

'You tried to start a new paper, but found all the doors closed in your face. Again Matoon, right?'

'Right.'

'In eighteen sixty-six your wife died. Shortly after that, you sold your house in Rochester –'

'*Had* to sell. Had to pay for the funeral. Had to pay school bills for the kids.'

'You moved to New York City, where you tried to find work on a newspaper. But you found that: a, no one wanted to hire a black man, even a well-known one, like yourself. And, b, no one wanted to hire a black man who drinks. How am I doing?'

Gilbert took the bottle from his hip pocket and pulled the cork.

'Beautiful,' he said. 'How do you like the recital, Flora? "Brief Biographies of Famous Living Men"?' He took a drink of whisky.

Lew watched. Then he continued, 'Two years ago, you came here to Washington. What little money you earn comes from adventure stories you write under a pen name. *When* you write.'

'My last successful piece of fiction was "Fearless Fred Faces the Canal Street Killer". I forget how it ends.'

Silence. Gilbert looked up at the man leaning against the wall.

'So?' he said. 'Now what? Flora tells me you want to hire me for something. Want a dime novel? I'll write you one for fifty dollars.'

'That's exactly what I want. "Fearless Gilbert Samson Faces the Matoon Gang". Except it won't be a dime novel. And I'll pay you ten thousand dollars a year.'

Gilbert laughed. 'This man's crazy,' he said.

'Could be. I'm negotiating to buy the Washington *Evening Banner*. Our first big campaign will be to expose the Matoon Gang. And I mean *expose*. The past as well as the present. I want you to be in charge of the past. I want you to dig up all the dirt on Ralph Matoon – every swindle he pulled when he was in the Department of War. I've got some leads for you . . . there's a company in Pittsburgh called the Kemp Armaments Company that Matoon ordered hand grenades from back in sixty-two. I think he and Kemp had a sweetheart deal. I want you to find out what the deal was, how much they milked the government for – I want it all. We're going to put together a dossier on Matoon that's going to spread out his whole rotten life, like a corpse. And then we're going to publish it.'

Gilbert sniffed. Then he took another drink of the whisky. Lew watched.

'Why me?' Gilbert said. 'Why would you hire a black man who drinks – assuming you're on the level, which is a pretty big assumption.'

'Because you're a first-rate newspaperman when you want to be. I've read some of the old copies of your paper. And because you have a personal stake in getting Matoon. He killed Christine Canrobert.'

Gilbert nodded. 'Yes, he killed her,' he said. 'I couldn't prove it, but he killed her. Her and her boy. Ran them down on the streets of New York. . . .' He thought a moment. Then he said, 'Why you, Mr Fraser? What's your personal stake?'

Lew was still leaning against the wall. 'In eighteen sixty-one Matoon ordered the death of his aide, a young lieutenant named Lew Crandall. Ever hear of him?'

'Sure. That was what started the whole thing in the first place. Christine wanted me to avenge his murder. She knew Matoon had had him killed.'

'How?'

'She heard him admit it to his wife. How did you know about Crandall?'

'I'm Lew Crandall,' he said quietly.

Gilbert Samson looked at him. Then he looked at Flora and held up the bottle.

'Jesus Christ,' he said, 'what's in this stuff?' He took another drink, then turned back to the man in the grey suit leaning against the wall. 'Lew Crandall's dead.'

'He's rejoined the living in a big way,' said Lew. 'And I hope you enjoyed that drink, Mr Samson. It was your last if you want to work for me.'

Gilbert frowned. He looked at Lew. He looked at the half-empty bottle. He looked at Flora. He looked back at Lew.

'Are you on the level?' he said.

Lew pulled his wallet from his coat. He took out five one-hundred-dollar bills. Then he came to Gilbert.

'Here's a five-hundred-dollar advance on your salary,' he said, holding out the money.

Gilbert was staring at the cash. Flora, in the door, was watching. There were tears in her eyes.

'Mr Fraser,' she said, 'don't give him that money. He'll just use it to buy more likker.'

Gilbert Samson stood up. He took the bottle across the room, then knelt down and pried up a loose floorboard. Holding the bottle upside down, he poured its contents through the hole onto the dirt beneath. Then he tossed the empty after it. He stood up.

'Let the cockroaches get drunk for a change. Mr Fraser – or Crandall, or whatever the hell your name is: you've got yourself a newspaperman.'

As Flora Marshall smiled and raised her apron to wipe her eyes, Lew brought the money over to Gilbert and gave it to him. Then they shook hands.

'Just to confuse you further, I'm staying at the Metropole Hotel under the name of Jardine.'

'Oh my God.'

'Well, there's a reason for Jardine. Anyway: be there at eight tonight. Go to the private dining room on the second floor. We'll have dinner and I'll tell you what I want you to do.'

Gilbert Samson knew the reason he specified the private dining room was that Gilbert Samson would not be allowed into the public one.

'I'll be there, Mr Fraser. And I'll be there sober.'

Lew smiled. 'Look: since I've got so many last names these days, why don't you just call me Lew?'

'Matoon's what I call a nickel-and-dime chiseler,' said Lew that night as he cut into his ham steak. 'He steals a little here, he steals a little there, and it all mounts up. At least, that's the way he operated when I was his moneybag man at the beginning of the war, and I have a theory that crooks don't change their methods. They may operate on a bigger scale, but they operate essentially the same.'

'I think you're right,' said Gilbert, taking a drink of milk and finding it surprisingly good. They were in a small room with Moroccan leather walls hung with paintings of florid nude nymphs gambolling in Arcadian pastures. 'But what do you mean, you were his moneybag man?'

'When I was his aide, he was stashing away his kickbacks under an account that was in my name. He thought I was too dumb to catch on, and when I did catch on, he tried to kill me. Now I believe that after he thought I'd gone to that big kickback in the sky, he must have looked for another patsy. Maybe his next aide. It might be worth while to try and find out who it was. You see, I think it's going to be difficult for us to find any correspondence that will prove anything. Matoon would have to be incredibly stupid to put anything on paper that could incriminate him, although you never know: he *might* have. He did keep that letter from Kemp I told you about. Still, our best bet is to find a witness who can testify. And the best witness would be his moneybag man.'

'Well, I'll look for him. But I'll tell you right now that I think raking over the war scandals is going to be a waste of time. After all, he already was investigated and cleared. And we're talking about seven or eight years ago.'

'I agree, but I want you to try, anyway. I think the way we're going to get him is to build up a picture of what he's currently up to. It'll be a nickel-and-dime picture, or, more likely by now, a hundred-dollar, thousand-dollar picture. It's going to take a lot of time and a lot of digging around, which is why I can't do it – I have to be getting back to Mexico soon. But I'm going to give you my private detectives. . . .'

'The men you hired to find out about me?'

'Right. They're Jim Hall and Frank Gilhooley. Do you know them?'

'Sure. They're the best in the business.'

'I've hired them on a retainer. Any time you want to use them, they're yours. Then there'll be Norbert Wilson, the editor of the *Banner*. He's first-rate, and he'll give you all the help you need – other reporters, whatever. By the way, I want to try to keep this as much under wraps as possible. I have a little scheme up my sleeve that's going to blow the whistle on Matoon soon, so he'll realize the *Banner* is out to get him, but that can't be helped. Also, I don't think I can go much longer before he starts to figure out who Peter Fraser really is. But even though he'll know the *Banner* is doing a hatchet job on him, I don't want him to know how we're going about it.'

'I understand. And how *are* we going about it?'

Lew drank some of his wine. He had purposely ordered wine to see how Gilbert would react. So far, Gilbert seemed happy with his milk and uninterested in the bottle of Burgundy by Lew's plate.

'Matoon,' he said, 'is on several key Senate committees. He's on the Pacific Railroad Committee and the Post Office Committee. Let's take railroads first. Last year I started buying stock in the Saint Louis–Denver Railroad. There were other reasons I bought it – business reasons – but mainly I bought to get on the Board of Directors because Matoon is a director. Well, I bought so much stock they had to put me on the board. I figured once I was in the inner circle, I could see if Matoon was playing games with the stock.'

'And? Is he?'

'No. At least, if he is, I haven't been able to spot it, and I've seen all the books. He may be playing games with Oakes Ames and the Crédit Mobilier boys, but I have an idea he's too smart to get involved with them in too big a way. And here we get back to his *modus operandi*: he's a nickel-and-dime man. That's how he's gotten away with it for so long – he doesn't do anything big. He stays small. So it's my feeling that railroads – where everyone is being a pig these days – aren't where we should look.'

'Which leaves post offices?'

'Exactly. And this is how I suggest you start. I think you should go through the *Congressional Record* and make a list of every bill Matoon has voted for. Every post office, primarily. But everything the government has been involved in in Pennsylvania. Schools, land-grant colleges, dams . . . whatever. Then when you've got that list, go to Pennsylvania and start checking them all out. Who built them? Who owned the land the government bought? Do you see what I'm after?'

'In other words, you think I'll find that Matoon's finger has been in each of these little pies?'

'Call them tarts for a bad joke. Exactly. I'll bet he owns the construction companies, or maybe the lumber-yards, or maybe the land. . . . Now, according to my theory, he may have stolen a little from each project – not enough for people to notice, or, if they did, to get excited about. But when we put together the whole picture, I think we'll see the nickels and dimes have added up to millions. Always by his using his position in the Senate to steer a government project to *his* land, *his* construction company – whatever it may have been. And I think when we plaster this all over the front page, we'll have enough to get a government investigation going.'

Gilbert thought about this as he chewed his steak.

'Well, that *may* work. But the public may not get all that riled up about a conflict-of-interest charge. They more or less assume it in politicians, as long as they don't get *too* greedy.'

'I know. That's why I'm hatching my other scheme. But I'm hoping we may get lucky. I'm hoping you'll turn up something really rotten that we can hang him with.'

'Like what?'

'I don't know. A faulty dam, maybe. Or' – he shrugged – 'I just don't know. But my hunch is if you dig hard enough, you'll hit pay dirt.'

'It's going to take a lot of time.'

'I'm giving you a lot of time. Till next spring.'

'What if we don't get lucky?'

'Then we'll cross that bridge when we get to it. Matoon is slippery, and he's powerful. It's not going to be easy to hang him. But I'm pouring a lot of money, a lot of time, and lot of effort into putting a noose around his fat neck. And I can assure you, Gilbert: he's going to hang.' He refilled his wine glass. 'For a second-rate hotel, this place has a good cellar. This Burgundy's excellent.'

Gilbert watched him drink the wine. Then he raised his glass. 'This milk's excellent, too. You know, you should watch your drinking. It can really creep up on you.'

He finished his milk, and Lew laughed.

'*Touché*.'

34

In the summer of 1870 a flashy, gaslit world came to an end. And the crash of the French Second Empire set in motion a chain of events which resulted in what Victor Hugo called 'The Terrible Year'. On the morning of 4 September there still seemed to be hope – some hope, even if it was a dim one. As Elizabeth Bramwell stood on the beach at Deauville, she kept telling herself there *had* to be hope. She looked at the sprawling hotel standing so proudly above the sand. How wonderful it looked! The Hôtel Beau Rivage was as wonderful as the architectural studies had promised: new white paint, broad verandas, a hundred windows reflecting the brilliant sunshine, towers with splendid banners snapping in the ocean breeze, lawns and gardens, a Chinese tea house, gaily painted bathing machines on the broad white beach. . . . The Hôtel Beau Rivage was everything she and Jefferson Kent had fought and prayed for these past four years. It *couldn't* fail because of this terrible, stupid war! There *had* to be hope!

If it failed, what would happen to Ward's trust fund?

The Philadelphia bankers who had handled the trust had objected strenuously to her letter. To use the trust as collateral for a sixty-thousand-dollar loan to invest in a *resort*? It was not only a dangerous speculation but it was illegal. Which was true. But it wasn't illegal by the much more flexible French banking laws, and nothing in Nicole Louise's will had precluded the executrix of the trust from placing it wherever she wanted. So Elizabeth, using her 'discretionary powers' as executrix, had transferred the trust to the Bank of France in Paris, which promptly loaned her three hundred thousand francs to invest in the Société des Plages Atlantiques, the president of which was Mr Jefferson Kent, Esquire. The officers of the Bank of France had thought the investment much less speculative than had the officers of the Philadelphia bank. How could the hotel possibly not succeed? Wasn't Deauville the most fashionable resort in France? Hadn't it been the favourite investment of the powerful Duc de Morny, the emperor's half-brother, who had poured millions into the town, building hotels, villas, a harbour, a church, public gardens, and, finally, in 1864, completing a railroad to bring the thousands of vacationing Parisians to the sea? Of course, the duke had died the next year, but still Deauville was a great success, and the Beau Rivage would be so also.

The hotel began to go up – the beautiful Hôtel Beau Rivage, with its great public rooms, its smartly furnished suites, its casino, its well-trained staff, its renowned chef, its gleaming tile bathrooms. Jeff's dream slowly became a reality. Its grand opening was announced for 23 July 1870.

On 19 July war was declared.

The war grew out of French fears of the growing might of Prussia, but its immediate cause was a vacancy on the Spanish throne. The Spanish authorities offered the throne to Prince Leopold of Hohenzollern, a member of the Prussian royal house. The Prussian chancellor, Bismarck, had long been itching to go to war with France in order to complete his unification of Germany, and he reasoned, correctly, that the French would not stand for a Hohenzollern on the Spanish throne at their back door. The announcement brought a howl of rage from the French, and Prince Leopold withdrew his candidacy. While this should have been enough to save French pride, certain overzealous members of the French Cabinet wanted Prussia to be made to eat crow. They insisted the Prussian King guarantee that Prince Leopold's candidacy would not be proposed again. The French ambassador went to the resort town of Ems, where King Wilhelm was taking the waters. The king saw him and politely refused to make such a guarantee. When the king sent a telegram to Bismarck informing him of his refusal, the Iron Chancellor, delighted with this opportunity to cause war, published his own version of the king's dispatch, which made the royal refusal seem more harsh than it had been. Louis Napoleon alone saw that war was madness. France, insulted, declared war. The rest of the country was beside itself with excitement. Paris roared with shouts of 'To Berlin!'

When the war was declared on 19 July, Jefferson Kent had had temporarily to postpone the grand opening of the Hôtel Beau Rivage. Surely the war would be won in a few weeks, and meanwhile the seaside resorts were emptying as everyone rushed back to Paris either to enlist or watch events. . . .

But the war wasn't won in a few weeks. Elizabeth and Jeff

agonized as the papers reported defeat after defeat. Each day that the hotel remained closed was costing a fortune. The staff had to be paid, the interest on the loans. . . . In mid-August, a sweating Jeff told Elizabeth he had to open the hotel soon or they would be ruined. But he kept postponing making a decision, hoping against hope that events would take a turn for the better. . . .

Now, on this morning of 4 September, he had gone into town to buy a newspaper while Elizabeth waited for him on the beach. The week before they had been forced to dismiss the staff, and the hotel was shuttered. But not *closed* . . . there was still a chance the staff could be rehired, the shutters opened. . . . There *had* to be a chance. If the sixty thousand dollars were lost, the principal would be taken from the trust, along with interest. . . . How could she have done it? Had she been mad? Had Jeff manipulated her all along, slowly winning her trust, pretending that he didn't want her to invest, and then . . . No, God no! That was unthinkable. No one could be that cynical, that conniving. He was too loving, too kind, too good to the children . . . certainly much better than Ben had been.

She saw his smartly turned-out landau pulling up to the hotel entrance. It was rented, of course, but he had to look the part of the prosperous developer. He got out of the carriage, and she watched him walking down the beach towards her. He played the part beautifully. The well-cut clothes, the confident manly stride, the healthy tan. He looked like a winner.

His eyes didn't. When he joined her, he didn't hand her the paper. He said, 'They got the news in Paris yesterday. There was a big battle up north in a town called Sedan. The French were wiped off the map. The emperor has abdicated.'

She was stunned.

'Then Prussia's won the war?'

'Prussia's won the war.'

He took the folded paper from under his arm and threw it with all his strength out to sea. He watched as it fell into the waves.

'Now what?' said Elizabeth.

'I don't know.' He stuck his hands in his pockets and watched the surf. 'There's no hope of opening the hotel for a while, anyway. Of all the rotten luck . . .'

She put her hand on his sleeve.

'I'm sorry, darling,' she said. 'I know what it means to you. I know what it means to *me*, as far as that goes. But at least the hotel's built, and now that the war's over . . . well, we can open next spring, can't we?'

'I suppose so. But meanwhile, there's no income. And even with the hotel closed, there's a lot of outgo. I don't know if I can hold out through the winter.'

He looked at her and forced a smile. 'Some investment I talked you into, wasn't it?'

She said nothing. The ocean breeze fluttered the flags.

'Shall we go back to Paris?' he said. 'There's nothing for us here.'

She took his arm, and they started walking slowly up the beach to the Hôtel Beau Rivage, which looked so beautiful in the summer sun.

When they arrived in Paris, they found the train station almost deserted.

'Where is everybody?' Jeff asked an aged porter.

'At the palace, monsieur. They're going to guillotine the empress!'

'You must be mistaken,' said a shocked Elizabeth.

The old man grinned a toothless grin. 'We did it before,' he said.

'Well, guillotine or no, get these bags in a cab,' said Jeff. The old man put the luggage on a cart, and they followed him to the front of the station, where there were only two cabs. Jeff hired the first one. After he and Elizabeth were inside, he said to the cabman, 'Number Six, rue la Pérousse. But take us by the palace first.'

'I'll get as close as possible, monsieur,' said the cabman. 'But there's a big crowd.'

'All right. As close as possible.'

'Jeff,' said Elizabeth, 'I'm not sure I want to see this.'

He settled back in his seat. 'It's history, Elizabeth. We

can't pass up a chance to see history. Besides, they won't guillotine Eugénie, but they may sack the Tuileries like they did when old Louis Philippe flew the coop. I wouldn't want to miss a palace-sacking. Might even pick up a few souvenirs. Wouldn't you like to have Eugénie's bedpan?'

'I think I could live without it.'

'You're losing your sense of humour.'

'You're incredible,' she sighed. 'Here we are with the hotel closed till next spring and France turning upside down, and you're not even worried. Happy as a lark!'

'Oh, I'm worried. But you have to take things as they come. We'll survive, and so will the hotel.'

He squeezed her hand.

They got no closer to the Place de la Concorde than a block away. The cab stopped on the Champs Elysées, and Jeff stuck his head out. He whistled.

'Look at that crowd! Come on, let's get out. . . .'

He opened the door and jumped down, turning to help Elizabeth to descend. It was a radiant day, and the trees along the spacious boulevard had never looked leafier. But the roar of the crowd was frightening. '*Dé-ché-ance! Dé-ché-ance! Dé-ché-ance!*'

Jeff climbed up to the driver's seat to get a better view. 'They're not very subtle about what they want, are they?' he said to the cabman.

'They want abdication.'

'Is she in the palace now?'

'That's what I hear. There was a big fracas at the Hôtel de Ville earlier. People say Favre has proclaimed a Republic, but who knows *what's* going on. Anyway, the crowd came over here about three. Don't know how long the National Guard can keep them from pushing through the gates. . . .'

He was stopped by a wild roar from the crowd. Jeff stood up on the seat. 'They're tearing the imperial eagles off the palace fence!' he yelled.

Though he seemed to find it exciting, the voice of the mob frightened Elizabeth. She felt sorry for the beautiful empress who was trapped in the elegant palace, whose world was tumbling in about her ears. No matter how many mistakes the Bonapartes had made, France had had eighteen glittering prosperous years. Did Eugénie deserve this finale? And if the crowd *did* break through the National Guard and got their hands on the 'Spanish woman', as they contemptuously called her, what then? Might not they tear her to pieces? Elizabeth shuddered at the thought.

'Jeff,' she called up, 'let's go home. I'm tired.'

Reluctantly he climbed down and helped her into the cab.

'I don't envy Eugénie,' he said, settling next to Elizabeth.

'Nor I. Poor woman.'

They rode in silence as the cab turned around and headed west towards the rue la Pérousse. As the shouts of the crowd ebbed, Jeff's excitement waned also. He fell into an unusual silence. Finally, just before they reached Elizabeth's house, he said, 'When are the kids leaving Philadelphia?'

'The day after tomorrow. They sail from New York Wednesday.'

'I think you should send your sister a cable and tell her to delay the sailing.'

'But they've been there all summer!'

'I know. But they're safe with your sister. I have a feeling things may get a little hair-raising around here.'

'What about their school? Ward's classes start next week, so he's missing two weeks as it is. . . .'

'Let him miss three.'

'But I miss them, Jeff. I want them home.'

'I miss them too. But I just don't think this is a good time to be bringing children into Paris. There's a lot of trouble in this city. A lot of discontent in Belleville and the other working-class districts. If this new republic gets off the ground, it's going to have a hard time keeping the workers quiet. . . .'

'I think you're being a bit alarmist.'

'Maybe. I still say, send the cable. They can wait another week. Listen: if I didn't love them like my own kids, I wouldn't say this.'

'I know.' The cab stopped in front of her house. 'Well, I suppose you're right. I'll send the cable.'

The cabman opened the door, and she climbed out. Jeff followed her. Since Ward and Pauline had gone to Philadelphia the previous May with Miss Pritchett to spend a summer with their American aunt Deborah – whom they had never met – Jeff had been living in Elizabeth's house. 'Why pay two rents when we don't have to?' had been his casual rationale. Elizabeth had agreed, although rather nervously. It was one thing for her to go to his flat to make love. But to have him move in to *her* house? Even with the children gone?

But, as usual, she had gone along with the charming redhead.

She sometimes asked herself whether she didn't go along with him too easily. But she didn't ask often.

They shared the same bed, and that night after dinner Jeff sprawled across it as Elizabeth sat in the next room brushing her hair. They were both naked.

'I'm going to Nice in the morning,' he called to her, inspecting a hangnail on his right thumb.

Elizabeth continued brushing.

'Oh? How long will you be gone?'

'A couple of days. I saw an ad for a beach property that's for sale in Cap d'Antibes. With the government fallen on its tail, I'll bet the real-estate prices will fall on their tail too. Maybe I can pick it up cheap.'

'But darling, what will you use for money?'

He bit the hangnail off, then spat it onto his naked belly, where he watched it go up and down as he wiggled his stomach muscles. Jeff was full of tricks.

'The same thing I always use: my matchless gift of gab.'

'I don't think real-estate prices are going down *that* far. And we have enough on our hands with the Beau Rivage. You wouldn't *seriously* consider taking on more debts?'

'Elizabeth, you don't understand real estate. The bigger you are, the safer you are. The more you owe, the more important it becomes for the banks to keep you afloat. Our corporation now owns one hotel. It's closed, so we're in trouble. But if we owned *two* hotels, one could balance out the other. See what I mean?'

'No.'

He lit a cigarette. 'We run the Deauville hotel in the summer, but we close it in the winter, right? But if we had a hotel at Cap d'Antibes, we could do the reverse: run it in the winter and close it in the summer. That way, there would be income all year round. Plus we're twice as big, twice as important – and the banks have twice as much to lose if we get in trouble.'

'But the Riviera is a summer resort. . . .'

'So we change the fashion. Make it a winter resort. It's too hot there in the summer anyway. I really think it's worth my going down to take a look. Besides, it will show the banks that we're not defeatist. When things are bad, *that's* when it's important to look aggressive.'

She came into the bedroom and looked at him. 'Really, you would have made a fantastic general. It's too bad poor Louis Napoleon didn't have *you* on his general staff.'

He smiled and held out his hand.

'Maybe I'll offer my services to the Prussians,' he said as she came to the bed and took his hand. 'It's important to stay on the winning side.'

He put his cigarette in the ash tray, then pulled her down into his arms and began making love.

'Let's forget the Prussians,' she whispered as she felt his lips on her neck. 'Let's forget everything.'

He rolled her over and got on top of her. And she forgot everything.

He left the next morning, and two days later sent her a cable saying he was staying in Nice till the end of the week. She was disappointed, but life seemed to be returning to normal after the upheavals of the previous weekend, and the weather was so spectacularly glorious it was difficult not to be in a cheery mood. The Parisians certainly seemed cheery. Despite the mortifying defeat of the French army, despite the fact that the Prussian armies were marching across the lush fields of France towards Paris, where, it was rumoured, they intended to dictate a ruinous peace to the new Republican government – despite all this, the Parisians walked about the boulevards of their beautiful city as if all were right with the world. There was widespread relief that the war was over, even though it had ended disastrously. The Parisians even seemed forgiving to the former imperial family. Eugénie had escaped the mob at the Tuileries and made her way to England with the help of her American dentist, Dr Evans (of all people, thought Elizabeth), and now that she was gone and the throne empty, Paris seemed ready to forgive and forget. Elizabeth began to think that Jeff's fears about bringing the children back had been groundless, and she looked up the sailing schedules to see which ship she should cable them to take. Besides, she knew that Debbie's husband of six months had won a seat in the House of Representatives in a special election, and they were moving to Washington at the end of the month, so she didn't want her sister to be burdened with Ward and Pauline during a move. Debbie's new husband was a lawyer named Courtney Biddle – Debbie had landed one of the Biddles, which was nice – and her sister was, according to her letters, deeply in love, which was also nice. Elizabeth had wanted to go back to Philadelphia for the wedding, but the hotel had held her in Paris. So she sent the children for the summer instead, deciding that it was time Ward and Pauline became acquainted not only with their aunt but also with their country. Ben had not been entirely wrong, she reflected. But now it was time to bring them home, for Paris *was* their home.

Then, Friday morning, a messenger arrived at 6 rue la Pérousse from the Bank of France, bearing a note for Madame Bramwell. Would it be convenient for her to present herself at the bank that afternoon at one o'clock? If so, would she tell the messenger? The note was signed by Philippe de la Gravière. Monsieur de la Gravière was the officer of the bank who handled Ward's trust. Wondering what had happened, she told the messenger that one o'clock would indeed be convenient.

M. de la Gravière was an elegant man whose manners matched the elegant quarters of the Bank of France, which was housed in the sumptuous palace that had been built by the Comte de Toulouse, one of Louis XIV's bastards. When last Elizabeth had seen M. de la Gravière, he had been wearing an imperial beard and moustache like the emperor's. Now, as she was ushered into his office with its *boiserie* walls and gilt sconces, she was amused to see that his thin face was clean-shaven.

'Madame Bramwell,' he said, kissing her hand, 'it is delightful to see you. Please come in.'

He ushered her to a chair in front of his ormolu desk.

'I see something is missing, monsieur,' she said, as he held the chair for her. 'Your beard.'

'Ah yes. Well' – he shrugged as he went around his desk – 'imperials are out of fashion. I thought I would wait to see what styles the Republican government adopts before I grow something new.' He sat down at his desk. 'These last few weeks have been terrible for France. I am sure you, who love our country even though you are an American, have suffered with us also.'

'That is true, monsieur. I stay out of French politics. But I was honoured to have met Their Majesties on several occasions, and I can feel only compassion for them at this terrible turn in their fortunes. And, of course, I am devoted to the Princess Mathilde.'

'Ah yes. You undoubtedly heard that she fled to Belgium?'

'Yes, I heard.'

'And what are your plans, madame?'

'My plans? Well, I have none.'

'You're staying here in Paris?'

'Of course. It's my home.'

'And your children?'

'They have been in America for the summer, but I was planning to bring them back soon. Do you see any reason why I shouldn't?'

M. de la Gravière adopted a very Gallic 'iffy' expression.

'Well, yes and no. I will tell you in confidence – since you are a valued client of the bank – that Herr Bismarck is planning to be very . . . shall we say, heavy-handed? in the peace negotiations. One of his generals is supposed to have said Prussia must teach France a lesson we won't forget for a hundred years. The bank is told by members of the government that Bismarck wants all of Alsace and most of Lorraine.'

'But that's French soil!'

De la Gravière nodded sadly.

'Exactly. The government will never agree to such a humiliation. Consequently, there is a possibility of a stalemate. There is even the possibility that the German armies are marching to Paris at this very moment with the intention of laying siege to the capital.'

'A siege? Of Paris? But that's impossible.'

He shrugged. 'It seems the Germans don't agree. Bismarck may actually try to starve the government into submission. It seems incredible, but I've come to think anything is possible after the past few months. Consequently, madame, I would think twice before bringing your children home. Perhaps they are better off in America.'

'But then' – she hesitated – 'then perhaps *I* should go back to America. At least until the Germans leave. . . .'

The banker nodded. 'Yes, I thought this might occur to you, which is why I thought I should make it *absolutely* clear to you what is the present position of your son's trust fund – particularly since Monsieur Kent told me you might be a little confused.'

She frowned. 'Jefferson's in Nice. . . .'

'Yes, I know. But he was here at the bank last Monday, when he transferred his shares to you.'

'What shares?'

The banker looked concerned. He leaned forward on the desk.

'His shares in the Société des Plages Atlantiques. At the promoter of the hotel venture, he owned ten per cent of the stock. Surely he told you he signed these over to your name?'

'Surely he *didn't* tell me!'

M. de la Gravière squirmed slightly.

'Madame, I was led to understand that you and Monsieur Kent are . . . intimate friends. . . .'

'That's true.'

'And he told me that since he was returning to America, he wanted you –'

'He *what*?'

'You didn't know he's going back to the United States?'

'No!'

'But madame –'

'Monsieur de la Gravière, exactly *what* has Jeff done?'

'Madame Bramwell, your friend has given you his shares in the company. His shares, combined with your own shares, now make you the largest stockholder in the Société des Plages Atlantiques.'

She was in a daze.

'But why wouldn't he have told me . . .?'

'He led us to believe he *had*, madame. As the major stockholder, you are of course responsible for the company's debts. . . . You, uh, *didn't* know that?'

Her daze was turning to fear.

'No . . .'

'In privately financed ventures of this sort, I'm afraid the stockholders are responsible. Of course, the hotel itself and its grounds are worth something, if you and the other stockholders decide to liquidate. But I wanted you to understand that until such time as you, the other stockholders, and the lending institutions involved can agree on a course of action, the Bank of France will be forced to hold the income from your son's trust in a sinking fund. Purely a formality, of course, but we do have a considerable investment at stake –'

'You mean,' she interrupted, 'you're stopping my income?'

'Unfortunately, that is what we are forced to do, madame. At least for the next several months.'

She leaned back in her chair and started laughing. The banker's eyebrows raised.

'Oh my God!' she exclaimed. 'What a joy ride he took me on!'

'I beg your pardon?'

'From the very beginning to the very end – a joy ride! And I believed every minute of it! No, not *every* . . . but practically every. Oh, what a laugh he must be having now on poor, stupid, blind Elizabeth! What a laugh!' She stopped laughing and started to cry. 'Stupid Elizabeth who loved him, who wanted to believe him. . . .'

M. de la Gravière watched with embarrassment as Madame Bramwell pulled a handkerchief from her purse and wiped her eyes. 'I did love him, you know.' She sniffed. 'He was kind to me. And he made me laugh and feel good. . . . He loved the children, too.' She sighed. 'And I was attracted to him. Yes, that was part of it. That was a big part of it. And all the time all he wanted was Ward's trust fund.' She wiped her nose. 'Well, in America we have a word for fools like me. We're called suckers.'

'Monsieur Kent is a clever speculator, madame, and Paris is full of speculators. Alas, like most of them, apparently his heart is in his wallet. Or, more accurately, in someone else's wallet.'

Elizabeth closed her eyes. Jeff – beautiful, red-haired Jeff – gone. Her children in America. Her income reduced to one-tenth its former size. The German army marching to lay siege to Paris.

'Monsieur,' she said, opening her eyes, 'I'm boxed into a corner. What am I going to do?'

'Perhaps, for the time being, nothing. Naturally, the bank will do everything to expedite matters. . . . You *do* have other sources of income?'

'Yes. My husband pays the household expenses and gives me a thousand francs a month. But I'm used to living on much more. . . .'

'Still, there is no immediate financial problem. I would suggest waiting for developments.'

She got out of her chair. 'Yes. I suppose so. Waiting. It's a sad, lonely word, isn't it?'

The banker was up, taking her to the door. 'There are sadder words, madame.' He kissed her hand. 'Believe me, I sympathize with your situation. And naturally, I am at your disposal at any time you need advice or help.'

'Thank you, monsieur. That seems the very least you can do – since you have my income.'

And she left the office.

When she got home, she threw herself on her bed and cried. When the hurt was somewhat out of her, she took the photograph of her first husband off the bed table and looked at it.

Oh God, she thought, why did You take him away from me? Lew dead, Ben gone, Jeff taken off and a swindler to boot. . . . Why?

She kissed the glass and then pressed the picture against her heart as she stared at the ceiling.

For the first time in years, she felt alone. Desperately alone.

10

ACID
1870–1871

35

On the night of 12 October 1870, Peter and Ysabel Fraser's carriage turned into the drive of the Matoon mansion. The weather had turned cold, and Ysabel was wearing the chinchilla-trimmed ermine coat her husband had given her the previous Christmas. Her blood-ruby eardrops accentuated the beauty of her white skin and her sleek black hair. Her black velvet evening dress beneath the white ermine accentuated the curves of her body and slimmed them flatteringly.

'You've never looked lovelier,' said her husband, kissing her hand.

She seemed nervous.

'Lew, I'm frightened.'

'Why? They've invited us to dinner. What's frightening about that?'

'I don't know. I just feel' – she looked out the window at the ugly mansion looming ahead of them – 'afraid.'

He squeezed her hand. 'Don't be.'

The carriage stopped under the porte-cochère, and two Negroes in livery opened the door. Ysabel stepped out, clutching her ermine and her velvet evening bag. Lew followed her up the steps to the etched-glass door, which was opened by a bowing Henry.

'Good evening, Mrs Fraser. Good evening, sir. Turned cold, hasn't it?'

'It has indeed.'

A footman took their coats and Lew's top hat. Then Henry led them to the walnut doors of the grand salon, which he slid open.

'Mr and Mrs Fraser,' he announced.

Rosemary Matoon turned and smiled. She was wearing a light-blue silk gown, and her long train rustled over the floor as she advanced to her guests.

'What a handsome couple!' she said as she extended her hand to Ysabel. 'You should always wear black, my dear. It is so becoming to you.'

'Thank you.'

'I'm sure you've been terribly upset after your robbery. . . . Is there any news of the diamond, Mr Fraser?'

'I'm afraid not. The police have contacted the authorities in New York, where they expect the stone will be taken. There are only a handful of fences in the world who could handle such a big diamond. Of course, the thieves may break it up.'

'What a pity if they do,' said Senator Matoon, joining them. 'A stone of that size and colour is a rarity, a real rarity. How are you, Mrs Fraser?' He kissed her hand. 'May I call you Ysabel? If there's anything I can't stand, it's formality. And we're just plain old Ralph and Rosemary.'

Ysabel smiled. 'Then we're delighted to be here, just plain old Ralph and Rosemary.'

'That's more like it. Say, we've got some nice people here we want you to meet. Come on over and say hello to Justice Wharton and his wife. . . .'

He led them across the room to the Renaissance fireplace in which two giant logs were burning and before which a group of people was seated. Now the men rose.

'Mr Justice Paul Wharton of the Supreme Court,' said Matoon, 'and Ida, his wife. Pete and Ysabel Fraser.'

Mr Justice Wharton was a tall, formal man with a full white beard. He shook Lew's hand, saying, 'Ah, the Mystery Man from Mexico. We've been reading about you in the papers. Delighted to meet you, sir. And you, madame.' He kissed Ysabel's hand.

'I'm afraid the only mystery about me,' said Lew, 'is why the papers seem to find me a mystery.'

'But you're so mysterious about your past,' Rosemary smiled. 'We all think there must be something quite sensational in your background.'

'Actually, there is.' He smiled back. Then he turned to Mrs Wharton and kissed her hand. 'Delighted to meet you, Mrs Wharton.'

'And I'm *thrilled* to meet you, sir!' gushed the older woman in an Ohio twang. 'Dear me, you're every bit as good-looking as I've heard! And I understand you've bought the *Evening Banner*?'

'That's correct.'

'I *do* hope you spice it up a bit! It's such a dull paper, and the society columnist – what's her name? Mrs Allen – is *so* far behind the times. All she writes about are dreary leftovers from the Fillmore administration, and I've always thought the Fillmore administration was dreary beyond description.'

'I couldn't agree more, Mrs Wharton, and I'm trying to find a replacement for Mrs Allen. We also hope to spice the *Banner* up, as you put it, with much more emphasis on the seamier side of politics.'

'Scandals!' she gasped. 'How thrilling! Everyone in Washington will hate you, dear Mr Fraser, except for me. I do *so* believe in a higher moral tone in our political life, but alas, it seems so elusive. And I fear dear Mr Grant – while such a kind man and, of course, a national treasure – seems curiously myopic about what goes on in his own administration.'

'Ida,' said her husband, clearing his throat, 'that will do.'

'Oh Paul, it will *not* do! My husband is always trying to shut me up –'

'Unsuccessfully, I might add,' interjected the justice.

'Nevertheless, a courageous newspaper publisher is *just* what Washington needs,' his wife went on, 'and I, for one, wish you great success, Mr Fraser. If you attack corruption with the zeal I feel certain is in you, you will have in me a devoted – I might almost say a passionate – reader.'

'Thank you, Mrs Wharton. I hope I live up to your expectations.'

Matoon guided him to the next couple.

'And this is the Assistant Attorney General, Tony Poindexter, and his wife, Faith.'

Lew shook hands with a thin young man with a blond beard.

'Glad to meet you, Mr Poindexter.'

'Glad to meet you, sir. And my sympathies about the theft of your wife's diamond. When the thief is caught, my office will be glad to do everything we can to assist in the prosecution.'

'Thank you. But I'm beginning to wonder if the thief will ever be caught. I have an idea he's clever.'

'Criminals are never clever enough, sir. Their moral depravity trips them up in the end.'

'Well, perhaps. This is my wife, Ysabel. . . .'

'How do you do?'

Lew kissed Mrs Poindexter's hand, then Matoon guided him and Ysabel to the last couple.

'And here are two new faces on the Washington scene, Pete. A young man from my own state who won old Phil Gridley's House seat in an off-election. Courtney Biddle, meet Pete Fraser.'

'How do you do?'

Courtney was a nice-looking man in his late twenties.

'And his wife, Deborah.'

Deborah Butterfield Biddle extended her hand to be kissed.

'Oh my God . . .' she gasped.

Lew stared at his former sister-in-law, who looked as if she had seen a ghost.

'Is something wrong, Mrs Biddle?' he said, telling himself to keep cool, keep cool. . . .

She was trembling.

'I'm . . . I'm terribly sorry, but for a moment I thought . . . oh, excuse me. . . .'

She leaned back in the brocade sofa, her hand on her heart. Her husband leaned over her.

'Are you all right, Debbie?' he asked, concerned.

'Yes, really. But this is so extraordinary!'

'*What* is extraordinary, Deborah?' asked Rosemary, who was watching intently.

'It's just that Mr Fraser looks so much like my sister's first husband that it gave me a terrible turn! I apologize. . . .'

'Where is your sister's first husband now?' said Matoon softly. He was watching Lew.

'He's dead. He was killed in the war, at the First Battle of Bull Run. That's why . . . I mean, it was like seeing a ghost! I'm really sorry about causing all this fuss. . . .'

'No, no,' said Matoon. 'No fuss. What was your sister's first husband's name?'

'Lew Crandall.'

'Lew Crandall?' said Matoon, his eyes on Lew. 'Now, isn't that a funny coincidence? I knew Lew Crandall. Knew him well. He was my aide when I was a general. Yes, sir. He died on the battlefield, and as fond as I was of him, I must say it's a good thing he died when he did.'

'Why, Senator!' exclaimed Debbie. 'How could you say such a terrible thing? Lew was a wonderful man, and he died a heroic death. . . .'

'I don't deny that, Mrs Biddle. But the fact is, young Crandall had committed a murder. . . .'

'A *murder*?' she exclaimed. 'Lew? Oh, I don't believe it!'

'Well, I'm afraid it's true, ma'am. He killed a man named Winkler on the morning of December twenty-first, eighteen-sixty.'

'But why?'

'Apparently it was a drunken brawl. It's odd you bring Crandall up, because my wife and I got interested in him lately, and Rosie took a trip to Philadelphia just last week. She even found a witness to the murder – an old darkie named Jethro. Well, Jethro didn't want to talk about it at first, but then my wife told him it was all in the interest of historical research and gave him some money, and the old fella told her the whole story. Even pointed out Winkler's grave in an apple orchard. Rosie checked out the statute of limitations on murder in Pennsylvania, and it turns out there isn't any. So if Pete Fraser *were* Lew Crandall, he'd be in a real fix, wouldn't he? Because he'd have to stand trial for murder.'

Matoon smiled at Lew. *Touché*, you fat bastard, Lew thought. *Touché*. You're using your head.

'Then,' he said aloud, 'it's a good thing I'm not Lew Crandall.'

'Isn't it?' Rosemary smiled. 'But it makes you all that more mysterious. Because, you see, I thought you were Lew Crandall, too. And now so does Mrs Biddle.' She turned to the assistant attorney general. 'What if Mr Fraser *were* a murderer, Mr Poindexter? As assistant attorney general, don't you find that rather fascinating?'

Tony Poindexter cleared his throat. 'Well, of course, murder is always fascinating, if morally reprehensible. But I'm a little confused about who's suppose to be who around here.'

Rosemary laughed. 'Yes, it is confusing, isn't it?'

Henry, the butler, slid open the doors.

'Dinner is served,' he announced.

'Shall we go to the dining room?' said Rosemary, taking Lew's arm. 'I do so want to hear about your newspaper, Pete.' She smiled. 'And your campaign against corruption. You must tell me all about it at dinner.'

And they slowly filed out of the room into the entrance hall.

Debbie Biddle couldn't take her eyes off Peter Fraser, who was seated next to her at the table. During the soup course she said, 'I can't believe what the senator was saying about Lew. I mean, about his having killed someone. If you'd known him, you wouldn't believe it either.'

'What was he like?'

'Oh, terribly nice. My sister was so in love with him – I was too, although I was only fourteen. I had a desperate crush on him! There really is a remarkable resemblance between you and him.'

'After ten years, how can you remember?'

'I remember,' she said softly.

'Where is your sister now?'

'She's in Paris. I'm awfully worried about her, with the Germans besieging the city. But Courtney says she'll be all right because she's an American. I certainly *hope* so . . . but I think it's a blessing her children are with me.'

Lew wiped his mouth with his napkin. 'Oh? How did that happen?'

'She sent them over to spend the summer with us. I'd never even *met* them, and of course I fell in love with them immediately. They're so adorable. . . .'

'How old are they?'

'Well, Ward – that's Lew's son – is almost ten. And Pauline – she's the daughter of my sister's second húsband – is six. They love America. They were supposed to go back to Paris last month, but Elizabeth asked me to keep them here until the trouble is resolved in France, and I must say they were thrilled. They just can't seem to get enough of America. Personally, I think my sister's been wrong keeping them abroad for so long, but she adores France, and –'

'Damn.'

He had knocked over his wine glass, and the wine was dripping in his lap.

'Excuse me. . . .'

He stood up, wiping his trousers with his napkin.

'Rosemary, I'm terribly sorry. . . .'

'Don't worry about the tablecloth,' said his hostess from the end of the table. 'It's white wine. I'm sure it will come out.'

'I got it on my shirt, too. . . .' He went to one of the footmen and said, in a low voice, 'Is there a bathroom?'

'Yes sir, right under the staircase.'

'Thanks.' He started for the door. Rosemary watched him a moment, then turned back to Mr Justice Wharton on her right. The justice lowered his voice.

'What *was* all that before dinner?' he said. 'All that business about this man Crandall? You and Ralph sounded as if you think this Fraser fellow is Crandall. . . .'

'Well,' said Rosemary carefully, 'we're not sure. But we thought we'd let Peter Fraser know we're suspicious.'

'But if he *is* Crandall, and Crandall committed a murder, shouldn't something be done about it?'

'Something *will* be done about it. But first, we have to make sure he's Crandall. Peter Fraser's a powerful man, and a clever one. He's covered his traces well, but he may make a false move, and then . . .' She smiled. 'But meanwhile,' she added, 'we thought we'd make him a little nervous. That's one of the reasons we wanted you and Tony Poindexter here tonight. We thought a Supreme Court justice and an assistant attorney general might make it a little warm for Mr Fraser – if he *is* Mr Crandall.'

'And here I thought you invited me for my ageing charm!'

Rosemary smiled and patted his sleeve. 'We always invite you for your charm, Paul. Which is eternally young.'

The footmen started removing the soup dishes.

Lew ran up the stairs and down the empty hall to the senator's office. He opened the door and hurried inside, closing the door behind him. Then he went to the safe, knelt down, and reached under it. His hand felt the bandage, glued to the safe bottom. He pulled the bandage off and drew his hand back from under the safe. Unfolding the stiff cotton, he looked at the Star of Mexico.

Now pray, he thought. Pray Matoon didn't change the combination.

He turned the dial to the right. He figured the boy would have told his father he thought someone had broken in the house that night. He figured Matoon would have looked in the safe. But since nothing had been taken from the safe, he figured Matoon would have concluded his son had been mistaken.

Apparently, he figured correctly. The tumblers clicked. He opened the safe door.

All the correspondence folders had been removed. So Matoon *had* suspected someone had opened his safe! But then why didn't he change the combination? And why did he remove the correspondence, and not the jewels? For the jewel collection was still there. . . .

He pulled out the wooden boxes and quickly opened them until he found the one holding the diamonds. He stuck the Star of Mexico in beside a pink diamond, then reclosed the box and put it back in the safe with the others. He spotted the envelope holding the Sonora Mining stock, pulled it from the safe, and stuffed it in his pocket. Good. We don't need those any more. They've served their purpose. . . .

Of course, he thought, as he locked the safe. They suspect I'm Lew Crandall, and they assume I'm not interested in the jewels, only the correspondence. . . . Well, they're in for a surprise. And how convenient the assistant attorney general is here to see it all happen! Not to mention a justice from the Supreme Court. . . .

He let himself out of the office, quietly closing the door, then hurried back down the hallway to the stairs, stuffing the cotton bandage in his hip pocket. A minute later, he walked back into the dining room.

'Did you get the wine off?' asked Ralph Matoon.

'Well, it didn't stain much. What bothers me is spilling all that excellent Chablis.'

'Ah, you like that?'

'It's first-rate, Ralph.'

Matoon signalled to Henry. 'Fill up Mr Fraser's glass.'

'Yes sir.'

After he had sat down again, Lew turned to his hostess. 'Ysabel and I are looking forward to seeing Ralph's jewel collection,' he said.

'Good. Ralph will give us a show after dinner.'

It's going to be a damned sight better show than the one he put on *before* dinner, thought Lew. And he smiled as he raised his wine glass.

'Look, Ysabel,' he said, an hour and a half later. 'The emeralds have been carved. Isn't that fascinating?'

The entire party was in the senator's office, standing around Matoon's desk as he proudly displayed the top box.

'Indian,' he said. 'The Indians do the best. That one you're holding came from Bombay. It's got a prayer on it.'

'Exquisite,' said Ysabel, holding up the cabochon emerald. 'I've never seen anything like it. And the colour is so beautiful!'

'May I see?' asked Debbie Biddle.

'Give her the whole box,' said Matoon.

Ysabel replaced the emerald, then handed the box to Tony Poindexter, who passed it to Debbie.

'They *are* exquisite!' she said.

'Aren't they?' said Lew. 'It's a good thing the man who stole my wife's diamond isn't here. He'd go crazy with this collection.'

Matoon laughed. 'Isn't that the truth? And speaking of diamonds, here are mine. All colours.' He unhooked the lid of the second box and raised it. 'Most people don't realize diamonds come in colours. . . .'

'My ring!' exclaimed Ysabel. 'Look! The Star of Mexico!'

She pointed at the box where the enormous blue-white diamond overwhelmed the pink one it was squeezed next to.

Matoon looked down. Then he looked up. His face was a study in bafflement.

'But . . .'

'It's the Star of Mexico!' cried Ysabel, taking the ring out of the box and holding it up. Then she turned angrily on Matoon. 'It was *you* who took it!'

'What do you mean? I didn't steal it!'

'Then how did it get in your jewel collection?'

'I . . . I don't know! This is incredible. . . .'

'Ralph,' said Lew, 'if you wanted it that badly, you could have *told* me. . . .'

'Goddamit, I didn't steal that diamond!' The senator was raging. 'If I'd stolen it, do you think I'd be so stupid as to show it off to its *owners*?'

Lew turned to Tony Poindexter. 'I don't know what to say. I can't believe Ralph would have done this to me, but' – he pointed to the box – 'there it was! What do you think I should do, Mr Poindexter? *Legally?*'

The assistant attorney general looked as baffled as everyone else.

'Well, I'm n-not quite sure,' he stammered. 'This is,

needless to say, highly unusual. . . . What is your explanation, Senator?'

Matoon was still in a rage. He pointed at Lew.

'That son of a bitch *planted* it on me!' he roared.

'Ralph!' said Rosemary. 'Be careful . . .'

'Careful? When this bastard is tryin' to frame me with this phony crime?'

'Sir!' said Mr Justice Wharton stiffly. 'Your language! There are ladies present!'

Matoon fumed. 'He . . . I *know* he did it! He sneaked in here two weeks ago and *planted* it!'

'Now, wait a minute,' said Lew. 'Are you accusing me of housebreaking?'

'Damned right I am!'

'You mean,' said Lew, confronting him across the desk, 'you think I broke into my own house, stole my wife's diamond – and remember, my safe was *broken* into! Why would I have broken into my own safe, when I had a key? Then I brought my own diamond here, broke into your house, and got it into your safe, which has obviously *not* been broken into?'

'That's *exactly* what I mean!' yelled Matoon.

'But Ralph, that makes no sense! Besides, the Star of Mexico is a *bit* noticeable, and you told me you spend hours with your jewels every day. . . . Do you expect us to believe that in two weeks' time, you didn't notice a thirty-carat diamond in your own jewel box?'

'But . . .' Matoon's face was red. 'The wine!' he cried. 'Tonight at dinner! You faked spilling the wine, then came up here and stuck that thing in the safe. . . .'

'How? I don't know the combination to your safe!'

'Well, you *must*!'

'Ralph, this is crazy! Do you have any witnesses to these accusations?'

'My son! My son heard you in here that night! My son heard you breathing!'

Lew shook his head sadly and turned to Mr Poindexter. 'This is embarrassing,' he said. 'Mr Poindexter, what should I do? I don't want to cause unnecessary trouble, but after all, that's a very valuable diamond. And the senator is making some highly slanderous remarks about me. . . .'

'I think,' said Tony Poindexter carefully, 'someone should go for the police.'

'Now wait a minute!' roared Matoon. 'I'm a United States senator, and by God, Tony Poindexter, you'd better not forget I voted for the confirmation of your boss as attorney general –'

'Ralph, shut up!' snapped Rosemary.

Senator Ralph Matoon leaned on his desk. He was breathing heavily. He stared at his wife, then at Mr Poindexter, whose face had gone stony.

'I repeat,' said Mr Poindexter slowly, 'someone should go for the police.'

'I will,' said Mr Justice Wharton. 'Come, Ida. I think you've heard enough of the senator's language for one evening.'

As they went to the door, Mrs Wharton touched Lew's arm.

'I'll certainly read your newspaper tomorrow evening, Mr Fraser,' she said softly. 'I assume this will be your lead story?'

'I think you're right, ma'am,' said Lew. 'And I think this story will sell a lot of papers.' He looked at Matoon.

As Mr Justice Wharton lead his wife out of the room, Ralph Matoon eased himself into the chair, staring at Lew.

'You won't get away with this, Crandall,' he said. 'You may try to pin this phony rap on me, but by God, I'll hang you with Winkler!'

'My name,' said Lew, 'is Peter Fraser. And, Ralph, I'm upset enough as it is without these insane insinuations of yours. Now, sir: I don't know if you stole my wife's diamond or not. But I do know that I'll be talking to my lawyers first thing in the morning. And even though I'm not a vindictive man, I can assure you that unless some *reasonable* explanation is offered me why my wife's diamond was found in your jewellery collection, I'm going to take this into a court of law. I think the public that reads my newspaper is going to *demand* I take it into a court of law! And Ralph, as your former friend, my advice to you at this moment is: *shut up*.' He looked over at Rosemary. 'Do you agree, Mrs Matoon?'

Her face was white, her lips tight, her eyes blazing.

Slowly, she nodded agreement.

Lew Crandall leaned back in his carriage seat and laughed.

'The look on his fat face when he saw your ring!' he exclaimed. 'That was worth a lot, Ysabel. My God, I'll never forget it.'

'And I'll never forget the look on his face when he said he'd hang you for Winkler,' said Ysabel, who was not laughing. It was two hours later. The police had come and taken down everyone's statement. Then they had taken temporary custody of the Star of Mexico, after which the guests had left. The Matoons had been as silent as frost.

'What do you mean?' said Lew.

'That look was *lethal*. That man hates you, darling, and it frightens me.'

'Of course he hates me, and of course he's lethal. I know how lethal he is better than anyone else. But now the world's going to know how lethal he is.'

'You *did* plant the diamond?' she asked.

'Yes, but Matoon's never going to be able to prove I did it.'

'But Lew, can you prove he stole it? After all, he's got a point: if he stole it, he would never have shown it off to us, of all people.'

'It doesn't matter whether I can prove it or not. The point is, every man, woman, and child in America is going to eat this story up for the next few weeks. It's got everything! A "mystery man from Mexico", a thirty-carat diamond, a powerful senator who loves jewels and opens up his collection – in front of a Supreme Court justice and an assistant attorney general, I might add! – and *voilà*! There's the missing Star of Mexico! The public will love it. And don't you think the American public is going to assume Ralph Matoon stole that diamond, whether we can prove it in court or not? Of course they will. And that was the point of the whole thing: to start the campaign against Matoon in the papers with a *flashy* crime – one that will grab the headlines. So that later, when we start publishing what he *really* did, which may not be so interesting to the general reader, the public will be howling for his scalp. And ultimately the public is going to have to hang Matoon. Not God, or me, but the public. The public is going to be made to see how rotten the Matoon Gang is, and the public is going to have to hound them out of office.'

'I suppose you're right. I never really thought of it that way. And as you say, having Mr Justice Wharton and Mr Poindexter there –'

'It was an opportunity I couldn't pass up. And the beautiful thing is, Matoon obviously invited them tonight to put the screws on *me*.'

'What about Winkler? Did you murder him?'

'I killed him in self-defence, which I could never prove. But it doesn't matter. They don't have a case. I told Jethro to tell them whatever he wanted. I knew that the moment they started to suspect I was Lew Crandall one of them would catch the first train for Philadelphia. I'll bet Jethro had fun pointing out Winkler's supposed "grave". He told me he'd use the place he buried his hound dog.'

'You mean, you went to Philadelphia –?'

'Six months ago. Mr Winkler's bones have long since been disposed of, and when you don't have a body, you don't have a murder charge. But I'll admit Matoon handled that fairly cleverly.' He hesitated, then added, 'The big surprise for me, though, was Debbie.'

'Do you think they invited her to see if she'd recognize you?'

'Of course. And that was a sticky moment. *Very* sticky. She told me my son is staying with her.'

She turned to look at her husband. It was too dark in the carriage for her to see his face well, but she could see enough. He looked troubled.

'Ward?'

He nodded.

'He's here, in Washington. I've never seen him.'

'And of course you want to . . .'

'Yes, very much. But I don't know if I should . . . I mean, if he finds out I'm his father – and he will, when "Peter Fraser" stops playacting – what will that do to him? What will he think of me? As far as that goes, what is Elizabeth going to think when she finds out I'm alive? This is the part I've dreaded. Matoon is one thing, but Elizabeth and Ward? That really frightens me.'

She reached over and took his hand.

'You know,' she said, 'how much I've been against your revenging yourself against Matoon. I suppose now I'm beginning to see that you probably have to. But darling, don't feel guilty about your son. After all, what happened wasn't your fault.'

'I know. But it wasn't Ward's fault, either. And he's never had a real father. Oh, I'm sure Ben has been wonderful to him, but it's not quite the same, is it? A stepfather? I don't know . . . I *think* I've done the right thing, or at least everything I could, under the circumstances. But I suppose I'll never really know.'

She didn't say anything for a while. Then, softly, 'Do you ever miss Elizabeth?'

'Yes, in a way. And I miss my past, my childhood. I miss not having been there when my son was born, not watching him grow up, start to talk. . . .' He leaned over and kissed her. 'That's why *our* children are so important to me. And that's why *you're* so important to me.'

She liked that. The carriage drove through the gates of West Wind. As it rattled up the long drive, she said, 'Lew?'

'Yes?'

'I wonder if we shouldn't hire guards. For us and for the children.'

He remembered Burt Thomson. He remembered the flash of the gun and the pain ripping into his chest. He remembered falling backward off the horse. He remembered the world going black. He remembered violence.

'I think,' he said, 'that's an excellent idea. I'll do it tomorrow.'

The carriage stopped in front of the columned veranda,

and Arturo got down to open the door. As Ysabel stepped out, she huddled against the cold night air in her ermines.

'I don't think I'll ever get used to these northern winters, will you, Arturo?' she said in Spanish.

'No, señora. I don't like the cold.'

They went inside the house. As Lew followed his wife up the curving stair, he suddenly said, 'No I've got a better idea.'

She turned to look down at him. 'What?'

'I'm really not needed here for a couple of months. Norbert Wilson knows what I want done to the *Banner*, and it's going to take some time for Gilbert Samson and the others to finish their research on Matoon . . . so why don't we go back to Mexico next week? That way, you and the children will *really* be safe. And it's been six months – there's a lot of business I should be seeing to down there. . . . Shall we go back to Mexico?'

She smiled. 'I won't give you much of an argument about that. I'd *love* to go back.'

He climbed two stairs and took her in his arms. 'You really are very important to me,' he whispered. 'And precious. You're *my* Star of Mexico.'

He kissed her. After a moment, he added, 'Guess what?'

'What?'

'I think the moon is exploding.'

'I *know* it is.'

He picked her up in his arms and began carrying her up the rest of the stairs. She put her arms around his neck.

'You've never done *this* before.' She purred.

'I know.'

He reached the top of the stairs and carried her to their bedroom.

36

The Washington *Evening Banner* had been founded in 1863 by an enterprising New Jersey businessman named Booker who had had the not unintelligent conviction that the nation's capital was a city with great growth potential. In 1866, still convinced of Washington's future, he bought a block on Connecticut Avenue and constructed a four-storey building that incorporated the most modern ideas and machinery in newspaper technology. The building was fire-proof, built of stone and iron, the exterior walls being made of a light olive-coloured stone brought down from Nova Scotia. It boasted an ornamental cast-iron pediment, and marble columns flanked its imposing door. Inside, the press rooms in the basement were the pride of the city. There were two rooms, each one hundred feet by twenty feet, each containing a Hoe's Lightning Power Press, one ten-cylinder, the other six. Behind the press rooms were the steam boilers and the engines. The rear of the building held an enormous paper-storage room, with generous space for folding and mailing.

On the first floor were the executive and editorial offices, plus the city room, with space for twenty desks. The upper three floors held more offices for specialty and feature writers. That all of this was more than adequate for a New York paper with the circulation of the *Times*, *Herald*, or *Tribune* was Mr Booker's boast. However, it quickly became his ruin. He had invested three hundred thousand dollars in his proud building, but Washington failed to live up to his expectations. Far from booming into a metropolis after the excitement of the war years, the nation's capital slowly slid back to something resembling its ante-bellum status of a small Southern town. True, the slaves were gone. True, more and more Americans were coming to Washington to suck at the Federal teat, and they generated business for the hotels, restaurants and gambling halls. But Washington had no industry except government, and government, while becoming somewhat more important to the nation, was still minor compared to the great industrial enterprises that were beginning to reshape America. Mr Booker found the *Banner* draining him. Its circulation hovered around an anaemic eighteen thousand. In 1869 he began looking for a buyer. By 1870 he was so desperate that Lew had been able to buy him out at forty cents on the dollar.

Along with a modern plant, Lew had also acquired an aggressive editor in the person of Norbert Wilson, whom Booker had hired away from the New York *Herald* in 1867. Wilson was a comfortable-looking man in his early forties, a native of Hartford, Connecticut, with a mild, almost sleepy approach to journalism that fooled many people into thinking he didn't care. Actually, he loved the business, had a sharp mind, and when he got his teeth into a good story, like a hungry dog he wouldn't let go until he had swallowed the whole thing. Norbert Wilson knew that his new employer from Mexico had a good story in the malodorous career of Senator Ralph Matoon. And the next morning, when Lew took him into his office and told him about the Star of Mexico, Norbert Wilson's sleepy eyes woke up.

'My God, it's beautiful,' he said. 'I'll write it myself.'

'Put out a special run,' said Lew. 'And don't worry about libel – let the bastard sue if he wants. I want it in big letters: "Senator *Steals*". It's the "steals" that's important. I want the whole country to soak in the idea that Matoon's a goddam thief.'

That afternoon the *Banner* hit the streets of Washington with a headline that screamed: 'Senator STEALS Diamond from Banner Publisher'. Meanwhile, Lew was meeting with his lawyers at the prestigious firm of Boatwright, Cummings, and Yeats. He told them he wanted a suit brought against Ralph Matoon. Their objection that suing a senator was fraught with legal difficulties he cut short. 'I know all that,' he said. 'I know it's going to take time and money. The point is to *harass* him. I don't give a damn if we win or lose: I want us barking at his heels. Later on, I've got some even bigger dogs I'll turn loose on him.'

The only other objection to his tactics came from an unlikely source. When Lew returned to the *Banner* building after meeting with his lawyers, he ran into Gilbert Samson.

'I want to talk to you,' said Gilbert.

'Come to my office.'

The two men went to the office of the publisher, a spacious room overlooking Connecticut Avenue with interior windows affording a view of the city room. Lew tossed his hat on the leather sofa and sat on the edge of his desk.

Gilbert closed the glass-windowed door and said, 'Why the hell are you attacking Matoon *now*?'

'Why not? The man stole my wife's diamond. What am I supposed to do, nominate him for the presidency of the Bible Society?'

'But no one's going to believe he stole that diamond! A two-ton senator climbs through a second-floor window, steals a diamond, then is stupid enough to show it off to the owner?'

'I don't give a damn if they believe it or not – and I'll bet a lot of them do. The point is, we start planting the idea in the public's mind that Matoon's a thief.'

Gilbert came up to him and studied his face. 'This was that scheme you told me about, isn't it? The one you had up your sleeve?'

'That's right.'

'Then *you* stole the diamond yourself.'

Lew smiled. 'Well now, Mr Samson, what a helluva thing to say about your employer.'

Gilbert shook his head with grudging admiration.

'You're one tricky white man,' he said.

'Shifty,' corrected Lew. 'I wouldn't trust me further than I can spit.'

Gilbert chuckled. 'Son of a bitch, I think you're right. Well, maybe you're right about turning this into a three-ring circus, too. It certainly makes better headlines than nickel-and-dime chiselling. But you're not making my job any easier. Before, we had the advantage of secrecy. Now whatever skeletons I might find are going to go dancing right back into the closets.'

'Maybe. But our biggest weapon against Matoon is sensation. If I have to frame a rape on him, I'll do it to keep the public reading. And meanwhile, while we're doing our fancy-dance on the front page, you can keep burrowing around in those closets. What have you found on Mr Kemp and the mysterious hand grenades?'

'Nothing. Mr Kemp is dead. He died two years ago, and the company was bought up by Dupont. The present management claims they keep files for only five years. So forget Mr Kemp and the hand grenades. I told you the war scandals would probably be a brick wall. By the way, are you above bribing?'

'Are you kidding? Me? To get Matoon, I'd bribe, steal – hell, I've already done that – or push a peanut with my nose up Pennsylvania Avenue in my underwear. Of course I'm not above bribing. In Mexico, it's a way of life. Got someone you want to bribe?'

'I may. I've gone through the *Congressional Record* for the past five years – that was fun. My God, reading that makes you seriously wonder about democracy as a viable form of government. Anyway, I've got every bill Matoon proposed and/or voted for. So tomorrow I head for Pennsylvania. It just occurred to me that a little money under the table here and there might be useful.'

'I think you're right. I'll tell Norbert to set up a bribe fund for you. We'll call it the Government Charities Fund. Bribe away!' He got up from the desk and extended his hand. 'My wife and I are going to Mexico in a few days, so I won't be seeing you for a while. I want to wish you good luck. I guess I don't have to remind you how important this is to me.'

'It's important to me, too.' They shook. 'You know,

Christine told me once you were the finest white man she ever knew.'

'She said that about *me*?' He looked surprised.

'Yes, she did.'

'If I was the best white man she ever met, that doesn't say much for the white race.'

Gilbert grinned. 'You said it, not me.'

They both laughed. Gilbert started for the door as Lew went around his desk.

'Send Norbert in, will you?'

'Right.'

Gilbert was at the door.

'By the way,' said Lew, 'congratulations.'

'For what?'

'All that tea you've been drinking.'

'Man, that oolong's got a real kick!'

He went out. A few minutes later, Norbert Wilson came in.

'You wanted to see me?'

'Yes. Take a seat.'

The editor sat down in front of the desk. Lew leaned back in his chair.

'You did a great job on the diamond story,' he said. 'How many papers did we sell?'

'I don't know yet, but I printed twenty-five thousand.'

'I told you I'd like to get our circulation up to thirty thousand by next year.'

'And I told you that's going to be tough. The New York *Times* only has a circulation of forty thousand.'

'But New York has fifteen dailies, while Washington has only four. Anyway, it's a goal. And to whet everyone's appetite, I'm putting through a ten per cent salary increase across the board. Everyone from the janitor on up to you.'

Norbert didn't look displeased. 'That's very generous, Lew.'

'It's not only that I think newspapermen are underpaid, which I do, but also I'm a little nervous about Matoon trying to buy information from some of our employees. The campaign we're going to launch against that man is going to make him desperate. He'll try anything. And if *I'm* not above bribing, I can assure you Matoon isn't. I think the ten per cent salary increase will help keep our people loyal.'

'It sure ought to help.'

'Now, I'm taking my wife and children back to Mexico, I'll probably be back after the New Year, and while I'm gone, I'm leaving everything in your hands. Speaking of bribes, Gilbert may have to do a little of that himself. So you'll see he gets whatever money he needs?'

'Yes sir.'

'I've told you everything I want done with the paper, and as far as I know, we see eye to eye on general policy. Am I right?'

'Absolutely.'

'Good.' He opened the right-hand desk drawer and pulled out a package wrapped in torn brown paper. He put it on the desk and looked at it a moment. Then he looked up at Norbert.

'You know,' he said, 'the war's been over more than five years now, and people are beginning to forget about it. I suppose that's natural, but there are hundreds of thousands of graves out there filled with men who'll never even know who won the damned thing. There was a lot of suffering in that war, Norbert.'

'I know. I was in it.'

'I think it's a newspaper's duty not only to report the news but also to jolt the public's memory whenever possible. I want us to do that, Norbert. I want us to remind the public of the suffering. I want the dead to talk to us, so to speak. I want to publish this.'

He handed the package across the desk. Norbert took it.

'Open it,' said Lew.

He tore off the brown wrapping paper and looked at the battered account book. He opened it and read the first entry:

'January twentieth, eighteen sixty-four. Belle Isle, Virginia. Swapped three onions for this account book with a fellow from Michigan this morning. Thought I'd try to keep a diary to fight off boredom and the blues. . . .'

Norbert looked up.

'Who's Henry Gaynor?' he asked.

'A kid from Indiana,' said Lew. 'I was in prison with him. A nice kid. I guess there wasn't anything unusual about him except that he kept a diary. He died at Andersonville, aged nineteen. Think of that, Norbert. Nineteen years old. Talk about being cheated out of life! And think about the hundreds of thousands of others who got cheated. We were the lucky ones, because we lived.'

'I know.'

'Anyway, I want to publish this in instalments. I've already gotten permission from his parents and arranged to pay them two thousand dollars for the serialization rights.'

'That's a lot of money.'

'Not for Hank Gaynor,' said Lew. 'You read it. I think you'll agree it's worth publishing.'

'I'll start it tonight. Anything else?'

'No, that's it for the time being. Except that I want to tell you again I think you did a terrific job on the diamond story.'

'Well,' and Norbert smiled as he got to his feet, 'the thief did most of our work for us.'

'You mean Matoon?' said Lew, with a wink.

'I've been wondering all day how he got that stomach of his through your bathroom window.'

Norbert carried the diary out of the office and closed the door. Lew swung around in his chair and looked out on Connecticut Avenue. Andersonville, Hank Gaynor. Wirz. Wirz had paid for his crimes. He had been hanged in Washington five years before as the onlookers at the execution chanted 'Remember Andersonville! Remember Andersonville!' Lew wondered how long people would remember Andersonville. He wondered if there would be other Andersonvilles in the future. Already it was being said in books that the Civil War was the first 'modern' war. The first war to use railroads, submarines, machine guns. The first war to be extensively photographed and reported. The first war to have casualties in the hundreds of thousands. Was it also the first war to have atrocities like Andersonville? First in carnage, first in horror? It was important the public didn't forget the horror, and maybe publishing Hank's diary would keep the memory alive.

Lew Crandall remembered the horror. And he remembered Hank Gaynor. Well, Hank, he thought, I told you I'd never forget, and I haven't.

I'll never forget.

As Lew stood at the front door of the pretty brick house in Georgetown, he listened to someone inside playing Mozart. Playing Mozart very well, in fact. In fact, playing Mozart amazingly well.

The door was opened by a coloured maid.

'Yes?' she said.

'Is Mrs Biddle home? My name is Peter Fraser.'

'She's back in the kitchen canning peaches. Come in on and I'll fetch her. Fraser, you said?'

'Yes. Peter Fraser.'

He came in the bright yellow-striped entrance hall and put his top hat on the bench above which hung a large sepia reproduction of Frith's 'Derby Day'. Then he looked into the drawing room, where the Mozart was coming from. To his surprise, a girl was playing. She couldn't have been more than six. She had rich brown hair with rolled-up pigtails, and was wearing a white dress with pink bows. Her booted feet dangled far above the pedals, but she didn't need pedals as her pudgy fingers raced with amazing accuracy across the keys. He watched and listened as she brought the difficult rondo to a flashy finale. Then he applauded.

'Bravo!'

Pauline Bramwell turned on the bench to look at the handsome man with the brown beard.

'Who are you?' she said.

'Mr Fraser. And something tells me you're Pauline.'

'That's right.' She climbed down. 'You shouldn't sneak in on people. That's not polite.'

'I'm sorry. Will you forgive me for not being polite? I'd hate to start things off with your being mad at me.'

She giggled.

'I'm not *really* mad,' she said.

'Good. You know, you play as well as your mother.'

'Do you know my mamma?'

'I knew her once, a long time ago. She's in Paris now, isn't she?'

'Yes, with all those horrid Germans all around her. I wish Clara Schumann weren't a German. I want to be like Clara Schumann when I grow up, but it's awfully hard liking her *now*.'

'Well, I don't think Frau Schumann approves of what's happening in France. Do you know you're a very pretty little girl?'

'Am I?' She blushed.

'Yes, you are. And I'll bet your parents are very proud of you.'

'Well, my mamma is. My father never comes to see us any more.'

'He doesn't? Why?'

'I don't know. I guess he doesn't love us. But we have Uncle Jeff! He's so nice!'

'Who's Uncle Jeff?'

'Mamma's friend.'

Friend? thought Lew. That's interesting. He heard a voice at the door say, 'Mr Fraser! What a pleasant surprise!' And he turned to see Debbie Biddle.

'Good afternoon, Mrs Biddle. I was just listening to your niece's concert. She's extremely good.'

'Isn't she? Pauline, dear, run upstairs to your room.'

'All right, Aunt Debbie. I was very glad to meet you, Mr Fraser.' She bobbed a curtsy.

'And I'm delighted to meet you, Pauline. How about a kiss?'

'All right.'

She ran to him. He picked her up and kissed her.

'Your beard tickles,' she said.

'Well, I may be getting rid of it pretty soon.'

He put her down, and she ran to the door. 'He used to know Mamma!' she said to her aunt as she went out the door.

Debbie looked at Peter Fraser.

'You *knew* Elizabeth?' she asked.

'I was married to her.'

Debbie's look turned to a stare. 'Then you *are* Lew Crandall?'

'Yes. I'm Lew Crandall.'

'But this is fantastic. . . . Why didn't you let my sister know you were alive?'

'It's a long story, Debbie. Shall we sit down?'

A half hour later, he finished. She said nothing for a while. Then: 'But – all other things aside – aren't you and Elizabeth both bigamists now?'

'No. I'm a Mexican citizen. Ysabel and I were married in the Catholic Church, which never recognized my marriage to Elizabeth in the first place. On top of which, my father-in-law – shall I say "arranged"? – to have my first marriage annulled by the Mexican authorities.'

'But what about Elizabeth?'

'As far as she knows, I'm legally dead. No court of law would ever challenge the legality of her marriage to Ben. Which, I gather from Pauline, isn't going as well as I thought.'

'It's not "going" at all. Ben left Elizabeth for some singer named Zaza. Then Elizabeth met an American named Jefferson Kent. . . .'

'That's "Uncle Jeff"?'

'That's "Uncle Jeff". And he swindled her. . . . Oh, Elizabeth has had a very *active* six years in Paris, let me tell you! Sometimes I wonder if she's the same Elizabeth I remember.'

'No one's the same. I'm certainly not.'

She looked at him.

'No,' she said. 'You've changed. It would be a miracle if you hadn't, after what you've gone through. But I dread to think how Elizabeth will react when she finds out you're alive.'

'I do too.'

Debbie sighed. 'Well, I suppose it can't be avoided. Are you going to tell Ward?'

'That's why I'm here. But I wanted to ask you first. Should I tell him?'

'Yes. Definitely. Shall I go get him? He's in the field next door playing lacrosse.'

Lew hesitated. Then he nodded. 'Yes, go get him.'

They both stood up, and Debbie started for the door.

'Debbie?'

'Yes?' She turned.

'What's he like?'

'He's very bright, very sensitive, and very nice. We adore him. I think you will, too.'

And she left the room. He stood by the sofa a few moments. Then, nervous, he went over to the piano and idly hit a note. The past. The present. And now, the future. His stomach was in knots.

He heard a high but firm voice say, 'Mr Fraser? My aunt said you wanted to see me.'

He turned and saw himself at the age of ten. Tall, a bit too skinny, just beginning to fill out. A head of thick yellow hair. Blue eyes. He was wearing dirty pants and a blue shirt. A baseball cap was on his head.

'Yes,' said Lew slowly. 'I wanted to see you very much.'

There was a long silence. Lew found himself at a total loss for words. The boy stood in the door looking at him, waiting for him to say something. Then, happily, Ward did the talking for him.

'Aιe you the Peter Fraser that Senator Matoon stole the diamond from?'

Lew nodded. 'Yes, that's me.'

'Boy, that was some story in the paper! Did he really tie a rope around your chimney and climb through your bathroom window? That must have been *something*!'

'Yes, it was.'

'Are you going to sue him?'

'Yes.'

'Well, I hope you put him in jail. Can you imagine a *senator* stealing a diamond like a common thief?'

'He stole a lot more from me than that diamond,' said Lew.

'He *did*? What else did he steal?'

'You.'

Ward looked at him strangely. 'I don't understand, sir.'

'Your father's name was Lew Crandall?'

'Yes sir. He was killed in the war.'

'No he wasn't.'

The boy looked confused. 'Excuse me, sir, is this some sort of joke?'

'No, it's not a joke. They thought I was dead, but the bullet didn't quite go where it was supposed to.'

He was trying to comprehend. 'You're saying . . . *you're* my father?'

'Yes.'

Debbie appeared beside him in the doorway and put her hand on his shoulder.

'It's true, darling,' she said softly. 'This man is your real father. He wasn't killed in the war the way we've thought all these years. He's lived through some terrible things, but now he's come back. And we're all very glad he's with us again.'

Ward looked back at Lew. 'Why didn't you come sooner?' he said.

'I couldn't. Also . . . I've been very nervous about this moment.'

'Why?'

'I'm afraid you're not going to like me. And I want you to like me.'

'Why wouldn't I like you?'

'At the age of ten, it's a little late to be meeting your father.'

Ward came across the room to him, looking at him with a mixture of curiosity and awe. Then, slowly, he extended his hand. Lew took it.

'You're *really* my father?' he said.

'Yes.'

He watched his son's face, which was beginning to pucker. So was his.

'Look,' said Lew, forcing a smile, 'I'm about to bawl like a baby. But I wish you'd do it first.'

The boy laughed and burst into tears at the same time. Then they embraced.

'I guess,' said Lew, tears rolling out of his eyes as he hugged his son, 'we've got a lot of catching up to do.'

'Yes sir.' Ward sniffed. 'A *lot*.'

37

Zaza d'Antibes looked at the upside-down man in the lens of her Scovill wet-plate camera and said, 'Hold it!' Her model was a Dutch ex-boxer named Bruno Zinh, and he was standing on a sheet-draped platform in her studio-apartment on the rue Dante holding a Roman spear in a martial pose. On his head was a Roman helmet, and around his middle hung the leather flaps of a Roman warrior's girdle. Roman sandals were strapped around his legs. Behind him was a scene-drop of classic Rome that Zaza had borrowed from the Théâtre du Vaudeville.

Zaza squeezed the bulb, then came out from under the canvas cloth and quickly removed the glass plate from her bulky Scovill. Zaza had acquired a passion for photography, but her hobby was hard work. The wet-plate method was the latest development, but it required the ability to move fast. Now she hurried to her darkroom.

'That was nice, Bruno. You can relax while I develop this.'

'Why don't you take some Eskimo shots?' said Bruno, rubbing his muscular arms. 'Then I could put on some bearskins. This place is freezing.'

'Go stand by the fire.'

And she disappeared through the curtains of her darkroom.

Bruno crossed the big and weirdly dramatic main room of the six-room duplex. Like everything else in her upside-down life, Zaza's apartment defied convention. Most Parisians who could afford it rented the bottom floors of houses: they were the fashionable floors for the obvious reason that one didn't have to climb steps. But not Zaza. She had wanted the top two floors of the building. Climbing stairs was good exercise, and besides, she wanted the skylight. And what a skylight it was! A great twenty-foot-square dome of glass and wrought iron that turned the big room into a magic bubble through which the sun could pour during the day and the moon at night – except on December days like this one when wet snowflakes turned the glass panes into rivulets of melting slush. Naturally, the dome offered terrible insulation, and the room was draughty anyway. Zaza didn't mind, but Bruno, clad in nothing but his sandals and leather flaps, was shivering. He stood before the snapping fire and called into the darkroom, 'Don't you catch pneumonia in here?'

'Never.' Her voice came through the dark curtains. 'Cold is good for the lungs.'

'I'll bet your palms think different.'

Beneath the dome was a jungle. Palms, ferns, and tropical trees were everywhere, planted in great clay pots. Among the foliage hung at least a dozen bird cages which she had bought in an Algerian boutique in Asnières. The cages were Arabian fantasies of curled steel, and inside them chirped, dozed, and preened an aviary of parrots, macaws . . . there was even a great, sulphur-crested cockatoo, the *Cacatua galerita*. Then there were the cats. Curled on the big Turkish divans with their mountains of coloured pillows. Dozing on the carpets of the floor beneath the big, *con brio* portrait of Zaza singing on the stage of the Théâtre du Vaudeville, costumed as a veiled houri. Two cats even slept on the iron steps of the spiral stair that led to the small iron gallery that ran around the room beneath the dome. The gallery was a Museum of

Zaza. Sketches of her on the wall. A vitrine holding scores of her hit songs, and some of her better-known props – the Spanish fan she had used in one skit set in Madrid, the fringed halter she had come *so* close to removing on stage during a scene set in a sultan's harem. Zaza's repertory never strayed far from the basic product she was selling to her adoring audience: sex. Or, more accurately, the suggestion of sex. Zaza never went too far in public. She knew that to show it all was to kill the mystery, and that it was the mystery that kept the customers returning for more. Zaza played on the Parisian's lust with the mastery of Franz Liszt playing the keyboard. Like Liszt, she never hit a wrong note in public.

But her private life was something else. Zaza showed it all in private. But there was also a mystery, and it was the mystery that plagued Bruno Zinh. Who stocked Zaza's kitchen with hams, cheeses, and African fruit when the rest of Paris was literally starving? The former boxer knew it wasn't Zaza's current lover, the playboy Prince de Lamballe. Even the prince, who was one of the richest men in Paris, couldn't buy prime cuts of beef like the steak he had seen in Zaza's kitchen two days before, when she had fed her model an excellent lunch after a posing session (part of Zaza's pay to her penniless model was good food. The rest was good sex. She didn't pay money. Zaza had lots of money, and one reason she had lots was that she was a skinflint). But if the Prince de Lamballe and his tony friends at the Jockey Club were buying elephant steaks as a delicacy (Castor and Pollux, the twin elephants at the zoo that had been the delight of a generation of Paris children, had been sold to a butcher), how did Zaza eat steak?

'What's for lunch?' he called, running in place to restore his circulation.

'Is all you think about food?'

'Yes. That's all *anyone* thinks about these days – except you.'

'What would you like?'

'I'd like to know where you get all the food you want when everyone else in Paris is eating cats and dogs.'

'And rats,' called out Zaza. 'I hear the rat-sellers are doing a big business.'

'You didn't answer my question.'

'And I'm not going to, so save your breath. I have a nice, fat chicken. Want a chicken?'

'I'd rather have a steak.'

'You're being offered a chicken.'

'I'll take a chicken.'

Stingy bitch, he thought. And the rotten Germans. When would this goddam siege be lifted so life could go back to normal? Wondering if the stingy bitch knew a rotten German (how else could she get food?), he picked a newspaper off the floor and scanned the front page. Nothing but news of the siege. What other news got into Paris? The city was cut off from the rest of the world by the Prussian armies that had entirely encircled the metropolis, creating a ring almost fifty miles in circumference. No one had thought it really possible, but the Germans seemed to thrive on the impossible these days. For three months now they had sat out there watching the city of two million souls be reduced to eating rats – although, with the Parisians' flare for cuisine, some ingenious recipes for rat had been concocted, and rat cookbooks, offering such delights as *salmis de rats*, were selling well. Three months! The siege had begun as something of a lark, then became a bore, and now a misery.

The commander of the French forces in Paris, General Trochu, had hoped the Germans would attack and had put thousands of men to work digging trenches in the Paris suburbs and throwing up barricades and fortifications. France's best hope, so the reasoning went, was that the Germans would try to storm the well-fortified city and, in the process, be decimated. But the Germans didn't attack. They sat and waited. Three months!

As the days passed, restlessness set in among the volatile Parisians; and, as the food supplies dwindled, drunkeness increased. Somehow, the supply of wine in the city seemed inexhaustible, and the thirty sous a day the government was paying the civilian-recruited National Guard bought plenty of cheap wine. Perhaps the most frustrating result of the siege was the lack of news. Balloons could carry messages out of the city, but no one seemed able to bring a balloon *into* the city, so rumours spread like brushfires: A great tunnel was being dug beneath the German lines to bring in a provincial army. The workers in Berlin were revolting against the king's government. The Germans were dying of cholera or smallpox or whatever. . . .

To make up for the lack of news, almost fifty newspapers sprang into print. Most of these were hand-printed, no more than leaflets, but they gave voice to the frustrations of the city, and almost all of them began to attack – not the Germans, but the government. Why was nothing being done? Why didn't the National Guard attack the Germans? Was France so weak and leaderless that it couldn't go on the offensive? And soon the radical papers began asking even more embarrassing questions. Such left-wing journals as *La Patrie en Danger*, edited by Diego Sanchez's hero, Auguste Blanqui, and *Le Réveil*, edited by Charles Delescluze, another professional and highly respected revolutionary, began charging that the lack of initiative on the part of the French authorities was a plot. The Paris bourgeoisie was more interested in saving its property from the destruction of war than it was in defeating the Germans. The Paris bourgeoisie was more terrified of the 'Red' regiments of the National Guard than it was of the besieging Huns. These papers began calling for a *levée en masse*, a rising of the Paris mob in the spirit of the Glorious French Revolution of 1789. The poor Parisians were the only true patriots. The poor Parisians alone could save Paris, save the Revolution, save French honour and pride. For the first time, a word began being whispered that chilled the blood of the middle class. A word that had been born eighty years before. A word that was mystical and magical. The word was 'Commune'. The Commune of 1792 had saved France from the foreign invaders that had tried to destroy the first revolution. A new Commune was needed now.

Meanwhile, the herds of sheep and oxen that had been brought into the Bois de Boulogne before the siege began dwindled to nothing. A wild inflation gripped the city, along with an equally wild terror of the unknown: what would happen? Was the world coming to an end? People began calculating the distance between their houses and the German guns that were ringing the city, and mattresses were lashed to rooftops to soften the impact of Herr Krupp's shells, which everyone assumed would, sooner or later, begin raining destruction on Paris. Wild schemes were hatched by the more ingenious to defeat the invaders. One scientist proposed bombarding the Prussians with bottles filled with smallpox germs. It was suggested that that staple of French cuisine, snails, could be trained to crawl messages through the German lines. A madman named Jules Allix proposed dipping pins in Prussic acid and arming the Paris women with these lethal *doigts Prussiques*. Everyone searched for some 'superexplosive' that would blast the Germans off the face of the earth. And now Bruno Zinh spotted the best suggestion of all.

'It's wonderful!' He laughed.

'What's wonderful?' called Zaza.

'Here in the paper! Someone has suggested a musical machine gun!'

'What in God's name is that?'

'It's a gun that plays Wagner and Schubert to lure the Germans out of their trenches. And then BANG! It mows 'em down.'

'Yes, that is wonderful,' said Zaza, coming out of her darkroom. She was wearing white trousers with a ruffled blouse and white satin pumps – for, like everything else in her life, Zaza's clothes were also upside down. In an age of feminine frills and wide skirts, Zaza – like George Sand before her – often dressed like a man. It had caused widespread publicity and packed more customers in at the box office. 'Want to see yourself?' she said. 'The picture came out well.'

The picture had come out very well, and Zaza had reason to be pleased with her expertise. The whole process could take no longer than ten minutes, which was why speed was so vital. First, she had to clean the glass plate in collodion, a mixture of sulphuric ether and ninety-five-proof alcohol.

Then she had had to bathe it in nitrate of silver. When the plate was ready for exposure, she had put it in a holder and placed it in the camera. Then she shot the picture, removed the plate, and returned to the darkroom for immediate development. The developer was sulphate of iron solution and acetic acid. After developing the plate, she had washed and fixed it with a solution of cyanide of potassium, which also removed the excess silver. Then came a final washing, drying, and varnishing.

Now she handed the plate to Bruno, who had come over from the fire place. He looked at himself. Every line, every muscle, even every hair of his body was in sharp detail. But Bruno wasn't interested in the photography.

'God,' he said, 'I'm beautiful.'

She laughed. 'That's your opinion.'

'But I am! I'm a Greek god!'

'You're a Dutch bum, and you know it. What do you want first, your lunch or your sex?'

He handed the glass plate back. 'Lunch.'

'All right. Let's go down to the kitchen. And take off that ridiculous helmet.'

'Don't you think I look like Mark Antony?'

'You may have his body, but you've got the brains of his horse. Come on.'

She went down the narrow wooden stair that led to the bottom floor of the apartment. He removed his helmet and put on a black robe, then followed her down. In the small kitchen, she had set a cold chicken on the wooden table along with a bottle of wine. Now she started carving the chicken as Bruno pulled up a chair.

'Why are you always saying I'm dumb?' he asked, pouring a glass of wine.

'Because, my sweet Bruno, you are.'

'I'm not so dumb that I haven't figured out that that chicken is delivered by a German grocery boy.'

'Oh? So you think I get my food from the Germans?'

'Where else? I hear they eat like kings at Versailles.'

'They should. That's where King Wilhelm is.'

'I mean the soldiers. The pickelhauben. They eat France

clean while Paris starves. You have a German lover, don't you?'

She smiled. 'Yes. His name is Bismarck. Want a leg?'

'I want the whole damned thing.'

'Then take it. I'm not hungry.'

'You're the only person in Paris who isn't.'

She sat down opposite him and poured a glass of wine as he picked up the whole chicken and started devouring it like a dog.

'You know,' he said between bites, 'if Paris found out the Great Zaza had a German lover, they'd tear you to pieces.'

'That's why I don't have a German lover. I've got *money*, dumb Bruno. And money can buy you anything.'

'Money can't buy steak. And you had a steak in here the other day. I saw it.'

'Last week, that "steak" was a wild boar in the Jardin des Plantes. I had to pay fifty francs a kilo for it, and it was stringy. Now listen: if you don't like this job, that's fine with me. There are plenty of out-of-work Greek gods around I can hire to pose for me. And if I hear any more about this phantom German lover, you can turn into the Flying Dutchman and fly right out of my window. *Verstehen Sie*?'

He looked at her over the half-eaten chicken and nodded. 'All right.'

'That's better.' She removed the lid of a small wooden box and took out a slim black cigarette. 'How's my old boy friend?' she asked, lighting it.

'Mr Bramwell? Same as always. Drunk.'

She exhaled. 'Poor Benjie. I almost feel sorry for him. Does he ever go out?'

'Oh yes. At night. He goes out and drinks.'

'Does he bring home whores?'

'All the time. Young ones.'

'He likes 'em young. That was his problem. He's a strange man. In some ways, he was sort of sweet. But he was terribly sad. I couldn't take more than six months of *that*, no matter how much money he gave me.'

'And he gave you a lot.'

'They *all* give Zaza a lot. Except you, Bruno. You get it free.'

'You think I'm handsome.'

She smiled. 'Oh sure. I never understood why Benjie didn't go back to his wife after I left him.'

'I think she had a lover.'

'You're not serious?'

'That's what I heard.'

She leaned back in her chair and laughed.

'What's so funny? he said.

'Oh, life. Madame Bramwell, the outraged wife, who caused such a stir in the Grand Seize! And she ends up with a lover. God, the Americans are no different than anyone else.'

'Did anyone say they were?'

'Oh, *they* do. They do all the time.'

'Well, he's the only American I've ever known. And I just see him when he comes in and out of the house. He never even says hello.'

She leaned across the table and smiled at him.

'But *I* said hello, didn't I?' she said.

He put down the carcass of the chicken and licked his fingers. 'Yes.'

'Hello Bruno, you big hunk of muscle. How's that big muscle between your legs? Ready for a little exercise?'

He grinned. 'Yes.'

'Then let's go back upstairs.'

She got up from the table and dropped her cigarette in her glass of wine.

Upstairs, she took off her clothes, kicking her pumps across the room, then peeling off her white trousers and throwing them on the floor. Then her blouse. She wore nothing underneath. She came over to Bruno, who was sitting on an ottoman still unstrapping his Roman sandles. She put her fingers in his brown hair and jerked his head back. He looked up at her. His face was anything but handsome. He had a pug nose, and there were fight scars all over it. Poor cretin, she thought. He can't stand to look in the mirror. Or maybe he does look in the mirror and keeps telling himself he's good-looking. She kissed his nose.

'Greek god my ass,' she said. 'No one ever saw that face in a museum.'

'I'm handsome.'

'All right, if you want to think so.'

'I *am* handsome. It's just that my nose got ruined in a prizefight.'

'Well, your nose isn't your meal ticket. Come on, hurry it up. I've got a rehearsal at two.'

'Are the theatres opening again?'

'There's talk about it. Anyway, I'm learning some new numbers. I've got a great new song – listen.' She went to one of the pillow-covered divans, humming a tune. 'Isn't that catchy?'

'Yes, it's nice.'

She lay down on the divan on her side, curling her beautiful legs under her and propping her child's face on her fist as she watched him take off his Roman girdle. When she saw his penis, she giggled.

'If Paris runs out of cats and rats, that thing could feed .he city for a couple of days.'

'At least. And your mouth would be there first.'

He came over to the divan and stood in front of her, his hands on his slim hips.

She sat up, kneeling on the divan, her eyes on his organ. Then she curled her arms around his thighs, leaned close, stuck out her tongue and started licking his penis. She licked it all over, then she licked his testicles. The penis grew stiff, glistening and slimy from her saliva. She removed a hair from her tongue, then opened her mouth and slid it over the crown of his penis. Expertly, she worked him. Slowly at first; then, as she felt him responding, more quickly, applying more pressure. He was panting now. She pushed her tongue against the base of his cock, engulfing almost the whole thing, or as much as she could get in her mouth.

When he exploded, she continued to apply the pressure. He was groaning, but she didn't let go. She started working him again. Again, he felt his organs responding. Again, he came in her mouth.

This time, she let go. She swallowed it all, then leaned back in the pillows and opened her arms.

'Now kiss me,' she said, with a smile.

And he did.

38

Two days after Christmas a French colonel named Heintzler and his wife sat down to a breakfast party for several friends at Avron, to the east of Paris. They had just opened their napkins when a Prussian black powder shell fell through the roof and blew all but the host and hostess to eternity. Thus began a new terror as the great German guns began to bombard the City of Light. Every night, starting at about ten, the shells would begin falling, and they wouldn't stop until three or four in the morning. Even though Elizabeth's house on the rue la Pérouse lay out of the shelling zone, the ceaseless noise, the booming and explosions and rumbles, made her nights a sleepless misery.

By the second week of January she was confronted with yet another horror. As if God were compounding the miseries of the Parisians, to the hunger and the devastation of the shelling was added the coldest winter in living memory. Supplies of coal gas had been exhausted by November, and the price of wood had become exorbitant. By January crowds of the starving poor were swarming out of Belleville to attack the trees of the fashionable boulevards, and board fences around the gardens of the rich were stolen in the night. The magnificent trees in the Bois de Boulogne were cut down for fuel. And when most of the trees were gone, saddened families, shivering in their shawls, began eyeing their furniture.

Thus it was that on 14 January 1871, the beginning of the eighteenth week of the siege, Elizabeth Bramwell stood in the drawing room of her icy house and looked at her piano. Then she looked at Gustave, her husky coachman, who was standing next to her. Gustave and Henriette, her maid, were the only two servants left in the house, since she had long since been forced to dismiss the others.

'Well, Gustave,' she sighed, 'the piano never made me a sou, but at least it can keep us warm. So kill it.'

Gustave raised his axe over his head and swung it with all his strength. The blade crashed into the gleaming top and, with a sad 'thunk' of a chord, the Pleyel died. An hour later, it had been converted to neatly stacked logs, and the three of them huddled around the fire in the kitchen. All the top floors of the house had been closed to conserve what little heat there was.

Elizabeth's bed had been moved to the dining room. Gustave and Henriette, who had been sleeping together furtively for months in the servants' rooms on the top floor, now slept together openly in the kitchen. Elizabeth didn't care any more. They were young and in love. Besides, they were practically her only company. The horrors of the siege kept her in her house most of the time.

'Does madame have any ideas for dinner?' asked Henriette rather timidly. Menus had become a delicate subject.

'Well,' said Elizabeth, 'I refuse to eat horse again this week. I caught myself whinnying the other day.' Henriette giggled. 'What about an omelette?'

'I bought four eggs this morning,' said Gustave, who did the shopping. 'But I don't guarantee how fresh they are.'

'Then we'll have a nice, stale omelette and a bottle of wine.'

'Does madame ever wish she were back in America?' asked Henriette.

Elizabeth smiled. 'Oh no. And miss all this fun? The coldest winter in forty years? No food? Bombs from the Germans every night to lull us to sleep? What could Philadelphia possibly offer that could even compare to all this delightful entertainment?'

'Is it true,' asked Gustave, 'that in America the streets are paved with gold?'

'No. A lot of them are paved with garbage. But it's a wonderful country. You'd like it.'

Gustave eyed his sweetheart. Then he took a deep breath. 'Henriette and I were talking about . . .' He stopped, his face turning red.

Elizabeth looked at him. 'About what?'

'Well, about perhaps going there some day.'

'Why, that would be wonderful!'

'That is, if we come out of all this in one piece. And, uh . . . if we ever could get the money together.'

'You see, madame,' said Henriette, 'Gustave and I are planning to get married some day. *Aren't* we, Gustave?'

She shot him a look.

'Oh yes.' He nodded quickly.

'And we thought we could make a better life for ourselves in America. That is, if we could borrow the money from someone. Of course, it's difficult when you're poor to borrow. . . .'

They were both looking at her.

'You know, Henriette – and you too, Gustave – I'd *give* you the money if I had it. But I just don't have it right now. It's all I can do to keep the three of us going.'

Henriette exchanged looks with Gustave. Then she said, 'Well, we were talking about *that*, too. And we wondered if perhaps you went to . . . Monsieur Bramwell. . . .'

'No!' said Elizabeth firmly.

'But madame, he is very rich. And perhaps if you told him how bad things are here, he would perhaps increase your allowance. . . .'

'No. I won't go crawling to him. He walked out on me.'

'But that was three years ago!'

'It doesn't matter. Now, I refuse to discuss it.'

'Very well, madame. But we thought we'd mention it. The food prices are getting *very* high.'

Elizabeth stared into the fire. Well, why shouldn't she go

see him? Could she afford to be so proud? God knows, the thousand francs a month melts like snow in June. . . .

'Oh, all right,' she sighed, 'I suppose it's worth a try. But how will I get there, since we ate our only form of transportation?'

Gustave shrugged sadly. 'I think madame will have to walk.'

Elizabeth nodded wearily as she got out of her chair. 'That's what I was afraid you'd say. All right, get me my sables.'

Gustave got up and pulled the horse blanket off his and Henriette's bed. Then he hurried to Elizabeth and put it around her shoulders.

'It's very chic, madame,' said Henriette.

Elizabeth laughed. 'Oh, Monsieur Worth would be stunned with admiration if he saw me! But – since the sables are in hock, along with everything else – Madame Bramwell will pay her husband a call in her horse blanket. And if *that* doesn't break his heart, nothing will.'

'Good luck.'

'I'll need it. I'll be back for dinner – for what *that's* worth.'

She left the kitchen and walked through the house to the front door to let herself out into the cold.

Outside, the wind was sweeping through the street, blowing up little whirlwinds of snow that were left over from the storm of three days before. She started towards the rue des Acacias, which was about a half mile distant, next to the Bois. Perhaps a ten-minute cab drive, but there were few cabs now and few carriages, most of the horses having been eaten. Even the thoroughbreds at the race tracks had been auctioned off and turned into *culotte de cheval à la mode* and *consommé de cheval*. How weird it all was, she reflected as she made her way across the icy street. And yet, in a way, she wouldn't have missed it. She could make light of her problems to Henriette and Gustave, even though the problems were monumental. Still, she took a certain pride in her ability to cope with them. The desperate loneliness she had felt after Jeff left her – as well as her despair at having

Ward's trust fund tied up in what now seemed a hopeless tangle as the finances of the plagued Société des Plages Atlantiques foundered on the rocks of war and the siege – all that now seemed somehow petty in comparison to the basic human needs of keeping warm and keeping fed. A year before, the thought of axing her piano into firewood would have horrified her. But today she had watched Gustave do it with barely a twinge of regret. Pianos were replaceable. Everything was replaceable except life. She was surviving in the most nightmarish of all possible worlds, and of that she was rather proud.

The once busy streets of her district were now eerily empty. It wasn't only the cold and the lack of transportation that kept people inside their houses – though that of course was part of it. It was also the fear of running into the gangs of the poor who had taken to roaming the streets of the fashionable districts. Some of them were only looking for whatever they could scavenge in the way of food or fuel. But others were known to attack people who looked worth attacking. At night no one went out; but she had heard stories of people being mugged even in the day. Often the muggers would accuse anyone well dressed of being a Prussian spy and then attack, though everyone knew this was a ploy. For that reason, anyone who had to go out took care to look as shabby as Possible. Paris, which such a short time before had been the fashion capital of the world, a city noted for its flamboyance and ostentation, now looked like a city of beggars. Elizabeth felt safe in her horse blanket and plain faded dress. Even if she hadn't pawned her sables, she would never have worn them.

The wind was biting her cheeks now, and she hugged the blanket around her. She had walked four blocks and encountered almost no one. A woman about her age carrying a bundle of twigs under her arm. An elderly gentleman she recognized as one of the better known *boulevardiers* of the previous regime, now still strolling his boulevard but looking calculatedly seedy in a frayed coat he probably had borrowed from his coachman. He recognized Elizabeth and tipped his worker's cap as if it were his accustomed top hat.

'*Bonjour, madame.*'

'*Bonjour, monsieur.*'

He strolled on. Eerie.

She was halfway to Ben's house when she passed a small private hospital run for the rich by nuns. It was a red brick building, rather grim by Paris standards, with tall windows that she was gratified to see were sparkling clean. Paris had become filthy, but it was nice that the Sisters of Charity refused to compromise their standards of hygiene. She saw a young man with a short black beard looking out one of the ground-floor windows. She was just thinking that it was a nice face when suddenly she slipped on a sheet of ice. Her feet zoomed out from under her, and she felt herself sailing. She landed on her back, her head whacking against the sidewalk. For a moment, she saw stars. Then she sat up, gingerly feeling the back of her skull. Her thick hair and the wool scarf she had tied around her head had cushioned the blow, but her skull was throbbing and she thought she would probably sprout a nice bump before long.

She started to get to her feet but slipped again, this time landing on her rump and twisting her left ankle. She looked at her boot, wondering if she had broken a bone. All she needed was a broken ankle.

Skating over the ice on her tail to an iron bench, she grabbed it and managed to get to her feet. She leaned against the back of the bench and put a little weight on her left ankle. It hurt, but she doubted it was broken.

'*Madame, permettez-moi de vous aider*,' said a voice with a heavy American accent. She looked up to see the young man with the short black beard running down the steps of the hospital. He hit the ice, slipped, went up in the air, landed on his back, and slid all the way to the bench. He looked so amazed that Elizabeth burst into laughter. She clapped her hand over her mouth, realizing she was being anything but polite to her would-be Galahad. He started to get to his feet, but, like Elizabeth, he again slipped. This sent her into new gales of laughter. She sat down on the bench and held out her hand.

'Hang on,' she said in English.

He looked surprised. 'How'd you know I was an American?'

'Because your accent's even worse than mine. Did you hurt your back?'

'I'll live.'

He took her hand and managed to make it to the bench, where he sat down next to her. He looked at the palm of his right hand, which had been skinned.

'Are you sure you're all right?' she said.

'Oh sure. I should have put on my gloves. . . . How about you?'

'I twisted my ankle, but I don't think I broke anything. And I'm sorry I laughed.'

'That's all right. I must have looked pretty stupid. Want me to look at the ankle? I'm a doctor.'

'I don't think that's necessary.'

'You never know with ankles. My office is on the first floor. It'll just take a minute. That is, *if* we can make it across the ice.'

'That's a big if.'

Hanging on to each other, they made it to the steps of the hospital. Then Elizabeth, leaning on him, started hobbling up the steps.

'Does it hurt?' he asked.

'When I put pressure on it.'

'A lot?'

'No.'

'Probably sprained it slightly. My name's Blake Foster. What's yours?'

'Elizabeth Bramwell.'

'You must be as crazy as I am to be in Paris.'

'I live here.'

'And I study here. There we go – the last step.'

He held the door, and she limped inside. He followed her, closing the door. They were in a high-ceilinged, tile-floored entrance hall. On one wall was a crucifix; opposite hung an official portrait of Eugénie. Elizabeth looked at it.

'Isn't that a bit out of date?'

'The empress used to be the patroness of the hospital,

and the nuns refuse to take her down. We can go in Sister Antoinette's office. I'm using it too, for the time being.'

He opened the door, and Elizabeth hobbled in to a small office, starkly furnished except for a portrait of Pope Pius IX. He helped her to a black sofa, where she sat down. She noticed that her breath, like his, was frosting in the air, just as it did outside.

'I take it you have no heat either?' she said.

'None. It's terrible for the patients. Not very good for me, either. Now let's look at that ankle.'

He knelt down and began unbottoning her left boot.

'Does that hurt?' he said.

'A little. Where's Sister Antoinette?'

'Upstairs in the ward. I was about to go to the American Ambulance when I saw you fall. You took quite a bump. I'll just slip this boot off nice and easy. . . .'

Gently he removed the boot. Elizabeth cringed as she realized there was a hole in the toe of her white silk stocking. He seemed to ignore it as he began feeling her ankle.

'Tell me what hurts.'

'Nothing so far.'

'It's swelling a little. I'm going to turn it. . . .' He twisted it slowly to the right.

'Ouch.'

'Bad?' he asked, looking up.

'Not too bad. I take it you're helping out at the American Ambulance?'

'Yes. Dr Swinburne's doing a wonderful job there. It's a funny thing to have patients *trying* to get into your hospital, but the French wounded beg to be taken to the American Ambulance. And no wonder! The French hospitals are losing four out of five amputees partly because they won't open windows. It's ridiculous. They haven't got any heat anyway, but they keep the windows closed, and the result is their hospitals are pesthouses. I'm going to put a bandage on this, then I think you'll be all right.'

He got up to go to a steel medicine cabinet with glass doors. As he opened the doors, she watched him. He was a little taller than she, slender, about twenty-eight, she guessed.

He spoke well with what she thought was a New York accent. He was wearing a rather shabby wool coat and had a red scarf wrapped around his neck, the end of which hung down his back.

'What does fresh air have to do with saving lives?' she asked.

'We learned in our war that what kills amputees is not only the gangrene but septicaemia, and septicaemia is caused by germs. Fresh air would help get the germs out, but the French won't believe it. Of course, a little cleanliness would help, and our French friends aren't too particular about keeping the wards clean. Either physically or morally. You may not believe this, but I've seen some nurses who are . . . well, how can I put it delicately? Retired *lorettes*.'

'Prostitutes?'

He came back with a bandage. 'That's putting it indelicately, but that's what I mean. And some of them aren't exactly retired, either. Their interest in the younger patients isn't entirely medical.'

'But that's shocking!'

'Isn't it. I'll put this around your stocking. . . . It's nice to see I'm not the only American with holes in my socks.'

She laughed. 'I was hoping you wouldn't notice.'

'Sort of hard not to. All right, now stand up. Here . . . lean on me. . . .'

She got to her feet.

'Put your weight on the foot.'

She did.

'How's that?' he asked.

'You're a miracle worker! It's much better.'

'Good. Sit down and I'll put your boot back on.'

She obeyed. As he slipped the boot on, he said, 'You should walk on this as little as possible for a few days. Where do you live?'

'On the rue la Pérouse.'

'That's too far for you to walk. I'll give you a lift.'

'You have a horse?' she asked, impressed.

'The sisters do. They let me use their buggy.'

'Actually, I was on my way to the rue des Acacias. Could you take me there instead?'

'I could, but how would you get home?'

'I don't know if my husband has a horse, but I'm sure he can arrange something for me.'

He stood up. 'Your husband doesn't live at the rue la Pérousse?'

'We're separated.' She got to her feet. 'I can practically do a jig,' she said.

'Well, don't.'

'You've been very kind. Could I . . .?'

He shook his head.

'On the house,' he said. 'The buggy's in the back.'

He went to the door and opened it. She walked out into the hall, limping slightly. Then he led her down the hall towards a rear door. She passed a number of closed doors with numbers on them. As they passed the door marked 3, someone started pounding on it. Blake Foster stopped.

'Excuse me a minute,' he said, pulling a key ring from his pocket. He chose one of the keys, unlocked the door, and pushed it open. She saw two hands jump out from behind the door and grab his throat.

'What's wrong, Ninon?' he said, calmly removing the hands. The bare arms looked wrinkled.

She heard a voice begin to sob. 'You're trying to poison me!'

Though Elizabeth couldn't see behind the door, it was the voice of an old woman.

'There was arsenic in my soup at lunch! You're trying to poison Ninon!'

'I'll admit the soup *tasted* like poison, but no one's trying to poison you. And we don't want any more pounding on the door. Understand?'

He was firm but gentle, as if talking to a naughty child.

'Yes.' Ninon sounded contrite.

'That's better.'

'Will you tell Sister Antoinette to stop putting snakes in my bed?'

'There aren't any snakes in your bed.'

'Yes there was! Last night! A ten-foot-long cobra! He almost bit me! Sister Antoinette put it there because she hates all of us.'

'All right. No more snakes. I'll tell her.'

'Thank you, Doctor. You're sweet to Ninon. Very sweet. Will you come sleep with me one night? It's so cold in my bed.'

'Maybe one night next week if you don't pound on the door.'

'Oh good. I'll remember!' She giggled coyly.

He came back into the hallway and locked the door. Then they continued towards the rear of the building.

'Ninon's got a crush on me,' he said. 'When she isn't trying to strangle me, she gets terribly romantic. I apologize.'

'What's wrong with the poor old thing?'

'She thinks the world is trying to kill her. Actually, from the life she's led, I don't blame her. And she's not old. She's only forty-one.'

'But those hands! And her voice . . .'

'I know. When you live in any asylum twenty years, you age fast.'

'But this isn't any asylum. . . .'

'It is now. The asylum I used to work at was hit by a Prussian shell ten nights ago. We transferred the patients who survived to this place, much against the wishes of Sister Antoinette, I might add.'

'Then you're a warden?'

'I am now. The warden was in the section the shell hit.'

He hung his key ring on a hook and opened the door. Elizabeth went out into a small courtyard.

'The stable's over here,' he said, pointing.

They crossed the courtyard to a wooden door.

'I came to Paris last year to study with Dr Peyerfitte, who was the warden. He had published some fascinating books on diseases of the mind, which is my field.'

'I never thought of the mind having "diseases". . . .'

'Most people don't. I hope to change that in my lifetime. Or at least help change it.' He opened the stable doors. She came in the stable and watched as he hitched the skinny horse to the buggy. Then he helped her up to the seat. He climbed in beside her, shook the reins, and the horse started out of the stable. 'The only thing that saved this horse from being turned into a sandwich is that he looks so tough the nuns decided they'd rather go hungry. Rue des Acacias?'

'Yes. Number twenty-five. Do you mean a brain can catch a disease by a germ?'

'No,' he said as the buggy rattled into the street. 'At least, we don't *think* so. But there have to be reasons why people go insane. It can't just *happen*, the way everyone assumes. It's not the full moon or a witch's curse. Dr Peyerfitte thought . . . oh well, I won't bore you.'

'I'm not bored – really! It's very interesting.'

'Well, he thought people are born rather like prisoners in a cell, the cell being their mind. Now, most people manage to get out of that cell fairly early in life. They have no trouble dealing with life, and as they learn more and more, the doors of their minds open up. But some people can't get the door open, for various reasons, and as they grow older and have less and less ability to deal with the rest of the world, the prison that is their mind becomes more and more impossible for them to escape from. So their brains start twisting. They hallucinate, like Ninon back there. And they become inhabitants of an unreal world. The real world calls them lunatics and locks them up in a real prison. But what Dr Peyerfitte was trying to do was to reach through into the prisons of their minds and try to free them. In other words, they aren't lunatics, they're invalids. The problem is to find the treatment to cure them.'

'Then could Ninon be cured?'

He shook his head. 'I doubt it. It's too late for her. But maybe by talking to her, I can learn something that may help me cure a future Ninon.'

'So you talk to her?'

'I used to. Every day, if I could. It's been a little too hectic lately, though, what with the American Ambulance and our German friends.'

They rode for a while in silence. Then Elizabeth said, 'How did you get interested in the mind?'

'My mother,' he said, 'died in an asylum, and no one knew why she had gone crazy. I was fifteen at the time, and it really tore me to pieces. So I told myself I was going to find out why people went crazy. It's fifteen years later and I don't know that much more, but I know a *little* more. And here we are: Number twenty-five, rue des Acacias. How's the ankle?'

'I've forgotten all about it.' She smiled at him. 'You've really been terribly kind, and I can't thank you enough. And it's been fascinating listening to you. I wish you great success.'

She held out her hand and he shook it.

'It's been a pleasure talking to a fellow American,' he said. 'It can get to be a little stultifying talking to Ninon.'

'I can imagine.'

'Are you sure you'll be able to get home from here?'

'I'll manage somehow.'

He started to say something else, then changed his mind. 'I'll help you down.'

He jumped down, came around the buggy, and held her hand as she climbed to the street.

'Well,' she said, 'thank you again.'

'I don't suppose . . .' He stopped.

'Yes?'

'Well, it's sort of ridiculous asking anyone to supper in Paris now, but I do know a restaurant where they serve a fairly good stew – as long as you don't ask too many questions about what's in it. Perhaps some night you'd like to have supper with me there?'

She studied his face a moment. Yes, she thought, I think he really is lonely.

'I'll do better than that,' she said. 'Why don't you come to my house for supper tomorrow night? My cook does miracles with onions, and I'd like to repay you for the miracle you did on my ankle. Could you come tomorrow?'

He smiled, and she liked his smile.

'I'd like to very much. What time?'

'Seven o'clock. Number six, rue la Pérouse.'

'I'll see you then. Good-bye.'

He climbed back in the buggy and shook the reins. She

waved to him as he drove off. Then she walked to the door of Number twenty-five. It wasn't until after she had rung the bell that she realized she had forgotten his name.

A man with a bashed-in nose answered the door. He was the janitor-porter-concierge of the building, and he wore a loose wool coat, baggy blue trousers, a black cap, and a green scarf.

'Yes?' said Bruno Zinh.

'I wanted to see Monsieur Bramwell. I'm his wife.'

Bruno looked surprised. 'His *wife*?'

'That's what I said. Is he in?'

'Yes.' He stood aside, and she entered the small hall. The private house was an elegant stone building that had been converted to apartments ten years before. The curving stone staircase had an elaborate wrought-iron balustrade. Beneath the stair was Bruno's small office.

He closed the door and pointed to two carved doors beyond the stair.

'That's his apartment. He's probably drunk.'

She gave the man a cool look. 'I don't think that's information you should know.'

He smiled. 'I deliver the brandy. The door's unlocked. Go on in.'

She went to the door and opened it. Bruno was right. She went into a foyer which gave into a large drawing room. She walked to the arch and looked around. The pale winter sunlight limped through tall windows looking onto a snowy garden. The room had pretensions to elegance. The high ceiling was elaborately plastered, and a rather splendid globed chandelier hung from the centre of it. The furniture was new – or at least its heavy gilt carving had been the height of fashion a few years before. But the coverings on the chairs and sofas were soiled and frayed. The chairs squatted sadly around the room, waiting for conversations that would never take place. Some lamps, some bad paintings, a tall gilt mirror over the mantel with a bottle of brandy reflected in its dusty recesses. A fire was burning – at least he had heat. A high-backed chair was in front of the fire. She saw an arm encased in a red velvet smoking jacket. The hand held a cigar.

'Ben?' she said. 'It's Elizabeth.'

The hand holding the cigar rose and disappeared from her view. Then a cloud of smoke rose lazily over the back of the chair.

'What do you want?' he said. His voice was neither surprised, hostile, nor friendly. She could have been anyone or no one.

'Money.'

'I figured the inflation would bring you around here sooner or later.'

'You might have sent some money without making me come and ask.'

'I might have done a lot of things.' The cigar pointed to a marble-topped commode with fancy brass handles. 'There's a chequebook and a pen in the top drawer. If you bring them to me, I'll write you a cheque. The Rothschild bank is still honouring cheques, though I don't know how long that will last. Pardon me for not getting up, but my good leg's got rheumatism.'

She went to the commode, took out the pen and chequebook, then brought them to the chair. When she saw his face, she winced. He looked ten years older. His hair had turned grey, and his skin was pallid, puffy, and wrinkled. He hadn't shaved for several days, and the shirt beneath his smoking jacket was dirty. A snifter of brandy was on the floor by his feet. So was a dish filled with cigar ashes. So was a half-empty bottle of brandy.

He looked at her with bloodshot eyes. 'Well, you haven't changed much, which is more than I can say for myself. I read about your Mr Kent in the papers. His timing for opening the hotel wasn't exactly brilliant, was it?'

'Not exactly.'

'Is he still living with you?'

'No, he went back to America.'

'Smart man. Why didn't you?'

'Because he stuck me with all the hotel's debts, and the Bank of France is holding Ward's trust fund until the debts are cleared.'

He blinked slowly. 'My God, he really suckered you in, didn't he?'

'Yes. But he was nice to me when you left. And I needed someone.'

He shrugged. 'Well, I don't blame you. Give me the chequebook.'

She handed it to him, with the pen. He thought a moment. Then he said, 'How much would it take to clear Ward's trust?'

'Ben, you don't have to do this. . . .'

'I'm his father, aren't I? How much?'

She hesitated. 'Well, I borrowed sixty thousand dollars from the Bank of France to invest in the hotel, using Ward's trust as collateral. I suppose if I paid back the sixty thousand and the interest due, they'd have to release the trust, wouldn't they?'

'They'd not only have to, they'd better. And if they don't, tell me and I'll put my bankers on them.' He started writing. Then he signed the cheque, tore it off, and handed it to her.

'Here's a half million francs,' he said. 'That will clear Ward's trust and leave you plenty extra to get through this rotten winter. What happened to your furs?'

'I pawned them.'

'You didn't have to do that. Why didn't you come to me sooner?'

'Pride. Plus the fact that I didn't like to admit I've been a fool. This is very generous of you, Ben. I appreciate it. I . . . wouldn't have come today except that things have gotten rather desperate.'

'I can see.'

She folded the cheque and put it in the pocket of her dress.

'You haven't asked about the children,' she said. 'Don't you care?'

He leaned over to flick his cigar ash in the dish. Then he picked up the brandy snifter.

'How are they?' he said.

'They're fine. They're with Debbie in Philadelphia.'

He sipped the brandy.

'Pauline's six now, isn't she?' he said.

'That's right. She's becoming very pretty. Why didn't you ever come to see them . . . or even write a note, or send a birthday present, or *something*?'

He looked up at her. 'Elizabeth, don't lecture me on what a rotten father and husband I've been. I know full well what a rotten father and husband I've been.'

'I'm not lecturing you. I'm in no position to lecture anyone. I'm just curious. I always thought you loved them.'

'I was afraid to see them,' he said. 'I felt guilty. I thought about sending presents, but then decided not to. I don't know why.'

'Was Zaza worth it?'

'What do you think?'

She shrugged.

'I have no idea, Ben. Maybe this is what you want out of life. You obviously didn't want me. And I'm not accusing you, because I don't feel bitter any more. I'm just stating a fact.'

He inhaled on his cigar. 'Was Zaza worth it? Well, that's a good question. Let me see if I can answer it. She gave me about three months of the most exciting physical passion I've ever known in my life. Then she gave me three months of violent quarrels that drove me practically crazy with jealousy – faithfulness, I need hardly mention, is not Zaza's long suit. Then she left me. This exhilarating experience cost me you, my children, my self-respect, and a considerable amount of money, and last, but not exactly least, my health. You see, Elizabeth, Zaza – or perhaps it was one of her replacements, but I tend to think it was Zaza – gave me a first-class case of syphilis.'

She drew in her breath.

'Oh yes, look shocked. I was too, when the first signs appeared. The doctors say three, maybe five years. Perhaps, if I'm lucky, ten. And it's not going to be a pleasant exit. So, was Zaza worth it? Well, what do you think?'

She put her hand on his shoulder, and there were tears in her eyes. 'Ben,' she whispered, 'I'm so sorry . . .'

'And I'm sorry for what I did to you. The problem is, being sorry never fixes anything, does it?'

'Perhaps it does, a little. I had no idea . . .'

'I didn't want you to. And I don't want Ward and Pauline to know. You won't tell them, will you?'

'Of course not. But maybe . . .'

'What?'

'Maybe you could come back. Maybe we could start over.'

'How? And I give it to you? No, it's too late for start-overs. Besides, I've given my life a great deal of thought lately. About two hundred bottles of brandy worth of thought. And I've about made up my mind, what I'm going to do.'

'What, Ben?'

'I'm going to pay off a little debt, then I'm going to help the French. Odd, isn't it? You were the one that loved Paris, and I was the one who wanted to go home. Now Paris fascinates me.'

'Why?'

'Because something's happening here that's . . . I don't know. It's the end of the old world, and the beginning of a new one.'

'Obviously it's the end of the old one, but what's the new one?'

'The Communards,' he said. 'They're something new. They fascinate me. What if they really do take over the city? What if the bottom of society becomes the top? Maybe things would be better. Did you ever think of that, Elizabeth?'

'I try to think of the Communards as little as possible. And I can assure you if they do take over, I'm going back to Philadelphia on the first boat. Don't get any romantic ideas about the poor, Ben. I feel sorry for them, but if they were running things, I think in the long run they'd end up no better than the people running things now.'

He smiled slightly. 'You're a political cynic? I never knew that, Elizabeth.'

'We never talked politics, Ben. Perhaps we never really talked at all.'

'Perhaps.'

She leaned down and kissed his forehead. Then she smoothed his hair a moment.

'Thank you,' she said, 'for all the good things you did for me. Those are the things I'll remember: not the bad.'

Then she started towards the door.

'Elizabeth.'

She turned to look at the back of the chair.

'Yes?'

'You and the children inherit everything. My lawyer in Philadelphia has the will.'

'Oh Ben, don't talk about wills yet! You still have years....'

'I just wanted you to know.'

'Well . . . thank you.' She started to leave, then remembered she had no transportation. 'By the way, do you have a carriage?'

'How did your horse taste?'

'Awful.'

'Mine was rather good. But I have one horse left. Tell Bruno to take you home. He's the porter. Tip him five francs. Better make it ten. He's a little punchdrunk, but he's harmless enough. Do you *have* ten francs?'

'Yes.'

She started into the foyer.

'Elizabeth?'

Again, she looked back at the chair before the fire.

'Yes?'

She watched the cigar go up in the direction of his mouth.

'I loved you very much. And I always will. Remember that too, will you?'

'Yes, Ben. I will.'

She looked at the smoke rising over the chair. Then she went into the foyer and let herself out.

Whatever bitterness she might have had was now gone. Syphilis! The scourge of Paris, what the moralists never tired of reminding the pleasure-loving, sex-mad Parisians was the penalty for their immorality. Thousands died of it, and there was no cure. Just a few years before, the brilliant poet Baudelaire had died of it. The previous June, Jules de Goncourt had died of it, leaving his older brother bereft with grief. She had dined with the Goncourt brothers at the Princess Mathilde's. She had had no idea one of them was riddled with what was now riddling her husband. Ben, Ben, Ben. Clumsy Ben. Faithless Ben. But somehow wonderful Ben, even with all his faults.

As she left the gloomy apartment, she felt nothing but an intense and poignant pity for him.

39

It was snowing the next evening when Blake Foster rang the bell at 6 rue la Pérouse. He didn't own dress clothes and wouldn't have worn them if he did because of the possibility of being mugged; but he had put on his best suit and bought a bottle of wine for his hostess. He felt more elated than he had for a long time. Meeting Elizabeth Bramwell the day before had been a much needed boost to his spirits. Life for the young doctor had not been particularly pleasant the past several months.

She opened the door herself, and he was surprised at the transformation. The woman in the black dress and horse blanket had been replaced by a woman in a lovely green silk dress with a white lace shawl. It had been a long time since Blake Foster had seen a pretty woman in a pretty dress.

'Good evening,' he said.

'Good evening. Come inside before we all freeze.'

He hurried in and she closed the door. He pulled a bottle of Beaujolais from his coat pocket.

'I don't know if this goes with onions, but it's last year's Beaujolais and should be good. And it's certainly chilled.'

'Oh, thank you! And we've had a bit of luck. Gustave, my coachman, found two rabbits in the market this morning.

Henriette's making a *lapin Coquibus,* so we'll have a feast tonight. And needless to say, I'm *hungry.*'

'So am I.'

'Let me take your coat. . . . You know, I have a terrible confession to make.'

'What's that?'

'I've forgotten your name.'

'Oh. Well, it's easy to forget, I guess. It's Blake Foster.'

She put his coat, scarf, and hat on a bench in the hall.

'Of course. And it's a very nice name. By the way, my ankle's much better.'

'Good.'

'Come in the drawing room. We have fires going in three rooms! It's a wonderful luxury, but tonight we're celebrating all sorts of things.'

'Oh? What?'

He followed her into the salon, where a fire was pumping heat into the chilly room.

'Well, today I straightened out my finances after four months of horrible complication, and I can't tell you what a relief that is. Then Gustave and Henriette, my servants, decided to become American citizens. . . .'

'Isn't that rather difficult in Paris?'

'I should have said they've decided to become *future* American citizens. I've arranged for them to go to America as soon as they can get out of Paris. And they were so excited about that, Henriette browbeat Gustave into proposing to her, so now we're going to have a wedding. Isn't that exciting?' She lowered her voice. 'I think Gustave isn't going to have too many surprises on the wedding night, *but* . . . at least now it's all going to be legal.'

He laughed as he warmed his hands at the fire.

'It all sounds very proper.'

'Well,' said Elizabeth, 'I don't think this house can be accused of having been *too* proper during the past few years.' She rang for Gustave, then sat down on a small sofa in front of the fire. He looked at her.

'I'm not quite sure how to interpret that,' he said.

'It's very easy, Dr Foster. After my husband left me several years ago, I met a charming young American who was a real-estate promoter, among other things. He took advantage of my loneliness, and I took advantage of his charm, because he became my lover. He's since decamped, as they say. But I wanted to make everything clear to you, in case you might have heard any stories about the wicked Mrs Bramwell. Ah, here's Gustave, our future Yankee Doodle. Gustave, this is Dr Foster, who has brought us a beautiful bottle of Beaujolais, which we'll have with the rabbit.'

She handed him the bottle.

'I understand you're to be congratulated?' said Blake.

Gustave grinned. 'Yes sir. Madame has made it possible for us to go to America. We're very grateful and happy.'

'Well, I hope America lives up to your expectations.'

'I know it will, sir. I know it's a wonderful country. It's the best country in the world!'

'Hear hear,' said Elizabeth. 'Tell Henriette we'll eat at eight. Would you like a glass of wine, Doctor? Or some sherry? We have some excellent Amontillado.'

'That sounds fine.'

'Gustave, bring us two glasses, please.'

'Yes, madame.'

Gustave hurried out.

'I can see why everyone's in such a good mood,' said Blake. 'It's nice to be in a cheery house for a change.'

'It's nice for us to be cheery. It hasn't been a very pleasant four months. Where do you live, Doctor?'

'I did live in the asylum,' he said, 'but since that got shelled, I've been sleeping in a room in the basement of the hospital. It's not very comfortable, but at least I'm near my patients.'

'I hope you have plenty of blankets.'

'Blankets we have. Where are you from originally, Mrs Bramwell?'

'Philadelphia. And you?'

'New York.'

'I thought so. You sound like a New Yorker. Do you miss it?'

'Very much. Particularly after this winter. I want to go

home as soon as the French and Germans come to some sort of agreement and we can get out. Of course, I'd have to make arrangements for my patients, which is something of a problem. But I'll work that out if I ever get enough time to think. How about you? Will you stay in Paris?'

She looked thoughtful.

'I don't know. Perhaps not. My husband used to say living abroad withers one's roots, and perhaps he's right. Maybe it's time for me to go home, too.'

Gustave brought in two glasses of sherry on a tray. Elizabeth took one and Blake the other. He raised his glass.

'Then, perhaps, we should drink to America?'

'A good idea,' said Elizabeth. 'No: wait. Gustave, pour yourself and Henriette a glass, then bring her in and we'll *all* toast America.'

Gustave looked surprised.

'Is madame *sure* . . .?'

'Gustave, we've been living in three rooms together for a month now. I think we can all have a drink together without the world coming to an end.'

'Very well. If madame says so.'

He hurried out, and Elizabeth lowered her voice.

'They have dreadful fights.'

'Oh?'

'She hen-pecks him, and he's lazy. It will be an *ideal* marriage.'

Blake laughed. 'Well, that's a new definition of domestic bliss.'

'It's old as the hills, Doctor.'

'Uh . . . my name is Blake.'

She smiled. 'I won't forget this time. And mine is Elizabeth.'

Gustave and Henriette came in the room, Henriette looking flustered. They both had glasses in their hands. Elizabeth turned.

'Ah, here she is! Our other Yankee Doodle. Henriette, Dr Foster and I were going to toast America, but then we decided you two were the obvious toasters, so we'll *all* drink. To America!'

She raised her glass.

'To America!' said Blake, raising his.

'To America!' exclaimed Gustave enthusiastically. 'Our new country.'

Silence. They were all looking at Henriette.

'Say the toast!' hissed her fiancé.

She bit her lip. 'I'm so happy,' she said, 'I think I'm going to cry. To America!'

She raised her glass. They all drank. Then Henriette burst into tears and fled from the room. Gustave groaned.

'She's impossible!'

And he hurried out after her.

Blake Foster laughed. 'Henriette is a bit emotional, I gather.'

He looked at Elizabeth. To his surprise, there were tears in her eyes, too.

'Is something wrong?' he asked.

She shook her head. 'No. It's just,' she said softly, 'I suddenly realized how much I miss home.'

Gustave had moved Elizabeth's bed out of the dining room for the dinner, and Henriette had pulled out the good china and silver. Now, as Gustave served the coffee, the candles in their silver sticks were low. Blake sighed with contentment.

'The rabbit was wonderful,' he said. 'And a vast improvement over horsemeat.'

'Wasn't it? And the Beaujolais was perfect with it. Do you mind if we have our coffee here? I think this room's warmer.'

'No, I'm very comfortable. Would you mind if I smoked?'

'Is it a cigar?'

He pulled a pipe from his pocket. She looked relieved.

'In that case,' she said, 'feel free. My husband is a cigar smoker, and I've developed a loathing for the smell of them.'

'How about your husband?' he said, puffing the pipe to life.

'Do you mean have I developed a loathing for him? No, far from it. I feel sorry for him. Now, anyway.'

'I know it's none of my business, but . . .'

She folded her hands, and he noticed how beautiful they were. They were ringless except for a diamond wedding band.

'You compared the mind to a prison,' she said. 'Well, my husband's prison was rather peculiar, though I know now it's not as peculiar as I once thought. He prefers young girls to mature women. He fell madly in love with a singer here in Paris and left me for her. Then the singer left him – it's hardly a new story. . . .'

'Hardly.'

'She also left him with a little present. One that will kill him.'

'Syphilis?'

She nodded. 'I think now he's cured of the singer. Unfortunately, he'll never be cured of the syphilis. Unless . . . there *is* a cure?'

He shook his head. 'Not that I know of. I've heard of a potassium iodide treatment, but I'm told it's painful and not reliable. I'm sorry for your husband. And you.'

She spread her hands. 'I'll survive. But Ben . . .' She shrugged.

'The moralists would say he got what he deserved,' said Blake, sipping his coffee. 'I say the whole thing could have been avoided. Perhaps.'

'How?'

'A less hypocritical attitude on everybody's part. Including that of your husband.'

'I don't see how he could have been less hypocritical. He left me and went to live with her. It seems to me he was wildly open about the whole thing.'

'Well, I didn't mean that, exactly. But I assume he didn't tell you he was interested in young girls until he took off with the singer?'

'Of course not.'

'Then he was being hypocritical. That's probably the wrong word. He was lying to society. And you. He was probably terrified of what he was feeling, and so he bottled it up until it finally exploded. Did he drink?'

'Yes. He still does.'

'Well, there's the explanation for the drinking. He desires

young girls. Society condemns his desire. To try to forget it, he drank. I'd bet a lot of money – if I had a lot of money to bet – that that's the truth.'

She thought about this. 'You may be right. Did you ever hear of a Professor Brandini?'

'The so-called faith healer? Yes.'

'Several years ago, I went to him about Ben's drinking problem. He was a fake, but I remember he said that greed and sex are the strongest urges in people. I suppose that's true, isn't it?'

'Well, it's true as far as it goes. I think human beings are a *little* more complicated than that. Will you try to divorce your husband?'

'I don't know. We have two children, and divorce is so incredibly complicated. . . .' She drank some coffee. 'Well, I've certainly been frank, haven't I? I've told you I had a lover, that my husband has syphilis . . . I guess I'm not exactly the discreet hostess, am I? But . . . I've been lonely. And I've enjoyed having you to talk to.'

'I've enjoyed listening.'

They looked at each other in silence. Then he said, 'May I be frank with you?'

'Of course.'

'I'd like very much to spend the night.'

She finished her coffee.

'Blake, I wouldn't blame you for thinking I'm a promiscuous woman – or at least hardly the model housewife. But I'm not quite *that* promiscuous.'

He smiled. 'I guess I didn't put that too well. What I meant was, I'd like to rent a room.'

'Oh. No, I guess you *didn't* put that too well.'

He leaned forward. 'That basement room in the hospital is not the ideal home by any means. And this is a big house within walking distance of the hospital. Would you consider renting me a room? I'm not the neatest man in the world, but most people I know think I'm fairly respectable. I don't throw wild parties. And I'd be very proper in a proper house like this.'

'Well, as I told you, we're not *all* that proper. But proper enough. I never thought of renting . . .'

'Mind you, I couldn't pay much. But – and I don't mean to scare you – Paris is a powder keg right now. You could do worse than to have an extra man around the house.'

'You mean the Communards?'

'Yes.'

She thought a moment. Then she picked up the silver bell and rang it. Gustave came in from the kitchen.

'Madame rang?'

'Gustave, we have a tenant.'

She gestured across the table at Blake Foster.

40

Bruno Zinh was worried about Monsieur Bramwell. For three days, ever since the unexpected appearance of Madame Bramwell, he had not drunk a drop. Bruno knew because there were no empties in the trash. Moreover, Monsieur Bramwell had not left the apartment, even to go to his favourite bistros. Bruno came to the conclusion that Monsieur Bramwell was drying out. Perhaps the visit from his wife was the reason.

On the fourth day, at noon, Monsieur Bramwell came out of his apartment. To Bruno's surprise, he was clean-shaven and clean, wearing a pressed suit. 'Bruno,' he said, 'are you free this afternoon? I need a driver and a bodyguard for about four hours. I'll pay you fifty francs an hour.'

Fifty francs! 'Yes sir,' said Bruno eagerly. 'I'll tell Madame Dulaage. She owes me some time off.'

Mme. Dulaage was the owner of the house, an elderly

widow who lived on the second floor. Bruno made the arrangements with her, then at two-thirty he pulled Ben's buggy up in front of the house. The weather had warmed up, and rain had replaced snow. It was pouring, and melting slush was clogging the sewers, turning the streets into small lakes. Ben came out of the house wearing a raincoat and holding an umbrella over his top hat. He limped slightly, as always, but Bruno thought there was almost a spring in his limp, if that were possible. Monsieur Bramwell looked positively jaunty.

He climbed in the buggy, folded his dripping umbrella, opened the window to the driver's seat, and said to Bruno, 'Our first stop is the Rothschild bank.'

Bruno snapped his whip, and the skinny horse sloshed into motion. Since there was hardly any traffic, they reached the bank in twenty minutes.

'I'll be about a half hour,' said Ben as he climbed out. He went in the bank and asked a guard to direct him to the office of Monsieur Lévy, the officer in charge of his account. The guard took him to M. Lévy's outer office, where a young male assistant gave him a seat.

'Monsieur Lévy will be with you in a moment, sir,' he said. 'We're all in a bit of an uproar today.'

'Because of the march on the Hôtel de Ville?' asked Ben.

'Exactly. The Reds – my God, they're getting nervier every day! Of course, I can hardly blame them, with the way things have been going. . . . You heard about General Trochu?'

'Yes. They finally got rid of him. About time, I'd say. If ever there was an incompetent commander in time of war . . .'

'True, but . . .' The young man rubbed his hands nervously. 'Still, to change commanders *now*, when everything is going wrong for us. . . .'

'Perhaps that's the best time to do it,' Ben said. 'You may remember that Mr Lincoln went through a number of generals until he found Grant. If I were running things here, I would have fired Trochu months ago.'

The young man nodded uncertainly. 'I suppose so. . . .

What's wrong with France?' he added miserably. 'Why can't we find a leader who will take us out of this mess? We need another Napoleon.'

'You had one,' Ben reminded him, 'and you threw him out.'

'Oh well . . . *him*. I meant his uncle. France needs a great man, but it seems all the great men are Germans these days. . . .'

M. Lévy bustled out of his office. He was a fat man with a bald scalp ringed with grey curls. He wore a pince-nez and looked as nervous as his assistant. 'Ah, Monsieur Bramwell!' he exclaimed, shaking Ben's hand. 'It's been a long time. Too long, sir! Come into my office. . . . Jules, get Monsieur Bramwell's file. . . .'

M. Lévy led Ben into a small office warmed by a small fire.

'Take a seat, sir. Perhaps my assistant mentioned that we're in a bit of an uproar today? The Reds! The damned Reds. . . . They are closing the clubs, I hear, and about time.'

'The Red cabarets?' said Ben.

M. Lévy went around his desk and sat down. 'Yes. Hotbeds of anarchy!'

'I hear they have some funny skits.'

'Oh yes, funny! France is dying, and the Reds make jokes. They're ghouls, monsieur. The vultures of the poor ready to pick the bones of the propertied classes clean. Ah, that I should have lived to see this *débâcle*! France going communist! I can't believe it. . . . Well, sir, you didn't come through all this rain to discuss politics, I'm sure. What can I do for you?'

'I want to make a withdrawal,' said Ben. 'In fact, I want to close my account.'

M. Lévy's bushy grey eyebrows rose.

'Close it, you say? Well, I suppose I can't blame you, under the circumstances. But Monsieur Bramwell, let me assure you that no matter what happens, the Rothschild family will stand behind its commitments. Even if Paris falls to these villains and they blow up our vaults, the other Rothschild banks abroad will replace all deposits lost.'

'I have no doubts of that, Monsieur Lévy. One thing I

have absolute faith in is the integrity of the Rothschilds, which is why I bank here. I'm closing my account for another reason. A private reason. You see, I'm going away.'

'Ah. Well, that's different. Have you managed to get a *laissez-passer* from your minister, Mr Washburne? I didn't know the Germans were letting anyone through the lines, not even the Americans. . . .'

'Let's say I've obtained a different sort of *laissez-passer*.'

'I see. No, I don't see, but . . . Jules! Ah, here he is. Give me the file.' The assistant handed him a file. Then M. Lévy lowered his voice. 'I can tell you something in confidence, monsieur, that might change your plans. Baron James has been told that Monsieur Favre is discussing surrender terms with Herr Bismarck at Versailles. . . . This horror may be over soon.'

'That would make no difference to my plans.'

'I see. Well . . .' He opened the folder on his desk and inspected the immaculately written entries. 'Yes . . . there was that large withdrawal earlier this week. The cheque to Madame Bramwell for a half million francs.'

'That's right.'

'Which leaves your current balance at one hundred and seventy-three thousand francs. Jules, Monsieur Bramwell is closing his account. Will you write him a cashier's cheque for the balance. . . .'

'I want cash,' said Ben.

M. Lévy looked at him. 'Cash? But surely not, sir. That is a very large sum. . . .'

'Cash. In fifty-franc notes, bundles of ten.'

M. Lévy leaned forward. 'Monsieur, may I remind you that Paris is extremely unsafe right now? Such an enormous sum of money . . .'

'Cash.'

M. Lévy gave up with a shrug.

'Cash,' he said to Jules. 'In fifty-franc notes, bundles of ten.'

'If I recall correctly,' added Ben, 'your couriers carry cash in leather attaché cases. I'd like the money packed in cases like them, if possible. You can deduct their cost from my withdrawal.'

Jules looked at his superior, who nodded yes. Then Jules left the office. M. Lévy turned back to his American client.

'May I ask, sir, what you intend to do with all this money?'

Ben smiled.

'Have a good time.'

M. Lévy wondered if Monsieur Bramwell were quite right in the head. All that drinking, after all . . .

A half hour later, a strange procession hurried out of the Rothschild bank through the rain to the waiting buggy. Four bank guards, two carrying black attaché cases apiece, the other two carrying guns. M. Lévy and Jules, holding umbrellas. Ben, holding his umbrella. Bruno Zinh watched as the guards stowed the four cases in the buggy. Then Ben shook hands with M. Lévy and climbed in with the attaché cases. He slid open the window, and Bruno looked back at him.

'Where now?' he asked.

'Belleville,' said Ben.

Bruno's eyes widened. '*Belleville*? Now wait a minute . . . I said I'd drive you, but I didn't know you wanted to go *there*. . . .'

Ben reached in his coat and pulled out a small revolver. He handed it through the window to Bruno, saying, 'Take this. I've got one, too. And I hired a bodyguard, not a tour guide.'

'But sir, the Reds . . .'

Ben put one of the attaché cases on his lap and opened the lid. Inside were packed banded stacks of fifty-franc notes, ten bills to the stack. He took one out and handed it through the window.

'Here's five hundred francs,' he said. 'Four hours' pay and a two-hundred-franc bonus. Now, take me to Belleville.'

He put a stack of bills in his own pocket, then closed the attaché case and sat back. Bruno stared at the money disbelievingly. Then he shoved it in his pocket.

'Belleville it is,' he said. 'Any particular place?'

'Go to the Boulevard Richard Lenoir first. Then we'll improvise.'

Bruno snapped his whip, and the buggy drove off in the rain, heading east towards the slums of Paris.

The buggy rolled down rabbit-warren streets and lanes. The streets were filthy. All the Paris streets were filthy, since the city had stopped cleaning them at the beginning of the siege, but these streets had never been clean to begin with. The dirt of centuries was grimed in the paving, and much of the paving had been torn up to build barricades. He passed a group of pinch-faced children leaving their school, holding their school boxes over their heads to keep off the rain. They looked hungry, and one dirty ten-year-old was smoking a cigarette. He passed a ragtail detachment of National Guards dragging half a dozen machine guns towards the ramparts of the city. Their red trousers were filthy, and they looked badly drilled.

He passed ragged foragers picking over the ruins of a burned-out building that had been the target of a Prussian shell. He passed two little girls carrying sacks of dirty laundry, their tensed bellies and thin thighs showing through their wet dresses. He passed a shoe-repair shop that had been converted into a fry shop. A hideous old woman was cooking something in the window, and a Zouave was her customer. Judging from the total absence of cats and dogs from the streets, he assumed she wasn't cooking roast beef.

He passed a stationery shop that was selling calendars printed with the *pluviôses* and *thermidors* of the revolutionaries. He passed beggars, whores, and ragmen. One ragman had a sackful of live rats that he was selling for one franc a kilo.

He passed dirty-looking cafés with fly-specked windows through which he could see workingmen drinking, smoking, and arguing. Bistros with crazy, sometimes obscene names. L'Abri des Voleurs. La Salle des Bonnets Rouges. Le Cul-de-Sac du Chien-Affamé. Le Cornet à Dés. Le Cul-de-Vache. Le Chat Qui Rit.

'That's it!' he said to Bruno, pointing to the seedy bistro. 'The Laughing Cat. Stop the buggy. We'll go in there.'

Bruno pulled over to the kerb. 'You want me to go in with you?' he asked.

'Yes. You take two of these, I'll take the other two.'

Bruno jumped down and opened the door. Ben handed him two of the attaché cases. Then he got out and took the others. They went into the café.

It was a small, low-ceilinged place filled with workers in elephant-legged trousers, dirty sashes, with dark scarves wrapped around their necks and shapeless caps on their uncut hair. They were sitting at wooden tables drinking cheap wine or marc. When they saw the top-hatted American in his well-cut suit holding the two shiny attaché cases, they fell silent and stared. A fat woman in a black dress and dirty slippers shuffled up to them.

'What do you want?' she said suspiciously.

'This table,' said Ben. He set one of the cases on an empty table next to the door. Then he pulled the five hundred francs from his pocket and handed them to her. She looked at the money.

'What's this for?'

'Rent.'

'Rent? I'm not renting this place!'

'Rent for this table.' He tapped the tabletop.

The woman gave him a look that said 'Crazy!' Then she looked at the money again. 'What is this – counterfeit?'

'It's right out of the vaults of the Rothschild bank.'

The woman turned to one of the tables behind her.

'Philippe,' she said, tossing the money to one of the drinkers, a skinny little man with a ferret face. 'Look at them.'

Philippe caught the money and pulled one of the bills out of the middle of the stack. He held it up and inspected it. Everyone else in the café respected his professionalism. They awaited his judgment silently.

He tossed the money back to the woman, pocketing the fifty-franc note he had inspected as a tip.

'It's good,' he said.

The woman caught the money and turned back to Ben. She still looked suspicious.

'Why would you "rent" a table when they're free?'

'I want to set up an office for the next hour.'

'An office? What are you selling?'

'I'm giving. I'm giving away money. Is this table all right?'

The fat woman shrugged. 'Why not? I think you're crazy, but for five hundred francs, I'll even toss in a drink on the house.'

'I don't drink any more,' he said, pulling out the chair and sitting down. Then he signalled Bruno to join him with the other attaché cases. He opened the first one, pulled out another stack of bills, and held it up. 'This is five hundred francs,' he announced. 'Who wants it?'

Silence. A big man with a doorknob of a nose got up from one of the tables and came to Ben.

'What is this?' he said. 'Some gag?'

'You can call it whatever you want. I'm giving away money. Five hundred francs a person until I run out.'

'No one gives away money without a reason.'

'I have a reason.'

'What?'

'All my life, I've looked for a purpose,' he said simply. Now I've found a purpose. It's to give away all my money.'

Doorknob sniffed suspiciously, eying the cash in the open attaché case.

'The purpose in life is to eat, drink, get drunk, get laid, have kids, fight with your wife, shit, get old, and die. Now that I've told you the purpose in life, keep your goddam money. We don't need rich Americans coming down here to make a sideshow out of us.'

'I'm not making a sideshow out of you. I'm giving away my money, five hundred francs per person. I have one hundred and seventy thousand francs in these attaché cases. And I don't give a damn what you think, my friend: I'm going to do it because I want to do it and doing it will give me a great deal of pleasure. Now, if you're not interested, I think someone else may be, so please get out of the way. Do I have any customers?' he shouted, holding up a stack of bills. 'Five hundred francs! Going once. Going twice. . . . Bruno, we may have to move to another café. There doesn't seem to be any action here. . . . Going three times –'

'WAIT!' yelled Philippe, the counterfeiter, jumping out of his chair. 'Jesus Christ, he *means* it! I'll take it, monsieur!' He was pushing his way through the chairs. 'I'll take it!' He reached Ben and took the bills. 'Beautiful!'

'They're marked,' said Doorknob. 'You dumb son of a bitch, don't you see this is a setup? The *flics* are probably down the street, waiting to arrest us. . . .'

'They're *not* marked!' said Philippe defiantly. 'I already checked. No one's ever given me anything in my life, and if you think I'm turning this down, your brain's in your *ass*!' He turned back to Ben. 'Only one per customer?'

'Only one.'

'Well, thanks for one.' He ran to the door, opened it, and ran out into the street yelling, 'They're giving away money! Some crazy American's giving away money at Le Chat Qui Rit!'

Suddenly, the others in the café began pushing back their chairs. There was a wild scramble as the shouting men pushed their way to Ben's table.

In forty minutes, all the money was gone. In forty minutes, a crowd of at least three hundred had jammed the street outside the café, ignoring the pelting rain as they tried to get into the Laughing Cat. Yet, with all the excitement, there was no attempt to riot. It was as if they knew a riot would break the magic spell. They waited, yelled, stood on their toes to try to see in. But no one rioted.

Then a great cheer as the men inside the café began to push out into the street. '*Vive l'Americain fou!*' 'Hurray for the crazy American!' Everyone took up the chant as Ben appeared in the doorway, his arms high over his head. He was grabbed and hoisted on the shoulders of two men, who began surging through the sea of people to the buggy. One boy tried to jump up for Ben's top hat, but he missed. Ben took it off and tossed it to him. Then he threw away his umbrella. As the crowd continued to cheer, he waved at them, his beaming face dripping rain. 'Hurray for the crazy American!' 'Hurray for the crazy American!'

When he reached the buggy, he signalled for silence. Slowly, the hubbub died.

'My friends,' he shouted, 'have fun with the money! Spend it, throw it away – whatever! But try to do better with it than I did.' A cheer. He signalled for silence again. 'My friends, I love you. I really do.' He paused as the rain ran down his face, mingling with tears. 'This,' he said, 'is the happiest day of my life.'

He blew them kisses. They cheered. The two men carrying him pushed him head-first through the buggy window. He landed unceremoniously, half on the seat, half off. He didn't care. He was laughing and crying, drunk with exhilaration. Somehow, Bruno made it to the driver's seat. He looked back. 'Where now?' he shouted over the noise.

'The rue Dante,' yelled Ben, getting up. Then he leaned out the window, blowing kisses to the crowd as the buggy slowly moved forward. It took them ten minutes to clear the block. Then, when the crowd fell behind them, still cheering, Ben sprawled back in his seat. He was soaked, and his suit was a mess.

But he was wildly, improbably happy. And he wasn't even sure why.

When they reached Zaza's block, the rain was tapering off and it had grown dark.

'There's someone parked in front of her house,' said Ben, looking out. He looked up and saw lights in her windows. 'Stop here and let's wait.'

Bruno obeyed. They sat in the buggy as the rain dripped. Bruno looked back through the window.

'What are you going to do?' he said.

'See Zaza. It's been a long time.' He lit a cigar.

'If,' said Bruno, 'you're going to try and make her your mistress again, you're wasting your time. She's got the Prince de Lamballe.'

'I know. I read the papers.'

'She's also got a German lover.'

'A German?' Ben sounded interested. 'How do you know?'

'You ought to see the food in her place. She *has* to have a German. No Parisian could bring her stuff like that.'

'So Zaza even sleeps with Germans. Well, it's all in character, isn't it?'

'Zaza's a terrific lay, but she'll sleep with anything.'

'I think you have a point.'

They waited ten minutes. Then Ben sat up. Someone was coming out of the house, hurrying across the sidewalk to the waiting carriage. Ben let out a low whistle. 'You're absolutely right, Bruno,' he whispered. 'Right on the button. She *does* have a German lover.'

Bruno looked back. His face was confused.

'But sir, that was a woman. . . .'

'Yes, and no German. That was the Marquise de Païva, who is the mistress of the richest man in Germany. I've read that they're out at Versailles with the German court. . . . So La Païva comes through the lines with goodies for her little Zaza. . . .'

'Then Zaza's a lesbian?' whispered Bruno, amazed.

'You put it better, Bruno,' he said, opening the buggy door and dropping his cigar in a puddle. 'She'll sleep with anything. If the price is right.'

He got out of the buggy, closed the door, and started limping down the sidewalk towards Zaza's entrance. The other carriage had pulled away. Now Bruno started the buggy. It lurched slowly forward. When he caught up with Ben, Bruno said, 'How long will you be?'

'You go home, Bruno,' said Ben. 'I'll be a while. No – better yet, come back in the morning. Pick me up then. Good night.'

He turned intoZaza's entrance, pushing open the glass-and-wrought-iron door. Bruno stopped the horse, watching Ben through the door as he began limping up the steep stairs.

Bruno started to go home, then changed his mind. I'll wait a while, he thought. There's something odd . . .

It was a difficult climb for Ben Bramwell with his wooden leg and rheumatism in his good leg. As he held on to the banister, pulling himself up step by painful step, he thought of Elizabeth and Pauline and Ward. He thought of Lew Crandall. He thought of Nicole Louise and that long-ago night in Philadelphia when she had turned on the stair and said, 'You hideous Jew.' He thought of Chancellorsville and the war. There had been a purpose to the war, hadn't there? Elizabeth, Pauline, Ward, Lew . . . he had betrayed them all. The people who had been dearest to him.

When he reached the top floor, he was panting. He limped to Zaza's door and knocked.

It was almost a minute before she answered. When she opened the door, she was wearing a white robe and eating a pear. She looked at him.

'Benjie!' she exclaimed. 'What in the world brings you here?'

'I was passing by and thought I'd say hello. It's been a long time. May I come in?'

'Why not?'

Taking another bite of the pear, she stood aside. He limped into the big, palm-filled room with its enormous skylight above. The rain was softly spattering on the many panes.

'You're soaked,' she said, closing the door. 'Don't you have an umbrella?'

'I threw it away.' He was looking around. 'I like to walk in the rain.' He looked at the bird cages with their colourful birds. He looked at the cats. Everywhere, the cats, sleeping, purring, stretching. 'I like your apartment, too.'

'Oh, thanks. I'd forgotten you've never been here. Would you like a drink?'

'No thanks. I quit.'

She crossed the carpets to a table holding several bottles, her bare feet sinking into the wool and the fur.

'Really? You're full of surprises, Benjie. An old toper like you? When did you stop?' She poured herself a glass of wine.

'Four days ago.'

'Oh well. Not exactly a world's record for temperance. You'll be back soon.'

'Maybe.'

She dropped the core of the pear in a wicker basket, then turned and leaned against the table.

'Well, you haven't gotten any better looking,' she said.

'No.' He smiled slightly. 'And I never will. You know, when I was younger I used to wish I were handsome. Now I don't particularly care.'

'Well, looks are only skin-deep, as they say. But a lot of people love that skin. You used to love mine, Benjie. Do you still?'

He blinked slowly, looking at her. The water dripped off his coat onto the floor as the rain dripped on the skylight above him.

'No, not any more, Zaza,' he said. 'I've come to kill you.'

She smiled. 'Oh? Well, you *are* full of surprises. Now, why would Benjie want to kill poor little Zaza?'

He pulled a revolver from his pocket and aimed at her. She looked at it as she sipped her wine.

'Because you're rotten,' he said matter-of-factly. 'I see, on top of everything else, you're sleeping with La Païva. She brought you that pear, didn't she?'

'What if she did?'

She set down the glass of wine. Then she smiled at him.

'Benjie, this is such a *sad* performance. You don't have the nerve to kill me. You didn't have the nerve to shoot *yourself* that night at La Païva's, much less me. You're just not a killer. I know you pretty well. You're a big oaf, but you're not a killer.' She started across the room to her darkroom. His gun followed her. 'I don't know what you're trying to prove with all this bravado. That you're a big, brave man? Well, you don't scare me. Nothing scares Zaza.'

He fired at her. Over her head. She looked at him, startled.

'The next time, I'm not going to aim high,' he said. The tropical birds in their elaborate Arabian cages started squawking as the jungle came to life.

She ran into the darkroom.

He limped across the room to the black curtains. Then he stopped, pointed the gun at them.

'You gave me syphilis, Zaza,' he said. 'You caused me to betray everything and everyone I love. You're rotten. You're the rot of Paris.'

He fired once through the curtains. Then again.

The birds screamed, and now the cats were meowing, running over the pillows of the divans, scampering up the iron steps to the gallery, then back down again.

Zaza lurched through the curtains. She was holding a big glass beaker filled with concentrated acetic acid. There was one red blotch on the front of her white robe. Her face was pure white marble, her eyes saucers. She hunched to one side slightly.

'This,' she whispered, staring at him, 'will develop *your* picture, Benjie.'

She started to throw it in his face, but he fired at her heart. She jerked to the left, then fell foward, sprawling on her stomach. The beaker dropped from her hands onto one of the wool carpets. The concentrated acetic acid spilled on the carpet and began smoking and sizzling.

Ben took a look at her. A long look. Then he raised the gun to his temple, closed his eyes, and pulled the trigger.

BANG!

He fell to the floor, dead.

The birds were screaming, the cats running all around the room in a frenzy . . .

The door burst open, and a panting Bruno ran in.

'Jesus Christ . . .'

He ran towards the two bodies. He had heard the shots below and guessed what had happened. But still, to *see* it . . .

'Zaza!'

He tripped over one of the squealing cats and fell on his face, landing in some liquid spilled on the rug. He felt something hot biting his skin. He sat up, putting his wet hands to his face. Now his palms were biting, as were his forehead, his cheek, his bashed-in nose. . . .

Then his eyes. Something bit into his eyes. He started moaning, trying to rub whatever it was off his face with his sleeve. What *was* it? The biting was worse, a million devils biting, burning, devouring him. . . .

He staggered to his feet, wiping desperately at his face with his sleeve, his eyes burning. . . .

And then, above the screeching of the birds and the squealing of the cats, came the screaming of Bruno Zinh.

11

NIGHTMARE
1871

41

The winter of 1870–71 was a happy time for Lew Crandall, even though he was aware that it was probably nothing but a lull in the storm of his life. Thanks to the opening of a telegraph line from Mexico City to the Texas border, he was able to keep abreast of events in Washington while at the same time he pursued his various business interests in Mexico. In December, Norbert Wilson informed him that Gilbert Samson was following up a number of leads in Pennsylvania, but that so far he had not been 'lucky' – which was their prearranged code word meaning that Gilbert had stumbled on something sensational. The *Banner* had continued to play up the incident of the theft of the Star of Mexico, but by Christmas Norbert informed Lew that that particular string had been pretty well played out and that, in fact, the publicity was having an adverse side effect. Matoon's colleagues in the Senate were stampeding to the senator's defence, and denunciations of the *Banner*'s 'smear' campaign were thundering from the Senate floor, along with orotund paeans celebrating Matoon's contributions to the war effort and his love of country, liberty, and motherhood. The other leading American newspapers, which had gleefully jumped into the Star of Mexico brouhaha in the wake of the *Banner*'s scoop, hooted and howled at these speeches as loudly as the *Banner*. But Norbert cabled that the public was beginning to tire of the whole thing. And Lew, realizing that he was flogging a dead horse, cabled back to keep

Matoon out of the paper for a while. It was better to give the public a respite before the major attack in the spring. Since his lawsuit against Matoon was hopelessly entangled in red tape and delaying tactics, he cabled his lawyers to drop that also. Its purpose had been achieved: the battle lines had been drawn. Now it was probably wiser for the publisher of the *Banner* to display magnaminity.

Meanwhile, he and Ysabel enjoyed a balmy winter with their children and their growing circle of friends in Mexico City and the Morelos Valley. To Lew's amusement, he was now invited regularly to the very houses that once, as El Juero, he had robbed. He was completely open about his former career as a jewel thief. There were some who found it outrageous, but they were too in awe of his present power and wealth (as well as his father-in-law's) to do much about it but grumble. Most, on the other hand, found it intriguing, and the very women he had robbed vied to be seated next to the dashing gringo ex-thief at dinner parties, hinting that they would not be at all dismayed if he climbed in their bedroom windows at night and lifted not only their jewellery but also their bedsheets. A bemused Lew took it all in his stride; secretly, he enjoyed his notoriety. Ysabel found it somewhat disturbing that her husband displayed no guilt at all over his criminal past, but she had become resigned to his, at best, equivocal morality. When he told her – as he often did – that it was much more exciting robbing the rich than dining with them, she sighed and changed the subject. She knew Lew Crandall had his own private code, and that he would never be entirely 'respectable'. Secretly, she rather admired it.

Nor was Ysabel entirely 'respectable'. Defying the custom of upper-class Mexican wives to live entirely in the shadows of their husbands, Ysabel became involved in charity work. The kernel that had been her desire to start a school for the children of the workers on her father's hacienda now sprouted into an active interest in national education, though most of her friends considered the peon as only slightly above the level of the cow. She began a series of dinner parties in the capital to which she invited politicians and educators, badgering them about the government's lack of commitment to a national school system. She also devoted her own time and money to individual schools. In all this Lew supported her wholeheartedly, giving large sums of his own money to his wife's projects. He admired Ysabel's compassion for the poor – which, having known poverty himself, he shared. Ysabel was vital and involved with life. Rather to his surprise, he was finding himself lonely when he wasn't with her, and he enjoyed nothing more than spending evenings talking to her about her projects and his. If, initially, he had not felt the passion for her that he had felt for Laura de Beaupré, he now found that Ysabel had become an indispensable part of his life. Some time in the middle of that idyllic winter, it occurred to him that this was probably really love, and that sex and the stormy passions of his youth, which he had always thought of as love, were only a part of the man-woman relationship; that mutual admiration, enjoyment, and common interests were as important as physical passion. If Lew Crandall would never be entirely 'respectable', as he passed his thirty-third birthday he was becoming very much the bourgeois family man. Ysabel blossomed under the sun of his affection. One blossom was another child. In January 1871 she told him she was, for the third time, pregnant.

Lew couldn't have been happier. Life with Ysabel was anything but dramatic. However, after years of drama, Lew longed for serenity. With Ysabel he found it. He also found happiness.

But he knew that the drama was not entirely over, for the final confrontation with Matoon still lay ahead. And in mid-February, when Norbert cabled him that Gilbert Samson had gotten 'lucky', Lew told Ysabel that it was time to return to Washington. On 20 February 1871 they left the capital for Veracruz, accompanied by governesses and nurses, the children, and mountains of luggage. At Veracruz they boarded the private yacht of Lord Roderick Despard, a wealthy English business associate of Lew's and an investor in his railroads. The yacht took them to Havana, where they spent a few days, then on to Washington where, on 4 March, they returned to West Wind. The estate was now guarded by round-the-clock armed guards, which Lew had cabled Norbert to hire for him. He knew that once the *Banner* began publishing, Matoon might well resort to the ultimate weapon: violence.

At ten o'clock on the morning of 5 March, Arturo deposited Lew at the door of the *Banner* building, and the publisher walked in. Many of his employees didn't recognize him. Gone was the beard and the brown hair. He had thrown away the dye and let his own blond hair grow back in. This, coupled with a Mexican suntan, gave him an entirely new look. When he stepped into Norbert's office, even his editor didn't recognize him at first. Then, realizing he knew few people with suntans, he got up. 'Lew!' he exclaimed, hurrying to shake his hand. 'Welcome back!'

'Thanks. It's good to see you, Norbert. And it's good to hear Gilbert's gotten "lucky".'

'Wait till you hear *how* lucky. You look quite a bit different.'

'Well, you'd better put out a memorandum to the staff that Peter Fraser caught a bad cold in Mexico and died. Poor man – his last hours were an agony. He left everything he had to Lew Crandall.'

'Then welcome back, Lew Crandall.'

'Is Gilbert here?'

'Yes.'

'Then why don't you bring him to my office, and you two can fill me in. Needless to say, I'm a bit anxious to hear.'

'When I first started going through the *Congressional Record*,' said Gilbert Samson twenty minutes later in Lew's office, 'and spotted that Matoon had been the sponsor of the bill that included funds for the building of the Harrisburg War Memorial Bridge, I thought that there was a place we might get lucky.'

'The bridge,' said Norbert, who was sitting next to Gilbert, 'was built in eighteen sixty-six by the Army Corps of Engineers.'

'Why?' said Lew. 'They don't build bridges, do they?'

'No, but they "improve rivers", quote unquote, and Matoon convinced the Senate that the Susquehannah needed a spillway at Harrisburg and fast-talked the boys into putting a bridge on top of it while they were at it. The bridge became a "river improvement" along with the spillway.'

'My God.'

'Right – it's rotten. The truth is, Harrisburg needed a bridge and didn't want to pay for it. So they called on their beloved ex-mayor, who got the bridge out of Uncle Sam.'

'A short canal was dug on the west side of the spillway so river traffic could get around it,' continued Gilbert, 'and the bridge spanned the canal too. The whole thing was over three hundred feet long. It was opened August tenth, eighteen sixty-seven. On September sixth, eighteen sixty-seven, a hurricane swung through Pennsylvania and wrecked hell out of the place. One of the casualties was the War Memorial Bridge. The wind tore the thing to pieces and it collapsed, washing out a big section of the spillway. This caused a flood in which forty-seven people were drowned. All this was less than a month after the damned thing was opened.'

'Of course, a howl went up, and there was a big investigation,' said Norbert.

'I read through the investigation, and it seemed to be thorough enough. The Corps of Engineers explained that they had miscalculated their stress tables, and the whole thing was blamed on God and the Army. Well, that looked *fairly* believable, so I kept looking elsewhere. I came across a lot of evidence of the fine hand of our friend, the fat senator. I have a list of projects he was involved with. Just as you suspected, he has a passion for post offices. A construction company he owns has built seventeen in Pennsylvania since the war. There have been other projects – it's all in here' – he tapped a pile of paper on Lew's desk – 'and Matoon made money off all of them. I've found plenty of shady practices – kickbacks, price-rigging. . . . And you were right, Lew. He does own a lumber company in Harrisburg, and guess who got most of the government business? Don't guess too hard. But while all this stank, none of it was headline stuff, and I kept thinking about that goddam bridge. I decided it was all too pat, so I went to Harrisburg for a week and started looking up the people who had testified at the investigation. And that's when I heard about George Denison.'

'Who's he?' said Lew.

'A former reporter on one of the Harrisburg papers. I was told he had wanted to testify at the investigation, but never did. So I looked him up. He was working as a clerk at a grocery store. I told him I was interested in the bridge story, and he began talking. Man, did he talk! It turned out he had found out the truth about the bridge, and everyone else who knew had been paid off to shut up. When he tried to print the truth in the paper, they fired him – Matoon has a lot of clout in Harrisburg – and he found he was blackballed in the newspaper business. So he ended up in a grocery store. And if you think *you* hate Matoon, talk to Mr Denison!'

'What was the truth?'

'One of Matoon's companies provided the cement for the spillway, and it was no good. This was all conveniently overlooked at the investigation. The cement company wasn't even mentioned, while the Army kept talking about stress tables. The company's called the Allegheny Cement Works, and Matoon's name isn't listed anywhere. But the biggest hunk of stock is owned by a certain Chester Twillingham, and guess who Chester Twillingham turns out to be?'

'I'll bite.'

'Matoon's drunk cousin.'

'In other words, he's the "moneybag man"?'

'Right. He holds the stock in his name, keeps ten per cent of the gravy as a fee, and passes on the rest to Cousin Ralph. So Cousin Ralph made a bundle off the Harrisburg bridge, the collapse of which cost forty-seven people their lives. And I think that, with everything else I dug up, puts the noose around Matoon's neck.'

'Will Denison testify?'

'He'll sign affadavits – anything to get Matoon.'

'How about Cousin Chester? How do we prove the connection between him and Matoon?'

'He used to live with a woman named Marie Forbes – Denison gave me her name, which is how I found out about Cousin Chester. Miss Forbes got in a fight with Chester and broke up with him, and she's willing to testify that she went with him several times to Washington and actually saw him pass the cash to Matoon at his house.'

Lew got up, came around his desk, and shook Gilbert's hand. 'I think you've done it,' he said, 'and I'm proud of you. Let's bring Denison to Washington, and you and he start working up the article. Think you can have it done by next week?'

'Yes.'

'Good. Then we'll print the whole thing. I want a big woodcut of Matoon in the centre of page one, and a headline like . . . any ideas?'

'How about "Matoon Connection to Harrisburg Bridge Disaster Revealed"?' said Norbert.

Lew shook his head. 'Too wordy.'

'"Senator's Empire of Fraud Exposed"?' suggested Gilbert.

'Lacks punch.'

Silence. Then Norbert said, 'How about two big words: "Matoon Murders!"'

Lew's face lit up.

'That's it, goddammit! Matoon Murders! I love it! And he did – he murdered those forty-seven people who drowned as well as if he'd slit their throats!'

'He murdered Christine,' said Gilbert.

'He tried to murder me,' said Lew. 'Gentlemen, we're in business. I congratulate both of you. Tomorrow night, I'll throw a little celebration, and we'll all drink to Matoon's hanging with champagne.'

'Except me,' said Gilbert, standing up. 'I'll drink milk. By the way, I thought you'd like to know: Flora and I got legal.'

'You were married?'

'Yep. We even bought ourselves a farm west of town. Thirty acres and the prettiest little house in Maryland.'

'Congratulations.'

Gilbert hesitated. 'Flora . . . well, she says we owe it all to you.'

'That's not true. I wouldn't have hired you if I hadn't thought you were good.'

'Well, she says . . . the drinking and everything. Anyway, she wanted to know if you and your wife would like to come to dinner some night? We'd love to show you the place. The thing is' – he looked Lew in the eye – 'we don't know whether you like Southern cooking.'

'I don't know much about Southern cooking.'

'Well, I meant . . . we're coloured.'

'I know what you meant. Listen, Gilbert: I've been a thief, a bandit; I've been on a chain gang, and I've killed people. On top of which, I'm a Frog married to a Spic. Now, it seems to me the question is whether you want disreputable people like me and my wife in your house?'

Gilbert smiled. 'Well . . . will you check your guns at the door?'

Lew laughed. 'Be glad to. When do you want us?'

'How about tomorrow night? Let Flora and me give the celebration for Matoon's hanging. Norbert, could you and your wife come?'

'Be delighted to.'

'You're on,' said Lew. 'And I'll bring the champagne. You can furnish the milk.'

'From my own cow!' Gilbert grinned.

Lew escorted them to the door. When they had left, he closed the door and stood a moment, thinking. Matoon. Yes, the Harrisburg bridge was perfect. After ten years, he had him.

It was a sweet feeling.

At four that afternoon, Lew's carriage pulled up in front of the Biddles' Georgetown house and Lew got out. He carried a large Mexican straw bag filled with presents. He told Arturo to wait for him and was starting towards the front door when he spotted his son kicking a ball in the empty lot next door. He headed for Ward instead. It was a cold day, with a strong March wind blowing, and Ward had on a thick sweater. He was by himself in the weed-grown lot and seemed listless. He kicked the ball towards two upright sticks at the end of the lot, then walked to retrieve it. As he picked it up, he saw his father. At least, he thought it was his father until he saw the blond hair.

'Yes, it's me,' said Lew, coming up to him.

'Is that a wig?' asked Ward, pointing to his hair.

'*This* is the real thing. Same colour as yours. How are you?'

'Oh, all right.' He spotted the straw bag. 'Are those for me?'

'Not all. Some are for your sister. We brought them from Mexico. Did you ever see a sombrero?'

He set down the bag and pulled a black sombrero from it.

'Is that what the Mexican cowboys wear?'

'Some of them. Here: try it on for size.'

He put the hat on Ward's head.

'How does it fit?'

'It feels all right. Thanks a lot.' Ward took the sombrero off and looked at it. Then he twisted it around.

'What's wrong?' asked Lew, who could sense a certain hostility. 'Aren't you glad to see me? I'm glad to see you.'

Ward forced a smile. 'Sure I'm glad to see you. You know that.'

'No, I don't know that. I don't know much about you at all, but I guess I know enough to realize something's bothering you. Are you mad at me?'

Ward looked up quickly. 'Oh no!' Then he changed his tune. 'Well, I am a little.'

'Because I went to Mexico?'

He nodded. 'There's something else,' he went on. 'We got a cable yesterday from Paris. The Germans and the French finally signed an armistice, so Mother could get word out to us.'

'Is she all right?'

'Yes. But our father . . . well, Pauline's father, anyway . . . committed suicide.'

Lew winced.

'Ben?'

Ward nodded, staring at his feet. 'I don't know why. The funny thing is, Pauline hardly remembers him, so she's not as upset as I am. But I *do* remember him, and he was always nice to me.' He looked up. 'He was my father until you came along. It's sort of crazy, isn't it? Did you know him very well? He told me once you were his best friend.'

'I was. We grew up together.'

'Then do you know why he killed himself? Oh, I know he was living with that singer . . . and I know he drank a lot, I guess. But still, why would he kill himself? He wasn't very old.'

A gust of wind blew his hair.

'I don't know, Ward. It's been so many years since I've even seen Ben, I have no idea. . . . He was a good man, though. And a good friend. He helped a lot of people when he was younger.'

'Did he? Who did he help?'

'He ran a station on the Underground Railroad. He helped a lot of runaway slaves.'

'No kidding? Gee, he never told me that. I knew he lost his leg in the war.'

They looked at each other, Ward's hair blowing in the wind.

'Last fall,' he said, 'you told me we had a lot of catching up to do. And then you went to Mexico. I still don't know very much about you except what Aunt Debbie told me. You've got another family, haven't you?'

Lew nodded.

'So where does that leave me?' asked Ward. 'Suddenly you appeared out of nowhere, and then you left again. And now you're back with a lot of presents. And my other father . . . well, he left Mother, and now he's dead. I'm sort of mixed up. It seems like my fathers come and go.'

Lew closed his eyes a moment. Then he opened them.

'Well,' he said, 'you've done what few people have been able to do. You've made me crawl with guilt.'

'I just asked a question,' said Ward. 'I didn't mean to make you feel guilty. It's not your fault. I just don't know where I am.'

Lew squatted down and took his hands. 'Look,' he said. 'I guess I've been the world's worst father – or at least the world's most absent father. But we're back in Washington for six months now, and I'm going to try and make up to you for all the time we've missed. I want to be your father, Ward. Or at least as much as I can be. Anyway, I want you to *think* of me as your father. That is, if you want to.'

'Of course I want to.'

'Last time I saw you, I said I was afraid you wouldn't like me. Well, now I not only want you to like me, I want you to love me. And any time you want me – any time you want to talk to me about anything, or whatever . . . any time you *need* me, I swear I'll drop anything I'm doing and come running. I want you to believe that, Ward.'

Ward nodded. 'I believe it.'

'You know, I've got twin boys. They're still only about three, but I'd like you to meet them. I'd like you to meet all my family. Would you like that?'

'Sure.'

'Then my wife and I will have to have you and Pauline out to West Wind.'

'What's West Wind?'

'That's our house over in Virginia. Maybe you could come spend a week or so with us. Is your mother coming back from Paris now?'

'I don't know. She didn't say anything about it in the cable.'

Lew stood up. 'Well, anyway, our house is your house. And I'm sorry you don't like the sombrero.'

Ward look surprised. 'I didn't say I didn't like it!'

'Oh. Well, you didn't look very enthusiastic. I was about to take all your presents back.'

Ward gaped. 'You'd better never!' he exclaimed. 'I want to see them!'

Lew laughed and gave him a Dutch rub.

'That's more like it. Come on let's go in and look at the loot from Mexico. It's Christmas all over again.'

He picked up the straw bag and started for the house. Ward gave his ball a quick kick towards the makeshift goal posts, then ran to catch up with his father. When he reached him, Lew put his hand around his shoulder. Ward put his arm around his waist. Then they went inside the Biddles' house.

Mrs Angela Allen, the society columnist of the *Banner*, was an imposing woman in her sixties who liked big hats, flowers, rich people, and dirt. Unfortunately, her dirt was so stale and inaccurate that 'Addled Angie', as she was known by the other people on the *Banner*, was anything but an asset to the newspaper, and Lew and Norbert had been looking for a replacement for her for some time. But that afternoon, as the cab let her out under the porte-cochère of the Matoon mansion, Addled Angie had some dirt that was neither stale nor inaccurate. It was also, she knew, pay dirt.

'Wait for me,' she told the cabman. Then she went to the front door and rang.

'Is the senator in?' she asked Henry when he answered.

'Yes ma'am.'

'Would you ask him if he could see Mrs Allen for a moment? It's important.'

'Yes ma'am. Come right in.'

Henry left her in the drawing room. Five minutes later, Matoon came in, closing the doors behind him.

'How are you, Angie?' he said, crossing the room to the fireplace, where she was standing.

Fine, Ralph. Mr Crandall's back, you know.'

'Yes, I heard.'

'They're publishing some time next week. Everything they have about you.'

'Have you been able to read it?'

'No. They're guarding it as if it were the crown jewels. But I know there's something about a bridge.'

Matoon looked at her.

'What bridge?'

'Some bridge in Harrisburg. I overheard that horrid black man say something about it to Mr Wilson. Personally, I can't understand how Mr Crandall could hire a Negro on a newspaper with the standing of the *Banner*.'

Matoon pulled an envelope from his coat pocket and handed it to her.

'This is for you, Angie. And you've done good work. I appreciate it.'

She put the envelope in her purse. 'Well, for a man who has done as much as you have for our country to be hounded and smeared by a vindictive person like Mr Crandall . . . well, it just strikes me as cruel, that's all. The man is obsessed with revenge! Personally, I think it's the influence of his wife. Those Mexicans! All they think about are vendettas. They're worse than the Italians.'

Matoon escorted her to the sliding doors. 'Lew Crandall is a pathetic person,' he said. 'I feel sorry for him. I think he's probably a little bit crazy in the head.'

'Oh, I agree absolutely. To hire a Negro? Well, my cab is waiting. Good night, Ralph.'

'Good night, Angie. And thanks again.'

When she got back in the cab, she pulled the envelope out and looked inside. One hundred dollars!

Addled Angie put the envelope back in her purse and smiled.

Ysabel looked down the polished table at her husband and said, 'What's wrong, darling?'

Lew straightened in his chair. 'My past is catching up with me.'

'Is it Ward?'

'Yes.'

They were in the dining room at West Wind, and outside the west wind was sweeping around the house. Draughts puffed the long blue silk curtains over the closed windows and flickered the candles in their tall Georgian sticks, making the light on the elegant Chinese landscape that papered the walls shimmer, bringing the stiff mandarins with their smiling concubines to ghostly life. A footman placed a plate in front of Lew, who looked without interest at the slice of pink roast.

When the footman had left the room, Ysabel said, 'Was he terribly upset about his stepfather's suicide?'

'Yes. He was also upset with me. I shouldn't have popped into his life last fall and then taken right off for Mexico.'

'You had good reasons.'

'I know, but . . . I'm telling you, Ysabel, if you'd seen his face when he said "It seems like my fathers come and go. . . ." Well, it broke my heart, and my heart doesn't break easily. And I don't know *what* Elizabeth's up to! Now that she can finally get out of Paris, why doesn't she come home? The boy's all alone! It's bad enough with his invisible father, but an invisible mother, too?'

'Well, it's possible she can't leave Paris yet.'

'Yes, it's possible.'

He started to cut the beef, but changed his mind and took a sip of the Burgundy instead. Then he slumped back in his chair again. 'It's Matoon again,' he said quietly. 'It's always Matoon.'

'Well, you can't blame Ward's loneliness on Matoon.'

'Can't I? Why didn't he ever have a real father? Wasn't it Matoon's fault?'

'I suppose so.'

'Well, Matoon's going to get his soon. But that doesn't help Ward. Would you mind if I brought him and Pauline out here for a while?'

'Of course not. I'd love it. I should have thought of it myself.'

'Then I'll make the arrangements with his aunt.' He sat up and cut into the meat. He took a bite and chewed. Then he washed it down with more Burgundy.

'If you could have seen his face . . .' he repeated, more to himself than to Ysabel.

42

Ned Norton watched his best friend twirling the lasso and groaned inwardly with envy.

'My father says they can jump in and out of the rope in Mexico,' said Ward, who had on the black *charro* outfit his father had brought him. Even though they were indoors, in Ned Norton's attic playroom, Ward still had on his black sombrero.

Now, as he twirled the lasso low, he tried jumping inside. He failed.

'Let me try!' said Ned, getting off the trunk he was sitting on. Ward gave him the rope and watched as Ned tried to twirl it.

'You're not doing it right,' said Ward. 'Here – let me show you.'

Ned was Ward's age and his best friend in Washington. The son of a lawyer, Ned lived three houses down from the Biddles.

'See? You've got to get it going. . . .'

Ward's new-found expertise with lasso-twirling impressed Ned, but what he really wanted was the *charro* outfit.

'Are you going to let me try on the sombrero?' he said.

'All right.' Ward put down the rope and took off his sombrero. He handed it to Ned, who looked at it with ill-disguised covetousness.

'Boy, it sure is beautiful.'

He put it on his head. 'How do I look?' he asked uncertainly.

'Well' – Ward inspected him sniffishly – 'you don't look very Mexican to me.'

'How about *you*? Whoever heard of a blond Mexican?'

'I'm a gringo!' announced Ward, bursting with pride at being able to show off his new word. 'Just like my father.'

'What's a gringo?'

'Boy, are you dumb. A gringo's an American, like you and me. That's what the Mexicans call us. Here, give me back my sombrero. . . .'

'Boys?' The voice of Ned's mother was heard at the bottom of the attic stairs. 'It's eight-thirty!'

Ned growled as he took off the sombrero.

'All right, Mother,' he called. He gave Ward the hat, whispering, 'Will you loan me the rope till tomorrow?'

'No!'

'I want to practise twirling it. Come on.'

'Oh, all right. Take it. But just till tomorrow.'

'Boy, are you stingy.'

'I'm leaving you the rope, aren't I? You're just jealous because you're father hasn't been in Mexico.'

'My father's been in England and all over Europe!' Ned fired back.

'Yeah, well that's not *Mexico*.'

Ned put out the light, then the two boys hurried down the stairs. When they reached the ground floor, Mrs Norton smiled at Ward.

'My, that's certainly a handsome outfit, Ward. What did you say they call it?'

'It's a *charro* outfit,' said Ward, again swelling with pride. 'It's what the cowboys wear, but only the rich ones. I don't know what the poor ones wear.'

'Are there rich cowboys in Mexico?'

'That's what my father said. He also said there are a lot of bandits. Boy, would I like to meet a bandit – wouldn't you, Ned?'

'Yeah.'

'Well, I'm not sure *I* would,' said Mrs Norton. 'You'd better get home now, Ward. It's Ned's bedtime.'

'All right. Good night, Mrs Norton. And Ned: don't lose that rope.'

'I won't. I never lose things.'

Ward went to the front door and opened it.

'If you meet any bandits on the way home,' said Ned, 'don't let them take your sombrero.'

'Are you kidding? Bandits wouldn't get anything from *me*. I'd shoot 'em down. Bang! Bang! Bang! Like that.'

He blew imaginary smoke from the end of his finger, then put his imaginary gun back in his imaginary holster and swaggered out to the dark street.

Mexico! Bandits! His father had told him just enough that afternoon to fire his imagination to white heat. Now he wasn't walking down the quiet Georgetown street. He was galloping across the plains of Mexico, firing at bandits who had seized the beautiful maiden. . . . 'Bang! Bang! Bang!' He fired his finger-gun into a rhododendron bush. 'Got you, you villain!' He was having such a wonderful time in Mexico that he didn't notice a buggy pulling up behind him. The buggy slowed, and a man jumped out. He had on a black suit and a black hat. He was in his thirties and sported a thick moustache.

'Bang! Bang! Bang!'

'Excuse me, young man.'

Ward turned and looked at the man. 'Yes sir?'

'Are you Ward Bramwell?'

'Yes sir.'

'Your father wants to see you.'

'He does? You mean now?'

'That's right. He sent us to bring you to him.'

Ward looked uncertainly at the buggy, which was driven by another man in a black suit. Then he turned to look down the street at the Biddles' house.

'I'd better tell my aunt first. . . .'

Something smashed down on his sombrero, and Ward's world turned off.

Flora Samson turned the two eggs over in the frying pan.

'I'm having chicken tonight,' she said to her husband, who was sitting behind her at the table in their cheerful kitchen. 'Do you think they'll like that? Or is chicken not fancy enough for the Crandalls?'

Gilbert was looking through the morning paper. 'Chicken'll be fine,' he said. 'I don't know about her, but Lew isn't that way.'

'You mean a snob?'

'That's right. Besides, the way you cook chicken, *anybody* would like it.'

'What's Mr Wilson's wife's name?'

'Helen.'

'Well, I'm going to have *some* day. Got to clean this place till it squeaks, got to set the table, got to cook the meal . . . what time are you bringing them out?'

Silence. She turned around to look at Gilbert. 'Honey, you listening to me?'

He put the paper on the table. 'I don't know if they'll be coming,' he said, getting up.

'What's wrong?'

'Something in the paper . . . I don't think there's going to be much celebrating tonight.' He kissed her cheek. 'I'd better get to town fast.'

'What's in the paper?'

'Read it. Page two. The boy in Georgetown.'

'But what about your breakfast, Gilbert?'

He had left the kitchen. Shaking her head, she went to the table and looked at page two. She saw the headline: 'Congressman's Nephew Reported Missing in Georgetown.'

She read it, then hurried through the house to the front door, where Gilbert was putting on his overcoat.

'Who's the boy that's missing?'

'Ward Bramwell is Lew's son by his first marriage. There's going to be a lot of trouble.'

'You think Matoon . . .?'

'Who else?'

He kissed her and hurried out of the house to the stable to hitch up his buggy.

Ralph Matoon had one of the more elaborately decorated offices in the Senate. A vast, globed gasolier hung from the frescoed ceiling, its hundreds of crystals reflecting in the enormous gold-framed mirror that rose almost to the ceiling behind his desk. Not an inch of the walls had been spared decoration: delicately painted flowers scrambled up and down with charming, if excessive exuberance. Flowers expanded on the thick carpet also, so that the clawed feet of the heavy leather chairs and sofas – as well as the feet of the senator himself – sank into an eternal meadow. Marble flowers garlanded the mantel, in which a fire was burning this chill March morning when Mr Gerald Dexter, the senator's secretary, came in the office.

'Mr Crandall is here,' said Mr Dexter, a slight man from Harrisburg. 'He wants to see you.'

Matoon was standing at the window. He didn't turn.

'Show him in,' he said.

'Yes sir.'

Dexter went out. Matoon moved quickly to his desk, sat down, opened a drawer, and pulled out a revolver. He checked to make sure it was loaded. Then he replaced it in the drawer, leaving the drawer half open.

Mr Dexter came back, followed by Lew Crandall. The publisher of the *Banner* was dressed in a checked suit and carried a bowler hat in his hand. Mr Dexter thought the suit was perhaps a bit loud for Washington, but he had to admit the tall man cut a dashing figure. His face, though, was stony. Mr Dexter left the room, wondering what was happening.

Senator Matoon smiled at Lew from his desk.

'Ah, Mr Fraser,' he said. 'Pardon me, it's Mr Crandall now, isn't it? You're such a chameleon, it's hard to keep up with you. What can I do for you, sir?'

'Where's my son?' His voice was almost a whisper.

'Yes,' said Matoon, 'I read about the disappearance of young Bramwell in the paper. Some scoundrel has abducted him, I gather. Shocking.'

'We received a note at the *Banner* an hour ago saying that if we publish what we have on you, my son will die. All right, Matoon: I've stopped the edition. But I want my son back.'

'So I take it you think *I* have abducted your son?'

'Don't play games with me, Matoon. I'm in no mood for games.'

'Assuming I had committed this dastardly deed – and by the way, I was at the British Legation last evening at a reception from seven till past one this morning, so I have plenty of witnesses to testify I had nothing to do with the abduction – but assuming I *had* what assurances would I have that you wouldn't publish this libellous trash about me after your son were returned?'

'What assurances would you want?'

'That you sell the *Banner* and return to Mexico. *Permanently*.'

Lew said nothing for a moment. Then: 'I'll have to think this over. Can I give you an answer in the morning?'

'Take your time,' said the senator. 'I'm in no hurry.'

'I'll be here at ten tomorrow. But Matoon: I give you my solemn word. If that boy is so much as scratched, I'll kill you.'

Matoon smiled. 'Such a bad temper, Lew, my boy. When you first came to work for me years ago, you were such a nice young man. It grieves me to see how you've changed.'

'The change, Matoon, has all been thanks to you, because when you walked into my life that nice young man you're talking about died. Sometime we'll have to have a long talk about it. I have *many* memories I'd love to share with you. Meanwhile, don't underestimate me. If Ward is hurt, you die.'

'Oh, I'd never underestimate you, Lew.' Matoon chuckled. 'Why, you keep turning up like a bad penny. And now that we're letting our hair down, so to speak, tell me: I've always been curious. What the hell happened that day at Bull Run? Did Burt Thomson shoot you, or didn't he?'

'You return my son,' said Lew softly, 'and I'll tell you all about it.'

He turned and walked out of the room, closing the door behind him.

Matoon slowly shut the desk drawer that held the revolver.

They had a meeting at West Wind that afternoon. Lew, Gilbert, Norbert, and Ysabel. They had a meeting in the library, and they were all seated. But no one said anything.

Lew was sitting on a bench in front of the fire. His left elbow was on his knee, and his chin rested on his fist as he stared at the design in the Oriental rug. Finally, Ysabel came across the room and put her hand on his shoulder.

'We know what you're going through, darling,' she said. 'But he's given us no choice.'

'I know.'

She ran her hand over his hair. 'Perhaps it's better if God punishes him.'

Lew said nothing. The tall grandfather clock in the corner ticked sleepily as its brass pendulum swung to and fro. He glanced up at its moon-bedecked face. Two minutes before three. Nineteen hours left.

'The damnable thing is,' he said, 'I never thought of Ward. This place crawls with guards, but Ward . . . I forgot about him. I *forgot* . . .' He closed his eyes.

Tick tock, tick tock. The Westminster chimes began striking the hour.

'Perhaps,' said Gilbert, 'the police will find him in time.'

'The police,' said Lew scornfully. 'What can they do? The Washington police force is a joke in the first place, and even if it weren't, where are they going to look? He could be anywhere. In the city, outside the city. . . . It's searching for a needle in a haystack. And there're only nineteen hours left.'

'Then,' said Norbert, 'agree to his terms.'

'Of course I'll agree to them in the end. But maybe . . .'

'Maybe what, darling?' said Ysabel.

'I don't know.'

The Westminster chimes fell silent. Norbert turned to Gilbert and said, 'Did you manage to get word to your wife about tonight?'

'Yes. I told her this morning the party was off.'

Another silence. Ysabel searched her mind for something to say to try to break these horrible silences, to try to relieve, even feebly, the agony her husband was going through. 'I was looking forward to seeing your place, Mr

Samson,' she said. 'My husband tells me it's in the country.'

'Yes. It's out in Maryland.'

'You were from Maryland originally, I believe?'

Gilbert nodded. 'From the Eastern Shore. I grew up on a plantation. I always wanted to farm . . . guess it's in my blood. Well, I haven't got a plantation, exactly, but I've got a farm. We love it.'

'Have you ever gone back to the Eastern Shore?'

'No, but I plan to one day. I've corresponded with Miss Julie – she was my owner.'

'That seems such an odd word to use now, doesn't it?'

'I know, but that's what she was. She owned me. In a way, it's rather ironic that we write each other occasional letters, since she taught me to read and write in the first place. In those days, it was a crime to teach slaves to read and write, but Miss Julie did it. She was quite a woman. Still is, for that matter.'

'Does she still own the plantation you grew up on?'

'Oh yes. It came through the war all right. She freed her slaves back in the fifties, which caused a ruckus.' He was remembering that night so many years ago when the men in the masks took him away from Billie Orton's. . . . He remembered even before then when he had stood in the library of Scarborough Hall and told Miss Julie he wanted to be free. He remembered the odd tension he had felt when he was around her, the way she had reached out and touched him that day she had come to Billie Orton's. He had never really understood what he felt then, but now, in retrospect, he realized he must have loved her. He wondered if she had loved him? 'She never married,' he added aloud.

'You mean Miss Julie?' asked Ysabel.

'Yes. She wrote me she's going to die an old maid, and she's glad of it. That's a long time ago. A long time . . .'

Tick tock, tick tock. Lew looked at the clock. Five minutes past three. He got up and went to one of the windows. He looked out over the lawn. It was a grey day, a miserable day. Yesterday's wind had abated somewhat, but the bare branches of the trees were still swaying, their fingers clawing the clouds. He saw a carriage pull into the drive. He watched as it approached the house, then stopped in front. The coachman got down and opened the door.

Rosemary Matoon stepped out. She was wearing a mink coat and matching hat, and as she climbed the steps of the veranda, Lew couldn't help but admire her looks.

'Ysabel,' he said, 'Mrs Matoon is here. See what the bitch wants.'

'Lew!' said his wife, going to the door. 'After all . . .'

Ysabel went out, closing the door behind her.

'The funny thing is,' he said, still at the window, 'I made love to that bitch once.'

'Rosemary Matoon?' said Norbert.

'Rosemary Matoon. Of course, there weren't many people in Washington who weren't making love to her. Rosemary Fletcher was her name, and she had a house on Third Street with a picture of Lincoln over her bed. What a farce.'

The door reopened, and Ysabel came in followed by Rosemary. Norbert and Gilbert got to their feet.

'Lew,' said Ysabel, 'Rosemary wants to talk to you.'

He turned around at the window. 'What do you want?'

Rosemary looked at the others, then at Lew. 'I know where your son is,' she said. 'They have him at the Cromwell Farm on Silver Spring Road.'

The men exchanged looks. Then Lew said, 'Wait a minute. What are you up to, Rosemary?'

'This isn't a trap, if that's what you're thinking,' she said coolly. 'I know my husband has done terrible things in his life. I have too, for that matter. But kidnapping a child is beyond the pale. I think he must be mad.'

'Who did the kidnapping?'

'Two men he brought up from Florida. He's been planning this for weeks, ever since he heard you were planning to expose him. He's paying them five thousand dollars apiece, and I have no doubt they're dangerous. But I think if you surround the farm, they'll give up peaceably. Why should they risk their necks for Ralph Matoon?'

'Maybe they'll give up, maybe they won't,' said Lew, starting for the door. Then he said to Gilbert, 'We can take my guards. They've got guns for all of us. Come on.'

He left the room. Gilbert and Norbert were right behind him. When they were gone, Ysabel turned to Rosemary.

'My husband called you a bad name before you came in,' she said. 'I think he must be quite wrong.'

'He's not wrong,' replied Rosemary. 'But I have a son, Mrs Crandall.'

Which was all she said. Then she walked out of the room.

John Neill was dealing. Now he put down the deck and picked up his hand. He and Willis Hammond were playing three-card draw, nothing wild. John Neill had a pair of nines.

'I'll open with a dollar,' said Willis Hammond, flipping a gold-piece on the wooden table. He was a heavy-set man with a jowly face and a bald spot.

John Neill stayed in the game. 'How many cards?' he asked, picking up the deck.

Willis discarded two, then looked over to the stone fireplace where the boy in the odd black suit was tied to a chair, a gag around his mouth. His eyes were watching them.

'Cute little rascal, ain't he?' said Willis, picking up his new cards. 'Smooth skin like a girl. Big blue eyes.'

'Pretty as a picture,' said John, discarding to his pair. He picked up three new cards. Hot damn, he thought. Another nine. Gives me three of a kind. . . .

'Ever do it with a boy?' said Willis, studying his hand.

'Naw. Too many girls around beggin' for it.'

'I did once. Sort of interestin'.' He turned and grinned at Ward. 'How about it, Blondie? Want to go to bed with me?'

'Are you playin' poker or courtin'?' said John.

'Maybe both. I'll bet five dollars.'

He pushed out the money. John studied his three nines. The son of a bitch drew two, he thought, so he must have three of a kind. On the other hand, he bluffs . . . I won't raise, but I'll stay.

'I'm in,' he said, putting the money on the table. 'What are you so proud of?'

Willis laid down a full house, jacks on sixes.

'Shit,' said John, throwing in his hand. 'That cleaned me out.' He got up and stretched. Then he looked at Ward.

'What are we gonna do with Junior? We can't leave him tied like that all night.'

'Why not?'

'It'll stop his circulation, won't it? And what if he has to pee?'

'We'll take him to the privy before we turn in. That'll let his blood get goin' again.'

John went over to Ward, grabbed his hair, and jerked his head back.

'You ain't scared of us, are you, boy?' he asked. Then he let him go. 'We won't hurt you none long as you don't give us no trouble. Should we take the gag off, Willis? Nobody's gonna hear him out here even if he yells.'

'No, leave it on for a while. He'll just be whinin' and cryin' and who needs to listen to that shit?'

'Well,' and John leered, 'you can't kiss him with a gag on.'

'Wasn't thinkin' 'bout *kissin'* him.'

John went to one of the dirty windows and looked out. The farm was a ramshackle building northeast of Washington. It had been deserted for four years, and Matoon had rented it the previous month for a song. The yard was filled with dead weeds. By the Silver Spring Road, two ancient trees stood, their branches touching. Across the road were empty fields.

'Goddam, this is the middle of *nowhere*,' said John Neill, who had served time for larceny. He had met Willis Hammond in the Florida State Pentitentiary, and when they had been released they had teamed up. 'How long do you think we'll be here?'

'Who knows?' said Willis, studying Ward. 'Maybe we'll be through tomorrow, but we've got grub for a month.'

'Jesus, I hate to think of rottin' out here for a whole *month.*'

'We're gettin' paid well, ain't we? And if we get bored, we got Blondie here to amuse us.' He flashed a grin at Ward, revealing brown teeth. Ward stared at him. He didn't know what they were talking about. Willis got up from the table and put his gun in his belt. 'I'm goin' out to get some more wood. It's gettin' cold in here.'

'Good idea.'

'Keep an eye on Junior.'

'He ain't goin' no place.'

Willis went into the kitchen, shoving the squeaking door closed behind him. John Neill walked back to the table in the centre of the room and picked up his gun.

'Don't worry,' he said to Ward. 'He's just sayin' all that stuff to scare you. He won't do nothin' to you.'

Ward watched him.

John came over to his chair. 'Are your arms all right?' he said. 'You want me to loosen you up a little?'

Ward nodded.

John put the gun in his holster, then went behind the chair and loosened the knots.

'No use makin' you uncomfortable,' he said. 'Besides, don't worry too much. You'll be out of here soon. I'll bet anything this whole thing'll be over by tomorrow. There. That better?'

Ward nodded.

'I've got my eye on you, so don't get tricky. Willis has got a mean temper, and I'm no angel of charity. Understand?'

Ward nodded.

John wandered back to the front window and looked out again. It was getting dark. Lonely, creepy place, he thought. My God, who'd want to be a farmer?

Ten minutes dragged by.

'Wonder what's keepin' Willis?' he said, turning away from the window. 'He could bring in a whole goddam forest by this time. Willis?' he yelled.

Silence. John Neill frowned as he listened. He drew his gun and started toward the kitchen door, which was next to the stone chimney. When he reached the door, he waited, listening. Ward turned his head to watch him.

John Neill listened almost a full minute. Then, holding his gun, he kicked open the kitchen door.

A barrage of bullets pitched him back into the room. His last living act was to squeeze the trigger of his gun.

Lew and Gilbert were the first into the room, followed by Norbert and three of Lew's guards.

'One dead kidnapper!' crowed Gilbert, looking at the bullet-ridden corpse that was staring at the ceiling. Then he heard a strange sound behind him, a noise that was half a cry of rage and half a sob of agony. He turned to see Lew Crandall staring at the boy in the chair. Gilbert watched as Lew went slowly over to the chair. Ward's face had dropped on his chest, but Gilbert could see the blood oozing out of the bullet hole in his right temple. Gilbert looked back at John Neill's corpse. His gun had fired as they shot him. Then Gilbert looked at Ward's temple.

'Oh Jesus,' he muttered.

Lew carefully untied the gag. Then, squatting down, he untied the ankles. Then, finally, the wrists. When Ward was free, he slumped forward. Lew caught him, then gently picked him up in his arms. The others were watching silently: Gilbert, Norbert, and the three guards. The fourth guard was outside with Willis, who they had surprised when he came out of the house for firewood. Then they had crept into the kitchen, waiting for the other man to appear, not daring to do anything while he was in the room with Ward. And then, finally, he had opened the door. . . .

Lew was crying as he held his dead son. He carried him over to a sagging sofa in the corner and laid him on it. Then he knelt beside him. Pulling a handkerchief from his pocket, he gently daubed the blood that was matting his hair. It had almost stopped coming out of the wound. Then he crossed Ward's hands over the the *charro* suit he had brought him from Mexico. Then he reached up and closed his eyes. Finally, he kissed his forehead.

When he stood up and turned around, Gilbert Samson had never seen a face so intense or eyes so full of burning hate.

'Bring my son to West Wind,' Lew said softly. 'I'm going back to Washington.'

He crossed the room towards the kitchen, stepping over John Neill's corpse. Gilbert said as he passed him, 'What are you going to do?'

'What I should have done in the first place.'

He walked into the kitchen.

Gilbert looked at Norbert.

'Stop him,' whispered Norbert.

Gilbert nodded and hurried into the kitchen. Lew was going out the back door. Gilbert followed him.

'Wait a minute. . . .'

He caught up with him outside the kitchen door. The back yard of the farm was weedy and strewn with junk: a rusted milk can on its side, a broken-down rotted wagon under a tree. Beside the barn, the fourth guard stood next to Willis Hammond, whose hands had been tied behind his back. In the woods behind the barn were tied the horses.

'Lew, don't do it,' said Gilbert.

Lew didn't stop. He was headed for the woods. Gilbert walked beside him.

'We've got this one,' he said, pointing to Willis. 'He'll testify that Matoon hired them. . . .'

'What would he get? Five years? And he'd be out in three. He's a senator.'

'All right, but we can publish now. . . .'

'You bet your ass we'll publish. It's still not enough. Matoon has to pay in kind.'

'Goddammit, use your head, man! You can't *murder* him!'

Lew said nothing. He just kept walking.

'I'm not going to let you do this,' said Gilbert.

'You can't stop me.'

Gilbert grabbed his arm, jerked him around, and smashed his fist into his jaw. Lew fell back in the weeds. He lay on his back a moment. Then he tried to sit up, rubbing his jaw.

'I'm not going to let you be *hanged*!' Gilbert roared.

Lew got to his feet slowly. He continued rubbing his jaw a moment. Then, fast, he slammed his right fist into Gilbert's stomach. As the black man doubled over, Lew gave him an uppercut. Gilbert staggered forward, then lunged for Lew's knees. He tackled him, bringing him down. They rolled around in the weeds, wrestling. Then Gilbert got on top of him, straddling him, pinioning his arms to the ground. Lew stared up at him, panting.

'Don't do this, Gilbert,' he said. 'Goddammit, don't *do* this!'

'You stupid son of a bitch, Matoon's done *enough* to you without putting a hangman's noose around your neck!'

'I don't *care*!' he roared, pushing with all his strength against the poweful ex-slave. 'I don't give a damn any more! Can't you understand that? Can't you *understand*?'

He was like a man possessed. Gilbert held onto him, forcing him down on the ground, but it was like riding a horse full of loco weed. Lew bucked, pushed, and shoved. Finally, he managed to get his left arm free. Grabbing Gilbert's neck in a hammerlock, he twisted him to the left. He rolled him over on his back. Then, fast, he climbed on his stomach and smashed his nose. As Gilbert groaned, Lew jumped off him and started running for the woods.

Gilbert, his nose bleeding, staggered to his feet. He picked up the rusted milk can with both hands, raised it over his head, and hurled it with all his strength at Lew. The pail glanced off the back of his head, then bonged on the ground as Lew stumbled forward, falling in the weeds on his face.

He lay still. Gilbert, panting, sweating, pulled a handkerchief from his pocket and held it to his nose. Then he went over to Lew. He stood over him a moment as the handkerchief slowly turned red. Lew had fallen on his right arm, and now Gilbert saw the arm move slightly. He knew what he was doing. He stepped back and reached for his own gun when Lew rolled over. He aimed his revolver at Gilbert.

Gilbert shook his head sadly.

'Oh man, *please* don't do this,' he said. '*Please* don't.'

'The only way you can stop me,' said Lew, as he got to his feet, 'is to kill me.'

He was backing towards the woods, keeping the gun on Gilbert. He was a mess. His suit bristled with weeds, his face was bruised and filthy, his hat was lost. He ran his free hand through his hair. Then, at the edge of the woods, he turned and ran for his horse.

Gilbert didn't try to stop him. He knew it was useless. But Gilbert Samson was crying as he watched the man who had rescued him from the gutter ride to his death.

When he galloped up the drive of Matoon's house, it was

six-thirty in the evening. The mansion blazed with gaslight. Lew jumped off his horse and ran to the front door. After smashing the etched glass with the butt of his revolver, he reached in, unlocked the door, and kicked it open. He came into the entrance hall and roared: 'MATOON!'

The name echoed around the enormous house. A frightened Henry appeared beside the staircase.

'Where is he?' said Lew.

Henry stared at the wild-eyed man with the gun. Then he looked at the broken glass behind him.

'Where *is* he?' Lew howled.

Henry was terrified. He pointed his finger to the second floor. Lew started up the stairs, the gun in his hand.

'Matoon!' he shouted. 'My son is dead! He's *dead*, Matoon, and you killed him. You're going to pay, Matoon. For everything. You're going to PAY!'

He was halfway up the red-carpeted stair. Now the hall below was filling with servants who were watching the man in the checked suit climbing the stairs. The man with the dirty face, the wild eyes, the shiny revolver. . . .

He reached the top of the stairs and looked to the right. At the end of the long corridor, Charles Matoon had come out of his playroom. He was standing, listening.

Lew stared at him. He put his free hand to his head, clutching his wind-messed, sweat-drenched hair, and looked at the blind boy.

He heard a shot behind him.

He turned. Then he started towards the other end of the long hall. He was aware of the servants climbing the stairs. As he broke into a run, he saw the door at the end of the hall opening. He saw a fat man in his underdrawers and a starched shirt stagger out of the bedroom. It was Matoon. He was clutching his chest, where blood was expanding on his dress shirt. His diamond cufflinks glittered in the gaslight as he looked at Lew.

'Rosemary . . .' he whispered. Then he pitched forward on his face.

Lew looked at him. He looked pathetic, even ridiculous, with his fat, hairy legs, his black silk socks and garters, his white, tentlike underdrawers embroidered with golden M's. This pathetic mound of flesh had twisted his entire life. . . .

Now he looked into the bedroom. Rosemary, looking starkly beautiful in a white peignoir, was standing by the bed, a pistol in her hand.

'I told him,' she said quietly, 'that if the boy died, I'd kill him.'

She tossed the gun on the bed and came to the door. She looked down at her husband. Then she looked at Lew. 'He did enough to you,' she said. 'So did I. Now the score is even.'

The servants were at the top of the stairs, watching with frightened faces. Rosemary stepped around her husband and started down the hall. She passed Lew, who was watching her with wonder in his eyes. When she reached Henry, she said, 'I killed the senator. Go for the police.'

Then she continued past Henry towards her son. She walked slowly, with the stateliness of a duchess. The servants watched. Lew watched. When she reached her son, she put her arms around him and kissed his eyes.

Then she took him inside his playroom.

43

On 1 March 1871 Elizabeth Bramwell and Dr Blake Foster were two of the many survivors of the siege of Paris to stand on the sidewalks of the Champs Elysées and watch thirty thousand picked troops of the victorious Prussian army stage its triumphal march through the once-proud capital of France. The victory march had been one of Bismarck's demands during the armistice negotiations; and while it might have seemed insignificant compared to the loss of Alsace and Lorraine and the incredible five-billion-franc indemnity saddled on the French, still, to the Parisians, the humiliation of watching the conquerors march through the city was an almost unbearable insult added to unbearable injury. Yet no one could deny it was a splendid show, and the sight of the Uhlans, with their flag-tipped spears stuck in their saddles, the Saxons with their light blue jackets, and the Bismarck cuirassiers with their white jackets, square hats, and waving plumes aroused grudging admiration in the hearts of the onlookers. This undeniably splendid army with its gleaming artillery had made mincemeat of the French. Perhaps the Germans, barbaric as they were, were the wave of the future. . . .

'You have to hand it to them,' said Blake. 'They look good.'

'Unfortunately, they *are* good,' said Elizabeth. 'Or at least efficient. Perhaps Ben was right.'

'What do you mean?'

'He said it was the beginning of a new age, and it looks as if it is. The Age of the Efficient Killers. I'm not sure it's a new age I particularly like.'

They watched for another half hour, listening to the drums, the trumpets, the military bands. Then they started walking back to the rue la Pérouse, since all vehicular traffic had been forced off the main streets by the parade. When they finally reached Elizabeth's house, they went into her drawing room and sat down to rest their feet.

'Well,' said Blake, 'now what? Are you going back to America?'

'I don't know,' she replied. 'First I have to send a cable to my sister to tell her I'm all right. Except I don't know whether to tell her about Ben. The children will have to know sooner or later, but to let them know by a cable seems so heartless. . . . On the other hand, Pauline hardly remembers him, and Ward was never that close to him, so perhaps . . . I don't know. What do you think I should do?'

'I'd let your sister tell the children. I don't see much point in not letting them know.'

'I suppose so.' She looked at her hands. 'I still don't understand it. Oh, I understand the suicide, I suppose, and killing Zaza. But that whole business before, when he gave away all that money . . . it just seemed so pointless. What good did it do anyone? Why didn't he give it to some charity?'

'I think I understand it. And I rather admire it. I have a feeling your husband was a romantic, and going into Belleville to give away all that money was a very romantic gesture.'

'Romantic? I don't see any romance in it.'

'I do. Perhaps there was a streak of the artist in him. Or the romantic rebel. Anyway, giving away the money was his final rebellion against a society he never really felt comfortable with, or fitted into.'

'Ben an artist? He never had any particular interest in the arts that I knew of.'

'That doesn't mean he couldn't have had the artist's personality – or the rebel's. You're taking me too literally. Let me put it this way. When I was a child, I read an old Norse folk tale about a beautiful young maiden that a polar bear fell in love with.'

Elizabeth laughed. 'Well, *that's* certainly romantic. I've always had a passion for polar bears.'

'Ah, but you see the polar bear was really a handsome prince who had had a spell put on him by his wicked stepmother.'

'Naturally. What else do wicked stepmothers do?'

'Exactly. Well, the polar bear worked out a deal with the beautiful maiden's father, who talked his daughter into going off to the polar bear's castle.'

'I see he was a rich polar bear.'

'That's right. And when she got there, she found out he was really a handsome prince, and she fell in love with him. But then the prince was whisked away to his wicked stepmother's castle, which lay east of the sun and west of the moon. And the poor girl was desolate because she couldn't get to the castle that lay east of the sun and west of the moon where her handsome prince was. But finally, to make a long story short, she made a deal with the north wind, who took her to the castle. And there she was reunited with her prince.'

'Ah, a happy ending. I like that. But I don't see what that has to do with Ben?'

'Ben was the polar bear, and the handsome prince was your first husband. And they both were taken away to the castle that lies east of the sun and west of the moon. And you're the lovely maiden who's trying to find the castle so you can be reunited with your prince.'

Elizabeth stared at him. 'But . . . what a cruel thing to say to me!'

'Why cruel? Don't you see, *everybody* has a castle that lies east of the sun and west of the moon. Ben had one. You have one. I do, for that matter. It's the castle of our dreams: the castle that represents happiness. And I suppose none of us ever really gets there except in fairy tales. Ben found a way to get there through suicide. . . .'

'Oh *stop*!' She got up and went to the window to look out on the street. 'Really, I'm surprised at you, being so morbid and tasteless.'

Blake looked confused. 'I didn't mean to be morbid. I was just trying to explain Ben's state of mind. . . .'

'You never even *knew* the man, so how can you presume to tell me, his widow, what really went on in his mind? Particularly with some ridiculous fairy story. . . .'

He got up and came to the window beside her.

'But it's true,' he said. 'And fairy stories are true, in a way, because they tell us what we're really like in our hearts. And all of us are looking for the unattainable. Most of us make compromises with reality. Some of us, like Ben, can't. They find life so ugly – so far from the ideal – that they refuse to continue living it. But we're all looking for the castle.'

She looked at the young man with the black beard. 'Are you?' she said.

'Of course. I'm looking for it in my work. And I'm looking

for it in my personal life. I think perhaps I've found it in my personal life.'

He took her hand and raised it to his lips to kiss. She watched him.

'Elizabeth,' he said, 'I've been a good tenant, haven't I?'

'Yes.' She sounded wary.

'This has been a very proper house. But I've been bottling up a lot of very improper thoughts, and they're all about you. I'm not exactly a polar bear, and I'm certainly not a handsome prince, but . . . I'm very much in love with you. Now that you're thinking about going back to America – well, I've been telling myself, I'd better do something fast or you'll slip away from me. So here goes. Is there any chance you'd consider being Mrs Blake Foster?'

He let her hand go. She turned back to the window.

'Are you going to carry me off to the castle that lies east of the sun and west of the moon?'

'We might find it together. Or at least come close.'

'But you see, Blake, your little story doesn't really apply to me. I've already been there, with my first husband . . . the handsome prince, as you say. And he was taken away from me, so I don't think I can ever go back. I tried with Ben, and I tried with Jeff. . . . And while I'm very fond of you – and I truly am – I don't think you're going to take me there either.'

'Would you let me try?'

'Marriage isn't something you "try".'

'Then let's forget marriage. Let's go away together for a while. God knows it would be a relief to get out of Paris after the past six months. . . . I'm pretty well free of my patients now that Dr Lebrun has taken them over. Let's go away together and see if it works between us.'

'Where would we go?'

'I don't know. Switzerland, Italy, the south of France . . . just to get away for a while. And see what happens.'

She looked into his brown eyes. It was tempting. . . .

'But I want to see my children. . . .'

'There'll be time for that. They're in school now in Washington, so they can't come back here. And it's important to me to be with you a while. I'd like to think perhaps it's important to you too.' He hesitated, then added, 'I don't have a lot of money, so I couldn't afford the best hotels.'

She studied his face. Was he another Jeff? No, she didn't think so. She really didn't think so.

'I'd pay my own way,' she said quietly.

He broke into a smile.

'Then you'll do it?' he said softly.

She smiled back. 'Where shall we go first: east of the sun, or west of the moon?'

Four weeks later, they were sipping coffee in front of a café overlooking the Mediterranean in Cagnes, a small village west of Nice. It was a spectacular spring day – the weather had been superb, as if God were making up for the cruel winter – and Elizabeth was wearing a white cotton dress, while Blake had taken off his jacket and tie. He was reading the morning paper. Now she leaned across the table and snatched it out of his hands.

'Hey –!'

'You're not going to read the paper!' she announced. 'You're going to talk to me and charm me and amuse me, or I'll turn you into a polar bear.'

He sighed. 'Well, I can see you've turned into the wicked stepmother.'

'I have *not*!' She put the paper under her chair. 'And I'm only two years older than you, so we'll have none of this "stepmother" business.'

He leaned across the table and took her hand. 'Happy?' he asked, with a smile.

'Yes. I'm quite, *quite* happy. I'm ridiculously happy. In fact . . . well, I won't say it. You'll get a swelled head.'

'Oh, say it. I want to have a swelled head.'

'All right. I'm very glad you admitted back in Paris that you had improper thoughts about me, because the truth is I'd had a *lot* of improper thoughts about you.'

'Aha! I see. Well now, Mrs Bramwell, the truth will out. And how long have you been having these improper thoughts?'

'Oh, practically from the moment I saw you.'

'Dear me. Shocking. And just how improper are you feeling this morning?'

'Deliciously improper. Outrageously improper. The same way I've felt every morning for the last month.'

'Uh huh. And what if I had the hotel make us up a picnic basket? And we took a bottle of wine, and I rented a dog-cart, and we went out in the countryside and found a lovely, secluded meadow and then had a highly improper picnic? What would you think of that?'

'I think it would be heaven. Improper, but heaven.'

'Well then.' He got up. 'Finish your coffee, and I'll make all the improper arrangements. Be back in a while.'

She watched him walk into the small hotel they had been staying at for the past four days. Then she stirred her coffee. How wonderful it had been! They had slowly made their way south from Paris, staying in villages for several days at a time, planning nothing, being alone, talking, eating, drinking, making love. . . . After the nightmare of the siege, it had been an idyllic vacation. The warm spring days and cool nights had passed by with the slow motion of dreams. He was a gentle but passionate lover, and she was finding that while there had been no more talk of marriage, she was thinking more and more about how alluring the idea of becoming Mrs Blake Foster was turning out to be. Her only regret was a nagging sense of guilt about her children. She had not told Debbie where she was going, mainly because she didn't know where they would be from one day to the next but also because she didn't want to tell her sister the truth, especially in a cable. 'Dear Debbie: am travelling through France with my tenant'? 'Dear Debbie: have fallen in love with the nicest young man and we are checking into hotels pretending to be married when we're really not'? She couldn't think of a way even to lie with reasonable respectability, so she had sent nothing, neither lie nor truth. All she did was cable about Ben's death. Much as she missed Pauline and Ward, she assumed they were all right with her sister. And Blake had been right: it turned out that it *was* important for her to be with him. After Ben, Zaza,

Jeff, and the siege, Elizabeth Bramwell needed to recuperate.

After she finished her coffee, she pulled the newspaper from under her chair and glanced at the headlines. She didn't like reading the papers these days. The headlines were anything but recuperative or reassuring.

Today, they were even less reassuring than usual. In fact they were frightening.

A few hours later, a white cow stood in a meadow looking with bovine boredom at a young woman in white who was seated in the grass looking back at her. 'Moo!' went Elizabeth. The cow shook its head and continued to stare. 'Moo, moo!' As if to say it thought the young woman was unbearably silly, the cow turned and moved away. Elizabeth laughed. 'Well, I'm getting nowhere with Madame Moo,' she said, curling her arms around her raised knees.

Blake was kneeling beside the stream washing the picnic dishes.

'What did you expect?' he said.

'Oh, a charming conversation in Moo Talk at the very least. *I* should be washing the dishes. You're spoiling me.'

'I like to spoil you.'

She watched as he got up to return to her with the dishes. He pulled out his shirt tail.

'Shall I dry them on my shirt?' he said.

'Why not?'

They had found a field that could hardly have been improved upon. Secluded, lined on one side with tall poplars and on the other bordered by the stream, filled with early spring flowers, it even came equipped with a herd of cows. As the sun poured down on them, she had never felt so close to nature or more in love with spring.

He wiped the plates on his shirt tail and stuck them back in the wicker basket. Then he stretched his arms to the sky.

'Oh God, that sun feels good!'

'Why don't you take your shirt off and get a nice tan?'

'Can I use you as a pillow?'

'Of course, darling. You know I'm a first-class pillow.'

He unbuttoned his shirt and took it off, throwing it

beside the basket. She admired his wiry torso with its thick black hair covering his chest. He was no handsome prince, but he was a very attractive man. He got down on his hands and knees, gave her a kiss, then turned over on his back and stretched out, his head in her lap. She picked a long-stemmed wildflower and tickled his nose with the petals. Then she leaned down and kissed the end of his nose.

'After much deliberation,' she said, 'I've come to the conclusion that you have the perfect nose.'

'I could have told you.'

'The rest of you is, alas, not perfect. Your ears are a tiny bit too big, and your eyes are a tiny bit too small. . . .'

'You make me sound like a mole.'

'They don't have any eyes, silly. But your nose is quite perfect. I think I am mad for your nose.'

'I'll leave it to you in my will.'

'What a grotesque idea.'

She ran the flower idly across his forehead as the sun baked his belly. 'We can't go back to Paris, can we?' she said.

'You read the paper?'

'Yes, much against my better judgment. It says the Reds have taken over the city. They've moved into the Hôtel de Ville and just taken over. It seems incredible.'

'I know.'

'And the National Guard is surrounding Paris . . . it's turned into a civil war, hasn't it?'

'Yes. Paris against France. The poor against the rich and the middle class.'

'And I thought it was all over! Well, thank heavens we got out of Paris in time. I want no part of the communists. Do you think the house is safe?'

'With Gustave there, yes. He'd kill anybody who tried to take something.'

'I suppose so. But since we can't go back, what should we do?'

He didn't answer for a while.

'Well,' he finally said, 'I cabled my father for some more money, because I'm practically broke. Assuming he sends me what I asked for, we could rent a cottage, settle in, and wait for the communists to be kicked out of Paris. What do you think of that?'

'I think it sounds even more improper than checking into hotels as Mr and Mrs Foster.'

'Of course, we could become Mr and Mrs Foster, and then everything would be so proper it would probably be stifling.'

She smiled. 'You don't make marriage sound very exhilarating.'

'I've never been married,' he said, looking up at her. 'But I can't believe it could be more fun than this.'

'It has been fun, hasn't it?'

He sat up and turned to her. 'It's been more than fun. It's been the best time of my life. How about it, darling? It does seem to be working, doesn't it? Shall we get married?'

She didn't answer. He took her in his arms and kissed her hungrily. Then, as she slowly rubbed her hands over his bare back, he eased her down into the grass.

'I love you,' he whispered. 'Say you'll marry me. Say you'll be my wife.'

Her heart was pounding wildly as she nodded yes. He said nothing. He began unbuttoning her dress as he kissed her neck. She felt his hand on her breast, then his other hand moving down her stomach. Now her dress was half off. He sat up to remove his trousers and drawers. She wriggled out of her dress, then pulled off her underskirt. They had long since taken off their shoes. Now, naked as God made them, facing each other as they kneeled in the grass, they embraced.

One of the cows stopped eating grass long enough to watch as Blake laid her gently down and eased himself on top of her.

The sun beat on their nakedness as they made love.

The cow shook its head to scare away a bumblebee and went back to its lunch.

They rented a small villa in Cagnes that had two tiny bedrooms, seemingly hundreds of potted flowers, and a breathtaking view of the sea. The floors were stone, the walls stucco, the roof orange tile, and there was a tiled terrace in back that perched on a cliff that dropped almost sheer to the water below. The villa belonged to the mayor of the town, a round little man named Monsieur Choufleur. He not only was named cauliflower, he rather resembled one, having a bald dome with enough bumps to enchant a phrenologist.

They were married in the American Consulate in Nice by a vacationing Presbyterian minister from Boston who was studying the Roman ruins at Nîmes. Blake wore a white suit and white hat. Elizabeth wore a white dress with a small bustle and a white plumed hat. She carried a bouquet of white daisies and a small white Bible. After the ceremony she was kissed by her husband, then by the minister, Dr Farquhar, and finally by the consul, Mr Porter. Afterward the Porters poured champagne and toasted the bride and groom. Then the conversation was brought around to the inevitable topic, Paris.

'I worry about Mr Washburne,' said Mr Porter, referring to the American minister in Paris.

'But surely the Communards wouldn't hurt a diplomat?' said Elizabeth.

Mr Porter shrugged. 'Who knows? They arrested the archbishop of Paris, and I understand they say they'll execute him as a reprisal for the execution of the Communards by the Nationals. If they'll execute an archbishop, they might execute a diplomat. Things are absolutely chaotic. You're very lucky to be out of Paris, madame.'

The bride smiled at the groom. 'That's Blake's doing,' she said. 'He talked me into leaving.'

'Are you worried about your house?'

'A little. But we left two servants there who I'm sure will take care of everything. Poor things, they were planning to go to America this month, and now they're stuck inside Paris, and we're stuck outside. . . .'

They rode back to Cagnes in an open carriage, Elizabeth holding a white lace parasol to keep the sun off. As she looked out at the sea, she said, 'It's so beautiful here, isn't it?'

'You're so beautiful,' he said, kissing her hand.

She turned to her husband. 'I was dying to tell Mr Porter we've already had our honeymoon. A six-week, *very* passionate honeymoon. Do you think he would have been shocked?'

'Oh, no question of it.'

'I wish I'd told him. Oh well. At least now I can tell Debbie where I am – now that I'm proper at long last. Oh Blake, I'm so eager for you to meet Ward and Pauline! I know you'll love them as I do . . . should we forget the things in Paris and go home? It may be months before we can get in the house, and I want to see my children. I want them to meet their new father!'

'Let's wait another few weeks,' he said. 'Then, if the Communards look as if they're in for the long haul, we'll go home. I want to write my father and see if he knows of any positions in New York I could apply for. You're sure you won't mind living in New York?'

'Why should I mind? New York will be exciting. Anywhere would be exciting with you. Did I tell you I'm very deeply in love with you?'

'Not in the last five minutes.'

'Well, I am. And I can hardly wait till we get home. I have a surprise for you, and if you don't like it, I'll throw myself into the sea.'

'Then I promise to like it. But it had better not be a wedding cake. Remember our vow: no cake, no supper, no servants. Just you and me alone.'

'Oh, I wouldn't do anything as unoriginal as a wedding cake. By the way, I think I'd better warn you: I'm an absolutely dreadful cook and have no intention of learning to be a good one. So even though we're on a tight budget, you'll have to let me hire a cook or we'll starve.'

'You may hire a cook.'

The surprise was a in a big box tied with red ribbons and bows. She carried it out to the terrace, where he was chilling a bottle of champagne.

'For my husband,' she said, handing it to him. 'You open it and I'll pour the champagne.'

He looked troubled, but said nothing. He put the box on

a table and untied the ribbons. He pulled off the lid. Inside was folded a brocade dressing gown. He pulled it out and held it up.

'Do you like it?' she said. 'Isn't it the most beautiful thing you've ever seen? I bought it in Nice at an adorable boutique –'

'Elizabeth,' he interrupted, 'it's beautiful, but it must have cost a fortune, and you *know* . . .'

She put her fingers against his mouth. 'We are *not* going to discuss money,' she said. 'I don't expect you to buy me anything, but there's no reason in the world why I can't buy my husband a present if I want to.'

He put the dressing gown over a chair and went to the stone balustrade. She watched him a moment. Then she poured two glasses of champagne and brought them over to him.

'Darling,' she said, 'please. Not on our wedding day.'

He turned to take the glass. 'May I make *one* remark about money?'

'All right, *one*.'

'My father is a wealthy man, and as soon as we get back to New York I'm going to have a talk with him about my miserable finances. But until then, you have money and I don't. So I would appreciate your living at *my* level of income, not the other way around.'

'That was three remarks, not one. And I still have the right to buy you a present.'

He shook his head, sighed, then smiled. 'You're incorrigible. All right, you win. Thanks for the robe. Now let's drink. To each other. To us. May we find the castle of happiness.'

They touched glasses.

'I think I already have,' she said softly. They kissed, then they drank. She set her glass down.

'Now: come here.' She took his hand and led him to the centre of the terrace. 'You stand right here and don't move.'

She unbuttoned his jacket.

'What are you going to do?' he asked.

'Take all your clothes off so you can put on the robe.'

'I'll take my own clothes off, thank you! And I won't do it out here!'

'No one can see us. Besides, I want to do it. You've taken my clothes off God knows how many times, now it's my turn to do it to you.'

'Elizabeth, this is crazy! Why do you want to do such a stupid thing?'

'I want to look at you, of course! And it's not stupid at all.'

'You've *seen* me. . . .'

'I want to see you again. And you're being very disagreeable for someone who's just been married. You may take off your shoes and socks. . . .'

'I will not! And I won't allow you to do this . . . this *vulgar* thing!'

She stepped back, her hands on her waist. 'Oh? When you do it to me it's perfectly all right, but when I do it to you it's "vulgar?" Well, Doctor, for a student of the mind, you have some very interesting views.'

'But . . . it's undignified!'

'For you? But not for me. Thank you, Doctor.'

She started into the house. He hurried after her.

'Elizabeth, wait a minute! Where are you going?'

'To my room to be by myself until you apologize.'

'Apologize for *what*?'

'For treating me like your wife instead of your equal.'

'But you *are* my wife!'

'Yes indeed, and I love you very much. But you are my third husband and not my first lover by a long shot. I've been made love to by a variety of people – some heavenly, some passable – but I have always been made love *to*. So this time I decided we would start things off on an equal footing and I would make love to *you*. However, since that seems to offend your male pride, I'm perfectly content to curl up on my wedding night with a good book.'

He stared at her. 'This is the most incredible thing I've ever heard!' he finally spluttered.

She smiled. 'Good. This way, our marriage will never be dull . . . or "stifling", as I think you put it. *À bientôt*.'

She blew him a kiss and went in the house, leaving him alone on the terrace. He fumed for a moment. Then he went back to the champagne and took a drink. Then he fumed. Then he leaned on the balustrade and stared at the sea. He fumed. Then he turned around and called, 'Elizabeth!'

She appeared at the door.

'Yes, dear?'

'You win.'

She smiled prettily. 'Good. Take off your shoes and socks, then come to the middle of the terrace.'

He sat on a chair and began untying his shoes. 'It's lucky for you I don't *have* much dignity,' he growled.

'Oh well, you have enough. Too much would be a bore.'

'I think you have an outrageous set of values.'

'They're getting more outrageous every year I live.'

'No lady would ever do this!'

'No lady would have slept halfway across France with the likes of you, my love.'

He pulled off his socks, then laughed. 'You're wild,' he said. 'Absolutely crazy. I think that's why I adore you.'

'Good. Come here.'

She pointed to the centre of the terrace. He came over. She kissed him. Then she took off his white jacket and put it on the table. She undid his tie, then unbuttoned his shirt.

'Mmm,' she said, 'such a nice chest. A bit bony, but I like bony chests.'

She unbuttoned his cuffs, then pulled the shirt tail out of his trousers.

'Hold out your arms.'

He did. She slipped the shirt off him and threw it on the jacket. Then she walked around him, inspecting him. 'Very nice,' she said. 'Very nice indeed. Now the trousers.'

She unbuckled his belt and unbuttoned his fly. The trousers fell to the floor.

'Ta ta!' she exclaimed, raising her hands dramatically. 'Oh, what legs! Absolutely gorgeous.'

'They're hairy and they're hideous.'

'That's *your* opinion, darling. I adore them. Now step out of your trousers.'

'I feel like an ass,' he growled, stepping out of them. She picked them up, folded them neatly, and draped them over a chair. Then she returned to him.

'You're *not* going to pull down my drawers,' he said.

'I wouldn't miss it for the world.'

She unbuttoned them and they dropped to the tiles. He put his hands over his genitals.

'Not fair,' she said, removing his hands. Then she looked him over, smiling.

'Perfection,' she said. She came up to him, put her hands on his cheeks, and pulled his face to hers. She kissed him. His hands crept around her waist.

'Now,' he whispered, removing his mouth from hers, 'I do it to you. That's only fair.'

'I can hardly wait.'

Three days later, she received a cable. She read it, then went out on the terrace, where Blake was sleeping in the sun.

'Darling, wake up,' she said.

He opened his eyes. 'What is it?'

'A cable just came from Debbie. She says we're to stay here, that a relative is coming to talk to me about Ben's will.'

'Who's the relative?'

'She doesn't say. I don't understand it. . . . She says it's very important we don't leave.'

'That's odd.'

'It's not only odd. It's a little frightening.'

That night she woke up screaming.

'Elizabeth, what is it?' He took her in his arms.

'Oh darling,' she sobbed, 'I had this horrible nightmare! Oh God, it was awful. . . .'

'Tell me.'

'It was all from that terrible story you told me . . . I was riding the north wind, except he looked like a polar bear. . . . And we were flying over the sea, which was filled with icebergs . . . and then . . .' She wiped her eyes with the pillowslip.

'Now calm down, darling.'

'Oh, I know it was only a dream, but it seemed so *real*. And then the north wind dived down into the sea and took me with him. And it was horribly cold and I couldn't breathe. . . .'

She sat up, running her hands through her hair. 'And then the polar bear was floating in front of me in the green water. . . .'

She stopped. He ran his hand over her arm.

'And then what?' he said.

She shuddered. 'Then the bear turned into a skeleton. It was horrible. Oh Blake, hold me. . . .'

He opened his arms and she went back into them. He smoothed her cheek as she listened to the tide outside their window.

'It's that cable,' she finally said. 'That cable from under the sea. Something's happened. I just *feel* it. Something we don't know about. . . .'

'You can't assume it's bad news just because of a dream.'

'Blake,' she said, after a while.

'What?'

'I love you with all my heart and soul. You know that, don't you?'

'Yes. And I love you with all my heart and soul.'

'Nothing will ever separate us, will it?'

'No, nothing.'

'I've lost so much in my life. I can't afford to lose you.'

'You won't lose me. Now go back to sleep. You're safe in my arms. I won't let any skeletons get you.'

'It wasn't funny.'

'I didn't say it was.'

'I love you.'

'And I love you.'

44

They were eating breakfast on the terrace in the first week in May when someone rang the front-door bell. Celestine, the plump cook they had hired, finished pouring the coffee, then went inside the house to answer the door. Elizabeth, who was wearing a blue skirt and white blouse, watched a seagull sail in the breeze. Blake was reading the paper.

'Madame,' said Celestine, 'there's a lady to see you. She says she is a relative.'

Blake put down the paper and exchanged looks with his wife. Then he said, 'Bring her out here, Celestine.'

'*Oui, monsieur*.' She went back in the house.

'Hold my hand,' whispered Elizabeth, reaching across the table. He took it and squeezed it.

A smartly dressed woman came onto the terrace. She wore a white travelling suit trimmed with green. She had jet-black hair and beautiful white skin. A bonnet of green silk bows was tied to her head.

'Mrs Foster?' she said.

Blake stood up.

'I'm Dr Foster. This is my wife.'

'My name is Ysabel Crandall.'

Elizabeth frowned slightly. 'Are you a relation of my first husband?'

'Yes. May I sit down?'

'Please.'

Blake held a chair for her. She sat at the table and removed her gloves.

'Some coffee?' asked Blake.

'No thank you. My husband and I are staying in Nice, and we've had breakfast. Your house is charming. What a lovely view.'

'Thank you.' Blake sat down.

'Are you the relative my sister cabled me about?' asked Elizabeth.

'Yes. First, let me tell you that your husband's will has been probated by his Philadelphia attorneys, and you have inherited everything. I believe it's quite a considerable sum.'

Silence. Elizabeth looked at Blake, then back to Ysabel.

'But surely you didn't come all the way from America just to tell me that?'

'No,' said Ysabel, 'we came for another reason. Mrs Foster, I have something to tell you that I fear may come as a shock to you. That's why my husband and I thought it imperative we tell you in person, rather than by a letter or cable.'

She was watching Elizabeth, who again reached out for her husband's hand. He took it.

'What is it?' she said quietly.

'Your first husband is alive.'

Elizabeth's eyes widened. 'Lew . . .?'

'Yes. He wasn't killed in the war.'

'But . . . ' She looked at Blake, trying to say something. He was looking at someone standing in the door. She turned and saw her first husband.

'Oh my God,' she whispered. 'Oh Blake, *do* something. . . . Oh God, I can't stand this . . . BLAKE!'

She began to scream. Blake jumped up and ran to her, holding her as she whimpered with fright, staring at the man in the white suit. The tall man with the blond hair and the face she had never forgotten.

An hour later she sat staring at him. He had told her almost everthing. Now all she said was, 'Ten years.'

'Ten years,' said Lew. 'Were we wrong to tell you this way?'

'I don't know. I suppose not.'

There was a long, awkward silence. Blake was watching his wife, who looked almost in shock. He said to Lew, 'Perhaps it would be better if you left us now.'

Lew stood up. 'I understand. We'll go back to Nice. We're going to be there for a few days, then we're going to Rome. Perhaps we could come back tomorrow?'

'No,' said Elizabeth dully. 'Don't come back. I don't want to see you again.'

He looked at his first wife. Then he looked at Ysabel and signalled her to stand up, which she did. Then he said to Elizabeth, 'I'm sorry.'

He put his hand on her shoulder a moment. Then he started for the house. 'Doctor,' he said, 'could I see you a moment?'

The Crandalls went inside the house. Blake paused by his wife. 'Why did you say that?' he whispered.

'I don't want to see him again. I hate him.'

He started to say something, then changed his mind. 'I'll be back in a moment.'

Blake left her staring at the sea.

Inside, Lew took him aside. 'There's something else,' he said quietly. 'But I think it's better if you tell her. Perhaps later . . . I think she's upset enough by seeing me.'

'What is it?'

'Our son,' said Lew. 'Ward Crandall. He was killed.'

'My God . . . how?'

'Matoon kidnapped him to pressure me. In the course of trying to free him, Ward was shot. I don't know . . . it's possible we shouldn't have tried it. . . .'

Ysabel put her hand on his arm.

Blake looked back at the terrace where Elizabeth was sitting, looking at the sea.

'I'll tell her,' he said. 'I don't know how, but I'll tell her.' He turned back to Lew.

'We were afraid she'd react this way,' said Ysabel.

'I want to do anything I can for her,' said Lew. 'I suppose it is better if we stay away for the time being. But if you need me, we'll be at the Grand Hotel in Nice.'

'All right.'

He opened the door and they started out. Lew paused.

'Tell her if you can,' he said, 'that it broke my heart too.'

Then he went out. Blake closed the door, then returned to the terrace. He watched his wife a moment. She was motionless, watching the sea. He came up behind her and put his hands on her shoulders. She turned around. Her face was cold.

'I hate him,' she said. 'If he'd loved me, he would have gotten word to me. . . .'

'That's not fair, darling. You heard him. It was impossible.'

'Nothing's impossible if you love someone. He could have done it some way. I *hate* him. I never want to see him again. I never even want to hear his name. Do you understand? *Never!*'

She got up and went into the house.

She locked herself in the bedroom most of the day. Several times he tried to talk to her through the door, but she told him to go away. He heard her crying. He went away.

Finally, at four o'clock, she came out. Her eyes were red, but she looked composed. She went to the kitchen and got an apple from Celestine. Then she went to the terrace, where Blake took her in his arms.

'Are you better?' he said.

'I'm hungry, so I must be better. I want to take a walk. Will you come with me?'

'Of course.'

They left the house and walked a while until they reached some steps leading down to the rocky beach. When they reached the beach, she took off her shoes and waded a few feet into the sea. She finished the apple and threw the core into the water. Blake took off his shoes and waded in beside her. The lazy surf swirled around their toes. He put his arm around her.

'It's time we went home,' she said. 'I want my children.'

He said nothing.

'Will you make the arrangements tomorrow?' she continued.

'What about Paris?'

'We'll send for the things. It's not that important. I miss my children. Seeing him made me realize just how much I *do* miss them.'

'Then we'll go home.'

The sea swirled around their toes.

'Elizabeth?'

'What?'

It was near midnight. They were in bed. He had been holding her in his arms, trying to decide whether to tell her. He knew he had to.

'There's something else.'

'What?'

'I want you to be very brave, darling. I want you to hold onto me and be very brave, because this is going to hurt.'

He felt her tense in his arms.

'What is it?'

'Ward is dead.'

Silence.

'He was kidnapped and somehow got shot.'

'Kidnapped by whom?' Her voice was a whisper.

'By the senator. Matoon. . . .'

He felt her twitching in his arms.

'You're lying,' she said. 'You must be lying. Why are you doing this to me?'

'I'm not lying. He was afraid to tell you. I guess they've all been afraid. But Ward is dead.'

She started struggling to free herself from him.

'I don't believe you!' she cried. 'I *don't*!'

'You have to believe me. It's true.'

'Ward *can't* be dead! He's my son! He *can't* be dead! Let me go!'

'Elizabeth –'

'Let me GO!'

He let her go. She climbed out of the bed and stumbled in the dark for her robe. Then she put it on and left the room. He got out of bed and put on the brocade robe she had given him as a wedding present. Then he hurried through the dark house.

'Elizabeth?' he called.

He saw her on the terrace standing by the balustrade in the moonlight. He came out to her. She was sobbing. He took her in his arms and held her. She pushed away from him, leaned over the balustrade, and began retching. When she was through, she sank down on the tiled floor, curled up against the balustrade, and whimpered.

He knelt beside her. 'Darling,' he whispered. 'Come back to bed. Let me hold you. It will be better.'

She said nothing. She continued to sob.

'Please . . . come with me. . . .'

'Go away.'

'I want to help. . . .'

'Leave me alone!'

Elizabeth . . .'

'Leave me *alone*!' she screamed hysterically.

He got up and backed away, staring at the huddled figure hiding in the shadow of the balustrade from the moonlight.

45

Bruno Zinh watched with fascination as the flames roared out of the windows of the Tuileries Palace, sending billowing clouds of fire and smoke up to the sky, frying heaven, turning night into day. Paris was burning. It had begun in the barricaded rue Royale when the retreating Communards had set fire to a house that obstructed their field of fire.

Paris, among its other troubles, had suffered near-drought conditions for a month, and so now the flames spread with frightening speed. Soon the fashionable jewellery shops and cafés of the famous street were burning like tinder.

What had begun as a military necessity soon became a revolutionary revel. The Commune was doomed. The thousands of soldiers of the national government situated outside Paris at Versailles were slowly pushing the Communards back towards the eastern slum of Belleville, where most of them had come from. The fighting was bitter and bloody. The progress of the Versaillais, the government troops, was made block by block, street by street. Yet their advance was inexorable, and the Communards knew it. They also knew what their fate would be when the revolution was crushed. They had no illusions that they would be treated with mercy by their captors; they faced certain death. Thus, as the flames spread down the rue Royale, the idea had spread with equal speed to burn Paris. If the Commune was doomed, so was the city that had been its breeding ground and the scene of its short triumph. A Communard named Jules Bergeret, who had been the first military commander of the Commune, now supervised the hauling of gunpowder into the enormous Salle des Maréchaux of the Tuileries, the scene of so many glittering balls during the Second Empire. The tapestries on the elegant walls were smeared with tar and petroleum. Then, at about ten in the evening of 23 May, flames leapt down the great halls of the palace. The gunpowder exploded with a shattering roar, and the central dome of the palace blew to the heavens.

Bruno Zinh, one of the crowd watching the spectacle, danced with glee. Some of the people near him shuddered as they saw his face in the light of the flames. It had been horribly burned by the acid. His forehead and upper right cheek were a mass of scar tissue, and his right eye had been partially blinded. Bruno didn't pay attention to the shudders. He was immune to them by now, because his brain had twisted to force himself to be immune. When he had first looked in a mirror, the shock had been so horrible he had crashed his fist into the glass. He had broken many mirrors since, but now he didn't look. He avoided mirrors like a vampire. And now, the flames of the Tuileries! The flames were eating the palace as the acid had eaten his face. It was a magical moment: let Paris burn! Corrupt, rotten Paris – let it burn, and let the scars of its gutted ruins be a permanent reminder to the world of the vengeful anger of the Commune, as the scars of his face were a permanent reminder to him of Zaza and Ben Bramwell.

He spent the rest of the night running around Paris, or that part of Paris it was still safe for him to be in, watching the spreading flames. They filled his heart with a weird joy: they were somehow a purge of his bitterness and anger. And, as if God were on the side of the Commune, in the early hours of the morning a mighty wind blew up, fanning the flames with near hurricane force and spreading them with even greater speed. The sky was an inferno; the Seine was a river of blood as the flames reflected off its turgid waters. The smoke could be seen for miles, and the air was filled with sparks and burning bits floating down like confetti from hell. Bruno loved it. It was the most exciting night of his life.

It was near dawn when he got his idea. He had seen people throwing bottles of petroleum through the windows of houses, setting them afire. Some of the throwers were women, fierce Amazons of the Commune filled with vengeance against a middle class that had condemned them to lives of squalor. Now was the hour of revenge! Destroy the bourgeoisie's beloved property, their real estate, their furniture, their draperies! Let it all be consumed in the cleansing flame of vengeance!

Mrs Bramwell. Ben was beyond his revenge, as was Zaza. But Mrs Bramwell's house on the rue la Pérouse wasn't beyond it. He had driven her there that day in January when she had visited Ben in the rue des Acacias. Yes, he remembered it well. He remembered *her*. Was it possible she was still there? Then it would be even sweeter to see her go up in flames as well as her house, see her burn as he had burned. . . . But even if she weren't there, he could burn her house. But could he get there? It would be dangerous. The west part of the city was in the hands of the Versaillais, and they were shooting anyone they suspected of being a Communard almost on sight. Dare he take the chance? But what was the alternative? He was doomed anyway. Certainly, if he stayed with the Commune he would be facing a firing squad sooner or later, so why not try it?

But how? The river! Yes, why not? He could swim downstream, bypass the worst of the fighting, make his way back to the rue des Acacias, where he was at least known. . . . Old Madame Dulaage, his former employer, had taken pity on him after his disfigurement. She would protect him from the Versaillais, and there were bottles in her basement, and lamp oil. . . .

He ran across the Place de la Concorde. The Tuileries was still smoking, the palace now a shell. He scurried down the steps of the quai to the Seine. Taking off his ragged jacket, he threw it on the stones. Then he pulled off his shoes. He looked up at the sky with his one good eye and laughed at the flames.

Then he jumped in the blood-red river.

The next day, the fire continued to spread, turning Paris into a suburb of hell. Besides the Tuileries and a large part of the Palais Royal, the Palais de Justice, the Prefecture of Police, the Cour des Comptes, the Légion d'Honneur, and the Conseil d'État had all gone up in flames. The rue de Lille and the rue de Rivoli were incendiary bombs, and the Ministry of Finance, on one wing of the Louvre, was ablaze. Whole blocks were burning. And by eleven that morning, one of the most historic buildings in the city succumbed to the flames as the medieval façade of the Hôtel de Ville – where the Commune had been proclaimed two months before – began blacking with smoke as fire licked its ancient stones.

As the fire spread, in the midst of the smoke the crack of rifles still filled the air as the Versaillais continued their slow advance. But now it was not only Communard versus Versaillais. Now the Communards were turning against each other in an orgy of blood lust. As if the ghosts of the first French Revolution were stalking the embattled streets of Paris, women with knitting needles in their aprons began accusing their fellow Communards of being traitors to the working class, spies, turncoats. . . . These unfortunates, including one renegade young count who had joined the Commune for romantic reasons, were shot on the spot. As blood flowed in the gutters, dripping into the elaborate sewer system built by Louis Napoleon, the archbishop of Paris was led from his tiny cell in the Roquette prison near Père Lachaise cemetery. Monsignieur Darboy was a frail old man with white hair. Yet as the Communards took him to an alley in the prison and lined him and several others up against a wall, the frail old man showed surprising spunk. Calmly, he bestowed the benediction on those who were to die with him – one of whom was the seventy-five-year-old former confessor of the Empress Eugénie. Then he faced the rifles of the belligerently anticlerical Communards. Whatever legitimate grievances the working class had against the French Church, executing the liberal archbishop was one of the Commune's most despicable acts, and the firing squad must have known it, because their aim was bad. Monseigneur Darboy was still standing after the first volley. He was finished off by revolver shots, then his body was gored by bayonets and tossed into a ditch in Père Lachaise.

On the rue la Pérouse, Gustave had just crawled into bed next to Henriette when he heard the crash of window glass. He jumped out of bed and ran to the window of his top-floor room. It was dark, but already flames were flickering out of the ground-floor window, and he could see the man on the street throw another bottle at the house. Crash!

'BASTARD!' roared Gustave.

The man looked up at him.

'Jesus,' muttered the coachman as he saw the hideous face of Bruno Zinh.

'What is it?' asked Henriette.

'The house is on fire. Go down the back stairs and stay in the garden. I'll see if I can put it out. . . .'

They ran out of the room in their nightclothes and hurried down the stairs.

'Was it a *petroleuse*?' asked Henriette, using the name Paris had given the bottle-throwing Amazons.

'It was a *petroleur*,' said Gustave, 'and the ugliest son of a bitch I've ever seen.'

When they reached the kitchen, he pushed his wife into the garden, then started filling two mop pails at the sink. Already smoke was curling under the dining-room door, and he could hear ominous snapping from the front of the house. He grabbed the pails, went to the door, and pushed it open.

Flames were licking the dining-room table, and the chairs were burning with luxuriant slowness, as if the fire were guest at some sedate dinner party. Beyond, past the open doors of the drawing room, the front room was already a mass of flames, and sparks were popping into the dining room, igniting the carpet, the curtains. . . . He threw the water on the smouldering carpet, then hurried back to the kitchen. There was no hope of firemen. With a city burning, there were no *pompiers* left over to fight a single fire in a house. Refilling the buckets, he ran back to the dining room and sloshed the water on the table and the chairs nearest the drawing-room doors. The room was filling with smoke so rapidly he could barely breathe. Besides, it was hopeless. The fire had spread too quickly for him to have a chance with his mop pails. He ran back into the kitchen and went out to the garden, where Henriette was waiting.

'It's no good,' he said. 'The whole house is going.'

They watched the smoke beginning to rise over the roof.

'Poor Madame Bramwell,' said Henriette. 'All her beautiful clothes and jewels . . . Do you think we should try and get some of the things out of her bedroom?'

'No. It's right above the drawing room. Too dangerous.'

'But she's paying our way to America. . . .'

'*No.*' Now he could see the fire in the kitchen. 'We'll pay her back when we get there. The important thing is to *get* there.'

On 10 June Blake and Elizabeth re-entered Paris.She had been sick for a month, causing them to postpone yet again their return to America. The sickness had grown from her hysteria that night on the terrace at Cagnes. The double shock of seeing her first husband return from the dead, then of learning about the death of her son, had precipitated a nervous breakdown. For a month Blake had nursed her back to health, or at least a saddened acceptance of reality. When she told him she was strong enough to travel, he asked her if they shouldn't return to Paris first. The Commune had been crushed, and the Communards executed – twenty-five thousand of them shot in one week – in an appalling burst of revenge on the part of the national government. But although Paris was a graveyard, Paris was at least open. So Elizabeth agreed they should return to the rue la Pérouse to pack their things before sailing to New York.

They took the train from Nice to Paris, then left the Gare de Lyon in a cab and headed west for the rue la Pérouse. As they passed the shell of the Tuileries, Elizabeth winced. She remembered the ball she had attended there so many years ago with Ben. What a fairyland it had been, with the coloured lanterns and the Bengal lights! How beautiful it had been! And how dead it was now. As dead as Ben. As dead as Ward. . . .

'What a waste,' she said.

She remembered watching the storming of the palace with Jeff, the angry mob yelling '*Dé-ché-ance! Dé-ché-ance!*' The palace was a symbol, true, but why destroy a symbol when the reality it symbolized was already dead? It was like burning a corpse. . . .

Blake was watching out the window, looking at block after block of gutted buildings.

'It's like sight-seeing in hell,' he observed. And he was right.

When the cab turned into the rue la Pérouse, Blake saw the house first.

'It's burned!'

'*Our* house?'

'Yes . . .'

When the cab stopped, he jumped down and looked at the mock-Renaissance façade, which was still standing. But its eyes were dead: the windows were smashed, their frames charred, their stone eyebrows black. Elizabeth got out and stood beside him.

'What do we do now?' she said.

'I guess we check into a hotel until our boat sails. Do you mind?'

'We don't have much choice, do we?'

Blake went up the steps and pushed open the front door. He looked inside, the entrance hall was piled with rubble, but some of it had been cleared. He made his way to the doors of the drawing room and looked in. The ceiling had collapsed, and the room was completely charred. He could smell the faint, acrid odour of burned wood.

He turned to see Elizabeth behind him. She was looking at the rubble with sadness.

'I hope Gustave and Henriette are all right,' she said.

'I do too.'

'I wonder what happened. None of the other houses on the block are burned.'

'Let me go next door and ask.'

He hurried out of the house, leaving Elizabeth alone. She looked at the rubble. There was no furniture left. She knew that whatever might have escaped the flames would have probably been carted off by looters. But she wondered if it were possible some of her jewels might still be buried beneath the plaster and lathing. Her bedroom had been above the drawing room, and when the ceiling collapsed, everything must have come crashing through. . . .

She went into the room to get a closer look. Beneath a burned beam she spotted a charred slipper stuck in a mass of crumbled plaster. She made her way to the dining-room door, her eyes looking everywhere, hoping to spot a gleam that might be a diamond or a topaz.

Near the door she saw a spark of light. It was the broken

glass of a picture. Stooping down, she pulled the photograph of Lew from the rubble, the one she had kept on her bed table. How many times had she looked at it and cried inwardly – sometimes outwardly. Now as she looked at the young lieutenant she did not cry. And yet the hatred she had felt for him a month before had abated. What Blake had said was true. It probably had been impossible for him to get word to her. She had never received the coded message he told her he had sent from Andersonville, but the knowledge that he had been in that horror was message enough. Whatever happiness Lew had now, he had paid for. Her attitude was softening.

She wiped the picture off, put it in her purse, and looked into the dining room, giving up for the time being the hope of spotting her jewellery. Here things weren't so bad. The ceiling was black, but it hadn't collapsed. Part of the table was still standing, the table where she and Ben had eaten so many meals and then, that night almost six months before, where she had had Blake to dinner and they had feasted on rabbit as the piano burned in the fireplace. Blake. How lucky she was to have him. He was the real jewel. But, she reflected, her happiness with him had been paid for, for she too had lived through horrors. . . .

She went through the dining room to the kitchen, passing the fireplace. The burning piano. Her career. Odd, but now she didn't regret her failure to become another Clara Schumann. Pauline promised to be a far better pianist than she, and she wondered if it weren't because Pauline had inherited Ben's romantic soul. For she had come to the conclusion that Blake was right. Ben had been a romantic of sorts. Now his daughter had inherited her mother's musical talent, which, combined with her father's romanticism, gave the daughter's music the soul the mother's music had lacked. What a nice legacy to the world if Ben's daughter became a great pianist. . . .

She went into the kitchen. This, too, had burned, but not as badly. She looked around. The zinc-topped table in the centre of the room had escaped harm. Odd. Its top was clean, and there was a half-empty bottle of wine standing on it. She went to the table and looked at the label. Château Lafite, 1848. One of Ben's . . .

The wine cellar. Ben's treasured cognacs, his Burgundies, his clarets, and champagnes. . . . Had looters taken them, even drunk them here in the kitchen? She went over to the cellar door and opened it.

A man with a hideous, half-burned face was grinning at her. She stepped back, stifling a scream of terror as Bruno Zinh stared at her with his one good eye and one milk-glazed half-blind eye.

'Who are you?' she gasped.

'I live here,' he said. 'In the basement. After the fire, I moved in. It's cool down there, and there's a lot of good wine.' He stepped up into the kitchen. She backed away. She wanted to take her eyes off his face, but she couldn't. It fascinated her even as it repelled her. 'I've been waiting for you,' he was saying, 'I knew you'd come back some day, Madame Bramwell.'

'How do you know who I am?'

'You don't remember me because I've changed. I was your husband's porter. I drove you home last January when you came to see your husband. But you don't remember Bruno because Bruno isn't handsome like he used to be. Bruno used to be a Greek god – that's what she called me.'

'Who?' She bumped against the table. He was standing a few feet away, grinning hideously at her.

'Zaza,' he said. 'Zaza used to take pictures of me. Sometimes with funny costumes and sometimes with nothing on at all. She loved my cock, Madame Bramwell. Would you like to see my cock?'

'Go away. . . .' She was shuddering, too terrified to move. 'Please go away. . . .'

He came closer.

'I was with your husband the night he murdered Zaza,' he was whispering. 'And that's when I had my accident. It was your husband's fault, Madame Bramwell. I can't do anything to him, but I can do something to you.'

She started to scream when he grabbed her, but he clapped his hand over her mouth, pressing her down against the table. His eyes were inches away from hers, one good, one milky. She tried to turn away, but he forced her face back.

'Look at Bruno,' he whispered. 'Bruno isn't handsome any more. But Bruno's cock is still beautiful.'

She struggled as he forced her onto the table and tore open her dress. She struggled, but he was too strong. The wine bottle fell over, spilling the Château Lafite in her hair. She was sick with terror. He ripped her petticoats open, then climbed on top of her. Now he took his hand off her mouth to tear open his fly, and she screamed.

'Blake! Blake! Oh God, he's raping me – Blake! Oh please . . . no, don't . . . please . . . BLAKE! Oh my God, my God . . . BLAKE . . . Lew . . . BLAKE!'

As he rammed into her, she managed to free one hand. She reached behind her, still screaming, trying to find the wine bottle. Her hand touched its neck. She grabbed it and swung it down on his skull. She hit him again and again until the bottle smashed.

Then everything was silent.

He slid off her onto the floor. Still sobbing, she struggled to a sitting position and looked down at him. She threw the neck of the bottle on the floor, then got off the table, clutching her torn clothes.

'Elizabeth . . .!'

She heard his voice, far away and distant. Whose voice was it? Lew's? No, no, he was dead. Ben's? No, that wasn't Ben's voice. Besides, Ben was dead too, wasn't he? Then whose voice was it?

She had backed against the stove. Now she saw someone in the doorway. A nice-looking young man with a beard. Who was he? Where was she? Who was the man on the floor?

The young man with the beard was kneeling beside the man on the floor, turning him over on his back. Was the man on the floor dead? No, he just moved. . . . how did he get there? How did she get there? Where was she? Who was she?

The young man with the beard was hugging her, saying

something to her. . . . What was he saying? She couldn't quite hear him. . . . Yes, something about am I all right. . . . Who is he? Is he the north wind? Where am I? East of the sun or west of the moon?

12

WEST OF THE MOON 1871

46

On 20 September 1871 Lew Crandall rang the bell of the front door of 133 East Thirty-eighth Street. The brownstone was in the fashionable Murray Hill section of Manhattan and belonged to Hubert Foster, a wealthy stockbroker who was Blake's father. The door was opened by an Irish maid.

'Yes?'

'I'm Mr Crandall. Dr Foster is expecting me.'

'Yes sir. Come right in, sir. Lovely weather, ain't it?'

'Very lovely.'

She took him into the comfortably furnished front parlour.

'I'll just go get the doctor for you, sir,' she said, bobbing a curtsy. Then she hurried out of the room.

Lew looked around. Nothing of particular interest except one table which was covered with family photographs. He went over to look at them. An early, faded photograph, taken some time in the 1850s, probably, of a family group. Mr and Mrs Foster and their three sons, stiffly posed. He wondered which one was Blake. Other photos of the three sons growing up. Then one of the sons in an Army uniform. Though the nice-looking young man in the uniform didn't have a beard, Lew thought it was probably Blake.

Then he spotted another photo of a man in a uniform. He picked it up and looked at himself. The glass had been repaired, but he was surprised that he was being displayed with the Foster family. . . .

'I put it there,' said a voice behind him.

He turned to see Blake Foster.

'Why?' He put the photograph back on the table.

'It was in Elizabeth's purse: She must have found it in the house in Paris. I had an idea she'd like it here. I appreciate your coming.'

Lew went over to shake his hand.

'Of course I'd come,' he said. 'Whatever has happened to Elizabeth is partially my fault.'

'I don't think you should blame yourself. . . .'

'I blame myself for a lot that's happened. My wife told me I should have let God pay Matoon back, but I wouldn't listen to her. I had to do it myself. Well, if I hadn't taken things into my own hands, Ward might be alive today. And from what you said in your letter, I gather the shock of learning about Ward's death was partially responsible for what's happened to her.'

'That's true. But I still think you're being hard on yourself. After all, we can't leave everything up to God, can we?'

'I don't know. All I know is, I've raged against heaven in my life, but heaven seems to be curiously deaf in my case. Anyway . . . what is it you want me to do?'

'Let's go upstairs. . . .'

Blake led him out of the room to the entrance hall. They started up the stairs.

'She's in a state we call catatonia,' he said. 'It's caused by a massive shock to the mind, as she had in Paris, and the result is that she's in a stupor. Sometimes she comes out of it and becomes hysterical for a brief time. But mostly she just sits by the window and stares out at the garden. It's as if her mind has forced out the real world and withdrawn into a secret hiding place of its own.'

'Is it curable?'

'Well, I hope so. I can't say for sure. I've been treating her as best I can. I've worked with some of these cases before, but it's touch and go.'

'I still don't see how *I* . . .'

'You're the past. I think one way to bring her back to the present may be to reintroduce her to the past. In other words, if she can accept the past, then perhaps, in time, she can accept the present.'

'What do you want me to do?'

'Just talk to her.'

'About what?'

'About when you were young together. When you were married to her. The good times . . . try to get some sort of response out of her.'

'I'll do my best.'

'That's all any of us can do.'

They had reached the top of the stairs. Now, Blake led him down a carpeted hall to the rear of the house, where he opened a door. He motioned to Lew to follow him in.

It was a cheerful bedroom with roses clambering over the wallpaper. A chenille-covered four-poster was against one wall opposite a wooden mantle. Two windows overlooked the rear garden. Sitting by one was Elizabeth. She wore a white dress, and her chestnut hair was pulled back in a chignon. When she heard them come in, she turned to look at them with blank eyes.

'Elizabeth,' said Blake, 'we've brought someone to talk to you. Someone you've known a long time. Do you remember him?' He took Lew's arm and guided him over to stand in front of her. She stared at him.

'Hello, Elizabeth,' said Lew.

Silence.

'She doesn't talk,' whispered Blake. 'You have to do it all on your own. Wait a minute: let me pull over a chair. . . .'

He grabbed a straight-backed chair next to the fireplace and carried it over in front of Elizabeth.

'Sit down,' he said.

Lew took the chair as Blake sat on the edge of the bed, watching his wife.

'I don't know where to begin,' said Lew, rather helplessly.

'Pick any time,' said Blake. 'Just start talking to her.'

Lew rubbed his hand slowly over his chin as he thought back in time.

'Do you remember that baseball game?' he finally said. 'The one you came to Princeton to watch when I was captain of the team? That was the last summer before the war, I think. Yes . . . I graduated that year. We won the game and you were so excited. . . .' He stopped. She was staring at him as before. He wasn't even sure if she had heard him. He turned to look at Blake, who gave him an encouraging nod.

'Go on,' he said.

Lew turned back to Elizabeth.

'Remember . . . that was the day I proposed to you. We were kissing in the grass by a pond, I think . . . yes, and your father had gone off to see somebody, and he left us alone for a while. My God, that *is* a long time ago. . . .' He thought for a moment. 'We were so young then,' he went on. 'The world seemed so beautiful that day. I remember I said I loved you . . . no, that wasn't it. I said, "I don't love you, I worship you". Something like that. And you were so excited. We both were excited. . . . Do you remember any of that, Elizabeth?'

Silence. No reaction. Again, he looked at Blake, who signalled him to go on.

'Then I remember you asked me if I was thinking about our marriage. And I, being conceited and more than a little unbearable as I recall, said no, I was thinking about how well I'd pitched that day. Do you remember that?'

'Look!' whispered Blake, pointing to her right eye.

A tear was forming.